PHOENIX II

Uncollected, Unpublished, and Other Prose Works by
D. H. LAWRENCE

*Collected and Edited with an
Introduction and Notes by*

WARREN ROBERTS *and* HARRY T. MOORE

New York / The Viking Press

Published in 1968 by The Viking Press, Inc.
625 Madison Avenue, New York, N.Y. 10022

Distributed in Canada by
The Macmillan Company of Canada Limited

Library of Congress catalog card number: 36-25253

PRINTED IN U.S.A.

CONTENTS

IV. REVIEWS AND INTRODUCTIONS

V. MISCELLANEOUS PIECES

VI. REFLECTIONS ON THE DEATH OF A PORCUPINE

VII. A PROPOS OF LADY CHATTERLEY'S LOVER

VIII. ASSORTED ARTICLES

INTRODUCTION

The essays and sketches of D. H. Lawrence take on a particular importance in any view of his imaginative, primary writings. Because his major achievements, his fiction and poetry, are so often prophetic— that is, closely related to Lawrence's passionately held beliefs—the secondary work is of greater significance than is the case with most writers. The material in the present volume, *Phoenix II*, offers special clues to Lawrence.

Many of his uncollected miscellaneous writings were skilfully put together by Edward D. McDonald in the large first *Phoenix* volume in 1936. That book appeared at a rather unfortunate time, when Lawrence's reputation was at low ebb. After his death in 1930, too many memoirs appeared which made him look foolish. He had impressed those who had met him, but what they remembered most was that he was a red-bearded man who often flew into rages. And most of the reminiscences were written by the weeping Marys of his entourage. The reading public tired of hearing about him, and his own books went unread. The depression was thriving, and a war seemed to be on the way—Lawrence seemed remote from such emergencies.

He was not, as a careful reading of *Phoenix* and his other writings would have shown. In New York, the reviewer for the *Nation* said *Phoenix* would be an influential book, as with the passing of the years it has become; long out of print in the United States, it is now much in demand there, and the new printing (which accompanies that of *Phoenix II*) is welcome. But when the first *Phoenix* appeared, it made little impression. Clifton Fadiman reviewed *Phoenix* in *The New Yorker*, which at the time of Lawrence's death had printed a preposterous legend to the effect that Lawrence was in the habit of stripping himself naked and climbing mulberry trees. In 1936, Clifton Fadiman could only find in *Phoenix* a cause for wonder: why had readers in the 1920s taken Lawrence seriously? A few years after the appearance of *Phoenix*, with the war succeeding the depression, Lawrence was almost entirely forgotten.

Then, a few years after the war, he had a marvellous resurrection. Readers began to see that he had written more trenchantly than most authors about the causes of modern evils, and that his books were an important statement about the problems of modern man. By the early 1950s the revival was well under way. Readers had also come to appreciate Lawrence's expressional powers, his vitally charged language. His books are now read widely, and *Phoenix II* is a contribution to this new appreciation of his work.

Lawrence made a positive statement about his philosophical writings, in the Foreword to *Fantasia of the Unconscious* (1922), where he playfully suggested that they might be called "pollyanalytics." What he said exactly was:

> ... This pseudo-philosophy of mine—"pollyanalytics," as one of my respected critics might say—is deduced from the novels and the poems, not the reverse. The novels and poems come unwatched out of one's pen. And then the absolute need which one has for some sort of satisfactory mental attitude towards oneself and things in general makes one try to abstract some definite conclusions from one's experiences as a writer and as a man. The novels and poems are pure passionate experience. These "pollyanalytics" are inferences made afterwards, from the experience.

For the most part this is true; there may be a few occasions on which Lawrence felt his way into fiction through an essay, but usually the essays are explanations of or commentaries on the imaginative work. This applies, for example, to "The Crown," which tells much about *The Rainbow*. Lawrence wrote "The Crown" (now part of the *Reflections on the Death of a Porcupine* collection) not long after he had completed *The Rainbow* in 1915. Similarly, the two essays he wrote in 1929, the year after the publication of *Lady Chatterley's Lover*, explains much of what he was trying to accomplish in that book. Those essays are "Pornography and Obscenity" and "A Propos of Lady Chatterley's Lover," the latter included in the present volume.

But even the secondary writings which bear no obvious relation to the primary are stimulating to read. Lawrence was never dull; at some times he was less brilliant than at others, but he always quickens the reader's consciousness.

In the first section of the present book, "Stories and Sketches," most of the material has not been collected before, and some of it has not previously been published. The Notes at the back of this book tell the history of these items.

Little sketches such as "A Prelude" and "A Fly in the Ointment" represent the very young Lawrence; the first of these is an early story indeed, interesting chiefly for the hints it contains as to Lawrence's later themes and attitudes. Yet, like all his work, it has a warmth to it. The next three little stories—"A Fly in the Ointment," "Lessford's Rabbits," and "A Lesson on a Tortoise"—date from Lawrence's Croydon period, autumn 1908–spring 1912, when he was a schoolmaster in the South London suburb. The first of these stories is set at his lodging house, the other two chiefly at the school. The last two sketches, along with several of Lawrence's poems of the time, tell us much about him as a young schoolmaster.

The next three stories—"A Chapel among the Mountains," "A Hay Hut among the Mountains," and "Once"—reflect Lawrence's meeting with Frieda Weekley-Richthofen in the spring of 1912 and his subsequent trip with her to the Continent. The two mountain sketches describe their walking tour from Germany to Italy, while "Once" is possibly based on an anecdote from Frieda's youth in Germany.

"The Thimble" is of particular interest because it is a first short version of one of Lawrence's striking long stories, "The Ladybird." Lawrence often took characters and situations from life, in the case of these stories Herbert Asquith (son of H. H. Asquith) and his wife, Lady Cynthia Asquith. "The Mortal Coil," written in 1916, has as its central character a young German officer. Lawrence called it one of his "purest creations." It was based on an experience of Frieda's father. "Delilah and Mr. Bircumshaw" is apparently an early (1912–1913?) comic story (part of the text is missing), and while not one of his best, it has some distinctly Lawrencean characteristics. The "Prologue" to *Women in Love* is a discarded section of an early version of the novel. It reveals much about Lawrence's attitude while he was writing that book, and serious readers will be interested to see what Lawrence finally omitted. "Mr. Noon" is an incomplete novel Lawrence wrote in 1920 and is evidently based on the same friend whom he used as the central figure of his play of 1912, "The Married Man."

The translation of the short story "The Gentleman from San Francisco," by Ivan Bunin, is an example of one of Lawrence's briefer translations. During his forty-four years, less than half of them spent as a professional writer, he turned various foreign works into English, including a novel and a number of tales from the Italian of Giovanni Verga, as well as "The Story of Doctor Manente," from the Italian of "Il Lasca." In these cases, Lawrence was a creative translator, bringing the material over into English in his own vital prose. He wrote the

"Introduction" to the translation by his friend S. S. Koteliansky of Shestov's *All Things Are Possible*. Long after Lawrence's death, the British bookseller Bertram Rota discovered that Lawrence had not only written the "Introduction" but had also collaborated on the translation. When Mr. Rota asked Koteliansky about this, Koteliansky explained that Lawrence in this instance wished to remain anonymous (as in the case of Dostoevsky's *The Grand Inquisitor*, which they also translated together) because he felt that if his name appeared too frequently as a translator it would damage his reputation with publishers. "The Gentleman from San Francisco" appeared as the title piece of a collection of Bunin's stories translated by Koteliansky and Leonard Woolf in 1922; the volume contained a tipped-in erratum slip which explained that "Owing to a mistake Mr. Lawrence's name has been omitted from the title page," where he should have been credited with translating the title story in collaboration with Koteliansky. Lawrence, who barely knew Russian, took the sense of the text from Koteliansky and then put it into English in his own way. As Bertram Rota reported after his conversation with Koteliansky, "In some cases Lawrence altered the sense, but when Koteliansky pointed this out Lawrence impatiently declared that he could not stand foolish things and had altered the original where he thought it necessary."

Among the essays, the first two—"Rachel Annand Taylor" and "Art and the Individual"—do not represent the distinctly original Lawrence of the later years. These two pieces are lectures the young schoolmaster read before a literary group in Croydon and, apparently, to a similar group in his native Eastwood during a visit home. These little lectures are, despite their crudeness, of interest to all students of Lawrence's development. They show the young writer's first amateurish attempts at criticism, and they reveal something about the background of the early poems—in the Taylor essay, for example, the link with the nineties and Pre-Raphaelitism. It is further interesting to note the young Lawrence's disgust for Whitman, who later (despite some reservations expressed in 1923 in *Studies in Classic American Literature*) was undoubtedly an important influence on Lawrence's poetry.

The other essays contained in this section are self-explanatory and need no comment. But there is a piquant story behind "On Coming Home," which appears here in full for the first time. It records Lawrence's reactions to England when he returned there from Mexico in 1923. Lawrence's friend John Middleton Murry, who had recently founded a journal, the *Adelphi*, to give Lawrence a platform, rejected "On Coming Home" lest it offend the *Adelphi*'s readers! In "Return to Bestwood" Lawrence refers to his native town of Eastwood as Best-wood—as he did in *Sons and Lovers.*

The reviews and introductions for the most part speak for themselves. The first two—the reviews of *The Oxford Book of German Verse* and of *The Minnesingers*—were recently discovered through the detective work of the Swiss scholar Armin Arnold, chairman of the Department of German at McGill University. Similarly, the review of *The Book of Revelation,* always a subject of compelling concern for Lawrence, was discovered by W. Forster of London. After the "Foreword" to *Women in Love* was privately printed in 1936, Bennett Cerf learned of its exist-ence and incorporated it into the Modern Library edition of the novel. It is particularly valuable because Lawrence so rarely commented on his own style of writing. The Introduction to Lawrence's translation of Verga's *Little Novels of Sicily* is different from and slightly longer than the original in the English edition, while the Introduction to Verga's *Mastro-don Gesualdo* printed here is far superior to the draft published in the first *Phoenix,* which is unaccountably reprinted in preference to the present version in Anthony Beal's selection of Law-rence's criticism. The Preface to Lawrence's play *Touch and Go* (1920) contains the ideas he then held concerning a "People's Theatre."

The "Preface" to *Black Swans,* not previously published, was writ-ten for a novel by Mollie L. Skinner, whose *The House of Ellis* Lawrence had rewritten as *The Boy in the Bush.*

The "miscellaneous piece," "A Britisher Has a Word with an Editor," was a commentary on what Harriet Monroe had written in the October 1923 issue of *Poetry: A Magazine of Verse.* The Introduction to *Memoirs of the Foreign Legion* is a character portrait, and a great one; Lawrence once spoke of it as his finest piece of writing, and it certainly stands high among his works. It is particularly important to bring this back into print again. The N— D— of the sketch, as everyone now knows, is Norman Douglas, and the M— is Maurice Magnus, whose foreign-legion reminiscences were published in 1924, four years after his death. They appeared in print only because of Lawrence's efforts and were accepted for publication only because of Lawrence's Introduction; Lawrence had to fight for Magnus's book because the publisher wanted to issue the Introduction as a single small volume. And although that Introduction is complete in itself, as a full sketch of Magnus, it needs a few words of introduction itself (*not* comment). Lawrence had gone to Florence in November 1919 after four and a half years away from Italy, and after having been confined in England dur-ing the war—a banned author with a German wife, he had a difficult time supporting himself with his writing. But when at last the authorities allowed him to leave England, he and Frieda scraped together a few pounds and went south; Frieda went first to Germany to visit her parents, later arranging to meet her husband in Florence. He had meanwhile got in touch with Norman Douglas, then living there, whom Lawrence had known when Douglas was helping Austin Harrison to edit the *English Review*. After Lawrence's lonely arrival, the meeting with Douglas in Florence, and with Magnus, and the events which grew out of this are magnificently narrated by Lawrence.

But the story needs an epilogue, part of which Lawrence himself wrote. After Lawrence had attended to the publication of Magnus's book, largely to help Magnus's Maltese creditors, Douglas launched an attack in a pamphlet, *D. H. Lawrence and Maurice Magnus: A Plea for Better Manners* (1924), which protested against the portraits of Douglas and Magnus and accused Lawrence of making money out of Magnus's literary remains—money which properly belonged to Douglas as his executor. Lawrence eventually replied to these charges, in a letter to the *New Statesman*. Quoting a 1921 letter from Douglas to himself, Lawrence used Douglas's own italics: "By all means do what you like with the MS. . . . *Pocket all the cash yourself.*"

Reflections on the Death of a Porcupine (1925) and *Assorted Articles* (1930) are two important volumes of essays by Lawrence. The opening piece in the *Porcupine* book—"The Crown"—has already been mentioned as having been written in 1915, shortly after Lawrence completed *The Rainbow*. The others date from the 1920s. They are all extremely valuable commentaries on Lawrence's imaginative work. "The Novel" is one of his great statements, and it probably explains more about his own writing than any other commentary. It further demonstrates, once again, Lawrence's critical vitality and brilliance.

"A Propos of Lady Chatterley's Lover," originally a small book (written in 1929, published in 1930) is, like "Pornography and Obscenity" (written and published in 1929), a discussion of *Lady Chatterley* and what it means. "A Propos" is probably Lawrence's most brilliant single essay.

The *Assorted Articles*, lively journalistic pieces dating from Lawrence's last year and a half of life, are easy expressions of some of his profoundest beliefs, and it is important to get these essays back into print. They form a kind of philosophical coda to Lawrence's life work. And some of them represent a new trend—"Insouciance," for example, which first appeared in a newspaper as "Over-Earnest Ladies." This is a comic little portrait of the intense old lady who shares Lawrence's balcony above a Swiss lake: she "cares" too much about issues. Only a short while before, Lawrence himself was caring intensely and wanted others to do likewise; but now the slowly dying man wants peace. His picture of the over-earnest little lady, however, is bright and amusing. Lawrence himself is now like the prophet in the short novel he had written not long before, *The Escaped Cock* (also known as *The Man Who Died*). The prophet, brought back to life after his crucifixion, wants only peace, desires to get away from doctrine. And this is how Lawrence now felt, though in his time he had uttered much doctrine, and a good part of it is represented here, along with some important sketches and the consummate portrait of Maurice Magnus. These pieces have been overlong in being republished, or in getting into print at all; but now here they are, in a book whose general title draws once again upon Lawrence's self-chosen symbol of continuing life.

Warren Roberts
University of Texas

Harry T. Moore
Southern Illinois University

I

Stories and Sketches

A Prelude

"Sweet is pleasure after pain . . ."

In the kitchen of a small farm a little woman sat cutting bread and butter. The glow of the clear, ruddy fire was on her shining cheek and white apron; but grey hair will not take the warm caress of firelight.

She skilfully spread the softened butter, and cut off great slices from the floury loaf in her lap. Already two plates were piled, but she continued to cut.

Outside the naked ropes of the creeper tapped and lashed at the window.

The grey-haired mother looked up, and, setting the butter on the hearth, rose and went to look out. The sky was heavy and grey as she saw it in the narrow band over the near black wood. So she turned and went to look through the tiny window which opened from the deep recess on the opposite side of the room. The northern sky was blacker than ever.

She turned away with a little sigh, and took a duster from the red, shining warming-pan to take the bread from the oven. Afterwards she laid the table for five.

There was a rumbling and a whirring in the corner, and the clock struck five. Like many clocks in farmers' kitchens it was more than half-an-hour fast. The little woman hurried about, bringing milk and other things from the dairy; lifting the potatoes from the fire, peeping through the window anxiously. Very often her neck ached with watching the gate for a sign of approach. There was a click of the yard gate. She ran to the window, but turned away again, and catching up the blue enamelled teapot, dropped into it a handful of tea from the caddy, and poured on the water. A clinking scrape of iron-shod boots sounded outside, then the door opened with a burst as a burly, bearded man entered. He drooped at the shoulders, and leaned forward as a man who has worked all his life.

"Hello, Mother," he said loudly and cheerfully. "Am I first? Aren't any of the lads down yet? Fred will be here in a minute."

"I wish they would come," said his wife, "or else it'll rain before they're here."

"Ay," he assented, "it's beginning, and it's cold rain an' all. Bit of sleet, I think," and he sat down heavily in his armchair, looking at his wife as she knelt and turned the bread, and took a large jar of stewed apples from the oven.

"Well, Mother," he said with a pleasant, comfortable little smile, "here's another Christmas for you and me. They keep passing us by."

"Ay," she answered, the effects of her afternoon's brooding now appearing. "They come and go, but they never find us any better off."

"It seems so," he said, a shade of regret appearing momentarily over his cheerfulness. "This year we've certainly had some very bad luck. But we keep straight . . . and we never regret that Christmas— see, it's twenty-seven years since . . . twenty-seven years."

"No, perhaps not, but there's Fred as hasn't had above three pounds for the whole year's work, and the other two at the pit."

"Well, what can I do? If I hadn't lost the biggest part of the hay, and them two beasts . . ."

"If . . . Besides, what prospects has he? Here he is working year in, year out for you and getting nothing at the end of it. When you were his age, when you were twenty-five, you were married and had two children. How can he ask anybody to marry him?"

"I don't know that he wants to. He's fairly contented. Don't be worrying about him and upsetting him. Besides, we may have a good year next year, and we can make this up."

"Ay, so you say."

"Don't fret yourself tonight, lass. It's true things haven't gone as we hoped they would. I never thought to see you doing all the work you have to do, but we've been very comfortable, all things considered, haven't we?"

"I never thought to see my first lad a farm labourer at twenty-five, and the other two in the pit. Two of my sons in the pit."

"I'm sure I've done what I could, and . . ." but he heard a scraping outside, and he said no more.

The eldest son tramped in, his great boots and his leggings all covered with mud. He took off his wet overcoat, and stood on the hearthrug, his hands spread out behind him in the warmth of the fire. Looking smilingly at his mother, as she moved about the kitchen, he said: "You do look warm and cosy, Mother. When I was coming up with the last load I thought of you trotting about in that big, white apron, getting tea ready, watching the weather. There are the lads. Aren't you quite contented now . . . perfectly happy?''

She laughed an odd little laugh, and poured out the tea. The boys came in from the pit, wet and dirty, with clean streaks down their faces where the rain had trickled. They changed their clothes and sat at the table. The elder was a big, heavy loosely-made fellow, with a long nose and chin, and comical wrinkling round his eyes. The younger, Arthur, was a handsome lad, dark-haired, with ruddy colour glowing through his dirt, and dark eyes. When he talked and laughed the red of his lips and the whiteness of his teeth and eyeballs stood out in startling contrast to the surrounding black.

"Mother, I'm glad to see thee," he said, looking at her with frank, boyish affection.

"There, Mother, what more can you want?" asked her husband.

She took a bite of bread and butter, and looked up with a quaint, comical glance, as if she were given only her just dues, but for all that it pleased and amused her, only she was half shy and a grain doubtful.

"Lad," said Henry, "it's Christmas Eve. The fire ought to burn its brightest."

"Yes, I will have just another potato, seeing as Christmas is the time for feeding. What are we going to do? Are we going to have a party, mother?"

"Yes, if you want one."

"Party," laughed the father, "who'd come?"

"We might ask somebody. We could have Nellie Wycherley who used to come, an' David Garton."

"We shall not do for Nellie nowadays," said the father. "I saw her on Sunday morning on the top road. She was drivin' home with another young woman, an' she stopped an' asked me if we'd got any holly with berries on, an' I said we hadn't."

Fred looked up from the book he was reading over tea. He had dark brown eyes, something like his mother's, and they always drew attention when he turned them on anyone.

"There is a tree covered in the wood," he said.

"Well," answered the irrepressible Henry, "that's not ours, is it? An' if she's got that proud she won't come near to see us, am I goin' choppin' trees down for her? If she'd come here an' say she wanted a bit, I'd fetch her half the wood in. But when she sits in the trap and looks down on you an' asks, 'Do you happen to hev a bush of berried holly in your hedges? Preston can't find a sprig to decorate the house, and I hev some people coming down from town,' then I tell her we're all crying because we've none to decorate ourselves, and we want it the more because nobody's coming, neither from the town nor th' country, an' we're likely to forget it's Christmas if we've neither folks nor things to remind us."

"What did she say?" asked the mother.

"She said she was sorry, an' I told her not to bother, it's better lookin' at folks than at bits o' holly. The other lass was laughing, an' she wanted to know what folks. I told her any as hadn't got more pricks than a holly bush to keep you off."

"Ha! ha!" laughed the father, "did she take it?"

"The other girl nudged her, and they both began a-laughing. Then Nellie told me to send down the guysers tonight. I said I would, but they're not going now."

"Why not?" asked Fred.

"Billy Simpson's got a gathered face, and Ward's gone to Nottingham."

"The company down at Ramsley Mill will have nobody to laugh at tonight," said Arthur.

"Tell you what," exclaimed Henry, "we'll go."

"How can we, three of us?" asked Arthur.

"Well," persisted Henry, "we could dress up so as they'd niver know us, an' hae a bit o' fun.

"Hey!" he suddenly shouted to Fred, who was reading, and taking no notice. "Hey, we're going to the Mill guysering."

"Who is?" asked the elder brother, somewhat surprised.

"You an' me, an' our Arthur. I'll be Beelzebub."

Here he distorted his face to look diabolic, so that everybody roared.

"Go," said his father, "you'll make our fortunes."

"What!" he exclaimed, "by making a fool of myself? They say fools for luck. What fools wise folk must be. Well, I'll be the devil— are you shocked, mother? What will you be, Arthur?"

"I don' care," was the answer. "We can put some of that red paint on our faces, and some soot, they'd never know us. Shall we go, Fred?"

"I don't know."

"Why, I should like to see her with her company, to see if she has very fine airs. We could leave some holly for her in the scullery."

"All right, then."

After tea all helped with the milking and feeding. Then Fred took a hedge knife and a hurricane lamp and went into the wood to cut some of the richly-berried holly. When he got back he found his brothers roaring with laughter before the mirror. They were smeared with red and black, and had fastened on grotesque horsehair moustaches, so that they were entirely unrecognisable.

"Oh, you are hideous," cried their mother. "Oh, it's shameful to disfigure the work of the Almighty like that."

Fred washed and proceeded to dress. They could not persuade him to use paint or soot. He rolled his sleeves up to the shoulder, and wrapped himself in a great striped horse rug. Then he tied a white cloth round his head, as the Bedouins do, and pulled out his moustaches to fierce points. He looked at himself with approval, took an old sword from the wall, and held it in one naked muscular arm.

"Decidedly," he thought, "it is very picturesque, and I look very fine."

"Oh, that is grand," said his mother, as he entered the kitchen. His dark eyes glowed with pleasure to hear her say it. He seemed somewhat excited, this bucolic young man. His tanned skin shone rich and warm under the white cloth, its coarseness hidden by the yellow lamplight. His eyes glittered like a true Arab's, and it was to be noticed that the muscles of his sun-browned arm were tense with the grip of the broad hand.

It was remarkable how the dark folds of the rug and the flowing burnous glorified this young farmer, who in his best clothes looked awkward and ungainly, and whose face in a linen collar showed coarse, owing to exposure from the weather, and long application to heavy labour.

They set out to cross the two of their own fields, and two of their neighbour's, which separated their home from the Mill. A few uncertain flakes of snow were eddying down, melting as they settled. The ground was wet, and the night very dark. But they knew the way well, and were soon at the gate leading to the mill yard. The dog began to bark furiously, but they called to him, "Trip, Trip," and, knowing their voices, he was quieted.

Henry gave a thundering knock, and bawled in stentorian tones, "Dun yer want guysers?"

A man came to the door, very tall, very ungainly, very swarthy.

"We non want yer," he said, talking down his nose.

"Here comes Beelzebub," banged away Henry, thumping a pan which he carried. "Here comes Beelzebub, an' he's come to th' right place."

A big, bonny farm girl came to the door.

"Who is it?" she asked.

"Beelzebub, you know him well," was the answer.

"I'll ask Miss Ellen if she wants you."

Henry winked a red and black wink at the maid, saying, "Never keep Satan on the doorstep," and he stepped into the scullery.

The girl ran away and soon was heard a laughing and bright talking of women's voices drawing nearer to the kitchen.

"Tell them to come in," said a voice.

The three trooped in, and glanced round the big kitchen. They could only see Betty, seated to them as near as possible on the squab, her father, black and surly, in his armchair, and two women's figures in the deep shadows of one of the great ingle-nook seats.

"Ah," said Beelzebub, "this is a bit more like it, a bit hotter. The Devils feel at home here."

They began the ludicrous old Christmas play that everyone knows so well. Beelzebub acted with much force, much noise, and some humour. St. George, that is Fred, played his part with zeal and earnestness most amusing, but at one of the most crucial moments he entirely forgot his speech, which, however, was speedily rectified by Beelzebub. Arthur was nervous and awkward, so that Beelzebub supplied him with most of the speeches.

After much horseplay, stabbing, falling on the floor, bangings of dripping-pans, and ludicrous striving to fill in the blanks, they came to an end.

They waited in silence.

"Well, what next?" asked a voice from the shadows.

"It's your turn," said Beelzebub.

"What do you want?"

"As little as you have the heart to give."

"But," said another voice, one they knew well, "we have no heart to give at all."

"You did not know your parts well," said Blanche, the stranger. "The big fellow in the blanket deserves nothing."

"What about me?" asked Arthur.

"You," answered the same voice, "oh, you're a nice boy, and a lady's thanks are enough reward for you."

He blushed and muttered something unintelligible.

"There'll be the Devil to pay," suggested Beelzebub.

"Give the Devil his dues, Nell," said Blanche, choking again with laughter. Nellie threw a large silver coin on the flagstone floor, but she was nervous, and it rolled to the feet of Preston in his armchair.

"'Alf-a-crern!" he exclaimed, "gie 'em thrippence, an' they're non worth that much."

This was too much for the chivalrous Saint George. He could bear no longer to stand in the ridiculous garb before his scornful lady-love and her laughing friend.

He snatched off his burnous and his robe, flung them over one arm, and with the other caught back Beelzebub, who would have gone to pick up the money. There he stood, St. George metamorphosed into a simple young farmer, with ruffled curly black hair, a heavy frown, and bare arms.

"Won't you let him have it?" asked Blanche. "Well, what do you want?" she continued.

"Nothing, thanks. I'm sorry we troubled you."

"Come on," he said, drawing the reluctant Beelzebub, and the three made their exit. Blanche laughed and laughed again to see the discomfited knight tramp out, rolling down his shirt sleeves.

Nellie did not laugh. Seeing him turn, she saw him again as a child, before her father had made money by the cattle-dealing, when she was a poor, wild little creature. But her father had grown rich, and the mill was a big farm, and when the old cattle dealer had died, she became sole mistress. Then Preston, their chief man, came with Betty and Sarah, to live in, and take charge of the farm.

Nellie had seen little of her old friends since then. She had stayed a long time in town, and when she called on them after her return found them cool and estranged. So she had not been again, and now it was almost a year since she had spoken many words to Fred.

Her brief meditations were disturbed by a scream from Betty in the scullery, followed by the wild rush of that damsel into the kitchen.

"What's up?" asked her father.

"There's somebody there got hold of my legs."

Nellie felt suddenly her own loneliness. Preston struck a match and investigated. He returned with a bunch of glittering holly, thick with scarlet berries.

"Here's yer somebody," said he, flinging the bunch down on the table.

"Oh, that is pretty," exclaimed Blanche. Nellie rose, looked, then hurried down the passage to the sitting-room, followed by her friend. There to the consternation of Blanche, she sat down and began to cry.

"Whatever is the matter?" asked Blanche.

It was some time before she had a reply, then, "It's so miserable and so lonely. I do think Will and Harry and Louie and all the others were mean not to come, then this wouldn't have happened. It was such a shame—such a shame."

"What was a shame?" asked Blanche.

"Why, when he had got me that holly, and come down to see . . ." she ended, blushing.

"Whom do you mean—the Bedouin?"

"And I had not seen him for months, and he will think I am just a mean, proud thing."

"You don't mean to say you care for him?"

Nellie's tears began to flow again. "I do, and I wish this miserable farm and bit of money had never come between us. He'll never come again, never, I know."

"Then," said Blanche, "you must go to him."

"Yes, and I will."

"Come along, then."

In the meantime the disappointed brothers had reached home. Fred had thrown down his Bedouin wardrobe, and put on his coat, muttering something about having a walk up the village. Then he had gone out, his mother's eyes watching his exit with helpless grief, his father looking over his spectacles in a half-surprised paternal sympathy. However, they heard him tramp down the yard and enter the barn, and they knew he would soon recover. Then the lads went out, and nothing was heard in the kitchen save the beat of the clock and the rustle of the newspaper, or the rattle of the board, as the mother rolled out paste for the mince-pies.

In the pitch-dark barn, the rueful Bedouin told himself that he expected no other than this, and that it was high time he ceased fooling himself with fancies, that he was well-cured, that even if she had invited himself to stay, how could he; she must think he wanted badly to become master of Ramsley Mill. What a fool he had been to go— what a fool!

"But," he argued, "let her think what she likes, I don't care. She may remember if she can that I used to sole her boots with my father's leather, and she went home in mine. She can remember that my mother taught her how to write and sew decently. I should say she must some-times." Then he admitted to himself that he was sure she did not forget. He could feel quite well that she was wishing that this long estrange-ment might cease.

"But," came the question, "why doesn't she end it? Pah, it's only my conceit; she thinks more of those glib, grinning fellows from the clerks' stools. Let her, what do I care!"

Suddenly he heard voices from the field at the back, and sat up listening.

"Oh, it's a regular slough," said someone. "We can never get through the gate. See, let us climb the stackyard fence. They've put some new rails in. Can you manage, Blanche? Here, just between the lilac bush and the stack. What a blessing they keep Chris at the front! Mind, bend under this plum tree. Dare we go, Blanche?"

"Go on, go on," whispered Blanche, and they crept up to the tiny window, through which the lamplight streamed uninterrupted. Fred stole out of the barn, and hid behind the great water-butt. He saw them stoop and creep to the window and peep through.

In the kitchen sat the father, smoking and appearing to read, but really staring into the fire. The mother was putting the top crusts on the little pies, but she was interrupted by the need to wipe her eyes.

"Oh, Blanche," whispered Nellie, "he's gone out."

"It looks like it," assented the other.

"Perhaps he's not," resumed the former bravely. "He's very likely only in the parlour."

"That's all right, then," said Blanche, "I thought we should have seen him looking so miserable. But, of course, he wouldn't let his mother see it."

"Certainly not," said Nellie.

Fred chuckled.

"But," she continued doubtfully, "if he has gone out, whatever shall we do? What can we tell his mother?"

"Tell her, we came up for fun."

"But if he's out?"

"Stay till he comes home."

"If it's late?"

"It's Christmas Eve."

"Perhaps he doesn't care after all."

"You think he does, so do I; and you're quite sure you want him?"

"You know I do, Blanche, and I always have done."

"Let us begin, then."

"What? Good King Wenceslas?"

The mother and father started as the two voices suddenly began to carol outside. She would have run to the door, but her husband waved her excitedly back. "Let them finish," his eyes shining, "let them finish."

The girls had retired from the window lest they should be seen, and stood near the water-butt. When the old carol was finished, Nellie began the beautiful song of Giordani's:—

Turn once again, heal thou my pain,
Parted from thee my heart is sore.

As she sang she stood holding a bough of the old plum tree, so close to Fred that by leaning forward he could have touched her coat. Carried away by the sweet pathos of her song, he could hardly refrain from rising and flinging his arms round her.

She finished; the door opened, showing a little woman holding out her hands.

Both girls made a motion towards her, but—

"Nell, Nell," he whispered, and caught her in his arms. She gave a little cry of alarm and delight. Blanche stepped into the kitchen and shut the door, laughing.

She sat in the low rocking-chair, swinging to and fro in a delighted excitement, chattering brightly about a hundred things. And with a keen woman's eye she noticed the mother put her hands on her husband's as she sat on the sofa by his chair, and saw him hold the shining stiffened hand in one of his, and stroke it with old undiminished affection.

Soon the two came in, Nellie all blushing. Without a word she ran and kissed the little mother, lingering a moment over her before she turned to the quiet embrace of the father. Then she took off her hat, and brushed back the brown tendrils all curled so prettily by the damp.

Already she was at home.

A Fly in the Ointment

(A Blot)

Muriel had sent me some mauve primroses, slightly weather-beaten, and some honeysuckle, twine threaded with grey-green rosettes, and some timid hazel catkins. They had arrived in a forlorn little cardboard box, just as I was rushing off to school.

"Stick 'em in water!" I said to Mrs. Williams, and I left the house. But those mauve primroses had set my tune for the day: I was dreamy and tender; school and the sounds of the boys were unreal, unsubstantial; beyond these were the realities of my poor winter—trodden primroses, and the pale hazel catkins that Muriel had sent me. Altogether the boys must have thought me a vacant fool; I regarded them as a punishment upon me.

I rejoiced exceedingly when night came, with the evening star, and the sky flushed dark blue, purple, over the golden pomegranates of the lamps. I was as glad as if I had been hurrying home to Muriel, as if she would open the door to me, would keep me a little while in the fire-glow, with the splendid purple pall of the evening against the window, before she laughed and drew up her head proudly and flashed on the light over the tea-cups. But Eleanor, the girl, opened the door to me, and I poured out my tea in solitary state.

Mrs. Williams had set out my winter posy for me on the table, and I thought of all the beautiful things we had done, Muriel and I, at home in the Midlands, of all the beautiful ways she had looked at me, of all the beautiful things I had said to her—or had meant to say. I went on imagining beautiful things to say to her looking at me with her wonderful eyes, from among the fir boughs in the wood. Meanwhile I talked to my landlady about the neighbours.

Although I had much work to do, and although I laboured away at it, in the end there was nothing done. Then I felt very miserable, and sat still and sulked. At a quarter to eleven I said to myself:

"This will never do," and I took up my pen and wrote a letter to Muriel.

"It was not fair to send me those robins"—we called the purple primroses 'robins', for no reason, unless that they bloomed in winter —"they have bewitched me. Their wicked, bleared little pinkish eyes follow me about and I have to think of you and home, instead of doing what I've got to do. All the time while I was teaching I got mixed up with you. 'If the interest on a certain Muriel be—' that was arithmetic. And I've read the miserable pieces of composition on 'Pancakes' over and over, and never seen them, thinking—'the primrose flowers because it is so sheltered under the plum-trees. They are black plums, with very gummy bark. She is fond of biting through a piece of hard bright gum. Then her lips get sticky'."

I will not say at what time I finished my letter. I can recall a sensation of being blind, dim, oblivious of everything, smiling to myself as I sealed the envelope; putting my books and papers in their places without the least knowledge of so doing, keeping the atmosphere of Strelley Mill close round me in my London lodging. I cannot remember turning off the electric light. The next thing of which I am conscious is pushing at the kitchen door.

The kitchen is at the back of the house. Outside in the dark was a little yard and a hand-breadth of garden backed up by the railway embankment. I had come down the passage from my room in the front of the house, and stood pushing at the kitchen door to get a glass for some water. Evidently the oilcloth had turned up a little, and the edge of the door was under it. I woke up irritably, swore a little, pushed the door harder, and heard the oilcloth rip. Then I bent and put my hand through the small space of the door to flatten the oilcloth.

The kitchen was in darkness save for the red embers lying low in the stove. I started, but rather from sleepy curiosity than anything else. Perhaps I ought to say that I opened my eyes a little. Pressing himself flat into the corner between the stove and the wall was a fellow. I did not feel alarmed: I was away in the Midlands still. So I stood looking in dull curiosity.

"Why?" I said quite mildly. I think this very mildness must have terrified him. Immediately he shrunk together, and began to dodge about between the table and stove, whining, snarling, with an incredibly mongrel sound:

"Don't yer touch me—don't yer come grabbin' at me—I'll hit yer between the eyes with this poker—I ain't done nothin' to you—don't yer touch me, yer bloody coward."

All the time he was writhing about in the space in which I had him trapped, between the table and stove. I was much too amazed to do anything but stare. Then my blood seemed to change its quality. It went cool and sharp with disgust. I was accustomed to displays of the kind in school, and I felt again the old misery of contempt and disgust. He dared not, I knew, strike, unless by trying to get hold of him I terrified him to the momentary madness of such a slum rat.

"Stop your row!" I said, standing still and leaving him his room. "Shut your miserable row. Do you want to waken the children?"

"Ah, but don't yer touch me, don't yer come no nearer!"

He had stopped writhing about, and was crouching at the defensive. The little frenzy too, had gone out of his voice.

"Put the poker down, you fool!"

I pointed to the corner of the stove, where the poker used to stand. I supplied him with the definite idea of placing the poker in the corner, and, in his crazy witless state, he could not reject it. He did as I told him, but indefinitely, as if the action were second-hand. The poker, loosely dropped into the corner, slid to the ground with a clatter. I looked from it to him, feeling further contempt for the nerveless knave. Yet my own heart had begun to beat heavily. His own indefinite clumsiness, and the jingle of the poker on the hearth, unnerved him still more. He crouched there abjectly.

I took a box of matches from the mantelpiece and lit the gas at the pendant that hung in the middle of the bare little room. Then I saw that he was a youth of nineteen or so, narrow at the temples with thin, pinched-looking brows. He was not ugly, nor did he look ill-fed. But he evidently came of the lowest breed. His hair had been cut close to his skull, leaving a tussocky fringe over his forehead to provide him with a "topping", and to show that it was no prison crop which had bared him.

"I wasn't doing no harm," he whined, resentfully, with still an attempt at a threat in his tones. "I 'aven't don nuffin' to you, you leave me alone. What harm have I done?"

"Shut up," I said. "Do you want to wake the baby and fetch everybody down? Keep your mouth shut!"

I went to the door and listened. No one was disturbed. Then I closed the door, and quietly pulled down the wide-opened window which was letting in the cold night air. As I did so I shivered, noting how chill and dreary the mangle looked in the yard, with the moonlight on its frosty cover.

The fellow was standing abjectly in the same place. He had evidently been rickety as a child. I sat down in the rocking-chair.

"What did you come in here for?" I asked, curious.

"Well," he retorted insolently "an' wouldn't you, if you 'adn't a place to go to of a night like this."

"Look here," I said coldly. "None of your sauce."

"Well, I only come in for a warm" he said, meekly.

"Nor blarney either," I replied. "You came to pinch something, it's no use saying you didn't. What should you have taken?" I asked, curiously. He looked back at me uneasily, then at his dirty hands, then at me again. He had brown eyes, in which low cunning floated like oil on the top of much misery.

"I might 'a took some boots" he said simply. For the moment he could not help speaking the truth.

"And what right have you to pinch boots from people who can't afford to buy any more?" I said.

"I ain't never done it before! This is the first time."

"You miserable creep!" I said. He looked at me with a flash of rat-fury.

"Where do you live?" I asked.

"Exeter Road."

"And do you do any work?"

"I couldn't never get a job—except I used to deliver laundry—"

"And they turned you off for stealing?"

He shifted and stirred uneasily in his chair. As he was so manifestly uncomfortable I did not press him.

"Who do you live with?"

"I live at 'ome."

"What does your father do?"

But he sat stubborn and would not answer. I thought of the gangs of youths who stood at the corner of the mean streets near the school, there all day long, month after month, fooling with the laundry girls, and insulting the passers-by.

"But," I said, "what's going to become of you?"

He hung his head again and fidgeted in his chair. Evidently what little thought he gave to the subject made him uncomfortable. He could not answer.

"Get a laundry girl to marry you and live on her?" I asked, sarcastically.

He smiled sicklily, evidently even a little bit flattered. What was the good of talking to him.

"You'll loaf at the street corner till you go rotten," I said.

He looked at me sullenly.

"Well, I can't get a job," he replied, with insolence. He was not hopeless, but like a man born without expectations, apathetic, looking to be provided for, sullenly allowing everything.

"But," I said, "if a man is worthy of his hire, the hire is worthy of a man—and I'm damned if you're one."

He grinned at me with sly insolence.

"It beats me that any woman 'ud let you touch her," I said.

And then he grinned slyly to himself, ducking his head to hide the joke. And I thought of the coloured primroses, and of Muriel's beautiful pensive face. Then of him with his dirty clothes and his nasty skin.

"Well," I said, "you're beyond me."

He gave me a narrow, leering look from his sore eyes.

"You don't know everything," he said, in contempt.

I sat and wondered. And I knew I could not understand him, that I had no fellow feeling with him. He was something beyond me.

"Well," I said, helplessly, "you'd better go. But for God's sake steal in different streets."

I rose, feeling he had beaten me. He could affect and alter me, I could not affect nor alter him. He shambled off down the path. I watched him skulk under the lamp-posts, afraid of the police. Then I shut the door.

In the silence of the sleeping house I stood quite still for some minutes, up against the impassable rock of this man, beyond which I could not get. Then I climbed the stairs. It was like a nightmare. I thought he was a blot, like a blot fallen on my soul, something black and heavy which I could not decipher.

As I hung up my coat I felt Muriel's fat letter in my pocket. It made me a trifle sick.

"No," I said, with a flush of rage against her perfect serene purity. "I don't want to think of her."

And I wound my watch up sullenly, feeling alone and wretched.

Lessford's Rabbits

On Tuesday mornings I have to be at school at half past eight to administer the free breakfasts. Dinners are given in the canteen in one of the mean streets, where the children feed in a Church Mission room appropriately adorned by Sunday School cartoons showing the blessing of the little ones, and the feeding of the five thousand. We serve breakfasts, however, in school, in the wood-work room high up under the roof.

Tuesday morning sees me rushing up the six short flights of stone stairs, at twenty-five minutes to nine. It is my disposition to be late. I generally find a little crowd of children waiting in the "art" room—so called because it is surrounded with a strip of blackboard too high for the tallest boy to reach—which is a sort of ante-room to the work-shop where breakfast is being prepared. I hasten through the little throng to see if things are ready. There are two big girls putting out the basins, and another one looking in the pan to see if the milk is boiling. The room is warm, and seems more comfortable because the windows are high up under the beams of the slanting roof and the walls are all panelled with ruddy gold, varnished wood. The work bench is in the form of three sides of a square—or of an oblong—as the dining tables of the ancients used to be, I believe. At one of the extremities are the three vises, and at the other the great tin pan, like a fish kettle, standing on a gas ring. When the boys' basins are placed along the outer edge of the bench, the girls' on the inner, and the infants' on the lockers against the wall, we are ready. I look at the two rows of assorted basins, and think of the three bears. Then I admit the thirty, who bundle to their places and stand in position, girls on the inside facing boys on the outside, and quaint little infants with their toes kicking the lockers along the walls.

Last week the infant mistress did not come up, so I was alone. She is an impressive woman, who always commands the field. I stand in considerable awe of her. I feel like a reckless pleasure boat with one extravagant sail misbehaving myself in the track of a heavy earnest coaster when she bears down on me. I was considerably excited to find myself in sole charge. As I ushered in the children, the caretaker, a little fierce-eyed man with hollow cheeks and walrus moustache, entered with the large basket full of chunks of bread. He glared around without bidding me good morning.

"Miss Culloch not come?" he asked.

"As you see," I replied.

He grunted, and put down the basket. Then he drew himself up like a fiery prophet, and stretching forth his hairy arm towards the opposite door, shouted loudly to the children:

"None of you's got to touch that other door there! You hear— you're to leave it alone!"

The children stared at him without answering.

"A brake as I'm making for these doors," he said confidentially to me, thrusting forward his extraordinarily hairy lean arms, and putting two fingers of one hand into the palm of the other, as if to explain his invention. I bowed.

"Nasty things them swing doors"—he looked up at me with his fierce eyes, and suddenly swished aside his right arm:

"They come to like *that*!" he exclaimed, "and a child's fingers is cut off—clean!"—he looked at me for ratification. I bowed.

"It'll be a good thing, I think," he concluded, considerably damped. I bowed again. Then he left me. The chief, almost the only duty of a caretaker, is to review the works of the head and of the staff, as a reviewer does books: at length and according to his superior light.

I told one of the girls to give three chunks of bread to each child, and, having fished a mysterious earwig out of the scalding milk, I filled the large enamelled jug—such as figures and has figured in the drawing lessons of every school in England, I suppose—and doled out the portions—about three-quarters of a pint per senior, and half a pint per infant. Everything was ready. I had to say grace. I dared not launch into the Infant mistress' formula, thanking the Lord for his goodness—, "and may we eat and drink to thine everlasting glory—Amen." I looked at the boys, dressed in mouldering garments of remote men, at the girls with their rat-tailed hair, and at the infants, quaint little mites on whom I wished, but could not bring myself, to expend my handkerchief, and I wondered what I should say. The only other grace I knew was "For these and for all good things may the Lord make us truly thankful." But I wondered whom we should thank for the bad things. I was becoming desperate. I plunged:

"Ready now—hands together, close eyes. 'Let us eat, drink and be merry, for tomorrow we die.'" I felt myself flushing with confusion— what did I mean? But there was a universal clink of iron spoons on the basins, and a snuffling, slobbering sound of children feeding. They had not noticed, so it was all right. The infants were kneeling and squalling by the lockers, the boys were stretching wide their eyes and their mouths at the same time, to admit the spoon. They spilled the milk on their jackets and wiped it off with their sleeves, continuing to eat all the time.

"Don't slobber, lads, be decent," I said, rebuking them from my superior sphere. They ate more carefully, glancing up at me when the spoon was at their mouths.

I began to count the number—nine boys, seven girls, and eleven infants. Not many. We could never get many boys to give in their names for free meals. I used to ask the Kelletts, who were pinched and pared thin with poverty:

"Are you sure you don't want either dinners or breakfasts, Kellett?"

He would look at me curiously, and say, with a peculiar small movement of his thin lips,

"No Sir."

"But have you plenty—quite plenty?"

"Yes Sir"—he was very quiet, flushing at my questions. None—or very few—of the boys could endure to accept the meals. Not many parents would submit to the indignity of the officer's inquirer and the boys, the most foolishly sensitive animals in the world, would, many of them, prefer to go short rather than to partake of charity meals of which all their school-mates were aware.

"Halket—where is Halket?" I asked.

"Please Sir, his mother's got work," replied Lessford, one of my own boys, a ruddy, bonny lad—many of those at breakfast were pictures of health. Lessford was brown-skinned and had fine dark eyes. He was a reticent, irresponsible creature, with a radical incapacity to spell and to read and to draw, but who sometimes scored at arithmetic. I should think he came of a long line of unrelievedly poor people. He was skilled in street lore, and cute at arithmetic, but blunt and blind to everything that needed a little delicacy of perception. He had an irritating habit of looking at me furtively, with his handsome dark eyes, glancing covertly again and again. Yet he was not a sneak; he gave himself the appearance of one. He was a well-built lad, and he looked well in the blue jersey he wore—there were great holes at the elbows, showing the whitish shirt and a brown bit of Lessford. At breakfasts he was a great eater. He would have five solid pieces of bread, and then ask for more.

We gave them bread and milk one morning, cocoa and currant bread the next. I happened to go one cocoa morning to take charge. Lessford,

I noticed, did not eat by any means so much as on bread mornings. I was surprised. I asked him if he did not care for currant loaf, but he said he did. Feeling curious, I asked the other teachers what they thought of him. Mr. Hayward, who took a currant bread morning, said he was sure the boy had a breakfast before he came to school;—Mr. Jephson, who took a milk morning, said the lad was voracious, that it amused him to try to feed him up. I watched—turning suddenly to ask if anyone wanted a little more milk, and glancing over the top of the milk pan as I was emptying it.

I caught him: I saw him push a piece of bread under his jersey, glancing furtively with a little quiver of apprehension up at me. I did not appear to notice, but when he was going downstairs I followed him and asked him to go into the class-room with me. I closed the door and sat down at my table: he stood hanging his head and marking with his foot on the floor. He came to me, very slowly, when I bade him. I put my hand on his jersey, and felt something underneath. He did not resist me, and I drew it out. It was his cap. He smiled, he could not help it, at my discomfiture. Then he pulled his lips straight and looked sulky. I tried again—and this time I found three pieces of bread in a kind of rough pocket inside the waist of his trousers. He looked at them blackly as I arranged them on the table before him, flushing under his brown skin.

"What does this mean?" I asked. He hung his head, and would not answer.

"You may as well tell me—what do you want this for?"

"Eat," he muttered, keeping his face bent. I put my hand under his chin and lifted up his face. He shut his eyes, and tried to move his face aside, as if from a very strong light which hurt him.

"That is not true," I said. "I know perfectly well it is not true. You have a breakfast before you come. You do not come to eat. You come to take the food away."

"I never!" he exclaimed sulkily.

"No," I said. "You did not take any yesterday. But the day before you did."

"I never, I never!!" he declared, more emphatically, in the tone of one who scores again. I considered.

"Oh no—the day before was Sunday. Let me see. You took some on Thursday—yes, that was the last time— You took four or five pieces of bread—" I hung fire; he did not contradict; "five, I believe," I added. He scraped his toe on the ground. I had guessed aright. He could not deny the definite knowledge of a number.

But I could not get another word from him. He stood and heard all I had to say, but he would not look up, or answer anything. I felt angry.

"Well," I said, "if you come to breakfasts any more, you will be reported."

Next day, when asked why he was absent from breakfast, he said his father had got a job.

He was a great nuisance for coming with dirty boots. Evidently he went roaming over fields and everywhere. I concluded he must have a strain of gipsy in him, a mongrel form common in the south of London. Halket was his great friend. They never played together at school, and they had no apparent common interests. Halket was a debonair, clever lad who gave great promise of turning out a neer-do-well. He was very lively, soon moved from tears to laughter; Lessford was an inveterate sulker. Yet they always hung together.

One day my bread-stealer arrived at half past two, when the register was closed. He was sweating, dishevelled, and his breast was heaving. He gave no word of explanation, but stood near the great blackboard, his head dropped, one leg loosely apart, panting.

"Well," I exclaimed, "this is a nice thing! What have you to say?" I rose from my chair.

Evidently he had nothing to say.

"Come on," I said finally. "No foolery! Let me hear it." He knew he would have to speak. He looked up at me, his dark eyes blazing:

"My rabbits has all gone!" he cried, as a man would announce his wife and children slain. I heard Halket exclaim. I looked at him. He was half-out of the desk, his mercurial face blank with dismay.

"Who's 'ad 'em?" he said, breathing the words almost in a whisper.

"Did you leave th' door open?" Lessford bent forward like a serpent about to strike as he asked this. Halket shook his head solemnly:

"No! I've not been near 'em today."

There was a pause. It was time for me to reassume my position of authority. I told them both to sit down, and we continued the lesson. Halket crept near his comrade and began to whisper to him, but he received no response. Lessford sulked fixedly, not moving his head for more than an hour.

At playtime I began to question Halket: "Please Sir— we had some rabbits in a place on the allotments. We used to gather manure for a man, and he let us have half of his tool-house in the garden—."

"How many had you—rabbits?"

"Please Sir—they varied. When we had young ones we used to have sixteen sometimes. We had two brown does and a black buck."

I was somewhat taken back by this.

"How long have you had them?"

"A long time now Sir. We've had six lots of young ones."

"And what did you do with them?"

"Fatten them, Sir"—he spoke with a little triumph, but he was reluctant to say much more.

"And what did you fatten them on?"

The boy glanced swiftly at me. He reddened, and for the first time became confused.

"Green stuff, what we had given us out of the gardens, and what we got out of the fields."

"And bread," I answered quietly.

He looked at me. He saw I was not angry, only ironical. For a few moments he hesitated, whether to lie or not. Then he admitted, very subdued:

"Yes Sir."

"And what did you do with the rabbits?"—he did not answer— "Come, tell me. I can find out whether or not."

"Sold them,"—he hung his head guiltily.

"Who did the selling?"

"I, Sir—to a greengrocer."

"For how much?"

"Eightpence each."

"And did your mothers know?"

"No Sir." He was very subdued and guilty.

"And what did you do with the money?"

"Go to the Empire—generally."

I asked him a day or two later if they had found the rabbits. They had not. I asked Halket what he supposed had become of them.

"Please Sir—I suppose somebody must 'a stole them. The door was not broken. You could open our padlock with a hair-pin. I suppose somebody must have come after us last night when we'd fed them. I think I know who it is, too, Sir." He shook his head widely— "There's a place where you can get into the allotments off the field——"

A Lesson on a Tortoise

It was the last lesson on Friday afternoon, and this, with Standard VI, was Nature Study from half-past three till half-past four. The last lesson of the week is a weariness to teachers and scholars. It is the end; there is no need to keep up the tension of discipline and effort any longer, and, yielding to weariness, a teacher is spent.

But Nature Study is a pleasant lesson. I had got a big old tortoise, who had not yet gone to sleep, though November was darkening the early afternoon, and I knew the boys would enjoy sketching him. I put him under the radiator to warm while I went for a large empty shell that I had sawn in two to show the ribs of some ancient tortoise absorbed in his bony coat. When I came back I found Joe, the old reptile, stretching slowly his skinny neck, and looking with indifferent eyes at the two intruding boys who were kneeling beside him. I was too good-tempered to send them out again into the playground, too slack with the great relief of Friday afternoon. So I bade them put out the Nature books ready. I crouched to look at Joey, and stroked his horny, blunt head with my finger. He was quite lively. He spread out his legs and gripped the floor with his flat hand-like paws, then he slackened again as if from a yawn, drooping his head meditatively.

I felt pleased with myself, knowing that the boys would be delighted with the lesson. "He will not want to walk," I said to myself, "and if he takes a sleepy stride, they'll be just in ecstasy, and I can easily calm him down to his old position." So I anticipated their entry. At the end of playtime I went to bring them in. They were a small class of about thirty—my own boys. A difficult, mixed class, they were, consisting of six London Home boys, five boys from a fairly well-to-do Home for the children of actors, and a set of commoners varying from poor lads who hobbled to school, crippled by broken enormous boots, to boys who brought soft, light shoes to wear in school on snowy days. The Gordons were a difficult set; you could pick them out: crop haired, coarsely dressed lads, distrustful, always ready to assume the defensive. They would lie till it made my heart sick, if they were charged with offence, but they were willing, and would respond beautifully to an appeal.

The actors were of different fibre: some gentle, a pleasure even to look at; others polite and obedient, but indifferent, covertly insolent and vulgar; all of them more or less gentlemanly.

The boys crowded round the table noisily as soon as they discovered Joe. "Is he alive?—Look, his head's coming out! He'll bite you?— He *won't*!"—with much scorn—"Please Sir, do tortoises bite?" I hurried them off to their seats in a little group in front, and pulled the table up to the desks. Joe kept fairly still. The boys nudged each other excitedly, making half audible remarks concerning the poor reptile, looking quickly from me to Joe and then to their neighbours. I set them sketching, but in their pleasure at the novelty they could not be still:

"Please Sir—shall we draw the marks on the shell? Please Sir, has he only got four toes?"—"Toes!" echoes somebody, covertly delighted at the absurdity of calling the grains of claws 'toes'. "Please Sir, he's moving—Please Sir!"

I stroked his neck and calmed him down:

"Now don't make me wish I hadn't brought him. That's enough. Miles—you shall go to the back and draw twigs if I hear you again! Enough now—be still, get on with the drawing, it's hard!"

I wanted peace for myself. They began to sketch diligently. I stood and looked across at the sunset, which I could see facing me through my window, a great gold sunset, very large and magnificent, rising up in immense gold beauty beyond the town, that was become a low dark strip of nothingness under the wonderful up-building of the western sky. The light, the thick, heavy golden sunlight which is only seen in its full dripping splendour in town, spread on the desks and the floor like gold lacquer. I lifted my hands, to take the sunlight on them, smiling faintly to myself, trying to shut my fingers over its tangible richness.

"Please Sir!"—I was interrupted—"Please Sir, can we have rubbers?"

The question was rather plaintive. I had said they should have rubbers no more. I could not keep my stock, I could not detect the thief among them, and I was weary of the continual degradation of bullying them to try to recover what was lost among them. But it was Friday afternoon, very peaceful and happy. Like a bad teacher, I went back on my word:

"Well—!" I said, indulgently.

My monitor, a pale, bright, erratic boy, went to the cupboard and took out a red box.

"Please Sir!" he cried, then he stopped and counted again in the box. "Eleven! There's only eleven, Sir, and there were fifteen when I put them away on Wednesday—!"

The class stopped, every face upturned. Joe sunk, and lay flat on his shell, his legs limp. Another of the hateful moments had come. The sunset was smeared out, the charm of the afternoon was smashed like a fair glass that falls to the floor. My nerves seemed to tighten, and to vibrate with sudden tension.

"Again!" I cried, turning to the class in passion, to the upturned faces, and the sixty watchful eyes.

"Again! I am sick of it, sick of it I am! A thieving, wretched set!—a skulking, mean lot!" I was quivering with anger and distress.

"Who is it? You must know! You are all as bad as one another, you hide it—a miserable—!" I looked round the class in great agitation. The "Gordons" with their distrustful faces, were noticeable:

"Marples!" I cried to one of them, "where are those rubbers?"

"I don't know where they are—I've never 'ad no rubbers"—he almost shouted back, with the usual insolence of his set. I was more angry:

"You must know! They're gone—they don't melt into air, they don't fly—who took them then? Rawson, do you know anything of them?"

"No Sir!" he cried, with impudent indignation.

"No, you intend to know nothing! Wood, have you any knowledge of these four rubbers?"

"No!" he shouted, with absolute insolence.

"Come here!" I cried, "come here! Fetch the cane, Burton. We'll make an end, insolence and thieving and all."

The boy dragged himself to the front of the class, and stood slackly, almost crouching, glaring at me. The rest of the "Gordons" sat upright in their desks, like animals of a pack ready to spring. There was tense silence for a moment. Burton handed me the cane, and I turned from the class to Wood. I liked him best among the Gordons.

"Now my lad!" I said. "I'll cane you for impudence first."

He turned swiftly to me; tears sprang to his eyes.

"Well," he shouted at me, "you always pick on the Gordons—you're always on to us—!" This was so manifestly untrue that my anger fell like a bird shot in a mid-flight.

"Why!" I exclaimed, "what a disgraceful untruth! I am always excusing you, letting you off—!"

"But you pick on us—you start on us—you pick on Marples, an' Rawson, an' on me. You always begin with the Gordons."

"Well," I answered, justifying myself, "isn't it natural? Haven't you boys stolen—haven't these boys stolen—several times—and been caught?"

"That doesn't say as we do now," he replied.

"How am I to know? You don't help me. How do I know? Isn't it natural to suspect you—?"

"Well, it's not us. We know who it is. Everybody knows who it is— only they won't tell."

"Who know?" I asked.

"Why Rawson, and Maddock, and Newling, and all of 'em."

I asked these boys if they could tell me. Each one shook his head, and said, "No Sir." I went round the class. It was the same. They lied to me every one.

"You see," I said to Wood.

"Well—they won't own up," he said. "I shouldn't 'a done if you hadn't 'a been goin' to cane me."

This frankness was painful, but I preferred it. I made them all sit down. I asked Wood to write his knowledge on a piece of paper, and I promised not to divulge. He would not. I asked the boys he had named, all of them. They refused. I asked them again—I appealed to them.

"Let them all do it then!" said Wood. I tore up scraps of paper, and gave each boy one.

"Write on it the name of the boy you suspect. He is a thief and a sneak. He gives endless pain and trouble to us all. It is your duty."

They wrote furtively, and quickly doubled up the papers. I collected them in the lid of the rubber box, and sat at the table to examine them. There was dead silence, they all watched me. Joe had withdrawn into his shell, forgotten.

A few papers were blank; several had "I suspect nobody"—these I threw in the paper basket; two had the name of an old thief, and these I tore up; eleven bore the name of my assistant monitor a splendid, handsome boy, one of the oldest of the actors. I remembered how deferential and polite he had been when I had asked him, how ready to make barren suggestions; I remembered his shifty, anxious look during the questioning; I remembered how eager he had been to do things for me before the monitor came in the room. I knew it was he—without remembering.

"Well!" I said, feeling very wretched when I was convinced that the papers were right. "Go on with the drawing."

They were very uneasy and restless, but quiet. From time to time they watched me. Very shortly, the bell rang. I told the two monitors to collect up the things, and I sent the class home. We did not go into prayers. I, and they, were in no mood for hymns and the evening prayer of gratitude.

When the monitors had finished, and I had turned out all the lights but one, I sent home Curwen, and kept my assistant-monitor a moment.

"Ségar, do you know anything of my rubbers?"

"No Sir"—he had a deep, manly voice, and he spoke with earnest protestation—flushing.

"No? Nor my pencils?—nor my two books?"

"No Sir! I know nothing about the books."

"No? The pencils then—?"

"No Sir! Nothing! I don't know anything about them."

"Nothing, Ségar?"

"No Sir."

He hung his head, and looked so humiliated, a fine, handsome lad, that I gave it up. Yet I knew he would be dishonest again, when the opportunity arrived.

"Very well! You will not help as monitor any more. You will not come into the classroom until the class comes in—any more. You understand?"

"Yes Sir"—he was very quiet.

"Go along then."

He went out, and silently closed the door. I turned out the last light, tried the cupboards, and went home.

I felt very tired, and very sick. The night had come up, the clouds were moving darkly, and the sordid streets near the school felt like disease in the lamplight.

A Chapel among the Mountains

It is all very well trying to wander romantically in the Tyrol. Sadly I sit on the bed, my head and shoulders emerging from the enormous overbolster like a cherub from a cloud, writing out of sheer exasperation, whilst Anita lies on the other bed and is amused.

Two days ago it began to rain. When I think of it I wonder. The gutter of the heavens hangs over the Tyrolese Alps.

We set off with the iridescent cloud of romance ahead, leading us southwards from the Isar towards Italy. We haven't got far. And the iridescent cloud, turned into a column of endless water, still endures around the house.

I omit the pathos of our setting forth, in the dimmery-glimmery light of the Isar Valley, before breakfast-time, with blue chicory flowers open like wonder on either side the road. Neither will I describe our crawling at dinner-time along the foot of the mountains, the rain running down our necks from the flabby straw hats, and dripping cruelly into one's boots from the pent-house of our rucksacks. We entered ashamed into a wayside inn, where seven ruddy, joyous peasants, three of them handsome, made a bonfire of their hearts in honour of Anita, whilst I sat in a corner and dripped. . . .

Yesterday I admit it was fine in the afternoon and evening. We made tea by a waterfall among yellow-dangling noli-me-tangere flowers, whilst an inquisitive lot of mountains poked their heads up to look, and a great green grasshopper, armoured like Ivanhoe, took a flying leap into eternity over a lovely, black-blue gentian. At least, I saw him no more.

They had told us there was a footpath over the mountain, three and a half hours to Glashütte. There *was* a faint track, and a myriad of strawberries like ruddy stars below, and a few dark bilberries. We climbed one great steep slope, and scrambled down beyond, into a pine wood. There it was damp and dark and depressing. But one makes the best of things, when one sets out on foot. So we toiled on for an hour, traversing the side of a slope, black, wet, gloomy, looking through the fir-trees across the gulf at another slope, black and gloomy and forbidding, shutting us back. For two hours we slipped and struggled, and still there we were, clamped between these two black slopes, listening to the water that ran uncannily, noisily along the bottom of the trap.

We grew silent and hot with exertion and the dark monotony of the struggle. A rucksack also has its moments of treachery, close friend though it seems. You are quite certain of a delicate and beautiful balance on a slippery tree-root; you take the leap; then the ironic rucksack gives you a pull from behind, and you are grovelling.

And the path *had* been a path. The side of the dark slope, steep as a roof, had innumerable little bogs where waters tried to ooze out and call themselves streams, and could not. Across these bogs went an old bed of fir-boughs, dancy and treacherous. So, there was a path! Suddenly there were no more fir-boughs, and one stood lost before the squalor of the slope. I wiped my brow.

"You so soon lose your temper," said Anita. So I stood aside, and yielded her the lead.

She blundered into another little track lower down.

"You *see!*" she said, turning round.

I did not answer. She began to hum a little tune, because her path descended. We slipped and struggled. Then her path vanished into the loudly-snorting, chuckling stream, and did not emerge.

"Well?" I said.

"But where is it?" she said with vehemence and pathos.

"You see even *your* road ends in nowhere," I said.

"I *hate* you when you preach," she flashed. "Besides it *doesn't* end in nowhere."

"At any rate," I said, "we can't sleep on the end of it."

I found another track, but I entered on it delicately, without triumph. We went in silence. And it vanished into the same loudly-snorting stream.

"Oh, don't look like that!" cried Anita. So I followed the bedraggled tail of her skirts once more up the wet, dark opposition of the slope. We found another path, and once more we lost the scent in the overjoyed stream.

"Perhaps we're supposed to go across," I said meekly, as we stood beside the waters.

"I—*why* did I take a damp match of a man like you!" she cried. "One could scratch you for ever and you wouldn't strike."

I looked at her, wondering, and turned to the stream, which was cunningly bethinking itself. There were chunks of rock, and spouts and combs and rattles of sly water. So I put my raincoat over my rucksack and ventured over.

The opposite bank was very steep and high. We were swallowed in this black gorge, swallowed to the bottom, and gazing upwards I set off on all fours, climbing with my raincoat over my rucksack, cloakwise, to leave me free. I scrambled and hauled and struggled.

And from below came shriek upon shriek of laughter. I reached the top, and looked down. I could see nothing, only the whirring of laughter came up.

"What is it?" I called, but the sound was lost amid the cackle of the waters. So I crawled over the edge and sat in the gloomy solitude, extinguished.

Directly I heard a shrill, frightened call:

"Where are you?"

My heart exulted and melted at the same moment.

"Come along," I cried, satisfied that there was one spot in this gloomy solitude to call to.

She arrived, scared with the steep climb, and the fear of loneliness in this place.

"I might never have found you again," she said.

"I don't intend you should lose me," I said. So she sat down, and presently her head began to nod with laughter, and her bosom shook with laughter, and she was laughing wildly without me.

"Well, what?" I said.

"You—you looked like a camel—with your hump—climbing up," she shrieked.

"We'd better be moving," I said. She slipped and laughed and struggled. At last we came to a beautiful savage road. It was the bed of some stream that came no more this way, a mass of clear boulders leading up the slope through the gloom.

"We are coming out now," said Anita, looking ahead. I also was quite sure of it. But after an hour of climbing, we were still in the bed of clear boulders, between dark trees, among the toes of the mountains.

Anita spied a hunter's hut, made of bark, and she went to investigate. Night was coming on.

"I can't get in," she called to me, obscurely.

"Then come," I said.

It was too wet and cold to sleep out of doors in the woods. But instead of coming, she stooped in the dark twilight for strawberries. I waited like the shadow of wrath. But she, unconcerned, careless and happy in her contrariety, gathered strawberries among the shadows.

"We *must* find a place to sleep in," I said. And my utter insistence took effect.

She realized that I was lost among the mountains, as well as she, that night and the cold and the great dark slopes were close upon us, and we were of no avail, even being two, against the coldness and desolation of the mountains.

So in silence we scrambled upwards, hand in hand. Anita was sure a dozen times that we were coming out. At last even she got disheartened.

Then, in the darkness, we spied a hut beside a path among the thinning fir-trees.

"It will be a woodman's hut," she said.

"A shrine," I answered.

I was right for once. It was a wooden hut just like a model, with a black old wreath hanging on the door. There was a click of the latch in the cold, watchful silence of the upper mountains, and we entered.

By the grey darkness coming in from outside we made out the tiny chapel, candles on the altar and a whole covering of ex-voto pictures on the walls, and four little praying-benches. It was all close and snug as a box.

Feeling quite safe, and exalted in this rare, upper shadow, I lit the candles, all. Point after point of flame flowed out on the night. There were six. Then I took off my hat and my rucksack, and rejoiced, my heart at home.

The walls of the chapel were covered close with naked little pictures, all coloured, painted by the peasants on wood, and framed with little frames. I glanced round, saw the cows and the horses on the green meadows, the men on their knees in their houses, and I was happy as if I had found myself among the angels.

"What wonderful luck!" I said to Anita.

"But what are we going to do?" she asked.

"Sleep on the floor—between the praying-desks. There's just room."

"But we can't sleep on a wooden floor," she said.

"What better can you find?"

"A hay hut. There must be a hay hut somewhere near. We *can't* sleep here."

"Oh yes," I said.

But I was bound to look at the little pictures. I climbed on to a bench. Anita stood in the open doorway like a disconsolate, eternal angel. The light of the six dusky tapers glimmered on her discontented mouth. Behind her, I could see tips of fir branches just illuminated, and then the night.

She turned and was gone like darkness into the darkness. I heard her boots upon the stones. Then I turned to the little pictures I loved. Perched upon the praying-desks, I looked at one, and then another. They were picture-writings that seemed like my own soul talking to me. They were really little pictures for God, because horses and cows and men and women and mountains, they are His own language. How should He read German and English and Russian, like a schoolmaster? The peasants could trust Him to understand their pictures: they were not so sure that He would concern Himself with their written script.

I was looking at a pale blue picture. That was a bedroom, where a woman lay in bed, and a baby lay in a cradle not far away. The bed was blue, and it seemed to be falling out of the picture, so it gave me a feeling of fear and insecurity. Also, as the distance receded, the bed-stead got wider, uneasily. The woman lay looking straight at me, from under the huge, blue-striped overbolster. Her pink face was round like a penny doll's, with the same round stare. And the baby, like a pink-faced farthing doll, also stared roundly.

"Maria hat geholfen E.G.—1777."

I looked at them. And I knew that I was the husband looking and wondering. G., the husband, did not appear himself. It was from the little picture on his retina that this picture was reproduced. He could not sum it up, and explain it, this vision of his wife suffering in child-birth, and then lying still and at peace with the baby in the cradle. He could not make head or tail of it. But at least he could represent it, and hang it up like a mirror before the eyes of God, giving the statement even if he could get no explanation. And he was satisfied. And so, per-force, was I, though my heart began to knock for knowledge.

The men never actually saw themselves unless in precarious con-ditions. When their lives were threatened, then they had a fearful flash of self-consciousness, which haunted them till they had represented it. They represented themselves in all kinds of ridiculous postures, at the moment when the accident occured.

Joseph Rieck, for example, was in a toppling-backward attitude rather like a footballer giving a very high kick and losing his balance. But on his left ankle had fallen a great grey stone, that might have killed him, squashing out much blood, orange-coloured—or so it looked by the candle-light—whilst the Holy Mary stood above in a bolster-frame of clouds, holding up her hands in mild surprise.

"Joseph Rieck
Gott sey Danck gasagt 1834."

It was curious that he thanked God because a stone had fallen on his ankle. But perhaps the thanks were because it had not fallen on his head. Or perhaps because the ankle had got better, though it looked a nasty smash, according to the picture. It didn't occur to him to thank God that all the mountains of the Tyrol had not tumbled on him the first day he was born. It doesn't occur to any of us. We wait till a big stone falls on our ankle. Then we paint a vivid picture and say: "In the midst of life we are in death," and we thank God that we've escaped. All kinds of men were saying: "Gott sey Danck"; either because big stones had squashed them, or because trees had come down on them whilst they were felling, or else because they'd tumbled over cliffs, or got carried away in streams: all little events which caused them to ejaculate: "God be thanked, I'm still alive".

Then some of the women had picture prayers that were touching, because they were prayers for other people, for their children and not for themselves. In a sort of cell kneeled a woman, wearing a Catherine of Russia kind of dress, opposite a kneeling man in Vicar of Wakefield attire. Between them, on the stone wall, hung two long iron chains with iron rings dangling at the end. Above these, framed in an oval of bolster-clouds, Christ on the Cross, and above Him, a little Maria, short in stature, something like Queen Victoria, with a very blue cloth over her head, falling down her dumpy figure. She, the Holy Mother of heaven, looked distressed. The woman kneeling in the cell put up her hands, saying:

"O Mutter Gottes von Rerelmos, Ich bitte mach mir mein Kind von Gefangenschaft los mach im von Eissen und Bandten frey wansz des Gottliche Willen sey.

Susanna Grillen 1783."

I suppose Herr Grillen knew that it was not the affair of the Mutter Gottes. Poor Susanna Grillen! It was natural and womanly in her to identify the powers that be with the eternal powers. What I can't see, is whether the boy had really done anything wrong, or whether he had merely transgressed some law of some duke or king or community. I suppose the poor thing did not know herself how to make the distinction. But evidently the father, knowing he was in temporal difficulty, was not very active in asking help of the eternal.

One must look up the history of the Tyrol for the 1783 period.

A few pictures were family utterances, but the voice which spoke was always the voice of the mother. Marie Schneeberger thanked God for healing her son. She kneeled on one side of the bedroom, with her three daughters behind her; Schneeberger kneeled facing her, with a space between them, and his one son behind him. The Holy Mary floated above the space of their thanks. The whole family united this time to bless the heavenly powers that the bad had not been worse. And, in the face of the divine power, the man was separate from the woman, the daughter from the son, the sister from the brother—one set on one side, one set on the other, separate before the eternal grace, or the eternal fear.

The last set of pictures thanked God for the salvation of property. One lady had six cows—all red ones—painted feeding on a meadow with rocks behind. All the cows I have seen in these parts have been dun or buff coloured. But these are red. And the goodwife thanks God very sincerely for restoring to her that which was lost for five days, viz. her six cows and the little cow-girl Kate. The little girl did not appear in the picture nor in the thanks: she was only mentioned as having been lost along with the cows. I do not know what became of her. Cows can always eat grass. I suppose she milked her beasts, and perhaps cranberries were ripe. But five days was a long time for poor Kathel.

There were hundreds of cattle painted standing on meadows like a child's Noah's Ark toys arranged in groups: a group of red cows, a group of brown horses, a group of brown goats, a few grey sheep; as if they had all been summoned into their classes. Then Maria in her cloud-frame blessed them. But standing there so hieroglyphic, the animals had a symbolic power. They did not merely represent property. They were the wonderful animal life which man must take for food. Arrayed there in their numbers, they were almost frightening, as if they might overthrow us, like an army.

Only one woman had had an accident. She was seen falling downstairs, just landing at the bottom into her peaceful kitchen where the kitten lay asleep by the stove. The kitten slept on, but Mary in a blue mantle appeared through the ceiling, mildly shocked and deprecating.

Alone among all the women, the women who had suffered childbirth or had suffered through some child of their own, was this housewife who had fallen downstairs into the kitchen where the cat slept peacefully. Perhaps she had not any children. However that may be, her position was ignoble, as she bumped on the bottom stair.

There they all were, in their ex-voto pictures that I think the women had ordered and paid for, these peasants of the valley below, pictured in their fear. They lived under the mountains where always was fear. Sometimes they knew it to close on a man or a woman. Then there was no peace in the heart of this man till the fear had been pictured, till he was represented in the grip of terror, and till the picture had been offered to the Deity, the dread, unnamed Deity; whose might must be acknowledged, whilst in the same picture the milder divine succour was represented and named and thanked. Deepest of all things, among the mountain darknesses, was the ever-felt fear. First of all gods was the unknown god who crushed life at any moment, and threatened it always. His shadow was over the valleys. And a tacit acknowledgment and propitiation of Him were the ex-voto pictures, painted out of fear and offered to Him unnamed. Whilst upon the face of them all was Mary the divine Succour, She, who had suffered, and knew. And that which had suffered and known, had prevailed, and was openly thanked. But that which had neither known nor suffered, the dread unnamed, which had aimed and missed by a little, this must be acknowledged covertly. For his own soul's sake, man must acknowledge his own fear, acknowledge the power beyond him.

Whilst I was reading the inscriptions high up on the wall, Anita came back. She stood below me in her weather-beaten panama hat, looking up dissatisfied. The light fell warm on her face. She was discontented and excited.

"There's a gorgeous hay hut a little farther on," she said.

"Hold me a candle a minute, will you?" I said.

"A great hay hut full of hay, in an open space. I climbed in——"

"Do you mind giving me a candle for a moment?"

"But no—come along——"

"I just want to read this—give me a candle." In a silence of impatience, she handed me one of the tapers. I was reading a little inscription.

"Won't you come?" she said.

"We could sleep well here," I said. "It is so dry and secure."

"Why!" she cried irritably. "Come to the hay hut and see."

"In one moment," I said.

She turned away.

"Isn't this altar adorable!" she cried. "Lovely little paper roses, and ornaments."

She was fingering some artificial flowers, thinking to put them in her hair. I jumped down, saying I must finish reading my pictures in the morning. So I gathered the rucksack and examined the cash-box by the door. It was open and contained six kreutzers. I put in forty pfennigs, out of my poor pocket, to pay for the candles. Then I called Anita away from the altar trinkets, and we closed the door, and were out in the darkness of the mountains.

A Hay Hut among the Mountains

I resented being dragged out of my kapelle into the black and dismal night. In the chapel were candles and a boarded floor. And the streams in the mountains refuse to run anywhere but down the paths made by man. Anita said: "You cannot imagine how lovely your chapel looked, as I came on it from the dark, its row of candles shining, and all the inside warm!"

"Then why on earth didn't you stay there?" I said.

"But think of sleeping in a hay hut," she cried.

"I think a kapelle is much more soul stirring," I insisted.

"But much harder to the bones," she replied.

We struggled out on to a small meadow, between the mountain tops. Anita called it a kettle. I presumed then that we had come in by the spout and should have to get out by the lid. At any rate, the black heads of the mountains poked up all round, and I felt tiny, like a beetle in a basin.

The hay hut stood big and dark and solid, on the clear grass.

"I know just how to get in," said Anita, who was full of joy now we were going to be uncomfortably situated. "And now we must eat and drink tea."

"Where's your water?" I asked.

She listened intently. There was a light swishing of pine-trees on the mountain side.

"I hear it," she said.

"Somewhere down some horrid chasm," I answered.

"I will go and look," she said.

"Well," I answered, "you needn't go hunting on a hillside where there isn't the faintest sign of a rut or watercourse."

We spoke *sotto voce*, because of the darkness and the stillness. I led down the meadow, nearly breaking my neck over the steepest places. Now I was very thirsty, and we had only a very little schnapps.

"There is sure to be water in the lowest place," I said.

She followed me stealthily and with glee. Soon we squelched in a soft place.

"A confounded marsh," I said.

"But," she answered, "I hear it trickling."

"What's the good of its trickling, if it's nasty."

"You *are* consoling," she mocked.

"I suppose," I said, "it rises here. So if we can get at the Quelle——"

I don't know why "Quelle" was necessary, instead of "source", but it was. We paddled up the wet place, and in the darkness found where the water welled out. Having filled our can, and our boots by the way, we trudged back. I slipped and spilled half the water.

"This," said Anita, "makes me perfectly happy."

"I wish it did me," I replied.

"Don't you like it, dear?" she said, grieved.

My feet were soddened and stone cold. Everywhere was wet, and very dark.

"It's all right," I said. "But the chapel——"

So we sat at the back of the hut, where the wind didn't blow so badly, and we made tea and ate sausage. The wind wafted the flame of the spirit lamp about, drops of rain began to fall. In the pitch dark, we lost our sausage and the packet of tea among the logs.

"At last I'm perfectly happy," Anita repeated.

I found it irritating to hear her. I was looking for the tea.

Before we had finished this precious meal, the rain came pelting down. We hurried the things into our rucksacks and bundled into the hut. There was one little bread left for morning.

The hut was as big as a small cottage. It was made of logs laid on top of one another, but they had not been properly notched, so there were stripes of light all round the Egyptian darkness. And in a hay hut one dares not strike a light.

"There's the ladder to the big part," said Anita.

The front compartment was only one-quarter occupied with hay: the back compartment was full nearly to the ceiling. I climbed up the ladder, and felt the hay, putting my hand straight into a nasty messy place where the water had leaked in among the hay from the roof.

"That's all puddly, and the man'll have his whole crop rotten if he doesn't watch it," I said. "It's a stinkingly badly-made hay hut."

"Listen to the rain," whispered Anita.

It was rattling on the roof furiously. Then, although there were slots of light, and a hundred horse-power draught tearing across the hut, I was glad to be inside the place.

"Hay," I remarked after a while, "has two disadvantages. It tickles like all the creeping insects, and it is porous to the wind."

"'Porous to the wind'," mocked Anita.

"It is," I said.

There was a great preparation. All valuables, such as hair-pins and garters and pfennigs and hellers and trinkets and collar studs, I carefully collected in my hat. It was pitch dark. I laid the hat somewhere. We took off our soddened shoes and stockings. Imagining they would somehow generate heat and dry better, I pushed the boots into the wall of hay. Then I hung up various draggled garments, hoping they would dry.

"I insist on your tying up your head in a hanky, and on my spreading my waistcoat for a pillow-cloth," I said.

Anita humbly submitted. She was too full of joy to refuse. We had no blankets, nothing but a Burberry each.

"A good large hole," I said, "as large as a double grave. And I only hope it won't be one."

"If you catch cold," said Anita, "I shall hate you."

"And if *you* catch cold," I answered, "I s'll nurse you tenderly."

"You dear!" she exclaimed, affectionately.

We dug like two moles at the grave.

"But see the mountains of hay that come out," she said.

"All right," I said, "you can amuse your German fancy by putting them back again, and sleeping underneath them."

"How lovely!" she cried.

"And how much lovelier a German fat bolster would be."

"Don't!" she implored. "Don't spoil it."

"I'd sleep in a lobster-pot to please you," I said.

"I don't want you to please me, I want you to be pleased," she insisted.

"God help me, I *will* be pleased," I promised.

At first it was pretty warm in the trough, but every minute I had to rub my nose or my neck. This hay was the most insidious, persistent stuff. However much I tried to fend it off, one blade tickled my nostrils, a seed fell on my eyelid, a great stalk went down my neck. I wrestled with it like a Hercules, to keep it at bay, but in vain. And Anita merely laughed at my puffs and snorts.

"Evidently," I said, "you have not so sensitive a skin as I."

"Oh no—not so delicate and fine," she mocked.

"In fact, you can't have," I said, sighing. But presently, she also sighed.

"Why," she said, "did you ,choose a waistcoat for a pillow? I've always got my face in one of the armholes."

"You should arrange it better," I said.

We sighed, and suffered the fiendish ticklings of the hay. Then I suppose we slept, in a sort of fitful fever.

I was awakened by the cracks of thunder. Anita clutched me. It was fearfully dark. Like a great whip clacking, the thunder cracked and spattered over our hut, seemed to rattle backwards and forwards from the mountain peaks.

"Something more for your money," I groaned, too sleepy to live.

"Does thunder strike hay huts?" Anita asked.

"Yes, it makes a dead set at them—simply preys on hay huts, does thunder," I declared.

"Now you needn't frighten me," she reproached.

"Go to sleep," I commanded.

But she wouldn't. There was Anita, there was thunder, and lightning, then a raging wind and cataracts of rain, and the slow, persistent, evil tickling of the hay seeds, all warring on my sleepiness. Occasionally I got a wink. Then it began to get cold, with the icy wind rushing in through the wide slots between the logs of the walls. The miserable hay couldn't even keep us warm. Through the chinks of it penetrated the vicious wind. And Anita would not consent to be buried, she would have her shoulders and head clear. So of course we had little protection. It grew colder and colder, miserably cold. I burrowed deeper and deeper. Then I felt Anita's bare feet, and they were icy.

"Woman," I said, "poke your wretched head in, and be covered up, and save what modicum of animal heat you can generate."

"I must breathe," she answered crossly.

"The hay is quite well aerated," I assured her.

At last it began to get dawn. Slots of grey came in place of slots of blue-black, all round the walls. There was twilight in the crate of a hay hut. I could distinguish the ladder and the rucksacks. Somewhere outside, I thought, drowsily, a boy was kicking a salmon tin down the street; till it struck me as curious, and I remembered it was only the sound of a cow-bell, or a goat-bell.

"It's morning," said Anita.

"Call this morning?" I groaned.

"Are you warm, dear?"

"Baked."

"Shall we get up?"

"Yes. At all events we can be one degree more wretched and cold."

"I'm perfectly happy," she persisted.

"You look it," I said.

Immediately she was full of fear.

"Do I look horrid?" she asked.

She was huddled in her coat: her tousled hair was full of hay.

I pulled on my boots and clambered through the square opening.

"But come and look!" I exclaimed.

It had snowed terrifically during the night; not down at our level, but a little higher up. We were on a grassy place, about half a mile across, and all round us was the blackness of pine-woods, rising up. Then suddenly in the middle air, it changed, and great peaks of snow balanced, intensely white, in the pallid dawn. All the upper world around us belonged to the sky; it was wonderfully white, and fresh, and awake with joy. I felt I had only to run upwards through the pine-trees, then I could tread the slopes that were really sky-slopes, could walk up the sky.

"No!" cried Anita, in protest, her eyes filling with tears. "No!"

We had quite a solemn moment together, all because of that snow. And the fearfully gentle way we talked and moved, as if we were the only two people God had made, touches me to remember.

"Look!" cried Anita.

I thought at least the Archangel Gabriel was standing beside me. But she only meant my breath, that froze while on the air. It reminded me.

"And the cold!" I groaned. "It fairly reduces one to an ash."

"Yes, my dear—we must drink tea," she replied solicitously. I took the can for water. Everything looked so different in the morning. I could find the marsh, but not the water bubbling up. Anita came to look for me. She was barefoot, because her boots were wet. Over the icy mown meadow she came, took the can from me, and found the spring. I went back and prepared breakfast. There was one little roll, some tea, and some schnapps. Anita came with water, balancing it gingerly. She had a distracted look.

"Oh, how it hurts!" she cried. "The ice-cold stubbles, like blunt icy needles, they did hurt!"

I looked at her bare feet and was furious with her.

"No one," I cried, "but a lunatic, would dream of going down there *barefoot* under these conditions——"

"'Under these conditions'," she mocked.

"It ought to have hurt you *more*," I cried. "There is no crime but stupidity."

"'Crime but stupidity'," she echoed, laughing at me.

Then I went to look at her feet.

We ate the miserable knob of bread, and swallowed the tea. Then I bullied Anita into coming away. She performed a beautiful toilet that I called the 'brave Tyrolese', and at last we set out. The snow all above us was laughing with brightness. But the earth, and our boots, were soddened.

"Isn't it wonderful!" cried Anita.

"Yes—with feet of clay," I answered. "Wet, raw clay!"

Sobered, we squelched along an indefinite track. Then we spied a little, dirty farm-house, and saw an uncouth-looking man go into the cow-sheds.

"This," I said, "is where the villains and robbers live."

Then we saw the woman. She was wearing the blue linen trousers that peasant women wear at work.

"Go carefully," said Anita. "Perhaps she hasn't performed her toilet."

"I shouldn't think she's got one to perform," I replied.

It was a deadly lonely place, high up, cold and dirty. Even in such a frost, it stank bravely beneath the snow peaks. But I went softly.

Seeing Anita, the woman came to the door. She was dressed in blue overalls, trousers and bodice, the trousers tight round the ankles, nearly like the old-fashioned leg-of-mutton sleeves. She was pale, seemed rather deadened, as if this continuous silence acted on her like a deadening drug. Anita asked her the way. She came out to show us, as there was no track, walking before us with strides like a man, but in a tired, deadened sort of way. Her figure was not ugly, and the nape of her neck was a woman's, with soft wisps of hair. She pointed us the way down.

"How old was she?" I asked Anita, when she had gone back.

"How old do you think?" replied Anita.

"Forty to forty-five."

"Thirty-two or three," answered Anita.

"How do you know, any more than I?"

"I am sure."

I looked back. The woman was going up the steep path in a mechanical, lifeless way. The brilliant snow glistened up above, in peaks. The hollow green cup that formed the farm was utterly still. And the woman seemed infected with all this immobility and silence. It was as if she were gradually going dead, because she had no place there. And I saw the man at the cow-shed door. He was thin, with sandy moustaches; and there was about him the same look of distance, as if silence, loneliness, and the mountains deadened him too.

We went down between the rocks, in a cleft where a river rushed. On every side, streams fell and bounded down. Some, coming over the sheer wall of a cliff, drifted dreamily down like a roving rope of mist. All round, so white and candid, were the flowers they call Grass of Parnassus, looking up at us, and the regal black-blue gentian reared themselves here and there.

[The following ending was erased.]

We ran ourselves warm, but I felt as if the fires had gone out inside me. Down and down we raced the streams, that fell into beautiful green pools, and fell out again with a roar. Anita actually wanted to bathe, but I forbade it. So, after two hours' running downhill, we came out in the level valley at Glashütte. It was raining now, a thick dree rain. We pushed on to a little Gasthaus, that was really the home of a forester. There the stove was going, so we drank quantities of coffee, ale, and went to bed.

"You spent the night in a hay hut," said I to Anita. "And the next day in bed."

"But I've done it, and I loved it," said she. "And besides, it's raining."

And it continued to pour. So we stayed in the house of the Jäger, who had a good, hard wife. She made us comfortable. But she kept her children in hand. They sat still and good, with their backs against the stove, and watched.

"Your children are good," I said.

"They are wild ones," she answered, shaking her head sternly. And I saw the boy's black eyes sparkle.

"The boy is like his father," I said.

She looked at him.

"Yes—yes! perhaps," she said shortly.

But there was a proud stiffness in her neck, nevertheless. The father was a mark-worthy man, evidently. He was away in the forests now for a day or two. But he had photos of himself everywhere, a good-looking, well-made, conceited Jäger, who was photographed standing with his right foot on the shoulder of a slaughtered chamois. And soon his wife had thawed sufficiently to tell me: "Yes, he had accompanied the Crown Prince to shoot his first chamois." And finally, she recited to us this letter, from the same Crown Prince:

"Lieber Karl, Ich möchte wissen wie und wann die letzte Gemse geschossen worden——"

Once

The morning was very beautiful. White packets of mist hung over the river, as if a great train had gone by leaving its steam idle, in a trail down the valley. The mountains were just faint grey-blue, with the slightest glitter of snow high up in the sunshine. They seemed to be standing a long way off, watching me, and wondering. As I bathed in the shaft of sunshine that came through the wide-opened window, letting the water slip swiftly down my sides, my mind went wandering through the hazy morning, very sweet and far-off and still, so that I had hardly wit enough to dry myself. And as soon as I had got on my dressing-gown, I lay down again idly on the bed, looking out at the morning that still was greenish from the dawn, and thinking of Anita.

I had loved her when I was a boy. She was an aristocrat's daughter, but she was not rich. I was simply middle-class, then. I was much too green and humble-minded to think of making love to her. No sooner had she come home from school than she married an officer. He was rather handsome, something in the Kaiser's fashion, but stupid as an ass. And Anita was only eighteen. When at last she accepted me as a lover, she told me about it.

"The night I was married," she said, "I lay counting the flowers on the wall-paper, how many on a string; he bored me so."

He was of good family, and of great repute in the Army, being a worker. He had the tenacity of a bulldog, and rode like a centaur. These things look well from a distance, but to live with they weary one beyond endurance, so Anita says.

She had her first child just before she was twenty: two years afterwards, another. Then no more. Her husband was something of a brute. He neglected her, though not outrageously, treated her as if she were a fine animal. To complete matters, he more than ruined himself owing to debts, gambling and otherwise, then utterly disgraced himself by using Government money and being caught.

"You have found a hair in your soup," I wrote to Anita.

"Not a hair, a whole plait," she replied.

After that, she began to have lovers. She was a splendid young creature, and was not going to sit down in her rather elegant flat in Berlin, to run to seed. Her husband was officer in a crack regiment. Anita was superb to look at. He was proud to introduce her to his friends. Then, moreover, she had her own relatives in Berlin, aristocratic but also rich, and moving in the first society. So she began to take lovers.

Anita shows her breeding: erect, rather haughty, with a good-humoured kind of scorn. She is tall and strong, her brown eyes are full of scorn, and she has a downy, warm-coloured skin, brownish to match her black hair.

At last she came to love me a little. Her soul is unspoiled. I think she has almost the soul of a virgin. I think, perhaps, it frets her that she never really loved. She has never had the real respect—*Ehrfurcht*—for a man. And she has been here with me in the Tyrol these last ten days. I love her, and I am not satisfied with myself. Perhaps I too shall fall short.

"You have never *loved* your men?" I asked her.

"I loved them—but I have put them all in my pocket," she said, with just the faintest disappointment in her good humour. She shrugged her shoulders at my serious gaze.

I lay wondering if I too were going into Anita's pocket, along with her purse and her perfume and the little sweets she loved. It would almost have been delicious to do so. A kind of voluptuousness urged me to let her have me, to let her put me in her pocket. It would be so nice. But I loved her: it would not be fair to her. I wanted to do more than give her pleasure.

Suddenly the door opened on my musing, and Anita came into my bedroom. Startled, I laughed in my very soul, and I adored her. She was so natural! She was dressed in a transparent lacy chemise, that was slipping over her shoulder, high boots, upon one of which her string-coloured stocking had fallen. And she wore an enormous hat, black, lined with white, and covered with a tremendous creamy-brown feather, that streamed like a flood of brownish foam, swaying lightly. It was an immense hat on top of her shamelessness, and the great, soft feather seemed to spill over, fall with a sudden gush, as she put back her head.

She looked at me, then went straight to the mirror.

"How do you like my hat?" she said.

She stood before the panel of looking-glass, conscious only of her hat, whose great feather-strands swung in a tide. Her bare shoulder glistened, and through the fine web of her chemise I could see all her body in warm silhouette, with golden reflections under the breasts and arms. The light ran in silver up her lifted arms, and the gold shadow stirred as she arranged her hat.

"How do you like my hat?" she repeated.

Then, as I did not answer, she turned to look at me. I was still lying on the bed. She must have seen that I had looked at her, instead of at her hat, for a quick darkness and a frown came into her eyes, cleared instantly, as she asked, in a slightly hard tone:

"Don't you like it?"

"It's rather splendid," I answered. "Where did it come from?"

"From Berlin this morning—or last evening," she replied.

"It's a bit huge," I ventured.

She drew herself up.

"Indeed not!" she said, turning to the mirror.

I got up, dropped off my dressing-gown, put a silk hat quite correctly on my head, and then, naked save for a hat and a pair of gloves, I went forward to her.

"How do you like my hat?" I asked her.

She looked at me and went off into a fit of laughter. She dropped her hat on to a chair, and sank on to the bed, shaking with laughter. Every now and then she lifted her head, gave one look from her dark eyes, then buried her face in the pillows. I stood before her clad in my hat, feeling a good bit of a fool. She peeped up again.

"You are lovely, you are lovely!" she cried.

With a grave and dignified movement I prepared to remove the hat, saying:

"And even then, I lack high-laced boots and one stocking."

But she flew at me, kept the hat on my head, and kissed me.

"Don't take it off," she implored. "I love you for it."

So I sat down gravely and unembarrassed on the bed.

"But don't you like my hat?" I said in injured tones. "I bought it in London last month."

She looked up at me comically, and went into peals of laughter.

"Think," she cried, "if all those Englishmen in Piccadilly went like that!"

That amused even me.

At last I assured her her hat was adorable, and, much to my relief, I got rid of my silk and into a dressing-gown.

"You *will* cover yourself up," she said reproachfully. "And you look so nice with nothing on—but a hat."

"It's that old Apple I can't digest," I said.

She was quite happy in her shift and her high boots. I lay looking at her beautiful legs.

"How many more men have you done that to?" I asked.

"What?" she answered.

"Gone into their bedrooms clad in a wisp of mist, trying a new hat on?"

She leaned over to me and kissed me.

"Not many," she said. "I've not been *quite* so familiar before, I don't think."

"I suppose you've forgotten," said I. "However, it doesn't matter." Perhaps the slight bitterness in my voice touched her. She said almost indignantly:

"Do you think I want to flatter you and make you believe you are the first that ever I really—*really*——"

"I don't know," I replied. "Neither you nor I are so easily deluded."

She looked at me peculiarly and steadily.

"I know all the time," said I, "that I am *pro tem.*, and that I shan't even last as long as most."

"You are sorry for yourself?" she mocked.

I shrugged my shoulders, looking into her eyes. She caused me a good deal of agony, but I didn't give in to her.

"I shan't commit suicide," I replied.

"*On est mort pour si longtemps,*" she said, suddenly dancing on the bed. I loved her. She had the courage to live, almost joyously.

"When you think back over your affairs—they are numerous, though you are only thirty-one——"

"Not numerous—only several—and you *do* underline the thirty-one——," she laughed.

"But how do you feel, when you think of them?" I asked.

She knitted her eyebrows quaintly, and there was a shadow, more puzzled than anything, on her face.

"There is something nice in all of them," she said. "Men are really fearfully good," she sighed.

"If only they weren't all pocket-editions," I mocked.

She laughed, then began drawing the silk cord through the lace of her chemise, pensively. The round caps of her shoulders gleamed like old ivory: there was a faint brown stain towards the arm-pit.

"No," she said, suddenly lifting her head and looking me calmly into the eyes, "I have nothing to be ashamed of—that is—no, I have nothing to be ashamed of!"

"I believe you," I said. "And I don't suppose you've done anything that even *I* shouldn't be able to swallow—have you?"

I felt rather plaintive with my question. She looked at me and shrugged her shoulders.

"I know you haven't," I preached. "All your affairs have been rather decent. They've meant more to the men than they have to you."

The shadows of her breasts, fine globes, shone warm through the linen veil. She was thinking.

"Shall I tell you," she asked, "one thing I did?"

"If you like," I answered. "But let me get you a wrap." I kissed her shoulder. It had the same fine, delicious coldness of ivory.

"No—yes, you may," she replied.

I brought her a Chinese thing of black silk with gorgeous embroidered dragons, green as flame, writhing upon it.

"How white against that black silk you are," I said, kissing the half globe of her breast, through the linen.

"Lie there," she commanded me. She sat in the middle of the bed, whilst I lay looking at her. She picked up the black silk tassel of my dressing-gown and began flattening it out like a daisy.

"Gretchen!" I said.

"'Marguerite with one petal'," she answered in French, laughing. "I am ashamed of it, so you must be nice with me——"

"Have a cigarette!" I said.

She puffed wistfully for a few moments.

"You've got to hear it," she said.

"Go on!"

"I was staying in Dresden in quite a grand hotel; which I rather enjoy: ringing bells, dressing three times a day, feeling half a great lady, half a cocotte. Don't be cross with me for saying it: look at me! The man was at a garrison a little way off. I'd have married him if I could——"

She shrugged her brown, handsome shoulders, and puffed out a plume of smoke.

"It began to bore me after three days. I was always alone, looking at shops alone, going to the opera alone—where the beastly men got behind their wives' backs to look at me. In the end I got cross with my poor man, though of course it wasn't his fault, that he couldn't come."

She gave a little laugh as she took a draw at her cigarette.

"The fourth morning I came downstairs—I was feeling fearfully good-looking and proud of myself. I know I had a sort of *café au lait* coat and skirt, very pale—and its fit was a *joy!*"

After a pause, she continued: "And a big black hat with a cloud of white ospreys. I nearly jumped when a man almost ran into me. O jeh! it was a young officer, just bursting with life, a splendid creature: the German aristocrat at his best. He wasn't over tall, in his dark blue uniform, but simply firm with life. An electric shock went through me, it slipped down me like fire, when I looked into his eyes. O jeh! they just flamed with consciousness of me—and they were just the same colour as the soft-blue revers of his uniform. He looked at me—ha!—and then, he bowed, the sort of bow a woman enjoys like a caress.

"'*Verzeihung, gnädiges Fräulein!*'

"I just inclined my head, and we went our ways. It felt as if something mechanical shifted us, not our wills.

"I was restless that day, I could stay nowhere. Something stirred inside my veins. I was drinking tea on the Brühler Terasse, watching the people go by like a sort of mechanical procession, and the broad Elbe as a stiller background, when he stood before me, saluting, and taking a seat, half apologetically, half devil-may-care. I was not nearly so much surprised at him, as at the mechanical parading people. And I could see he thought me a cocotte——"

She looked thoughtfully across the room, the past roused dangerously in her dark eyes.

"But the game amused and excited me. He told me he had to go to a Court ball tonight—and then he said, in his nonchalant yet pleadingly passionate way:

"'And afterwards——?'

"'And afterwards——!' I repeated.

"'May I——?' he asked.

"Then I told him the number of my room.

"I dawdled to the hotel, and dressed for dinner, and talked to somebody sitting next to me, but I was an hour or two ahead, when he would come. I arranged my silver and brushes and things, and I had ordered a great bunch of lilies of the valley; they were in a black bowl. There were delicate pink silk curtains, and the carpet was a cold colour, nearly white, with a tawny pink and turquoise ravelled border, a Persian thing, I should imagine. I know I liked it. And didn't that room feel fresh, full of expectation, like myself!

"That last half-hour of waiting—so funny—I seemed to have no feeling, no consciousness. I lay in the dark, holding my nice pale blue gown of *crêpe de Chine* against my body for comfort. There was a fumble at the door, and I caught my breath! Quickly he came in, locked the door, and switched on all the lights. There he stood, the centre of everything, the light shining on his bright brown hair. He was holding something under his cloak. Now he came to me, and threw on me from out of his cloak a whole armful of red and pink roses. It was delicious! Some of them were cold, when they fell on me. He took off his cloak. I loved his figure in its blue uniform; and then, oh jeh! he picked me off the bed, the roses and all, and kissed me—*how* he kissed me!"

She paused at the recollection.

"I could feel his mouth through my thin gown. Then, he went still and intense. He pulled off my *saut-de-lit*, and looked at me. He held me away from him, his mouth parted with wonder, and yet, as if the gods would envy him—wonder and adoration and pride! I liked his worship. Then he laid me on the bed again, and covered me up gently, and put my roses on the other side of me, a heap just near my hair, on the pillow.

"Quite unashamed and not the least conscious of himself, he got out of his clothes. And he *was* adorable—so young, and rather spare, but with a *rich* body, that simply glowed with love of me. He stood looking at me, quite humbly; and I held out my hands to him.

"All that night we loved each other. There were crushed, crumpled little rose-leaves on him when he sat up, almost like crimson blood! Oh, and he was fierce, and at the same time, tender!"

Anita's lips trembled slightly, and she paused. Then, very slowly, she went on:

"When I woke in the morning he was gone, and just a few passionate words on his dancing-card with a gold crown, on the little table beside me, imploring me to see him again in the Brühler Terasse in the afternoon. But I took the morning express to Berlin——"

We both were still. The river rustled far off in the morning.

"And——?" I said.

"And I never saw him again."

We were both still. She put her arms round her bright knee, and caressed it, lovingly, rather plaintively, with her mouth. The brilliant green dragons on her wrap seemed to be snarling at me.

"And you regret him?" I said at length.

"No," she answered, scarcely heeding me. "I remember the way he unfastened his sword-belt and trappings from his loins, flung the whole with a jingle on the other bed——"

I was burning now with rage against Anita. Why should she love a man for the way he unbuckled his belt!

"With him," she mused, "everything felt so inevitable."

"Even your never seeing him again," I retorted.

"Yes!" she said, quietly.

Still musing, dreaming, she continued to caress her own knees.

"He said to me: 'We are like the two halves of a walnut'." And she laughed slightly. "He said some lovely things to me—'Tonight, you're an Answer'. And then: 'Whichever bit of you I touch seems to startle me afresh with joy'. And he said he should never forget the velvety feel of my skin.—Lots of beautiful things he told me."

Anita cast them over pathetically in her mind. I sat biting my finger with rage.

"—And I made him have roses in his hair. He sat so still and good while I trimmed him up, and was quite shy. He had a figure nearly like yours——"

Which compliment was a last insult to me.

"And he had a long gold chain, threaded with little emeralds, that he wound round and round my knees, binding me like a prisoner, never thinking."

"And you wish he had kept you prisoner," I said.

"No," she answered. "He couldn't!"

"I see! You just preserve him as the standard by which you measure the amount of satisfaction you get from the rest of us."

"Yes," she said, quietly.

Then I knew she was liking to make me furious.

"But I thought you were rather ashamed of the adventure?" I said.

"No," she answered, perversely.

She made me tired. One could never be on firm ground with her. Always, one was slipping and plunging on uncertainly. I lay still, watching the sunshine streaming white outside.

"What are you thinking?" she asked.

"The waiter will smile when we go down for coffee."

"No—tell me!"

"It is half past nine."

She fingered the string of her shift.

"What were you thinking?" she asked, very low.

"I was thinking, all you want, you get."

"In what way?"

"In love."

"And what do I want?"

"Sensation."

"Do I?"

"Yes."

She sat with her head drooped down.

"Have a cigarette," I said. "And are you going to that place for sleighing today?"

"Why do you say I only want sensation?" she asked quietly.

"Because it's all you'll take from a man.—You *won't* have a cigarette?"

"No thanks—and what else could I take——?"

I shrugged my shoulders.

"Nothing, I suppose," I replied.

Still she picked pensively at her chemise string.

"Up to now, you've missed nothing—you haven't felt the lack of anything—in love," I said.

She waited awhile.

"Oh yes, I have," she said gravely.

Hearing her say it, my heart stood still.

The Thimble

She had not seen her husband for ten months, not since her fortnight's honeymoon with him, and his departure for France. Then, in those excited days of the early war, he was her comrade, her counterpart in a sort of Bacchic revel before death. Now all that was shut off from her mind, as by a great rent in her life.

Since then, since the honeymoon, she had lived and died and come to life again. There had been his departure to the front. She had loved him then.

"If you want to love your husband," she had said to her friends, with splendid recklessness, "you should see him in khaki." And she had really loved him, he was so handsome in uniform, well-built, yet with a sort of reserve and remoteness that suited the neutral khaki perfectly.

Before, as a barrister with nothing to do, he had been slack and unconvincing, a sort of hanger-on, and she had never come to the point of marrying him. For one thing they neither of them had enough money.

Then came the great shock of the war, his coming to her in a new light, as lieutenant in the artillery. And she had been carried away by his perfect calm manliness and significance, now he was a soldier. He seemed to have gained a fascinating importance that made her seem quite unimportant. It was she who was insignificant and subservient, he who was dignified, with a sort of indifferent lordliness.

So she had married him, all considerations flung to the wind, and had known the bewildering experience of their fortnight's honeymoon, before he left her for the front.

And she had never got over the bewilderment. She had, since then, never thought at all, she seemed to have rushed on in a storm of activity and sensation. There was a home to make, and no money to make it with: none to speak of. So, with the swift, business-like aptitude of a startled woman, she had found a small flat in Mayfair, had attended sales and bought suitable furniture, had made the place complete and perfect. She was satisfied. It was small and insignificant, but it was a complete unity.

Then she had had a certain amount of war-work to do, and she had kept up all her social activities. She had not had a moment which was not urgently occupied.

All the while came his letters from France, and she was writing her replies. They both sent a good deal of news to each other, they both expressed their mutual passion.

Then suddenly, amid all this activity, she fell ill with pneumonia and everything lapsed into delirium. And whilst she was ill, he was wounded, his jaw smashed and his face cut up by the bursting of a shell. So they were both laid by.

Now, they were both better, and she was waiting to see him. Since she had been ill, whilst she had lain or sat in her room in the castle in Scotland, she had thought, thought very much. For she was a woman who was always trying to grasp the whole of her context, always trying to make a complete thing of her own life.

Her illness lay between her and her previous life like a dark night, like a great separation. She looked back, she remembered all she had done, and she was bewildered, she had no key to the puzzle. Suddenly she realized that she knew nothing of this man she had married, he knew nothing of her. What she had of him, vividly, was the visual image. She could *see* him, the whole of him, in her mind's eye. She could remember him with peculiar distinctness, as if the whole of his body were lit up by an intense light, and the image fixed on her mind.

But he was an impression, only a vivid impression. What her own impression was, she knew most vividly. But what *he* was *himself*: the very thought startled her, it was like looking into a perilous darkness. All that she knew of him was her own affair, purely personal to her, a subjective impression. But there must be a *man*, another being, somewhere in the darkness which she had never broached.

The thought frightened her exceedingly, and her soul, weak from illness, seemed to weep. Here was a new peril, a new terror. And she seemed to have no hope.

She could scarcely bear to think of him as she knew him. She could scarcely bear to conjure up that vivid image of him which remained from the days of her honeymoon. It was something false, it was something which had only to do with herself. The man himself was something quite other, something in the dark, something she dreaded, whose coming she dreaded, as if it were a mitigation of her own being, something set over against her, something that would annul her own image of herself.

Nervously she twisted her long white fingers. She was a beautiful woman, tall and loose and rather thin, with swinging limbs, one for whom the modern fashions were perfect. Her skin was pure and clear, like a Christmas rose, her hair was fair and heavy. She had large, slow, unswerving eyes, that sometimes looked blue and open with a childish candor, sometimes greenish and intent with thought, sometimes hard, sea-like, cruel, sometimes grey and pathetic.

Now she sat in her own room, in the flat in Mayfair, and he was coming to see her. She was well again: just well enough to see him. But she was tired as she sat in the chair whilst her maid arranged her heavy, fair hair.

She knew she was a beauty, she knew it was expected of her that she should create an impression of modern beauty. And it pleased her, it made her soul rather hard and proud: but also, at the bottom, it bored her. Still, she would have her hair built high, in the fashionable mode, she would have it modelled to the whole form of her head, her figure. She lifted her eyes to look. They were slow, greenish, and cold like the sea at this moment, because she was so perplexed, so heavy with trying, all alone, always quite coldly alone, to understand, to understand and to adjust herself. It never occurred to her to expect anything of the other person: she was utterly self-responsible.

"No," she said to her maid, in her slow, laconic, plangent voice, "don't let it swell out over the ears, lift it straight up, then twist it under—like that—so it goes clean from the side of the face. Do you see?"

"Yes, my lady."

And the maid went on with the hair-dressing, and she with her slow, cold musing.

She was getting dressed now to see her bridegroom. The phrase, with its association in all the romances of the world, made her snigger involuntarily to herself. She was still like a schoolgirl, always seeing herself in her part. She got curious satisfaction from it, too. But also she was always humorously ironical when she found herself in these romantic situations. If brigands and robbers had carried her off, she would have played up to the event perfectly. In life, however, there was always a certain painful, laborious heaviness, a weight of self-responsibility. The event never carried her along, a helpless protagonist. She was always responsible, in whatever situation.

Now, this morning, her husband was coming to see her, and she was dressing to receive him. She felt heavy and inert as stone, yet inwardly trembling convulsively. The known man, he did not affect her. Heavy and inert in her soul, yet amused, she would play her part in his reception. But the unknown man, what was he? Her dark, unknown soul trembled apprehensively.

At any rate he would be different. She shuddered. The vision she had of him, of the good-looking, lean, slightly tanned, attractive man, ordinary and yet with odd streaks of understanding that made her ponder, this she must put away. They said his face was rather horribly cut up. She shivered. How she hated it, coldly hated and loathed it, the thought of disfigurement. Her fingers trembled, she rose to go downstairs. If he came he must not come into her bedroom.

So, in her fashionable but inexpensive black silk dress, wearing her jewels, her string of opals, her big, ruby brooch, she went downstairs. She knew how to walk, how to hold her body according to the mode. She did it almost instinctively, so deep was her consciousness of the impression her own appearance must create.

Entering the small drawing-room she lifted her eyes slowly and looked at herself: a tall, loose woman in black, with fair hair raised up, and with slow, greenish, cold eyes looking into the mirror. She turned away with a cold, pungent sort of satisfaction. She was aware also of the traces of weariness and illness and age, in her face. She was twenty-seven years old.

So she sat on the little sofa by the fire. The room she had made was satisfactory to her, with its neutral, brown-grey walls, its deep brown, plain, velvety carpet, and the old furniture done in worn rose brocade, which she had bought from Countess Ambersyth's sale. She looked at her own large feet, upon the rose-red Persian rug.

Then nervously, yet quite calm, almost static, she sat still to wait. It was one of the moments of deepest suffering and suspense which she had ever known. She did not want to think of his disfigurement, she did not want to have any preconception of it. Let it come upon her. And the man, the unknown strange man who was coming now to take up his position over against her soul, her soul so naked and exposed from illness, the man to whose access her soul was to be delivered up! She could not bear it. Her face set pale, she began to lose her consciousness.

Then something whispered in her:

"If I am like this, I shall be quite impervious to him, quite oblivious of anything but the surface of him." And an anxious sort of hope sent her hands down onto the sofa at her side, pressed upon the worn brocade, spread flat. And she remained in suspense.

But could she bear it, could she bear it? She was weak and ill in a sort of after-death. Now what was this that she must confront, this other being? Her hands began to move slowly backwards and forwards on the sofa bed, slowly, as if the friction of the silk gave her some ease.

She was unaware of what she was doing. She was always so calm, so self-contained, so static; she was much too stoically well-bred to allow these outward nervous agitations. But now she sat still in suspense in the silent drawing-room, where the fire flickered over the dark brown carpet and over the pale rose furniture and over the pale face and the black dress and the white, sliding hands of the woman, and her hands slid backwards and forwards, backwards and forwards like a pleading, a hope, a tension of madness.

Her right hand came to the end of the sofa and pressed a little into the crack, the meeting between the arm and the sofa bed. Her long white fingers pressed into the fissure, pressed and entered rhythmically, pressed and pressed further and further into the tight depths of the fissure, between the silken firm upholstery of the old sofa, whilst her mind was in a trance of suspense, and the fire-light flickered on the yellow chrysanthemums that stood in a jar in the window.

The working, slow, intent fingers pressed deeper and deeper in the fissure of the sofa, pressed and worked their way intently, to the bottom. It was the bottom. They were there, they made sure. Making sure, they worked all along, very gradually, along the tight depth of the fissure.

Then they touched a little extraneous object, and a consciousness awoke in the woman's mind. Was it something? She touched again. It was something hard and rough. The fingers began to ply upon it. How firmly it was embedded in the depths of the sofa-crack. It had a thin rim, like a ring, but it was not a ring. The fingers worked more insistently. What was this little hard object?

The fingers pressed determinedly, they moved the little object. They began to work it up to the light. It was coming, there was success. The woman's heart relaxed from its tension, now her aim was being achieved. Her long, strong, white fingers brought out the little find.

It was a thimble set with brilliants; it was an old, rather heavy thimble of tarnished gold, set round the base with little diamonds or rubies. Perhaps it was not gold, perhaps they were only paste.

She put it on her sewing finger. The brilliants sparkled in the fire-light. She was pleased. It was a vulgar thing, a gold thimble with ordinary pin-head dents, and a belt of jewels around the base. It was large too, big enough for her. It must have been some woman's embroidery thimble, some bygone woman's, perhaps some Lady Ambersyth's. At any rate, it belonged to the days when women did stitching as a usual thing. But it was heavy, it would make one's hand ache.

She began to rub the gold with her handkerchief. There was an engraved monogram, an Earl's, and then Z, Z, and a date, 15 Oct., 1801. She was very pleased, trembling with the thought of the old romance. What did Z. stand for? She thought of her acquaintances, and could only think of Zouche. But he was not an Earl. Who would give the gift of a gold thimble set with jewels, in the year 1801? Perhaps it was a man come home from the wars: there were wars then.

The maid noiselessly opened the door and saw her mistress sitting in the soft light of the winter day, polishing something with her handkerchief.

"Mr. Hepburn has come, my lady."

"Has he!" answered the laconic, slightly wounded voice of the woman.

She collected herself and rose. Her husband was coming through the doorway, past the maid. He came without hat or coat or gloves, like an inmate of the house. He was an inmate of the house.

"How do you do?" she said, with stoic, plangent helplessness. And she held out her hand.

"How are *you*?" he replied, rather mumbling, with a sort of muffled voice.

"All right now, thanks," and she sat down again, her heart beating violently. She had not yet looked at his face. The muffled voice terrified her so much. It mumbled rather mouthlessly.

Abstractedly, she put the thimble on her middle finger, and continued to rub it with her handkerchief. The man sat in silence opposite, in an arm-chair. She was aware of his khaki trousers and his brown shoes. But she was intent on burnishing the thimble.

Her mind was in a trance, but as if she were on the point of waking, for the first time in her life, waking up.

"What are you doing? What have you got?" asked the mumbling, muffled voice. A pang went through her. She looked up at the mouth that produced the sound. It was broken in, the bottom teeth all gone, the side of the chin battered small, whilst a deep seam, a deep, horrible groove ran right into the middle of the cheek. But the mouth was the worst, sunk in at the bottom, with half the lip cut away.

"It is treasure-trove," answered the plangent, cold-sounding voice. And she held out the thimble.

He reached to take it. His hand was white, and it trembled. His nerves were broken He took the thimble between his fingers.

She sat obsessed, as if his disfigurement were photographed upon her mind, as if she were some sensitive medium to which the thing had been transferred. There it was, her whole consciousness was photographed into an image of his disfigurement, the dreadful sunken mouth that was not a mouth, which mumbled in talking to her, in a disfigurement of speech.

It was all accident, accident had taken possession of her very being. All she was, was purely accidental. It was like a sleep, a thin, taut, over-filming sleep in which the wakefulness struggles like a thing as yet un-born. She was sick in the thin, transparent membrane of her sleep, her overlying dream-consciousness, something actual but too unreal.

"How treasure-trove?" he mumbled. She could not understand.

She felt his moment's hesitation before he tried again, and a hot pain pierced through her, the pain of his maimed, crippled effort.

"Treasure-trove, you said," he repeated, with a sickening struggle to speak distinctly.

Her mind hovered, then grasped, then caught the threads of the conversation.

"I found it," she said. Her voice was clear and vibrating as bronze, but cold. "I found it just before you came in."

There was a silence. She was aware of the purely accidental condition of her whole being. She was framed and constructed of accident, accidental association. It was like being made up of dream-stuff, without sequence or adherence to any plan or purpose. Yet within the imprisoning film of the dream was herself, struggling unborn, struggling to come to life.

It was difficult to break the inert silence that had succeeded between them. She was afraid it would go on forever. With a strange, convulsive struggle, she broke into communication with him.

"I found it here, in the sofa," she said, and she lifted her eyes for the first time to him.

His forehead was white, and his hair brushed smooth, like a sick man's. And his eyes were like the eyes of a child that has been ill, blue and abstract, as if they only listened from a long way off, and did not see any more. So far-off he looked, like a child that belongs almost more to death than to life. And her soul divined that he was waiting vaguely where the dark and the light divide, whether he should come in to life, or hesitate, and pass back.

She lowered her eyelids, and for a second she sat erect like a mask, with closed eyes, whilst a spasm of pure unconsciousness passed over her. It departed again, and she opened her eyes. She was awake.

She looked at him. His eyes were still abstract and without answer, changing only to the dream-psychology of his being. She contracted as if she were cold and afraid. They lit up now with a superficial over-flicker of interest.

"Did you really? Why, how did it come there?"

It was the same voice, the same stupid interest in accidental things, the same man as before. Only the enunciation of the words was all mumbled and muffled, as if the speech itself were disintegrating.

Her heart shrank, to close again like an over-sensitive new-born thing, that is not yet strong enough in its own being. Yet once more she lifted her eyes, and looked at him.

He was flickering with his old, easily roused, spurious interest in the accidentals of life. The film of separateness seemed to be coming over her. Yet his white forehead was somewhat deathly, with its smoothly brushed hair. He was like one dead. He was within the realm of death. His over-flicker of interest was only extraneous.

"I suppose it had got pushed down by accident," she said, answering from her mechanical mind.

But her eyes were watching him who was dead, who was there like Lazarus before her, as yet unrisen.

"How did it happen?" she said, and her voice was changed, pene-trating with sadness and approach. He knew what she meant.

"Well, you see I was knocked clean senseless, and that was all I knew for three days. But it seems that it was a shell fired by one of our own fellows, and it hit me because it was faultily made."

Her face was very still as she watched.

"And how did you feel when you came round?"

"I felt pretty bad, as you can imagine; there was a crack on the skull as well as this on the jaw."

"Did you think you were going to die?"

There was a long pause, whilst the man laughed self-consciously. But he laughed only with the upper part of his face: the maimed part re-mained still. And though the eyes seemed to laugh, just as of old, yet underneath them was a black, challenging darkness. She waited whilst this superficial smile of reserve passed away.

Then came the mumbling speech, simple, in confession.

"Yes, I lay and looked at it."

The darkness of his eyes was now watching her, her soul was exposed and new-born. The triviality was gone, the dream-psychology, the self-dependence. They were naked and new-born in soul, and depended on each other.

It was on the tip of her tongue to say: "And why didn't you die?" But instead, her soul, weak and new-born, looked helplessly at him.

"I couldn't while you were alive," he said.

"What?"

"Die."

She seemed to pass away into unconsciousness. Then, as she came to, she said, as if in protest:

"What difference should *I* make to you! You can't live off me."

He was watching her with unlighted, sightless eyes. There was a long silence. She was thinking, it was not her consciousness of him which had kept *her* alive. It was her own will.

"What did you hope for, from me?" she asked.

His eyes darkened, his face seemed very white, he really looked like a dead man as he sat silent and with open, sightless eyes. Between his slightly-trembling fingers was balanced the thimble, that sparkled sometimes in the firelight. Watching him, a darkness seemed to come over her. She could not see, he was only a presence near her in the dark.

"We are both of us helpless," she said, into the silence.

"Helpless for what?" answered his sightless voice.

"To live," she said.

They seemed to be talking to each other's souls, their eyes and minds were sightless.

"We are helpless to live," he repeated.

"Yes," she said.

There was still a silence.

"I know," he said, "we are helpless to live. I knew that when I came round."

"I am as helpless as you are," she said.

"Yes," came his slow, half-articulate voice. "I know that. You're as helpless as I am."

"Well then?"

"Well then, we are helpless. We are as helpless as babies," he said.

"And how do you like being a helpless baby," came the ironic voice.

"And how do *you* like being a helpless baby?" he replied.

There was a long pause. Then she laughed brokenly.

"I don't know," she said. "A helpless baby can't know whether it likes being a helpless baby."

"That's just the same. But I feel *hope*, don't you?"

Again there was an unwilling pause on her part.

"Hope of what?"

"If I am a helpless baby now, that I shall grow into a man."

She gave a slight, amused laugh.

"And I ought to hope that I shall grow into a woman," she said.

"Yes, of course."

"Then what am I now?" she asked, humorously.

"Now, you're a helpless baby, as you said."

It piqued her slightly. Then again, she knew it was true.

"And what was I before—when I married you?" she asked, challenging.

"Why, then—I don't know what you were. I've had my head cracked and some dark let in, since then. So I don't know what you were, because it's all gone, don't you see."

"I see."

There was a pause. She became aware of the room about her, of the fire burning low and red.

"And what are we doing together?" she said.

"We're going to love each other," he said

"Didn't we love each other before?" challenged her voice.

"No, we couldn't. We weren't born."

"Neither were we dead," she answered.

He seemed struck.

"Are we dead now?" he asked in fear.

"Yes, we are."

There was a suspense of anguish, it was so true.

"Then we must be born again," he said.

"Must we?" said her deliberate, laconic voice.

"Yes, we must—otherwise—" He did not finish.

"And do you think we've got the power to come to life again, now we're dead?" she asked.

"I think we have," he said.

There was a long pause.

"Resurrection?" she said, almost as if mocking. They looked slowly and darkly into each other's eyes. He rose unthinking, went over and touched her hand.

"'Touch me not, for I am not yet ascended unto the Father,'" she quoted, in her level, cold-sounding voice.

"No," he answered; "it takes time."

The incongruous plainness of his statement made her jerk with laughter. At the same instant her face contracted and she said in a loud voice, as if her soul was being torn from her:

"Am I going to love you?"

Again he stretched foward and touched her hand, with the tips of his fingers. And the touch lay still, completed there.

Then at length he noticed that the thimble was stuck on his little finger. In the same instant she also looked at it.

"I want to throw it away," he said.

Again she gave a little jerk of laughter.

He rose, went to the window, and raised the sash. Then, suddenly with a strong movement of the arm and shoulder, he threw the thimble out into the murky street. It bounded on the pavement opposite. Then a taxi-cab went by, and he could not see it any more.

The Mortal Coil

I

She stood motionless in the middle of the room, something tense in
her reckless bearing. Her gown of reddish stuff fell silkily about her feet;
she looked tall and splendid in the candlelight. Her dark-blond hair was
gathered loosely in a fold on top of her head, her young, blossom-fresh
face was lifted. From her throat to her feet she was clothed in the ele-
gantly-made dress of silky red stuff, the colour of red earth. She looked
complete and lovely, only love could make her such a strange, complete
blossom. Her cloak and hat were thrown across a table just in front of
her.

Quite alone, abstracted, she stood there arrested in a conflict of emotions. Her hand, down against her skirt, worked irritably, the ball of the
thumb rubbing, rubbing across the tips of the fingers. There was a slight
tension between her lifted brows.

About her the room glowed softly, reflecting the candlelight from
its whitewashed walls, and from the great, bowed, whitewashed ceiling curving down on either side, so that both the far walls were low.
Against one, on one side, was a single bed, opened for the night, the
white over-bolster piled back. Not far from this was the iron stove. Near
the window closest to the bed was a table with writing materials, and a
handsome cactus-plant with clear scarlet blossoms threw its bizarre
shadow on the wall. There was another table near the second window,
and opposite was the door on which hung a military cloak. Along the
far wall, were guns and fishing-tackle, and some clothes too, hung on
pegs—all men's clothes, all military. It was evidently the room of a
man, probably a young lieutenant.

The girl, in her pure red dress that fell about her feet, so that she
looked a woman, not a girl, at last broke from her abstraction and went
aimlessly to the writing-table. Her mouth was closed down stubbornly,
perhaps in anger, perhaps in pain. She picked up a large seal made of
agate, looked at the ingraven coat of arms, then stood rubbing her
finger across the cut-out stone, time after time. At last she put the seal
down, and looked at the other things—a beautiful old beer-mug used

as a tobacco-jar, a silver box like an urn, old and of exquisite shape, a bowl of sealing wax. She fingered the pieces of wax. This, the dark-green, had sealed her last letter. Ah, well! She carelessly turned over the blotting book, which again had his arms stamped on the cover. Then she went away to the window. There, in the window-recess, she stood and looked out. She opened the casement and took a deep breath of the cold night air. Ah, it was good! Far below was the street, a vague golden milky way beneath her, its tiny black figures moving and cross-ing and re-crossing with marionette, insect-like intentness. A small horse-car rumbled along the lines, so belittled, it was an absurdity. So much for the world! . . . he did not come.

She looked overhead. The stars were white and flashing, they looked nearer than the street, more kin to her, more real. She stood pressing her breast on her arms, her face lifted to the stars, in the long, an-guished suspense of waiting. Noises came up small from the street, as from some insect-world. But the great stars overhead struck white and invincible, infallible. Her heart felt cold like the stars.

At last she started. There was a noisy knocking at the door, and a female voice calling:

"Anybody there?"

"Come in," replied the girl.

She turned round, shrinking from this intrusion, unable to bear it, after the flashing stars.

There entered a thin, handsome dark girl dressed in an extravagantly-made gown of dark purple silk and dark blue velvet. She was followed by a small swarthy, inconspicuous lieutenant in pale-blue uniform.

"Ah *you*! . . . alone?" cried Teresa, the newcomer, advancing into the room. "Where's the Fritz, then?"

The girl in red raised her shoulders in a shrug, and turned her face aside, but did not speak.

"Not here! You don't know where he is? Ach, the dummy, the lout!" Teresa swung round on her companion.

"Where is he?" she demanded.

He also lifted his shoulders in a shrug.

"He said he was coming in half an hour," the young lieutenant replied.

"Ha!—half an hour! Looks like it! How long is that ago—two hours?"

Again the young man only shrugged. He had beautiful black eye-lashes, and steady eyes. He stood rather deprecatingly, whilst his girl, golden like a young panther, hung over him.

"One knows where he is," said Teresa, going and sitting on the opened bed. A dangerous contraction came between the brows of Marta, the girl in red, at this act.

"Wine, Women and Cards!" said Teresa, in her loud voice. "But they prefer the women on the cards.

> 'My love he has four Queenies,
> Four Queenies has my lo-o-ove,' "

she sang. Then she broke off, and turned to Podewils. "Was he winning when you left him, Karl?"

Again the young baron raised his shoulders.

"Tant pis que mal," he replied, cryptically.

"Ah, *you*!" cried Teresa, "with your *tant pis que mal*! Are *you* tant pis que mal?" She laughed her deep, strange laugh. "Well," she added, "he'll be coming in with a fortune for you, Marta—"

There was a vague, unhappy silence.

"I know his fortunes," said Marta.

"Yes," said Teresa, in sudden sober irony, "he's a horse-shoe round your neck, is that young jockey.—But what are you going to do, Matzen dearest? You're not going to wait for him any longer?—Don't dream of it! The idea, waiting for that young gentleman as if you were married to him!—Put your hat on, dearest, and come along with us . . . Where are we going, Karl, you pillar of salt?—Eh?—Geier's?—To Geier's, Marta, my dear. Come, quick, up—you've been martyred enough, Marta, my martyr—haw!—haw!!—put your hat on. Up—away!"

Teresa sprang up like an explosion, anxious to be off.

"No, I'll wait for him," said Marta, sullenly.

"Don't be such a fool!" cried Teresa, in her deep voice. "Wait for him! *I'd* give him wait for him. Catch this little bird waiting." She lifted her hand and blew a little puff across the fingers. "Choo-fly!" she sang, as if a bird had just flown.

The young lieutenant stood silent with smiling dark eyes. Teresa was quick, and golden as a panther.

"No, but really, Marta, you're not going to wait any more—really! It's stupid for you to play Gretchen—your eyes are much too green. Put your hat on, there's a darling."

"No," said Marta, her flower-like face strangely stubborn. "I'll wait for him. He'll have to come some time."

There was a moment's uneasy pause.

"Well," said Teresa, holding her shoulders for her cloak, "so long as you don't wait as long as Lenora-fuhr-ums-Morgenrot—! Adieu, my dear, God be with you."

The young lieutenant bowed a solicitous bow, and the two went out, leaving the girl in red once more alone.

She went to the writing-table, and on a sheet of paper began writing her name in stiff Gothic characters, time after time:

Marta Hohenest

Marta Hohenest

Marta Hohenest.

The vague sounds from the street below continued. The wind was cold. She rose and shut the window. Then she sat down again.

At last the door opened, and a young officer entered. He was buttoned up in a dark-blue great-coat, with large silver buttons going down on either side of the breast. He entered quickly, glancing over the room, at Marta, as she sat with her back to him. She was marking with a pencil on paper. He closed the door. Then with fine beautiful movements he divested himself of his coat and went to hang it up. How well Marta knew the sound of his movements, the quick light step! But she continued mechanically making crosses on the paper, her head bent forward between the candles, so that her hair made fine threads and mist of light, very beautiful. He saw this, and it touched him. But he could not afford to be touched any further.

"You have been waiting?" he said formally. The insulting futile question! She made no sign, as if she had not heard. He was absorbed in the tragedy of himself, and hardly heeded her.

He was a slim, good-looking youth, clear-cut and delicate in mould. His features now were pale, there was something evasive in his dilated, vibrating eyes. He was barely conscious of the girl, intoxicated with his own desperation, that held him mindless and distant.

To her, the atmosphere of the room was almost unbreathable, since he had come in. She felt terribly bound, walled up. She rose with a sudden movement that tore his nerves. She looked to him tall and bright and dangerous, as she faced round on him.

"Have you come back with a fortune?" she cried, in mockery, her eyes full of dangerous light.

He was unfastening his belt, to change his tunic. She watched him up and down, all the time. He could not answer, his lips seemed dumb. Besides, silence was his strength.

"Have you come back with a fortune?" she repeated, in her strong, clear voice of mockery.

"No," he said, suddenly turning. "Let it please you that—that I've come back at all."

He spoke desperately, and tailed off into silence. He was a man doomed. She looked at him: he was insignificant in his doom. She turned in ridicule. And yet she was afraid; she loved him.

He had stood long enough exposed, in his helplessness. With difficulty he took a few steps, went and sat down at the writing-table. He looked to her like a dog with its tail between its legs.

He saw the paper, where her name was repeatedly written. She must find great satisfaction in her own name, he thought vaguely. Then he picked up the seal and kept twisting it round in his fingers, doing some little trick. And continually the seal fell on to the table with a sudden rattle that made Marta stiffen cruelly. He was quite oblivious of her.

She stood watching as he sat bent forward in his stupefaction. The fine cloth of his uniform showed the moulding of his back. And something tortured her as she saw him, till she could hardly bear it: the desire of his finely-shaped body, the stupefaction and the abjectness of him now, his immersion in the tragedy of himself, his being unaware of her. All her will seemed to grip him, to bruise some manly nonchalance and attention out of him.

"I suppose you're in a fury with me, for being late?" he said, with impotent irony in his voice. Her fury over trifles, when he was lost in calamity! How great was his real misery, how trivial her small offendedness!

Something in his tone burned her, and made her soul go cold.

"I'm not exactly pleased," she said coldly, turning away to a window.

Still he sat bent over the table, twisting something with his fingers. She glanced round on him. How nervy he was! He had beautiful hands, and the big topaz signet-ring on his finger made yellow lights. Ah, if only his hands were really dare-devil and reckless! They always seemed so guilty, so cowardly.

"I'm done for now," he said suddenly, as if to himself, tilting back his chair a little. In all his physical movement he was so fine and poised, so sensitive! Oh, and it attracted her so much!

"Why?" she said, carelessly.

An anger burned in him. She was so flippant. If he were going to be shot, she would not be moved more than about half a pound of sweets.

"Why!" he repeated laconically. "The same unimportant reason as ever."

"Debts?" she cried, in contempt.

"Exactly."

Her soul burned in anger.

"What have you done now?—lost more money?"

"Three thousand marks."

She was silent in deep wrath.

"More fool you!" she said. Then, in her anger, she was silent for some minutes. "And so you're done for, for three thousand marks?" she exclaimed, jeering at him. "You go pretty cheap."

"Three thousand—and the rest," he said, keeping up a manly *sang froid*.

"And the rest!" she repeated in contempt. "And for three thousand —and the rest, your life is over!"

"My career," he corrected her.

"Oh," she mocked, "only your career! I thought it was a matter of life and death. Only your career? Oh, only that!"

His eyes grew furious under her mockery.

"My career is my life," he said.

"Oh, is it!—You're not a *man* then, you are only a career?"

"I am a gentleman."

"Oh, are you! How amusing! How very amusing, to be a gentleman and not a man!—I suppose that's what it means, to be a gentleman, to have no guts outside your career?"

"Outside my honour—none."

"And might I ask what *is* your honour?" She spoke in extreme irony.

"Yes, you may ask," he replied coolly. "But if you don't know without being told, I'm afraid I could never explain it."

"Oh, you couldn't! No, I believe you—you are incapable of explaining it, it wouldn't bear explaining." There was a long, tense pause. "So you've made too many debts, and you're afraid they'll kick you out of the army, therefore your honour is gone, is it?—And what then— what after that?"

She spoke in extreme irony. He winced again at her phrase "kick you out of the army." But he tilted his chair back with assumed nonchalance.

"I've made too many debts, and I *know* they'll kick me out of the army," he repeated, thrusting the thorn right home to the quick. "After that—I can shoot myself. Or I might even be a waiter in a restaurant —or possibly a clerk, with twenty-five shillings a week."

"Really!—All those alternatives!—Well, why not, why not be a waiter in the Germania? It might be awfully jolly."

"Why not?" he repeated ironically. "Because it wouldn't become me."

She looked at him, at his aristocratic fineness of physique, his extreme physical sensitiveness. And all her German worship for his old, proud family rose up in her. No, he could not be a waiter in the Germania: she could not bear it. He was too refined and beautiful a thing.

"Ha!" she cried suddenly. "It wouldn't come to that, either. If they kick you out of the army, you'll find somebody to get round—you're like a cat, you'll land on your feet."

But this was just what he was not. He was not like a cat. His self-mistrust was too deep. Ultimately he had no belief in himself, as a separate isolated being. He knew he was sufficiently clever, an aristo-crat, good-looking, the sensitive superior of most men. The trouble was, that apart from the social fabric he belonged to, he felt himself nothing, a cipher. He bitterly envied the common working-men for a certain manly aplomb, a grounded, almost stupid self-confidence he saw in them. Himself—he could lead such men through the gates of hell—for what did he care about danger or hurt to himself, whilst he was lead-ing? But—cut him off from all this, and what was he? A palpitating rag of meaningless human life.

But she, coming from the people, could not fully understand. And it was best to leave her in the dark. The free indomitable self-sufficient being which a man must be in his relation to a woman who loves him—this he could pretend. But he knew he was not it. He knew that the world of man from which he took his value was his mistress beyond any woman. He wished, secretly, cravingly, amost cravenly, in his heart, it was not so. But so it was.

Therefore, he heard her phrase "you're like a cat," with some bitter envy.

"Whom shall I get round?—some woman, who will marry me?" he said.

This was a way out. And it was almost the inevitable thing, for him. But he felt it the last ruin of his manhood, even he.

The speech hurt her mortally, worse than death. She would rather he died, because then her own love would not turn to ash.

"Get married, then, if you want to," she said, in a small broken voice.

"Naturally," he said.

There was a long silence, a foretaste of barren hopelessness.

"Why is it so terrible to you," she asked at length, "to come out of the army and trust to your own resources? Other men are strong enough."

"Other men are not me," he said.

Why would she torture him? She seemed to enjoy torturing him. The thought of his expulsion from the army was an agony to him, really worse than death. He saw himself in the despicable civilian clothes, engaged in some menial occupation. And he could not bear it. It was too heavy a cross.

Who was she to talk? She was herself, an actress, daughter of a tradesman. He was himself. How should one of them speak for the other? It was impossible. He loved her. He loved her far better than men usually loved their mistresses. He really cared.—And he was strangely proud of his love for her, as if it were a distinction to him . . . But there was a limit to her understanding. There was a point beyond which she had nothing to do with him, and she had better leave him alone. Here in this crisis, which was *his* crisis, his downfall, she should not presume to talk, because she did not understand.—But she loved to torture him, that was the truth.

"Why should it hurt you to work?" she reiterated.

He lifted his face, white and tortured, his grey eyes flaring with fear and hate.

"Work!" he cried. "What do you think I am worth?—Twenty-five shillings a week, if I am lucky."

His evident anguish penetrated her. She sat dumbfounded, looking at him with wide eyes. He was white with misery and fear; his hand, that lay loose on the table, was abandoned in nervous ignominy. Her mind filled with wonder, and with deep, cold dread. Did he really care so much? But did it *really* matter so much to him? When he said he was worth twenty-five shillings a week, he was like a man whose soul is pierced. He sat there, annihilated. She looked for him, and he was nothing then. She looked for the man, the free being that loved her. And he was not, he was gone, this blank figure remained. Something with a blanched face sat there in the chair, staring at nothing.

His amazement deepened with intolerable dread. It was as if the world had fallen away into chaos. Nothing remained. She seemed to grasp the air for foothold.

He sat staring in front of him, a dull numbness settled on his brain. He was watching the flame of the candle. And, in his detachment, he realized the flame was a swiftly travelling flood, flowing swiftly from the source of the wick through a white surge and on into the darkness above. It was like a fountain suddenly foaming out, then running on dark and smooth. Could one dam the flood? He took a piece of paper, and cut off the flame for a second.

The girl in red started at the pulse of the light. She seemed to come to, from some trance. She saw his face, clear now, attentive, abstract, absolved. He was quite absolved from his temporal self.

"It isn't true," she said, "is it? It's not so tragic, really?—It's only your pride is hurt, your silly little pride?" She was rather pleading.

He looked at her with clear steady eyes.

"My pride!" he said. "And isn't my pride *me*? What am I without my pride?"

"You are *yourself*," she said. "If they take your uniform off you, and turn you naked into the street, you are still *yourself*."

His eyes grew hot. Then he cried:

"What does it mean, *myself*! It means I put on ready-made civilian clothes and do some dirty drudging elsewhere: that is what *myself* amounts to."

She knitted her brows.

"But what you are *to me*—that naked self which you are to me—that is something, isn't it?—everything," she said.

"What is it, if it means nothing?" he said. "What is it, more than a pound of chocolate *dragées*?—It stands for nothing—unless as you say, a petty clerkship, at twenty-five shillings a week."

These were all wounds to her, very deep. She looked in wonder for a few moments.

"And what does it stand for now?" she said. "A magnificent second-lieutenant!"

He made a gesture of dismissal with his hand.

She looked at him from under lowered brows.

"And our love!" she said. "It means nothing to you, nothing at all?"

"To me as a menial clerk, what does it mean? What does love mean! Does it mean that a man shall be no more than a dirty rag in the world?—What worth do you think I have in love, if in life I am a wretched inky subordinate clerk?"

"What does it matter?"

"It matters everything."

There was silence for a time, then the anger flashed up in her.

"It doesn't matter to you what *I* feel, whether *I* care or not," she cried, her voice rising. "They'll take his little uniform with buttons off him, and he'll have to be a common little civilian, so all he can do is to shoot himself!—It doesn't matter that I'm there—"

He sat stubborn and silent. He thought her vulgar. And her raving did not alter the situation in the least.

"Don't you see what value you put on *me*, you clever little man?" she cried in fury. "I've loved you, loved you with all my soul, for two years—and you've lied, and said you loved me. And now, what do I get? He'll shoot himself, because his tuppenny vanity is wounded.—Ah, *fool*—!"

He lifted his head and looked at her. His face was fixed and superior.

"All of which," he said, "leaves the facts of the case quite untouched!"

She hated his cool little speeches.

"Then shoot yourself," she cried, "and you'll be worth *less* than twenty-five shillings a week!"

There was a fatal silence.

"*Then* there'll be no question of worth," he said.

"Ha!" she ejaculated in scorn.

She had finished. She had no more to say. At length, after they had both sat motionless and silent, separate, for some time, she rose and went across to her hat and cloak. He shrank in apprehension. Now, he could not bear her to go. He shrank as if he were being whipped. She put her hat on, roughly, then swung her warm plaid cloak over her shoulders. Her hat was of black glossy silk, with a sheeny heap of cocksfeathers, her plaid cloak was dark green and blue, it swung open above her clear harsh-red dress. How beautiful she was, like a fiery Madonna!

"Good-bye," she said, in her voice of mockery. "I'm going now."

He sat motionless, as if loaded with fetters. She hesitated, then moved towards the door.

Suddenly, with a spring like a cat, he was confronting her, his back to the door. His eyes were full and dilated, like a cat's, his face seemed to gleam at her. She quivered, as some subtle fluid ran through her nerves.

"Let me go," she said dumbly. "I've had enough." His eyes, with a wide, dark electric pupil, like a cat's, only watched her objectively. And again a wave of female submissiveness went over her.

"I want to go," she pleaded. "You know it's no good.—You know this is no good."

She stood humbly before him. A flexible little grin quivered round his mouth.

"You know you don't want me," she persisted. "You know you don't really want me.—You only do this to show your power over me—which is a mean trick."

But he did not answer, only his eyes narrowed in a sensual, cruel smile. She shrank, afraid, and yet she was fascinated.

"You won't go yet," he said.

She tried in vain to rouse her real opposition.

"I shall call out," she threatened. "I shall shame you before people."

His eyes narrowed again in the smile of vindictive, mocking indifference.

"Call then," he said.

And at the sound of his still, cat-like voice, an intoxication ran over her veins.

"I *will*," she said, looking defiantly into his eyes. But the smile in the dark, full, dilated pupils made her waver into submission again.

"Won't you let me go?" she pleaded sullenly.

Now the smile went openly over his face.

"Take your hat off," he said.

And with quick, light fingers he reached up and drew out the pins of her hat, unfastened the clasp of her cloak, and laid her things aside.

She sat down in a chair. Then she rose again, and went to the window. In the street below, the tiny figures were moving just the same. She opened the window, and leaned out, and wept.

He looked round at her in irritation as she stood in her long, clear-red dress in the window-recess, leaning out. She was exasperating.

"You will be cold," he said.

She paid no heed. He guessed, by some tension in her attitude, that she was crying. It irritated him exceedingly, like a madness. After a few minutes of suspense, he went across to her, and took her by the arm. His hand was subtle, soft in its touch, and yet rather cruel than gentle.

"Come away," he said. "Don't stand there in the air—come away."

He drew her slowly away to the bed, she sat down, and he beside her.

"What are you crying for?" he said in his strange, penetrating voice, that had a vibration of exultancy in it. But her tears only ran faster.

He kissed her face, that was soft, and fresh, and yet warm, wet with tears. He kissed her again, and again, in pleasure of the soft, wet saltness of her. She turned aside and wiped her face with her handkerchief, and blew her nose. He was disappointed—yet the way she blew her nose pleased him.

Suddenly she slid away to the floor, and hid her face in the side of the bed, weeping and crying loudly:

"You don't love me—Oh, you don't love me—I thought you did, and you let me go on thinking it—but you don't, no, you don't, and I can't bear it.—Oh, I can't bear it."

He sat and listened to the strange, animal sound of her crying. His eyes flickered with exultancy, his body seemed full and surcharged with power. But his brows were knitted in tension. He laid his hand softly on her head, softly touched her face, which was buried against the bed.

She suddenly rubbed her face against the sheets, and looked up once more.

"You've deceived me," she said, as she sat beside him.

"Have I? Then I've deceived myself." His body felt so charged with male vigour, he was almost laughing in his strength.

"Yes," she said enigmatically, fatally. She seemed absorbed in her thoughts. Then her face quivered again.

"And I loved you so much," she faltered, the tears rising. There was a clangor of delight in his heart.

"I love *you*," he said softly, softly touching her, softly kissing her, in a sort of subtle, restrained ecstasy.

She shook her head stubbornly. She tried to draw away. Then she did break away, and turned to look at him, in fear and doubt. The little, fascinating, fiendish lights were hovering in his eyes like laughter.

"Don't hurt me so much," she faltered, in a last protest.

A faint smile came on his face. He took her face between his hands and covered it with soft, blinding kisses, like a soft, narcotic rain. He felt himself such an unbreakable fountain-head of powerful blood. He was trembling finely in all his limbs, with mastery.

When she lifted her face and opened her eyes, her face was wet, and her greenish-golden eyes were shining, it was like sudden sunshine in wet foliage. She smiled at him like a child of knowledge, through the tears, and softly, infinitely softly he dried her tears with his mouth and his soft young moustache.

"You'd never shoot yourself, because you're mine, aren't you!" she said, knowing the fine quivering of his body, in mastery.

"Yes," he said.

"Quite mine?" she said, her voice rising in ecstasy.

"Yes."

"Nobody else but mine—nothing at all—?"

"Nothing at all," he re-echoed.

"But me?" came her last words of ecstasy.

"Yes."

And she seemed to be released free into the infinite of ecstasy.

2

They slept in fulfilment through the long night. But then strange dreams began to fill them both, strange dreams that were neither waking nor sleeping;—only, in curious weariness, through her dreams, she heard at last a continual low rapping. She awoke with difficulty. The rapping began again—she started violently. It was at the door—it would be the orderly rapping for Friedeburg. Everything seemed wild and unearthly. She put her hand on the shoulder of the sleeping man, and pulled him roughly, waited a moment, then pushed him, almost violently, to awake him. He woke with a sense of resentment at her violent handling. Then he heard the knocking of the orderly. He gathered his senses.

"Yes, Heinrich!" he said.

Strange, the sound of a voice! It seemed a far-off tearing sound. Then came the muffled voice of the servant.

"Half-past four, Sir."

"Right!" said Friedeburg, and automatically he got up and made a light. She was suddenly as wide awake as if it were daylight. But it was a strange, false day, like a delirium. She saw him put down the match, she saw him moving about, rapidly dressing. And the movement in the room was a trouble to her. He himself was vague and unreal, a thing seen but not comprehended. She watched all the acts of his toilet, saw all the motions, but never saw him. There was only a disturbance about her, which fretted her, she was not aware of any presence. Her mind, in its strange, hectic clarity, wanted to consider things in absolute detachment. For instance, she wanted to consider the cactus plant. It was a curious object with pure scarlet blossoms. Now, how did these scarlet blossoms come to pass, upon that earthly-looking unliving creature? Scarlet blossoms! How wonderful they were! What were they, then, how could one lay hold on their being? Her mind turned to him. Him, too, how could one lay hold on him, to have him? Where was he, what was he? She seemed to grasp at the air.

He was dipping his face in the cold water—the slight shock was good for him. He felt as if someone had stolen away his being in the night, he was moving about a light, quick shell, with all his meaning absent. His body was quick and active, but all his deep understanding, his soul was gone. He tried to rub it back into his face. He was quite dim, as if his spirit had left his body.

"Come and kiss me," sounded the voice from the bed. He went over to her automatically. She put her arms round him, and looked into his face with her clear brilliant, grey-green eyes, as if she too were looking for his soul.

"How are you?" came her meaningless words.

"All right."

"Kiss me."

He bent down and kissed her.

And still her clear, rather frightening eyes seemed to be searching for him inside himself. He was like a bird transfixed by her pellucid, grey-green, wonderful eyes. She put her hands into his soft, thick, fine hair, and gripped her hands full of his hair. He wondered with fear at her sudden painful clutching.

"I shall be late," he said.

"Yes," she answered. And she let him go.

As he fastened his tunic he glanced out of the window. It was still night: a night that must have lasted since eternity. There was a moon in the sky. In the streets below the yellow street-lamps burned small at intervals. This was the night of eternity.

There came a knock at the door, and the orderly's voice.

"Coffee, Sir."

"Leave it there."

They heard the faint jingle of the tray as it was set down outside.

Friedeburg sat down to put on his boots. Then, with a man's solid tread, he went and took in the tray. He felt properly heavy and secure now in his accoutrement. But he was always aware of her two wonderful, clear, unfolded eyes, looking on his heart, out of her uncanny silence.

There was a strong smell of coffee in the room.

"Have some coffee?" His eyes could not meet hers.

"No, thank you."

"Just a drop?"

"No, thank you."

Her voice sounded quite gay. She watched him dipping his bread in the coffee and eating quickly, absently. He did not know what he was doing, and yet the dipped bread and hot coffee gave him pleasure. He gulped down the remainder of his drink, and rose to his feet.

"I must go," he said.

There was a curious, poignant smile in her eyes. Her eyes drew him to her. How beautiful she was, and dazzling, and frightening, with this look of brilliant tenderness seeming to glitter from her face. She drew his head down to her bosom, and held it fast prisoner there, murmuring with tender, triumphant delight: "Dear! Dear!"

At last she let him lift his head, and he looked into her eyes, that seemed to concentrate in a dancing, golden point of vision in which he felt himself perish.

"Dear!" she murmured. "You love me, don't you?"

"Yes," he said mechanically.

The golden point of vision seemed to leap to him from her eyes, demanding something. He sat slackly, as if spellbound. Her hand pushed him a little.

"Mustn't you go?" she said.

He rose. She watched him fastening the belt round his body, that seemed soft under the fine clothes. He pulled on his greatcoat, and put on his peaked cap. He was again a young officer.

But he had forgotten his watch. It lay on the table near the bed. She watched him slinging it on his chain. He looked down at her. How beautiful she was, with her luminous face and her fine, stray hair! But he felt far away.

"Anything I can do for you?" he asked.

"No, thank you—I'll sleep," she replied, smiling. And the strange golden spark danced on her eyes again, again he felt as if his heart were gone, destroyed out of him. There was a fine pathos too in her vivid, dangerous face.

He kissed her for the last time, saying:

"I'll blow the candles out, then?"

"Yes, my love—and I'll sleep."

"Yes—sleep as long as you like."

The golden spark of her eyes seemed to dance on him like a destruction, she was beautiful, and pathetic. He touched her tenderly with his finger-tips, then suddenly blew out the candles, and walked across in the faint moonlight to the door.

He was gone. She heard his boots click on the stone stairs—she heard the far below tread of his feet on the pavement. Then he was gone. She lay quite still, in a swoon of deathly peace. She never wanted to move any more. It was finished. She lay quite still, utterly, utterly abandoned.

But again she was disturbed. There was a little tap at the door, then Teresa's voice saying, with a shuddering sound because of the cold:

"Ugh!—I'm coming to you, Marta my dear. I can't stand being left alone."

"I'll make a light," said Marta, sitting up and reaching for the candle. "Lock the door, will you, Resie, and then nobody can bother us."

She saw Teresa, loosely wrapped in her cloak, two thick ropes of hair hanging untidily. Teresa looked voluptuously sleepy and easy, like a cat running home to the warmth.

"Ugh!" she said, "it's cold!"

And she ran to the stove. Marta heard the chink of the little shovel, a stirring of coals, then a clink of the iron door. Then Teresa came running to the bed, with a shuddering little run, she puffed out the light and slid in beside her friend.

"So cold!" she said, with a delicious shudder at the warmth. Marta made place for her, and they settled down.

"Aren't you glad you're not them?" said Resie, with a little shudder at the thought. "Ugh!—poor devils!"

"I am," said Marta.

"Ah, sleep—sleep, how lovely!" said Teresa, with deep content. "Ah, it's so good!"

"Yes," said Marta.

"Good morning, good night, my dear," said Teresa, already sleepily.

"Good night," responded Marta.

Her mind flickered a little. Then she sank unconsciously to sleep. The room was silent.

Outside, the setting moon made peaked shadows of the high-roofed houses; from twin towers that stood like two dark, companion giants in the sky, the hour trembled out over the sleeping town. But the footsteps of hastening officers and cowering soldiers rang on the frozen pavements. Then a lantern appeared in the distance, accompanied by the rattle of a bullock wagon. By the light of the lantern on the wagon-pole could be seen the delicately moving feet and the pale, swinging dewlaps of the oxen. They drew slowly on, with a rattle of heavy wheels, the banded heads of the slow beasts swung rhythmically.

Ah, this was life! How sweet, sweet each tiny incident was! How sweet to Friedeburg, to give his orders ringingly on the frosty air, to see his men like bears shambling and shuffling into their places, with little dancing movements of uncouth playfulness and resentment, because of the pure cold.

Sweet, sweet it was to be marching beside his men, sweet to hear the great thresh-thresh of their heavy boots in the unblemished silence, sweet to feel the immense mass of living bodies co-ordinated into oneness near him, to catch the hot waft of their closeness, their breathing.

Freideburg was like a man condemned to die, catching at every impression as at an inestimable treasure.

Sweet it was to pass through the gates of the town, the scanty, loose suburb, into the open darkness and space of the country. This was almost best of all. It was like emerging in the open plains of eternal freedom.

They saw a dark figure hobbling along under the dark side of a shed. As they passed, through the open door of the shed, in the golden light were seen the low rafters, the pale, silken sides of the cows, evanescent. And a woman with a red kerchief bound round her head lifted her face from the flank of the beast she was milking, to look at the soldiers threshing like multitudes of heavy ghosts down the darkness. Some of the men called to her, cheerfully, impudently. Ah, the miraculous beauty and sweetness of the merest trifles like these!

They tramped on down a frozen, rutty road, under lines of bare trees. Beautiful trees! Beautiful frozen ruts in the road! Ah, even, in one of the ruts there was a silver of ice and of moon-glimpse. He heard ice tinkle as a passing soldier purposely put his toe in it. What a sweet noise!

But there was a vague uneasiness. He heard the men arguing as to whether dawn were coming. There was the silver moon, still riding on the high seas of the sky. A lovely thing she was, a jewel! But was there any blemish of day? He shrank a little from the rawness of the day to come. This night of morning was so rare and free.

Yes, he was sure. He saw a colourless paleness on the horizon. The earth began to look hard, like a great, concrete shadow. He shrank into himself. Glancing at the ranks of his men, he could see them like a company of rhythmic ghosts. The pallor was actually reflected on their livid faces. This was the coming day! It frightened him.

The dawn came. He saw the rosiness of it hang trembling with light, above the east. Then a strange glamour of scarlet passed over the land. At his feet, glints of ice flashed scarlet, even the hands of the men were red as they swung, sinister, heavy, reddened.

The sun surged up, her rim appeared, swimming with fire, hesitating, surging up. Suddenly there were shadows from trees and ruts, and grass was hoar and ice was gold against the ebony shadow. The faces of the men were alight, kindled with life. Ah, it was magical, it was all too marvellous! If only it were always like this!

When they stopped at the inn for breakfast, at nine o'clock, the smell of the inn went raw and ugly to his heart: beer and yesterday's tobacco!

He went to the door to look at the men biting huge bites from their hunks of grey bread, or cutting off pieces with their clasp-knives. This made him still happy. Women were going to the fountain for water, the soldiers were chaffing them coarsely. He liked all this.

But the magic was going, inevitably, the crystal delight was thawing to desolation in his heart, his heart was cold, cold mud. Ah, it was awful. His face contracted, he almost wept with cold, stark despair.

Still he had the work, the day's hard activity with the men. Whilst this lasted, he could live. But when this was over, and he had to face the horror of his own cold-thawing mud of despair: ah, it was not to be thought of. Still, he was happy at work with the men: the wild desolate place, the hard activity of mock warfare. Would to God it were real: war, with the prize of death!

By afternoon the sky had gone one dead, livid level of grey. It seemed low down, and oppressive. He was tired, the men were tired, and this let the heavy cold soak in to them like despair. Life could not keep it out.

And now, when his heart was so heavy it could sink no more, he must glance at his own situation again. He must remember what a fool he was, his new debts like half thawed mud in his heart. He knew, with the cold misery of hopelessness, that he would be turned out of the army. What then?—what then but death? After all, death was the solution for him. Let it be so.

They marched on and on, stumbling with fatigue under a great leaden sky, over a frozen dead country. The men were silent with weariness, the heavy motion of their marching was like an oppression. Friedeburg was tired too, and deadened, as his face was deadened by the cold air. He did not think any more; the misery of his soul was like a frost inside him.

He heard someone say it was going to snow. But the words had no meaning for him. He marched as a clock ticks, with the same monotony, everything numb and cold-soddened.

They were drawing near to the town. In the gloom of the afternoon he felt it ahead, as unbearable oppression on him. Ah the hideous suburb! What was his life, how did it come to pass that life was lived in a formless, hideous grey structure of hell! What did it all mean? Pale, sulphur-yellow lights spotted the livid air, and people, like soddened shadows, passed in front of the shops that were lit up ghastly in the early twilight. Out of the colourless space, crumbs of snow came and bounced animatedly off the breast of his coat.

At length he turned away home, to his room, to change and get warm

and renewed, for he felt as cold-soddened as the grey, cold, heavy bread
which felt hostile in the mouths of the soldiers. His life was to him like
this dead, cold bread in his mouth.

As he neared his own house, the snow was peppering thinly down. He
became aware of some unusual stir about the house-door. He looked—
a strange, closed-in wagon, people, police. The sword of Damocles that
had hung over his heart, fell. O God, a new shame, some new shame,
some new torture! His body moved on. So it would move on through
misery upon misery, as is our fate. There was no emergence, only this
progress through misery unto misery, till the end. Strange, that human
life was so tenacious! Strange, that men had made of life a long, slow
process of torture to the soul. Strange, that it was no other than this!
Strange, that but for man, this misery would not exist. For it was not
God's misery, but the misery of the world of man.

He saw two officials push something white and heavy into the cart,
shut the doors behind with a bang, turn the silver handle, and run
round to the front of the wagon. It moved off. But still most of the
people lingered. Friedeburg drifted near in that inevitable motion
which carries us through all our shame and torture. He knew the people
talked about him. He went up the steps and into the square hall.

There stood a police-officer, with a note-book in his hand, talking to
Herr Kapell, the housemaster. As Friedeburg entered through the swing
door, the housemaster, whose brow was wrinkled in anxiety and pertur-
bation, made a gesture with his hand, as if to point out a criminal.

"Ah!—the Herr Baron von Friedeburg!" he said, in self-exculpa-
tion.

The police-officer turned, saluted politely, and said, with the
polite, intolerable *suffisance* of officialdom:

"Good evening! Trouble here!"

"Yes?" said Friedeburg.

He was so frightened, his sensitive constitution was so lacerated, that
something broke in him, he was a subservient, murmuring ruin.

"Two young ladies found dead in your room," said the police-
official, making an official statement. But under this cold impartiality
of officialdom, what obscene unction! Ah, what obscene exposures
now!

"Dead!" ejaculated Friedeburg, with the wide eyes of a child. He
became quite child-like, the official had him completely in his power.
He could torture him as much as he liked.

"Yes." He referred to his note-book. "Asphyxiated by fumes from
the stove."

Friedeburg could only stand wide-eyed and meaningless.

"Please—will you go upstairs?"

The police-official marshalled Friedeburg in front of himself. The youth slowly mounted the stairs, feeling as if transfixed through the base of the spine, as if he would lose the use of his legs. The official followed close on his heels.

They reached the bedroom. The policeman unlocked the door. The housekeeper followed with a lamp. Then the official examination began.

"A young lady slept here last night?"

"Yes."

"Name, please?"

"Marta Hohenest."

"H-o-h-e-n-e-s-t," spelled the official. "—And address?"

Friedeburg continued to answer. This was the end of him. The quick of him was pierced and killed. The living dead answered the living dead in obscene antiphony. Question and answer continued, the note-book worked as the hand of the old dead wrote in it the replies of the young who was dead.

The room was unchanged from the night before. There was her heap of clothing, the lustrous, pure-red dress lying soft where she had carelessly dropped it. Even, on the edge of the chair-back, her crimson silk garters hung looped.

But do not look, do not see. It is the business of the dead to bury their dead. Let the young dead bury their own dead, as the old dead have buried theirs. How can the dead remember, they being dead? Only the living can remember, and are at peace with their living who have passed away.

Delilah and Mr. Bircumshaw

"He looked," said Mrs. Bircumshaw to Mrs. Gillatt, "he looked like a positive saint: one of the noble sort, you know, that will suffer with head up and with dreamy eyes. I nearly died of laughing."

She spoke of Mr. Bircumshaw, who darted a look at his wife's friend. Mrs. Gillatt broke into an almost derisive laugh. Bircumshaw shut tight his mouth, and set his large, square jaw. Frowning, he lowered his face out of sight.

Mrs. Bircumshaw seemed to glitter in the twilight. She was like a little, uncanny machine, working unheard and unknown, but occasionally snapping a spark. A small woman, very quiet in her manner, it was surprising that people should so often say of her, "She's *very* vivacious." It was her eyes: they were brown, very wide-open, very swift and ironic. As a rule she said little. This evening, her words and her looks were quick and brilliant. She had been married four years.

"I was thankful, I can tell you, that you didn't go," she continued to Mrs. Gillatt. "For a church pageant, it was the most astonishing show. People blossomed out so differently. *I* never knew what a fine apostle was lost in Harry. When I saw him, I thought I should scream."

"You looked sober enough every time I noticed you," blurted Harry, in deep bass.

"You were much too rapt to notice *me*," his wife laughed gaily. Nevertheless, her small head was lifted and alert, like a fighting bird's. Mrs. Gillatt fell instinctively into rank with her, unconscious of the thrill of battle that moved her.

Mr. Bircumshaw, bowing forward, rested his arms on his knees, and whistled silently as he contemplated his feet. Also, he listened acutely to the women. He was a large-limbed, clean, powerful man, and a bank clerk. Son of a country clergyman, he had a good deal of vague, sensuous, religious feeling, but he lacked a Faith. He would have been a fine man to support a cause, but he had no cause. Even had he been forced to work hard and unremittingly, he would have remained healthy in spirit. As it was, he was a bank clerk, with a quantity of unspent energy turning sour in his veins, and a fair amount of barren leisure torturing his soul. He was degenerating: and now his wife turned upon him.

She had been a schoolteacher. He had had the money and the position. He was inclined to bully her, when he was not suited: which was fairly often.

"Harry was one of the 'Three Wise Men.' You should have seen him, Mrs. Gillatt. With his face coming out of that white forehead band, and the cloth that hung over his ears, he looked a picture. Imagine him—!"

Mrs. Gillatt looked at Bircumshaw, imagining him. Then she threw up her hands and laughed aloud. It *was* ludicrous to think of Bircumshaw, a hulking, frequently churlish man, as one of the Magi. Mrs. Gillatt was a rather beautiful woman of forty, almost too full in blossom. Better off than the Bircumshaws, she assumed the manner of patron and protector.

"Oh," she cried, "I can *see* him—I can see him looking great and grand—Abraham! Oh, he's got that grand cut of face, and plenty of size."

She laughed rather derisively. She was a man's woman, by instinct serving flattery with mockery.

"That's it!" cried the little wife, deferentially. "Abraham setting out to sacrifice. He marched—his march was splendid."

The two women laughed together. Mrs. Gillatt drew herself up superbly, laughing, then coming to rest.

"And usually, you know," the wife broke off, "there's a good deal of the whipped schoolboy about his walk."

"There is, Harry," laughed Mrs. Gillatt, shaking her white and jewelled hand at him. "You just remember that for the next time, my lad." She was his senior by some eight years. He grinned sickly.

"But now," Mrs. Bircumshaw continued, "he marched like a young Magi. You could see a look of the Star in his eyes."

"Oh," cried Mrs. Gillatt. "Oh! the look of the Star—!"

"Oftener the look of the Great Bear, isn't it?" queried Mrs. Bircumshaw.

"That is quite true, Harry," said the elder woman, laughing.

Bircumshaw cracked his strong fingers, brutally.

"Well, he came on," continued the wife, "with the light of the Star in his eyes, his mouth fairly sweet with Christian resignation—"

"Oh!" cried Mrs. Gillatt, "oh—and he beats the baby. Christian resignation!" She laughed aloud. "Let me hear of you beating that child again, Harry Bircumshaw, and I'll Christian-resignation you—"

Suddenly she remembered that this might implicate her friend. "I came in yesterday," she explained, "at dinner. 'What's the matter, baby?' I said, 'what are you crying for?' 'Dadda beat baby—naughty baby.' It was a good thing you had gone back to business, my lad, I can tell you. . . ."

Mrs. Bircumshaw glanced swiftly at her husband. He had ducked his head and was breaking his knuckles tensely. She turned her head with a quick, thrilled movement, more than ever like a fighting bird.

"And you know his nose," she said, blithely resuming her narrative, as if it were some bit of gossip. "You know it usually looks a sort of 'Mind your own business or you'll get a hit in the jaw' nose?"

"Yes," cried Mrs. Gillatt, "it does—" and she seemed unable to contain her laughter. Then she dropped her fine head, pretending to be an angry buffalo glaring under bent brows, seeking whom he shall devour, in imitation of Harry's nose.

Mrs. Bircumshaw bubbled with laughter.

"Ah!" said Mrs. Gillatt, and she winked at her friend as she sweetened Harry's pill, "I know him—I know him." Then: "And what *did* his nose look like?" she asked of the wife.

"Like Sir Galahad on horseback," said Ethel Bircumshaw, spending her last shot.

Mrs. Gillatt drew her hand down her own nose, which was straight, with thin, flexible nostrils.

"How does it feel, Harry," she asked, "to stroke Galahad on horseback?"

"I don't know, I'm sure," he said icily.

"Then stroke it, man, and tell me," cried the elder woman: with which *her* last shot was sped. There was a moment of painful silence.

"And the way the others acted—it was screamingly funny," the wife started. Then the two women, with one accord, began to make mock of the other actors in the pageant, people they knew, ridiculing them, however, only for blemishes that Harry had not, pulling the others to pieces in places where Harry was solid, thus leaving their man erect like a hero among the litter of his acquaintances.

This did not mollify him: it only persuaded him he was a fine figure, not to be carped at.

Suddenly, before the women had gone far, Bircumshaw jumped up. Mrs. Gillatt started. She got a glimpse of his strict form, in its blue serge, passing before her, then the door banged behind him.

Mrs. Gillatt was really astonished. She had helped in clipping this ignoble Samson, all unawares, from instinct. She had no idea of what she had been doing. She sat erect and superb, the picture of astonishment that is merging towards contempt.

"Is it someone at the door?" she asked, listening.

Mrs. Bircumshaw, with alert, listening eyes, shook her head quickly, with a meaning look of contempt.

"Is he mad?" whispered the elder woman. Her friend nodded. Then Mrs. Gillatt's eyes dilated, and her face hardened with scorn. Mrs. Bircumshaw had not ceased to listen. She bent forward.

"Praise him," she whispered, making a quick gesture that they should play a bit of fiction. They rose with zest to the game. "Praise him," whispered the wife. Then she herself began. Every woman is a first-rate actress in private. She leaned forward, and in a slightly lowered yet very distinct voice, screened as if for privacy, yet penetrating clearly to the ears of her husband—he had lingered in the hall, she could hear—she said:

"You know Harry really acted splendidly."

"I know," said Mrs. Gillatt eagerly. "I know. I know he's a really good actor."

"He is. The others did look paltry beside him, I have to confess."

Harry's pride was soothed, but his wrath was not appeased.

"Yes," he heard the screened voice of his wife say. "But for all that, I don't care to see him on the stage. It's not manly, somehow. It seems unworthy of a man with any character, somehow. Of course it's all right for strangers—but for anyone you care for—anyone *very* near to you—"

Mrs. Gillatt chuckled to herself: this was a thing well done. The two women, however, had not praised very long—and the wife's praise was sincere by the time she had finished her first sentence—before they were startled by a loud "Thud!" on the floor above their heads. Both started. It was dark, nearly nine o'clock. They listened in silence. Then came another "Thud!"

Mrs. Bircumshaw gave a little spurt of bitter-contemptuous laughter.

"He's not—?" began Mrs. Gillatt.

"He's gone to bed, and announces the fact by dropping his boots as he takes them off," said the young wife bitterly.

Mrs. Gillatt was wide-eyed with amazement. "You don't mean it!" she exclaimed.

Childless, married to an uxorious man whom she loved, this state of affairs was monstrous to her. Neither of the women spoke for a while. It was dark in the room. Then Mrs. Gillatt began, sotto voce:

"Well, I could never have believed it, no, not if you'd told me forever. He's always so fussy—"

So she went on. Mrs. Bircumshaw let her continue. A restrained woman herself, the other's outburst relieved her own tension. When she had sufficiently overcome her own emotion, and when she knew her husband to be in bed, she rose.

"Come into the kitchen, we can talk there," she said. There was a new hardness in her voice. She had not "talked" before to anyone, had never mentioned her husband in blame.

The kitchen was bare, with drab walls glistening to the naked gas-jet. The tiled floor was uncovered, cold and damp. Everything was clean, stark, and cheerless. The large stove, littered with old paper, was black, black-cold. There was a baby's high chair in one corner, and a teddy-bear, and a tin pigeon. Mrs. Bircumshaw threw a cloth on the table that was pushed up under the drab-blinded window, against the great, black stove, which radiated coldness since it could not radiate warmth.

"Will you stay to supper?" asked Mrs. Bircumshaw.

"What have you got?" was the frank reply.

"I'm afraid there's only bread and cheese."

"No thanks then. I don't eat bread and cheese for supper, Ethel, and you ought not."

They talked—or rather Mrs. Gillatt held forth for a few minutes, on suppers. Then there was a silence.

"I never knew such a thing in my life," began Mrs. Gillatt, rather awkwardly, as a tentative: she wanted her friend to unbosom. "Is he often like it?" she persisted.

"Oh yes."

"Well, I can see now," Mrs. Gillatt declared, "I can understand now. Often have I come in and seen you with your eyes all red: but you've not said anything, so I haven't liked to. But I know now. Just fancy—the brute!—and will he be all right when you go to bed?"

"Oh no."

"Will he keep it up tomorrow?" Mrs. Gillatt's tone expressed nothing short of amazed horror.

"Oh yes, and very likely for two or three days."

"Oh the brute! the brute!! Well, this *has* opened my eyes. I've been watching a few of these men lately, and I tell you—. You'll not sleep with him tonight, shall you?"

"It would only make it worse."

"Worse or not worse, I wouldn't. You've got another bed aired—you had visitors till yesterday—there's the bed—take baby and sleep there."

"It would only make it worse," said Mrs. Bircumshaw, weariedly. Mrs. Gillatt was silent a moment.

"Well—you're better to him than I should be, I can tell you," she said. "Ah, the brute, to think he should always be so fair and fussy to my face, and I think him so nice. But let him touch that child again—! Haven't I seen her with her little arms red? 'Gentlemanly'—so fond of quoting his 'gentlemanly'! Eh, but this has opened my eyes, Ethel. Only let him touch that child again, to my knowledge. I only wish he would."

Mrs. Bircumshaw listened to this threat in silence. Yet she did wish she could see the mean bully in her husband matched by this spoiled, arrogant, generous woman.

"But tell him, Ethel," said Mrs. Gillatt, bending from her handsome height, and speaking in considerate tones, "tell him that I saw nothing —nothing. Tell him I thought he had suddenly been called to the door: tell him that—and that I thought he'd gone down the 'Drive' with a caller—say that—you can do it, it's perfectly true—I did think so. So tell him—the brute!"

Mrs. Bircumshaw listened patiently, occasionally smiling to herself. She would tell her husband nothing, would never mention the affair to him. Moreover, she intended her husband to think he had made a fool of himself before this handsome woman whom he admired so much.

Bircumshaw heard his wife's friend take her leave. He had been in torment while the two women were together in the far-off kitchen. Now the brute in him felt more sure, more triumphant. He was afraid of *two* women: he could cow one. He felt he had something to punish: that he had his own dignity and authority to assert: and he was going to punish, was going to assert.

"I should think," said Mrs. Gillatt in departing, "that you won't take him any supper."

Mrs. Bircumshaw felt a sudden blaze of anger against him. But she laughed deprecatingly.

"You *are* a silly thing if you do," cried the other. "My word, I'd starve him if I had him."

"But you see you haven't got him," said the wife quietly.

"No, I'm thankful to say. But if I had—the brute!"

He heard her go, and was relieved. Now he could lie in bed and sulk to his heart's content, and inflict penalties of ill-humour on his insolent wife. He was such a lusty, emotional man—and he had nothing to do.

What was his work to him? Scarcely more than nothing. And what was to fill the rest of his life—nothing. He wanted something to do, and he thought he wanted more done for him. So he got into this irritable, sore state of moral debility. A man cannot respect himself unless he does something. But he can do without his own positive self-respect, so long as his wife respects him. But when the man who has no foothold for self-esteem sees his wife and his wife's friend despise him, it is hell: he fights for very life. So Bircumshaw lay in bed in this state of ignoble misery. His wife had striven for a long time to pretend he was still her hero: but he had tried her patience too far. Now he was confounding heroism, mastery, with brute tyranny. He would be a tyrant, if not a hero.

She, downstairs, occasionally smiled to herself. This time she had given him his dues. Though her heart was pained and anxious, still she smiled: she had clipped a large lock from her Samson. Her smile rose from the deep of her woman's nature.

After having eaten a very little supper, she worked about the house till ten o'clock. Her face had regained that close impassivity which many women wear when alone. Still impassive, at the end of her little tasks she fetched the dinner joint and made him four sandwiches, carefully seasoned and trimmed. Pouring him a glass of milk, she went upstairs with the tray, which looked fresh and tempting.

He had been listening acutely to her last movements. As she entered, however, he lay well under the bedclothes, breathing steadily, pretending to sleep. She came in quite calmly.

"Here is your supper," she said, in a quiet, indifferent tone, ignoring the fact that he was supposed to be asleep. Another lock fell from his strength. He felt virtue depart from him, felt weak and watery in spirit, and he hated her. He made no reply, but kept up his pretence of sleep.

She bent over the cot of the sleeping baby, a bonny child of three. The little one was flushed in her sleep. Her fist was clenched in a tangle of hair over her small round ear, whilst even in sleep she pouted in her wilful, imperious way. With very gentle fingers the mother loosened the bright hair and put it back from the full, small brow, that reminded one of the brow of a little Virgin by Memling. The father felt that he was left out, ignored. He would have wished to whisper a word to his wife, and so bring himself into the trinity, had he not been so wroth. He retired further into his manly bulk, felt weaker and more miserably insignificant, at the same time more enraged.

Mrs. Bircumshaw slipped into bed quietly, settling to rest at once, as far as possible from the broad form of her husband. Both lay quite still, although, as each knew, neither slept. The man felt he wanted to move, but his will was so weak and shrinking, he could not rouse his muscles. He lay tense, paralyzed with self-conscious shrinking, yet bursting to move. She nestled herself down quite at ease. She did not care, this evening, how he felt or thought: for once she let herself rest in indifference.

Towards one o'clock in the morning, just as she was drifting into sleep, her eyes flew open. She did not start or stir; she was merely wide awake. A match had been struck.

Her husband was sitting up in bed, leaning forward to the plate on the chair. Very carefully, she turned her head just enough to see him. His big back bulked above her. He was leaning forward to the chair. The candle, which he had set on the floor, so that its light should not penetrate the sleep of his wife, threw strange shadows on the ceiling, and lighted his throat and underneath his strong chin. Through the arch of his arm, she could see his jaw and his throat working. For some strange reason, he felt that he could not eat in the dark. Occasionally she could see his cheek bulged with food. He ate rapidly, almost voraciously, leaning over the edge of the bed and taking care of the crumbs. She noticed the weight of his shoulder muscles at rest upon the arm on which he leaned.

"The strange animal!" she said to herself, and she laughed, laughed heartily within herself.

"Are they nice?" she longed to say, slyly.

"Are they nice?"—she must say it—"are they nice?" The temptation was almost too great. But she was afraid of this lusty animal startled at his feeding. She dared not twit him.

He took the milk, leaned back, almost arching backwards over her as he drank. She shrank with a little fear, a little repulsion, which was nevertheless half pleasurable. Cowering under his shadow, she shrugged with contempt, yet her eyes widened with a small, excited smile. This vanished, and a real scorn hardened her lips: when he was sulky his blood was cold as water, nothing could rouse it to passion; he resisted caresses as if he had thin acid in his veins. "Mean in the blood," she said to herself.

He finished the food and milk, licked his lips, nipped out the candle, then stealthily lay down. He seemed to sink right into a grateful sleep.

"Nothing on earth is so vital to him as a meal," she thought.

She lay a long time thinking, before she fell asleep.

Prologue to *Women in Love*

The acquaintance between the two men was slight and insignificant. Yet there was a subtle bond that connected them.

They had met four years ago, brought together by a common friend, Hosken, a naval man. The three, Rupert Birkin, William Hosken, and Gerald Crich had then spent a week in the Tyrol together, mountain-climbing.

Birkin and Gerald Crich felt take place between them, the moment they saw each other, that sudden connection which sometimes springs up between men who are very different in temper. There had been a subterranean kindling in each man. Each looked towards the other, and knew the trembling nearness.

Yet they had maintained complete reserve, their relations had been, to all knowledge, entirely casual and trivial. Because of the inward kindled connection, they were even more distant and slight than men usually are, one towards the other.

There was, however, a certain tenderness in their politeness, an almost uncomfortable understanding lurked under their formal, reserved behaviour. They were vividly aware of each other's presence, and each was just as vividly aware of himself, in presence of the other.

The week of mountain-climbing passed like an intense brief lifetime. The three men were very close together, and lifted into an abstract isolation, among the upper rocks and the snow. The world that lay below, the whole field of human activity, was sunk and subordinated, they had trespassed into the upper silence and loneliness. The three of them had reached another state of being, they were enkindled in the upper silences into a rare, unspoken intimacy, an intimacy that took no expression, but which was between them like a transfiguration. As if thrown into the strange fire of abstraction, up in the mountains, they knew and were known to each other. It was another world, another life, transfigured, and yet most vividly corporeal, the senses all raised till each felt his own body, and the presence of his companions, like an essential flame, they radiated to one enkindled, transcendent fire, in the upper world.

Then had come the sudden falling down to earth, the sudden extinction. At Innsbruck they had parted, Birkin to go to Munich, Gerald Crich and Hosken to take the train for Paris and London. On the station they shook hands, and went asunder, having spoken no word and given no sign of the transcendent intimacy which had roused them beyond the everyday life. They shook hands and took leave casually, as mere acquaintances going their separate ways. Yet there remained always, for Birkin and for Gerald Crich, the absolute recognition that had passed between them then, the knowledge that was in their eyes as they met at the moment of parting. They knew they loved each other, that each would die for the other.

Yet all this knowledge was kept submerged in the soul of the two men. Outwardly they would have none of it. Outwardly they only stiffened themselves away from it. They took leave from each other even more coldly and casually than is usual.

And for a year they had seen nothing of each other, neither had they exchanged any word. They passed away from each other, and, superficially, forgot.

But when they met again, in a country house in Derbyshire, the enkindled sensitiveness sprang up again like a strange, embarrassing fire. They scarcely knew each other, yet here was this strange, unacknowledged, inflammable intimacy between them. It made them uneasy.

Rupert Birkin, however, strongly centred in himself, never gave way in his soul, to anyone. He remained in the last issue detached, self-responsible, having no communion with any other soul. Therefore Gerald Crich remained intact in his own form.

The two men were very different. Gerald Crich was the fair, keen-eyed Englishman of medium stature, hard in his muscles and full of energy as a machine. He was a hunter, a traveller, a soldier, always active, always moving vigorously, and giving orders to some subordinate.

Birkin on the other hand was quiet and unobtrusive. In stature he was long and very thin, and yet not bony, close-knit, flexible, and full of repose, like a steel wire. His energy was not evident, he seemed almost weak, passive, insignificant. He was delicate in health. His face was pale and rather ugly, his hair dun-coloured, his eyes were of a yellowish-grey, full of life and warmth. They were the only noticeable thing about him, to the ordinary observer, being very warm and sudden and attractive, alive like fires. But this chief attraction of Birkin's was a false one. Those that knew him best knew that his lovable eyes were, in the last issue, estranged and unsoftening like the eyes of a wolf. In the last issue he was callous, and without feeling, confident, just as Gerald Crich in the last issue was wavering and lost.

The two men were staying in the house of Sir Charles Roddice, Gerald Crich as friend of the host, Rupert Birkin as friend of his host's daughter, Hermione* Roddice. Sir Charles would have been glad for Gerald Crich to marry the daughter of the house, because this young man was a well-set young Englishman of strong conservative temperament, and heir to considerable wealth. But Gerald Crich did not care for Hermione Roddice, and Hermione Roddice disliked Gerald Crich.

She was a rather beautiful woman of twenty-five, fair, tall, slender, graceful, and of some learning. She had known Rupert Birkin in Oxford. He was a year her senior. He was a fellow of Magdalen College, and had been, at twenty-one, one of the young lights of the place, a coming somebody. His essays on Education were brilliant, and he became an inspector of schools.

Hermione Roddice loved him. When she had listened to his passionate declamations, in his rooms in the Blackhorse Road, and when she had heard the respect with which he was spoken of, five years ago, she being a girl of twenty, reading political economy, and he a youth of twenty-one, holding forth against Nietzsche, then she devoted herself to his name and fame. She added herself to his mental and spiritual flame.

Sir Charles thought they would marry. He considered that Birkin, hanging on year after year, was spoiling all his daughter's chances, and without pledging himself in the least. It irked the soldierly knight considerably. But he was somewhat afraid of the quiet, always-civil Birkin. And Hermione, when Sir Charles mentioned that he thought of speaking to the young man, in order to know his intentions, fell into such a white and overweening, contemptuous passion, that her father was nonplussed and reduced to irritated silence.

"How vulgar you are!" cried the young woman. "You are not to dare to say a word to him. It is a friendship, and it is not to be broken-in upon in this fashion. Why should you want to rush me into marriage? I am more than happy as I am."

Her liquid grey eyes swam dark with fury and pain and resentment, her beautiful face was convulsed. She seemed like a prophetess violated. Her father withdrew, cold and huffed.

So the relationship between the young woman and Birkin continued. He was an inspector of schools, she studied Education. He wrote also harsh, jarring poetry, very real and painful, under which she suffered; and sometimes, shallower, gentle lyrics, which she treasured as drops of manna. Like a priestess she kept his records and his oracles, he was like a god who would be nothing if his worship were neglected.

* Lawrence substituted the name *Hermione* in place of the name *Ethel.*

Hermione could not understand the affection between the two men. They would sit together in the hall, at evening, and talk without any depth. What did Rupert find to take him up, in Gerald Crich's conversation? She, Hermione, was only rather bored, and puzzled. Yet the two men seemed happy, holding their commonplace discussion. Hermione was impatient. She knew that Birkin was, as usual, belittling his own mind and talent, for the sake of something that she felt unworthy. Some common correspondence which she knew demeaned and belied him. Why would he always come down so eagerly to the level of common people, why was he always so anxious to vulgarize and betray himself? She bit her lip in torment. It was as if he were anxious to deny all that was fine and rare in himself.

Birkin knew what she was feeling and thinking. Yet he continued almost spitefully against her. He *did* want to betray the heights and depths of nearly religious intercourse which he had with her. He, the God, turned round upon his priestess, and became the common vulgar man who turned her to scorn. He performed some strange metamorphosis of soul, and from being a pure, incandescent spirit burning intense with the presence of God, he became a lustful, shallow, insignificant fellow running in all the common ruts. Even there was some vindictiveness in him now, something jeering and spiteful and low, unendurable. It drove her mad. She had given him all her trembling, naked soul, and now he turned mongrel, and triumphed in his own degeneration. It was his deep desire, to be common, vulgar, a little gross. She could not bear the look of almost sordid jeering with which he turned on her, when she reached out her hand, imploring. It was as if some rat bit her, she felt she was going insane. And he jeered at her, at the spiritual woman who waited at the tomb, in her sandals and her mourning robes. He jeered at her horribly, knowing her secrets. And she was insane, she knew she was going mad.

But he plunged on triumphant into intimacy with Gerald Crich, excluding the woman, tormenting her. He knew how to pitch himself into tune with another person. He could adjust his mind, his consciousness, almost perfectly to that of Gerald Crich, lighting up the edge of the other man's limitation with a glimmering light that was the essence of exquisite adventure and liberation to the confined intelligence. The two men talked together for hours, Birkin watching the hard limbs and the rather stiff face of the traveller in unknown countries, Gerald Crich catching the pale, luminous face opposite him, lit up over the edge of the unknown regions of the soul, trembling into new being, quivering with new intelligence.

To Hermione, it was insupportable degradation that Rupert Birkin should maintain this correspondence, prostituting his mind and his understanding to the coarser stupidity of the other man. She felt confusion gathering upon her, she was unanchored on the edge of madness. Why did he do it? Why was he, whom she knew as her leader, star-like and pure, why was he the lowest betrayer and the ugliest of blasphemers? She held her temples, feeling herself reel towards the bottomless pit.

For Birkin did get a greater satisfaction, at least for the time being, from his intercourse with the other man, than from his spiritual relation with her. It satisfied him to have to do with Gerald Crich, it fulfilled him to have this other man, this hard-limbed traveller and sportsman, following implicitly, held as it were consummated within the spell of a more powerful understanding. Birkin felt a passion of desire for Gerald Crich, for the clumsier, cruder intelligence and the limited soul, and for the striving, unlightened body of his friend. And Gerald Crich, not understanding, was transfused with pleasure. He did not even know he loved Birkin. He thought him marvellous in understanding, almost unnatural, and on the other hand pitiful and delicate in body. He felt a great tenderness towards him, of superior physical strength, and at the same time some reverence for his delicacy and fineness of being.

All the same, there was no profession of friendship, no open mark of intimacy. They remained to all intents and purposes distant, mere acquaintances. It was in the other world of the subconsciousness that the interplay took place, the interchange of spiritual and physical richness, the relieving of physical and spiritual poverty, without any intrinsic change of state in either man.

Hermione could not understand it at all. She was mortified and in despair. In his lapses, she despised and revolted from Birkin. Her mistrust of him pierced to the quick of her soul. If his intense and pure flame of spirituality only sank to this guttering prostration, a low, degraded heat, servile to a clumsy Gerald Crich, fawning on a coarse, unsusceptible being, such as was Gerald Crich and all the multitudes of Gerald Criches of this world, then nothing was anything. The transcendent star of one evening was the putrescent phosphorescence of the next, and glory and corruptibility were interchangeable. Her soul was convulsed with cynicism. She despised her God and her angel. Yet she could not do without him. She believed in herself as a priestess, and that was all. Though there were no God to serve, still she was a priestess. Yet having no altar to kindle, no sacrifice to burn, she would be barren and useless. So she adhered to her God in him, which she claimed almost violently, whilst her soul turned in bitter cynicism from the prostitute man in him. She did not believe in him, she only believed in that which she could gather from him, as one gathers silk from the corrupt worm. She was the maker of gods.

So, after a few days, Gerald Crich went away and Birkin was left to Hermione Roddice. It is true, Crich said to Birkin: "Come and see us, if ever you are near enough, will you?", and Birkin had said yes. But for some reason, it was concluded beforehand that this visit would never be made, deliberately.

Sick, helpless, Birkin swung back to Hermione. In the garden, at evening, looking over the silvery hills, he sat near to her, or lay with his head on her bosom, while the moonlight came gently upon the trees, and they talked, quietly, gently as dew distilling, their two disembodied voices distilled in the silvery air, two voices moving and ceasing like ghosts, like spirits. And they talked of life, and of death, but chiefly of death, his words turning strange and phosphorescent, like dark water suddenly shaken alight, whilst she held his head against her breast, infinitely satisfied and completed by its weight upon her, and her hand travelled gently, finely, oh, with such exquisite quivering adjustment, over his hair. The pain of tenderness he felt for her was almost unendurable, as her hand fluttered and came near, scarcely touching him, so light and sensitive it was, as it passed over his hair, rhythmically. And still his voice moved and thrilled through her like the keenest pangs of embrace, she remained possessed by him, possessed by the spirit. And the sense of beauty and perfect, blade-keen ecstasy was balanced to perfection, she passed away, was transported.

After these nights of superfine ecstasy of beauty, after all was consumed in the silver fire of moonlight, all the soul caught up in the universal chill-blazing bonfire of the moonlit night, there came the morning, and the ash, when his body was grey and consumed, and his soul ill. Why should the sun shine, and hot gay flowers come out, when the kingdom of reality was the silver-cold night of death, lovely and perfect.

She, like a priestess, was fulfilled and rich. But he became more hollow and ghastly to look at. There was no escape, they penetrated further and further into the regions of death, and soon the connection with life would be broken.

Then came his revulsion against her. After he loved her with a tenderness that was anguish, a love that was all pain, or else transcendent white ecstasy, he turned upon her savagely, like a maddened dog. And like a priestess who is rended for sacrifice, she submitted and endured.

She would serve the God she possessed, even though he should turn periodically into a fierce dog, to rend her.

So he went away, to his duties, and his work. He had made a passionate study of education, only to come, gradually, to the knowledge that education is nothing but the process of building up, gradually, a complete unit of consciousness. And each unit of consciousness is the living unit of that great social, religious, philosophic idea towards which mankind, like an organism seeking its final form, is laboriously growing. But if there *be* no great philosophic idea, if, for the time being, mankind, instead of going through a period of growth, is going through a corresponding process of decay and decomposition from some old, fulfilled, obsolete idea, then what is the good of educating? Decay and decomposition will take their own way. It is impossible to educate for this end, impossible to teach the world how to die away from its achieved, nullified form. The autumn must take place in every individual soul, as well as in all the people, all must die, individually and socially. But education is a process of striving to a new, unanimous being, a whole organic form. But when winter has set in, when the frosts are strangling the leaves off the trees and the birds are silent knots of darkness, how can there be a unanimous movement towards a whole summer of florescence? There can be none of this, only submission to the death of this nature, in the winter that has come upon mankind, and a cherishing of the unknown that is unknown for many a day yet, buds that may not open till a far off season comes, when the season of death has passed away.

And Birkin was just coming to a knowledge of the essential futility of all attempt at social unanimity in constructiveness. In the winter, there can only be unanimity of disintegration, the leaves fall unanimously, the plants die down, each creature is a soft-slumbering grave, as the adder and the dormouse in winter are the soft tombs of the adder and the dormouse, which slip about like rays of brindled darkness, in summer.

How to get away from this process of reduction, how escape this phosphorescent passage into the tomb, which was universal though unacknowledged, this was the unconscious problem which tortured Birkin day and night. He came to Hermione, and found with her the pure, translucent regions of death itself, of ecstasy. In the world the autumn was setting in. What should a man add himself on to?—to science, to social reform, to aestheticism, to sensationalism? The whole world's constructive activity was a fiction, a lie, to hide the great process of decomposition, which had set in. What then to adhere to?

He ran about from death to death. Work was terrible, horrible because he did not believe in it. It was almost a horror to him, to think of going from school to school, making reports and giving suggestions, when the whole process to his soul was pure futility, a process of mechanical activity entirely purposeless, sham growth which was entirely rootless. Nowhere more than in education did a man feel the horror of false, rootless, spasmodic activity more acutely. The whole business was like dementia. It created in him a feeling of nausea and horror. He recoiled from it. And yet, where should a man repair, what should he do?

In his private life the same horror of futility and wrongness dogged him. Leaving alone all ideas, religious or philosophic, all of which are mere sounds, old repetitions, or else novel, dexterous, sham permutations and combinations of old repetitions, leaving alone all the things of the mind and the consciousness, what remained in a man's life? There is his emotional and his sensuous activity, is not this enough?

Birkin started with madness from this question, for it touched the quick of torture. There was his love for Hermione, a love based entirely on ecstasy and on pain, and ultimate death. He *knew* he did not love her with any living, creative love. He did not even desire her: he had no passion for her, there was no hot impulse of growth between them, only this terrible reducing activity of phosphorescent consciousness, the consciousness ever liberated more and more into the void, at the expense of the flesh, which was burnt down like dead grey ash.

He did not call this love. Yet he was bound to her, and it was agony to leave her. And he did not love anyone else. He did not love any woman. He *wanted* to love. But between wanting to love, and loving, is the whole difference between life and death.

The incapacity to love, the incapacity to desire any woman, positively, with body and soul, this was a real torture, a deep torture indeed. Never to be able to love spontaneously, never to be moved by a power greater than oneself, but always to be within one's own control, deliberate, having the choice, this was horrifying, more deadly than death. Yet how was one to escape? How could a man escape from being deliberate and unloving, except a greater power, an impersonal, imperative love should take hold of him? And if the greater power should not take hold of him, what could he do but continue in his deliberateness, without any fundamental spontaneity?

He did not love Hermione, he did not desire her. But he wanted to force himself to love her and to desire her. He was consumed by sexual desire, and he wanted to be fulfilled. Yet he did not desire Hermione.

She repelled him rather. Yet he *would* have this physical fulfilment, he would have the sexual activity. So he forced himself towards her.

She was hopeless from the start. Yet she resigned herself to him. In her soul, she knew this was not the way. And yet even she was ashamed, as of some physical deficiency. She did not want him either. But with all her soul, she *wanted* to want him. She would do anything to give him what he wanted, that which he was raging for, this physical fulfilment he insisted on. She was wise; she thought for the best. She prepared herself like a perfect sacrifice to him. She offered herself gladly to him, gave herself into his will.

And oh, it was all such a cruel failure, just a failure. This last act of love which he had demanded of her was the keenest grief of all, it was so insignificant, so null. He had no pleasure of her, only some mortification. And her heart almost broke with grief.

She wanted him to take her. She wanted him to take her, to break her with his passion, to destroy her with his desire, so long as he got satisfaction. She looked forward, tremulous, to a kind of death at his hands, she gave herself up. She would be broken and dying, destroyed, if only he would rise fulfilled.

But he was not capable of it, he failed. He could not take her and destroy her. He could not forget her. They had too rare a spiritual intimacy, he could not now tear himself away from all this, and come like a brute to take its satisfaction. He was too much aware of her, and of her fear, and of her writhing torment, as she lay in sacrifice. He had too much deference for her feeling. He could not, as she madly wanted, destroy her, trample her, and crush a satisfaction from her. He was not experienced enough, not hardened enough. He was always aware of *her* feelings, so that he had none of his own. Which made this last love-making between them an ignominious failure, very, very cruel to bear.

And it was this failure which broke the love between them. He hated her, for her incapacity in love, for her lack of desire for him, her complete and almost perfect lack of any physical desire towards him. Her desire was all spiritual, all in the consciousness. She wanted him all, all through the consciousness, never through the senses.

And she hated him, and despised him, for his incapacity to wreak his desire upon her, his lack of strength to crush his satisfaction from her. If only he could have taken her, destroyed her, used her all up, and been satisfied, she would be at last free. She might be killed, but it would be the death which gave her consummation.

It was a failure, a bitter, final failure. He could not take from her what he wanted, because he could not, bare-handed, destroy her. And she despised him that he could not destroy her.

Still, though they had failed, finally, they did not go apart. Their relation was too deep-established. He was by this time twenty-eight years old, and she twenty-seven. Still, for his spiritual delight, for a companion in his conscious life, for someone to share and heighten his joy in thinking, or in reading, or in feeling beautiful things, or in knowing landscape intimately and poignantly, he turned to her. For all these things, she was still with him, she made up the greater part of his life. And he, she knew to her anguish and mortification, he was still the master-key to almost all life, for her. She wanted it not to be so, she wanted to be free of him, of the strange, terrible bondage of his domination. But as yet, she could not free herself from him.

He went to other women, to women of purely sensual, sensational attraction, he prostituted his spirit with them. And he got *some* satisfaction. She watched him go, sadly, and yet not without a measure of relief. For he would torment her less, now.

She knew he would come back to her. She knew, inevitably as the dawn would rise, he would come back to her, half-exultant and triumphant over her, half-bitter against her for letting him go and wanting her now, wanting the communion with her. It was as if he went to the other, the dark, sensual, almost bestial woman thoroughly and fully to degrade himself. He despised himself, essentially, in his attempts at sensuality, she knew that. So she let him be. It was only his rather vulgar arrogance of a sinner that she found hard to bear. For before her, he wore his sins with braggadocio, flaunted them a little in front of her. And this alone drove her to exasperation to the point of uttering her contempt for his childishness and his instability.

But as yet, she forbore, because of the deference he still felt towards her. Intrinsically, in his spirit, he still served her. And this service she cherished.

But he was becoming gnawed and bitter, a little mad. His whole system was inflamed to a pitch of mad irritability, he became blind, unconscious to the greater half of life, only a few things he saw with feverish acuteness. And she, she kept the key to him, all the while.

The only thing she dreaded was his making up his mind. She dreaded his way of seeing some particular things vividly and feverishly, and of his acting upon this special sight. For once he decided a thing, it became a reigning universal truth to him, and he was completely inhuman.

He was, in his own way, quite honest with himself. But every man has his own truths, and is honest with himself according to them. The terrible thing about Birkin, for Hermione, was that when once he decided upon a truth, he acted upon it, cost what it might. If he decided that his eye did really offend him, he would in truth pluck it out. And this seemed to her so inhuman, so abstract, that it chilled her to the depths of her soul, and made him seem to her inhuman, something between a monster and a complete fool. For might not she herself easily be found to be this eye which must needs be plucked out?

He had stuck fast over this question of love and of physical fulfilment in love, till it had become like a monomania. All his thought turned upon it. For he wanted to keep his integrity of being, he would not consent to sacrifice one half of himself to the other. He would not sacrifice the sensual to the spiritual half of himself, and he could not sacrifice the spiritual to the sensual half. Neither could he obtain fulfilment in both, the two halves always reacted from each other. To be spiritual, he must have a Hermione, completely without desire: to be sensual, he must have a slightly bestial woman, the very scent of whose skin soon disgusted him, whose manners nauseated him beyond bearing, so that Hermione, always chaste and always stretching out her hands for beauty, seemed to him the purest and most desirable thing on earth.

He knew he obtained no real fulfilment in sensuality, he became disgusted and despised the whole process as if it were dirty. And he knew that he had no real fulfilment in his spiritual and aesthetic intercourse with Hermione. That process he also despised, with considerable cynicism.

And he recognized that he was on the point either of breaking, becoming a thing, losing his integral being, or else of becoming insane. He was now nothing but a series of reactions from dark to light, from light to dark, almost mechanical, without unity or meaning.

This was the most insufferable bondage, the most tormenting affliction, that he could not save himself from these extreme reactions, the vibration between two poles, one of which was Hermione, the centre of social virtue, the other of which was a prostitute, anti-social, almost criminal. He knew that in the end, subject to this extreme vibration, he would be shattered, would die, or else, worse still, would become a mere disordered set of processes, without purpose or integral being. He knew this, and dreaded it. Yet he could not save himself.

To save himself, he must unite the two halves of himself, spiritual and sensual. And this is what no man can do at once, deliberately. It must happen to him. Birkin willed to be sensual, as well as spiritual, with Hermione. He might will it, he might act according to his will, but he did not bring to pass that which he willed. A man cannot create desire in himself, nor cease at will from desiring. Desire, in any shape or form, is primal, whereas the will is secondary, derived. The will can destroy, but it cannot create.

So the more he tried with his will, to force his senses towards Hermione, the greater misery he produced. On the other hand his pride never ceased to contemn his profligate intercourse elsewhere. After all, it was *not* that which he wanted. He did not want libertine pleasures, not fundamentally. His fundamental desire was, to be able to love completely, in one and the same act: both body and soul at once, struck into a complete oneness in contact with a complete woman.

And he failed in this desire. It was always a case of one or the other, of spirit or of senses, and each, alone, was deadly. All history, almost all art, seemed the story of this deadly half-love: either passion, like Cleopatra, or else spirit, like Mary of Bethany or Vittoria Colonna.

He pondered on the subject endlessly, and knew himself in his reactions. But self-knowledge is not everything. No man, by taking thought, can add one cubit to his stature. He can but know his own height and limitation.

He knew that he loved no woman, that in nothing was he really complete, really himself. In his most passionate moments of spiritual enlightenment, when like a saviour of mankind he would pour out his soul for the world, there was in him a capacity to jeer at all his own righteousness and spirituality, justly and sincerely to make a mock of it all. And the mockery was so true, it bit to the very core of his righteousness, and showed it rotten, shining with phosphorescence. But at the same time, whilst quivering in the climax-thrill of sensual pangs, some cold voice could say in him: "You are not really moved; you could rise up and go away from this pleasure quite coldly and calmly; it is not radical, your enjoyment."

He knew he had not loved, could not love. The only thing then was to make the best of it, have the two things separate, and over them all, a calm detached mind. But to this he would not acquiesce. "I should be like a Neckan," he said to himself, "like a sea-water being, I should have no soul." And he pondered the stories of the wistful, limpid creatures who watched ceaselessly, hoping to gain a soul.

So the trouble went on, he became more hollow and deathly, more like a spectre with hollow bones. He knew that he was not very far from dissolution.

All the time, he recognized that, although he was always drawn to women, feeling more at home with a woman than with a man, yet it was for men that he felt the hot, flushing, roused attraction which a man is supposed to feel for the other sex. Although nearly all his living interchange went on with one woman or another, although he was always terribly intimate with at least one woman, and practically never intimate with a man, yet the male physique had a fascination for him, and for the female physique he felt only a fondness, a sort of sacred love, as for a sister.

In the street, it was the men who roused him by their flesh and their manly, vigorous movement, quite apart from all the individual character, whilst he studied the women as sisters, knowing their meaning and their intents. It was the men's physique which held the passion and the mystery to him. The women he seemed to be kin to, he looked for the soul in them. The soul of a woman and the physique of a man, these were the two things he watched for, in the street.

And this was a new torture to him. Why did not the face of a woman move him in the same manner, with the same sense of handsome desirability, as the face of a man? Why was a man's beauty, the beauté mâle, so vivid and intoxicating a thing to him, whilst female beauty was something quite unsubstantial, consisting all of look and gesture and revelation of intuitive intelligence? He thought women beautiful purely because of their expression. But it was plastic form that fascinated him in men, the contour and movement of the flesh itself.

He wanted all the time to love women. He wanted all the while to feel this kindled, loving attraction towards a beautiful woman, that he would often feel towards a handsome man. But he could not. Whenever it was a case of a woman, there entered in too much spiritual, sisterly love; or else, in reaction, there was only a brutal, callous sort of lust.

This was an entanglement from which there seemed no escape. How can a man *create* his own feelings? He cannot. It is only in his power to suppress them, to bind them in the chain of the will. And what is suppression but a mere negation of life, and of living.

He had several friendships wherein this passion entered, friendships with men of no very great intelligence, but of pleasant appearance: ruddy, well-nourished fellows, good-natured and easy, who protected him in his delicate health more gently than a woman would protect him. He loved his friend, the beauty of whose manly limbs made him tremble with pleasure. He wanted to caress him.

But reserve, which was as strong as a chain of iron in him, kept him from any demonstration. And if he were away for any length of time from the man he loved so hotly, then he forgot him, the flame which invested the beloved like a transfiguration passed away, and Birkin remembered his friend as tedious. He could not go back to him, to talk as tediously as he would have to talk, to take such a level of intelligence as he would have to take. He forgot his men friends completely, as one forgets the candle one has blown out. They remained as quite extraneous and uninteresting persons living their life in their own sphere, and having not the slightest relation to himself, even though they themselves maintained a real warmth of affection, almost of love for him. He paid not the slightest heed to this love which was constant to him, he felt it sincerely to be just nothing, valueless.

So he left his old friends completely, even those to whom he had been attached passionately, like David to Jonathan. Men whose presence he had waited for cravingly, the touch of whose shoulder suffused him with a vibration of physical love, became to him mere figures, as non-existent as is the waiter who sets the table in a restaurant.

He wondered very slightly at this, but dismissed it with hardly a thought. Yet, every now and again, would come over him the same passionate desire to have near him some man he saw, to exchange intimacy, to unburden himself of love to this new beloved.

It might be any man, a policeman who suddenly looked up at him, as he inquired the way, or a soldier who sat next to him in a railway carriage. How vividly, months afterwards, he would recall the soldier who had sat pressed up close to him on a journey from Charing Cross to Westerham; the shapely, motionless body, the large, dumb, coarsely-beautiful hands that rested helpless upon the strong knees, the dark brown eyes, vulnerable in the erect body. Or a young man in flannels on the sands at Margate, flaxen and ruddy, like a Viking of twenty-three, with clean, rounded contours, pure as the contours of snow, playing with some young children, building a castle in sand, intent and abstract, like a seagull or a keen white bear.

In his mind was a small gallery of such men: men whom he had never spoken to, but who had flashed themselves upon his senses unforgettably, men whom he apprehended intoxicatingly in his blood. They divided themselves roughly into two classes: these white-skinned, keen-limbed men with eyes like blue-flashing ice and hair like crystals of winter sunshine, the northmen, inhuman as sharp-crying gulls, distinct like splinters of ice, like crystals, isolated, individual; and then the men with dark eyes that one can enter and plunge into, bathe in, as in a liquid darkness, dark-skinned, supple, night-smelling men, who are the living substance of the viscous, universal heavy darkness.

His senses surged towards these men, towards the perfect and beautiful representatives of these two halves. And he knew them, by seeing them and by apprehending them sensuously, he knew their very blood, its weight and savour; the blood of the northmen sharp and red and light, tending to be keenly acrid, like cranberries, the blood of the dark-limbed men heavy and luscious, and in the end nauseating, revolting.

He asked himself, often, as he grew older, and more unearthly, when he was twenty-eight and twenty-nine years old, would he ever be appeased, would he ever cease to desire these two sorts of men. And a wan kind of hopelessness would come over him, as if he would never escape from this attraction, which was a bondage.

For he would never acquiesce to it. He could never acquiesce to his own feelings, to his own passion. He could never grant that it should be so, that it was well for him to feel this keen desire to have and to possess the bodies of such men, the passion to bathe in the very substance of such men, the substance of living, eternal light, like eternal snow, and the flux of heavy, rank-smelling darkness.

He wanted to cast out these desires, he wanted not to know them. Yet a man can no more slay a living desire in him, than he can prevent his body from feeling heat and cold. He can put himself into bondage, to prevent the fulfilment of the desire, that is all. But the desire is there, as the travelling of the blood itself is there, until it is fulfilled or until the body is dead.

So he went on, month after month, year after year, divided against himself, striving for the day when the beauty of men should not be so acutely attractive to him, when the beauty of woman should move him instead.

But that day came no nearer, rather it went further away. His deep dread was that it would always be so, that he would never be free. His life would have been one long torture of struggle against his own innate desire, his own innate being. But to be so divided against oneself, this is terrible, a nullification of all being.

He went into violent excess with a mistress whom, in a rather anti-social, ashamed spirit, he loved. And so for a long time he forgot about this attraction that men had for him. He forgot about it entirely. And then he grew stronger, surer.

But then, inevitably, it would recur again. There would come into a restaurant a strange Cornish type of man, with dark eyes like holes in his head, or like the eyes of a rat, and with dark, fine, rather stiff hair, and full, heavy, softly-strong limbs. Then again Birkin would feel the desire spring up in him, the desire to know this man, to have him, as it were to eat him, to take the very substance of him. And watching the strange, rather furtive, rabbit-like way in which the strong, softly-built man ate, Birkin would feel the rousedness burning in his own breast, as if this were what he wanted, as if the satisfaction of his desire lay in the body of the young, strong man opposite.

And then in his soul would succeed a sort of despair, because this passion for a man had recurred in him. It was a deep misery to him. And it would seem as if he had always loved men, always and only loved men. And this was the greatest suffering to him.

But it was not so, that he always loved men. For weeks it would be all gone from him, this passionate admiration of the rich body of a man. For weeks he was free, active, and living. But he had such a dread of his own feelings and desires, that when they recurred again, the interval vanished, and it seemed the bondage and the torment had been continuous.

This was the one and only secret he kept to himself, this secret of his passionate and sudden, spasmodic affinity for men he saw. He kept this secret even from himself. He knew what he felt, but he always kept the knowledge at bay. His a priori were: "I *should not* feel like this," and "It is the ultimate mark of my own deficiency, that I feel like this." Therefore, though he admitted everything, he never really faced the question. He never accepted the desire, and received it as part of himself. He always tried to keep it expelled from him.*

Gerald Crich was the one towards whom Birkin felt most strongly that immediate, roused attraction which transfigured the person of the attracter with such a glow and such a desirable beauty. The two men had met once or twice, and then Gerald Crich went abroad, to South America. Birkin forgot him, all connection died down. But it was not finally dead. In both men were the seeds of a strong, inflammable affinity.

Therefore, when Birkin found himself pledged to act as best man at the wedding of Hosken, the friend of the mountain-climbing holiday, and of Laura Crich, sister of Gerald, the old affection sprang awake in a moment. He wondered what Gerald would be like now.

Hermione, knowing of Hosken's request to Birkin, at once secured for herself the position of bridesmaid to Laura Crich. It was inevitable. She and Rupert Birkin were running to the end of their friendship. He was now thirty years of age, and she twenty-nine. His feeling of hostility towards Hermione had grown now to an almost constant dislike.

---

* At one time the Prologue chapter ended here, for the next page of the manuscript is headed *Chapter II The Wedding*. This heading is cancelled and the direction "Run on" is twice inserted.

Still she held him in her power. But the hold became weaker and weaker. "If he breaks loose," she said, "he will fall into the abyss."

Nevertheless he was bound to break loose, because his reaction against Hermione was the strongest movement in his life, now. He was thrusting her off, fighting her off all the while, thrusting himself clear, although he had no other foothold, although he was breaking away from her, his one rock, to fall into a bottomless sea.

Mr. Noon

1. ATTACK ON MR. NOON

Her very stillness, as she sat bent upon her book, gradually made him uncomfortable. He twisted over, sprawling in his armchair, and pretended to go on with his perusal of the *New Age*. But neither Mr. Orage nor Miss Tina could carry him on the wings of the spirit this afternoon. He kept glancing at his wife, whose intensified stillness would have told a cuter man that she knew he was fidgeting, and then glancing at the window and round the room. It was a rainy, dark Sunday afternoon. He ought to be very cosy, in the quiet by the roasting fire. But he was bored, and he wanted to be amused.

He perched his pince-nez on his nose and looked with an intellectual eye on his paper once more. Perhaps the light was fading. He twisted to look at the window. The aspidistras and ferns were not inspiring; it was still far from nightfall. He twisted the other way, to look at the little round clock on the mantelpiece. No use suggesting a meal, yet. He gave a heavy sigh, and rattled the leaves of the *New Age*.

But no response! no response! The little red metal devils frisked as ever on the mantelpiece, his own pet devils. Having gone back on the Lord, he signified his revolt by establishing a little company of scarlet, tail-flourishing gentry on his sitting-room mantelpiece. But it was only half-past three, and there was nothing to be done. He would not insult himself by nodding off to sleep. So again he perched his pince-nez on his nose, and began to have a grudge against his wife. After all, what was she so absorbed in?

She was a woman of about forty, stoutish, with very dark glossy brown hair coiled on her head. She sat sunk deep in a chair, with her feet on a little footstool, and her spectacles right away on the tip of her nose. He, of course, did not observe that she never turned the page of her absorbing book.

His blue eyes strayed petulantly to the fire. Ah-ha! Here he was in demand. In the well of the grate a mass of fire glowed scarlet like his devils, with a dark, half-burnt coal resting above. He crouched before the curb and took the poker with satisfaction. Biff! A well-aimed blow; he could congratulate himself on it. The excellent coal burst like magic into a bunch of flames.

"That's better!" he said heartily.

And he remained crouching before the fire, in his loose homespun clothes. He was handsome, with a high forehead and a small beard; a socialist; something like Shakespeare's bust to look at, but more refined. He had an attractive, boyish nape of the neck, for a man of forty-five, no longer thin.

So he crouched gazing into the hot, spurting, glowing fire. He was a pure idealist, something of a Christ, but with an intruding touch of the goat. His eyelids dropped oddly, goat-like, as he remained abstracted before the fire.

His wife roused, and cleared her throat.

"Were you sleeping, Missis?" he asked her in a jocular manner of accusation, screwing round to look at her. She had a full, soft, ivory-pale face, and dark eyes with heavy shadows under them. She took her spectacles off her nose-tip.

"No," she said, in the same sparring humour. "I was *not*."

"May I ask you what was the last sentence you read?"

"You may ask. But you mayn't expect me to answer."

"I'll bet not," he laughed. "It would be the tail-end of a dream, if you did."

"No, it would *not*," she said. "Not even a day-dream."

"What, were you as sound as all that?" he said.

But she began rustling her book, rather ostentatiously. He crouched, watching her. The coil of hair was rust-brown on her dark, glossy head. Her hair became reddish towards the ends. It piqued him still, after twenty years of marriage. But since the top of her head was all she showed him, he went back to his big chair, and screwed himself in with his legs underneath him, though he was a biggish man, and once again settled his pince-nez. In a man who doesn't smoke or drink, an eye-glass or a pair of pince-nez can become a vice.

"Ay-y-y!" he sighed to himself, as he tried to find excitement in the well-filled pages of the *New Statesman*. He kept his quick ears attentive to the outside. The church clock sounded four. Some people passed, voices chattering. He got up to look. Girls going by. He would have liked a chat, or a bit of fun with them. With a longing, half-leering eye he looked down from the window.

"It's about lighting-up time, Mrs. Goddard, isn't it?" he said to his wife.

"Yes, I suppose it is," she said abstractedly.

He bustled round with the matches, lit three gas-jets, drew the curtains, and rocked on his heels with his hands in his pockets and his back to the fire. This was the precious Sunday afternoon. Every week-day he was at the office. Sunday was a treasure-day to the two of them. They were socialists and vegetarians. So, in fine weather, they tramped off into the country. In bad weather they got up late, had a substantial meal towards the end of the morning, and another in the early evening. None of the horrors of Sunday joints.

Lewis rocked on his heels on the hearth, with his back to the fire and his hands in his pockets, whistling faintly.

"You might chop some wood," said Patty.

"I was just thinking so," he said, with rather a resentful cheerfulness in his acquiescence.

However, off he went to the back yard, and Patty could hear him letting off some of his steam on the wood, whilst he kept up all the time a brilliant whistling. It wouldn't be Lewis if he didn't make himself heard wherever he was.

She mused on, in the brilliantly-lighted, hot room. She seemed very still, like a cat. Yet the dark lines under her eyes were marked. Her skin was of that peculiar transparency often noticed in vegetarians and idealists. Her husband's was the same; as if the blood were lighter, more limpid, nearer to acid in the veins. All the time, she heard her husband so plainly. He always sounded in her universe: always. And she was tired; just tired. They were an ideal married couple, she and he. But something was getting on her nerves.

He appeared after a time.

"Can't see any more," he said. "Beastly rain still. The Unco Guid will want their just umbrellas tonight. I'm afraid there'll be a fair amount of pew-timber showing beneath the reverend eyes, moreover. There's nothing parsons hate more than the sight of bare pew-timber. They don't mind a bare bread-board half as much. That reminds me, Mrs. Goddard, what about tea?"

"What about it?" she answered, screwing up her face at him slightly, in a sort of smile. He looked down at her from under his eyelids.

"Is that intended as a piece of cheek?" he asked.

"Yes, it might be," she said.

"I won't stand it."

"I wouldn't. I wouldn't. No man ever does," she quizzed.

"When a woman begins to give her husband cheek—"

"Go and put the kettle on."

"*I've* got to go and get the tea, have I?" he asked.

"Yes, if you want it so early, you have. It's only five o'clock."

"The wiles and circumventions of a woman's heart, not to mention her tongue, would cheat ten Esaus out of ten birthrights a day."

"All right, then put the kettle on."

"You have any more of your impudence, Patty Goddard, and *I* won't, so I tell you straight."

"I'm dumb," she said.

"My word, then I'll make haste and clear out, while the victory is yet mine."

So he retreated to the kitchen, and his brilliant whistling kept her fully informed of his existence down the long length of the passage. Nay, even if he went out of actual earshot, he seemed to be ringing her up all the time on some viewless telephone. The man was marvellous. His voice could speak to her across a hundred miles of space; if he went to America, verily, she would hear him invisibly as if he was in the back kitchen. The connection between a mother and her infant was as nothing compared to the organic or telepathic connection between her and Lewis. It was a connection which simply was never broken. And not a peaceful, quiet unison. But unquiet, as if he was always talking, always slightly forcing her attention, as now by his whistling in the kitchen. When he was right away from her, he still could make some sort of soundless noise which she was forced to hear and attend to. Lewis, Lewis, her soul sounded with the noise of him as a shell with the sea. It excited her, it pleased her, it saved her from ever feeling lonely. She loved it, she felt immensely pleased and flattered. But the dark lines came under her eyes, and she felt sometimes as if she would go mad with irritation.

He was fumbling at the door, and she knew he was balancing the full tray on his knee whilst he turned the door-handle. She listened. He was very clever at these tricks, but she must listen, for fear.

"Well, of all the idle scawd-rags!" he said as he entered with the tray.

"I'm the idlest, I know it," she said, laughing. She had in fact known that she ought to spread the cloth in readiness for his coming. But today a kind of inertia held her.

"How much does that admission cost you?" bantered Lewis, as he flapped the white cloth on to the round table.

"Less than the effort of getting up and laying the cloth," she laughed.

"Ay, such a lot," he said. He liked doing things, really, on these days when the work-woman was absent.

There were buttered eggs in little casseroles; there was a Stilton cheese, a salad, a pudding of chestnuts and cream, celery, cakes, pastry, jam, and preserved ginger; there were delicate blue Nankin cups, and berries and leaves in a jar. It had never ceased to be a delightful picnic *à deux*. It was so this evening, still. But there was an underneath strain, unaccountable, that made them both listen for some relief.

They had passed the eggs and cheese and pudding stage, and reached the little cakes and tarts, when they heard the front gate bang.

"Who's this?" said Lewis, rising quickly and going to light the hall lamp. The bell pinged.

Patty listened with her ears buttoned back.

"I wondered if you'd be at home . . ." a man's bass voice.

"Ay, we're at home. Come in." Lewis's voice, heartily. He was nothing if not hospitable. Patty could tell he did not know who his visitor was.

"Oh, Mr. Noon, is it you? Glad to see you. Take your coat off. Ay? Are you wet? Have you walked? You've just come right for a cup of tea. Ay, come in."

Mr. Noon! Patty had risen hastily, hearing the name. She stood in the sitting-room doorway in her soft dress of dark-brown poplin trimmed with silk brocade in orange and brown. She was waiting. The visitor came forward.

"How nice of you to come," she said. "Where have you been for so long? We haven't seen you for ages. You're sure your feet aren't wet? Let Lewis give you a pair of slippers."

"Ay, come on," said Lewis heartily.

Mr. Noon, in a bass voice, said he had come on the motor-bicycle, and that he had left his overalls at the Sun. He was a young man of twenty-five or twenty-six, with broad, rather stiff shoulders and a dark head somewhat too small for these shoulders. His face was fresh, his mouth full and pursed, his eye also rather full, dark-blue, and abstracted. His appearance was correct enough, black coat and a dark-blue tie tied in a bow. He did not look like a socialist.

The whole character of the room was now changed. It was evident the Goddards were pleased, rather flattered to entertain their visitor. Yet his hands were red, and his voice rather uncouth. But there was a considerable force in him. He ate the food they gave him as if he liked it.

"Now tell us," said Patty, "what brings you to Woodhouse on a night like this."

"Not any desire to sit at the feet of one of our famous administers of the gospel, I'll warrant," said Lewis.

"No," said Noon. "I'd got an appointment and was here a bit too soon, so I wondered if you'd mind if I called."

"Ah!" exclaimed Patty. His answer was hardly flattering. "Of course, of course! You may just as well wait here as at a street-corner, or in a public-house."

"The public-houses, my dear Patty, don't open till half-past six, so that they shan't get an unfair start on the House of the Lord," said Lewis.

"No, of course," said Patty. "But you won't have to hurry away at once, I hope?" she added, to Gilbert Noon.

"I can stop till about half-past seven," said that gentleman.

"Till chapel comes out," said Lewis drily.

"Ha-a-a!" laughed Patty, half-scornfully, half-bitterly, as if she had found him out.

"That's it," said Mr. Noon, getting rather red.

"Which of the tabernacles is it, then?" asked Lewis. "We'd better know, to start you off in good time. Pentecost is half an hour earlier than the others, and Church is about ten minutes before the Congregational. Wesleyan is the last, because the Reverend Mr. Flewitt is newly arrived on the circuit, and wants to sweep the chapel very clean of sin, being a new broom."

"Congregational," said Mr. Noon.

"Ha-ha! Ha-ha!" said Patty teasingly. She was really rather chagrined. "You're quite sure the fair flame will have come out on such a night?"

"No, I'm not sure," said Mr. Noon, rather awkwardly.

"Many waters cannot quench love, Patty Goddard," said Lewis.

"They can put a considerable damper on it," replied Patty.

Gilbert Noon laughed.

"They can that," he replied.

"You speak as if you knew," laughed Patty, knitting her brows.

But Gilbert only shook his head.

"Ah, well," said Patty, looking at the clock. "We can just clear away and settle down for an hour's talk, anyhow. I've a lot of things to ask you. Do smoke, if you care to."

Lewis, a non-smoker, hurried up with a box of cigarettes. But the young man preferred a pipe. They were soon all seated round the fire.

The reason the Goddards made so much of Gilbert Noon was because he was so clever. His father owned a woodyard in Whetstone, six miles away, and was comfortably well-off, but stingy. Gilbert, the only son, had started his career as an elementary school-teacher, but had proved so sharp at mathematics, music and science that he had won several scholarships, had gone up to Cambridge, and might have had a Fellowship if only he had stayed and worked. But he would neither work nor stay at the University, although he was accounted one of the most brilliant of the young mathematicians. He came back to Whetstone with his degree, and started the old round of Whetstone life, carousing in common public-houses, playing his violin for vulgar dances— "hops," as they were called—and altogether demeaning himself. He had a post as Science Master in Haysfall Technical School, another five miles from Whetstone, and, so far, Haysfall shut its ears to Whetstone misdemeanours. Gilbert's native town, a raw industrial place, was notorious for its roughs.

Occasionally Mr. Noon, being somewhat of a celebrity in the countryside, would give popular lectures on scientific subjects. Lewis Goddard was secretary for the Woodhouse Literary Society, and as such had had much pride in securing Gilbert on several occasions. Gilbert's lectures to the people were really excellent: so simple, and so entertaining. His account of Mars, with lantern-slides, thrilled Woodhouse to the marrow. And particularly it thrilled Patty. Mars, its canals, and its inhabitants and its what-not: ah, how wonderful it was! And how wonderful was Mr. Noon, with his rough bass voice, roughly and laconically and yet with such magic and power landing her on another planet. Mephistopheles himself, in a good-natured mood, could not have been more fascinating than the rough young man who stood on the rostrum and pointed at the lantern sheet with a long wand, whose ruddy face was lit up by his dark-lantern, as he glanced at his notes.

So had started the Noon-Goddard acquaintance, which had not as yet ripened into a friendship. The Goddards warmly invited Gilbert, but he rarely came. And his social uncouthness, though acceptable in the Midlands as a sign of manliness, was rather annoying sometimes to a woman.

He sat now with a big pipe in his fist, smoking clouds of smoke and staring abstractedly into the fire. He wore a ring with a big red stone on one finger. Patty wondered at him, really. He made no effort to be pleasant, so his hostess fluttered her two neat little feet on her footstool, settled herself deep in her chair, and lifted her sewing from under a cushion. She perched her spectacles away on the slope of her nose, then looked up at Gilbert from under her dark eyebrows.

"You won't be shocked if I stitch on the Sabbath, and sew clothes for the devil?" she asked.

"Me?" said Gilbert. "Better the day, better the deed."

"So they say," retorted Patty sarcastically. But it was lost on him.

"I'd rather clothe the devil than those up aloft," said Lewis. "He stands more need. Why, he's never a rag to his back. Not even a pair of bathing-drawers, much less an immortal mantle. Funny thing that."

"Beauty is best unadorned," said Patty.

"Then the angels and the Lord must be pretty unbeautiful, under all their robes and spangles," said Lewis.

But Mr. Noon was not attentive. Patty called a sort of hush. From the midst of it she inquired in a small, searching voice:

"And what are you doing with yourself these days, Mr. Noon?"

"Me? Making stinks at Haysfall."

"Chemical, I hope, not moral," said Lewis.

"And what are you doing at Whetstone?" asked Patty.

Gilbert took his pipe from his mouth and looked at her.

"Pretty much as usual," he said.

She laughed quickly.

"And what is that?" she said. "Are you working at anything?"

He reached forward and knocked his pipe on the fire-bar.

"I'm doing a bit," he said.

"Of what?" she asked.

"Oh—thesis for my M.A.—maths.—And composing a bit as well."

"Composing music? But how splendid! What is it?"

"A violin concerto."

"Mayn't we hear it?"

"It wouldn't mean anything to you—too abstract."

"But mayn't we hear it?"

"Ay—you might, sometime—when I can arrange it."

"Do arrange it! Do!"

"Yes, do," put in Lewis.

"It's not finished," said Gilbert.

"But when it is," said Patty. "You *will* finish it, won't you?"

"I hope so, some day."

She stuck her needle in her sewing, and looked up, and mused.

"I think of all the wonderful things to create," she said, "music is the most difficult. I can never understand how you begin. And do you prefer music to your mathematics?"

"They run into one another—they're nearly the same thing," he said. "Besides, it isn't any good. It's too abstract and dry for anybody but me, what I write."

"Can't you make it less abstract?" she said.

He looked at her.

"Somehow I can't," he said; and she saw a flutter of trouble in him.

"Why?" she asked.

"I don't know, I'm sure. I know it hasn't got the right touch. It's more a musical exercise than a new piece of work. I only do it for a bit of pastime. It'll never amount to anything."

"Oh, surely not. You who have such talents . . ."

"*Who?*" said Gilbert scoffingly.

"You. You have wonderful talents."

"I'm glad to hear it. Where are they?" asked Gilbert.

"In your head, I suppose."

"Ay, and there they can stop, for all they're worth."

"Nay, now . . ." began Lewis.

"But why? But why?" rushed in Patty. "Don't you *want* to make anything of your life? Don't you want to produce something that will help us poor mortals out of the slough?"

"Slough?" said Gilbert. "What I should do would only make the slough deeper."

"Oh, come! Come! Think of the joy I got out of your lecture."

He looked at her, smiling faintly.

"A pack of lies," he said.

"What?" she cried. "*Didn't* I get joy out of it?"

He had got his pipe between his pouting lips again, and had closed his brow.

"What is lies?" she persisted.

"Mars," he said. "A nice little fairy-tale. You only like it better than 'Arabian Nights'."

"Oh, *come* . . . !" she cried in distress.

"Ay, we like it better than 'Arabian Nights,'" said Lewis.

"I know you do," said Gilbert. "I'll tell you another, some time."

"Oh, but *come!*—come!" said Patty. "Is nothing real? Is nothing true?"

"Not that I know of," said Gilbert. "In that line."

"Why, dear me, how surprising!" said Patty, puzzled. "Surely you believe in your own work?"

"Yes, I believe in mathematics."

"Well, then . . ." she said.

He took his pipe from his mouth, and looked at her.

"There isn't any *well then*," he said.

"Why not?"

"Mathematics is mathematics, the plane of abstraction and perfection. Life is life, and is neither abstraction nor perfection."

"But it has to do with both," she protested.

"*Art* has. Life hasn't."

"Life doesn't matter to you then?"

"No. Why should it?"

The answer staggered her.

"How can anything matter, if life doesn't matter?" she said.

"How could anything matter, if life mattered?" he replied. "Life is incompatible with perfection, or with infinity, or with eternity. You've got to turn to mathematics, or to art."

She was completely bewildered.

"I can't believe it," she cried.

"Ay, well," he retorted, knocking out his pipe.

"You're young yet. You'll find that life matters before you've done," she said.

"I'm quite willing," he said.

"No," she said, "you're not." Suddenly her ivory face flushed red. "Indeed you're not willing. When do you ever give life a chance?"

"Me?" he said. "Always."

"No, you don't. Excuse my contradicting you. You *never* give life a chance. Look how you treat women!"

He looked round at her in wonder.

"How do I?" he said. "What women?"

"Yes, how do you!" She stumbled, and hesitated. "Confess it's a girl you're going to meet tonight," she continued, plunging. "I'm old enough to be able to speak. You've never really had a mother. You don't know how you treat women. Confess you're going to meet a girl."

"Yes—what by that?"

"And confess she's not your equal."

"Nay, I don't see it."

"Yes, you do. Yes, you do. How do you look on her? Do you look on her as you do on your mathematics? Ha!—you know what a difference there is."

"Bound to be," he said. "Bound to be a difference."

"Yes, bound to be. And the girl bound to be an inferior—a mere plaything—not as serious as your chemical apparatus, even."

"Different," protested Gilbert. "All the difference in the world."

"Of course," said Patty. "And who sinks down in the scale of difference? Who does? The girl . . . I won't ask you who the girl is—I know nothing about her. But what is she to you? A trivial Sunday-night bit of fun! Isn't she?—isn't she, now?"

"Ay, she's good fun, if I must say it."

"She is! Exactly! She's good fun," cried Patty bitterly. "Good fun, and nothing else. What a humiliation for her, poor thing!"

"I don't think she finds it so," said Gilbert.

"No, I'll bet she doesn't," laughed Lewis, with his goat's laugh.

"She doesn't. She doesn't," cried Patty. "But how cruel that she doesn't! How cruel for her!"

"I don't see it at all. She's on the look-out for me as much as I am for her," said Gilbert.

"Yes, probably. Probably. And perhaps even more. And what is her life going to be afterwards? And you, what is your life going to be? What are you going to find in it, when you get tired of your bit of fun, and all women are trivial or dirty amusements to you? What then?"

"Nay, I'll tell you when I know," he answered.

"You won't. You won't. By that time you'll be as stale as they are, and you'll have lost everything but your mathematics and science— even if you've not lost them. I pity you. I pity you. You may well despise life. But I pity you. Life will despise *you*, and you'll know it."

"Why, where am I wrong?" asked Gilbert awkwardly.

"Where! For shame! Isn't a woman a human being? And isn't a human being more than your science and stuff?"

"Not to me, you know," he said. "Except in one way."

"Ay," laughed Lewis. "There's always the exception, my boy." There was a moment's pause.

"Well," said Patty, resuming her sewing. "For your mother's sake, I'm glad she can never hear you, never know. If she was a woman, it would break her heart."

But Gilbert could not see it. He smoked obstinately until Lewis reminded him that he must depart for his rendezvous.

Patty smiled at him as she shook hands, but rather constrainedly.

"Come in whenever you are near, and you feel like it,"she said.

"Thank you."

Lewis sped his parting guest, and had full sympathy with him, saying: "I'm all for a bit of fun, you know."

2. SPOON

Patty stitched on in silence, angry and bitter. Lewis fidgeted and whistled.

"He's got his human side to him right enough," he said, to make a breach in Patty's silence, which buzzed inaudibly and angrily on the atmosphere.

"*Human!*" she repeated. "Yes, call it *human!* A yellow dog on the streets has more humanity."

"Nay—nay," said Lewis testily. "Don't get your hair off, Mrs. Goddard. We aren't angels yet, thank heaven. Besides, there's no harm in it. A young chap goes out on Sunday night for a bit of a spoon. What is it but natural?"

He rocked easily and fussily on the hearth-rug, his legs apart. She looked up, quite greenish in her waxen pallor, with anger.

"You think it natural, do you?" she retorted. "Then I'm sorry for you. *Spoon!* A bit of a *spoon!*" She uttered the word as if it was full of castor-oil.

Her husband looked down on her with a touch of the old goat's leer.

"Don't forget you've been spoony enough in your day, Patty Goddard," he said.

She became suddenly still, musing.

"I suppose I have. I suppose I have," she mused, with disgust. "And I can't bear myself when I think of it."

"Oh, really!" said her husband sarcastically. "It's hard lines on *you*, all of a sudden, my dear." He knew that if she had been spoony with anybody, it was with him.

But, yellow-waxy with distaste, she put aside her sewing and went out. He listened, and followed her in a few minutes down to the kitchen, hearing dishes clink.

"What are you doing?" he asked her.

"Washing-up."

"Won't Mrs. Prince do it tomorrow?"

And to show his anger, he went away without drying the pots for her.

Spoon! "You've been spoony enough in your day, Patty Goddard!" Spoony! Spooning! The very mental sound of the word turned her stomach acid. In her anger she felt she could throw all her past, with the dish-water, down the sink. But, after all, if Gilbert Noon had been spooning with *her* instead of with some girl, some bit of fluff, she might not have felt such gall in her veins.

She knew all about it, as Lewis had said. She knew exactly what Sunday night meant, in the dark, wintry, rainy Midlands. It meant all the young damsels coming out of chapel or of church, brazen young things from fifteen upwards, and being accompanied or met by young louts who would touch their exaggerated caps awkwardly; it meant strolling off to some dark and sheltered corner, passage, entry, porch, shop-door, shed, anywhere where two creatures might stand and squeeze together and *spoon*. Yes, spoon. Not even kiss and cuddle, merely: *spoon*. Spooning was a fine art, whereas kissing and cuddling are calf-processes.

Mr. Gilbert had gone off for his Sunday-night's spoon, and her veins, the veins of a woman of forty, tingled with rage against him. She knew so much more.

But Sunday night, oh Sunday night; how she loathed it! There was a sort of Last Day suspense about it. Monday and Monday morning's work-day grip was very near. The iron hand was open to seize its subjects. And the emotional luxury and repletion of Sunday deepened into a sort of desperation as the hour of sleep and Monday approached. There must be a climax—there must be a consummation. Chapel did not finish it off sufficiently. The elder men dashed off for a drink, the women went to each other's houses for an intense gossip and a bit of supper, the young people went off for a spoon. It was the recognized thing to do—only very stiff-necked parents found any fault. The iron grip of Monday was closing. Meanwhile, dear young things, while the *frisson* of approaching captivity goes through you, to add an intenser sting to your bliss, spoon, dears, spoon.

Mr. Noon waited on the edge of the kerb, on the side of the road opposite the chapel. They were late coming out. The big but rather flimsy stained-glass window shed its colours on the muddy road, and Gilbert impassively contemplated the paucity of the geometric design of the tracery. He had contemplated it before. He contemplated it again as he stood in the rain with his coat-collar turned up and listened to the emotional moan of the vesper-verse which closed the last prayer. He objected to the raspberry-juice aerated-water melody and harmony, but had heard it before. Other louts were lurking in the shelter like spiders, down the road, ready to pounce on the emerging female flies.

Yes, the congregation was beginning to filter out; the spider-youths who scorned to go to chapel emerged from their lairs. Their cigarette-ends, before only smellable, now became visible. The young dogs waited to snap up their fluffy rabbits.

People oozed through the chapel gateway, expanded into umbrellas, and said of the rain: "Well, I never! It's as hard as ever!" and called "Good-night, then. So long! See you soon! Too-ra-loo! Keep smiling!"—and so on. Brave young dogs of fellows sniffed across the road. Sanctioned young hussies seized the arm of the "boy" who had his cap over his nose, his cigarette under his nose, and his coat-collar turned up;

and they set off down the road. Trickling dark streams of worshippers ebbed in opposite directions down the rainy night.

Mr. Noon was a stranger, and really too old for this business of waiting at the chapel gates. But since he had never got fixed up with a permanent girl, what was he to do? And he had the appointment. So, feeling rather self-conscious, he loitered like a pale ghost on the edge of the chapel stream.

She did not appear. It suddenly occurred to him that young people were emerging from the darkness of the tiny gateway at the other end of the chapel shrubbery, where there was no light. Sure enough, through that needle's eye the choir were being threaded out, and he remembered she was in the choir. He strolled along on the pavement opposite.

Of course he heard her voice.

"It's fair sickening. You'd think the Lord *liked* rain, for it pours every blessed Sunday. There comes Freddy! Oh, Agatha, you *are* short-sighted—can't see your own boy! Hello, Fred."

A tall youth in a bowler hat had stalked up to the two girls, who were dim under the trees on the wet pavement.

"Hellow, you two. How's things?"

"Oh, swimming," came Emmie's voice.

"You don't mean to say you're on the shelf tonight, Emmie?" sounded the young man's resonant voice.

"'Pears as if I am; though it's not the oven-shelf this time, my lad. What?"

"But aren't you expecting anybody?"

"Shut up. Well, good-night, Agatha—see you Wednesday. Good-night, Freddy. Lovely night for ducks."

"Ay, an' tadpoles," came Freddy's guffaw. "So long."

She had caught sight of Gilbert on the opposite pavement, and came prancing across the muddy road to him, saying in a guarded voice:

"Hello! Thought you hadn't come."

"Yes, I'm here."

"Hold on a minute."

She darted from him and went to speak to another girl. In a moment she was back at his side.

"Come on," she said. "I don't want our Dad to see me. I just said to our Sis I was going to Hackett's for a book. Come on."

She tripped swiftly along the pavement. She was a little thing, in a mackintosh and a black velvet cap. A lamp's light showed her escaping fair hair, which curled more in the wet. She carried an umbrella.

"Coming under?" she said to him, half raking him in with the umbrella. He avoided her.

"No. I don't want it all down my neck."

"All right. Stop where you are. Goodness, aren't we late! I thought father Dixon was never going to dry up. Have you been waiting long?"

"No. I went to Lewis Goddard's."

"Did you? Isn't he soft? But I like Lewis."

They passed along the pavement for two hundred yards, till they came to the big dark windows of the Co-operative Stores. In the midst of the range of dark buildings was a great closed doorway, where on week-days the drays entered to the yard and the storehouse.

Emmie put down her umbrella, and glanced along the road.

"Half a tick," she said.

She went to the big doors, and pushed her finger through a round hole. A latch clicked, and she opened a sort of little wicket in the big doors. It was left open for the bakers.

"Come on," she said.

And stepping through, she disappeared in the darkness. He stepped after her, and she closed the door behind him.

"All right here," she whispered, drawing him on.

He found himself in the wide passage or archway between the two departments of the stores, where the vans unloaded. Beyond was rainy darkness, brilliant lights of a smallish building in the near distance, down the yard, lights which emanated and revealed ghosts of old packing-cases and crates in the yard's chaos. Inside the passage it was very dark. Emmie piloted him to the further end, then she climbed a step into a doorway recess.

"Come up," she said, tugging his arm.

He came up, and they stowed themselves in the doorway recess for the spoon.

He realized, whilst she was stuffing her velvet cap in her pocket, that there were other couples in the entry—he became aware of muffled, small sounds, and then of bits of paleness and deeper darkness in the dark corners and doorway recesses. They were not alone in their spooning, he and Emmie. Lucky they had found an empty corner. He liked the invisible other presences, with their faint, ruffling sounds. The outside light from the street-lamps showed faintly under the great doors, there was a continuous echo of passing feet. Away in the yard, the wind blew the rain, and sometimes the broken packing-cases rattled hollowly, and sometimes a wet puff caught him and Emmie. There were sounds from the brilliantly-lighted bakery in the small distance.

Emmie, in her wet mackintosh, cuddled into his arms. He was famous as a spooner, and she was famous as a sport. They had known each other, off and on, for years. She was a school-teacher, three years his junior; he had seen her first at the Pupil Teacher's Centre. Both having a sort of reputation to keep up, they were a little bit excited.

A small, wriggling little thing, she nestled up to him in the darkness, and felt his warm breath on her wet frizzy hair. She gave a convulsive little movement, and subsided in his embrace. He was slowly, softly kissing her, with prefatory kisses. Yes, his reputation as a spoon would not belie him. He had lovely lips for kissing; soft, hardly touching you, and yet melting you. She quivered with epicurean anticipation.

As a matter of fact, he had that pouting mouth which is shown in Shelley's early portraits, and of which the poet, apparently, was rather proud.

He was continually touching her brow with his mouth, then lifting his face sharply, as a horse does when flies tease it, putting aside her rainy, fine bits of hair. Soft, soft came his mouth towards her brow, then quick he switched his face, as the springy curls tickled him.

"Half a mo," she said suddenly.

She unfastened his wet overcoat, and thrust her hands under his warm jacket. He likewise unfastened her mackintosh, and held her warm and tender. Then his kisses began again, wandering along the roots of her hair, on her forehead, his mouth slowly moving forward in a browsing kind of fashion. She sighed with happiness, and seemed to melt nearer and nearer to him. He settled her in his arms, whilst she clung dreamily to the warmth of his shoulders, like a drowsy fly on the November window-pane.

Since the spoon is one of the essential mysteries of modern love, particularly English modern love, let us clasp our hands before its grail-like effulgence. For although all readers belonging to the upper classes —and what reader *doesn't* belong to the upper classes?—will deny any acquaintance with any spoon but the metallic object, we regret to have to implicate the whole of the English race, from princes downwards, in the mystic business.

Dear reader, have we not all left off believing in positive evil? And therefore is it not true that the seducer, invaluable to fiction, is dead? The seducer and the innocent maid are no more. We live in better days.

There are only spooners now, a worldful of spoons. Those wicked young society people, those fast young aristocrats, ah! how soft as butter their souls are really, tender as melted butter their sinfulness, in our improved age. Don't talk of lust; it isn't fair. How can such creamy feelings be lustful? And those Oxfordly young men with their chorus-girls—ah! God, how wistful their hearts and pure their faces, really!—not to speak of their minds. Then look at young colliers and factory-lasses, they fairly reek with proper sentiment.

It doesn't matter what you do—only how you do it. Isn't that the sincerest of modern maxims?—And don't we all do it nicely and *con molto espressione*? You know we do. So little grossness nowadays, and so much dear reciprocal old-beaniness! How can there be any real wrong in it? Old wives' tales! There is no wrong in it. We are all so perfectly sweet about it all, and on such a sympathetic plane.

Why bother about spades being spades any more? It isn't the point. Adam no more delves that Eve spins, in our day. *Nous avons changé tout cela.* Call a spoon a spoon, if you like. But don't drag in garden implements. It's almost as bad as the Greeks with their horrid plough metaphor.

Ah, dear reader, you don't need me to tell you how to sip love with a spoon, to get the juice out of it. You know well enough. But you will be obliged to me, I am sure, if I pull down that weary old scarecrow of a dark designing seducer, and the alpaca bogey of lust. There is no harm in us any more, is there now? Our ways are so improved; so spiritualized, really. What harm is there in a bit of a spoon? And if it goes rather far; even very far; well, what by that? As we said before, it depends *how* you go, not where you go. And there is nothing *low* about our goings, even if we go to great lengths. A spoon isn't a spade, thank goodness. As for a plough—don't mention it! No, let us keep the spoon of England bright, between us.

Mr. Noon was a first-rate spoon—the rhyme is unfortunate, though, in truth, to be a first-rate spoon a man must be something of a poet. With his mouth he softly moved back the hair from her brow, in slow, dreamy movements, most faintly touching her forehead with the red of his lips, hardly perceptible, and then drawing aside her hair with his firmer mouth, slowly, with a long movement. She thrilled delicately, softly tuning up, in the dim, continuous, negligent caress. Innumerable pleasant flushes passed along her arms and breasts, melting her into a sweet ripeness.

Let us mention that this melting and ripening capacity is one of the first qualities for a good modern daughter of Venus, a perfect sweetness in a love-making girl, the affectionate comradeship of a dear girl deepening to a voluptuous enveloping warmth, a bath for the soft Narcissus, into which he slips with voluptuous innocence.

His mouth wandered, wandered, almost touched her ear. She felt the first deep flame run over her. But no—he went away again; over her brow, through the sharp roughness of her brows, to her eyes. He closed her eyes, he kissed her eyes shut. She felt her eyes closing, closing, she felt herself falling, falling, as one falls asleep. Only she was falling deeper, deeper than sleep. He was kissing her eyes slowly, drowsily, deeply, soft, deep, deep kisses. And she was sinking backward, and swaying, sinking deep, deep into the depths beyond vision; and swaying, swaying, as a stone sways as it sinks through deep water. And it was delicious; she knew how delicious it was. She was sunk below vision, she swayed suspended in the depths, like a stone that can sink no more.

He was kissing her, she hardly knew where. But in her depths she quivered anew, for a new leap, or a deeper plunge. He had found the soft down that lay back beyond her cheeks, near the roots of her ears. And his mouth stirred it delicately, as infernal angels stir the fires with glass rods, or a dog on the scent stirs the grass till the game starts from cover.

A little shudder ran through her, and she seemed to leap nearer to him, and then to melt in a new fusion. Slowly, slowly she was fusing once more, deeper and deeper, enveloping him all the while with her arms as if she were some iridescent sphere of flame half-enclosing him; a sort of Watts picture.

A deep pulse-beat, a pulse of expectation. She was waiting, waiting for him to kiss her ears. Ah, how she waited for it! Only that. Only let him kiss her ears, and it was a consummation.

But no! He had left her, and wandered away to the soft little kiss-curls in the nape of her neck; the soft, warm, sweet little fibrils of her hair. She contracted with a sharp convulsion, like tickling. Delicious thrills ran down her spine, before he gave her the full assurance, and kissed her soft, deep, full among the fine curls centred in the nape of her neck. She seemed to be lifted into the air as a bit of paper lifts itself up to a piece of warm amber. Her hands fluttered, fluttered on his shoulders; she was rising up on the air like Simon Magus. Let us hope Mr Noon will not let her down too sharp.

No! No! Even as she rose in the air she felt his breath running warm at the gates of her ears. Her lips came apart; she panted with acute anticipation. Ah!—Ah!—and softly came his full, fathomless kiss; softly her ear was quenched in darkness. He took the small, fine contours subtly between his lips, he closed deeper, and with a second reeling swoon she reeled down again and fell, fell through a deeper, darker sea. Depth doubled on depth, darkness on darkness. She had sunk back to the root-stream, beyond sight and hearing.

Now surely it was finished. Occultists tell us that hearing is the most radical of all the senses; that, at a crisis, all sensation can be summed up in the perfected sensation of sound. Surely then it was accomplished. At each new phase she felt she had melted, had sunk to the very bottom. And every time, oh, bliss of it, came a new crisis, and she swooned downwards, down a deeper depth, to a new, fathomless, oscillating rest. Oscillating at the deeps of intoxication, as now.

Yet still there was a tiny core of unquenched desire. She seemed to melt and become tinier; and yet she swung in an immeasurable, hungry rhythm, like a meteorite that has fallen through worlds of space, yet still swings, not yet burnt out, caught in some unstable equilibrium between the forces of the planets. So she hung and quivered in immeasurable space.

For sometimes it seemed to her drunken consciousness that she was high, high in space, yet not beyond all worlds, the net of the stars. And sometimes it seemed she was sunk, sunk to immeasurable depths, yet not quite to extinction.

His mouth was coming slowly nearer to her mouth; and yet not approaching. Approaching without disclosing its direction. Loitering, circumventing, and then suddenly taking the breath from her nostrils. For a second she died in the strange sweetness and anguish of suffocation. He had closed her nostrils for ever with a kiss and she was sleeping, dying in sweet fathomless insentience. Death, and the before-birth sleep.

Yet, not quite. Even now, not quite. One spark persisted and waited in her. Frail little breaths came through her parted lips. It was the brink of ecstasy and extinction. She cleaved to him beyond measure, as if she would reach beyond herself. With a sudden lacerating motion she tore her face from his, aside. She held it back, her mouth unclosed. And obedient down came his mouth on her unclosed mouth, darkness closed on darkness, so she melted completely, fused, and was gone.

She sank, sank with him, right away. Or rising, he lifted her into the oneness with him, up, up, and beyond, into the infinite. It seemed to him she was the heavier, rounded breath which he enwreathed in the perfected bubble flame of himself. So they floated as a perfect bubble, beyond the reach even of space. Beyond height and depth, beyond gravitation. Out in the beyond, suspended in the perfection.

Who knows if they breathed, if they lived?

But all the time, of course, each of them had a secondary mundane consciousness. Each of them was aware of the entry, the other spooners, and the passers-by outside. Each of them attended minutely when one pair of spooners crept through the gap in the big doors, to go home. They were all there, mark you. None of your bestial loss of faculties.

We have risen to great heights, dear reader, and sunk to great depths. Yet we have hardly fathomed the heights and depths of the spoon in the Co-op. entry. Don't you wish you were as good at it as Noon and Emmie! Practise, then; and you too may swing suspended in the heights, or depths, of infinity, like the popular picture we used to see over the railway bookstalls, winged spooners mid-heaven in the blue ether. Ah, we are all so clean, nowadays; fine clean young men, infinitely spoony, and clean young spoony maidens to match. Nothing earthy; not we. All in mid-air, our goings-on.

Till her mouth fell away and her head fell aside. He turned his face aside from her, and they breathed their slow, inert breaths apart. They kept their faces apart from each other. And gradually conscious sight returned into the open mirrors of her eyes, gradually wakeful discrimination busied itself in the re-echoing cavities of her ears. Noises which she had heard all the time she now admitted into her audience. Gradually. It could not be done, or should not be done, all in a smack.

Ah, the spoon, the perfect spoon! In its mystic bowl all men are one, and so are all women. Champagne and shoulders, poetry and long scarves, loftiness, altruism, souls, hard work, conscience, sacrifice, all fuse into perfect oneness in the spoon. All Whitman's Songs of Himself and Other People lie in the hollow of a spoon. If you seek the Infinite and the Nirvana, look not to death nor the after-life, nor yet to pure abstraction; but into the hollow spoon.

Gilbert was staring down the opposite direction under lifted, Mephistophelian brows. And seeing, of course, the ghostly chaos of packing-cases in the rain, and the strong beams from the bakery windows.

The small sound of church chimes in the night! Emmie broke away from him abruptly.

"I s'll have to be going. I s'll cop it from my Dad."

He lost his balance and stepped down from the step of the doorway embrasure with a jerk, cramped. He felt rather vague and uncomfortable.

She was pushing at her hair, and pulling her cap on. There was a flutter and rustle of her mackintosh. She stepped down from the step, and shook herself. He would move towards the door.

"My gamp!" she said quickly, snatching the article out of a corner in the recess. Then briskly she went forward to the dark wall of the doors. The little round hole showed. In an instant he saw a framed

picture of wet pavements and passers-by, and a scarlet cart, which he
knew carried the mail, splashing phantom through the mud.

Ah, dear reader, I hope you are not feeling horribly superior. You
would never call an umbrella a brolly, much less a gamp. And you have
never so much as seen a Co-op. entry. But don't on this small account
sniff at Emmie. No; in that notorious hour when a woman is alone with
her own heart, really enjoying herself, ask yourself if your spoon is
brighter than Emmie's, if your spooner is better than Gilbert. Nay, if
you prefer *love* and *lover*, say love and lover to yourself. It all amounts
to the same. But in communion with your naked heart, say whether you
have reached Gilbertian heights and Emmelian profundities of the
human kiss—or whether you have something to learn even from our
poor pair.

3. GILBERT LICKS THE SPOON

Let none complain that I pry indecently into the privacies of the
spoon. A spoon is an open mirror, necessarily a public concern. I do but
walk down the public road, past the Co-op. entry, and see Emmie and
Mr. Noon stepping guiltlessly forth through the aperture in the big
doors, as integral a part of the Sunday night as is the darkness itself, or
me in my after-service expansion of soul, and since all is told to me, in
the innocent act of slipping through the Co-op. aperture, I tell all
again including the innocence.

Neither let the experts and *raffinés* of the spoon object that my
account is but the bare outline of what actually is. I insist that this is
the summary and essence of all that is above-board in spooning. There
are variations on the spoon. There are tricks, dear reader. In the old
days, wicked black silk bed-sheets, for example. Ah, but mere inter-
larded tricks. Different seasoning, the soup is the same. I have heard,
too, of Frenchy, and even of Neopolitan spooning, which I should not
like to speak of from hearsay. There are all kinds of kissings. Every
nation, every city, every individual introduces a special and individual
touch. There are dodges and peculiarities which I leave to experience
and to other novelists. I concern myself with the essential English kiss,
within the spoon. Yes, and with the basis of the essential; in short, the
radical Co-op. entry spoon of the common people, that has neither
champagne nor shoulders, nor yet cocktails and *fard* to embellish it and
to obscure its pure simplicity. I am no dealer in abnormalities. Far

from it. I take the thing at its best, as one should. I speak of the spoon
pure and simple, the spoon of our clean-minded age, from which we sip
love's limpidest sweets. Ah, infinite spoon moments! dear spoon-
memories!

Mr. Noon, however, was in no such complacent mood as ours.

"It's not raining so much; I shan't bother with the brolly," said
Emmie, turning her Noon-kissed face to the dim moist heavens. "That
was half-past I heard strike. I s'll be in a row with our Dad if I don't
hop it."

She spoke rather breathlessly as she tripped along.

"Why, what's the matter with *him*?" asked Gilbert irritably, turning traitor to the spoon-grail in the very moment when he had quaffed
his dose.

"Because he's a wire-whiskered nuisance, and I've got to be in by
quarter to ten, because he's on night-duty."

"What would he do if you weren't in by quarter to ten?"

"Ah, you *ask* me! Make my life a blooming hell—Oh!" and she
stopped for a second in the road. "*Now* I haven't got a book, and I told
our Sis I was calling for one. Little fool! Little fool I am! *Drat!*"
And she stamped her foot. "You haven't got a book on you? He's sure
to twig. Oh, what a bally nuisance!"

Gilbert fortunately had in his pocket a volume on Conic Sections,
and this Emmie at once appropriated, hugging it under her arm.

She ran tripping forward, Gilbert strode beside her. She lived down
in the valley, about a mile out of Woodhouse. She was uneasy now because of her father, and had almost forgotten Mr. Noon at her side.

He, however, had not forgotten her. A black vindictiveness had come
over him.

"What time does your father go to work?" he asked. He knew that
Mr. Bostock had a job on the railway.

"Ten. He's on duty at ten; and it takes him quarter of an hour to
get there, or he says so. It would take me about five minutes. Like him
to make a mountain of it."

"Come out a bit after he's gone," suggested Gilbert.

"Go on!" said Emmie, with a suggestive sharpness.

Now this was not the first of Emmie's spoons—even with Gilbert.
And she was quite prepared for after-spoon developments—even
naughty ones. So that when she said "Go on!" she was merely non-
committal.

She knew that young men would frequently follow up a nice innocent lovely spoon with a certain half-tiresome persistence in going

further. Half-tiresome, because it is the last step which may cost. And yet rather wickedly nice, you know. Remember that Emmie is a sport, and that in defiance of father and stone tablets there is also bliss. And moreover the man who is a true and faithful spoon makes this ultimate so dear, such a last clean sweep in sympathy! Ah, talk of grossness in this soft and sympathising conjunction! Don't you agree, dear reader?

"You'll come, won't you?" said Gilbert.

"Let's see how the land lies, first," she replied. "You needn't wait if I don't come out and cooey."

By *Cooey* she meant call a soft, lurking *Coo-ey!* to him.

Gilbert was behaving in the accepted way—or one of the ways—of after-spoon, and she took no alarm. He was quiet, and seemed persuasive. His silence came suggestive and rather pleading to her, as they hurried down the hill. She was a sport—and liked a man who could come on; one who pressed on, a Galahad of sentiment, to the bitter end. Bitter? Well, bitter-sweet. Oh, gentle joust of ultimate sentiment, oh, last sweet throw of love, wherein we fall, spoon-overthrown! Shall I be Minnesinger of the spoon?

But, alas, there is a fly in the ointment. There is a snake in the grass. It is in Gilbert's mood. Alas, poor Emmie. She is mistaken about his soft, sweet, sinful coming-on. Instead of being in the melting stage, just ready to melt right down with her, the final fuse within the spoon, he is horrid. Ah, in the last coming-on, how gentle is the Galahad of kisses, how subtle his encroachment to the goal! But Gilbert was a snake in the grass. He was irritable, in a temper, and would not let her go though he did not really want her. Why he was in a temper, and why he hated her he did not know. Doubtful if he ever knew his own state of feelings. Beware, gentle reader! For if in the course of soft and kissy love you once get out of the melting spoon-mood, there is hell to pay, both for you and for her.

Emmie's garden-gate opened from a little path between two hedges that led from the high-road between cottage gardens to the field stile. The two arrived at the bottom of the hill and crossed the road to where the path, called a twitchel, opened between thick hedges.

"Don't come down the twitchel," she said to him in a low tone. "I'll bet he's watching. If I can slip out when he's gone I shall cooey. Au revoy."

She disappeared between the dark hedges of the twitchel, and shortly he heard her gate clash. He loitered about again, and was in a temper because he was kept waiting. He was in a rage with himself, so turned his wrath against circumstance.

He was in a rage. He did really like women—so he put it to himself. There was nothing he liked better than to have one in his arms—his own phraseology again. And Emmie was a regular little sport, a regular little sport. He admired her. And he fidgeted about in a temper waiting for her. Black devils frisked in his veins, and pricked him with their barbed tails. He was full of little devils. Alas, he had fallen from the white election of the spoon. He plunged into the twitchel, saw the row of cottages, of which hers was the end one; saw the lighted window, heard voices, heard a man's voice from the back premises, from the back door, and plunged on. He clambered over the stile and went forward from the black muddy field-path towards the canal. No good going very far, however.

He heard a step behind him, and listened. Her father, ten to one. He loitered on the dark, open field. The man came nearer. Glancing round, Gilbert saw the dark whiskers on the pallid face, and sent out a wave of hatred. He loitered whilst her father strode past him, on into the night. Then he turned back towards the cottage.

He had been in a similar situation more than once. Nay, for the young fellows of the colliery-places like Whetstone and Woodhouse, for the young bloods who had a bit of dash of warmth about them, the situation was almost traditional. Bostock, Emmie's father, had done the same, and worse, many a time in his day. So had old Noon, Gilbert's father. Gilbert was but keeping up a human tradition. And yet he was in a temper about it. He sort of felt himself in a ready-made circumstance, going through a ready-made act, and he was thoroughly annoyed with everything. Yes, he was, in Woodhouse phraseology, a womanizer; and he knew it; and he meant to be a womanizer. So why make any bones about his present situation? But his temper mounted. Yes, he *would* be a womanizer. He prided himself on it. Wasn't "Down Among the Dead Men" one of his favourite songs? A fine tune, too.

> And may Confusion still pursue
> The senseless woman-hating crew . . .

Alas, he would be a womanizer. Yet he kicked with fury against the universal spoon. He fought like a fly in oil.

Meanwhile Emmie indoors was going through her own little act. She enjoyed play-acting. She had lied like a little trooper to her father, having a sulky, innocence-suspected look which he exacted, and a pert tongue which he threatened with extraction. For Alf Bostock had been a womanizer both before and after his marriage to his mild, lax Jinny; and him a man with a swarm of little children. She had no rosy time of it. Till he got kicked out of his job, and suddenly became religious, with all the ferocity of narrow-pathdom. His poor Jinny was always wax, but his own offspring tended to bristle. And Emmie, who was perhaps his favourite—a pretty, taking, sharp-answering little thing, with a way of her own—she was his special enemy as she grew up. A roaming bitch, he called her in his wrath. And it was curiously appropriate, for she had the alert, inquisitive, tail-in-the-air appearance of a bitch who has run away and finds the world an adventure, as she tripped the streets.

Once the tyrant was gone, Emmie was quite equal to any occasion. She had retreated upstairs, as if to bed, before his departure. Now down she came again.

"Hoy, our mother, I'll have my supper now in peace," she said, taking a knife and going into the pantry for bread and cheese and cake.

"There's a bit of apple-pie if you'd like it," said her indulgent, easy mother.

Emmie walked out with the pie-dish, and sat scraping it with a spoon.

"I've got my lessons to do yet," she said cheerfully.

"Be ashamed," said her mother. "Last minute."

"Make use of my fag-ends of time," said Emmie.

"Ay, fag-ends," said her mother.

Emmie spread her books on the table under the lamp, to write the Compulsory notes for the morrow's lessons. She pulled her hair untidy on her brow as she did so.

"Go to bed, Mother Bostock," she said to her mother. "Don't sit dropping off in that chair. How do you think anybody can make notes, when they have to watch for your head dropping on to the floor? Get up. Go on."

"Ay," said her mother amiably. "How long shall you be?"

"About twenty minutes, I should think. Go on now—go to bed. You know you'll get a crick in your neck."

"Ay, you'd like to think so," said her mother, weakly, rising and obeying. "I shall listen for you, now," she added from the foot of the stairs.

"Go on—I shan't be a minute, if you leave me in peace."

And Mrs. Bostock slowly mounted the creaky stairs.

Emmie scribbled away in her flighty fashion for some time, pausing occasionally to listen. At length she shut her books and stretched her arms. Then with startling suddenness she blew out the lamp. After which she stood in the darkness and listened.

All seemed quiet. She slipped to the back door and pushed away the bar. Closing the door behind her, she sauntered down the front path with all her leisurely assurance and bravado. The sense of danger was salt to her. The rain was now only very slight. Glancing over the hedge on the left, she could see, through the clearing darkness, the far-off lamps of the station and the junction sidings where her father would by now be safely occupied. So much for him.

She reached the gate and peered down the dark twitchel.

"Coo-ee!" she called, very softly.

And the dark shadow of Gilbert was approaching.

"Think I was never coming?" she said.

"I wondered," he answered.

They stood for a moment with the gate between them.

"How are you feeling?" she asked.

"All right. Coming out?"

"No; you come in." And she opened the gate for him to enter the dark garden.

"Ma's put her light out. Sleeping the sleep of the nagged by now, I bet. My Dad's gone."

"I'm not going in the house," said Gilbert suspiciously.

"Nobody asked you."

She led him down the little winding side-path, in the wintry garden, between the currant-bushes, to a little greenhouse. The door was locked, but the key was on the nail. She knew the greenhouse of old. It was pretty small, but she knew how to move the plants and arrange things. Luckily there were not many plants to move.

"Hold on a bit," she whispered to Gilbert, who hung in the doorway whilst she made a place.

Meanwhile, we are sorry to say, the enemy was on their tracks. Alf Bostock should not have been a railwayman, but a policeman. Now that he was a reformed character, the policeman in him had no rest. Before Emmie arrived home, at a quarter to ten, he had been in the back yard listening for her. He had heard her voice speaking to Mr. Noon, though he had not caught what she said. But he had smelled a rat. And he was a very keen rat-catcher these days.

Therefore he did nothing that could betray his suspicions, and he set off to work a few minutes earlier than he need in order that he might turn back and do a bit of spying. When he passed the more-than-doubtful figure of Mr. Noon in the field the smell of the rat was very hot in his nostrils. Like the wicked, he exulted, and said Ha-ha! He let Gilbert return towards the cottage.

And then the reformed parent swerved from his way to his work, made a bend over the sodden field in the black darkness, and came to the big hedge at the bottom of his garden, near the summer house. There, among the old nettle-stalks he crouched and watched. He heard Gilbert champing in the twitchel and away on the high-road, and prepared the net for the bird. He saw his wife's candle go upstairs, and at once supposed that she, poor thing, was conniving at her daughter's shame. He saw his wife's candle go out—heard Mr. Gilbert champ and chafe and light a pipe—and at last, ah-ha!—saw the kitchen go suddenly dark.

Yes, there she was, the little bitch, prancing her shadowy, leisurely way towards the gate, and staring at the hedge where he crouched as if she too could smell a rat. He ducked low and watched.

"Coo-ee!"

He heard it, and his veins tingled. He'd give her *Coo-ee*, else his name wasn't Alfred.

Up comes the Johnny to the gate. Who could he be? But wait a bit. Wait a bit. He'd follow soon and find out.

Hush! He strained his ears in vain to hear what they were murmuring. He rose to his feet, and cracked a stick. He would stalk them. Then all at once he ducked again under the hedge. Inside the garden, they were coming towards him. His nerves were keen on the alert, to gather if they had heard him.

But they, poor darlings, were all unsuspecting. Alf Bostock crouched on his heels. His greenhouse! His little glasshouse! She was opening the door with the key. Well, of all the evil, low little bitches, if she wasn't a sly one! For a second his mind reverted to youthful escapades, and the girls he despised so much for escapading with him. For it is a peculiarity of his type that the more they run after sin, the more contempt they feel for their partner in sinning, the more insufferably superior they rise in their own esteem. Till nowadays, he would spoon with nobody but his Saviour. In religion he was, still, oh, so spoony. So spoony, listening to the sermon, so spoony saying his prayers. Ah, such relish! With women he had always been rather gross. No wonder he hated Emmie for bringing it home to him again, now that his higher nature had triumphed.

He'd kill her. He'd flay her. He'd torture her. Wouldn't he! My word, wouldn't he! What? Was she going to shame him, her father? Was he going to be shamed and disgraced by her? His indignation rose to an inquisitional pitch. At the thought of the shame and disgrace *he* might incur through her he could have burnt her at the stake cheerfully, over a slow fire. *Him* to be shamed and disgraced by a girl of his! Was anything on earth more monstrous? The strumpet. The bitch. Hark at her clicking the flower-pots, shifting the plants. He'd give her shift the plants! He'd show her! He longed to torture her. Back went his mind over past events. Now he knew. Now he knew how the pink primulas had been smashed and re-potted before he got home. Now he knew a thousand things. If his daughter had been the Whore of Babylon herself her father could not have painted her with a more livid striping of sin. She was a marvel of lust and degradation, and defamation of *his* fair repute. But he'd show her.

They had gone into the greenhouse and shut the door on themselves. Well and good—they had fastened themselves in their own trap. He straightened his creaking knees and drew himself upright. He was cold, damp, and cramped; and all this added venom to his malignancy.

Lurching awkwardly, he shambled along the grass to the stile, climbed, and went along the twitchel to his own gate. If it cost him his job once more, he'd settle this little game. *Wouldn't* he, just! He'd show them. He'd show them.

He was in such a rage, as he drew near the greenhouse, he went so slowly, on tiptoe, that he seemed to emanate in hate rather than to walk to the threshold of the poor little place. He got there, and stood still. He stood evilly and malignantly still, and listened; listened, with all his cute attention and shameful old knowledge.

Poor Emmie! She thought she'd got a demon inside the greenhouse; she little suspected a devil outside. Gilbert did not make her happy any more. Instead of being nice and soft and spoony, and pleasant in his coming-on, he was rough and hard. She was startled, jarred in her rather melty mood. She hadn't bargained for this. If she had not possessed a rather catty courage, she would have cried out. But her soul rose against him, and she hated him.

And then, at an awful moment, the door slowly opened, and she gave an awful, stifled yell.

"What's going on in there?" came a beastly policeman's voice.

Emmie heard it, and seemed to fall for a moment into a fit, paralysed. Gilbert was arrested, perfectly still.

"You're coming out there, aren't you?" said the voice. "Come on; let's see who you are."

And there was a little rattling sound of a box of matches. He was going to strike a light. Emmie was making a funny little sound, as if she had fallen into icy water. Gilbert, on his knees, turned. He saw the stooping figure, stooping policeman-like in the doorway, and black rage burst his head like a bomb. He crouched and leapt like a beast, but aimed too high, and only caught the cap and hair of his assailant. The two men went down with a crash upon a gooseberry bush.

Emmie had leaped to her feet with another hoarse cry. The men were a confused heap. She heard gurgling curses from her father. She gave a third raven-like cry, and sped straight down the garden, through the gate, and away into the night.

A window had opened, and a frightened voice was saying:

"What's amiss? Who is it? Is it you, Emmie? Who is it?"

Children's voices were calling, "Mother! Mother!"

Gilbert had risen to his feet, but the other man clung after him, determined not to let him go, frenzied like some lurking creature of prey. In a convulsion of revolt, Gilbert flung the gripping horror from him, madly; flung himself free, and turned blindly to escape. He was through the gate, down the twitchel and over the stile in one moment, making for the dark country, whereas Emmie had made for the lights of Woodhouse.

The disorder of his clothing impeded his running. He heard the other man rushing to the stile. He turned, in the darkness of the open field, and said loudly:

"Come on, and I'll kill you."

By the sound of his voice, he probably would have done so.

Women and children were screaming from the house.

The other man thought better of it, and turned back.

Gilbert, standing there on the defensive, adjusted himself and waited. No one came. He walked away into the night. He had lost his cap in the fray.

4. APHRODITE AND THE COW

During the week that followed, Gilbert heard nothing of Emmie or of the Sunday-night affair. He was busy at Haysfall during the day, and during some of the evenings. He might have made an opportunity for running over to Woodhouse; but he didn't.

Sunday came again; a fine day for once, dim-blue and wintry. Gilbert looked out of his window upon it when he got up, and after breakfast went out into the wood-yard. Tall yellow timbers reared up into the sky, leaning to one another and crossing in the air. Planks, correctly arranged in squares, with a space between each plank, stood seasoning.

In the shed were planks and poles in solid piles. Near a chopping-block was a pile of split faggots, while huge trunks of trees, oak and elm, stripped of branches, lay aside like swathed corpses. Gilbert noticed the star-shaped cracks that ran from the centres of the trunk-bottoms, thought of the plant-histology, and in a dim sort of way calculated the combination of forces that had brought about the fissures. He ran his finger over a heavy-grained oak surface, and to him it was an exquisite pleasure, vibrating in his veins like music, to realize the flexible but grandly-based rhythm in the morphological structure of the tree, right from the root-tip through the sound trunk, right out to a leaf-tip; wonderful concatenation and association of cells, incalculable and yet so genetic in their rhythm, unfolding the vast unsymmetrical symmetry of the tree. What he loved so much in plant morphology was that, given a fixed mathematical basis, the final evolution was so incalculable. It pleased him to trace inherent individual qualities in each separate organic growth, qualities which were over and above the fixed qualities belonging to the genus and the species, and which could not really be derived by a chain of evolutionary cause-and-effect. Could they? Could the individual peculiarities all derive from the chain of cause and effect? He mused abstractedly. The question piqued him. He had almost decided not. The one little element of individuality, not attributable to any cause, fascinated him always in plants and trees. He longed to make quite sure of it. He longed to feel it musically. In plants it seemed to him so profoundly suggestive, the odd aloneness of the separate self in each specimen. He longed to hear the new note of this in music. But his longing was vague, far removed from the intensity of action.

He dawdled the morning away, with his pipe. There were things he ought to do. But he could not begin. He sat in the kitchen by the fire, glancing over the large pages of *Lloyd's Weekly*, the lurid Sunday newspaper, whilst the woman made pies and an apple-dumpling, and continually pushed past him to the oven; whilst the saucepans bubbled and sent off first a smell of pudding-cloth, then a scent of vegetable-steam; whilst the meat sizzled in the oven, and his father came and went, fidgety, and drank a glass of beer between-whiles.

Between father and son there was not much correspondence. The old man was mean, and he kept his heart also to himself. He looked with a jealous eye on his son, half-scorning him because he did no real work, nothing in the wood-yard, for example, and in the other half admiring him for being so clever. At the bottom he was domineeringly grateful to have the lad at home, though he found every manner of fault with him.

His only other child, a girl, a woman now, was married, with children of her own, and because she needed a little more money, the old man was secretly determined to leave all to Gilbert.

A few instincts Gilbert had of a gentleman so-called. He could not bear to sit down to dinner unshaven and with no collar on, as his father did. So, judging from the smell of the sirloin that it was nearly done, he went upstairs to his room and shaved and dressed. His bedroom was bare and tidy. There was not a picture, not a book. From the window he looked down on the wood-yard. But next to his bedroom was a sort of study, with many books, and a piano, a violin and music-stand, piles and sheets of music. This room, too, was tidy and clean, though Gilbert tidied and cleaned it all himself.

Being dressed, he went and touched his violin; but he did not want to play. He turned over a sheet of music; but did not want to look at it. He waited for the woman to call him to dinner.

After dinner, he had still his mind to make up. He went out to his motor-cycle and got it ready. He went indoors and put on his rubbers. He pushed off, and was running noiselessly down Whetstone's steep main street, past tram-cars and saunterers, before he knew where he was going.

And then, after all, he turned towards Woodhouse. In half an hour he was there, and had put up his cycle. Coming out, brushed and tidy, on to the Knarborough Road, he hesitated which way to turn. Therefore he did not turn, but walked forward.

And whom should he see but Patty Goddard walking down the rather empty street; it was too soon for the afternoon chapel people, and the men were having a last drink before half-past two. Patty in a dark wine-coloured coat and skirt and dark silk hat, with grey gloves and very carefully-chosen shoes, walking by herself with her pale, full, ivory face towards the afternoon sun! She smiled across the road to him, and nodded. He strode over to her.

"Oh! I thought you might come this afternoon or evening," she said, and he felt a touch of significance in her voice, and was uncomfortable.

"Is Lewis there?" he asked, jerking his head in the direction of the house.

"No. He's gone to an I.L.P. meeting in Knarborough. I expect him back about six. Did you want him?" Again her dark eyes seemed to glance up at him with a certain mocking spite.

"No—no," said Gilbert.

"Another appointment, perhaps?" smiled Patty maliciously.

"No, I haven't. I've got nothing to do."

"Oh, well, then, if you'd care to take a walk. I'm just enjoying the sun while it lasts."

"Yes, if you don't mind."

And he took his place at her side. She was pleased. But today her pleasure was qualified, though she kept the qualification a secret. She made no more mention of the previous Sunday, and the conversation between them was rather lame.

They descended the hill in the pleasant afternoon, and came to the damp, mossy old park wall, under the trees. Patty stopped before the unimposing, wooden park gate.

"I thought I'd walk across the park," she said. "Lewis has managed to get the key."

So Gilbert opened the gate, and they walked along the pink-coloured drive, between the greenish winter grass. The old hall was shut up; everywhere seemed abandoned in the wintry sunshine of the afternoon. Just before they came to the second gate, the gate of the forlorn garden, Patty went to a huge beech tree, and smilingly took out a pair of rubber over-shoes.

"We keep all kinds of surprises here," she said. "But I love to walk across the grass past the brook. I love the sound of water so much, and the berries are so beautiful this year."

It was true. The dark, shaggy, hairy hawthorn trees had a purplish-burning look; they were still so heavy with haw. They stood about fairly numerous in the near part of the park. Gilbert and Patty walked along the crest of the stagnant, artificial ponds that lay melancholy in their abandon below the old house. Then Patty led the way across the rough grass, to the brook which rattled and clucked under deep hedges. Gilbert helped her to pick scarlet rose-berries, and black privet berries, and white snow-berries from the bushes that grew rampant down by the brook. Patty flushed with exercise and pleasure. She was happy gathering the wet, bright, cold berries on their twigs and branches. She was excited being helped by the young man near her. It was such a pungent, chill isolation, this of theirs down in the hollow of the forsaken park, the open country, pathless, stretching in the dim beyond.

"Aren't they beautiful? Aren't they lovely?" said Patty, holding out the bunch between her white hands. The scarlet and black and white heavy berries looked well in her hands. Her pale face was almost like an ivory snow-berry itself, set with dark, half-tired, half-malicious eyes. Her mouth set in an odd way, a slight grimace of malice against life. She had had such a happy married life, such a perfect love with Lewis.

"Tell me, now," she said to him, with her intensive seriousness of a franchised woman, "how *you* look on marriage." And she glanced at him furtively, a touch of unconscious, general malevolence between her brows.

"Marriage? Me? Why, I don't know," came Gilbert's gruff voice. Then he stood still, to ponder. She watched his face. He looked forwards and upwards, into space. "I shall marry some day," he said.

"You will? But what sort of woman? What sort of marriage will it be?"

He pondered still.

"Why," he said, "a woman with brains, I think. A woman who could stand on her own feet, not one who would cling to me. I shouldn't mind, you know, what she did. If she liked another man, all right. We should be good pals. Oh, I should want a woman to do as she liked."

Patty watched him sardonically, then strode on a few paces.

"You would? You think you would?" she replied, and the sardonic touch sounded in her voice. She was thinking how young he was, and how full of mental conceit. He glanced down at her, and his full, dark-blue eyes met her brown, onyx-bright eye. A flush came over her face, and a doubt over his mind, or his spirit, rather.

"I think so," he said.

"Yes, you think so," she replied quietly, walking on. He followed in silence.

"Why?" he said. "Don't you?"

She stopped, and turned round to him, smiling suddenly, her face seeming to flicker all over with a strange, ivory-coloured flame, amid which her eyes showed dark.

"Ah!" she said. "What a difference there is between what you think now and what you'll think afterwards!"

She was usually rather uncouth in expressing herself, and he, for the moment, was dazzled, had lost his feet. He only looked at her, at her strange, changed, almost uncanny face, so tense in its laughing. Something stirred in his veins. Something completely unusual awoke in him.

He had never had any real contact with a woman; only with tarts and bits of girls and sports like Emmie. Other women, such as Patty, had always been to him dresses with faces. And now, to his terror, something else seemed to be emerging from her face, a new Aphrodite from the stiff dark sea of middle-aged matronliness, an Aphrodite drenched with knowledge, rising in a full ivory-soft nudity, infinitely more alluring than anything flapperdom could offer. Some veil was rent in his consciousness, and he remained a moment, lost, open-mouthed. Patty dropped her eyes, and her smile became small and a little weary.

She had *had* to try to beat the flappers and the sports. She had *had* to try to break the spoon-spell; which was the spell of her marriage, alas. And she saw the beginnings of victory. But she was frightened. After all, she too was very fixed in her old way of life, up to the neck in the stiff wave of her fine serge dress. And to rise like Aphrodite—ah, after all—! There were so many considerations. Perhaps she was more frightened even than he.

He remained bemused, suddenly realizing the soft, full Aphrodite steeped in the old sea of matrimony, and ready to rise, perhaps; rise from the correct, wine-coloured coat and skirt of fine serge in all her exquisite fulness and softness of forty years, and all the darkness of a finished past in her eyes. A finished past. The sense of it came over him with a shock. He looked at her, but she was walking slowly, with bent head. He saw the outline of her forty-year-old cheek, full and ivory-white; he saw the bowed head. And in the flame that ran from his feet to his head all the Emmies of the world withered and were gone like so many shavings.

"What do you think of marriage yourself?" he blurted out.

"Ah!" she only half-looked at him, funking the question, and answering archly: "I *don't* think about it, for myself. I have it behind me. You have it ahead of you. There's a difference."

He watched her, puzzling over her. She would not look at him, except with a screwed-up, baffling sort of smile. He pondered in his logical way.

"But what you have behind you, have I got that in front of me?" he asked, putting himself in Lewis's place for all the past years, and not feeling himself fit.

Patty was caught in the net of her own words.

"No," she said, seriously, becoming again the clumsy, thinking woman. "No. You're a generation younger than that. You're bound to start different from where *we* started. But you've *got* to start somewhere."

Her phrases came out clumsily.

"Perhaps where you left off," he said, inspired.

She flushed suddenly like a red camellia flower. She was very like a camellia flower; usually creamy-white, now rose.

"Yes," she said, in her suffragette voice now. "Very probably." She was retreating on to safe ground; the platform of Woman. He felt it; and still, in his one-sighted way, was looking for the full, soft, pale Aphrodite.

"Then I should want a woman who's been through it all," he said, logically infallible. She winced, and retreated further on to the dry boards of the theoretic platform.

"I don't know. I shouldn't like to be so sure. There are many kinds of women in the world; many more than you have ever dreamed of. You don't see them—but they're there. You see little—remarkably little, if I may have the impudence to say so."

And she smiled at him in the old, matronly, woman-who-thinks fashion. But it had no effect this time, because, between the blinkers of his logical concentration, he was looking ahead along his own road.

"Yes—I think that's true. I think that's true. But you won't get me to believe that you can find me a girl, a woman under thirty, who can start where a woman of your age and experience leaves off. You won't get me to believe it."

"Why not?" she cried. "Can *you*, of all men, judge? Can you even have any idea where it *is* that a woman of my age and experience leaves off? How do you know?"

Now she was fencing with other weapons, trying to flirt with him. But she had reckoned without her host. She was not prepared for the blinkers of concentration which shut out from this Balaam's ass of a mathematician all the side-tracks into which she would cajole him, and sent him straight ahead with his nose against the opposing angel.

He looked straight down on her, with full, dark-blue eyes. And she, suddenly caught as by an apparition, was so startled that she let the crinkly smile fall from her face, and the fencing cunning drop like a mask from her eyes. For a second she met his look of strange enquiry, and it was more than she could bear. Her heart ceased beating; she wilted backwards. Mercifully, he began to speak.

"I've just realized something," he said. "And you can't make me believe different till I realize something else."

What she heard in this speech was that he loved her; loved not the girl in her, nor the independent, modern, theorizing woman Lewis had loved; not that, but the soft, full, strange, unmated Aphrodite of forty, who had been through all ideal raptures of love and marriage and modern motherhood, through it all, and through the foam of the fight for freedom, the sea of ideal right and wrong, and now was emerging, slowly, mysteriously, ivory-white and soft, woman still, leaving the sea of all her past, nay, the sea of all the extant human world behind her, and rising with dark eyes of age and experience, and a few grey hairs among the dark; soft, full-bodied, mature, and woman still, unpossessed, unknown of men, unfathomed, unexplored, belonging nowhere and to no one, only to the unknown distance, the untrodden shore of all the sea of all the unknown knowledge. Aphrodite, mistress, mother of all the worlds of unknown knowledge that lie over our horizon, she felt him looking at her with strange, full eyes, seeing her in her unguessed ivory-soft nudity, the darkness of her promise in her eyes, the woman of forty, and desiring her with a profound desire that seemed like a deep, far-off bell booming, or a sea coming up.

And her strength ebbed; it was too much for her.

"Hadn't we better be turning home?" she asked, wide-eyed and pathetic.

"Ay, I suppose we had," he answered automatically.

And they veered on the wintry grass, in the pale-coloured wintry afternoon. They had walked to the far end of the park, where it was open like a wide, rough meadow. At this end some rather shaggy cattle were out to pasture, winter-rough creatures. Some rough horses were in a far corner, by the fence. Patty was looking round her, with a sort of anxious look on her face. She wanted to get back, back on to the road; above all, back into her own pleasant room, with her feet on her own hassock.

"You don't mind cows, do you?" asked Gilbert, noticing her anxiety.

"No. I don't *like* them, though—not too near. I didn't know these were here."

"They're all right," said Gilbert.

"Oh, yes, I'm sure they are," she said. But she hurried rather nervously. Glancing round, she said anxiously:

"Do you think that one means mischief?"

He saw a heifer putting her head down.

"No," he said negligently. He had no natural fear of cattle.

"She *does*," said Patty vehemently. "She's coming."

"Not she," said Gilbert easily.

But Patty was looking round in fear.

"Where can I go?" she cried.

"Don't bother," he said.

But she glanced round and gave a cry.

"She's coming!" And she started running forward, blindly, with little, frightened steps. Patty was making for the brook, as the nearest safety.

Gilbert turned round. And, sure enough, the heifer, with her head down, was running forward in that straight line of vicious intent which cows have when they *do* mean mischief. Gilbert was startled. Patty's nervousness unnerved him also. His instinct was to take to his heels. But he remained where he was, in a moment of stupefaction.

The heifer was going for Mrs. Goddard. She was a dark-red creature with sharp horns. Gilbert gave a shout, and running forward to the vicious, disagreeable-tempered beast, he flung his cherry-wood walking-stick at her. It caught her on the neck and rattled in her horns. She wavered, shook her head, and stopped. Gilbert took off his overcoat, and whirling it by the sleeve, walked towards her. She watched—snorted—suddenly, with a round swerve, made off, galloping into the distance, her tail in the air, female and defiant.

"She's gone. Don't run. She's all right," he called to the speeding Patty.

Patty glanced round with a white face of anguish.

"No. She'll come again," she said, in a stifled voice. And she pressed forward.

"She won't. You needn't hurry," said Gilbert, hastening after the dark little form of the woman, who pressed forward blindly, with hurried steps. He followed at some distance behind her, having recovered his stick.

The cow had stopped, and was watching. When he looked again, she had her head down and was coming on again.

"Damn the thing!" he exclaimed, in nervousness and anger. And stick in one hand, overcoat in the other, he started walking towards the animal, like some nervous toreador.

The cow ran at him. He threw his overcoat right in her face, and turned and ran also for a few paces. When he looked round, the cow was galloping in a funny, jerky zigzag, with his overcoat hanging on one horn, stumbling, snorting, shaking her head. There went his overcoat.

Patty was at the brook, climbing down among the bushes. The cow was prancing and jerking in the near distance, floundering with the black overcoat. He stood with his stick, and waited. He wanted his coat.

So he set off after the cow. She was a rare scarecrow, plunging and ducking in fear and fury. He pursued her as she dodged, shouting after her. At last she trod on the coat and got it off her horn, and went galloping away. He recovered his garment, and returned after Patty.

She had scrambled through the deep brook and up the other bank, and was leaning against a tree, with her eyes shut, faint. Her feet were full of water, there was brown earth on her skirt at the knee, where she had scrambled, and her breast was heaving. She could not speak.

When he came up, he was filled with consternation.

"Has it upset you?" he asked, not knowing what to do.

"Frightened me," she murmured, gasping. She was ill. She could not stand up. She subsided at the foot of the tree, with her head dropped.

He stood near, looking on in distress and anxiety. He did not know in the least what to do. He wanted to put his coat for her to sit on, but did not like to disturb her. Her head was dropped as if she was unconscious, but her bosom laboured.

He waited, in nervous, irritable suspense. Her breathing seemed to be quieter. At last she lifted her head. Her face was paper-white, there were dark lines under her eyes, her eyes seemed dimmed.

"I'm sorry to give you so much trouble," she said, rather ghostily. "But it's my heart. It gives way—on these occasions."

She seemed a shattered, elderly woman. He felt pity, distress, shame, and irritation.

At last she put her hand on the earth to rise. He assisted her, and steadied her. He had seen her overshoes full of water.

"Let me take off your galoshes," he said.

She leaned against the tree as he did so. He saw her nice shoes were wet too. And he wiped her skirt with his handkerchief where it was soiled.

"Thank you. Thank you," she said. "It's awfully weak of me. But I can't help it." She closed her eyes, haggardly.

"Don't you bother. Let me do what I can for you," he said sympathetically.

At last she drew herself together, haggard-looking.

"I'll see if I can walk," she said, her mouth thin and pinched and frightened. He held her by the arm to support her, and wished they were both out of the situation.

So they crossed the meadow, crept through a fence into a bit of an orchard, and through the orchard gate into the road. She suffered agonies of self-consciousness because people saw them, and agonies of self-consciousness all the way home, because of her appearance. It seemed a cruel long way. And Gilbert at her side took step after step, and thought to himself his luck was out as regards women. As a matter of fact, the accident of the cow was rather a bitter blow to him, though he formulated nothing in his consciousness. Still, he felt that his heart had wakened and risen, and been knocked back again with a mallet-stroke. But he took it rather for granted that life was like that.

As for poor Patty, she felt humiliated, and was rather petulant. She recovered from her shock as she walked home, but her face did not lose all its haggardness and its broken look. And she wanted Lewis. She badly wanted Lewis to come home. She wanted him to be there. The presence of this other man was a strain on her. She wanted her husband.

5. CHOIR CORRESPONDENCE

This same evening, Emmie sat in the choir loft in chapel and warbled with her pleasant little voice. She was looking rather nipped, having had a bad week of it. But tonight she was on the wing again, and perking up her indomitable little head under her jaunty brown velour hat. Still, it was rather an effort. The enemy sat below, inimical. His stiff, thin figure rose at the end of the family pew; he looked as if butter wouldn't melt in his mouth, he sat so meek and still, with such a pietistic look on his face as he gazed up to the pulpit. Anyone would have imagined that the plump minister, in a black B.A. gown, shed out some mild incandescent light as he fluttered his plump hands, such a wistful effulgence seemed to linger on Alf Bostock's rapt, black-whiskered face. He looked almost lovely, the demon; he was rather good-looking. Emmie spitefully itched to throw things in his rapt mug. But her hate went deep just now—down to rebellion-level. The poor mother sat next the father, rather reddish and mottled in complexion, of no particular expression at all, except that she appeared submissive and seemed to be taking a rest, just sitting still. Her lilac hat looked as if it had been in the weather; a look her hats were apt to get, in spite of all her daughters could do. After the mother came a row of Bostocks, dear little Fra-Angelico-faced girls and rather long-nosed sons. The biggest son sat at the remote end of the pew, a long lad of nineteen, mild-looking, balancing the sermon-imbibing father who sat next the aisle, with his hands folded in his black-trousered lap.

Emmie was struggling hard to spread her game little wings. But they felt rather numb, after the treatment she had undergone. She watched the little minister. He was very plump, and rather ridiculous, perched on a stool in the pulpit and gyrating his pretty hands, as his voice soared or sank in leisurely, elegant measure. He was rather a comic; but Emmie liked him. He was nothing if not indulgent and good-natured. She would almost have liked to flirt with him. He *loved* his preaching, seemed to be swimming like some elegant little merman in the waters of his eloquence. A spirit of mischief spread its spoiled, storm-beaten wings in her eyes.

Just in front of her, among the altos, sat Agatha Sharp, next to Alvina Houghton. Agatha was one of Emmie's pals, a school-teacher like herself, but much better-behaved. Tall and slim, the girl in the altos sat looking her best, her boy being in a pew away below, facing her.

Emmie twitched and fidgeted, glanced bird-like down on the bonnets and parted hair in the chapel and shifted on her seat like a fidgety bird on a bough, looking down on a motionless congregation, sermon-drugged. She knocked down her anthem-sheet, and picked it up again; sat with it in her lap; took a hymn-book, fished a stump of pencil from her pocket and began to scribble on her anthem-sheet, on the back:

"Lovely spoon last week with G. N. Eh, what do you think. Wire-whiskers came back from work and caught us. Oh ay, Agatha, I nearly had a fit. G. N. and W. W. went for one another, and I ran off— thought I was never going back home."

She folded down the anthem-sheet like a game of consequences and poked her friend in the back. Agatha looked round. Emmie gave her the paper and pencil. Agatha, flushing and looking demure, bowed her head to read the paper. Then she, too, put the pencil to her lips, scribbled, and put her hand behind her back without turning round. Emmie fished up the paper and pencil.

"Do you mean after chapel? Wherever did you go?"

Emmie sucked her pencil and scribbled.

"About half-past ten. He caught us in our greenhouse. I'd got no hat on nor anything. I ran without knowing where I was going, to Lewis Goddard's."

She poked Agatha in the back. Instead of looking round, Agatha curled her hand behind her. Emmie deposited the paper in the fingers of her friend. Alvina Houghton, who disapproved of Emmie, looked round rather snappishly. Emmie turned up her nose.

Back came the paper.

"You bad wench. How did you go home? Have you seen G. N. since?"

Emmie snatched the paper, sucked her pencil, and scribbled hastily.

"I stopped all night at Goddard's. Mrs. G. rather snipey. Lewis went down home and told our Dad a thing or two. I was awfully bad—they thought I was going to be really badly. So did I. I didn't go to school Monday—stopped in bed at Goddard's, and went home in the afternoon. Our Dad hasn't spoken to me since."

Again Agatha felt a poke in the back. Again she curled her hand behind her. And again Alvina Houghton glanced round, frowning coldly, while Cissy Gittens glanced inquiringly over her shoulder. The choir was beginning to concentrate upon this correspondence. Even some of the audience were noticing a new centre of disturbance. And the clergyman, poor man, was becoming decidedly irritable in his delivery, fidgeting on his foot-stool.

Back came the paper from Agatha.

"You *are* an awful bad catamaran. Haven't you seen G. N. since?"

Emmie got the paper, and industriously popped her pencil to her lips.

"No, I've never been out. He wouldn't let me. Never saw you Wednesday. He's trying his hardest to get G. N.'s name. He's got his cap. But he's never asked *me*. He bothers our mother, and the others. He'd better not ask *me*."

The paper went, and returned.

"This will be a lesson to you, my lady. What will he do if he gets G. N.'s name? Did they really hit one another? Didn't he see G. N.? Oh I *do* think it's awful."

Emmie seized this message, and wrote:

"They were down in a gooseberry-bush when I scooted for my life. Look at the scratches on W. W.'s ear. It was pitch-dark. He says I'm never going to be out again after dark. *Aren't I?* I'm not frightened of him. But he's not going to get Great Northern's name. Our mother doesn't know either. They're all trying to guess. Do you think he'll come tonight? Can't see him if he does. You'll have to tell him, Agatha. He's the best spoon out. But tell him not to come again—not just yet. I'm going to be a reformed character, and stick to Walter George. What? See me—"

A poke in Agatha's back.

And at the same time the minister raised his fat, near-sighted, pince-nezed face, that was red as a boiled shrimp. Agatha was reading in sublime unconsciousness, when the whole congregation woke from its sermonial somnolence with a shudder as if someone had scratched on a slate a long shriek with a screeching pencil. So did the changed note in the minister's sweet-oil voice set their teeth on edge like vinegar.

"I should be glad if the interruption from the choir could be brought to an end. I have continued as long as I could without observation, but further continuance is impossible. Either the unseemly correspondence in the choir gallery must cease, or I must close for this evening."

A moment's pause and re-adjustment.

"*Please* let the passing of papers cease," continued the all-forgiving minister. "I should be extremely sorry to hurt any individual feelings. But I speak out of painful necessity, after considerable endurance. And I cannot continue under the strain of the previous distraction."

He was nettled, but with Christian forbearance already rubbed dock-leaves on the sting, adjusted his eye-glasses, looked down at his notes, and, still red as a boiled shrimp, picked up his oratorical voice, which somehow he seemed to have dropped and left in the distance. The sermon began to trickle its suave flow again.

But the congregation! The congregation was electrified. Every eye was on the choir-gallery, except only the eyes of those who sat in the rather select pews beneath the said gallery. And these, the nobs, so far forgot themselves as to screw their necks and look up at the sloping roof near above them, as if their x-ray eyes could pierce the flooring and distinguish the offender by his, or her, shoe-soles. Sternly and indignantly they stared at the little roof over their heads, above which roof, they knew, were perched the choral angels of the chapel. Fallen angels indeed.

In the choir itself consternation and indignation struggled in every breast. As the Roman emperors were jealous and suspicious of any society which leagued itself together within the body-politic, so are Christian ministers obliged to beware of the wheels within wheels of their church. A choir is an unpaid independent body, highly oligarchic and given to insubordination. For music, said to be a soothing art, produces the most wayward members of the Christian community. If the army caused the fall of emperor after emperor, how many Christian ministers are unpleasantly thrown from the pulpit in these self-governing churches by the machinations of the obstreperous choir! So little Daddy Dixon, as he was half-affectionately called, had better beware how he rushes with his angry lamb's bleat of expostulation into this mountainous nest of bears and she-bears.

From consternation the choir quickly passed to indignation. Poor Agatha sat with her crimson face buried in her bosom, screened by her broad black hat. Emmie, the impudent, sat with her nose in the air, looking guilty. Alvina Houghton and Cissie Gittens kept glancing round at her, damnatory. The other members glanced at Emmie, and then turned their indignant looks to one another, before they directed them in a volume against the little minister, perched there just beneath them on his little stool, continuing his little sermon, mildly flourishing his deprecating, plump hand out of the black wing of his gown. Emmie might be guilty of slight misdemeanour. But then, was she not an old member of the sacred choral college? And was this privileged body to be submitted to the injury and ignominy of a public rebuke from the pulpit? From Daddy Dixon, moreover, that plump lamb! Bears and she-bears uttered inaudible growls, and flounced on their seats, crackled their music-sheets, and altogether behaved like a mutiny on the upper deck.

Alf Bostock, however, sat with a wolf's eye glaring greenly up at his perky daughter. Mrs. Bostock's brows were knitted with ancient perplexity, as she too looked upwards, on her right. The boy Bostocks had gone red to their ears, of course. They seized every available opportunity of going red to the ears.

Came the closing hymn, sung by the choir as if they had grit between their teeth. Meanwhile the poor parson sat in the pulpit, with his brow in his hand, drawing upon himself the full and vicious flow of sympathy from the congregation, the extra venom of the choir, who stood upright in their dimmish loft like a crowd of demons on the war-path.

Poor Norman Dixon prayed, in the final prayer, that hearts might be kept from anger and turned away from wrath, and oh, if we, whose sacred duty it is to guide the way along the path of Right, if we should stumble and catch our feet against the stones of passion, may we in our humble repentance before Thee beseech that our stumbling shall not cause others to fall, but shall rather show them the difficulties of the way, and assist them to walk in uprightness and love, remembering that each has his own burden to bear along the difficult journey of life, and that he who adds weight to his brother's burden does not thereby make lighter his own, but brings weariness and sorrow where before was joy. For oh, let us beware of our own thoughtlessness . . .

This homily, though intended of course for the Almighty, the choir set down to their own account, and determined not to be mollified all at once. No, indeed. If Norman Dixon stumbled it was his own toe he must blame, not somebody else's stone that lay in the way. Let him pick his way through the stones. What else was he a minister of the gospel for? And the congregation half agreed. After all, he could have spoken later on, in private, and not have caused a public scandal. Everybody is so eager to pull the chair of authority from under the poor devil whom they have chosen to sit down in it.

Only one member of the congregation agreed, and more than agreed, with plump Norman Dixon in the pulpit. We know who this member was. He proceeded to gnash his teeth in preparation.

Emmie knew well enough the fat was in the fire, and therefore she was dumb when the choir rather guiltily moaned the emotional vesper:

Lord, keep us safe this night,
Secure from all our fears.
May angels guard us while we sleep,
Till morning light appears.

The bass curved up and the treble curved down in the luscious melody, and Emmie tried to gather her wits. Things were already at a break-ing-point between her and her pa.

As the choir trooped down the stairs after service, venting their indignation, Emmie hurried and caught her friend by the arm.

"Oh, I say, Agatha, damn Norman Dixon. What had *he* got to go and put his foot in it for? I say, if he's waiting—you know—you'll tell him, won't you? Oh, an' I say, I've got a book of his. Tell him I s'll leave it for him at Lewis Goddard's, shall you. I fair forgot it till to-night, when I was thinking of last week. Oh, I'm fair sick of things, Agatha. I'm sure I wish I was dead, I'm that persecuted. You know my Dad's made my mother swear she'll tell him everything what I do. She told me herself he had. And what do you think, he can wring anything out of her, the inquisition devil. He'd better not try it on me, though, or he'll get more than he's bargained for. I tell you what, Agatha, I could fair jump in the cut, I could, I'm that harassed and tormented. And all by that old fool. And what's more, what right has he? I'm over twenty-one. I hope his rabbits'll die, for I hate him. Eh, Agatha. And tell *him*—you know—that I can't get his cap back for him. My father's got it, trying to get a clue from it. But he won't then, because it was bought at Parker's in Knarborough and hasn't got a name or anything in. I got it out of my mother, all that. But Lewis Goddard'll stand by me. An' I shall run away to our Fan's if he gives me any more bother."

They had reached the needle's-eye gate by which the choir emerged from the chapel precincts. Emmie glanced swiftly round. Yes, there was Gilbert on the opposite pavement. She pinched Agatha's arm excitedly.

"He's come, Agatha. You tell him. And if he wants to see me, tell him—"

"You're coming, there, aren't you?" said a policeman-like voice. We know whose.

"Yes, I am," said Emmie sullenly. Then: "Good-night, Agatha. Hope I shall see you Wednesday."

And she followed her irate parent, who joined her forlorn mother at the big gate, and the family trailed off in a disconsolate Sunday-night crowd.

Agatha meanwhile went across the road.

"Good evening, Mr. Noon. Excuse me. Emmie can't come tonight. She told me about last week. You know, don't you . . ."

"Yes," said Gilbert. "Mr. Goddard told me about it. Hasn't she been to chapel, then? Wasn't that she?"

"Yes. Her father made her go home. He's in another of his tantrums now. Oh—here's my boy. Can I introduce you . . ."

And Agatha went on to communicate all Emmie's commissions.

"All right," said Gilbert. "Give her these when you see her. I shall go to Goddard's for the book."

He gave Agatha the inevitable packet of chocolates, and turned away. Ah, spoony chocolates! 'Tis you who have made the cocoa fortunes. And now Gilbert will buy no more. Lewis had given him a lively description of Emmie's plight on the previous Sunday night; how she seemed to be losing her reason; and all the things *he*, Lewis, had said to her father, first oil, then vinegar; and how Bostock had been brought to promise to say nothing to the girl; how he had kept his promise, but had been up to Patty to find out if *she* could tell him what the fellow's name was. Of course she couldn't. Of course Emmie hadn't mentioned the name to *them*. This with one of Lewis's side-looks, which told Gilbert that the Goddards knew only too well. Moreover, he remembered that Emmie was going to leave the book for *him* at Lewis's. Whereupon he had something else to put in his pipe and smoke. And Alf Bostock was a nasty customer, Lewis said; one of your reformed ones.

6. THE SACK

Meanwhile a pretty kettle of fish was preparing for Mr. Noon. He smelled nothing of it for some days. Neither did he go over to Woodhouse, but let matters remain where they were. He was annoyed and irritated by the whole business. The thought of Emmie now gave him a prickly sensation in his skin and made him knit his brows irritably. He had been relieved that he could not see her on the Sunday evening, and after receiving her message he hoped the whole affair was finished. Never would he start such a mess again; never. For the whole world of spooning, bits of fluff, jolly good sports, bits of hot stuff and the like he now felt a prickly repulsion, an irritable distaste. No more of that for *him*.

But wait a bit. Let him not holloa till he is out of the wood.

He did not go to the Goddards' either, because he felt that Patty had been making a butt of him. Yes, while he was feeling such a hero in the park, she was laughing up her sleeve at him.

"While from the dark park, hark. . ." The ridiculous Tom Hood line ran in his mind. Yes, he was a fool, a born fool and a made fool, both, and he felt in a state of intense irritation against everybody he knew and the whole circumstances of his life.

To crown which, on Thursday he received a note, at school, requesting him to attend a meeting *in camera* of the Higher Grade Committee at Knarborough, at seven in the evening—signed M. Britten.

Haysfall Technical School was under the control of the Education Committee, which had its seat in the county town of Knarborough. *M. Britten* was Minnie Britten, secretary for the above; and secretary for everything else into which she could poke her nose. Gilbert knew her; a woman with grey hair and a black hat, in a tremendous hurry of mental responsibility and importance, always scuffling in when she wasn't wanted and setting all the leaves fluttering with her strained sense of duty and her exaggerated sense of importance. Heaven knows how much she cost the county in petrol, for she was not out of the official motor-car ever for a longer space than half-an-hour. Her superior, Jimmy Blount, a youngish bald man with an eyeglass, Clerk for Education for the County, let her flutter the dovecotes at will. He, poor devil, was harassed by the officious interference of the innumerable little gods who have education at heart and can make an official's chair uncomfortable. Mrs. Britten, then—we forgot to mention she was married— darted about the county wherever she felt she was in request, like some spider dashing from the centre of its web along the lines every time it feels or imagines it feels a disturbance. Of course Mrs. Britten did actually rush into a lot of educational bothers; which proves, of course, that the bothers existed. Whether her rushes made matters any better, we leave to the imagination of any individual who has ever had the misfortune and humiliation to be connected with our educational system.

Mrs. Britten, then; she was a B.A. also, and felt that her education was unquestionable. She wrote pamphlets on Education, and was surprised, yes, surprised, if at least every head-teacher in every school did not show an acquaintance with their contents. She was Secretary for the Children's Holiday Fund, and an assiduous collector therefor. A footpad, even a burglar with a revolver, is answerable. But Mrs. Britten was unanswerable, especially to poor quaking elementary school-teachers, to whom she was the *Deus ex machina*. She forced the reluctant sixpences out of them, and let her sun shine on schools whose contribution to the Fund was highest. She was an opponent of Feeding the Children—we must refer to her pamphlet on the subject for the reason why. In fact, she was for or against innumerable things, so that it was a wonder her hair hadn't all disappeared, instead of being merely stone-grey at forty. She was honest, of course. She was kind, as goes without saying. She was hard and straightforward and downright enough. Wonderful what a lot of virtues she managed to have in a hurry. Though she wasn't at all a new broom, she swept the dust from pillar to post, and left everybody spitting, till some poor devil got the dust-pan and collected the dirt.

Mr. Noon knew her. We've all known her. Such conscientious people don't let themselves remain unknown. She rather approved of Mr. Noon —because he was so clever, and had brought the remnants of such a reputation with him from Cambridge. She even rather toadied to him —in a mental kind of way. Spiteful female teachers said she wouldn't at all mind setting her black hat at him; but this isn't true. Mrs. Britten was merely Minerva extending her grace and craving a little adulation in return. She heard—oh, yes, she heard of his peccadilloes. What escaped her? But, curiously enough, she was rather more indulgent to him because of them. If he had been so brilliant and impregnable, her wing might not have covered him. But if not her intellectual, at least he might be her moral chicken.

Therefore Gilbert felt no particular qualm when he received the note summoning him to the meeting *in camera*. Rather he poured a little ointment on his prickly, nettle-rashed vanity, and concluded they were going to consult him, privately, upon some matter connected with the school—probably the fitting-up of a laboratory for technical chemistry.

So he put his best suit on, tied his tie to his taste, and whizzed over on the motor-cycle to the county town. When he arrived at the town hall, the porter told him the meeting was already sitting. He went to the waiting-room, and there sat cooling his heels. Doubtful if even now he smelled the above-mentioned fish, which were stewed and nearly ready for him in the next room.

A bell rang. A clerk went into the meeting-room, returned and ushered in Mr. Noon. Mrs. Britten was at the head of a long table round which were seated the various members of the committee, mostly fat fossils and important persons of complete insignificance. Mrs. Britten rose to her feet.

"Ah, good evening, Mr. Noon. Will you sit *there*?"—and she indicated a chair at the doorwards end of the table, opposite herself. Gilbert said good evening, and, looking very fresh and spruce, seated himself in the chair indicated. Meanwhile, down either side of the black-leathered table the members of the committee, their faces very distinct owing to the shaded lights that hung over the table and cast all the glow down on them, looked steadfastly at Mr. Noon, as if they had expected some inhabitant of Mars to make his appearance. Gilbert suddenly felt like a baby that has fallen to the bottom of the sea and finds all the lobsters staring at him in the undersea light. So they stared, like enquiring lobsters, and he felt like a baby, with his fresh face and pouting mouth.

But Mrs. Britten had seated herself once more, and stretching out her arms on the table in a very-much-herself fashion, she held certain papers within the full glare of the lamp, and began:

"We are sorry, Mr. Noon, to have to call this meeting tonight to consider the subject in hand. Yesterday, a formal report was made and signed in my presence which, although it does not directly affect the concerns of this Committee, yet may prejudice your successful work in the Haysfall Technical School seriously. Is not that so, gentlemen?"

The lobsters buzzed and nodded in the sub-marine. They no longer looked at Mr. Noon, but studiously away from him. He sat looking rather wonder-stricken and stupid, with his pouting mouth a shade open.

"Therefore we have decided to put the matter before you openly, and hear your account. We are sorry to have to intrude on your private life, but we do feel that the interests of the school where you are doing such good work are at stake."

"Quite!" said one of the lobsters distinctly and emphatically. Gilbert's eyes strayed wonderingly to him.

"We are met here *in camera*, even without a clerk. If we can clear the matter up satisfactorily, nothing more shall be heard of it. We are prepared to forget all about it."

"Oh, certainly, certainly," barked a couple of lobsters.

At this time Mr. Noon's attention was interrupted by his recalling the story about a certain French poet who was seen slowly leading a lobster by a blue ribbon along one of the boulevards. When a friend asked him why, why? the poet replied wistfully: "You see, they don't bark."

Gilbert wondered if they really did never bark, or if, under-water, they rushed out of their rock-kennels and snapped and yapped at the heels of the passing fishes. This fancy caused him to hear only a wave-lapping sound for a few moments, which wave-lapping sound was actually Mrs. Britten's going-on. He came to himself when she flapped a paper to attract his rather vacant-looking attention. He stared alert at the paper, and heard her portentous reading.

"I wish to make known to the Members of the Knarborough Education Committee that Gilbert Noon, science-teacher in Haysfall Technical School, has been carrying on with my daughter, Emma Grace Bostock, and has had criminal commerce with her. He has got my daughter into trouble, and ruined her life. I wish to know whether such a man is fit to be a teacher of young boys and girls, and if nothing is going to be done in the matter by the Knarborough Education Committee. Signed—Alfred Wright Bostock."

Mrs. Britten's level voice came coldly to an end, and she looked keenly at Mr. Gilbert. He sat staring at some invisible point above the middle of the table, and was quite inscrutable.

"We feel," said Mrs. Britten, "how delicate the matter is. We wish above all things not to trespass. But we find we must have an answer from your own mouth. The meeting is private—everything will be kept in strictest privacy. Will you tell us, please, whether this statement by the man Bostock is altogether false?"

Gilbert still stared at the invisible point and looked absent. There was a dead silence which began to get awkward.

"Yes or no, Mr. Noon?" said Mrs. Britten gently.

Still the vacant Gilbert stared at a point in space, and the lobsters began to squiggle in their arm-chairs.

"We have your interest at heart, Mr. Noon. Please believe it. But we are bound, *bound* to have the interest of your school and scholars also at heart. If the matter had not been formally forced upon our attention, as I may say, we might have let gossip *continue* its gossiping. But the man Bostock seems to be a determined individual, capable of creating considerable annoyance. We thought it best to try to settle the matter quietly and as privately as possible. We have the greatest possible esteem for your services; we would not like to lose them. And so we are met here tonight to do what we can.

"Answer, then, simply, yes or no. Is this statement made by the man Bostock utterly false, or must we consider it? Is it completely false? Yes?"

The lobsters glued their eyes on Mr. Noon's face. He looked up and along at Mrs Britten; surely she was a Jewess by birth. A thousand to one on it she was a benevolent Jewess by birth.

"All right, then," he said gruffly, leaning forward on the table and half-rising, pushing his chair scraping back; "I'll send in my resignation."

He stood leaning forward for one second at the table, looking at the confounded lobsters.

"No, no, Mr. Noon! Please! Please sit down. Please! Please! Do sit down. Please do! Please!" Mrs Britten had risen to her feet in her earnest agitation. She seemed really *so* concerned for his welfare that he wavered, and half sat down.

"Certainly! Take your seat, young man," said one of the lobsters, who evidently owned employees.

"I'll send in my resignation," barked Gilbert, sending his chair back with a jerk and opening the door before any lobster could disentangle himself from his lobster-pot of a round official chair.

"Oh, *don't* let him go!" cried Mrs. Britten, with a wail of distress. There was a clinking and scraping of lobster-pots, and one lobster-voice shouted: "Here! Here, you!" But Gilbert—Gilbert was going down the wide, dim stone stairs three at a time, not running, but lunging down, smack, smack, smack, three steps at a time. He bumped aside the porter and took his hat and coat, and in another second was going out of the front door of the Town Hall, hearing the last of Mrs. Britten's voice wailing from the semi-darkness up aloft the stairs:

"Please, Mr. Noon! *Please* come back!"

All her nice little game of that evening was spoilt. Oh, what a temper she was in, and how she longed to box the ears of all the lobsters, particularly the one who had "young-manned" the truant. Oh, how she hated the lobsters, over whom she queened it so regally. Oh, how she itched to smack their faces and tell them what she thought of them. A Jewess born!

But she did none of these things. She only said:

"He will send in his resignation tomorrow."

"And it will be accepted," barked a lobster.

"*Sine die*," yapped another, though nobody knew what he meant by it, or whether it was English which they hadn't quite caught.

7. JAW

Gilbert's kettle of fish had been all lobsters but one; but that didn't make it any the sweeter.

The next day was Saturday; half-day at school. His one fear was that Mrs. Britten would pounce on him. If she did, he would put her off with vague promises and sweetnesses. For he was determined to have done with Haysfall, Whetstone, Woodhouse, Britten women, Goddard women, Emmie women, all his present life and circumstance, all in one smack. Men at some times are masters of their fates, and this was one of Gilbert's times. The wonder is he did not break his neck at it, or get locked up, for he rode his motor-cycle at many forbidden miles an hour, so anxious he was to get home. He was so anxious to have between his fingers the Lachesis shears of his thread of fate, in the shape of a fountain-pen. He could snip off the thread of his Haysfall life in about three strokes—"I beg to resign my post in Haysfall Technical School, and wish to leave at the very earliest opportunity." That was all he would say. And he was itching to say it. His motor-cycle fairly jumped over the dark roads from Knarborough to Whetstone.

He arrived, wrote out his resignation, and sat down to think.

In the first place, he was clearing out. He was going to Germany, as he had often said he would, to study for his doctorate.

That was settled.

But . . .

And there were rather serious "buts."

Criminal correspondence with Emmie had *got her into trouble* and *ruined her life.* Did that mean she was going to have a baby? Lord save us, he hoped not. And even if she was, whose baby was it going to be? He felt in no mood at all for fatherhood, but decided, since he was running away, he had better see Emmie again and make it as square with her as possible.

Which meant also going to the Goddards.

And would that damned Mrs. Britten fasten on him tomorrow? He knew she would on Monday, if not tomorrow. Saturday morning, he knew, she was busier and fuller up than ever, if that were possible. The thing was, to get away without seeing her. Could he clear out after tomorrow morning? Not put in any further appearance after the morrow?

That remained to decide.

Then, money. He had no money. He never had any money, though his father said that when *he* was his age, meaning Gilbert's, he had saved a hundred and seventy pounds out of thirty shillings a week. Gilbert would have been glad of the hundred and seventy pounds if he'd saved them, but he hadn't. How was he to clear out with about fifty-five shillings, which was all he had?

He must get something out of his father, that was all. And sell his motor-cycle. Ay, sell his motor-cycle. Leave that also for the morrow. Sufficient unto the day, etc.

Of course he'd brought it all on himself. And he didn't seriously care, either. One must bring one thing or another on oneself.

There was his father just come in from having half-a-pint at the Holly Bush. Down he went. His father was sitting in the many-staved arm-chair, almost a lobster-pot, the throne of the home. Gilbert sat on the sofa opposite. The father began to unfasten his boots.

"Father," said Gilbert, "I'm chucking Haysfall Technical."

"Oh, ay," replied his parent.

"I'm thinking of going to Germany."

"Are you?"

"I'm going to work there for my doctorate."

"Doctorate? Oh, yes."

"Doctor of Science, you know."

"Ay! Ay!"

"It would do me a lot of good, you know."

"It would, would it?"

"I should get a much better job than ever I can get now."

"Yes—yes."

"The only thing is funds."

"Funds. Yes."

"It'll cost me a bit at first; only at first."

"Where? In Germany? Oh, yes."

"Yes."

"Ay."

This passionate conversation between father and son was drawing to an inevitable close.

"You don't see your way to helping me a bit, Dad?"

"Helping you, child! I'm always helping you."

"Yes, but a bit extra."

"Nay, how can I help you if you go to foreign parts?"

"By setting me up with a few quid."

"A few quid? Why—you can stop at home an' have board an' lodging for nothing. What'st want to be goin' to Germany for?"

"For my doctorate."

"Doctrat be—hanged."

"Nay, father."

"Thou'rt doing right enough as t'art."

"No; I'm going to Germany."

"Tha art?"

"Yes."

"Oh—all right."

"You see, father, I want a few quid to start off with."

"Save 'em, then, my boy."

"I haven't saved them, Dad, and you have. So you give me a few."

"Tha does talk."

"Ay—what else should I do?"

"Save thy wind."

"Like you save your money."

"Ay—t'same."

"And you won't give me any?"

"Tha'lt get the lot when I'm gone."

"But I don't want you gone, and I want a little money."

"Want. Want. What art doin' wi' wants? Tha should ha'e th' fulness, not th' want."

"So I should if you'd give it to me."

"Nay, I can nivir put th' fat off my own belly on to thine."

"I don't want your fat—I want about fifty pounds."

"That *is* my fat."

"You know it isn't."

"I know it is."

"Won't you give them me?"

"Tha'lt get all when I've gone."

"I want it now."

"Aye, me an' all. I want it now."

Whereupon Gilbert rose and went upstairs again. His father was a lobster.

The next morning passed without any descent of Mrs. Britten. He got on his bicycle, and left Haysfall for good, taking his few personal possessions with him from the big red school.

Arriving at Whetstone at one o'clock, he immediately went and bargained with an acquaintance who, he knew, wanted his motorcycle. The man offered fifteen pounds. The thing was worth a good forty.

"Give me twenty, or I'll ride it to London and sell it there."

It was agreed he was to have twenty, and hand over the cycle the next day, Sunday. So he went home for dinner, did not speak to his father, with whom he was angry, hurried through his meal, and shoved off with his motor-bike again.

8. HIS MIGHT-HAVE-BEEN MOTHER-IN-LAW

At Woodhouse, Patty opened the door to him. She started, and looked embarrassed.

"Is it you, Mr. Noon! Come in." Then, in a low tone: "I've got Mrs. Bostock here. Poor thing, I'm sorry for her. But perhaps you'd rather not see her."

"What do you think?" he said.

Patty pursed up her mouth.

"Oh—as you please. She's quite harmless."

"All right."

He took off his hat, and marched into the room. Mrs. Bostock fluttered from her chair. Patty came in wagging herself fussily as she walked, and arching her eyebrows with her conspicuously subtle smile.

"What a coincidence, Mrs. Bostock! This is Mr. Noon."

Mrs. Bostock, who at a nearer view was seen to have a slip-shod, amiable cunning in her eyes, shook hands and said she hoped she saw him well. Patty settled herself with her ivory hands in her dark-brown lap, and her ivory face flickering its important smile, and looked from one to the other of her guests.

"How remarkable you should have come just at this minute, Mr. Noon! Mrs. Bostock has just brought this book of yours. I believe you lent it Emmie."

Gilbert eyed the treatise on Conic Sections.

"Yes," he said. "I did."

"It was my mistake as did it," said Mrs. Bostock with that slip-shod repentance of her nature. "I picked it up and said, 'Whose is this book about Comic Sections?' I thought it was a comic, you see, not noticing. And our Dad twigged it at once. 'Give it here,' he said. And he opened it and saw the name. If I'd seen it I should have put it back on the shelf and said nothing."

"How very unfortunate," Patty said. "May I see?"

She took the book, read the title, and laughed sharply.

"A mathematical work?" she said, wrinkling up her eyes at Gilbert. Not that she knew any more about it, really, than Mrs. Bostock did. She saw the Trinity College stamp, and the name, Gilbert Noon, written on the fly-leaf.

"What a curious handwriting you have, Mr. Noon," she said, looking up at him from under her dark brows. He did not answer. People had said so, often. He wrote in an odd, upright manner, rather as if his letter was made up out of crochets and quavers and semibreves, very picturesque and neat.

"If I'd opened it I should have guessed, though I didn't know the name any more than he did. But he was too sharp for me. I tried to pass it off. It was no good, though," said Mrs. Bostock. She had a half-amused look, as if the intrigue pleased her.

"So it all came out?" asked Patty.

"Ay, I'm sorry to say. As soon as our Emmie came in he showed it to her and said, 'I'm goin' to Haysfall Technical with this.' And she, silly-like, instead of passing it off, flew at him and tried to snatch it from him. That just pleased our Dad. I said to her after: 'Why, you silly thing, what did you let on for? Why didn't you make out you knew nothing?' And then she flew at me."

"You must have had a trying time between the two," said Patty, wrinkling her brows at Noon.

"Oh, I have, I can tell you. He vowed he'd go up to the Tech. with the book, and she said if he did she'd jump in the cut. I kept saying to her, 'Why didn't you pass it off with a laugh?' But she seemed as if she'd gone beyond it. So he kept the book till this morning. She told me she'd promised to leave it here."

"You knew," said Patty, "that Emmie had run away?"

"No," said Gilbert.

"Gone to our Fanny's at Eakrast," said Mrs. Bostock. "I had a letter from our Fanny next day, saying she was bad in bed. I should have gone over, but I've got Elsie with measles."

"You have your hands full," said Patty.

"I have, I tell you. I said to our Dad, 'You can do nothing but drive things from bad to worse.' Our Fanny has had the doctor in to her, and he says it's neuralgia of the stomach. Awful, isn't it? I know neuralgia of the face is bad enough. I said to our Dad, 'Well,' I said, 'I don't know whether she's paying for her own wickedness or for your nasty temper to her, but she's paying, anyhow.'"

"Poor Emmie. And she's such a gay thing by nature," said Patty.

"Oh, she's full of life. But a wilful young madam, and can be snappy enough with the children. I've said to her many a time, 'You're like your Dad; you keep your smiles in the crown of your hat, and only put 'em on when you're going out.' She can be a cat, I tell you, at home. She makes her father worse than he would be."

"I suppose she does," said Patty.

"Oh, he gets fair wild, and then tries to blame me. I say to him,

'She's your daughter; I didn't whistle her out o' th' moon.' He's not bad, you know, if you let him be. He wants managing, then he's all right. Men doesn't have to be told too much, and it's no good standing up to them. That's where our Emmie makes her mistake. She *will* fly back at him, instead of keeping quiet. I'm sure, if you answer him back, it's like pouring paraffin to put a fire out. He flares up till I'm frightened."

"I'm afraid," laughed Patty grimly, "I should have to stand up to him."

"That's our Emmie. I tell him, if he will make school-teachers of them, he must expect them to have tongues in their heads." Then she turned to Gilbert. "He never did nothing about your book, did he?"

"Yes," said Gilbert. "I've got the sack."

"Oh, how disgusting!" cried Patty.

"Ay, a lot of good that'll do," said Mrs. Bostock. "It's like him, though. He'll pull the house down if the chimney smokes."

"When are you leaving?" said Patty.

"This week-end."

"Can you believe it!" said Mrs. Bostock.

Patty mused for a time.

"Well," she said, "I must say, your husband has caused a marvellous lot of mischief, Mrs. Bostock. He's fouled his own nest, indeed he has; done a lot of damage to others, and no good to himself."

"No; it's just like him—but there you are. Those that won't be ruled can't be schooled."

"What is Emmie going to do, then?" Gilbert asked.

"Don't ask me, Mr. Noon. She'll come back when she's better, I should think: silly thing she is, going off like it."

"What is her address?"

"Were you thinking of going over on your motor-bike? Well, I'll back she'll be pleased. Care of Mrs. Harold Wagstaff, Schools House, Eakrast. He's one of the schoolmasters, Fanny's husband. A clever young fellow, come out first at college. I'm sure you'd get on with him. It's the fourth house down the lane after the church-house and school combined. You can't miss it. But it's a very quiet place, you know. I bet they're not sorry for a bit of company."

Gilbert looked down his nose rather, for Mrs. Bostock continually glanced sideways at him, approvingly, and he knew she was quite comfortable, assuming in him a prospective, or at least a possible, son-in-law. Not that she was making any efforts herself towards the status of mother-in-law. But there was never any knowing what the young people would do, and she was quite willing, whichever way it was. She was quite ready to be agreeable, whichever way things went.

And this was almost as disconcerting to Mr. Gilbert as the old man's tantrum of hostility had been. Moreover that neuralgia of the stomach was worrying him. How easily it might mean an incipient Noon—or, since it is a wise father that knows his own child—an incipient little Emmie, an Emmeling. The thought of this potential Emmeling was rather seriously disconcerting to our friend. He had certain standards of his own, one of them being a sort of feeling that if you put your foot in it, you must clean your own shoe, and not expect someone else to do it. At the same time, he was determined to clear out of the whole show.

Mrs. Bostock rose, and must be hurrying back to her home. Gilbert rose too.

"Oh, but you'll stay and have a cup of tea?" Patty cried. "You're sure you can't stay, Mrs. Bostock?"

"I can't, thank you. I s'll have our master home at half-past five, and the children's tea to get, besides our Elsie. Thank you all the same, I'm sure. I'm sure you and Mr. Goddard have been very kind to our Emmie. I'm sure I don't know what she'd have done without Mr. Goddard."

"Oh, he's a friend in need," said Patty, with a curl of the lip.

"He is, bless him."

And the mother of the Bostocks took her leave.

Patty rang at once for tea, and sat herself down by the fire in the twilight. Gilbert had remained. It was too late to get to Eakrast that night.

"Well," said Patty, settling her skirts over her knees in a way she had; "you've had quite an adventure." And she smiled her wrinkled smile. She reminded Gilbert for a moment of one of those wrinkle-faced ivory demons from China. But that was because he was in a temper, and rather in a funk.

"If you look on it as an adventure," he said.

"Well—how else? Not as a tragedy, I hope. And not altogether a comedy. Too many people have had to smart. I guess Emmie Bostock feels anything but comic at this moment." This in an admonitory tone.

"Why?" said Gilbert.

"Why!" replied Patty, curling her lip in some scorn of such a question. "I should have thought it was very obvious. A poor girl lying ill—"

"What of?"

"Well—neuralgia of the stomach, they say. I expect it's some sort of gastritis . . ."

"You don't think it's a baby?"

Even Patty started at the bluntness of the question.

"No. I can't say. I've had no suggestion of such a thing. I hope not, indeed. That *would* be a calamity. Did you say you were going over?"

"Yes. I'm going to ask her."

"Yes. So you should. And if it were so—would you marry her?"

"What do you think?"

"I don't know. What do you *feel*?"

"Me? Nothing very pleasant."

"No—so I should imagine, so I should imagine. You've got yourself into a nasty position—"

"Not I. If a lot of fools make a lot of fuss, why should I blame myself for something that's only natural, anyhow?"

"Natural?—yes—maybe. But if Emmie Bostock is going to become a mother, and you're not going to marry her—or perhaps you are?—"

"No, I'm not."

"No, you're not! Well, then!"

"I can't help it," said Gilbert.

"That is no solution of her problem," said Patty.

"I didn't invent the problem," said Gilbert.

"Who did, then?"

"Her father, society, and fools."

"You had no hand in it, then? You had no finger in the pie?"

"Be hanged to fingers," said Gilbert.

"Well, then!" said Patty, starting and looking round as the woman came in with the tray.

"Do you mind lighting up, Mrs. Prince?"

Then, changing the subject slightly, she spoke of Lewis and his doings, until the woman went out of the room.

"Mind," said Patty, pouring out the tea, "I'm not so foolish as to think that you *ought* to marry the girl, if she is in trouble."

"Thank you," said Gilbert, taking his cup.

"No. I think that would be throwing good money after bad, so to speak. But surely *some* of the responsibility is yours? The woman isn't going to be left to suffer everything?"

"What a damned lot of fool's rot it is!" said Gilbert, becoming angry as he felt the crown of fatherhood being pressed rather prickly on his brow.

"Yes, it is! It is! There should be a provision for the woman in these matters. There should be a State Endowment of Motherhood; there should be a removal of the disgraceful stigma on bastardy. There *should* be. But there isn't. And so what are you going to do?''

"Find out first," said Gilbert, rising and buttoning his coat.

"Oh, but finish your tea," said Patty.

"I've done, thank you."

"But you can't ride to Eakrast tonight."

"Yes, I can."

"Dear me. But leave it till tomorrow—do. Wait till Lewis comes."

"No, thanks. I'll go and make sure, anyhow."

As a matter of fact, State Endowment of Motherhood and the stigma of bastardy had done for him. The wind had gone out of his sails as completely as if Patty had put two cannon-balls through him, and the ship of his conversation could make no more headway on the ruffled waters of her tea-table. Was he to lie there like a water-logged hulk? Was he to sit in that smothering arm-chair, with his cup on his knee and a scone in his fingers, sinking deeper and deeper through the springs of the chair like a leaky wreck foundering? Thank goodness his legs had taken the matter into their own hands—pardon the Irishism—and had jerked him on to his feet.

9. EMMIE AT EAKRAST

Emmie, we had forgotten to say, was engaged to Walter George all the time she was carrying-on with Mr. Noon. The fact so easily slipped her memory that it slipped ours. We ought to have mentioned it sooner, for the sake of Alfred Bostock, even.

To be sure, Emmie had been engaged several times. She got engaged in peace-time as easily as other women do in war-time. On every possible occasion she accepted a ring; varying in value from ten shillings to three pounds. Almost every time she sent the ring back when the affair was over. Twice the young men had generously said she could keep it. Hence the three ornaments which decked her fingers, and of which she was justly proud.

One she wore ostentatiously on her engagement-finger. It was one of those re-made rubies, quite red and nice, and Emmie felt she could honestly say it was a real stone. It tied her to Walter George quite closely. She had shown it with pleasure to Gilbert, and told him its history. And he had wondered if he was bound by the laws of Emmiegallantry to offer himself as an engagee. There wouldn't be much harm in it. And Emmie would so lightly commit pre-wedding bigamy, and there is safety in numbers.

But he hadn't gone so far, and Emmie had no ring of his. These rings, she loved them; they were her trophies and her romances, her scalp-fringe and her forget-me-not wreaths, her dried roses pressed into sound L.s.d.

Walter George was quite a nice boy; we are going to make his acquaintance. He was a clerk, and quite a gentleman. Let us say it softly, for fear of offending a more-than-sacred institution, he was a bank-clerk. He had walked out with Emmie all the time he was in Woodhouse, and she had hardly found an opportunity for a stroll with anyone else. Cruel authority, however, had moved him to the newly-opened branch of the London and Provincial Bank in Warsop. He departed, deeply regretting the soft and cuddly Emmie, who made love an easy and simple path for him. For the ease and simplicity of his paths of love he was wise enough to be thankful. Therefore, when rumour whispered poison-gas in his ear, he looked at other maidens, and imagined himself cuddling with *them* in a dark entry, and wiped his ears. Emmie was Emmie. So far, she belonged to herself. His nature, being easy, like hers, though less flighty, comprehended her sufficiently to realize that she was sipping all the flowers in her singleness in order to store the honey-jars of connubial felicity for him. The honey might be no more than golden syrup, but he would never know the difference. And therefore, so long as Emmie had the decency not to offend him too openly, he had the sense not to peep round the corner after her when she left him.

Some men want the path of love to run pleasantly between allotment-gardens stocked with cabbages and potatoes and an occasional sweet-william; some men want rose-avenues and trickling streams, and so scratch themselves and get gnat-bitten; some want to scale unheard-of-heights, roped to some extraordinary female of their fancy. *Chacun à son gout.* Walter George was born in the era of allotment-gardens, and thus Providence had provided for his marital Saturday afternoons, which is saying a good deal. He was a bank-clerk, too, and wanted to have an easy conscience and a dressy spouse. Church parade every Sunday morning was an institution to him. And he had quite a lot of cuddly lovey-doveyness. If anyone can mention to me a better recipe for a husband, I shall be glad to write it down.

Emmie took him seriously. Roses and rapture were good fun, but the cauliflower was the abiding blossom. Co-op. entries might have their thrill, but she was not one of those whose fanatic idealism insists on spending a lifetime in such places. No; she would rather forfeit her chances of heaven than her chance of a home of her own, where she could keep warm like a cat, and eat her cauliflower of a Sunday dinner.

In short, Emmie was *au fond* very sensible, much more sensible than her father. She knew even better than he that the cauliflower is the flower of human happiness, and that rose-leaves act like senna. All very well to purge off the follies of youth with red, or, better still, with pink roses. And she was sooner purged than her father. If only he had understood, he would have slept better in his bed. But, seeing his own more frenzied colics revived in the vagaries of his Emmie, he reacted more violently than he need have done, and that largely from fear. Once his daughter had run away, he began to realize this.

Having thus apologized for our characters, and demonstrated that they have a bed-rock of common-sense; having revealed their acquaintance with the fact that rose-leaves bring belly-aches, and that cauliflowers are delicious, and that Sunday dinner is the key-stone of the domestic arch on which repeated arches all society rests; having proved, in short, that the Bostocks are of the bulldog breed, full of sound British sense, let us go on with our story with more self-satisfaction than heretofore.

Emmie arrived at her sister Fanny's with real pains rending her. She knew it was rose-leaves, but blamed her father. In fact, she was in a state of subdued hysteria. So she took to her bed, and decided to turn over a new leaf. No, not a rose-leaf. She decided, if possible, to open the last long chapter of a woman's life, headed Marriage. She intended it to be a long and quite banal chapter, cauliflower and lovey-doves. Having at the moment a variety of pains in her inside, dubbed neuralgia of the stomach, she developed some of her own father's re-actionary hatred against the immortal rose. And though her hatred would lose its violence as the pains passed off; though it would decline into mere indifference, like her mother's, except she would retain a little crisp flirtiness of manner, to show she kept her end up; still, this sound and sensible emotion, this fundamental detestation of rose-leaves because she knew what rose-leaves were (just like her father: a piece of impudent assurance, too); this dislike of the immortal rose, and a consequent exaltation of the solid cauliflower would henceforth be the directing force of her life.

Warsop—and with this word the story gets on its feet again—lies but ten miles from Eakrast, across the forest. After two days of temper, hysteria, neuralgia of the stomach, after-effect of rose-leaves, or whatever it may have been, Emmie began to recover her commonsense. She had eaten the rose, and would make an ass of herself no more. So she lay and plotted for settling down in life.

The school and school-house were one building. In the front, the long school-room faced the road: at the back, the house-premises and garden looked to the fields and the distant forest.

Fanny, Emmie's sister, was a dark, rather big-nosed girl, very goodnatured. She had been married for a year, and had a baby. She received Emmie without too much surprise or consternation. In Fanny's sky the weather always blew over.

"Don't bother. It'll blow over," she said to Emmie, as she said all her life to herself.

She put her sister on the sofa, covered her up, and gave her a hot cup of tea; then she waited for Harold to come in. Emmie could hear Harold, on the other side of the wall, talking away at the scholars.

"Now then, Salt, what river comes next? Withan, Welland, Nen and Great Ouse—what comes after that? Don't you know? Do you know what your own name is? What? Oh, you do, do you? What is it? What? Salt? And if the Salt hath lost its savour . . . ? You don't know, do you? No, you wouldn't. Tell him what river comes next, Poole."

Emmie guessed it was Geography; therefore probably near the end of the afternoon. Listening, she could occasionally hear a shrill word from the assistant teacher, a girl, who was apparently taking sewing. There were only about forty-five scholars in the whole school.

The itch came over the rose-leaf-griped girl to be down in the schoolroom taking a lesson. She longed to begin with a "Now then . . ." Fanny had been a teacher, and had helped Harold till the advent of the baby. When the baby was a bit older, she would get a servant and go into the school again with Harold. It was so handy. You could just pop in and turn the pudding while the children were doing their drawing. You could pop in and put the kettle on at half-past three, and at four o'clock you would find it singing nicely.

Emmie envied Fanny her little school and school-house. As for Harold, he was all right. He was very respectable and a bit of a mardy, perhaps . . . but he was all right.

"Hello, Emmie. We weren't expecting you," he said, when he came in from school and found her at tea with Fanny and the baby. He talked in the rather mouthing fashion which teachers often have in the Midlands. "Have you got holidays at Woodhouse then?" he continued, his first thought, of course, being school.

"No; I've come away from our Dad for a bit."

"Oh! I thought perhaps you'd closed for measles. We've twelve absent this afternoon. What's amiss, then?"

"Oh, same old song. Our Dad nagging the life out of me till I can't put up with it. I thought I'd come here a bit, if you'd have me."

"Yes, you're welcome. But won't your dad be more wild than ever? What about school?"

"I've sent to tell them I'm bad. And I am an' all. I'm feeling damn bad, Harold!"

"Are you? Why, what's wrong?"

"I've got a cramp in my inside till I don't know what to do with myself. I had to sit down about six times coming from the station."

"And she's not eaten a thing," said Fanny.

"Looks to me as if she'd better go to bed," said the sympathetic Harold. "I've had sore throat for this last week. I've been thinking, Fanny—have you got that linseed in th' oven?"

Fanny had.

"You'd better look at it an' see it's not too dry. I sent Bentley for a stick of Spanish juice. You'd perhaps have some of that, Emmie. I know it's an old-fashioned remedy, but it does me more good than these modern preparations like aspirin and camphorated chlorodyne and such."

Fanny meanwhile was at the oven, looking into a steamy stew-jar, from which came a strange odour of flax-seeds. She stirred the brown, pulpy, porridgy mass, and Harold came to look.

"It would do with a drop more water, dear; don't you think it would?" he said to Fanny, putting his arm round her neck as they both stared into the stew-jar, she crouching on the hearth-rug.

"Just a drop," said Fanny. "Take it from the kettle."

And between them they concocted the mess.

On the other side of the tall range which prevented, or which was to prevent, the baby from walking into the fire, in future days, the bedding was airing.

"Should you like to go to bed now, Emmie?" asked Harold in concern.

"Oh, I can wait," said Emmie.

"You needn't wait," said Harold, disturbed to see her sitting there mute, with a pinched-up face, doubling herself over as twinges caught her.

"I'll make your bed directly I've fed baby," said Fanny, picking up the infant that was crying crossly for food.

"I can do it," said Harold. Like a good, economical soul and husband, he had taken off his jacket when he came in, and was in his shirt-sleeves. "I'll take th' oven-shelf up, Fanny," he added.

"Take the bottom one," said Fanny, who was faintly squeezing her breast between two fingers as she directed the nipple to the infant. "It's not so red-hot as the top one."

Harold wrapped the oven-shelf in an old piece of blanket, and took it upstairs with him and the candle, for a bed-warmer. In the spare bedroom he went methodically about, making up the bed.

"I tell you what," he said, as he came down, "I'll put that oil-stove up there a bit, to warm the air. It comes rather cold."

And he rubbed his arms, through his shirt-sleeves.

Another half-hour, then, saw Emmie in a warm bed, in company of the oven-shelf, against which she knew she'd knock her toe. She screwed herself up upon her pains, which, though genuine enough, seemed to proceed from a sort of crossness which she could not get over. The little paraffin-stove shed its low light and its curious, flat, oil-flame warmth across the atmosphere. Harold appeared with a cup of the brown, steaming linseed-and-liquorice stew and pressed her to drink it.

"I take a lot of it, and find it does me worlds of good. I think it's the oil, myself. I'm sure it's better than codliver oil. Your skin gets so nice and soft if you take it regular."

But Emmie, her naturally fluffy hair rather astray over the pillow, her little brows rather tense, would not look at it.

"Don't come near me, my lad. I don't want to be looked at," she said, half hiding her crossness in a sort of gruffness.

"Is it all that bad? I'll go down and make you a bran-bag, should I? You've not lost your good looks, anyway. But should I make a bran-bag for you?"

"Ay," said Emmie.

Down he went, found there was no bran, put his hat and coat on, and went down the lane to borrow some; returned, and stuffed it into a flat flannel bag; put this between two plates in the oven, to heat, and finally carried it, piping-hot, up to Emmie, who gratefully hugged it against her.

"Thank you, my old chuck," she said to him. "It's rosy, that is."

"Perhaps that'll shift it," said Harold.

"Ay—perhaps."

But she had her pains all through the night, and said in the morning she hadn't slept a wink. She looked peaked, and Harold was bothered, so he sent a note for the doctor: much against Emmie's will. The doctor said it was neuralgia of the stomach, and Emmie said it felt like it. Harold made Fanny write to Woodhouse, and in the schoolroom, from time to time, he would raise his voice a little and say:

"Less noise there, down at the end. You know what I've told you. You know how poorly Miss Bostock is, in bed in the house. Think of others besides yourselves."

And the scholars duly hushed themselves, and felt important, having somebody poorly in bed in the school-house.

That evening Harold came up to Emmie for a fatherly talk.

"What's wrong between you an' Dad more than usual?" he asked.

"Oh, nothing," said Emmie.

"Nay, come, it's not nothing. It must be something rather special, if you've not told Fanny."

"I don't feel like talking, either," she said.

"You'd better tell us. You'd feel better if you got it off your chest."

"There's nothing to tell," said Emmie.

"Nay," expostulated the young man. "If that's the way you feel towards me and Fanny, then we know how matters stand."

Emmie sulked in bed with her new bran-bag, and Harold sat in the chair beside the little oil-stove—there was no fireplace in the bedroom—and felt offended.

"Oh, damn you," said Emmie. "You're an old nuisance."

"Ay, I know I'm an old nuisance, if I don't please you altogether," said Harold, rather flattered than otherwise. "But it's for your own good I ask you. It's nothing to me personally—except I always want to do my best for you and for all of you for Fanny's sake. Though it isn't so very much I can do. Still, I'll do my bit whenever I get a chance."

There was a slight pause after this ovation.

"I had a walk with Gilbert Noon, if you want to know," said Emmie.

"What, with Gilbert Noon from Haysfall Technical? I should have thought he'd have known better. And did your Dad catch you?"

"Yes."

"And what did he say?"

"He knocked Gilbert Noon's cap off, and had his own cap knocked off back again, and they both fell down in the dark in a gooseberry-bush, and all the blame laid on me, of course."

"You don't mean to say so! Did they go for one another?"

"I didn't stop to look. Our Dad's a devil—an interfering, spying devil. He'll kill me before he's done."

And Emmie pulled the sheet over her face and blubbered underneath it. Poor Harold, who was in a whirlpool of emotion, sat pale as death in the chair, and felt like offering himself up as a burnt-offering, if he could but find an altar with a fire going.

"Well, now," he said at length. "You shouldn't let it get on your nerves. Dad means well, I suppose, only he goes a funny way about it. What do you take it to heart for? You can stop here for a bit till things blow over. Have you written to Walter George?"

He waited with beating heart for an answer. No answer: though a certain stilling of the under-sheet waters.

"Have you written to Walter George, Emmie?" asked Harold once more, in an excruciating gentle and pained voice.

A sniff from under the sheet.

"No"—from under the sheet.

Harold watched the sheet-top, which had grown damp during the bad weather, and to its mournful blotting-paper blankness he said, tender, anxious, treading gingerly on the hot bricks of emotion:

"And aren't you going to?"

No answer from under the sheet.

"You're going to, aren't you, Emmie?"

No action from under the winter-landscape of a sheet.

"You're not in love with Gilbert Noon, are you, Emmie? You'd never make such a mistake."

"No, I'm not, fathead."

This barked out from under the sheet gave Harold hopes of the re-emergence of the crocuses and scilla of Emmie's head. Surely a thaw had set in beneath the damp snowscape of the sheet.

"Well, I'm glad to hear that, at any rate. Because I'm sure it would be a mistake. I'm sure Walter George is the man for you, Emmie; though I must say your treatment of him is such as most men wouldn't stand. I know I shouldn't. But he hasn't got a jealous nature, and that's why he's the right sort for you.—My word, if your Fanny treated me as you treat him, there'd be some fat in the fire, I can tell you. Somebody would have to look out. But different men, different ways. He's not a jealous nature, thank goodness."

Out popped crocuses, scillas, Christmas roses and japonica buds in one burst from beneath the wintry landscape. In short, Emmie's head came out of the sheet, and her nose was so red with crying that we felt constrained to make the japonica flower too early.

"Different men have different ways of showing it, you mean," she snapped. "He won't have any occasion to be jealous, once he isn't a hundred miles off. So there! I know what I'm doing."

"Well, I've always said so. I've said to him more than once: 'She'll be as true as wax once the knot is tied, Walter George, but she's not the one to leave at a loose end.' And he sees it plain enough. Only he doesn't think he's in a position yet . . .

"But I tell you what! Why don't you come here and help me? Miss Tewson is leaving at the end of February. You come here and help me, and you could see a bit more of one another while you made your minds up."

Harold had his little plan. Indeed, life is made up of little plans which people manufacture for one another's benefit. But this little plan Emmie had fore-ordained herself. It had occurred to her when she heard Miss Tewson's treble chiming after Harold's baritone in the school beneath. She wanted a little peace.

And so she began to feel somewhat better, and the pains began to diminish.

"You write him a note," said Harold, "and I'll ride over tomorrow night and take it him, and ask him to come over for the week-end. How about that, now? Does that suit?"

"I'll see," said Emmie.

But Harold knew the victory was won, and he went to bed with his Fanny as pleased as if all the angels were patting him on the back. And his Fanny was quite content that the marigolds of his self-satisfaction should shed themselves in her lap.

In the morning Emmie wrote to Walter George.

"Dear old bean-pod,

Lo and behold I'm at our Fanny's, and bad in bed, and that mad with myself I could swear like a trooper. Come over and cheer me up a bit, if you can. If you can't, come over to the funeral. Ollivoy! E. B."

"Ollivoy" was Emmie's little pleasantry, substituted for *au revoir*. Sometimes she wrote *olive-oil* instead.

The day was Friday. She listened to the business of the school, and at last felt happier in bed. She felt what a luxury it was, to lie in bed and hear school going on: hateful school. She heard the children go shouting out at midday, into the rain. There was rain on the window and on the wet, bare creeper-stalks. She wondered if Harold would ride ten miles through the weather.

Listening, she heard thud-thud-thud, and realized it was Fanny knocking with the poker on the fire-back downstairs, to summon Harold in from the schoolroom. This was Fanny's wireless message to her overdue schoolmaster. Presently the sister, rather blowsy but pleasant-looking, came up with stewed rabbit and a baked onion.

Harold had thought out the baked onion. It was such a good recipe for earache and neuralgia of the face—a hot onion placed against the ear: therefore why not just as good taken internally, for neuralgia of the stomach? Nourishing, as well. He explained to the two sisters, who had been school-teachers as well as he, what proportion of sugar there was in onions, and what proportion of other matter: something very encouraging, though we forget exactly the ratio. So Emmie plunged her fork into the nutritious bulb, which sent its fumes wildly careering round the room, and even tickled the nostrils of afternoon scholars, so that they became hungry again at five-past two. We little know the far-reaching results of our smallest actions.

10. INTRODUCES WALTER GEORGE

The afternoon, thank goodness, cleared up, and Harold prepared his acetylene lamp, till the whole village knew he was going to ride on his bicycle, and wondered if Miss Bostock was taken worse, you know.

He reached Warsop by half-past six, having ridden against the wind. Walter George did not come in till seven, because the bank was doing overtime. When he came, Harold greeted him as man to man, and met with a similar greeting back again.

Walter George—his family name was Whiffen, since trifles matter—was a nice, well-built, plump lad of twenty-one, with round, rosy cheeks and neat hair cut rather long and brushed carefully sideways: *not* backwards: who looked exactly like a choir-boy grown into a bank-clerk, and a bank-clerk just budding for a nice, confidential, comfortable-looking, eminently satisfactory manager of a little bank in some little industrial place in the provinces. Already he inspired confidence, he looked so like the right kind of choir-boy grown into the right kind of high-school boy, the kind that mothers find so satisfactory as a product of their own.

And indubitably he was gone on Emmie. We prefer the slang, as having finer shades than the cant though correct phrase *in love with*. *In-love-with* means just anything. But to be gone on somebody is quite different from being smitten by her, or sweet on her, or barmy over her. Walter George was gone on Emmie, and he was neither smitten by her nor barmy over her.

"Hello, Harold. You're a stranger."

Walter George Whiffen was just a tinge patronizing towards the bicycle-bespattered, wind-harrowed young schoolmaster.

"You've not ridden over from Eakrast?"

Why, you bank-clerk, do you think he'd flown over, with bicycle-clips round his trouser-ankles and spots of mud on his nose?

"Yes, I've come with a message for you."

"For me?"

Immediately Walter George's rosy face looked anxious.

"We've got Emmie bad at our house."

The choir-boy—he was not more at this moment—looked with round eyes on Harold.

"Bad?" he re-echoed. "How long?"

"Oh, since Tuesday. She's been in a rare way, I tell you: awful amount of pain."

"Where?"

"Why, the doctor says neuralgia of the stomach, but I say it was more like cramp of the stomach. We were up half the night two nights, with hot bran-bags. I thought she'd go off any minute, as true as I'm here I did. Cramp of the stomach catches you, and you die like a fly, almost before you know where you are. I was thankful when she came round a bit, with hot bran-bags and hot-water-bottles to her feet, I can tell you."

The choir-boy stood with his mouth open and his eyes blue and round, and did not say a word for some moments.

"Had she got it when she came?" he asked at length.

"Bad, she had. She'd got it bad when I came in and found her at tea-time. It took her I don't know how long to walk from the station. She had to keep sitting down by the roadside, and going off in a dead faint. —It's a thousand wonders she ever got to our house: our Fanny says so an' all."

The choir-boy's pleasant mouth, that still looked more like chocolate than cigarettes, began to quiver, and he turned aside his face as his eyes filled with tears. Harold, also moved too deeply, turned his pale and hollow face in the opposite direction, and so they remained for some minutes like a split statue of Janus, looking two ways.

"Did she ask for me?" quavered the choir-boy's voice in the east.

"She did," sounded the schoolmaster's voice from the west. "She sent you a note." And he took the missive from his pocket.

Then the two halves of the Janus statue turned to one another, as if for the first time, and the choir-boy wiped his eyes with a dashing and gentlemanly silk handkerchief which he had bought for himself at the best shop in Warsop. Having wiped his eyes, he took the letter. Having read the contents, he looked at the envelope. After which he kissed the notepaper, and let Harold see him do it. Harold approved heartily and knew that was how he himself would feel if it was Fanny. The hearts of the two young men beat as one.

"Poor little child," said the high-school boy, wiping his eyes again. "How did she get it?"

"It's nerves, you know. She's a bundle of nerves—I know from Fanny. She lives on her spirit, till her nerves break down. And she'd had a row with her father again. He doesn't understand her a *bit*." This last from the psychological schoolmaster with some spleen.

"Has he been tormenting her?" asked the bank-clerk.

"Why, he makes her life a misery," said the schoolmaster, with a curl of the lip.

The bank-clerk, almost a man now, looked aside and became red with profound indignation.

"She's only a bit of a thing, you know," he said brokenly.

"I tell you," rejoined Harold, "she ran away to Fanny and me for a bit of protection."

"Damned devil!" murmured the bank-clerk, making his brows heavy against the bugbear.

"Oh, but she's a king to what she was," said Harold. "And that's one thing—she'll be better nearly as sudden as she got bad. I'm hoping so, anyhow. She's eating a bit today. She seemed fair comforted when I told her to ask you over for the week-end, and when I said she could stop with us and take Miss Tewson's place. Don't you think that would be better all round?"

"Yes . . ." But the young gentleman wasn't listening. "I'll ride back with you tonight."

"Oh, I shouldn't," said Harold. "Can't you come tomorrow and stop over Sunday? That's what we were counting on."

"Yes, I shall be only too glad. But I'll see her tonight."

The high-school boy had no sooner uttered this resolve, and was fixing his clouded brow like another Roland, than his landlady tapped at the door and hovered half-way into the little parlour. She was a nice old lady with a lace cap.

"Your pardon, young gentlemen—but tea is ready for you."

"Oh!" and the high-school boy became the incipient bank-manager. He put his hand lightly through Harold's arm. "Come on. We have dinner at one o'clock here, and a late tea. Mrs. Slater can't cope with dinner at night. We'll sit down, shall we?" And he led the half-willing Harold to the door.

"No, thanks," said Harold. "I'll be off. I had my tea before I came. I'd better be getting back."

"Oh, no, you won't—not till you've had a cup of tea." And he led his friend hospitably across the little hall or entrance-passage, to where his landlady stood hovering in the doorway of the little dining-room.

"Mrs. Slater—you know Mr. Wagstaff, don't you?"

"Indeed I do. Indeed I do. Come and sit down, both of you."

She spoke in a small, piping voice, quite briskly for the sake of the young men. But her face looked remote, as if she hardly belonged. She seemed to be looking across the gulfs which separates us from early Victorian days, a little dazedly and wanly.

Walter George, of course, did not dream of going without his tea. He ate large quantities of toast and bloater-paste and jam and cake, and Harold tucked in too. And the little woman in a lace cap looked at them from far away behind the teapot—not that it was geographically far away, only ethnologically—and was glad they were there, but seemed a little bewildered, as if she could hardly understand their language.

Harold, as appetite began to be appeased, demonstrated methodically to the bank-clerk that it was no use his, Walter George's, riding to Eakrast tonight, that he would only knock himself up for tomorrow and spoil Emmie's chance of a perfect recovery and her bliss in a perfect meeting. Of which the young gentleman allowed himself to be convinced. Therefore he begged to be allowed to write a line in answer to Emmie's. Therefore Harold sat on pins-and-needles while the young Tristan covered much paper. Harold, of course, was thinking of Fanny and the baby, and how they'd be getting nervous, etc., etc.

But at length Walter George sealed his letter and addressed it to Miss E. Bostock. He wrung Harold's hand in the highroad, and watched the acetylene flare elope down the hill.

11. LOVERS' MEETING

My precious, poor little thing,

I felt my heart was breaking when Harold told me the news. Little was I expecting such a shock as I came in late from the bank, where we are doing overtime for the next fortnight. Little did I think you were so near, and in such a condition. I almost broke down completely when Harold told me. I wanted to come at once, but by the time I had had my tea and given Harold a cup it was after eight o'clock, and he said you'd be settling down for the night before I could get to Eakrast. Not wishing to imperil your night's rest, I have put off coming to my own little angel till tomorrow, but ah, I don't know how I keep away, for I feel my heart torn for you. I have never had a greater shock than when I heard of your illness. I picture you so small and fragile, with your beautiful baby face, and could kill myself to think of all you have had to suffer. Why these things should be, I don't know. I only know it shall not happen again if I can help it.

Well, my darling little treasure, Harold is waiting for this, so I must not keep him. What a splendid fellow he is! How thankful I am to heaven that you have his roof to shelter you and his arm to sustain you. He is indeed a man in a thousand, in a million I might say. I shall never be sufficiently grateful to him for taking care of you at this critical juncture. But when I think of your father I feel that never can the name of father cross my lips to him. He is not my idea of a father, though unfortunately his type is only too common in the world. Why are children given to such men, who are not fit even to have a dog?

Oh, my little child-love, I long to see your flower-face again. If I am not unexpectedly detained I shall be at Eakrast by three o'clock tomorrow, but don't be anxious if I am a little later. Man proposes, God disposes—unless there is really the devil having a share in the matter, which I believe sincerely there is, otherwise you would not be suffering as you are. I hope the pains are gone, or at least diminished by now. I cannot bear to think of you in agony, and am afraid Mrs. Slater may see in my face what I feel.

Well, good-bye, my own sweetest little kitten and angel. I feel I can't wait till tomorrow to fold you in arms and tell you once more how I love you. Oh, if we could only unite our perfect love and be as happy as Harold and Fanny. I feel we must risk it very soon, funds or no funds. This kind of thing must not and shall not continue.

With one last kiss from your unhappy lover, and one last hug before you go to sleep,

I am your own ever-loving
WALTER GEORGE WHIFFEN.

Emmie read this effusion once more when she woke in the morning, and was satisfied. It was what she expected, in the agreeable line, and what can woman have more? What can satisfy her better than to get what she expects? Emmie, moreover, knew what to expect, for she had had various such letters from various authors. Walter George was perhaps the most elegant of her correspondents, though not the lengthiest. She had known one young collier who would run to six pages of his own emotions over her baby-face, etc. Oh, she knew all about her baby-face and "our perfect love." This same perfect love seemd to pop up like a mushroom, even on the shallow soil of a picture-postcard from the sea-side. Oh, we little know, we trembling fiction-writers, how much perfect love there is in the post at this minute. A penny stamp will carry it about hither and thither like a dust-storm through our epistolary island. For in this democratic age love dare not show his face, even for five minutes, not even to a young tram-conductor, unless in the light of perfection.

So Emmie took her perfect love with her breakfast bacon, and remembered that morning had been at seven some little while back, at which hour God is particularly in His heaven, and that hence, according to Mr. Browning, all was well with the world. Like any other school-teacher, she had a number of "repetition" odds and ends of poetry in her stock-cupboard. So why shouldn't she, as well as some Earl's daughter, enrich the dip of her bacon with Browning?—to borrow Hood's pun.

The day was fine, and her only problem was whether to get up or not. She would have had no problem if only she had brought her sky-blue woolly dressing-jacket along with her. Failing this, how would she manage in a white shetland shawl of baby's, and Fanny's best nighty? She decided she would manage.

The morning was fine. Harold went pelting off on his bicycle to buy a few extra provisions. Emmie had the baby in bed with her, and smelt Fanny's cakes and pies cooking down below. Dinner was a scratch meal of sausages, and Emmie had an egg instead.

Harold brought her some sprigs of yellow jasmine to put by her bed, and titivated up the room a bit, according to his and her fancy. Then he left her with her toilet requisites. She was a quick, natty creature. She washed and changed in a few minutes, and did her hair. When Harold tapped, to carry away the wash-water, asking if he could come in, she answered yes, and went on with her job.

She was propped up in bed, with a silver-backed mirror propped facing her, against her knees, and she was most carefully, most judiciously powdering her face and touching up her lips with colour. Harold stood with the pail in his hand and watched her.

"Well, if you don't take the biscuit!" he said.

"Which biscuit?" she said absorbedly. "Hand me the towel." And she concentrated once more on her nose, which was her Achilles' heel, her sore point.

"You fast little madam," said Harold. His Fanny never "made up." He wouldn't have stood it. But he quite liked it in Emmie. And he loved being present during the mysteries of the process.

"Go on," she said. "I feel so bare and brazen without a whiff of powder on my nose."

He gave a shout of laughter.

"I like that!" he said.

"It's a fact, though. I feel as uncomfortable without a bit of powder as if I'd forgot to put my stockings on."

"Well, it never struck me in that light before. We live and learn. I bet you think other women barefaced hussies, if they don't powder."

"They are. They don't know how to make the best of themselves, and then they show the cheek of the Old Lad."

She put her head sideways, screwed her mouth a little, and carefully, very carefully put on a stroke of rouge.

"You think it improves you, do you?" he asked, standing with the pail in his hand, and watching curiously.

"Why," she said, not taking her eyes off the mirror, "what do you think yourself?"

"Me? Nay, I'm no judge."

"Oh, well, now you've said it. People who are no judge generally do the judging."

He felt pinched in his conscience.

"Ay, well—I think I like the genuine article best," he said, walking away.

"Go on; you're no judge," she said coldly.

She finished her toilet, disposed her shawl carefully, and proceeded to the last task of polishing her nails. She looked at her hands. How beautiful they had become whilst she was in bed; how white and smooth! What lovely little hands she had! She thought to herself she had never seen such beautiful hands on anybody else. She looked at them, and polished her small fingernails with consummate satisfaction. Then she tried her rings first on one finger and then on another, and thought the bits of gold and colour showed up the loveliness of the skin. She enjoyed herself for half-an-hour, fiddling with her own hands and admiring them and wondering over their superiority to all other hands.

We feel bound to show our spite by saying her hands were rather meaningless in their prettiness.

While thus engaged, she heard a loud prrring-prrring of a bicycle-bell outside in the road. Heavens! And it was only a quarter to four. She hastily dropped her scissors into the little drawer, and took the sevenpenny copy of *The Girl of the Limberlost* into one hand and her best hanky in the other. So equipped, and framed behind by the linen and crochet-edging of one of Fanny's best pillow-slips, she was prepared.

She heard voices and heavy feet on the stairs. It was her Childe Rolande to the dark tower come, ushered up by Harold.

She looked for him as he crossed the threshold. Never was so mutual a greeting of tender faces. He was carrying a bunch of pheasant's eye narcissus and mimosa; luckily it was Saturday, and he could get them at the shop.

"Hello, old thing!" sounded his overcharged voice.

"Hello!"—her deep, significant brevity.

And he bent over the bed, and she put her arms round his shoulders, and they silently kissed, and Harold in the doorway felt how beautiful and how right it was. We only wish there might be a few more *ands*, to prolong the scene indefinitely.

But Walter George slowly disengaged himself and stood up, whilst she gazed up at him. His hair was beautifully brushed and parted at the side, and he looked down at her. Their looks indeed were locked. He silently laid the flowers at her side, and sank down on one knee beside the bed. But the bed was rather high, and if he kneeled right down he was below the emotional and dramatic level. So he could only sink down on one poised foot, like a worshipper making his deep reverence before the altar, in a Catholic church, and staying balanced low on one toe. It was rather a gymnastic feat. But then, what did Walter George do his Sandow exercises for in the morning, if not to fit him for these perfect motions?

So he springily half-kneeled beside the bed, and kept his face at the true barometric level of tenderness. His one arm was placed lightly around her, his other gently held her little wrist. She lay rather side-ways, propped on her pillows, and they looked into each other's eyes. If Harold had not been there to spectate they would have done just the same for their own benefit. Their faces were near to one another; they gazed deep into each other's eyes. Worlds passed between them, as goes without saying.

"Are you poorly, my love?" asked Walter George Whiffen, in a tone so exquisitely adjusted to the emotional level as to bring tears to the eyes.

"Getting better," she murmured, and Harold thought that never, never would he have thought Emmie's little voice could be so rich with tenderness.

He was turning to steal away, feeling he could no longer intrude in the sacred scene, and the two dramatists were just feeling disappointed that he was going, when fate caused a rift in the lute.

Fanny, like a scientific school-teacher, polished her bedroom floors. The mat on which Childe Rolande was so springily poised on one foot slid back under the pressure of the same foot, so his face went floundering in the bed. And when, holding the side of the bed, he tried to rise on the same original foot, the mat again wasn't having any, so his head ducked down like an ass shaking flies off its ears. When at last he scrambled to his feet he was red in the face, and Emmie had turned and lifted the beautiful flowers between her hands.

"I tell our Fanny we shall be breaking our necks on these floors before we've done," said Harold, pouring his ever-ready spikenard.

"Don't they smell lovely!" said Emmie, holding up the flowers to the nose of Walter George.

"They aren't too strong for you, are they?"

"They might be at night."

"Should I put them in water for you?" interrupted Harold.

"Ay, do, my dear," said Emmie benevolently to him. And he went away for a jar, pleased as a dog with two tails. When the flowers were arranged, he spoke for the last time.

"You don't feel this room cold, do you, Walter George?"

"Not a bit," said Walter George.

"Then I'll go and see what Fanny is doing."

Now the perfect lovers were left together, and tenderness fairly smoked in the room. They kissed, and held each other in their arms, and felt superlative. Walter George had been wise enough to take a chair, abandoning that kneeling, curtseying-knight posture. So he was at liberty to take Emmie right in his arms, without fear of the ground giving way beneath him. And he folded her to his bosom, and felt he was shielding her from the blasts of fate. Soft, warm, tender little bud of love, she would unfold in the greenhouse of his bosom. Soft, warm, tender through her thin nighty, she sent the blood to his head till he seemed to fly with her through dizzy space, to dare the terrors of the illimitable. Warm, and tender, and yielding, she made him so wildly sure of his desire for her that his manliness was now beyond question. He was a man among men henceforth, and would not be abashed before any of the old stagers. Heaven save and bless us, how badly he did but want her, and what a pleasure it was to be so sure of the fact.

"I tell you what," he said. "We'll get married and risk it."

"Risk what?"

"Why, everything. We will, shall we? I can't stand it any longer."

"But what about everybody?" said Emmie.

"Everybody can go to hell."

And here we say, as Napoleon said of Goethe:

"*Voilà un homme!*"

He held her in his arms. And this was serious spooning. This was actual love-making, to develop into marriage. It was cuddly rather than spoony; the real thing, and they knew it. Ah, when two hearts mean business, what a different affair it is from when they only flutter for sport! From the budding passion in the Eakrast bedroom many a firm cauliflower would blossom, in after-days, many a Sunday dinner would ripen into fruit!

The lovers were very cosy, murmuring their little conversation between their kisses. The course of their true love was as plain as a pike-staff. It led to a little house in a new street, and an allotment-garden not far off. And the way thither, with kisses and the little plannings, was as sweet as if it had led to some detached villa, or even to one of the stately homes of England. It is all the same in the end; safe as houses, as the saying goes. Emmie was now taking the right turning, such as you have taken, gentle reader, you who sit in your comfortable home with this book on your knee. Give her, then, your blessing, for she hardly needs it any more, and play a tune for her on the piano:

> The cottage homes of England,
> How thick they crowd the land.

Or, if that isn't good enough for you:

> The stately homes of England
> Are furnished like a dream.

Play the tune, and let that be your portion, for you are not going to take any part in the burning bliss of buying the furniture, or the tragedy of the wedding-presents.

> There's a little grey home in the west.

Pleasantly the hours passed. The party gathered for a common chat in Emmie's bedroom before supper. The table was laid downstairs, and there was polony as well as cheese and cocoa, all waiting invitingly, the cocoa still in its tin but standing at attention on the table. The clock ticked, the baby was in bed, the kitchen was a cosy feast, if only they would come down and tackle it. The clock struck ten.

And still the party in the bedroom did not break up. Still the supper waited below. Emmie was making her droll speeches, Harold was exercizing his dry wit, and the high-school boy was laughing out loud, and Fanny was saying: "Oh my word! what about baby?" Whereupon they all lifted a listening ear.

12. THE INTERLOPER

In one of these moments of strained attention a motor-cycle was heard slowly pulsing down the road outside. It came to a stop. The strength of its white lights showed under the bedroom blind, in spite of Emmie's lamp. She knew at once what it was, and restraint came over her.

In another minute there was the crunching of a footstep on the path below, and a loud knock at the back door. The company in the bedroom looked at one another in consternation, even affright. Harold summoned his master-of-the-house courage and went downstairs. The three in the bedroom listened with beating hearts.

"Is this Mr. Wagstaff's?"

"Yes."

"Is Miss Bostock here?"

"Yes."

"Can I see her?"

"She's in bed."

"Ay, her mother told me she was bad. Is she asleep?"

"No, she's not asleep."

"Can I speak to her a minute?"

"Who is it?"

"Gilbert Noon."

"Oh! Is it anything particular?"

"No. But I just want to speak to her. Just tell her, will you?"

Harold was so flustered he went upstairs and said:

"Gilbert Noon wants to see Emmie."

Childe Rolande and Fanny stood open-mouthed.

"All right; let him come up, then," said Emmie sharply.

"Should I?" said Harold.

"Don't look so 'ormin'. Let him come up," repeated Emmie in the same sharp tone.

Harold looked at her strangely, looked round the room in bewilderment. They listened while he went downstairs. Gilbert still stood outside in the dark.

"Shall you come up?" said Harold.

And after a moment:

"There's the stair-foot here. Let me get a candle."

"I can see," said the bass voice.

The light of the little bedroom lamp showed on the landing at the top of the stairs.

Heavy feet were ascending. Emmie gathered her shawl on her breast. Gilbert appeared in his rubber overalls in the doorway, his face cold-looking, his hair on end after having taken his cap off.

"Good evening," he said, standing back in the doorway at the sight of the company.

"Do you know Mr. Whiffen, Mr. Noon?" said Emmie sharply. "My elect, so to speak."

Gilbert shook hands with Childe Rolande, then with Fanny, whom he knew slightly, and then with Harold, to whom he was now introduced. Harold had gone rather stiff and solemn, like an actor in a play.

There was a moment's pause.

"Well, how are we?" said Gilbert rather awkwardly to Emmie.

"Oh, just about in the pink, like," she replied. She was cross, and showed it.

He was rather disconcerted.

"I saw your mother this afternoon," he began.

"Where?" she snapped. "Sit down, some of you, and make a bit of daylight. It's like being in a wood."

Fanny handed Gilbert a chair, Childe Rolande sat assertively on the bed, at the foot, and Harold went to the next bedroom and was heard bumping the legs of a chair as he carried it in, while Fanny looked agonies for baby.

"Where did you see mother?" asked Fanny pleasantly.

"At Lewis Goddard's."

"And she was all right?"

"Yes—seemed so. Worried, you know."

"What, about Emmie?"

"Yes—and one of the children with measles; but getting better, I believe."

"Tissie hasn't got them, then?" asked Fanny.

"I didn't hear your mother say so."

"Because, when they start, they usually go through the house. I hope baby won't catch them."

"There's no reason why she should, is there?"

"Oh, they're very bad in Eakrast . . ."

And Emmie, Walter George and Harold sat like stuffed ducks while this conversation wound its way through all the circumstances of measles in the Warsop Vale region.

Emmie had not told Walter George about Gilbert and the *fracas*. She had warned the other two not to speak of it. And now she was in such a temper she could not, for her life, think of anything to say. She sat propped up in bed, looking very blooming, but with a frown between her little brows. She twisted and twisted her ring with its big ruby round and round her finger, and grew more tense as she felt the Fanny-Gilbert conversation running down. She had asked Harold to bring Gilbert up because she always preferred to trust rather to her ready wit than to her powers for inventing a plausible lie in answer to troublesome questions. And now she was as stupid as a stuffed owl, and couldn't say a word. The conversation died; there was an awful vacuum of a pause. Meanwhile Emmie sat in the bed, with her head dropped, twisting and twisting her ring. In another minute she would be flying into tears; and Walter George sat near her feet, worse than a monument.

Harold Hardraada lifted his head.

"You came on a motor-bike, didn't you, Mr. Noon?"

"Yes," said Gilbert.

"I thought I heard one come up the lane."

"I lost my way the other side of Blidworth, and got to Sutton before I knew where I was. And then, coming through Huthwaite, I had something wrong with my engine, and had to stop and have that seen to."

"My word, you have had a journey. What time did you start?"

"Why, I was coming down Woodhouse hill at a quarter-to-six."

"My word, and it's after ten! You've been out of your road some."

"I have. I don't know these roads round here, and it's like riding in a puzzle."

"Oh, the roads through the forest and round-about, they're very misleading. You'd best have come through Thoresby, you know. It's a bit longer, but it's a better road. What made you go Blidworth way?"

Started an itinerary conversation between the motor-cyclist and the push-cyclist, whilst Emmie turned her ring, and Childe Rolande stared

inquiringly and rather mortifiedly at the newcomer. He resented the
intrusion deeply. Not only was he forced to smell a rat, but even he
must have the rat thrust under his nostrils. He sat rather stiff on the
bed, and turned the side of his rosy cheek unrelentingly towards the
bothered Emmie.

The itinerary conversation slowed down, and Fanny felt she must get
out of it. She couldn't stand it.

"I'll go and make the cocoa," she said, rising. "You'll have a cup of
cocoa, won't you, Mr. Noon?"

"No, thanks; I won't trouble you."

"Yes, do. It's no trouble. I'll make you one, then. Harold, you'll go
to baby if he cries?"

"All right," said Harold.

And when Fanny departed, a hoar-frost of silence once more settled
on the dislocated party. Harold began to get a resigned, martyr-at-the-
stake look, Walter George was becoming thoroughly sulky, and Emmie
was breathing short. Gilbert sat looking rather vacant—a trick he had
when he was ill at ease.

Suddenly came a thin wail from the unknown.

"There's baby!" said Harold, and with all the alacrity of a young
husband he quitted the room.

The frost now became a black frost. It seemed as if each of the three
of them remaining in the bedroom would have been killed rather than
utter a word to either of the others. A deadlock! Lips and hearts were
padlocked. The trinity sat as if enchanted in a crystal pillar of dense
and stupid silence. Emmie felt the pains coming on again, Gilbert felt
how cold his feet were with the cycling, and Walter George felt that a
can-opener would never open *his* heart or lips again. He was soldered
down.

From the next bedroom they could hear all the soothing sounds of
the young husband, sounds anything but soothing to one who is not a
first-born and an infant-in-arms. From below they heard the clink of
tea-spoons and smelled the steam of stirring cocoa. And suddenly Gilbert lifted his head.

"What ring is that?" he asked.

Emmie started, and stared defiantly.

"What, this? It's my engagement ring."

"Mine," said Childe Rolande, with a sulky yelp. Whereupon he became nearly as red as the re-composed ruby.

And immediately the frost settled down again, the padlocks snapped
shut, and the solder went hard in the burning lid-joints of Walter

George's heart. For a few seconds, Gilbert went to sleep, the cold air having numbed him. Walter George sat on the edge of the bed and looked blackly at his toe-tips. Emmie tried to scheme, and almost got hold of the tail of a solution, when it evaded her again.

A soft, very soft, fear-of-waking-baby voice floated like a vapour up the stairs.

"Cocoa's ready."

Gilbert woke and looked round at the door, but did not stir. Childe Rolande did not bend his gloomy looks, but stretched his neck downwards over the bed-edge and stubbornly contemplated his nice brown shoes as if he had heard no sound.

"Go and have your cocoa," said Emmie, speaking to t'other-or-which, as the saying is. But she was completely ineffectual. Gilbert sat dreamily, vacantly on, and Childe Rolande sank his chin nearer and nearer his knees, as he perched on the edge of the bed like some ungraceful bird.

Emmie now gave way to resignation. Was she not the base of this obtuse-angled triangle, this immortal trinity, this framework of the universe? It was not for her to break the three-cornered tension. Let fate have its way. If Gilbert had not given himself to vacancy the problem might seriously have concerned him; how to resolve an obtuse-angled triangle into a square of the same dimensions. But he was glotzing, if we may borrow the word.

But eternity has rested long enough on this tripod footing; the universe has been framed quite long enough inside a triangle, and the doctrine of the trinity has had its day. Time, now, the sacred figure, which magicians declare to be malevolent, dissolved into its constituents, or disappeared in a resultant of forces.

Oh, *Deus ex machina*, get up steam and come to our assistance, for this obtuse-angled triangle looks as if it would sit there stupidly forever in the spare bedroom at Eakrast. Which would be a serious misfortune to us, who have to make our bread-and-butter chronicling the happy marriage and the prize-taking cauliflower of Emmie and Walter George, and the further lapses of Mr. Noon.

So, *Deus ex machina*, come. Come, god in the machine, come. Be invoked! Puff thy blessed steam, or even run by electricity, but come, O Machine-God, thou Wheel of Fate and Fortune, spin thy spokes of destiny and roll into the Eakrast bedroom, lest Time stand still and Eternity remain a deadlock.

Is our prayer in vain? We fear it is. The god in the machine is perhaps too busy elsewhere. Alas, no wheel will incline its axis in our direc-

tion, no petrol will vaporize into spirit for our sakes. Emmie, and Childe
Rolande and Mr. Noon may sit forever in the Eakrast bedroom.

Well, then, let them. Let them go to hell. We can at least be as manly
as Walter George, in our heat of the moment.

Gentle reader, this is the end of Mr. Noon and Emmie. If you really
must know, Emmie married Walter George, who reared prime cauliflowers, whilst she reared dear little Georgian children, and all went
happy ever after.

As for Mr. Noon. Ah, Mr. Noon! There is a second volume in store
for you, dear reader. Pray heaven there may not be a third.

But the second volume is in pickle. The cow in this vol. having
jumped over the moon, in the next, the dish, dear reader, shall run
away with the spoon. Scandalous the elopement, and a *decree nisi* for
the fork. Which is something to look forward to.

II
Translation

THE GENTLEMAN FROM SAN FRANCISCO

by Ivan Bunin

The Gentleman from San Francisco

"Woe to thee, Babylon, that mighty city!"
APOCALYPSE

The gentleman from San Francisco—nobody either in Capri or Naples ever remembered his name—was setting out with his wife and daughter for the Old World, to spend there two years of pleasure.

He was fully convinced of his right to rest, to enjoy long and comfortable travels, and so forth. Because, in the first place he was rich, and in the second place, notwithstanding his fifty-eight years, he was just starting to live. Up to the present he had not lived, but only existed; quite well, it is true, yet with all his hopes on the future. He had worked incessantly—and the Chinamen whom he employed by the thousand in his factories knew what that meant. Now at last he realized that a great deal had been accomplished, and that he had almost reached the level of those whom he had taken as his ideals, so he made up his mind to pause for a breathing space. Men of his class usually began their enjoyments with a trip to Europe, India, Egypt. He decided to do the same. He wished naturally to reward himself in the first place for all his years of toil, but he was quite glad that his wife and daughter should also share in his pleasures. True, his wife was not distinguished by any marked susceptibilities, but then elderly American women are all passionate travellers. As for his daughter, a girl no longer young and somewhat delicate, travel was really necessary for her: apart from the question of health, do not happy meetings often take place in the course of travel? One may find one's self sitting next to a multi-millionaire at table, or examining frescoes side by side with him.

The itinerary planned by the Gentleman of San Francisco was extensive. In December and January he hoped to enjoy the sun of southern Italy, the monuments of antiquity, the tarantella, the serenades of vagrant minstrels, and, finally, that which men of his age are most susceptible to, the love of quite young Neapolitan girls, even when the love is not altogether disinterestedly given. Carnival he thought of spending in Nice, in Monte Carlo, where at that season gathers the most select society, the precise society on which depend all the blessings of civilization—the fashion in evening dress, the stability of thrones, the declaration of wars, the prosperity of hotels; where some devote themselves passionately to automobile and boat races, others to roulette, others to what is called flirtation, and others to the shooting of pigeons which beautifully soar from their traps over emerald lawns, against a background of forget-me-not sea, instantly to fall, hitting the ground in little white heaps. The beginning of March he wished to devote to Florence, Passion Week in Rome, to hear the music of the Miserere; his plans also included Venice, Paris, bull-fights in Seville, bathing in the British Isles; then Athens, Constantinople, Egypt, even Japan . . . certainly on his way home. . . . And everything at the outset went splendidly.

It was the end of November. Practically all the way to Gibraltar the voyage passed in icy darkness, varied by storms of wet snow. Yet the ship travelled well, even without much rolling. The passengers on board were many, and all people of some importance. The boat, the famous *Atlantis*, resembled a most expensive European hotel with all modern equipments: a night refreshment bar, Turkish baths, a newspaper printed on board; so that the days aboard the liner passed in the most select manner. The passengers rose early, to the sound of bugles sounding shrilly through the corridors in that grey twilit hour, when day was breaking slowly and sullenly over the grey-green, watery desert, which rolled heavily in the fog. Clad in their flannel pyjamas, the gentlemen took coffee, chocolate, or cocoa, then seated themselves in marble baths, did exercises, thereby whetting their appetite and their sense of well-being, made their toilet for the day, and proceeded to breakfast. Till eleven o'clock they were supposed to stroll cheerfully on deck, breathing the cold freshness of the ocean; or they played table-tennis or other games, that they might have an appetite for their eleven o'clock refreshment of sandwiches and bouillon; after which they read their newspaper with pleasure, and calmly awaited luncheon—which was a still more varied and nourishing meal than breakfast. The two hours which followed luncheon were devoted to rest. All the decks were crowded with lounge chairs on which lay passengers wrapped in plaids, looking at the mist-heavy sky or the foamy hillocks which flashed behind the bows, and dozing sweetly. Till five o'clock, when, refreshed and lively, they were treated to strong, fragrant tea and sweet cakes. At seven bugle-calls announced a dinner of nine courses. And now the Gentleman from San Francisco, rubbing his hands in a rising flush of vital forces, hastened to his state cabin to dress.

In the evening, the tiers of the *Atlantis* yawned in the darkness as with innumerable fiery eyes, and a multitude of servants in the kitchens, sculleries, wine-cellars, worked with a special frenzy. The ocean heaving beyond was terrible, but no one thought of it, firmly believing in the captain's power over it. The captain was a ginger-haired man of monstrous size and weight, apparently always torpid, who looked in his uniform with broad gold stripes very like a huge idol, and who rarely emerged from his mysterious chambers to show himself to the passengers. Every minute the siren howled from the bows with hellish moroseness, and screamed with fury, but few diners heard it—it was drowned by the sounds of an excellent string band, exquisitely and untiringly playing in the huge two-tiered hall that was decorated with marble and covered with velvet carpets, flooded with feasts of light from crystal chandeliers and gilded girandoles, and crowded with ladies in bare shoulders and jewels, with men in dinner-jackets, elegant waiters and respectful *maîtres d'hôtel*, one of whom, he who took the wine-orders only, wore a chain round his neck like a lord mayor. Dinner-jacket and perfect linen made the Gentleman from San Francisco look much younger. Dry, of small stature, badly built but strongly made, polished to a glow and in due measure animated, he sat in the golden-pearly radiance of this palace, with a bottle of amber Johannisberg at his hand, and glasses, large and small, of delicate crystal, and a curly bunch of fresh hyacinths. There was something Mongolian in his yellowish face with its trimmed silvery moustache, large teeth blazing with gold, and strong bald head blazing like old ivory. Richly dressed, but in keeping with her age, sat his wife, a big, broad, quiet woman. Intricately, but lightly and transparently dressed, with an innocent immodesty, sat his daughter, tall, slim, her magnificent hair splendidly done, her breath fragrant with violet cachous, and the tenderest little rosy moles showing near her lip and between her bare, slightly powdered shoulder-blades. The dinner lasted two whole hours, to be followed by dancing in the ball-room, whence the men, including, of course, the Gentleman from San Francisco, proceeded to the bar; there, with their feet cocked up on the tables, they settled the destinies of nations in the course of their political and stock-exchange conversations, smoking meanwhile Havana cigars and drinking liqueurs till they were crimson in the face, waited on all the while by negroes in red jackets with eyes like peeled, hard-boiled eggs. Outside, the ocean heaved in black mountains; the snow-storm hissed furiously in the clogged cordage; the steamer trembled in every fibre as she surmounted these watery hills and struggled with the storm, ploughing through the moving masses which every now and then reared in front of her, foam-crested. The siren, choked by the fog, groaned in mortal anguish. The watchmen in the look-out towers froze with cold, and went mad with their super-human straining of attention. As the gloomy and sultry depths of the inferno, as the ninth circle, was the submerged womb of the steamer, where gigantic furnaces roared and dully giggled, devouring with their red-hot maws mountains of coal cast hoarsely in by men naked to the waist, bathed in their own corrosive dirty sweat, and lurid with the purple-red reflection of flame. But in the refreshment bar men jauntily put their feet up on the tables, showing their patent-leather pumps, and sipped cognac or other liqueurs, and swam in waves of fragrant smoke as they chatted in well-bred manner. In the dancing hall light and warmth and joy were poured over everything; couples turned in the waltz or writhed in the tango, while the music insistently, shamelessly, delightfully, with sadness entreated for one, only one thing, one and the same thing all the time. Amongst this resplendent crowd was an ambassador, a little dry modest old man; a great millionaire, clean-shaven, tall, of an indefinite age, looking like a prelate in his old-fashioned dress-coat; also a famous Spanish author, and an inter-national beauty already the least bit faded, of unenviable reputation; finally an exquisite loving couple, whom everybody watched curiously because of their unconcealed happiness: *he* danced only with *her*, and sang, with great skill, only to *her* accompaniment, and everything about them seemed so charming!—and only the captain knew that this couple had been engaged by the steamship company to play at love for a good salary, and that they had been sailing for a long time, now on one liner, now on another.

At Gibraltar the sun gladdened them all: it was like early spring. A new passenger appeared on board, arousing general interest. He was a hereditary prince of a certain Asiatic state, travelling incognito: a small man, as if all made of wood, though his movements were alert; broad-faced, in gold-rimmed glasses, a little unpleasant because of his large black moustache which was sparse and transparent like that of a corpse; but on the whole inoffensive, simple, modest. In the Mediter-ranean they met once more the breath of winter. Waves, large and florid as the tail of a peacock, waves with snow-white crests heaved under the impulse of the tramontane wind, and came merrily, madly rushing towards the ship, in the bright lustre of a perfectly clear sky. The next day the sky began to pale, the horizon grew dim, land was approaching: Ischia, Capri could be seen through the glasses, then Naples herself, looking like pieces of sugar strewn at the foot of some dove-coloured mass; whilst beyond, vague and deadly white with snow, a range of distant mountains. The decks were crowded. Many ladies and gentlemen were putting on light fur-trimmed coats. Noiseless Chinese servant boys, bandy-legged, with pitch-black plaits hanging down to their heels, and with girlish thick eyebrows, unobtrusively came and went, carrying up the stairways plaids, canes, valises, hand-bags of crocodile leather, and never speaking above a whisper. The daughter of the Gentleman from San Francisco stood side by side with the prince, who, by a happy circumstance, had been introduced to her the previous evening. She had the air of one looking fixedly into the distance towards something which he was pointing out to her, and which he was explaining hurriedly, in a low voice. Owing to his size, he looked amongst the rest like a boy. Altogether he was not handsome, rather queer, with his spectacles, bowler hat, and English coat, and then the hair of his sparse moustache just like horse-hair, and the swarthy, thin skin of his face seeming stretched over his features and slightly varnished. But the girl listened to him, and was so excited that she did not know what he was saying. Her heart beat with incomprehensible rapture because of him, because he was standing next to her and talking to her, to her alone. Everything, everything about him was so unusual—his dry hands, his clean skin under which flowed ancient, royal blood, even his plain, but somehow particularly tidy European dress; everything was invested with an indefinable glamour, with all that was calculated to enthrall a young woman. The Gentleman from San Francisco, wearing for his part a silk hat and grey spats over patent-leather shoes, kept eyeing the famous beauty who stood near him, a tall, wonderful figure, blonde, with her eyes painted according to the latest Parisian fashion, holding on a silver chain a tiny, cringing, hairless little dog, to which she was addressing herself all the time. And the daughter, feeling some vague embarrassment, tried not to notice her father.

Like all Americans, he was very liberal with his money when travelling. And like all of them, he believed in the full sincerity and good-will of those who brought his food and drinks, served him from morn till night, anticipated his smallest desire, watched over his cleanliness and rest, carried his things, called the porters, conveyed his trunks to the hotels. So it was everywhere, so it was during the voyage, so it ought to be in Naples. Naples grew and drew nearer. The brass band, shining with the brass of their instruments, had already assembled on deck. Suddenly they deafened everybody with the strains of their triumphant rag-time. The giant captain appeared in full uniform on the bridge, and like a benign pagan idol waved his hands to the passengers in a gesture of welcome. And to the Gentleman from San Francisco, as well as to every other passenger, it seemed as if for him alone was thundered forth that rag-time march, so greatly beloved by proud America; for him alone the Captain's hand waved, welcoming him on his safe arrival. Then, when at last the *Atlantis* entered port and veered her many-tiered mass against the quay that was crowded with expectant people, when the gangways began their rattling—ah, then what a lot of porters and their assistants in caps with golden galloons, what a lot of all sorts of commissionaires, whistling boys, and sturdy ragamuffins with packs of postcards in their hands rushed to meet the Gentleman from San Francisco with offers of their services! With what amiable contempt he grinned at those ragamuffins as he walked to the automobile of the very same hotel at which the prince would probably put up, and calmly muttered between his teeth, now in English, now in Italian—"Go away! Via!"

Life at Naples started immediately in the set routine. Early in the morning, breakfast in a gloomy dining-room with a draughty damp wind blowing in from the windows that opened on to a little stony garden: a cloudy, unpromising day, and a crowd of guides at the doors of the vestibule. Then the first smiles of a warm, pinky-coloured sun, and from the high, overhanging balcony a view of Vesuvius, bathed to the feet in the radiant vapours of the morning sky, while beyond, over the silvery-pearly ripple of the bay, the subtle outline of Capri upon the horizon! Then nearer, tiny donkeys running in two-wheeled buggies away below on the sticky embankment, and detachments of tiny soldiers marching off with cheerful and defiant music.

After this a walk to the taxi-stand, and a slow drive along crowded, narrow, damp corridors of streets, between high, many-windowed houses. Visits to deadly-clean museums, smoothly and pleasantly lighted, but monotonously, as if from the reflection of snow. Or visits to churches, cold, smelling of wax, and always the same thing: a majestic portal, curtained with a heavy leather curtain: inside, a huge emptiness, silence, lonely little flames of clustered candles ruddying the depths of the interior on some altar decorated with ribbon: a forlorn old woman amid dark benches, slippery gravestones under one's feet, and somebody's infallibly famous "Descent from the Cross." Luncheon at one o'clock on San Martino, where quite a number of the very selectest people gather about midday, and where once the daughter of the Gentleman from San Francisco almost became ill with joy, fancying she saw the prince sitting in the hall, although she knew from the

newspapers that he had gone to Rome for a time. At five o'clock, tea
in the hotel, in the smart salon where it wàs so warm, with the deep
carpets and blazing fires. After which the thought of dinner—and again
the powerful commanding voice of the gong heard over all the floors,
and again strings of bare-shouldered ladies rustling with their silks on
the staircases and reflecting themselves in the mirrors, again the wide-
flung, hospitable, palatial dining-room, the red jackets of musicians on
the platform, the black flock of waiters around the *maître d'hôtel*, who
with extraordinary skill was pouring out a thick, roseate soup into soup-
plates. The dinners, as usual, were the crowning event of the day. Every
one dressed as if for a wedding, and so abundant were the dishes, the
wines, the table-waters, sweetmeats, and fruit, that at about eleven
o'clock in the evening the chamber-maids would take to every room
rubber hot-water bottles, to warm the stomachs of those who had dined.

None the less, December of that year was not a success for Naples.
The porters and secretaries were abashed if spoken to about the
weather, only guiltily lifting their shoulders and murmuring that they
could not possibly remember such a season; although this was not the
first year they had had to make such murmurs, or to hint that "everywhere something terrible is happening." . . . Unprecedented rains and
storms on the Riviera, snow in Athens, Etna also piled with snow and
glowing red at night; tourists fleeing from the cold of Palermo. . . . The
morning sun daily deceived the Neapolitans. The sky invariably grew
grey towards midday, and fine rain began to fall, falling thicker and
colder. The palms of the hotel approach glistened like wet tin; the city
seemed peculiarly dirty and narrow, the museums excessively dull;
the cigar-ends of the fat cab-men, whose rubber rain-capes flapped like
wings in the wind, seemed insufferably stinking, the energetic cracking
of whips over the ears of thin-necked horses sounded altogether false,
and the clack of the shoes of the signorini who cleaned the tram-lines
quite horrible, while the women, walking through the mud, with their
black heads uncovered in the rain, seemed disgustingly short-legged: not
to mention the stench and dampness of foul fish which drifted from the
quay where the sea was foaming. The gentleman and lady from San
Francisco began to bicker in the mornings; their daughter went about
pale and head-achey, and then roused up again, went into raptures over
everything, and was lovely, charming. Charming were those tender,
complicated feelings which had been aroused in her by the meeting
with the plain little man in whose veins ran such special blood. But
after all, does it matter *what* awakens a maiden soul—whether it is
money, fame, or noble birth? . . . Everybody declared that in Sorrento,

or in Capri, it was quite different. There it was warmer, sunnier, the
lemon-trees were in bloom, the morals were purer, the wine unadul-
terated. So behold, the family from San Francisco decided to go with
all their trunks to Capri, after which they would return and settle down
in Sorrento: when they had seen Capri, trodden the stones where stood
Tiberius' palaces, visited the famous caves of the Blue Grotto, and
listened to the pipers from Abruzzi, who wander about the isle during
the month of the Nativity, singing the praises of the Virgin.

On the day of departure—a very memorable day for the family from
San Francisco—the sun did not come out even in the morning. A heavy
fog hid Vesuvius to the base, and came greying low over the leaden
heave of the sea, whose waters were concealed from the eye at a distance of half a mile. Capri was completely invisible, as if it had never
existed on earth. The little steamer that was making for the island
tossed so violently from side to side that the family from San Francisco
lay like stones on the sofas in the miserable saloon of the tiny boat,
their feet wrapped in plaids, and their eyes closed. The lady, as she
thought, suffered worst of all, and several times was overcome with sick-
ness. It seemed to her that she was dying. But the stewardess who came
to and fro with the basin, the stewardess who had been for years, day
in, day out, through heat and cold, tossing on these waves, and who
was still indefatigable, even kind to every one—she only smiled. The
younger lady from San Francisco was deathly pale, and held in her
teeth a slice of lemon. Now not even the thought of meeting the prince
at Sorrento, where he was due to arrive by Christmas, could gladden
her. The gentleman lay flat on his back, in a broad overcoat and a flat
cap, and did not loosen his jaws throughout the voyage. His face grew
dark, his moustache white, his head ached furiously. For the last few
days, owing to the bad weather, he had been drinking heavily, and had
more than once admired the "tableaux vivants." The rain whipped on the
rattling window-panes, under which water dripped on to the sofas, the
wind beat the masts with a howl, and at moments, aided by an onrush-
ing wave, laid the little steamer right on its side, whereupon something
would roll noisily away below. At the stopping places, Castellamare,
Sorrento, things were a little better. But even there the ship heaved
frightfully, and the coast with all its precipices, gardens, pines, pink and
white hotels, and hazy, curly green mountains swooped past the window, up and down, as it were on swings. The boats bumped against
the side of the ship, the sailors and passengers shouted lustily, and somewhere a child, as if crushed to death, choked itself with screaming. The
damp wind blew through the doors, and outside on the sea, from a reel-

ing boat which showed the flag of the Hotel Royal, a fellow with
guttural French exaggeration yelled unceasingly: "Rrroy-al! Hotel
Rrroy-al!" intending to lure passengers aboard his craft. Then the
Gentleman from San Francisco, feeling, as he ought to have felt, quite
an old man, thought with anguish and spite of all these "Royals,"
"Splendids," "Excelsiors," and of these greedy, good-for-nothing,
garlic-stinking fellows called Italians. Once, during a halt, on opening
his eyes and rising from the sofa he saw under the rocky cliff-curtain
of the coast a heap of such miserable stone hovels, all musty and
mouldy, stuck on top of one another by the very water, among the
boats, and the rags of all sorts, tin cans and brown fishing-nets, and,
remembering that this was the very Italy he had come to enjoy, he
was seized with despair. . . . At last, in the twilight, the black mass of
the island began to loom nearer, looking as if it were bored through at
the base with little red lights. The wind grew softer, warmer, more
sweet-smelling. Over the tamed waves, undulating like black oil, there
came flowing golden boa-constrictors of light from the lanterns of the
harbour. . . . Then suddenly the anchor rumbled and fell with a splash
into the water. Furious cries of the boatmen shouting against one another came from all directions. And relief was felt at once. The electric
light of the cabin shone brighter, and a desire to eat, drink, smoke,
move once more made itself felt. . . . Ten minutes later the family from
San Francisco disembarked into a large boat; in a quarter of an hour
they had stepped on to the stones of the quay, and were soon seated in
the bright little car of the funicular railway. With a buzz they were
ascending the slope, past the stakes of the vineyards and wet, sturdy
orange-trees, here and there protected by straw screens, past the thick
glossy foliage and the brilliancy of orange fruits. . . . Sweetly smells the
earth in Italy after rain, and each of her islands has its own peculiar
aroma.

The island of Capri was damp and dark that evening. For the
moment, however, it had revived, and was lighted up here and there as
usual at the hour of the steamer's arrival. At the top of the ascent, on
the little piazza by the funicular station stood the crowd of those whose
duty it was to receive with propriety the luggage of the Gentleman
from San Francisco. There were other arrivals too, but none worthy of
notice: a few Russians who had settled in Capri, untidy and absent-
minded owing to their bookish thoughts, spectacled, bearded, half-
buried in the upturned collars of their thick woollen overcoats. Then a
group of long-legged, long-necked, round-headed German youths in
Tirolese costumes, with knapsacks over their shoulders, needing no

assistance, feeling everywhere at home and always economical in tips. The Gentleman from San Francisco, who kept quietly apart from both groups, was marked out at once. He and his ladies were hastily assisted from the car, men ran in front to show them the way, and they set off on foot, surrounded by urchins and by the sturdy Capri women who carry on their heads the luggage of decent travellers. Across the piazza, that looked like an opera scene in the light of the electric globe that swung aloft in the damp wind, clacked the wooden pattens of the women-porters. The gang of urchins began to whistle to the Gentleman from San Francisco, and to turn somersaults around him, whilst he, as if on the stage, marched among them towards a mediæval archway and under huddled houses, behind which led a little echoing lane, past tufts of palm-trees showing above the flat roofs to the left, and under the stars in the dark blue sky, upwards towards the shining entrance of the hotel. . . . And again it seemed as if purely in honour of the guests from San Francisco the damp little town on the rocky little island of the Mediterranean had revived from its evening stupor, that their arrival alone had made the hotel proprietor so happy and hearty, and that for them had been waiting the Chinese gong which sent its howlings through all the house the moment they crossed the doorstep.

The sight of the proprietor, a superbly elegant young man with a polite and exquisite bow, startled for a moment the Gentleman from San Francisco. In the first flash, he remembered that amid the chaos of images which had possessed him the previous night in his sleep, he had seen that very man, to a *t* the same man, in the same full-skirted frock-coat and with the same glossy, perfectly smoothed hair. Startled, he hesitated for a second. But long, long ago he had lost the last mustard-seed of any mystical feeling he might ever have had, and his surprise at once faded. He told the curious coincidence of dream and reality jest-ingly to his wife and daughter, as they passed along the hotel corridor. And only his daughter glanced at him with a little alarm. Her heart suddenly contracted with home-sickness, with such a violent feeling of loneliness in this dark, foreign island, that she nearly wept. As usual, however, she did not mention her feelings to her father.

Reuss XVII, a high personage who had spent three whole weeks on Capri, had just left, and the visitors were installed in the suite of rooms that he had occupied. To them was assigned the most beautiful and expert chambermaid, a Belgian with a thin, firmly corseted figure, and a starched cap in the shape of a tiny indented crown. The most experienced and distinguished-looking footman was placed at their service, a coal-black, fiery-eyed Sicilian, and also the smartest waiter,

the small, stout Luigi, a tremendous buffoon, who had seen a good deal
of life. In a minute or two a gentle tap was heard at the door of the
Gentleman from San Francisco, and there stood the *maître d'hôtel*, a
Frenchman, who had come to ask if the guests would take dinner, and
to report, in case of answer in the affirmative—of which, however, he
had small doubt—that this evening there were Mediterranean lobsters,
roast beef, asparagus, pheasants, etc., etc. The floor was still rocking
under the feet of the Gentleman from San Francisco, so rolled about
had he been on that wretched, grubby Italian steamer. Yet with his
own hands, calmly, though clumsily from lack of experience, he closed
the window which had banged at the entrance of the *maître d'hôtel*,
shutting out the drifting smell of distant kitchens and of wet flowers in
the garden. Then he turned and replied with unhurried distinctness,
that they would take dinner, that their table must be far from the door,
in the very centre of the dining-room, that they would have local wine
and champagne, moderately dry and slightly cooled. To all of which
the *maître d'hôtel* gave assent in the most varied intonations, which conveyed that there was not and could not be the faintest question of the
justness of the desires of the Gentleman from San Francisco, and that
everything should be exactly as he wished. At the end he inclined his
head and politely inquired:

"Is that all, sir?"

On receiving a lingering "Yes," he added that Carmela and Giuseppe, famous all over Italy and "to all the world of tourists," were
going to dance the tarantella that evening in the hall.

"I have seen picture-postcards of her," said the Gentleman from
San Francisco, in a voice expressive of nothing. "And is Giuseppe her
husband?"

"Her cousin, sir," replied the *maître d'hôtel*.

The Gentleman from San Francisco was silent for a while, thinking
of something, but saying nothing; then he dismissed the man with a
nod of the head. After which he began to make preparations as if for
his wedding. He turned on all the electric lights, and filled the mirrors
with brilliance and reflection of furniture and open trunks. He began
to shave and wash, ringing the bell every minute, and down the corridor raced and crossed the impatient ringings from the rooms of his
wife and daughter. Luigi, with the nimbleness peculiar to certain stout
people, making grimaces of horror which brought tears of laughter to
the eyes of chambermaids dashing past with marble-white pails, turned
a cart-wheel to the gentleman's door, and tapping with his knuckles, in
a voice of sham timidity and respectfulness reduced to idiocy, asked:

"Ha suonato, Signore?"

From behind the door, a slow, grating, offensively polite voice:

"Yes, come in."

What were the feelings, what were the thoughts, of the Gentleman from San Francisco on that evening so significant to him? He felt nothing exceptional, since unfortunately everything on this earth is too simple in appearance. Even had he felt something imminent in his soul, all the same he would have reasoned that, whatever it might be, it could not take place immediately. Besides, as with all who have just experienced sea-sickness, he was very hungry, and looked forward with delight to the first spoonful of soup, the first mouthful of wine. So he performed the customary business of dressing in a state of excitement which left no room for reflection.

Having shaved, washed, and dexterously arranged several artificial teeth, standing in front of the mirror, he moistened his silver-mounted brushes and plastered the remains of his thick pearly hair on his swarthy yellow skull. He drew on to his strong old body, with its abdomen protuberant from excessive good living, his cream-coloured silk underwear, put black silk socks and patent-leather slippers on his flat-footed feet. He put sleeve-links in the shining cuffs of his snow-white shirt, and bending forward so that his shirt front bulged out, he arranged his trousers that were pulled up high by his silk braces, and began to torture himself, putting his collar-stud through the stiff collar. The floor was still rocking beneath him, the tips of his fingers hurt, the stud at moments pinched the flabby skin in the recess under his Adam's apple, but he persisted, and at last, with eyes all strained and face dove-blue from the over-tight collar that enclosed his throat, he finished the business and sat down exhausted in front of the pier glass, which reflected the whole of him, and repeated him in all the other mirrors.

"It is awful!" he muttered, dropping his strong, bald head, but without trying to understand or to know what was awful. Then, with habitual careful attention examining his gouty-jointed short fingers and large, convex, almond-shaped finger-nails, he repeated: "It is awful. . . ."

As if from a pagan temple shrilly resounded the second gong through the hotel. The Gentleman from San Francisco got up hastily, pulled his shirt-collar still tighter with his tie, and his abdomen tighter with his open waistcoat, settled his cuffs and again examined himself in the mirror. . . . "That Carmela, swarthy, with her enticing eyes, looking like a mulatto in her dazzling-coloured dress, chiefly orange, she must be an extraordinary dancer—" he was thinking. So, cheerfully leaving his room and walking on the carpet to his wife's room, he called to ask if they were nearly ready.

"In five minutes, Dad," came the gay voice of the girl from behind the door. "I'm arranging my hair."

"Right-o!" said the Gentleman from San Francisco.

Imagining to himself her long hair hanging to the floor, he slowly walked along the corridors and staircases covered with red carpet, downstairs, looking for the reading-room. The servants he encountered on the way pressed close to the wall, and he walked past as if not noticing them. An old lady, late for dinner, already stooping with age, with milk-white hair and yet *decolletée* in her pale grey silk dress, hurried at top speed, funnily, henlike, and he easily overtook her. By the glass-door of the dining-room, wherein the guests had already started the meal, he stopped before a little table heaped with boxes of cigars and cigarettes, and taking a large Manila, threw three liras on the table. After which he passed along the winter terrace, and glanced through an open window. From the darkness came a waft of soft air, and there loomed the top of an old palm-tree that spread its boughs over the stars, looking like a giant, bringing down the far-off smooth quivering of the sea. . . . In the reading-room, cosy with the shaded reading-lamps, a grey, untidy German, looking rather like Ibsen in his round silver-rimmed spectacles and with mad astonished eyes, stood rustling the newspapers. After coldly eyeing him, the Gentleman from San Francisco seated himself in a deep leather arm-chair in a corner, by a lamp with a green shade, put on his pince-nez, and, with a stretch of his neck because of the tightness of his shirt-collar, obliterated himself behind a newspaper. He glanced over the headlines, read a few sentences about the never-ending Balkan war, then with a habitual movement turned over the page of the newspaper—when suddenly the lines blazed up before him in a glassy sheen, his neck swelled, his eyes bulged, and the pince-nez came flying off his nose. . . . He lunged forward, wanted to breathe—and rattled wildly. His lower jaw dropped, and his mouth shone with gold fillings. His head fell swaying on his shoulder, his shirt-front bulged out basket-like, and all his body, writhing, with heels scraping up the carpet, slid down to the floor, struggling desperately with some invisible foe.

If the German had not been in the reading-room, the frightful affair could have been hushed up. Instantly, through obscure passages the Gentleman from San Francisco could have been hurried away to some dark corner, and not a single guest would have discovered what he had been up to. But the German dashed out of the room with a yell, alarming the house and all the diners. Many sprang up from the table, upsetting their chairs, many, pallid, ran towards the reading-room, and in every language it was asked: "What—what's the matter?" None answered intelligibly, nobody understood, for even today people are more surprised at death than at anything else, and never want to believe it is true. The proprietor rushed from one guest to another, trying to keep back those who were hastening up, to soothe them with assurances that it was a mere trifle, a fainting-fit that had overcome a certain Gentleman from San Francisco. . . . But no one heeded him. Many saw how the porters and waiters were tearing off the tie, waistcoat, and crumpled dress-coat from that same gentleman, even, for some reason or other, pulling off his patent evening-shoes from his black-silk, flat-footed feet. And he was still writhing. He continued to struggle with death, by no means wanting to yield to that which had so unexpectedly and rudely overtaken him. He rolled his head, rattled like one throttled, and turned up the whites of his eyes as if he were drunk. When he had been hastily carried into room No. 43, the smallest, wretchedest, dampest, and coldest room at the end of the bottom corridor, his daughter came running with her hair all loose, her dressing-gown flying open, showing her bosom raised by her corsets: then his wife, large and heavy and completely dressed for dinner, her mouth opened round with terror. But by that time he had already ceased rolling his head.

In a quarter of an hour the hotel settled down somehow or other. But the evening was ruined. The guests, returning to the dining-room, finished their dinner in silence, with a look of injury on their faces, whilst the proprietor went from one to another, shrugging his shoulders in hopeless and natural irritation, feeling himself guilty through no fault of his own, assuring everybody that he perfectly realized "how disagreeable this is," and giving his word that he would take "every possible measure within his power" to remove the trouble. The tarantella had to be cancelled, the superfluous lights were switched off, most of the guests went to the bar, and soon the house became so quiet that the ticking of the clock was heard distinctly in the hall, where the lonely parrot woodenly muttered something as he bustled about in his cage preparatory to going to sleep, and managed to fall asleep at length with his paw absurdly suspended from the little upper perch. . . . The Gentleman from San Francisco lay on a cheap iron bed under coarse blankets on to which fell a dim light from the obscure electric lamp in the ceiling. An ice-bag slid down on his wet, cold forehead; his blue, already lifeless face grew gradually cold; the hoarse bubbling which came from his open mouth, where the gleam of gold still showed, grew weak. The Gentleman from San Francisco rattled no longer; he was no more—something else lay in his place. His wife, his daughter, the doctor, and the servants stood and watched him dully. Suddenly that which they feared and expected happened. The rattling ceased. And slowly, slowly under their eyes a pallor spread over the face of the deceased, his features began to grow thinner, more transparent . . . with a beauty which might have suited him long ago. . . .

Entered the proprietor. "Gia, e morto!" whispered the doctor to him. The proprietor raised his shoulders, as if it were not his affair. The wife, on whose cheeks tears were slowly trickling, approached and timidly asked that the deceased should be taken to his own room.

"Oh no, madame," hastily replied the proprietor, politely, but coldly, and not in English, but in French. He was no longer interested in the trifling sum the guests from San Francisco would leave at his cash desk. "That is absolutely impossible." Adding by way of explanation, that he valued that suite of rooms highly, and that should he accede to madame's request, the news would be known all over Capri and no one would take the suite afterwards.

The young lady, who had glanced at him strangely all the time, now sat down in a chair and sobbed, with her handkerchief to her mouth. The elder lady's tears dried at once, her face flared up. Raising her voice and using her own language she began to insist, unable to believe that the respect for them had gone already. The manager cut her short with polite dignity. "If madame does not like the ways of the hotel, he dare not detain her." And he announced decisively that the corpse must be removed at dawn: the police had already been notified, and an official would arrive presently to attend to the necessary formalities. "Is it possible to get a plain coffin?" madame asked. Unfortunately not! Impossible! And there was no time to make one. It would have to be arranged somehow. Yes, the English soda-water came in large strong boxes—if the divisions were removed.

The whole hotel was asleep. The window of No. 43 was open, on to a corner of the garden where, under a high stone wall ridged with broken glass, grew a battered banana tree. The light was turned off, the door locked, the room deserted. The deceased remained in the darkness, blue stars glanced at him from the black sky, a cricket started to chirp with sad carelessness in the wall. . . . Out in the dimly-lit corridor two chambermaids were seated in a window-sill, mending something. Entered Luigi, in slippers, with a heap of clothes in his hand.

"Pronto?" he asked, in a singing whisper, indicating with his eyes the dreadful door at the end of the corridor. Then giving a slight wave thither with his free hand: "Patenza!" he shouted in a whisper, as though sending off a train. The chambermaids, choking with noiseless laughter, dropped their heads on each other's shoulders.

Tip-toeing, Luigi went to the very door, tapped, and cocking his head on one side asked respectfully, in a subdued tone:

"Ha suonato, Signore?"

Then contracting his throat and shoving out his jaw, he answered himself in a grating, drawling, mournful voice, which seemed to come from behind the door:

"*Yes, come in. . . .*"

When the dawn grew white at the window of No. 43, and damp wind began rustling the tattered fronds of the banana tree; as the blue sky of morning lifted and unfolded over Capri, and Monte Solaro, pure and distinct, grew golden, catching the sun which was rising beyond the far-off blue mountains of Italy; just as the labourers who were mending the paths of the islands for the tourists came out for work, a long box was carried into room No. 43. Soon this box weighed heavily, and it painfully pressed the knees of the porter who was carrying it in a one-horse cab down the winding white high-road, between stone walls and vineyards, down, down the face of Capri to the sea. The driver, a weakly little fellow with reddened eyes, in a little old jacket with sleeves too short and bursting boots, kept flogging his wiry small horse that was decorated in Sicilian fashion, its harness tinkling with busy little bells and fringed with fringes of scarlet wool, the high saddle-peak gleaming with copper and tufted with colour, and a yard-long plume nodding from the pony's cropped head, from between the ears. The cabby had spent the whole night playing dice in the inn, and was still under the effects of drink. Silent, he was depressed by his own debauchery and vice: by the fact that he gambled away to the last far-thing all those copper coins with which his pockets had yesterday been full, in all four lire, forty centesimi. But the morning was fresh. In such air, with the sea all round, under the morning sky headaches evaporate, and man soon regains his cheerfulness. Moreover, the cabby was cheered by this unexpected fare which he was making out of some Gentleman from San Francisco, who was nodding with his dead head in a box at the back. The little steamer, which lay like a water-beetle on the tender bright blueness which brims the bay of Naples, was already giving the final hoots, and this tooting resounded again cheerily all over the island. Each contour, each ridge, each rock was so clearly visible in every direction, it was as if there were no atmosphere at all. Near the beach the porter in the cab was overtaken by the head porter dashing down in an automobile with the lady and her daughter, both pale, their eyes swollen with the tears of a sleepless night. . . . And in ten minutes the little steamer again churned up the water and made her way back to Sorrento, to Castellamare, bearing away from Capri for ever the family from San Francisco. . . . And peace and tranquillity reigned once more on the island.

On that island two thousand years ago lived a man entangled in his own infamous and strange acts, one whose rule for some reason extended over millions of people, and who, having lost his head through the absurdity of such power, committed deeds which have established him for ever in the memory of mankind; mankind which in the mass now rules the world just as hideously and incomprehensibly as he ruled it then. And men come here from all quarters of the globe to look at the ruins of the stone house where that one man lived, on the brink of one of the steepest cliffs in the island. On this exquisite morning all who had come to Capri for that purpose were still asleep in the hotels, although through the streets already trotted little mouse-coloured donkeys with red saddles, towards the hotel entrances where they would wait patiently until, after a good sleep and a square meal, young and old American men and women, German men and women would emerge and be hoisted up into the saddles, to be followed up the stony paths, yea to the very summit of Monte Tiberio, by old persistent beggar-women of Capri, with sticks in their sinewy hands. Quieted by the fact that the dead old Gentleman from San Francisco, who had intended to be one of the pleasure party but who had only succeeded in frightening the rest with the reminder of death, was now being shipped to Naples, the happy tourists still slept soundly, the island was still quiet, the shops in the little town not yet open. Only fish and greens were being sold in the tiny piazza, only simple folk were present, and amongst them, as usual without occupation, the tall old boatman Lorenzo, thorough debauchee and handsome figure, famous all over Italy, model for many a picture. He had already sold for a trifle two lobsters which he had caught in the night, and which were rustling in the apron of the cook of that very same hotel where the family from San Francisco had spent the night. And now Lorenzo could stand calmly till evening, with a majestic air showing off his rags and gazing round, holding his clay pipe with its long reed mouth-piece in his hand, and letting his scarlet bonnet slip over one ear. For as a matter of fact he received a salary from the little town, from the commune which found it profitable to pay him to stand about and make a picturesque figure—as everybody knows. . . . Down the precipices of Monte Solaro, down the stony little stairs cut in the rock of the old Phoenician road came two Abruzzi mountaineers, descending from Anacapri. One carried a bagpipe under his leather cloak, a large goat skin with two little pipes; the other had a sort of wooden flute. They descended, and the whole land, joyous, was sunny beneath them. They saw the rocky, heaving shoulder of the island, which lay almost entirely at their feet, swimming in the fairy blueness of the water. Shining morning vapours rose over the sea to the east, under a dazzling sun which already burned hot as it rose higher and higher; and there, far off, the dimly cerulean masses of Italy, of her near and far mountains, still wavered blue as if in the world's morning, in a beauty no words can express. . . . Half-way down the descent the pipers slackened their pace. Above the road, in a grotto of the rocky face of Monte Solaro stood the Mother of God, the sun full upon her, giving her a splendour of snow-white and blue raiment, and royal crown rusty from all weathers. Meek and merciful, she raised her eyes to heaven, to the eternal and blessed mansions of her thrice-holy Son. The pipers bared their heads, put their pipes to their lips: and there streamed forth naïve and meekly joyous praises to the sun, to the morning, to Her, Immaculate, who would intercede for all who suffer in this malicious and lovely world, and to Him, born of Her womb among the caves of Bethlehem, in a lowly shepherd's hut, in the far Judean land. . . .

And the body of the dead old man from San Francisco was returning home, to its grave, to the shores of the New World. Having been subjected to many humiliations, much human neglect, after a week's wandering from one warehouse to another, it was carried at last on to the same renowned vessel which so short a time ago, and with such honour, had borne him living to the Old World. But now he was to be hidden far from the knowledge of the voyagers. Closed in a tar-coated coffin, he was lowered deep into the vessel's dark hold. And again, again the ship set out on the long voyage. She passed at night near Capri, and to those who were looking out from the island, sad seemed the lights of the ship slowly hiding themselves in the sea's darkness. But there aboard the liner, in the bright halls shining with lights and marble, gay dancing filled the evening, as usual. . . .

The second evening, and the third evening, still they danced, amid a storm that swept over the ocean, booming like a funeral service, rolling up mountains of mourning darkness silvered with foam. Through the snow the numerous fiery eyes of the ship were hardly visible to the Devil who watched from the rocks of Gibraltar, from the stony gateway of two worlds, peering after the vessel as she disappeared into the night and storm. The Devil was huge as a cliff. But huger still was the liner, many storeyed, many funnelled, created by the presumption of the New Man with the old heart. The blizzard smote the rigging and the funnels, and whitened the ship with snow, but she was enduring, firm, majestic—and horrible. On the topmost deck rose lonely amongst the snowy whirlwind the cosy and dim quarters where lay the heavy master of the ship, he who was like a pagan idol, sunk now in a light, uneasy slumber. Through his sleep he heard the sombre howl and furious screechings of the siren, muffled by the blizzard. But again he re-assured himself by the nearness of that which stood behind his wall, and was in the last resort incomprehensible to him: by the large, apparently armoured cabin which was now and then filled with a mysterious rumbling, throbbing, and crackling of blue fires that flared up explosive around the pale face of the telegraphist who, with a metal hoop fixed on his head, was eagerly straining to catch the dim voices of vessels which spoke to him from hundreds of miles away. In the depths, in the under-water womb of the *Atlantis*, steel glimmered and steam wheezed, and huge masses of machinery and thousand-ton boilers dripped with water and oil, as the motion of the ship was steadily cooked in this vast kitchen heated by hellish furnaces from beneath. Here bubbled in their awful concentration the powers which were being transmitted to the keel, down an infinitely long round tunnel lit up and brilliant like a gigantic gun-barrel, along which slowly, with a regularity crushing to the human soul, revolved a gigantic shaft, precisely like a living monster coiling and uncoiling its endless length down the tunnel, sliding on its bed of oil. The middle of the *Atlantis*, the warm, luxurious cabins, dining-rooms, halls, shed light and joy, buzzed with the chatter of an elegant crowd, was fragrant with fresh flowers, and quivered with the sounds of a string orchestra. And again amidst that crowd, amidst the brilliance of lights, silks, diamonds, and bare feminine shoulders, a slim and supple pair of hired lovers painfully writhed and at moments convulsively clashed. A sinfully discreet, pretty girl with lowered lashes and hair innocently dressed, and a tallish young man with black hair looking as if it were glued on, pale with powder, and wearing the most elegant patent-leather shoes and a narrow, long-tailed dress coat, a beau resembling an enormous leech. And no one knew that this couple had long since grown weary of shamly tormenting themselves with their beatific love-tortures, to the sound of bawdy-sad music; nor did any one know of that thing which lay deep, deep below at the very bottom of the dark hold, near the gloomy and sultry bowels of the ship that was so gravely overcoming the darkness, the ocean, the blizzard. . . .

III

Essays

Rachel Annand Taylor

(A Lecture Delivered in Croydon)

"Mrs. Rachel Annand Taylor is not ripe yet to be gathered as fruit for lectures and papers. She is young, not more than thirty; she has been married and her husband has left her, she lives in Chelsea, visits Professor Gilbert Murray in Oxford, and says strange, ironic things of many literary people in a plaintive peculiar fashion.

"This then is raw green fruit to offer you, to be received with suspicion, to be tasted charily and spat out without much revolving and tasting. It is impossible to appreciate the verse of a green fresh poet. He must be sun-dried by time and sunshine of favourable criticism, like muscatels and prunes: you must remove the crude sap of living, then the flavour of his eternal poetry comes out unobscured and unpolluted by what is temporal in him—is it not so?

"Mrs. Taylor is, however, personally, all that could be desired of a poetess: in appearance, purely Rossettian: slim, svelte, big beautiful bushes of reddish hair hanging over her eyes which peer from the warm shadow; delicate colouring, scarlet, small, shut mouth; a dark, plain dress with a big boss of a brooch in the bosom, a curious carven witch's brooch; then long, white, languorous hands of the correct, subtle radiance. All that a poetess should be.

"She is a Scotch-woman. Brought up lonelily as a child, she lived on the Bible, on the 'Arabian Nights,' and later, on Malory's 'King Arthur.' Her upbringing was not Calvinistic. Left to herself, she developed as a choice romanticist. She lived apart from life, and still she cherishes a yew-darkened garden in the soul where she can remain withdrawn, sublimating experience into odours.

"This is her value, then: that to a world almost satisfied with the excitement of Realism's Reign of Terror, she hangs out the flag of Romance, and sounds the music of citterns and viols. She is mediæval; she is pagan and romantic as the old minstrels. She belongs to the company of Aucassin and Nicolette, and to no other.

"The first volume of poems was published in 1904. Listen to the titles of the poems: 'Romances,' 'The Bride,' 'The Song of Gold,'

'The Queen,' 'The Daughter of Herodias,' 'Arthurian Songs,' 'The Knights at Kingstead,' 'Devotional,' 'Flagellants,' 'An Early Christian,' 'Rosa Mundi,' 'An Art-lover to Christ,' 'Chant d'Amour,' 'Love's Fool to His Lady,' 'Saint Mary of the Flowers,' 'The Immortal Hour,' 'Reveries,' 'The Hostel of Sleep.'

"I will read you four of the love songs. Against the first, in the book Mrs. Taylor gave me, I found a dried lily of the valley, that the author had evidently overlooked. She would have dropped it in the fire, being an ironical romanticist. However, here is the poem, stained yellow with a lily: it is called 'Desire.'

"That is the first of the love songs. The second is called 'Surrender.' The third, which is retrospective, is 'Unrealized,' and the fourth is 'Renunciation.' There is the story of Mrs. Taylor's married life, that those who run may read. Needless to say, the poetess' heart was broken.

"'There is nothing more tormenting,' I said to her, 'than to be loved overmuch.'"

" 'Yes, one thing more tormenting,' she replied.

"'And what's that?' I asked her.

"'To love,' she said, very quietly.

"However, it is rather useful to a poetess or poet to have a broken heart. Then the rare fine liquor from the fragile vial is spilled in little splashes of verse, most interesting to the reader, most consoling to the writer. A broken heart does give colour to life.

"Mrs. Taylor, in her second volume, 'Rose and Vine,' published last year, makes the splashes of verse from her spilled treasure of love. But they are not crude, startling, bloody drops. They are vermeil and gold and beryl green. Mrs. Taylor takes the pageant of her bleeding heart, first marches ironically by the brutal daylight, then lovingly she draws it away into her magic, obscure place apart where she breathes spells upon it, filters upon it delicate lights, tricks it with dreams and fancy, and then re-issues the pageant.

"'Rose and Vine' is much superior to the Poems of 1904. It is gorgeous, sumptuous. All the full, luscious buds of promise are fullblown here, till heavy, crimson petals seem to brush one's lips in passing, and in front, white blooms seem leaning to meet one's breast. There is a great deal of sensuous colour, but it is all abstract, impersonal in feeling, not the least sensual. One tires of it in the same way that one tires of some of Strauss' music—'Electra,' for instance. It is emotionally insufficient, though splendid in craftsmanship.

"Mrs. Taylor is, indeed, an exquisite craftsman of verse. Moreover, in her metres and rhythms she is orthodox. She allows herself none of the modern looseness, but retains the same stanza form to the end of a lyric. I should like more time to criticize the form of this verse.

"However, to turn to 'Rose and Vine.' There is not much recognizable biography here. Most of the verses are transformed from the experience beyond recognition. A really new note is the note of motherhood. I often wonder why, when a woman artist comes, she never reveals the meaning of maternity, but either paints horses, or Venuses or sweet children, as we see them in the Tate Gallery, or deals with courtship, and affairs, like Charlotte Brontë and George Eliot. Mrs. Taylor has a touch of the mother note. I read you 'Four Crimson Violets' and now 'A Song of Fruition' ('An October Mother'). What my mother would have said to that when she had me, an Autumn baby, I don't know!

"A fine piece of thoughtful writing is 'Music of Resurrection,' which significantly opens the 'Rose and Vine' volume.

"That was last year. This year came the 'Hours of Fiammetta'—a sonnet sequence. There are sixty-one sonnets in the Shakespeare form, and besides these, a 'Prologue of Dreaming Women,' an 'Epilogue of Dreaming Women' and an Introduction. In the Introduction Mrs. Taylor says there are two traditions of women—the Madonna, and the dreaming woman.

"The latter is always, the former never, the artist: which explains, I suppose, why women artists do not sing maternity. Mrs. Taylor represents the dreaming woman of today—and she is almost unique in her position, when all the women who are not exclusively mothers are suffragists or reformers.

"Unfortunately, Mrs. Taylor has begun to dream of her past life and of herself, very absorbedly; and to tell her dreams in symbols which are not always illuminating. She is esoteric. Her symbols do not show what they stand for of themselves: they are cousins of that Celtic and French form of symbolism which says—'Let X = the winds of passion, and Y = the yearning of the soul for love.'

"*Now the dim, white petalled Y*
Draws dimly over the pallid atmosphere
The scalded kisses of X.

"Mrs. Taylor has begun the same dodge.

"*Since from the subtle silk of agony*
Our lamentable veils of flesh are spun.

"'Subtle silk of agony' may claim to sound well, but to me it is meaningless.

"But I read you the 'Prologue of Dreaming Women,' which surely is haunting: . . .*

"How dare a woman, a woman, sister of Suffragists and lady doctors, how dare she breathe such a thing! But Mrs. Taylor is bolder still. Listen to the 'Epilogue of Dreaming Women.' It is, I think, a very significant poem, to think over and to think of again when one reads 'Mrs. Bull.'*

"But these are not Fiammetta. They are her creed. Her idiosyncrasies are in the sonnets, which, upon close acquaintance, are as interesting, more interesting far to trace than a psychological novel. I read you only one, No. 18. Some of these sonnets are very fine: they stand apart in an age of 'open road' and Empire thumping verse."

* At this point Lawrence read aloud the poem mentioned. Eds.

Art and the Individual

"These Thursday night meetings are for discussing social problems with a view to advancing a more perfect social state and to our fitting ourselves to be perfect citizens—communists—what not. Is that it? I guess in time we shall become expert sociologists. If we would live a life above the common ruck we must be experts at something—must we not? Besides, we have peculiar qualities which adapt us for particular parts of the social machine. Some of us make good cranks, doubtless each of us would make a good hub of the universe. They have advanced the question in education— 'Where in the school shall we begin to specialize?' Specialize, that's the word! This boy has a strong, supple wrist; let him practise pulling pegs out of a board like a Jap dentist's apprentice, then he'll be an expert tooth puller. Under Socialism every man with the spirit of a flea will become a specialist—with such advantages it were disgraceful not to cultivate that proverbial one talent, and thus become a shining light on some tiny spot. It will take some four hundred specialists to make a normal family of four. However!

"Now listen to the text which describes the ultimate goal of education. 'The ultimate goal of education is to produce an individual of high moral character.' Take that on the authority of the great expert. Moral character consists, I suppose, in a good sense of proportion, a knowledge of the relative effects of certain acts or influences, and desire to use that knowledge for the promoting of happiness. The desire you may easily possess. We are all altruists. But what about the knowledge, the sense of proportion? How can you have an idea of proportional values unless you have an extensive knowledge of or at least acquaintance with the great influences which result in action. Here is the immediate goal of education—and our real purpose of meeting here, after that of making ourselves heard, is to educate ourselves. The immediate goal of education is to gain a wide sympathy, in other words a *many-sided interest*.

"Let us look at Herbart's classification of interests, adding one that he overlooked."

Interest arising from	Knowledge Intellectual	1. Empirical 2. Speculative 3. Aesthetic
	Sympathy Emotional	4. Sympathetic 5. Social 6. Religious
	Action	

EMPIRICAL:

Interest in concrete individual things (I see a swan—it sails up to me and attracts my attention. I notice how it shows itself off to me—it pecks under the water—it swims nearer—I observe its wings magnificently arched)—(evening flowers).

SPECULATIVE:

Interest in deeper connections and causes of events—scientific and philosophic interests (it is remarkable that the swan should raise its wings so proudly—why can it be—evening flowers).

AESTHETIC:

Interest aroused neither by phenomena nor causes as such, but by the approval which their harmony and adaptability to an end win from me. (The swan is very beautiful—the moon-light on the flowers is lovely—why does it move me so?)

SYMPATHETIC:

Social: Growing comprehension of the incorporation of the individual in the great social body whose interests are large beyond his personal feelings. He is a unit, working with others for a common welfare, like a cell in a complete body.

RELIGIOUS:

When this extended sympathy is directed to the history (origin) and destiny of mankind, when it reverentially recognizes the vast scope of the laws of nature, and discovers something of intelligibility and consistent purpose working through the whole natural world and human consciousness, the religious interest is developed and the individual loses for a time the sense of his own and his day's importance, feels the wonder and terror of eternity with its incomprehensible purposes. This, I hold it, is still a most useful and fruitful state. Note parallelism of 1, 2, 3,—4, 5, 6,—increasing height of planes.

"Which of these forms of interest are we most likely to neglect? Consider—the aesthetic is our present consideration. Since we have accepted the Herbartian broad interpretation, we must take a broad view of Art to fit it, since Aestheticism embraces all art. Examine the definition, 'The Approval which the Harmony and Adaptability to an end win from us.'

"It is vague and unsatisfactory. Look closely. 'Approval of Harmony'—That is a pleasurable experience. We see or hear something that gives us pleasure—we call it harmony—invert it—we see or hear harmonious blendings—we feel pleasure. We are not much further, except that we recognize that the ultimate test of all harmony, beauty, whatever you call it, is in *personal feeling*. This would place aesthetic interest under the emotional group. Look at it again. 'Approval of adaptability of things to an end.' Here is harmony again—but it is more comprehensible, more intellectual. We see a good purpose in sure and perhaps uninterrupted process of accomplishment. It is gratifying —we are glad—why? Because, I believe, we are ourselves almost unconscious agents in a great inscrutable purpose, and it gives us relief and pleasure to consciously recognize that power working out in things beyond and apart from us. But that is aside.

"There have been two schools of Aesthetic thought since the beginning of such thought.

"(1) Art. Beauty is the expression of the perfect and divine Idea. This is the mystic Idea, held by Hegel, 'Beauty is the shining of the Idea through matter.'

"(2) a. Art is an activity arising even in the animal kingdom and springing from sexual desire and propensity to play (Darwin, Schiller, Spencer) and it is accompanied by pleasurable excitement.

"b. Art is the external manifestation by lines, colour, words, sounds, movements of emotion felt by man.

"c. Art is the production of some permanent object or passing action filled to convey pleasurable impression quite apart from personal advantage.

"In the interpretation we have accepted, these two, the mystical and the sensual ideas of Art are blended. Approval of Harmony—that is sensual—approval of Adaptation—that is mystic—of course none of this is rigid. Now apply the case to our swan.

I. Approval of Harmony (Beauty we will say)—there is the silken whiteness, the satisfying curve of line and mass. Why do these charm us? I cannot answer.

"Turn to Adaptation: Now we might say that we love the silken whiteness and the grandly raised wings because they are the expression of the great purpose which leads the swan to raise itself as far as possible to attract a mate, the mate choosing the finest male that the species may be reproduced in its most advantageous form. That you must sift for yourselves. But there is a sense (perhaps unconscious) of exquisite harmony and adaptation to an end when we feel the boat-like build of the bird, the strength of those arched wings, the suppleness of the long neck which we have seen waving shadowily under the water in search of food. Contrast the quaint gobbling, diving ducks. Think too of our positive pain in seeing the great unwieldy body of the bird, standing on the bank supported by ugly black legs. Why is it ugly? Because a structure like that could *not* walk with ease or grace—it is unfitted to its surroundings. The legs are hateful because, being black, they are too violent a contrast to the body which is so white—they are clammy looking too—and what sense is 'clammy' applied to? Think of evening primroses in the moonlight and in the noonday. Flowers and insects have evolved side by side.

"This is Beauty in Nature—but does the same hold good when we turn to the human productions of Art? Often it does. But think of the works of Poe, of Zola, de Maupassant, Maxim Gorky, Hood's 'Song of the Shirt'—think of Watts' Mammon (if that is Art), of the Laocoön, the Outcasts of Luke Filde. Do you experience any 'pleasure' in these? Do they excite 'pleasurable feelings'? Do they show Divine purpose? Yet they are Art. Why? Somebody would say, 'They are so true.' But they are not necessarily true, in the strict sense of the word. Not true, except that they have been felt, experienced as if they were true. They express—as well perhaps as is possible—the real *feelings* of the artist. Something more, then, must be added to our idea of Art—it is the medium through which men express their deep, real feelings. By ordinary words, common speech, we transmit thoughts, judgments, one to another. But when we express a true emotion, it is through the medium of Art.

"When Carlyle said that a hero could hardly express himself otherwise than through song, he meant that the vigorous emotion so moulded the speech of his hero—Mahomet, Dante, Burns—that this speech became Art. So Art is the second great means of communication between man and man, as Tolstoi says. Intellectual Art, which has no emotion, but only wit, has cold barren effect. Think of Pope and the great Encyclopedists. This means of communication of emotion is in three ways—by form and colour (as in all painting, sculpture, weaving, building)—by sound (music)—by ideas through words—all literature down to the graphic, moving tale told by a boy to his mates. The picture words, the thrilling voice, the animated face and lively gestures, all go to make up the art of story-telling. The English, whatever is said of them, are a truly poetic people, if reserved. Look at our words— words like 'flash', 'laughter', 'wonder'. Compare Latin and French, 'rideo' and 'rire'.

"The essence then of true human art is that it should convey the emotions of one man to his fellows. It is a form of sympathy, and sympathy is in some measure harmony and unity, and in harmony and unity there is the idea of consistent purpose, is there not? So it works back to the old definition. But, you will say, there are emotions desirable and undesirable—and Art may transmit the undesirable. Exactly —then it is bad Art. According to the feeling that originated it, Art may be bad, weak, good, in all shades. So Tolstoi says that all nude study is bad art—Honi soit qui mal y pense.

"This might lead you to reflect that anyone who feels deeply must be an artist. But there you must consider that not one person in a thousand can express his emotions. We are most of us dumb, there, or we can only talk to a few who understand our mute signs, and the peculiar meanings we give to the words we use. The same sentence in ten different mouths has ten different meanings. We can feel, but we cannot transmit our feelings—we can't express ourselves. When you have tried, when you have felt compelled to write to somebody, for you could not contain yourself, what sort of a letter has it appeared when written? Weak, maudlin, ridiculous—Why? You didn't feel ridiculous. But you did not understand what effect certain words have on readers. You didn't find the picture word, you didn't use a quick, spirited, vigorous style, so your letter is *not* art, for it does *not* express anything adequately.

"This brings us to the technique of art. This again seems to be mostly a question of pleasurable feeling. Take these examples—of drawing—the physiological aspect—of music—of colour—the common basis. Now we are in a position to attempt criticism. Take Leighton's 'Wedded' and Watts' 'Mammon.' We can excellently well criticize what we call the 'spirit' of the thing—look! But we are not so well able to understand, or even to appreciate, the technique. That needs study. 'The chief triumph of art,' says Hume, 'is to insensibly refine the temper and to point out to us those dispositions which we should endeavour to attain by constant *bent* of mind and by repeated *habit*.'

"If we bend our minds, not so much to things beautiful, as to the beautiful aspect of things, then we gain this refinement of temper which can *feel* a beautiful thing. We are too gross—a crude emotion carries us away—we cannot feel the beauty of things. It is so in Socialism as in everything. You must train yourself to appreciate beauty or Art—refine yourself, or become refined, as Hume puts it. And what is refinement? It is really delicate sympathy. What then is the mission of Art? To bring us into sympathy with as many men, as many objects, as many phenomena as possible. To be in sympathy with things is to some extent to acquiesce in their purpose, to help on that purpose. We want, we are for ever trying to unite ourselves with the whole universe, to carry out some ultimate purpose—evolution, we call one phase of the carrying out. The passion of human beings to be brought into sympathetic understanding of one another is stupendous; witness it in the eagerness with which biographies, novels, personal and subjective writings are read. Emotion tends to issue in action.

"In Socialism you have the effort to take what is general in the human character and build a social state to fit it. In Art is revealed the individual character. After all the part of a man's nature which is roughly common to all his fellows is only a small part of his nature. He must be more than that—more refined, to understand the host of the particular qualities which go to make up the human character and are influences in the progress of things. So, though art is general, it is also particular. Socialism is general.

"Think, we can still feel the arms of Ruth round the neck of Naomi, we can feel the tears in the women's eyes. We too, can love and suffer at parting. We still count the story of David and Jonathan one of the finest in the world. There are other tales incomprehensible to us; and only a few can recognize the ideal, the noble emotion which many medieval artists expressed so perfectly in their Madonnas—moon faced Madonnas, we say, and turn aside. But with a little thought and study you might feel a sympathy grow up for these Madonnas, and understand. So through Art we may be brought to live many lives, taking a commonplace life as a unit, and each may have so many fields of life to wander in as never to feel wretched and empty. These things are not obvious and immediate, so we are apt to despise them. But above all things we must understand much if we would do much.

"In conclusion, I would like to suggest that whatever be the subject for discussion, everyone should try and make some study of it, think about it, and, if there is anything they feel inclined to say, say it. It would be a good idea, too, to take a book, socialistic essays, an essay of Mill or Spencer or anybody, something that costs little, and study it for full discussion one evening, someone presiding. We might at rare intervals, take a poet, painting, or a novel, or a play."

The Two Principles

After Hawthorne come the books of the sea. In Dana and Herman Melville the human relationship is no longer the chief interest. The sea enters as the great protagonist.

The sea is a cosmic element, and the relation between the sea and the human psyche is impersonal and elemental. The sea that we dream of, the sea that fills us with hate or with bliss, is a primal influence upon us beyond the personal range.

We need to find some terms to express such elemental connections as between the ocean and the human soul. We need to put off our personality, even our individuality, and enter the region of the elements.

There certainly does exist a subtle and complex sympathy, correspondence, between the plasm of the human body, which is identical with the primary human psyche, and the material elements outside. The primary human psyche is a complex plasm, which quivers, sense-conscious, in contact with the circumambient cosmos. Our plasmic psyche is radio-active, connecting with all things, and having first-knowledge of all things.

The religious systems of the pagan world did what Christianity has never tried to do: they gave the true correspondence between the material cosmos and the human soul. The ancient cosmic theories were exact, and apparently perfect. In them science and religion were in accord.

When we postulate a beginning, we only do so to fix a starting-point for our thought. There never was a beginning, and there never will be an end of the universe. The creative mystery, which is life itself, always was and always will be. It unfolds itself in pure living creatures.

Following the obsolete language, we repeat that in the beginning was the creative reality, living and substantial, although apparently void and dark. The living cosmos divided itself, and there was Heaven and Earth: by which we mean, not the sky and the terrestrial globe, for the Earth was still void and dark; but an inexplicable first duality, a division in the cosmos. Between the two great valves of the primordial universe, moved "the Spirit of God," one unbroken and indivisible heart of creative being. So that, as two great wings that are spread, the living cosmos stretched out the first Heaven and the first Earth, terms of the inexplicable primordial duality.

Then the Spirit of God moved upon the face of the waters. As no "waters" are yet created, we may perhaps take the mystic "Earth" to be the same as the Waters. The mystic Earth is the cosmic Waters, and the mystic Heaven the dark cosmic Fire. The Spirit of God, moving between the two great cosmic principles, the mysterious universal dark Waters and the invisible, unnameable cosmic Fire, brought forth the first created apparition, Light. From the darkness of primordial fire, and the darkness of primordial waters, light is born, through the intermediacy of creative presence.

Surely this is true, scientifically, of the birth of light.

After this, the waters are divided by the firmament. If we conceive of the first division in Chaos, so-called, as being perpendicular, the inexplicable division into the first duality, then this next division, when the line of the firmament is drawn, we can consider as horizontal: thus we have the ⊕, the elements of the Rosy Cross, and the first enclosed appearance of that tremendous symbol, which has dominated our era, the Cross itself.

The universe at the end of the Second Day of Creation is, therefore, as the Rosy Cross, a fourfold division. The mystic Heaven, the cosmic dark Fire is not spoken of. But the firmament of light divides the waters of the unfathomable heights from the unfathomable deeps of the other half of chaos, the still unformed earth. These strange unfathomable waters breathe back and forth, as the earliest Greek philosophers say, from one realm to the other.

Central within the fourfold division is the creative reality itself, like the body of a four-winged bird. It has thrown forth from itself two great wings of opposite Waters, two great wings of opposite Fire. Then the universal motion begins, the cosmos begins to revolve, the eternal flight is launched.

Changing the metaphors and attending to the material universe only, we may say that sun and space are now born. Those waters and that dark fire which are drawn together in the creative spell impinge into one centre in the sun; those waters and that fire which flee asunder in the creative spell form space.

So that we have a fourfold division in the cosmos, and a fourfold travelling. We have the waters under the firmament and the waters above the firmament: we have the fire to the left hand and the fire to the right hand of the firmament; and we have each travelling back and forth across the firmament. Which means, scientifically, that invisible waters steal towards the sun, right up to feed the sun, whilst new waters are shed away from the sun, into space; whilst invisible dark fire rolls its waves to the sun, and new fire floods out into space. The sun is the great mystery-centre where the invisible fires and the invisible waters roll together, brought together in the magnificence of the creative spell of opposition, to wrestle and consummate in the formation of the orb of light. Night, on the other hand, is Space presented to our consciousness, that space or infinite which is the travelling asunder of the primordial elements, and which we recognize in the living darkness.

So the ancient cosmology, always so perfect theoretically, becomes, by the help of our scientific knowledge, physically, actually perfect. The great fourfold division, the establishment of the Cross, which has so thrilled the soul of man from ages far back before Christianity, far back in pagan America as well as in the Old World, becomes real to our reason as well as to our instinct.

Cosmology, however, considers only the creation of the material universe, and according to the scientific idea life itself is but a product of reactions in the material universe. This is palpably wrong.

When we repeat that on the First Day of Creation God made Heaven and Earth we do not suggest that God disappeared between the two great valves of the cosmos once these were created. Yet this is the modern, scientific attitude. Science supposes that once the first forces was in existence, and the first motion set up, the universe produced itself automatically, throwing off life as a by-product, at a certain stage.

It is such an idea which has brought about the materialization and emptiness of life. When God made Heaven and Earth, that is, in the beginning when the unthinkable living cosmos divided itself, God did not disappear. If we try to conceive of God, in this instance, we must conceive some homogeneous rare *living* plasm, a *living* self-conscious ether, which filled the universe. The living ether divided itself as an egg-cell divides. There is a mysterious duality, life divides itself, and yet life is indivisible. When life divides itself, there is no division in life. It is a new life-state, a new being which appears. So it is when an egg divides. There is no split in life. Only a new life-stage is created. This is the eternal oneness and magnificence of life, that it moves creatively on in progressive being, each state of being whole, integral, complete.

But as life moves on in creative singleness, its substance divides and subdivides into multiplicity. When the egg divides itself, a new stage of creation is reached, a new oneness of living being; but there appears also a new differentiation in inanimate substance. From the new life-being a new motion takes place: the inanimate reacts in its pure polarity, and a third stage of creation is reached. Life has now achieved a third state of being, a third creative singleness appears in the universe; and at the same time, inanimate substance has re-divided and brought forth from itself a new creation in the material world.

So creation goes on. At each new impulse from the creative body, All comes together with All: that is, the one half of the cosmos comes together with the other half, with a dual result. First issues the new oneness, the new singleness, the new life-state, the new being, the new individual; and secondly, from the locked opposition of inanimate dual matter, another singleness is born, another creation takes place, new matter, a new chemical element appears. Dual all the time is the creative activity: first comes forth the living apparition of new being, the perfect and indescribable singleness; and this embodies the single beauty of a new substance, gold or chlorine or sulphur. So it has been since time began. The gems of being were created simultaneously with the gems of matter, the latter inherent in the former.

Every new thing is born from the consummation of the two halves of the universe, the two great halves being the cosmic waters and the cosmic fire of the First Day. In procreation, the two germs of the male and female epitomize the two cosmic principles, as these are held within the life-spell. In the sun and the material waters the two principles exist as independent elements. Life-plasm mysteriously corresponds with inanimate matter. But life-plasm, in that it lives, is itself identical with being, inseparable from the singleness of a living being, the indivisible oneness.

Life can never be produced or made. Life is an unbroken oneness, indivisible. The mystery of creation is that new and indivisible being appears forever within the oneness of life.

In the cosmic theories of the creation of the world it has been customary for science to treat of life as a product of the material universe, whilst religion treats of the material universe as having been deliberately created by some will or idea, some sheer abstraction. Surely the universe has arisen from some universal living self-conscious plasm, plasm which has no origin and no end, but is life eternal and identical, bringing forth the infinite creatures of being and existence, living creatures embodying inanimate substance. There is no utterly immaterial existence, no spirit. The distinction is between living plasm and inanimate matter. Inanimate matter is released from the dead body of the world's creatures. It is the static residue of the living conscious plasm, like feathers of birds.

When the living cosmos divided itself, on the First Day, then the living plasm became twofold, twofold supporting a new state of singleness, new being; at the same time, the twofold living plasm contained the finite duality of the two unliving, material cosmic elements. In the transmutation of the plasm, in the interval of death, the inanimate elements are liberated into separate existence. The inanimate material universe is born through death from the living universe, to co-exist with it for ever.

We know that in its essence the living plasm is twofold. In the same way the dynamic elements of material existence are dual, the fire and the water. These two cosmic elements are pure mutual opposites, and on their opposition the material universal is established. The attraction of the two, mutually opposite, sets up the revolution of the universe and forms the blazing heart of the sun. The sun is formed by the impinging of the cosmic water upon the cosmic fire, in the stress of opposition. This causes the central blaze of the universe.

In the same way, mid-way, the lesser worlds are formed; as the two universal elements become entangled, swirling on their way to the great central conjunction. The core of the worlds and stars is a blaze of the two elements as they rage interlocked into consummation. And from the fiery and moist consummation of the two elements all the material substances are finally born, perfected.

This goes on however, mechanically now, according to fixed, physical laws. The plasm of life, the state of living potentiality exists still central, as the body of a bird between the wings, and spontaneously brings forth the living forms we know. Ultimately, or primarily, the creative plasm has no laws. But as it takes form and multiple wonderful being, it keeps up a perfect law-abiding relationship with that other half of itself, the material inanimate universe. And the first and greatest law of creation is that all creation, even life itself, exists within the strange and incalculable balance of the two elements. In the living creature, fire and water must exquisitely balance, commingle, and consummate, this in continued mysterious process.

So we must look for life midway between fire and water. For where fire is purest, this is a sign that life has withdrawn itself, and is withheld. And the same with water. For by pure water we do not mean that bright liquid rain or dew or fountain stream. Water in its purest is water most abstracted from fire, as fire in its purest must be abstracted from water. And so, water becomes more essential as we progress through the rare crystals of snow and ice, on to that infinitely suspended invisible element which travels between us and the sun, inscrutable water such as life can know nothing of, for where it is, all life has long ceased to be. This is the true cosmic element. Our material water, as our fire, is still a mixture of fire and water.

It may be argued that water is proved to be a chemical compound, composed of two gases, hydrogen and oxygen. But is it not more true that hydrogen and oxygen are the first naked products of the two parent-elements, water and fire. In all our efforts to decompose water we do but introduce fire into the water, in some naked form or other, and this introduction of naked fire into naked water *produces* hydrogen and oxygen, given the proper conditions of chemical procreation. Hydrogen and oxygen are the first fruits of fire and water. This is the alchemistic air. But from the conjunction of fire and water within the living plasm arose the first matter, the Prima Materia of a living body, which, in its dead state, is the alchemistic Earth.

Thus, at the end of what is called the Second Day of Creation, the alchemistic Four Elements of Earth, Air, Fire, and Water have come into existence: the Air and the Earth born from the conjunction of Fire and Water within the creative plasm. Air is a final product. Earth is the incalculable and indefinable residuum of the living plasm. All other substance is born by the mechanical consummation of fire and water within this Earth. So no doubt it is the fire and water of the swirling universe, acting upon that Earth or dead plasm which results at the end of each life-phase, that has brought the solid globes into being, invested them with rock and metal.

The birth of the chemical elements from the grain of Earth, through the consummation of fire and water, is as magical, as incalculable as the birth of men. For from the material consummation may come forth a superb and enduring element, such as gold or platinum, or such strange, unstable elements as sulphur or phosphorus, phosphorus, a sheer apparition of water, and sulphur a netted flame. In phosphorus the water principle is so barely held that at a touch the mystic union will break, whilst sulphur only waits to depart into fire. Bring these two unstable elements together, and a slight friction will cause them to burst spontaneously asunder, fire leaping out; or the phosphorus will pass off in watery smoke. The natives of Zoruba, in West Africa, having the shattered fragments of a great pagan culture in their memory, call sulphur the dung of thunder: the fire-dung, undigested excrement of the fierce consummation between the upper waters and the invisible fire.

The cosmic elements, however, have a two-fold direction. When they move together, in the mystic attraction of mutual unknowing, then, in some host, some grain of Earth, or some grain of living plasm, they embrace and unite and the fountain of creation springs up, a new substance, or a new life-form. But there is also the great centrifugal motion, when the two flee asunder into space, into infinitude.

This fourfold activity is the root-activity of the universe. We have first the mystic dualism of pure otherness, that which science will not admit, and which Christianity has called "the impious doctrine of the two principles." This dualism extends through everything, even through the *soul* or *self* or *being* of any living creature. The self or soul is single, unique, and undivided, the gem of gems, the flower of flowers, the fulfilment of the universe. Yet *within* the self, which is single, the principle of dualism reigns. And then, consequent upon this principle of dual *otherness*, comes the scientific dualism of polarity.

So we have in creation the two life-elements coming together within the living plasm, coming together softly and sweetly, the kiss of angels within the glimmering place. Then newly created life, new being arises. There comes a time, however, when the two life-elements go asunder, after the being has perfected itself. Then there is the seething and struggling of inscrutable life-disintegration. The individual form disappears, but the being remains implicit within the intangible life-plasm.

Parallel to this, in the material universe we have the productive coming-together of water and fire, to make the sun of light, the rainbow, and the perfect elements of Matter. Or we have the slow activity in disintegration, when substances resolve back towards the universal Prima Materia, primal inanimate ether.

Thus all creation depends upon the fourfold activity. And on this root of four is all law and understanding established. Following the perception of these supreme truths, the Pythagoreans made their philosophy, asserting that all is number, and seeking to search out the mystery of the roots of three, four, five, seven, stable throughout all the universe, in a chain of developing phenomena. But our science of mathematics still waits for its fulfilment, its union with life itself. For the truths of mathematics are only the skeleton fabric of the living universe.

Only symbolically do the numbers still live for us. In religion we still accept the four Gospel Natures, the four Evangels, with their symbols of man, eagle, lion, and bull, symbols parallel to the Four Elements, and to the Four Activities, and to the Four Natures. And the Cross, the epitome of all this fourfold division, still stirs us to the depths with unaccountable emotions, emotions which go much deeper than personality and the Christ drama.

The ancients said that their cosmic symbols had a sevenfold or a five-fold reference. The simplest symbol, the divided circle, ⊖, stands not only for the first division in the living cosmos and for the two cosmic elements, but also, within the realms of created life, for the sex mystery; then for the mystery of dual psyche, sensual and spiritual, within the individual being; then for the duality of thought and sensation—and so on, or otherwise, according to varying exposition. Having such a clue, we can begin to find the meanings of the Rosy Cross, the ⊕; and for the ankh, the famous Egyptian symbol, called the symbol of life, the cross or Tau beneath the circle ☥, the soul undivided resting upon division; and for the so-called symbol of Aphrodite, the circle resting upon the complete cross, ♀. These symbols too have their multiple reference, deep and far-reaching, embracing the cosmos and the indivisible soul, as well as the mysteries of function and production. How foolish it is to give these great signs a merely phallic indication!

The sex division is one of the Chinese three sacred mysteries. Vitally, it is a division of pure otherness, pure dualism. It is one of the first mysteries of creation. It is parallel with the mystery of the first division in chaos, and with the dualism of the two cosmic elements. This is not to say that the one sex is identical with fire, the other with water. And yet there is some indefinable connection. Aphrodite born of the waters, and Apollo the sun-god, these give some indication of the sex distinction. It is obvious, however, that some races, men and women alike, derive from the sun and have the fiery principle predominant in their constitution, whilst some, blonde, blue-eyed, northern, are evidently water-born, born along with the ice-crystals and blue, cold deeps, and yellow, ice-refracted sunshine. Nevertheless, if we must imagine the most perfect clue to the eternal waters, we think of woman, and of man as the most perfect premiss of fire.

Be that as it may, the duality of sex, the mystery of creative *otherness*, is manifest, and given the sexual polarity, we have the fourfold motion. The coming-together of the sexes may be the soft, delicate union of pure creation, or it may be the tremendous conjunction of opposition, a vivid struggle, as fire struggles with water in the sun. From either of these consummations birth takes place. But in the first case it is the birth of a softly rising and budding soul, wherein the two principles commune in gentle union, so that the soul is harmonious and at one with itself. In the second case it is the birth of a disintegrative soul, wherein the two principles wrestle in their eternal opposition: a soul finite, momentaneous, active in the universe as a unit of sundering. The first kind of birth takes place in the youth of an era, in the mystery of accord; the second kind preponderates in the times of disintegration, the crumbling of an era. But at all times beings are born from the two ways, and life is made up of the duality.

The latter way, however, is a way of struggle into separation, isolation, psychic disintegration. It is a continual process of sundering and reduction, each soul becoming more mechanical and apart, reducing the great fabric of co-ordinate human life. In this struggle the sexes act in the polarity of antagonism or mystic opposition, the so-called sensual polarity, bringing tragedy. But the struggle is progressive. And then at last the sexual polarity breaks. The sexes have no more dynamic connection, only a habitual or deliberate connection. The spell is broken. They are not balanced any more even in opposition.

But life depends on duality and polarity. The duality, the polarity now asserts itself within the individual psyche. Here, in the individual, the fourfold creative activity takes place. Man is divided, according to old-fashioned phraseology, into the upper and lower man: that is, the spiritual and sensual being. And this division is physical and actual. The upper body, breast and throat and face, this is the spiritual body; the lower is the sensual.

By spiritual being we mean that state of being where the self excels into the universe, and knows all things by passing into all things. It is that blissful consciousness which glows upon the flowers and trees and sky, so that I am sky and flowers, I, who am myself. It is that movement towards a state of infinitude wherein I experience my living oneness with all things.

By sensual being, on the other hand, we mean that state in which the self is the magnificent centre wherein all life pivots, and lapses, as all space passes into the core of the sun. It is a magnificent central positivity, wherein the being sleeps upon the strength of its own reality, as a wheel sleeps in speed on its positive hub. It is a state portrayed in the great dark statues of the seated lords of Egypt. The self is incontestable and unsurpassable.

Through the gates of the eyes and nose and mouth and ears, through the delicate ports of the fingers, through the great window of the yearning breast, we pass into our oneness with the universe, our great extension of being, towards infinitude. But in the lower part of the body there is darkness and pivotal pride. There in the abdomen the contiguous universe is drunk into the blood, assimilated, as a wheel's great speed is assimilated into the hub. There the great whirlpool of the dark blood revolves and assimilates all unto itself. Here is the world of living dark waters, where the fire is quenched in watery creation. Here, in the navel, flowers the water-born lotus, the soul of the water begotten by one germ of fire. And the lotus is the symbol of our perfected sensual first-being, which rises in blossom from the unfathomable waters.

In the feet we rock like the lotus, rooted in the under-mud of earth. In the knees, in the thighs we sway with the dark motion of the flood, darkly water-conscious, like the thick, strong, swaying stems of the lotus that mindlessly answer the waves. It is in the lower body that we are chiefly blood-conscious.

For we assert that the blood has a perfect but untranslatable consciousness of its own, a consciousness of weight, of rich, down-pouring motion, of powerful self-positivity. In the blood we have our strongest self-knowledge, our most powerful dark conscience. The ancients said the heart was the seat of understanding. And so it is: it is the seat of the primal sensual understanding, the seat of the passional self-consciousness.

In the nerves, on the other hand, we pass out and become the universe. But even this is dual. It seems as if from the tremendous sympathetic centres of the breast there ran out a fine, silvery emanation from the self, a fine silvery seeking which finds the universe, and by means of which we *become* the universe, we have our extended being. On the other hand, it seems as if in the great solar plexus of the abdomen were a dark whirlwind of pristine force, drawing, whirling all the world darkly into itself, not concerned to look out, or to consider beyond itself. It is from this perfect self-centrality that the lotus of the navel is born, according to Oriental symbolism.

But beyond the great centres of breast and bowels, there is a deeper and higher duality. There are the wonderful plexuses of the face, where our being runs forth into space and finds its vastest realization; and there is the great living plexus of the loins, there where deep calls to deep. All the time, there is some great incomprehensible balance between the upper and the lower centres, as when the kiss of the mouth accompanies the passionate embrace of the loins. In the face we live our glad life of seeing, perceiving, we pass in delight to our greater being, when we are one with all things. The face and breast belong to the heavens, the luminous infinite. But in the loins we have our unbreakable root, the root of the lotus. There we have our passionate self-possession, our unshakable and indomitable being. There deep calls unto deep. There in the sexual passion the very blood surges into communion, in the terrible sensual oneing. There all the darkness of the deeps, the primal flood, is perfected, as the two great waves of separated blood surge to consummation, the dark infinitude.

When there is balance in first-being between the breast and belly, the loins and face, then, and only then, when this fourfold consciousness is established within the body, then, and only then, do we come to full consciousness in the mind. For the mind is again the single in creation, perfecting its finite thought and idea as the chemical elements are perfected into finality from the flux. The mind brings forth its gold and its gems, finite beyond duality. So we have the sacred pentagon, with the mind as the conclusive apex.

In the body, however, as in all creative forms, there is the dual polarity as well as the mystic dualism of *otherness*. The great sympathetic activity of the human system has the opposite pole in the voluntary system. The front part of the body is open and receptive, the great valve to the universe. But the back is sealed, closed. And it is from the ganglia of the spinal system that the *will* acts in direct compulsion, outwards.

The great plexuses of the breast and face act in the motion of oneing, from these the soul goes forth in the spiritual oneing. Corresponding to this, the thoracic ganglion and the cervical ganglia are the great centres of spiritual compulsion or control or dominion, the great *second* or negative activity of the spiritual self. From these ganglia go forth the motions and commands which *force* the external universe into that state which accords with the spiritual will-to-unification, the will for equality. Equality, and religious agreement, and social virtue are enforced as well as found. And it is from the ganglia of the upper body that this compulsion to equality and virtue is enforced.

In the same way, from the lumbar ganglion and from the sacral ganglion acts the great sensual will to dominion. From these centres the soul goes forth haughty and indomitable, seeking for mastery. These are the great centres of activity in soldiers, fighters: as also in the tiger and the cat the power-centre is at the base of the spine, in the sacral ganglion. All the tremendous sense of power and mastery is located in these centres of volition, there where the back is walled and strong, set blank against life. These are the centres of negative polarity of our first-being.

So the division of the psychic body is fourfold. If we are divided horizontally at the diaphragm, we are divided also perpendicularly. The upright division gives us our polarity, our for and against, our mystery of right and left.

Any man who is perfect and fulfilled lives in fourfold activity. He knows the sweet spiritual communion, and he is at the same time a sword to enforce the spiritual level; he knows the tender unspeakable sensual communion, but he is a tiger against anyone who would abate his pride and his liberty.

Certain Americans and an Englishman

I arrive in New Mexico at a moment of crisis. I suppose every man always does, here. The crisis is a thing called the Bursum bill, and it affects the Pueblo Indians. I wouldn't know a thing about it if I needn't.

But it's Bursum, Bursum, Bursum! the Bill, the Bill, the Bill! Twitchell, Twitchell, Twitchell! O Mr. Secretary Fall, Fall, Fall! O Mr. Secretary Fall, you bad man, you good man, you Fall, you Rise, you Fall! The Joy Survey, Oh, Joy, No Joy, Once Joy, Now Woe! Woe! Whoa, Bursum! Whoa, Bill! Whoa-a-a!—like a Vachel Lindsay Boom-Boom bellowing, it goes on in my unwonted ears, till I have to take heed.

And then I sit down solemnly in a chair and read the Bill, the Bill, the printed Bursum bill, Section one—two—three—four—five—six —seven, whereas and wherefore and heretobefore, right to the damned and distant end. Then I start the insomuch-as of Mr. Francis Wilson's Brief concerning the Bill. Then I read Mr. C.'s passionate article against, and Mrs. H.'s hatchet-stroke summary against, and Mr. M.'s sharp-knife jugglery for the Bill. After which I feel I'm getting mixed up. Then, lamb-like, ram-like, I feel I'll do a bit of butting, too, on a stage where every known animal butts.

But first I toddle to a corner and, like a dog when music is going on in the room, put my paws exasperatedly over my ears, and my nose to the ground, and groan softly. So doing, I try to hypnotize myself back into my old natural world, outside the circus tent, where horses don't buck and prance so much, and where not every lady is leaping through the hoop and crashing through the paper confines of the universe at every hand's turn.

Try to extricate my lamb-like soul into its fleecy isolation, and then adjust myself. Adjust myself to that much-talked-of actor in the Wild West show, the Red Indian.

Don't imagine, indulgent reader, that I'm talking at you or down to you; or trying to put something over on you. No, no; imagine me, lamb-like and bewildered, muttering softly to myself, between soft groans, trying to make head or tail of myself in my present situation. And then you'll get the spirit of these effusions.

The Indian is not an American citizen. He is apparently in the position of a defenceless nation protected by a benevolent Congress. He is an American subject, but a member of a dominated, defenceless nation which Congress undertakes to protect and cherish. The Indian Bureau is supposed to do the cherishing.

Around about the pueblos live Mexican and American settlers who are American citizens, who do pay taxes and who do vote. They have cattle ranches, sheep ranches, little farms, and so on, and are most of them in debt.

These are the first two items: the dark spots of the protected pueblos; the hungry, unscrupulous frontier population squatting, rather scattered and rather impoverished, around.

There is plenty of land: sage brush desert. All depends on water. The pueblos, of course, are pitched upon the waters. The beautiful Taos Valley culminates in Taos Pueblo. The ranches and farms straggle round and try to encroach on this watered place. Six miles away is a deserted Mexican village, waterless.

Already you have a situation.

Now, when the United States took over New Mexico in 1848, Congress decided to abide by all the conditions established by Spain and old Mexico in this State. Congress also, apparently, decreed that to each pueblo belonged the four square leagues of land surrounding the pueblo; whether in accordance with ancient Spanish grant or not, isn't for me to say. Anyhow, there it is. Taos Pueblo owning four square leagues, which is thirty-six square miles of land immediately surrounding the pueblo; measuring a league in each direction from the centre of the pueblo. There are 800 Indians in the pueblo. But much of the land is dry desert or stony hill. True, some of the desert might be irrigated —if the water were there to irrigate it with, or if the Indians would make the effort.

At the same time Congress will abide by all the old Spanish or Mexican grants, titles, and so forth, which were in existence at the time of the taking over of this territory.

Immediately a problem. Because the Indian four square leagues has been much of it for centuries occupied by Spanish or Mexican or white settlers. There they sit. Taos Plaza, that is the white village of Taos, stands itself entirely within the four square leagues decreed to Taos Pueblo. There are Spanish grants from governors; there are Mexican grants; and there are forged grants, forged deeds. Well, then, a terrible problem. For Taos Plaza has probably been standing for at least 200 years. Almost as old as New York.

Terrible problem! Why hasn't the place run with blood? Because the Indian never measured any leagues, but tilled his land around the pueblo itself. Much of the space intervening between the pueblo and the plaza is just sage desert. And this definite uncontested Indian land—uncontested for the moment, that is, so long as there is no Bursum bill—lies between plaza and pueblo as a sort of frontier. Nobody cut anybody's throat, because the occasion didn't arrive. Many squatters squat within the bounds of these four square leagues, but they are beyond a no man's land still of sage desert, away from the heart where the pueblo rises, among the cotton-wood trees, and tills its land around the waters.

Thus the situation.

Then the highbrows come and say: "Poor Indian, dear Indian! why, *all* America ought to belong to him! Why look you now at the injustice that has been done to him! Not only has *all* America been snatched from him, but even his four square leagues are invaded by vile white men, greedy white men, hateful white men!"

So sing the highbrow palefaces. Till the Indian gradually begins to get his tail up.

Luckily for us he is few; unluckily for himself. Because if the tiny prairie dog yaps too hard at the western American airedale, alas for prairie dogs!

Now things begin to stir. It is time this business of grants and titles was settled. Old Spanish grants to Spaniards versus these four square leagues. Taos Plaza versus Taos Pueblo. Spanish grants, Mexican titles, forged deeds suddenly fluttering into life in a breath of hot wind of contest. Four square leagues flying away on the wings of old Spanish grants, which Congress is bound to validify, and the Indian perching on his big toe end, trying to poise on four square inches. Or, vice versa, an appeal to Congress, and Congress is sovereign majesty, and the Indians can come and take their brooms and sweep old José or old Fernandez or old Maria, with all Taos village, pell-mell over the border of the four square leagues, into limbo.

Not that the Indian is likely to take Congress by the ear and do it. The Indian is afflicted with the lovable malady of laissez-faire. But then you never know what some of those white highbrows will be up to, these palefaces who love the dear Indian, the poor Indian, and who would like to see all America restored to him, let alone four square leagues, which is thirty-six square miles.

Now I believe the lands of some of the pueblos, sadly, very sadly enough, have been eaten right up by encroachments. But let me not be very sad. Taos isn't sad. Let me stay by Taos.

It will be obvious to everybody that a move had to be made about these leagues and these grants. And New Mexico made the move. Senator Bursum is the black knight who has hopped on to the four leagues. His famous Bursum bill has passed the Senate and comes before the House, presumably this month (December).

And here is the Bursum bill: an absolute checkmate to Pueblo, highbrow and all. It is the frontiersman biting off as much as he can chew.

"A bill to ascertain and settle land claims of persons not Indian, within Pueblo Indian land, land grants, and reservations in the State of New Mexico."

1. A court called the District Court of the United States for the District of New Mexico shall assume jurisdiction over all crimes, offenses, etc., committed within the areas of pueblo grants, by any person, Indian or non-Indian, so long as the Indians are occupying that land or claim that land.

(So this nice New Mexico court, which knows just what it wants for itself, takes a first modest step.)

2. This court shall have exclusive original jurisdiction in all suits of a civil nature, in all suits involving any right or title to any land within the said pueblo reservations, also in all suits involving property of Indians, also in all suits involving any question of internal government of any of the said pueblos.

(Which means that the old, autonomous tribal body of the pueblo is placed at the mercy of this distant district court.)

4. All persons or corporations who have had possession of lands within the pueblo grants since prior to the Guadalupe Hidalgo Treaty of 1848 shall be entitled to a decree in their favour for all lands so possessed. In proof, secondary evidence shall be admissible and competent.

5. All persons who have held possession of lands within the pueblo grants for more than ten years previous to July, 1910, without colour of title * * * shall be entitled to a decree in their favour for all lands so possessed. But in return to the Indians, the secretary of the Interior shall have some other bit of adjacent land allotted to the pueblo if any such land be available. (None of the available land is any good.) Otherwise the pueblo shall be compensated in cash, as the Secretary thinks fit.

6. Pueblos shall have the right to the use of just as much water as they use at this minute (even though this amount be sadly insufficient

to irrigate the present fields). But if any dam or reservoir be made, damming up the pueblo supplies, then all the surplus water and the control thereof shall be adjudicated according to the laws of the State of New Mexico.

7. All proceedings under this act shall be without cost to parties.

8. All suits under this act must be brought within five years.

9. The "Joy Surveys" (which were made to give evidence as to how Indian lands had been wrongly invaded) shall be accepted as prima facie evidence.

12. That any person or persons making any claim whatsoever to any lands within pueblo grants, whether they squatted on it only yesterday, may, with approval of the court, purchase the land at the court's valuation, and the money paid shall be held by the Secretary of the Interior on behalf of the Indians. (Which means that if I want a chunk of pueblo land I put a fence around it and pay the Secretary of the Interior a sum which the court will, if it likes me, kindly make as small as possible, and the Indian sits staring at the Charybdis of me and the Scylla of Mr. Secretary Fall and holding out his hand for a bit of charity bread.)

It is obvious this means the scattering of the pueblos. The squatters and Mexicans interested—and where land grabbing is the game, every neighbour is interested—openly declare that the pueblos will be finished in ten years. That is, five years for the claims to be all made and five for their final enforcement. And then the Indians will have merged. They will be scattered day labourers through the States and the nucleus will be broken.

The great desire to turn them into white men will be fulfilled as far as it can be fulfilled. They will all be wage earners, and that's enough. For the rest, lost, mutilated intelligences.

As it is, the pueblos are slowly disbanding; there are the Indian schools, a doom in themselves. The young men all speak American. They go as hired labourers. And man is like a dog—he believes in the hand that feeds him. He belongs where he is fed.

The end of the pueblos. But at least let them die a natural death. To me the Bursum bill is amusing in its bare-facedness—a cool joke. It startles any English mind a little to realize that it may become law.

Let the pueblos die a natural death. The Bursum bill plays the Wild West scalping trick a little too brazenly. Surely the great Federal Government is capable of instituting an efficient Indian Commission to inquire fairly and settle fairly. Or a small Indian office that knows what it's about. For Heaven's sake keep these Indians out of the clutches of politics.

Because, finally, in some curious way, the pueblos still lie here at the core of American life. In some curious way, it is the Indians still who are American. This great welter of whites is not yet a nation, not yet a people.

The Indians keep burning an eternal fire, the sacred fire of the old dark religion. To the vast white America, either in our generation or in the time of our children or grandchildren, will come some fearful convulsion. Some terrible convulsion will take place among the millions of this country, sooner or later. When the pueblos are gone. But oh, let us have the grace and dignity to shelter these ancient centres of life, so that, if die they must, they die a natural death. And at the same time, let us try to adjust ourselves again to the Indian outlook, to take up an old dark thread from their vision, and see again as they see, without forgetting we are ourselves.

For it is a new era we have now got to cross into. And our own electric light won't show us over the gulf. We have to feel our way by the dark thread of the old vision. Before it lapses, let us take it up.

Before the pueblos disappear, let there be just one moment of reconciliation between the white spirit and the dark.

And whether there be this moment of reconciliation or not, let us prevent Jack Grab and Juan Arrapar from putting their foot on the pueblos.

Besides, if the Bursum bill passes, what a lively shooting match will go on between all the Jacks and the Juans who claim the bits of land in question, ten claimants to every inch!

And then, again, what business is it of mine, foreigner and newcomer?

[Germans and English]

Yesterday, in Florence, in the flood of sunshine on the Arno at evening, I saw two German boys steering out of the Por Santa Maria, on to the Ponte Vecchio, passing for a moment in the bright sun, then gone again in shadow. The glimpse made a strong impression on me. They were dark-haired, not blond, but otherwise the true Wandervogel type: thick boots, heavy Rucksack, hatless, with shirt-sleeves rolled back above brown, muscular arms, and shirt-breast open from the scorched breast, and face and neck glowing sun-darkened as they strode into the flood of evening sunshine, out of the dark gulf of the street. They were talking loudly to one another in German, as if oblivious of their surroundings, in the thronged crossing of the Ponte Vecchio. And they leaned forward in the surge of travel, marching with long strides, heedless, past the Italians, as if the Italians were but shadows. Travelling so intently, bent a little forward from the Rucksacks in the plunge of determination to urge onwards, looking neither to right nor left, conversing in strong voices only with one another, as if the world around were unreal, where were they going, in the last golden sun-flood of evening, over the Arno? Were they leaving town, at this hour? Were they pressing on, to get out of the Porta Romana before nightfall, going south?

In spite of the fact that one is used to these German boys, in Florence especially, in summer, still the mind calls a halt, each time they appear and pass by. If swans, or wild geese flew low, honking over the Arno in the evening light, moving with that wedge-shaped, intent, unswerving progress that is so impressive, they would create something of the same impression on one. They would bring that sense of remote, northern lands, and the mystery of strange, blind, instinctive purpose in migration, which these Germans give.

Now no one knows better than I do that Munich and Frankfurt and Berlin are heavily civilized cities; they are not at all remote and lonely homes of the wild swan; and that these boys are not mysteriously migrating, they are only just wandering out of restlessness and need to move. Perhaps an instinct carries them south, once more to Rome, the old centre point. But in absolute fact, the Wandervogel is not very different from any other tourist.

Then why does he create such a strong and almost startling impression, here in the streets of Florence, or in Rome? There are Englishmen who go with knapsacks and sleeves rolled up; there are even Italians. But they look just what they are, men taking a walking tour. Whereas when I see the Wandervogel pushing at evening out of the Por Santa Maria, across the blaze of sun and into the Ponte Vecchio, then Germany becomes again to me what it was to the Romans: mysterious, half-dark land of the north, bristling with gloomy forests, resounding to the cry of the wild geese and swans, the land of the bear and the stork, the Drachen and the Greifen.

I know it is not so. I know Germany is the land of steel and of ordered civilization. Yet the old impression comes over me, as I see the youths pressing heedlessly past. And I know the Italians have something of the same feeling. They see again the Goths and the Vandals passing with loud and guttural speech, *i barbari*. That is the look in the eyes of the little policeman in his peaked cap and belt, as he watches the boys from the north go by: *i barbari!* Not a look of dislike or contempt; on the contrary. It is the old weird wonder. So he might look up at wild swans flying over the bridge: strangers!

There are English strangers too, of course, and American and Swedish and all sorts. They are all a bit fantastic to the Italian policeman. All nations find all other nations ridiculous. That is not the point. The point is, that though the English and American and Swede may be ridiculous to the Italian policeman, they are all, as it were, compatible, they are all part of the show, and we must expect them.

Whereas the Wandervogel is incompatible, you can't expect him, he is strictly not in the game. He has got a game of his own up his sleeve, like a predative old Goth in the sixth century. And he brings with him such a strong feeling of somewhere else, somewhere *outside* our common circle. That was the impression the Russians used to give so vividly: the impression of another country, outside the group. The impression of a land still unknown and unencircled, large and outside. Now the Russians have disappeared, or have lost their dynamic vibration. And now it is the Wandervogel alone who trail with them the feeling of a far country, outside the group, a northland still unknown. The impression is there in spite of facts.

How wonderful it must have been, at the end of the Roman Empire, to see the big, bare-limbed Goths with their insolent-indifferent blue eyes, pass through the Roman market-place, or stand looking on, with the little Germanic laugh, part derision, part admiration and wonder, part uneasy, at the doings of the little, fussy natives! They were like a vision. *Non angli sed angeli*, we are told the first great Pope said of the British slave-children in the slave-market. Creatures from the beyond, presaging another world of men.

Coming home, I found books from Germany, and among them: *Zeit und Stunde*, by Karl Scheffler. The first essay, called *Der Einsame Deutsche*, at once brought back to me the Wandervogel, and reminded me of the problem: Where are they going? What are they making for? And there on the first page of Scheffler's book, there is the answer: "Weil sie—eine Welt der reinen Idee brauchen."

Was that why those boys were steering so intent out of town, in the evening? Was it that they were seeking for a world of the pure idea? Or, which amounts to the same thing, as Scheffler says, because they were steering impatiently away from all forms that have already been developed, all the ideas that have already been made explicit? Were they rushing towards what shall be, in their queer haste at nightfall? Or were they rushing away from all that is?

It looked much like the latter. They seemed to be rushing away from Germany, much more positively than rushing to Rome. Perhaps they want to touch the centre stone, there in the Roman Forum, to see if there is still virtue in it. Probably they'll find it dead, like a dead heart. As the German boy said to me, in the tombs at Tarquinia, speaking of his travels in Italy and Tunis: It's all *mehr Schrei wie Wert*. If not something much worse. One day, as Scheffler says, the German desire for a world of pure idea led the Germans to invent militarism; the next day, it was industrialism. If that isn't enough to cure any man of wanting a world of pure idea, I don't know what is.

Herr Scheffler advises the Germans to accept their race-destiny as the heaviest of all destinies. "Die Einsamkeit in der Welt und im eigenen Volk ertragen lernen: das ist der Sieg. Swindelfrei, wie die Geflügelte Göttin auf der Kugel, das Ganze überschauen, den Graus der Geschichte mit derselben Gefasstheit und ehrfürchtigen Neugier erleben, wie er in besseren Zeiten nur gedacht worden ist, an die Weltmission deutscher Problematik, an die höhere Sittlichkeit scheinbarer Charakterlosigkeit, an die Kraft in der Schwäche glauben, und alles das tätig tun, jeden Tag für verloren halten, an dem nicht irgend etwas getan worden ist: das ist, das sei das irdische Glück des in der Welt und im eigenen Land einsamen Deutschen."

That sounds fine and heroic, especially the Goddess on the globe, but to a mere outsider and Englishman, a little unnecessary. Those boys crossing the Ponte Vecchio, I am sure, had no need to learn all those difficult things. It seemed to me, they had really learned intuitively what they had to learn, already. They had such a look of bolting away from Germany to escape any further coil of "pure ideas," that it seemed to me they were all right.

What has ruined Europe, but especially northern Europe, is this very "pure idea." Would to God the "Ideal" had never been invented. But now it's got its claws in us, and we must struggle free. The beast we have to fight and to kill is the Ideal. It is the worm, the foul serpent of our epoch, in whose coils we are strangled.

But this very German unrest that seems so lamentable is just a healthy instinct fighting off the coils of the beast. The Germans are more frantically entangled up in the folds of the serpent of the Ideal than any people; except, perhaps, the Russian intelligents. But also, the Germans are much more lusty, fighting the beast. The German has a strong primitive nature still, unexploited by civilization. And this primitive nature has an intuitive wisdom of its own, an intuitive ethic also, much deeper than the ideal ethic. When the German learns to trust his own intuitive wisdom, and his own intuitive ethic, then he will have slain the ideal dragon, for the rest of Europe as well as for himself. But it needs a very high sense of responsibility and a deep courage, to depend on the intuitive wisdom and ethic, instead of on the ideal formula.

This is the point that Herr Scheffler makes in the very interesting essay: "Warum Wir den Krieg Verloren Haben." He links together instinct, intuition, and imagination a little confusingly. But it certainly was for lack of these three things that Germany lost the war; and for lack of the same three things, in the other nations, there was a war at all. It is not only Germany, it is our whole civilization that is damned by the "Ideal," and by the lack of trust in the intuitive, instinctive, imaginative consciousness in ourselves.

Herr Scheffler's essay on the Englishman is also very amusing. And possibly, from the outside, it is quite true. That is obviously how the Englishman *looks* to any foreigner who only sees him from the outside But from the inside, the story is a different one.

The clue to the Englishman is the curious radical isolation, or instinct of isolation, which every born native of my country has at the core of him. We are little islands, each one of us is a tiny island to himself, and the immutable sea washes between us all. That is the clue to the Englishman. He is born alone. He is proud of the fact. And he is proud of the fact that he belongs to a nation of isolated individuals. He is proud of being one island in the great archipelago of his nation.

But it is the fact of his own consciousness of isolation that makes the Englishman such a good citizen. He wants no one to touch him, and he wants not to touch anybody. Hence the endless little private houses of England, and the fierce preservation of the privacy.

The Englishman, however, is not bourgeois. Myself, I could never understand what *bourgeois* meant, till I went abroad, and saw Germans and Frenchmen and Italians. They have a bourgeoisie, because they have had bourgs for centuries. In England, there are no bourgs.

So the Englishman is not bourgeois. But he is hopelessly civilly disciplined, with a discipline he has imposed on himself. He is an islander, an individualist. What has carried the Englishman abroad, what has made him "imperial"—though the word means very little to an Englishman—is his fatal individualism. The Englishman, *alone*, is fatally and fantastically individualistic. That is, he is aware of his own isolation almost to excruciation. So he disciplines himself almost to extinction, and is the most perfect civilian on earth. But scratch one of these civilian, made-to-pattern Englishmen, and you will find him fantastic, almost a caricature. Hence his endless forbearing, and at the same time, his absolute resistance to tyranny. He is an island to himself.

Perhaps it was the mixture of Germanic with celtic British blood that produced this Hamletish-Falstaffian sense of being distinct from the body of mankind, which is the glory and the torture of the Englishman. The Englishman *cannot not* be alone. He is essentially always apart. For this reason he seems a hypocrite. His nature is so private to him, that he leaves it out in most of his social dealings. He expects other people to do the same, and it seems to him a lack of breeding when the others don't do it.

But nowadays, the Englishman has so disciplined himself to the social ideals, that he has almost killed himself. He is almost a walking pillar of society, as dead and stiff as a pillar. He has crucified himself on the social ideal most effectively, and has a terrible moment ahead of him, when he cries *consummatum est*, and the life goes out of him. There is something spectral about the British people.

Cut off! That is the inner tragedy of the English. They are cut off from the flow of life. Nowhere are the classes so absolutely cut off from touch, from living contact, as in England. It is inhuman, it is almost ghoulish.

As for the English not being revolutionary—they made the first great European revolution, and it is highly probable that among them is preparing the last. The English will bear anything, till the sense of injustice really enters into them. And then nothing will stop them. But it needs that fatal sense of injustice. Only that can make them see red, and blind them to that fetish of theirs, "the other fellow's point of view".

So it is. We all have our own Völkerschicksale. At the same time, we are all men, and we can all have some glimpse of realization of one another, if we use imagination and intuition and *all* our instincts, instead of just one or two. And the fate of all nations in Europe hangs together. We have our separate Völkerschicksale. But there is over and above a human destiny, and a European destiny.

On Coming Home

Breathes there a man with soul so dead
Who never to himself hath said
This is my own, my native land—

With a vengeance!

It is four years since I saw, under a little winter snow, the death-grey coast of Kent go out. After four years, down, down on the horizon, with the last sunset still in the west, right down under the eyelid of the shut cold sky, the faintest spark, like a message. It is the Land's End light. And I, who am a bit short-sighted, saw it almost first. One sees by divination. The infinitesimal sparking of the Land's End light, so absolutely remote, as one approaches from over the sea, from the Gulf of Mexico, after sunset.

I won't pretend my heart was dead. It exploded again in my chest. "This is my own, my native land!" My God, what lies behind that spark of light!

One goes out on deck again, two hours later, to find a vast light towering out of the dark, as if someone were swinging an immense white beam of communication in the black boughs of the tree of night. And the ship creeps invisible under the pure white branches of the light of men, down on the little lustre of the sea. We are entering Plymouth Sound.

"Breathes there a man with soul so dead—?"

There are the small lights on the soft blackness that must be land. Far off, ahead, a tiny row of lights that must be the Hoe. And the ship slowly pulses forward, at half speed, venturing in.

England! So still! So remote-seeming! Across what mysterious belt of isolation does England lie! "It doesn't seem like a big civilized country," says the Cuban behind me. "It seems as if there were no people in it."

"Yes!" cries the German woman. "So still! So still! As if one could never come to it."

And that is how it seems, as you slowly steam up the Sound in the night, and watch the little lights that must be land, on the unspeaking darkness. The darkness doesn't speak, as the darkness of the coast of

America, or of Spain for example, speaks in the night when you are passing.

Slowly the ship lapses to silence in mid-water. A tender lit up with red and white and yellow lights—the German woman calls it the Christmas-tree boat—hovers round the stern and comes up on the lee-ward side. It looks curiously empty, in spite of its lights. And with strange quick quietness, the English sailors make fast. Queer to hear English voices below on the tender, so curiously quiet and withheld, against the noise of Spanish and German we are used to on board.

It is the same with English voices of sailors making fast the ropes, as with the sight of land. They do not stir the darkness. They do not come through. Quickly, quietly, the ladder is put up. Quickly, quietly, the police and passport people come on board. All is strangely still, and the ship, which at tea-time was still lively with mixed nationalities, seems deserted. England is on board—everything has fallen silent.

Quietly, quickly, softly, everything is done, and we are landed. There is a strange absence of something, an absentness is felt in everything and in everybody. I think, in the ordinary come-and-go of life, only the Englishman is really civilized. So, the soft, quiet, vague landing, the vague looking at the luggage, the vague finding oneself in the hotel in Plymouth. Everything soft, vague, with the quiet of accomplished civil-ization. Accomplished, that is, in these matters of landing from a ship and finding oneself in an hotel.

And it is the first night ashore, in the curious stillness. I cannot say wherein lies the almost deathly sense of stillness one gets, returning to England from the west. Landing in San Francisco gave me the feeling of intolerable crackling noise. But London gives me a dead muffled sense of stillness, as if nothing had any resonance. Everything muffled, or muted, and no sharp contact, no sharp reaction anywhere. As if all the traffic went on deep sand, heavily, straining the heart, and hushed.

I must confess, this curious mutedness of my native land frightens me more than the noise of New York or of Mexico City. Since the sparking of the Lands End light, and the great strong beaming of the lighthouse overhead, tall overhead like a great tree, at the entrance to the Sound, I have not had one single sharp impression in England. Everything seems sand-bagged, like when a ship hangs bags of sand over her side to deaden the bump with the wharf. So it is here. Every impact, every contact is sand-bagged, deadened. Everything that every-body says is modified beforehand, to prevent any kind of bump. Everything that everybody feels is keyed down, and muted, so as not to impinge on anybody else's feelings.

And this, in the end, becomes a madness. One sits in the breakfast car in the train, coming to London. There is a strange tension. What is the curious unease that holds the car spell-bound? In America the Pullmans, being much heavier, don't shake like our cars. And there seems more room, inside and out, morally and physically. It is possible the American manners are not so good, though I doubt if I agree, even there. The silent bad manners of the Englishman when he happens to decide that he is not among his own "sort," take a lot of beating. But of course, he never says or does anything, so he is perfectly safe and proper in his circumstance.

But there one sits in a breakfast car on the Great Western. The train shakes terribly. The waiters are quick and soft and attentive, but the food isn't very good, and one feels as if one were some sort of ghost being waited on by men who have long ago gone to sleep, and are serving one in their sleep. The place feels tight: one would like to smash something. Outside, a tight little landscape goes by, just unbelievable, with sunshine like thin water, a horizon half a mile away, and everything crowded forward into one's face till one gasps for space and breath, and tries to jerk one's head back, as one does when someone pushes his face right under one's hat-brim. Too horribly close!

Inside, we eat kippers and bacon. The place is full. The other people, mostly men, all keep themselves modified and muted, as if they didn't want their aura to stray beyond the four legs of their chair. Inside this charmed circle of their self-constraint they seem to sit and smile with pleasant English faces. And, of course, they are all trying to be a bit "grander" than they really are: to give the impression that they have more servants in the kitchen than they really have, and so on. That is part of the English naïveté! If they have two servants, they want to give the impression of four: not less than four.

Essentially, however, and apart from being "grand," each one of them sits complacent inside a crystal bubble, smiling and eating and sprinkling sugar on porridge, and then half-furtively glancing through the transparency of their bubble, to see if there is anything outside. They will never allow anything outside: except, of course, other bubbles of varying "grandness."

In the small things of life, the Englishman is the only perfectly civilized being. But God save me from such civilization. God in heaven deliver me. The trick lies in tensely withholding oneself, tensely withholding one's aura, till it forms a perfect and transparent little globe around one. At the centre of this little globe sits the Englishman, his own little god unto himself, terribly complacent, and at the same time, terribly self-deprecating. He seems to say: My dear man, I know I am no more than what I am. I wouldn't trespass on what you are, not for worlds. Oh, not for worlds! Because when all's said and done, what you are means nothing to me. I am god inside my own crystal world, the strictly limited domain of myself, which after all no one can deny is my own. I am only god within the bubble of my own self-contained being, dear sir; but there, god I am, so how could I possibly desire to trespass? I only urge that all other people shall be as self-contained and as little inclined to trespass. And they may be gods inside their own bubbles if they like.

Hence the feeling of intolerable shut-in-edness. One enters from the open sea, to the Channel: first box. Into Plymouth Sound: second box. Into the customs place: third box. Into the hotel: fourth. Into the dining car of the train: fifth. And so on and so on, like those Chinese boxes that fit one inside the other, and at the very middle is a tiny porcelain figure half an inch long. That is how one feels. Like a tiny porcelain figure shut in inside box after box of repeated and intensified shut-in-edness. It is enough to send one mad.

That is coming home, home to one's fellow countrymen! In one sense—the small ways of life—they are the nicest and most civilized people in the world. But there they are: each one of them a perfect little accomplished figure, enclosed first and foremost within the box, or bubble, of his own self-contained ego, and afterwards in all the other boxes he has made for himself, for his own safety.

At the centre of himself he is complacent, and even "superior." It strikes one very hard, coming home, that every Englishman sits there feeling subtly "superior." He wouldn't impose anything on anybody, dear me no. That is part of his own superiority. He is too superior to make any imposition of himself in any way. But like a pleased image, there he sits at the centre of his own bubble, and feels superior. Superior to what? Oh, nothing in particular, don't you know. Just superior. And well—if you press him—superior to everything. Just damn superior to everything. There inside the bubble of his own self-constraint, his own illusion, the strange germ of his unnatural conceit.

This is my own, my native land.

He seems to have accomplished the trick of being at his ease, the gentleman in the breakfast car, sprinkling sugar on his porridge. He knows he has a pretty way of sprinkling sugar on porridge: he knows he can put the spoon back prettily into the sugar-bowl: he knows his voice is cultured and his smile charming, compared to the rest of the world. It is quite obvious he means no one ill. Surely it is obvious he would like to give every man the best that man could have. If it were his, to give, which it isn't. And finally he knows he is able to contain himself. He is an Englishman and he is himself, he is able to contain and to constrain himself, and to live within the unbroken bubble of his own self-constraint, without letting his aura stray and get at cross-purposes with other people's auras. The dear, dangerless patrician!

Yet something does stray out of him. Look into his nice, bright, apparently-smiling English eyes. They are not smiling. And look again at his nice fresh English face, that seems so pleased with life. It also is not smiling, any more than Mr. Lloyd George is really smiling. The eyes are not really at ease, and the nice, fresh face is not at ease either. At the centre of the eyes, where the smile twinkles, there is fear. Even at the middle of this amiable and all-tolerant English complacency, there is fear. And the smile-wrinkles on the fresh, pleased face, they give odd quivers, and look like spite wrinkles. There strays out of him, in spite of all his self-constraining, the faint effluence of fear, and the sense of impotence, and a quiver of spite, of subdued malice. Underneath the soft civilizedness of him, fear, impotence, and malice.

> Whose heart within him ne'er hath burned
> As home his wandering steps he turned
> From travelling in a foreign land.

That's how one finds the Englishman at home. And then one understands the bitterness of Englishmen abroad in the world, especially Englishmen in responsible positions.

There is no denying this: that since the war, England's prestige has declined terribly, all over the world. Ah, says the Englishman, that's because America has the dollars. And there you hear the voice of England's own downfall.

England's prestige wasn't based on money. It was based on the imagination of men. England was supposed to be proud, and at the same time, free. Proud in her freedom, and free, to a certain extent generous, truly generous, in her pride.

This was the England that led the world. Myself, I think this was a true conception of England at her best. This was how the other nations accepted her: at her best. And the individual Englishman got his certain honour, in the world, on the strength of it.

Now? Now he still receives the remnants of honour, but mockingly, as poor Russian counts receive a little mocking distinction, now that they have to sell newspapers. The real English pride has gone, and "superiority" takes its place: a really imbecile superiority, which the world laughs at.

As far as the wide world is concerned, England is anything but superior. She is just humiliated. From day to day she makes a more humiliated spectacle of herself in the eyes of the world. Weak, vacillating, without purpose or policy, without even the last vestige of pride, she continues to apologize and deprecate on the platform of the world.

And of course individual Englishmen abroad feel it. You rarely meet an Englishman far from home, but he is burning with impatience, disgust, and even contempt, of home. Home seems a shoddy place. And when you get here, it's even shoddier than it seems from afar.

If, abroad, you meet an Englishman in office, he is speechless, almost cynical with rage. "What can I do!" he says. "What can I do, against the orders from home. I get orders that I must give no loop-hole for offence against America. All I have to do is to guard against giving offence, above all to America. I must be on my knees all the time, in front of America, begging her not to take offence, when she hasn't the faintest intention even of taking offence."

This is from a man who has lived out in the world, and who knows that the moment you go down on your knees to a man, he spits on you: and quite right too. Men have no business on their knees.

"I have an Englishman wants to go into the United States: Washington has given him a visa, and said: Yes, you can enter whenever you like. Comes a cable from London: Prevent this man from crossing into the United States, Washington might not like it. What can one do?"

The same story everywhere. A man is building a railway with nigger labour. Some insolent Jamaica nigger—British subject, larger than life—brings a charge against his boss. Solemn trial by the British, influence from the government, the Englishman is reprimanded, and nigger smiles and spits in his face.

Long live the bottom dog! May he devour us all.

Same story from India, from Egypt, from China. At home, a lot of queer, insane, half-female-seeming men, not quite men at all, and certainly not women! The women would be far braver. Then abroad, a few Englishmen still struggling.

England seems to me the one really soft spot, the rotten spot in the empire. If ever men had to think in world terms, they have to think in world terms today. And here you get an island no bigger than a back garden, chock-full of people who never realize there is anything outside their back garden, pretending to direct the destinies of the world. It is pathetic and ridiculous. And the "superiority" is bathetic to lunacy.

These poor "superior" gentry, all that is left to them is to blame the Americans. It amazes me, the rancour with which English people speak of Americans. Just because the republican eagle of the west doesn't choose to be a pelican for other people's convenience. Why should it?

After all, rancour is a bad sign in a superior person. It is a sign of impotence. The superior Englishman feels impotent against the American dollar, so he is wildly rancorous, in private, when America can't hear him.

Now I am an Englishman. And I know that if my countrymen still have a soul to sell, they'll sell it for American dollars, and drive a hard bargain.

Which is what I call being truly superior to the dollar.

This is my own, my native land.*

It was such a brave country, for so many years: the old brave, reckless, manly England. Even a man with dyed whiskers, like Palmerston. Too brave and reckless to be treacherous. My England.

Look at us now. Not a man left inside all the millions of pairs of trousers. Not a man left. A host of would-be-amiable cowards shut up each in his own bubble of conceit, and the whole lot within box after box of safeguards.

One could shout with laughter at the figures inside these endless safety boxes. Except that one is still English, and therefore flabbergasted. My own, my native land just leaves me flabbergasted.

* Lawrence has misquoted Scott's *The Lay of the Last Minstrel*. The accepted reading of these first six lines of Canto VI is: 'Breathes there the man, with soul so dead,/Who never to himself hath said,/This is my own, my native land!/Whose heart hath ne'er within him burn'd,/As home his footsteps he hath turn'd,/From wandering on a foreign strand!' Eds.

[Return to Bestwood]

I came home to the Midlands for a few days, at the end of September. Not that there is any home, for my parents are dead. But there are my sisters, and the district one calls home; that mining district between Nottingham and Derby.

It always depresses me to come to my native district. Now I am turned forty, and have been more or less a wanderer for nearly twenty years, I feel more alien, perhaps, in my home place than anywhere else in the world. I can feel at ease in Canal Street, New Orleans, or in the Avenue Madero, in Mexico City, or in George Street, Sydney, in Trincomallee Street, Kandy, or in Rome or Paris or Munich or even London. But in Nottingham Road, Bestwood, I feel at once a devouring nostalgia and an infinite repulsion. Partly I want to get back to the place as it was when I was a boy, and I waited so long to be served in the Co-op I remember our Co-op number, 1553A.L., better than the date of my birth—and when I came out hugging a string net of groceries. There was a little hedge across the road from the Co-op then, and I used to pick the green buds which we called bread-and-cheese. And there were no houses in Gabes Lane. And at the corner of Queen Street, Butcher Bob was huge and fat and taciturn.

Butcher Bob is long dead, and the place is all built up. I am never quite sure where I am, in Nottingham Road. Walker Street is not very much changed, though, because the ash tree was cut down when I was sixteen, when I was ill. The houses are still only on one side the street, the fields on the other. And still one looks across at the amphitheatre of hills which I still find beautiful, though there are new patches of reddish houses, and a darkening of smoke. Crich is still on the sky line to the west, and the woods of Annesley to the north, and Coney Grey Farm still lies in front. And there is still a certain glamour about the country-side. Curiously enough, the more motor-cars and tram-cars and omnibuses there are rampaging down the roads, the more the country retreats into its own isolation, and becomes more mysteriously inaccessible.

When I was a boy, the whole population lived very much more *with* the country. Now, they rush and tear along the roads, and have joy-rides and outings, but they never seem to touch the reality of the country-side. There are many more people, for one thing: and all these new contrivances, for another.

The country seems, somehow, fogged over with people, and yet not really touched. It seems to lie back, away, unreached and asleep. The roads are hard and metalled and worn with everlasting rush. The very field-paths seem wider and more trodden and squalid. Wherever you go, there is the sordid sense of humanity.

And yet the fields and the woods in between the roads and paths sleep as in a heavy, weary dream, disconnected from the modern world.

This visit, this September, depresses me peculiarly. The weather is soft and mild, mildly sunny in that hazed, dazed, uncanny sunless sunniness which makes the Midlands peculiarly fearsome to me. I cannot, cannot accept as sunshine this thin luminous vaporousness which passes as a fine day in the place of my birth. Oh Phœbus Apollo! Surely you have turned your face aside!

But the special depression this time is the great coal strike, still going on. In house after house, the families are now living on bread and margarine and potatoes. The colliers get up before dawn, and are away into the last recesses of the country-side, scouring the country for blackberries, as if there were a famine. But they will sell the blackberries at fourpence a pound, and so they'll be fourpence in pocket.

But when I was a boy, it was utterly *infra dig.* for a miner to be picking blackberries. He would never have demeaned himself to such an unmanly occupation. And as to walking home with a little basket—he would almost rather have committed murder. The children might do it, or the women, or even the half grown youths. But a married, manly collier!

But nowadays, their pride is in their pocket, and the pocket has a hole in it.

It is another world. There are policemen everywhere, great big strange policemen with faces like a leg of mutton. Where they come from, heaven only knows: Ireland or Scotland, presumably, for they are no Englishmen. And they exist, along the country-side, in thousands. The people call them "blue-bottles," and "meat-flies." And you can hear a woman call across the street to another: "Seen any blow-flies about?"—Then they turn to look at the alien policemen, and laugh shrilly.

And this in my native place! Truly, one no longer knows the palm of his own hand. When I was a boy, we had our own police sergeant, and two young constables. And the women would as leave have thought of calling Sergeant Mellor a "blue-bottle" as calling Queen Victoria one. The Sergeant was a quiet, patient man, who spent his life trying to keep people out of trouble. He was another sort of shepherd, and the miners and their children were a flock to him. The women had the utmost respect for him.

But the women seem to have changed most in this, that they have no respect for anything. There was a scene in the market-place yesterday, a Mrs Hufton and a Mrs Rowley being taken off to court to be tried for insulting and obstructing the police. The police had been escorting the black-legs from the mines, after a so-called day's work, and the women had made the usual row. They were two women from decent homes. In the past they would have died of shame, at having to go to court. But now, not at all.

They had a little gang of women with them in the market-place, waving red flags and laughing loudly and using occasional bad language. There was one, the decent wife of the post-man. I had known her and played with her as a girl. But she was waving her red flag, and cheering as the motor-bus rolled up.

The two culprits got up, hilariously, into the bus.

"Good luck, old girl! Let 'em have it! Give it the blue-bottles in the neck! Tell 'em what for! Three cheers for Bestwood! Strike while the iron's hot, girls!"

"So long! So long, girls! See you soon! Merry home coming, what, eh?"

"Have a good time, now! Have a good time! Stick a pin in their fat backsides, if you can't move 'em any other road. We s'll be thinking of you!"

"So long! So long! See you soon! Who says Walker!"

"E-eh! E-eh!"

The bus rolled heavily off, with the shouting women, amid the strange hoarse cheering of the women in the little market-place. The draughty little market-place where my mother shopped on Friday evenings, in her rusty little black bonnet, and where now a group of decent women waved little red flags and hoarsely cheered two women going to court!

O mamma mia!—as the Italians say. My dear mother, your little black bonnet would fly off your head in horrified astonishment, if you saw it now. You were so keen on progress: a decent working man, and a good wage! You paid my father's union pay for him, for so many years! You believed so firmly in the Co-op! You were at your Women's

Guild when they brought you word your father, the old tyrannus, was dead! At the same time, you believed so absolutely in the ultimate benevolence of all the masters, of all the upper classes. One had to be grateful to them, after all!

Grateful! You can have your cake and eat it, while the cake lasts. When the cake comes to an end, you can hand on your indigestion. Oh my dear and virtuous mother, who believed in a Utopia of goodness, so that your own people were never quite good enough for you—not even the spoiled delicate boy, myself!—oh my dear and virtuous mother, behold the indigestion we have inherited, from the cake of perfect goodness you baked too often! Nothing was good enough! We must all rise into the upper classes! Upper! Upper! Upper!

Till at last the boots are all uppers, the sole is worn out, and we yell as we walk on stones.

My dear, dear mother, you were so tragic, because you had nothing to be tragic about! We, on the other side, having a moral and social indigestion that would raise the wind for a thousand explosive tragedies, let off a mild crepitus ventris and shout: Have a good time, old girl! Enjoy yourself, old lass!

Nevertheless, we have all of us "got on." The reward of goodness, in my mother's far-off days, less than twenty years ago, was that you should "get on." *Be good, and you'll get on in life.*

Myself, a snotty-nosed little collier's lad, I call myself at home when I sit in a heavy old Cinquecento Italian villa, of which I rent only half, even then—surely I can be considered to have "got on." When I wrote my first book, and it was going to be published—sixteen years ago—and my mother was dying, a fairly well-known editor wrote to my mother and said, of me: "By the time he is forty, he will be riding in his carriage."

To which my mother is supposed to have said, sighing, "Ay, if he lives to be forty!"

Well, I am forty-one, so there's one in the eye for that sighing remark. I was always weak in health, but my life was strong. Why had they all made up their minds that I was to die? Perhaps they thought I was too good to live. Well, in that case they were had!

And when I was forty, I was not even in my own motor-car. But I did drive my own two horses in a light buggy (my own) on a little ranch (also my own, or my wife's, through me) away on the western slope of the Rocky Mountains. And sitting in my corduroy trousers and blue shirt, calling: "Get up Aaron! *Ambrose!*" then I thought of Justin Harrison's prophecy. Oh Oracle of Delphos! Oracle of Dodona!

"Get up, Ambrose!" Bump! went the buggy over a rock, and the pine-needles slashed my face! See him driving in his carriage, at forty! —driving it pretty badly too! Put the brake on!

So I suppose I've got on, snotty-nosed little collier's lad, of whom most of the women said: "He's a *nice* little lad!" They don't say it now: if ever they say anything, which is doubtful. They've forgotten me entirely.

But my sister's "getting on" is much more concrete than mine. She is almost on the spot. Within six miles of that end dwelling in The Breach, which is the house I first remember—an end house of hideous rows of miners' dwellings, though I loved it, too—stands my sister's new house, "a lovely house!"—and her garden: "I wish mother could see my garden in June!"

And if my mother did see it, what then? It is wonderful the flowers that bloom in these Midlands, in June. A northern Persephone seems to steal out from the Plutonic, coal-mining depths and give a real hoot of blossoms. But if my mother *did* return from the dead, and see that garden in full bloom, and the glass doors open from the hall of the new house, what then? Would she then say: It is reached! Consummatum est!

When Jesus gave up the ghost, he cried: It is finished. Consummatum est! But was it? And if so, what? What was it that was consummate?

Likewise, before the war, in Germany I used to see advertised in the newspapers a moustache-lifter, which you tied on at night and it would make your moustache stay turned up, like the immortal moustache of Kaiser Wilhelm II, whose moustache alone is immortal. This moustache-lifter was called: Es ist erreicht! In other words: It is reached! Consummatum est!

Was it? Was it reached? With the moustache-lifter?

So the ghost of my mother, in my sister's garden. I see it each time I am there, bending over the violas, or looking up at the almond tree. Actually an almond tree! And I always ask, of the grey-haired, good little ghost: "Well what of it, my dear? What is the verdict?"

But she never answers, though I press her:

"Do look at the house, my dear! Do look at the tiled hall, and the rug from Mexico, and the brass from Venice, seen through the open doors, beyond the lilies and the carnations of the lawn beds! Do look! And do look at me, and see if I'm not a gentleman! Do say that I'm almost upper class!"

But the dear little ghost says never a word.

"Do say we've got on! Do say we've arrived. Do say it is reached, es ist erreicht, consummatum est!"

But the little ghost turns aside, she knows I am teasing her. She gives me one look, which is a look I know, and which says: "I shan't tell you, so you can't laugh at me. You must find out for yourself." And she steals away, to her place, wherever it may be.—"In my father's house are many mansions. If it were not so, I would have told you."

The black-slate roofs beyond the wind-worn young trees at the end of the garden are the same thick layers of black roofs of blackened brick houses, as ever. There is the same smell of sulphur from the burning pit bank. Smuts fly on the white violas. There is a harsh sound of machinery. Persephone couldn't quite get out of hell, so she let Spring fall from her lap along the upper workings.

But no! There are no smuts, there is even no smell of the burning pit bank. They cut the bank, and the pits are not working. The strike has been going on for months. It is September, but there are lots of roses on the lawn beds.

"Where shall we go this afternoon? Shall we go to Hardwick?"

Let us go to Hardwick. I have not been for twenty years. Let us go to Hardwick:

> Hardwick Hall
> More window than wall.

Built in the days of good Queen Bess, by that other Bess, termagant and tartar, Countess of Shrewsbury.

Butterley, Alfreton, Tibshelf—what was once the Hardwick district is now the Notts-Derby coal area. The country is the same, but scarred and splashed all over with mines and mining settlements. Great houses loom from hill-brows, old villages are smothered in rows of miners' dwellings, Bolsover Castle rises from the mass of the colliery village of Bolsover.—Böwser, we called it, when I was a boy.

Hardwick is shut. On the gates, near the old inn, where the atmosphere of the old world lingers perfect, is a notice: "This park is closed to the public and to all traffic until further notice. No admittance."

Of course! The strike! They are afraid of vandalism.

Where shall we go? Back into Derbyshire, or to Sherwood Forest.

Turn the car. We'll go on through Chesterfield. If I can't ride in my own carriage, I can still ride in my sister's motor-car.

It is a still September afternoon. By the ponds in the old park, we see colliers slowly loafing, fishing, poaching in spite of all notices.

And at every lane end there is a bunch of three or four policemen, "blue-bottles," big, big-faced, stranger policemen. Every field path, every stile seems to be guarded. There are great pits, coal mines, in the fields. And at the end of the paths coming out of the field from the colliery, along the high-road, the colliers are squatted on their heels, on the wayside grass, silent and watchful. Their faces are clean, white, and all the months of the strike have given them no colour and no tan. They are pit-bleached. They squat in silent remoteness, as if in the upper galleries of hell. And the policemen, alien, stand in a group near the stile. Each lot pretends not to be aware of the others.

It is past three. Down the path from the pit come straggling what my little nephew calls "the dirty ones." They are the men who have broken strike, and gone back to work. They are not many: their faces are black, they are in their pit-dirt. They linger till they have collected, a group of a dozen or so "dirty ones," near the stile, then they trail off down the road, the policemen, the alien "blue-bottles," escorting them. And the "clean ones," the colliers still on strike, squat by the wayside and watch without looking. They say nothing. They neither laugh nor stare. But here they are, a picket, and with their bleached faces they see without looking, and they register with the silence of doom, squatted down in rows by the road-side.

The "dirty ones" straggle off in the lurching, almost slinking walk of colliers, swinging their heavy feet and going as if the mine-roof were still over their heads. The big blue policemen follow at a little distance. No voice is raised: nobody seems aware of anybody else. But there is the silent, hellish registering in the consciousness of all three groups, clean ones, dirty ones and blue-bottles.

So it is now all the way into Chesterfield, whose crooked spire lies below. The men who have gone back to work—they seem few, indeed —are lurching and slinking in quiet groups, home down the high-road, the police at their heels. And the pickets, with bleached faces, squat and lean and stand, in silent groups, with a certain pale fatality, like Hell, upon them.

And I, who remember the homeward-trooping of the colliers when I was a boy, the ringing of the feet, the red mouths and the quick whites of the eyes, the swinging pit bottles, and the strange voices of men from the underworld calling back and forth, strong and, it seemed to me, gay with the queer, absolved gaiety of miners—I shiver, and feel I turn into a ghost myself. The colliers were noisy, lively, with strong underworld voices such as I have never heard in any other men, when I was a boy. And after all, it is not so long ago. I am only forty-one.

But after the war, the colliers went silent: after 1920. Till 1920 there was a strange power of life in them, something wild and urgent, that one could hear in their voices. They were always excited, in the afternoon, to come up above-ground: and excited, in the morning, at going down. And they called in the darkness with strong, strangely evocative voices. And at the little local foot-ball matches, on the damp, dusky Saturday afternoons of winter, great, full-throated cries came howling from the foot-ball field, in the zest and the wildness of life.

But now, the miners go by to the foot-ball match in silence like ghosts, and from the field comes a poor, ragged shouting. These are the men of my own generation, who went to the board school with me. And they are almost voiceless. They go to the welfare clubs, and drink with a sort of hopelessness.

I feel I hardly know any more the people I come from, the colliers of the Erewash Valley district. They are changed, and I suppose I am changed. I find it so much easier to live in Italy. And they have got a new kind of shallow consciousness, all newspaper and cinema, which I am not in touch with. At the same time, they have, I think, an underneath ache and heaviness very much like my own. It must be so, because when I see them, I feel it so strongly.

They are the only people who move me strongly, and with whom I feel myself connected in deeper destiny. It is they who are, in some peculiar way, "home" to me. I shrink away from them, and I have an acute nostalgia for them.

And now, this last time, I feel a doom over the country, and a shadow of despair over the hearts of the men, which leaves me no rest. Because the same doom is over me, wherever I go, and the same despair touches my heart.

Yet it is madness to despair, while we still have the course of destiny open to us.

One is driven back to search one's own soul, for a way out into a new destiny.

A few things I know, with inner knowledge.

I know that what I am struggling for is life, more life ahead, for myself and the men who will come after me: struggling against fixations and corruptions.

I know that the miners at home are men very much like me, and I am very much like them: ultimately, we want the same thing. I know they are, in the life sense of the word, good.

I know that there is ahead the mortal struggle for property.

I know that the ownership of property has become, now, a problem, a religious problem. But it is one we can solve.

I know I want to own a few things: my personal things. But I also know I want to own no more than those. I don't want to own a house, nor land, nor a motor-car, nor shares in anything. I don't want a fortune—not even an assured income.

At the same time, I don't want poverty and hardship. I know I need enough money to leave me free in my movements, and I want to be able to earn that money without humiliation.

I know that most decent people feel very much the same in this respect: and the indecent people must, in their indecency, be subordinated to the decent.

I know that we could, if we would, establish little by little a true democracy in England: we could nationalise the land and industries and means of transport, and make the whole thing work infinitely better than at present, *if we would*. It all depends on the spirit in which the thing is done.

I know we are on the brink of a class war.

I know we had all better hang ourselves at once, than enter on a struggle which shall be a fight for the ownership or non-ownership of property, pure and simple, and nothing beyond.

I know the ownership of property is a problem that may have to be fought out. But beyond the fight must lie a new hope, a new beginning.

I know our vision of life is all wrong. We must be prepared to have a new conception of what it means, *to live*. And everybody should try to help to build up this new conception, and everybody should be prepared to destroy, bit by bit, our old conception.

I know that man cannot live by his own will alone. With his soul, he must search for the sources of the power of life. It is life we want.

I know that where there is life, there is essential beauty. Genuine beauty, which fills the soul, is an indication of life, and genuine ugliness, which blasts the soul, is an indication of morbidity.—But prettiness is opposed to beauty.

I know that, first and foremost, we must be sensitive to life and to its movements. If there is power, it must be sensitive power.

I know that we must look after the quality of life, not the quantity. Hopeless life should be put to sleep, the idiots and the hopeless sick and the true criminal. And the birth-rate should be controlled.

I know we must take up the responsibility for the future, now. A great change is coming, and must come. What we need is some glimmer of a vision of a world that shall be, beyond the change. Otherwise we shall be in for a great débâcle.

What is alive, and open, and active, is good. All that makes for inertia, lifelessness, dreariness, is bad. This is the essence of morality.

What we should live for is life and the beauty of aliveness, imagination, awareness, and contact. To be perfectly alive is to be immortal.

I know these things, along with other things. And it is nothing very new to know these things. The only new thing would be to act on them.

And what is the good of saying these things, to men whose whole education consists in the fact that twice two are four?—which, being interpreted, means that twice tuppence is fourpence. All our education, the whole of it, is formed upon this little speck of dust.

IV
Reviews and Introductions

A Review of *The Oxford Book of German Verse* edited by H. G. Fiedler

This book seems to us extraordinarily delightful. From Walther von der Vogelweide onwards, there are here all the poems in German which we have cherished since school days. The earlier part of the book seems almost like a breviary. It is remarkable how near to the heart many of these old German poems lie; almost like the scriptures. We do not question or examine them. Our education seems built on them.

> Geh aus, mein Herz, und suche Freud,
> In dieser lieben Sommerzeit
> An deines Gottes Gaben . .

Then again, so many of the poems are known to us as music, Beethoven, Schubert, Schumann, Brahms and Wolf, that the earlier part of the book stands unassailable, beyond question or criticism.

There are very few of the known things that we may complain of missing. Heine's "Thalatta" is not included—but it is foolish to utter one's personal regrets, when so much of the best is given.

For most of us, German poetry ends with Heine. If we know Mörike we are exceptional. In this anthology, however, Heine is finished on page 330, while the last poem in the book, by Schaukal, is on page 532; that is, two hundred pages of nineteenth-century verse. It is a large proportion. And it is this part of the book that, whilst it interests us absorbingly, leaves us in the end undecided and unsatisfied.

Lenau, Keller, Meyer, Storm, Mörike are almost classics. Over the seven pages of Paul Heyse we hesitate uncertainly; would we not rather have given more space to Liliencron, and less to Heyse?—although Liliencron is well represented. But this soldier poet is so straight, so free from the modern artist's hyper-sensitive self-consciousness, that we would have more of him. We wish England had a poet like him, to give grit to our modern verse.

TOD IN ÄHREN

> Im Weizenfeld, in Korn und Mohn
> Liegt ein Soldat, unaufgefunden,
> Zwei Tage schon, zwei Nächte schon,
> Mit schweren Wunden, unverbunden.

Durstüberquält und fieberwild,
Im Todeskampf den Kopf erhoben.
Ein letzter Traum, ein letztes Bild,
Sein brechend Auge schlägt nach oben.

Die Sense sirrt im Ährenfeld,
Er sieht sein Dorf im Arbeitsfrieden.
Ade, ade du Heimatwelt—
Und beugt das Haupt und ist verschieden.

The selections from Dehmel are not so satisfactory. It is not at all certain whether these poems are altogether representative of the author of "Aber die Liebe" and the "Verwandlungen der Venus." Dehmel is a fascinating poet, but he for ever leaves us doubtful in what rank to place him. He is turgid and violent, his music is often harsh, usually discomforting. He seems to lack reserve. It is very difficult to decide upon him. Then suddenly a fragment will win us over:—

NACH EINEM REGEN

Sieh, der Himmel wird blau;
Die Schwalben jagen sich
Wie Fische über den nassen Birken.
Und du willst weinen?

In deiner Seele werden bald
Die blanken Bäume und blauen Vögel
Ein goldnes Bild sein.
Und du weinst?

Mit meinen Augen
Seh' ich in deinen
Zwei kleine Sonnen,
Und du lächelst.

Hauptmann is dramatic and stirring, Bierbaum sings pleasantly, Max Dauthendey's brief, impersonal sketches have a peculiar power; one returns to them, and they remain in mind. Hofmannsthal, the symbolist, has three very interesting poems. There are many other names, some quite new, and one's interest is keenly roused. It is a question, where so many are admitted, why Geiger and Peter Baum and Elsa Lasker-Schüle have been excluded. But nothing is so easy as to carp at the compiler of an anthology; and no book, for a long time, has given us the pleasure that this has given.

A Review of *The Minnesingers*
by Jethro Bithell

This is a rather large, important-looking volume of translations with a few comparative footnotes, and a brief appendix which is scarcely scholarly, but shows the author has read widely in verse. It is to be followed next autumn by a second volume, a history of Minnesong as compared with the old lyrical poetry of Provence, Portugal and Italy. This second volume, we are told in the preface, is to be the "pièce de résistance."

"These translations," we read, "may be regarded as the by-products of a more painful process—the extraction of parallel passages. The two volumes should, by rights, have appeared together, but the translations were easier, and are finished first."

This considerably damps our ardour. "The translations were easier." It is a phrase that pricks the gay bladder of our enthusiasm.

The book is issued as an independent volume. It is not a scholastic work. It is an anthology, selected at the author's discretion, of translations of the chief of the Minnesong. That is, it is issued to us as a book of poetry. And instead of a book of poetry, we have a book of by-products.

"The translations were easier. . . ." As a result, we have a volume of crude, careless English verse which is not often poetry. Nevertheless, the author is so blithe and unconcerned and facile at his task, that the book has a certain charm.

The method of translation, we are told, is the "plaster-cast": that is, the outward form is strictly preserved. Also the author has striven to be "Sinngetreu" rather than "Wortgetreu"; to be true to the poet's thought rather than to his phrasing. But it is not so easy to be "Sinngetreu." The earlier Minnesingers especially are so naïve and winsome in the expression of their sentiment, that they are not to be translated off-hand. Take the very first verse in the book, and put it side by side with the original—none of the German originals, by the way, are included in this book:

Dû bist mîn, ich bin dîn: Mine thou art, thine am I:
Des solt dû gewis sîn.   Deem not that in this I lie.
Dû bist beslozzen   Locked thou art
In mînem herzen: In my heart:
Verlorn is das slüzzelîn: Never canst thou thence depart:
Dû muost immer drinne sîn.   For the key is lost, sweetheart.

The translation may be "Sinngetreu," but it has lost all poetry by the way. Then take the first stanza of Walther von der Vogelweide's well-known "Tantaradei," or "Unter den Linden."

On the heather-lea,
In the lime-tree bower,
There of us twain was made the bed:
There you may see
Grass-blade and flower
Sweetly crushed and shed.
By the forest, in a dale,
Tantaradei!
Sweetly sang the nightingale.

The translation certainly seems to have been easy, and in making it the author will have made enemies of all who remember the original.

Nevertheless, this blithe facility and unconcern on the author's part does give the book a certain quality, almost a charm of its own. And as the Minnesong goes on, becomes more narrative, more ballad-like, less delicately lyrical, it is easier to translate. There is solid stuff of narrative and of dramatic emotion, that does not vanish away in being conveyed from one language to another. And these later translations are often made very attractive by the author's irresponsible, artless manner.

In among the Minnesong is a good proportion of Volkslied. A bookful of courtly, mediæval love-song soon cloys. The lays of Marie de France sicken in the end. So the inclusion of coarse, harsh folksong among so much sugar-cream of sentimental love is welcome.

The book is very interesting, in spite of its faults.

A Review of *The Book of Revelation* by Dr. John Oman

The Apocalypse is a strange and mysterious book. One therefore welcomes any serious work upon it. Now Dr. John Oman (*The Book of Revelation*, Cambridge University Press, 7s. 6d. net) has undertaken the rearrangement of the sections into an intelligible order. The clue to the order lies in the idea that the theme is the conflict between true and false religion, false religion being established upon the Beast of world empire. Behind the great outward happenings of the world lie the greater, but more mysterious happenings of the divine ordination. The Apocalypse unfolds in symbols the dual event of the crashing-down of world empire and world civilization, and the triumph of men in the way of God.

Doctor Oman's rearrangement and his exposition give one a good deal of satisfaction. The main drift we can surely accept. John's passionate and mystic hatred of the civilization of his day, a hatred so intense only because he knew that the living realities of men's being were displaced by it, is something to which the soul answers now again. His fierce, new usage of the symbols of the four Prophets of the Old Testament gives one a feeling of relief, of release into passionate actuality, after the tight pettiness of modern intellect.

Yet we cannot agree that Dr. Oman's explanation of the Apocalypse is exhaustive. No explanation of symbols is final. Symbols are not intellectual quantities, they are not to be exhausted by the intellect.

And an Apocalypse has, must have, is intended to have various levels or layers or strata of meaning. The fall of World Rule and World Empire before the Word of God is certainly one stratum. And perhaps it would be easier to leave it at that. Only it is not satisfying.

Why should Doctor Oman oppose the view that, besides the drama of the fall of World Rule and the triumph of the Word, there is another drama, or rather several other concurrent dramas? We gladly accept Dr. Oman's interpretation of the two Women and the Beasts. But why should he appear so unwilling to accept any astrological reference?

Why should not the symbols have an astrological meaning, and the drama be also a drama of cosmic man, in terms of the stars?

As a matter of fact, old symbols have many meanings, and we only define one meaning in order to leave another undefined. So with the meaning of the Book of Revelation. Hence the inexhaustibility of its attraction.—L. H. DAVIDSON.

Foreword to *Women in Love*

This novel was written in its first form in the Tyrol, in 1913. It was altogether re-written and finished in Cornwall in 1917. So that it is a novel which took its final shape in the midst of the period of war, though it does not concern the war itself. I should wish the time to remain unfixed, so that the bitterness of the war may be taken for granted in the characters.

The book has been offered to various London publishers. Their almost inevitable reply has been "We should like very much to publish, but feel we cannot risk a prosecution." They remember the fate of "The Rainbow," and are cautious. This book is a potential sequel to "The Rainbow."

In England, I would never try to justify myself against any accusation. But to the Americans, perhaps I may speak for myself. I am accused, in England, of uncleanness and pornography. I deny the charge, and take no further notice.

In America the chief accusation seems to be one of "Eroticism." This is odd, rather puzzling to my mind. Which Eros? Eros of the jaunty "amours," or Eros of the sacred mysteries? And if the latter, why accuse, why not respect, even venerate?

Let us hesitate no longer to announce that the sensual passions and mysteries are equally sacred with the spiritual mysteries and passions. Who would deny it any more? The only thing unbearable is the degradation, the prostitution of the living mysteries in us. Let man only approach his own self with a deep respect, even reverence for all that the creative soul, the God-mystery within us, puts forth. Then we shall all be sound and free. Lewdness is hateful because it impairs our integrity and our proud being.

The creative, spontaneous soul sends forth its promptings of desire and aspiration in us. These promptings are our true fate, which is our business to fulfil. A fate dictated from outside, from theory or from circumstance, is a false fate.

This novel pretends only to be a record of the writer's own desires, aspirations, struggles; in a word, a record of the profoundest experiences in the self. Nothing that comes from the deep, passional soul is bad, or can be bad. So there is no apology to tender, unless to the soul itself, if it should have been belied.

Man struggles with his unborn needs and fulfilment. New unfoldings struggle up in torment in him, as buds struggle forth from the midst of a plant. Any man of real individuality tries to know and to understand what is happening, even in himself, as he goes along. This struggle for verbal consciousness should not be left out in art. It is a very great part of life. It is not superimposition of a theory. It is the passionate struggle into conscious being.

We are now in a period of crisis. Every man who is acutely alive is acutely wrestling with his own soul. The people that can bring forth the new passion, the new idea, this people will endure. Those others, that fix themselves in the old idea, will perish with the new life strangled unborn within them. Men must speak out to one another.

In point of style, fault is often found with the continual, slightly modified repetition. The only answer is that it is natural to the author: and that every natural crisis in emotion or passion or understanding comes from this pulsing, frictional to-and-fro, which works up to culmination.

Note on Giovanni Verga

Giovanni Verga, the Sicilian novelist and playwright, is surely the greatest writer of Italian fiction, after Manzoni.

Verga was born in Catania, Sicily, in 1840, and died in the same city, at the age of eighty-two, in January, 1922. As a young man he left Sicily to work at literature and mingle with society in Florence and Milan, and these two cities, especially the latter, claim a large share of his mature years. He came back, however, to his beloved Sicily, to Catania, the seaport under Etna, to be once more Sicilian of the Sicilians and spend his long declining years in his own place.

The first period of his literary activity was taken up with "Society" and elegant love. In this phase he wrote the novels *Eros, Eva, Tigre Reale, Il Marito di Elena*, real Italian novels of love, intrigue and "elegance": a little tiresome, but with their own depth. His fame, however, rests on his Sicilian works, the two novels: *I Malavoglia* and *Mastro-don Gesualdo*, and the various volumes of short sketches, *Vita dei Campi (Cavalleria Rusticana), Novelle Rusticane*, and *Vagabondaggio*, and then the earlier work *Storia di una Capinera*, a slight volume of letters between two schoolgirls, somewhat sentimental and once very popular.

The libretto of *Cavalleria Rusticana*, the well-known opera, was drawn from the first of the sketches in the volume *Vita dei Campi*.

As a man, Verga never courted popularity, any more than his work courts popularity. He kept apart from all publicity, proud in his privacy: so unlike D'Annunzio. Apparently he was never married.

In appearance, he was of medium height, strong and straight, with thick white hair, and proud dark eyes, and a big reddish moustache: a striking man to look at. The story "Across the Sea," playing as it does between the elegant life of Naples and Messina, and the wild places of south-east Sicily, is no doubt autobiographic. The great misty city would then be Milan.

Most of these sketches are said to be drawn from actual life, from the village where Verga lived and from which his family originally came. The landscape will be more or less familiar to anyone who has gone in the train down the east coast of Sicily to Syracuse, past Etna and the Plains of Catania and the Biviere, the Lake of Lentini, on to the hills again. And anyone who has once known this land can never be quite free from the nostalgia for it, nor can he fail to fall under the spell of Verga's wonderful creation of it, at some point or other.

The stories belong to the period of Verga's youth. The King with the little Queen was King Francis of Naples, son of Bomba. Francis and his little northern Queen fled before Garibaldi in 1860, so the story "So Much for the King" must be dated a few years earlier. And the auto-biographical sketch "Across the Sea" must belong to Verga's first man-hood, somewhere about 1870. Verga was twenty years old when Garibaldi was in Sicily and the little drama of "Liberty" took place in the Village on Etna.

During the 'fifties and 'sixties, Sicily is said to have been the poorest place in Europe: absolutely penniless. A Sicilian peasant might live through his whole life without ever possessing as much as a dollar, in hard cash. But after 1870 the great drift of Sicilian emigration set in, towards America. Sicilian young men came back from exile rich, accor-ding to standards in Sicily. The peasants began to buy their own land, instead of working on the half-profits system. They had a reserve fund for bad years. And the island in the Mediterranean began to prosper as it prospers still, depending on American resources. Only the gentry decline. The peasantry emigrate almost to a man, and come back as gentry themselves, American gentry.

Novelle Rusticane was first published in Turin, in 1883.

Introduction to *Mastro-don Gesualdo*
by Giovanni Verga

Giovanni Verga was born in the year 1840, and he died at the beginning of 1922, so that he is almost as much of a contemporary as Thomas Hardy. He seems more remote, because he left off writing many years before he died. He was a Sicilian from one of the lonely little townships in the south of the island, where his family were provincial gentlefolk. But he spent a good deal of his youth in Catania, the city on the sea, under Etna, and then he went to Naples, the metropolis; for Sicily was still part of the Bourbon kingdom of Naples.

As a young man he lived for a time in Milan and Florence, the intellectual centres, leading a more or less fashionable life and also practising journalism. A real provincial, he felt that the great world must be conquered, that it must hold some vital secret. He was apparently a great beau, and had a series of more or less distinguished love affairs, like an Alfred de Vigny or a Maupassant. In his early novels we see him in this phase. *Tigre Reale,* one of his most popular novels, is the story of a young Italian's love for a fascinating but very enigmatical (no longer so enigmatical) Russian countess of great wealth, married, but living in distinguished isolation alone in Florence. The enigmatical lady is, however, consumptive, and the end, in Sicily, is truly horrible, in the morbid and deathly tone of some of Matilde Serao's novels. The southerners seem to go that way, macabre. Yet in Verga the savage, manly tone comes through the morbidity, and we feel how he must have loathed the humiliation of fashionable life and fashionable love affairs. He kept it up, however, till after forty, then he retired back to his own Sicily, and shut himself up away from the world. He lived in aristocratic isolation for almost another forty years, and died in Catania, almost forgotten. He was a rather short, broad-shouldered man with a big red moustache.

It was after he had left the fashionable world that he wrote his best work. And this is no longer Italian, but Sicilian. In his Italian style, he manages to get the rhythm of colloquial Sicilian, and Italy no longer exists. Now Verga turns to the peasants of his boyhood, and it is they who fill his soul. It is their lives that matter.

There are three books of Sicilian sketches and short stories, very brilliant, and drenched with the atmosphere of Sicily. They are *Cavalleria Rusticana*, *Novelle Rusticane*, and *Vagabondaggio*. They open out another world at once, the southern, sun-beaten island whose every outline is like pure memory. Then there is a small novel about a girl who is condemned to a convent: *Storia di una Capinera*. And finally, there are the two great novels, *I Malavoglia* and *Mastro-don Gesualdo*. The sketches in *Cavalleria Rusticana* had already established Verga's fame. But it was *I Malavoglia* that was hailed as a masterpiece, in Paris as well as in Italy. It was translated into French by Jose-Maria de Heredia, and after that, into English by an American lady. The English translation, which weakens the book very much, came out in America in the 'nineties, under the title *The House by the Medlar Tree*, and can still be procured.

Speaking, in conversation, the other day about Giovanni Verga, in Rome, one of the most brilliant young Italian literary men said: There is Verga, ah yes! *Some* of his things! But a thing like the *Storia di una Capinera*, now, that is ridiculous.—And it was so obvious, the young man thought all Verga a little ridiculous. Because Verga *doesn't* write about lunatics and maniacs, like Pirandello, therefore he is ridiculous. It is the attitude of the smart young. They find Tolstoi ridiculous, George Eliot ridiculous, everybody ridiculous who is not "disillusioned."

The *Story of a Blackcap* is indeed sentimental and overloaded with emotion. But so is Dickens' *Christmas Carol*, or *Silas Marner*. They do not therefore become ridiculous.

It is a fault in Verga, partly owing to the way he had lived his life, and partly owing to the general tendency of all European literature of the eighteen-sixties and thereabouts, to pour too much emotion, and especially too much pity, over the humble poor. Verga's novel *I Malavoglia* is really spoilt by this, and by his exaggeration of the tragic fate of his humble fisher-folk. But then it is characteristic of the southerner, that when he has an emotion he has it wholesale. And the tragic fate of the humble poor was the stunt of that day. *Les Misérables* stands as the great monument to this stunt. The poor have lately gone rather out of favour, so Hugo stands at a rather low figure, and Verga hardly exists. But when we have got over our reaction against the pity-the-poor stunt, we shall see that there is a good deal of fun in Hugo, and that *I Malavoglia* is really a very great picture of Sicilian sea-coast life, far more human and *valid* than Victor Hugo's picture of Paris.

The trouble with the Italians is, they do tend to take over other people's stunts and exaggerate them. Even when they invent a stunt of their own, for some mysterious reason it *seems* second-hand. Victor Hugo's pity-the-poor was a real Gallic gesture. Verga's pity-the-poor is just a bit too much of a good thing, and it doesn't seem to come *quite* spontaneously from him. He had been inoculated. Or he had reacted.

In his last novel, *Mastro-don Gesualdo*, Verga has slackened off in his pity-the-poor. But he is still a realist, in the grim Flaubertian sense of the word. A realism which, as every one now knows, has no more to do with reality than romanticism has. Realism is just one of the arbitrary views man takes of man. It sees us all as little ant-like creatures toiling against the odds of circumstance, and doomed to misery. It is a kind of aeroplane view. It became the popular outlook, and so today we actually are, millions of us, little ant-like creatures toiling against the odds of circumstance, and doomed to misery; until we take a different view of ourselves. For man always becomes what he passionately thinks he is; since he is capable of becoming almost anything.

Mastro-don Gesualdo is a great realistic novel of Sicily, as *Madame Bovary* is a great realistic novel of France. They both suffer from the defects of the realistic method. I think the inherent flaw in *Madame Bovary*—though I hate talking about flaws in great books; but the charge is really against the realistic method—is that individuals like Emma and Charles Bovary are too insignificant to carry the full weight of Gustave Flaubert's profound sense of tragedy; or, if you will, of tragic futility. Emma and Charles Bovary are two ordinary persons, chosen because they *are* ordinary. But Flaubert is by no means an ordinary person. Yet he insists on pouring his own deep and bitter tragic consciousness into the little skins of the country doctor and his dissatisfied wife. The result is a certain discrepancy, even a certain dishonesty in the attempt to be too honest. By choosing *ordinary* people as the vehicles of an extraordinarily passionate feeling of bitterness, Flaubert loads the dice, and wins by a trick which is sure to be found out against him.

Because a great soul like Flaubert's has a pure satisfaction and joy in its own consciousness, even if the consciousness be only of ultimate tragedy or misery. But the very fact of being so marvellously and vividly *aware*, awake, as Flaubert's soul was, is in itself a refutation of the all-is-misery doctrine. Since the human soul has supreme joy in true, vivid consciousness. And Flaubert's soul has this joy. But Emma Bovary's soul does not, poor thing, because she was deliberately chosen because her soul was ordinary. So Flaubert cheats us a little, in his doctrine, if not in his art. And his art is biased by his doctrine as much as any artist's is.

The same is true of *Mastro-don Gesualdo*. Gesualdo is a peasant's son, who becomes rich in his own tiny town through his own force and sagacity. He is allowed the old heroic qualities of force and sagacity. Even Emma Bovary has a certain extraordinary female energy of restlessness and unsatisfied desire. So that both Flaubert and Verga allow their heroes something of the hero, after all. The one thing they deny them is the consciousness of heroic effort.

Now Flaubert and Verga alike were aware of their own heroic effort to be truthful, to show things as they are. It was the heroic impulse which made them write their great books. Yet they deny to their protagonists any inkling of the heroic effort. It is in this sense that Emma Bovary and Gesualdo Motta are "ordinary." Ordinary people don't have much sense of heroic effort in life; and by the heroic effort we mean that instinctive fighting for more life to come into being, which is a basic impulse in more men than we like to admit; women too. Or it used to be. The discrediting of the heroic effort has almost extinguished that effort in the young, hence the appalling "flatness" of their lives. It is the parents' fault. Life without the heroic effort, and without *belief* in the subtle, life-long validity of the heroic impulse, is just stale, flat and unprofitable. As the great realistic novels will show you.

Gesualdo Motta has the makings of a hero. Verga had to grant him something. I think it is in *Novelle Rusticane* that we find the long sketch or story of the little fat peasant who has become enormously rich by grinding his labourers and bleeding the Barons. It is a marvellous story, reeling with the hot atmosphere of Sicily, and the ironic fatalism of the Sicilians. And that little fat peasant must have been an actual man whom Verga knew—Verga wasn't good at inventing, he always had to have a core of actuality—and who served as the idea-germ for Gesualdo. But Gesualdo is much more attractive, much nearer the true hero. In fact, with all his energy and sagacity *and* his natural humaneness, we don't see how Gesualdo quite escaped the heroic consciousness. The original little peasant, the prototype, was a mere frog, a grabber and nothing else. He had none of Gesualdo's large humaneness. So that Verga brings Gesualdo much nearer to the hero, yet denies him still any spark of the heroic consciousness, any spark of awareness of a greater impulse within him. Men naturally have this spark, if they are the tiniest bit uncommon. The curious thing is, the moment you deny the spark, it dies, and then the heroic impulse dies with it.

It is probably true that, since the extinction of the pagan gods, the countries of the Mediterranean have never been aware of the heroic impulse in themselves, and so it has died down very low, in them. In Sicily, even now, and in the remoter Italian villages, there is what we call a low level of life, appalling. Just a squalid, unimaginative, heavy, petty-fogging, grubby sort of existence, without light or flame. It is the absence of the heroic awareness, the heroic hope.

The northerners have got over the death of the old Homeric idea of the hero, by making the hero self-conscious, and a hero by virtue of suffering and awareness of suffering. The Sicilians may have little spasms of this sort of heroic feeling, but it never lasts. It is not natural to them.

The Russians carry us to great lengths of introspective heroism. They escape the non-heroic dilemma of our age by making every man his own introspective hero. The merest scrub of a pickpocket is so phenomenally aware of his own soul, that we are made to bow down before the imaginary coruscations of suffering and sympathy that go on inside him. So is Russian literature.

Of course, your soul will coruscate with suffering and sympathy, if you think it does: since the soul is capable of anything, and is no doubt full of unimaginable coruscations which far-off future civilizations will wake up to. So far, we have only lately wakened up to the sympathy-suffering coruscation, so we are full of it. And that is why the Russians are so popular. No matter how much of a shabby little slut you may be, you can learn from Dostoevsky and Tchekov that you have got the most tender, unique soul on earth, coruscating with sufferings and impossible sympathies. And so you may be most vastly important to yourself, introspectively. Outwardly, you will say: Of course I'm an ordinary person, like everybody else.—But your very saying it will prove that you think the opposite: namely, that everybody on earth is ordinary, *except* yourself.

This is our northern way of heroism, up to date. The Sicilian hasn't yet got there. Perhaps he never will. Certainly he was nowhere near it in Gesualdo Motta's day, the mediæval Sicilian day of the middle of the last century, before Italy existed, and Sicily was still part of the Bourbon kingdom of Naples, and about as remote as the kingdom of Dahomey.

The Sicilian has no soul, except that funny little naked man who hops on hot bricks, in purgatory, and howls to be prayed out into paradise; and is in some mysterious way an *alter ego*, my me beyond the grave. This is the catholic soul, and there is nothing to do about it but to pay, and get it prayed into paradise.

For the rest, in our sense of the word, the Sicilian doesn't have any soul. He can't be introspective, because his consciousness, so to speak, doesn't have any inside to it. He can't look inside himself, because he is, as it were, solid. When Gesualdo is tormented by mean people, atrociously, all he says is: I've got bitter in my mouth.—And when he is dying, and has some awful tumour inside, he says: It is all the bitterness I have known, swelled up inside me.—That is all: a physical fact! Think what even Dmitri Karamazov would have made of it! And Dmitri Karamazov doesn't go half the lengths of the other Russian soul-twisters. Neither is he half the man Gesualdo is, although he may be much more "interesting," if you like soul-twisters.

In *Mastro-don Gesualdo* you have, in a sense, the same sort of tragedy as in the Russians, yet anything more un-Russian could not be imagined. Un-Russian almost as Homer. But Verga will have gods neither above nor below.

The Sicilians today are supposed to be the nearest descendants of the classic Greeks, and the nearest thing to the classic Greeks in life and nature. And perhaps it is true. Like the classic Greeks, the Sicilians have no insides, introspectively speaking. But, alas, outside they have no busy gods. It is their great loss. Because Jesus is to them only a wonder-man who was killed by foreigners and villains, and who will help you to get out of Hell, perhaps.

In the true sense of the word, the Sicily of Gesualdo is drearily godless. It needs the bright and busy gods outside. The inside gods, gods who have to be inside a man's soul, are distasteful to people who live in the sun. Once you get to Ceylon, you see that even Buddha is purely an outside god, purely objective to the natives. They have no conception of his being inside themselves.

It was the same with the Greeks, it is the same today with the Sicilians. They aren't *capable* of introspection and the inner Jesus. They leave it all to us and the Russians.

Save that he has no bright outside gods, Gesualdo is very like an old Greek: the same energy and quickness of response, the same vivid movement, the same ambition and real passion for wealth, the same easy conscience, the same queer openness, without ever really openly committing himself, and the same ancient astuteness. He is prouder, more fearless, more frank, yet more subtle than an Italian; more on his own. He is like a Greek or a traditional Englishman, in the way he just goes ahead by himself. And in that, he is Sicilian, not Italian.

And he is Greek above all, in having no inside, in the Russian sense of the word.

The tragedy is, he has no heroic gods or goddesses to fix his imagination. He has nothing, not even a country. Even his Greek amibitious desire to come out splendidly, with a final splendid look of the thing and a splendid final ring of words, turns bitter. The Sicilian aristocracy was an infinitely more paltry thing than Gesualdo himself.

It is the tragedy of a man who is forced to be ordinary, because all visions have been taken away from him. It is useless to say he should have had the northern inwardness and the Russianizing outlet. You might as well say the tall and reckless asphodel of Magna Græcia should learn to be a snowdrop. "I'll learn you to be a toad!"

But a book exists by virtue of the vividness, the aliveness and powerful pulsing of its life-portrayal, and not by vitue of the pretty or unpretty things it portrays. *Mastro-don Gesualdo* is a great undying book, one of the great novels of Europe. If you cannot read it because it is à *terre*, and has neither nervous uplift nor nervous hysteria, you condemn yourself.

As a picture of Sicily in the middle of the last century, it is marvellous. But it is a picture done from the inside. There are no picturepostcard effects. The thing is a heavy, earth-adhering organic whole. There is nothing showy.

Sicily in the middle of the last century was an incredibly poor, lost, backward country. Spaniards, Bourbons, one after the other they had killed the life in her. The Thousand and Garibaldi had not risen over the horizon, neither had the great emigration to America begun, nor the great return, with dollars and a newish outlook. The mass of the people were poorer even than the poor Irish of the same period, and save for climate, their conditions were worse. There were some great and wealthy landlords, dukes and barons still. But they lived in Naples, or in Palermo at the nearest. In the country, there were no roads at all for wheeled vehicles, consequently no carts, nothing but donkeys and pack-mules on the trails, or a sick person in a mule litter, or armed men on horseback, or men on donkeys. The life was mediæval as in Russia. But whereas the Russia of 1850 is a vast flat country with a most picturesque life of nobles and serfs and soldiers, open and changeful, Sicily is a most beautiful country, but hilly, steep, shut-off, and abandoned, and the life is, or was, grimly unpicturesque in its dead monotony. The great nobles shunned the country, as in Ireland. And the people were sunk in bigotry, suspicion, and gloom. The life of the villages and small towns was of an incredible spiteful meanness, as life always is when there is not enough change and fresh air; and the conditions were sordid, dirty, as they always are when the human spirits sink below a certain level. It is not in such places that one looks for passion and colour. The passion and colour in Verga's stories come in the villages near the east coast, where there is change since Ulysses sailed that way. Inland, in the isolation, the lid is on, and the intense watchful malice of neighbours is infinitely worse than any police system, infinitely more killing to the soul and the passionate body.

The picture is a bitter and depressing one, while ever we stay in the dense and smelly little streets. Verga wrote what he knew and felt. But when we pass from the habitations of sordid man, into the light and marvellous open country, then we feel at once the undying beauty of Sicily and the Greek world, a morning beauty, that has something miraculous in it, of purple anemones and cyclamens, and sumach and olive trees, and the place where Persephone came above-world, bringing back spring.

And we must remember that eight-tenths of the population of Sicily is maritime or agricultural, always has been, and therefore practically the whole day-life of the people passes in the open, in the splendour of the sun and the landscape, and the delicious, elemental aloneness of the old world. This is a great *unconscious* compensation. But what a compensation, after all!—even if you don't know you've got it; as even Verga doesn't quite. But he puts it in, all the same, and you can't read *Mastro-don Gesualdo* without feeling the marvellous glow and glamour of Sicily, and the people throbbing inside the glow and the glamour like motes in a sunbeam. Out of doors, in a world like that, what is misery, after all! The great freshness keeps the men still fresh. It is the women in the dens of houses who deteriorate most.

And perhaps it is because the outside world is so lovely, that men in the Greek regions have never become introspective. They had not been driven to *that* form of compensation. With them, life pulses outwards, and the positive reality is outside. There is no turning inwards. So man becomes purely objective. And this is what makes the Greeks so difficult to understand: even Socrates. We don't understand him. We just translate him into another thing, our own thing. He is so peculiarly *objective* even in his attitude to the soul, that we could never get him if we didn't translate him into something else, and thus "make him our own."

And the glorious objectivity of the old Greek world still persists, old and blind now, among the southern Mediterranean peoples. It is this decayed objectivity, not even touched by mediæval mysticism, which makes a man like Gesualdo so simple, and yet so incomprehensible to us. We are apt to see him as just meaningless, just stupidly and meaninglessly getting rich, merely acquisitive. Yet, at the same time, we see him so patient with his family, with the phthisical Bianca, with his daughter, so humane, and yet so desperately enduring. In affairs, he has an unerring instinct, and he is a superb fighter. Yet in life, he seems to do the wrong thing every time. It is as if, in his life, he has no driving motive at all.

He should, of course, by every standard we know, have married Diodata. Bodily, she was the woman he turned to. She bore him sons. Yet he married her to one of his own hired men, to clear the way for his, Gesualdo's, marriage with the noble but merely pathetic Bianca Trao. And after he was married to Bianca, who was too weak for him, he still went back to Diodata, and paid her husband to accommodate him. And it never occurs to him to have any of this on his conscience. Diodata has his sons in her house, but Gesualdo, who has only one daughter by the frail Bianca, never seems to interest himself in his boys at all. There is the most amazing absence of a certain range of feeling in the man, especially feeling about himself. It is as if he had no inside. And yet we see that he most emphatically has. He has a warm and attractive presence. And he suffers bitterly, bitterly. Yet he blindly brings most of his sufferings on himself, by doing the wrong things to himself.

The idea of living for love is just entirely unknown to him, unknown as if it were a new German invention. So is the idea of living for sex. In that respect, woman is just the female of the species to him, as if he were a horse, that jumps in heat, and forgets. He never really thinks about women. Life means something else to him.

But what? What? It is so hard to see. Does he just want to *get on*, in our sense of the word? No, not even that. He has not the faintest desire to be mayor, or podesta, or that sort of thing. But he does make a duchess of his daughter. Yes, Mastro-don Gesualdo's daughter is a duchess of very aristocratic rank.

And what then? Gesualdo realizes soon enough that she is not happy. And now he is an elderly, dying man, and the impetuosity of his manhood is sinking, he begins to wonder what he should have done. What was it all about?

What *did* life mean to him, when he was in the impetuous tide of his manhood? What was he unconsciously driving at? Just blindly at nothing? Was that why he put aside Diodata, and brought on himself all that avalanche of spite, by marrying Bianca? Not that his marriage was a failure. Bianca was his wife, and he was unfailingly kind to her, fond of her, her death was bitter to him. Not being under the tyrannical sway of the idea of "love," he could be fond of his wife, and he could be fond of Diodata, and he needn't get into a stew about any of them.

But what was he under the sway of? What was he blindly driving at? We ask, and we realize at last that it was the old Greek impulse towards splendour and self-enhancement. Not ambition, in our sense of the word, but something more personal, more individual. That which swayed Achilles and swayed Pericles and Alcibiades: the passionate desire for individual splendour. We now call it vanity. But in the countries of the sun, where the whole outdoors consists in the splendour of the sun, it is a real thing to men, to try to make themselves splendid and like suns.

Gesualdo was blindly repeating, in his own confused way, the magnificent old gesture. But ours is not the age for splendour. We have changed all that. So Gesualdo's life amounts to nothing. Yet not, as far as I can see, to any less than the lives of the "humble" Russians. At least he lived his life. If he thought too little about it, he helps to counterbalance all those people who think too much. Because he never has any "profound" talk, he is not less a man than Myshkin or a Karamazov. He is possibly not more a man, either. But to me he is less distasteful. And because his life all ends in a mistake, he is not therefore any more meaningless than Tolstoi himself. And because he simply has no idea whatsoever of "salvation," whether his own or anybody else's, he is not therefore a fool. Any more than Hector and Achilles were fools; for neither of them had any idea of salvation.

The last forlorn remnant of the Greeks, blindly but brightly seeking for splendour and self-enhancement, instead of salvation, and choosing to surge blindly on, instead of retiring inside himself to twist his soul into knots, Gesualdo still has a lovable glow in his body, the very reverse of the cold marsh-gleam of Myshkin. His life ends in a tumour of bitterness. But it was a life, and I would rather have lived it than the life of Tolstoi's Pierre, or the life of any Dostoevskian hero. It was not Gesualdo's fault that the bright objective gods are dead, killed by envy and spite. It was not his fault that there was no real splendour left in our world for him to choose, once he had the means.

Preface to *Touch and Go*

A nice phrase: "A People's Theatre." But what about it? There's no such thing in existence as a People's Theatre: or even on the way to existence, as far as we can tell. The name is chosen, the baby isn't even begotten: nay, the would-be parents aren't married, nor yet courting.

A People's Theatre. Note the indefinite article. It isn't The People's Theatre, but A People's Theatre. Not The people: il popolo, le peuple, das Volk, this monster is the same the world over: Plebs, the proletariat. Not the theatre of Plebs, the proletariat, but the theatre of A People. What people? Quel peuple donc?—A People's Theatre. Translate it into French for yourself.

A People's Theatre. Since we can't produce it, let us deduce it. Major premiss: the seats are cheap. Minor Premiss: the plays are good. Conclusion: A People's Theatre. How much will you give me for my syllogism? Not a slap in the eye, I hope.

We stick to our guns. The seats are cheap. That has a nasty proletarian look about it. But appearances are deceptive. The proletariat isn't poor. Everybody is poor except Capital and Labour. Between these upper and nether millstones great numbers of decent people are squeezed.

The seats are cheap: in decency's name. Nobody wants to swank, to sit in the front of a box like a geranium on a window-sill—"the cynosure of many eyes." Nobody wants to profiteer. We all feel that it is as humiliating to pay high prices as to charge them. No man consents in his heart to pay high prices unless he feels that what he pays with his right hand he will get back with his left either out of the pocket of a man who isn't looking, or out of the envy of the poor neighbour who *is* looking, but can't afford the figure. The seats are cheap. Why should A People, fabulous and lofty giraffe, want to charge or to pay high prices? If it were *the people* now.—But it isn't. It isn't Plebs, the proletariat. The seats are cheap.

The plays are good. Pah!—this has a canting smell. Any play is good to the man who likes to look at it. And at that rate *Chu Chin*

Chow is extra-super-good. What about your *good* plays? Whose good? *Pfui* to your goodness!

That minor premiss is a bad egg: it will hatch no bird. Good plays? You might as well say mimsy bomtittle plays, you'd be saying as much. The plays are—don't say good or you'll be beaten. The plays—the plays of A People's Theatre are—oh heaven, what are they?—not popular nor populous nor plebeian nor proletarian nor folk nor parish plays. None of that adjectival spawn.

The only clue-word is People's, for all that. A People's —— Chaste word, it will bring forth no adjective. The plays of A People's Theatre are People's plays. The plays of A People's Theatre are plays about people.

It doesn't look much, at first sight. After all—people! Yes, people! Not *the people*, *i.e.* Plebs, nor yet the Upper Ten. People. Neither Piccoli nor Grandi in our republic. People.

People, ah God! Not mannequins. Not lords nor proletariats nor bishops nor husbands nor co-respondents nor virgins nor adulteresses nor uncles nor noses. Not even white rabbits nor presidents. People.

Men who are somebody, not men who are something. Men who *happen* to be bishops or co-respondents, women who happen to be chaste, just as they happen to freckle, because it's one of their innumerable odd qualities. Even men who happen, by the way, to have long noses. But not noses on two legs, not burly pairs of gaiters, stuffed and voluble, not white meringues of chastity, not incarnations of co-respondence. Not proletariats, petitioners, presidents, noses, bits of fluff. Heavens, what an assortment of bits! And aren't we sick of them!

People, I say. And after all, it's saying something. It's harder to be a human being than to be a president or a bit of fluff. You can be a president, or a bit of fluff, or even a nose, by clockwork. Given a rôle, a *part*, you can play it by clockwork. But you can't have a clockwork human being.

We're dead sick of parts. It's no use your protesting that there is a man behind the nose. We can't see him, and he can't see himself. Nothing but nose. Neither can you make us believe there is a man inside the gaiters. He's never showed his head yet.

It may be, in real life, the gaiters wear the man, as the nose wears Cyrano. It may be Sir Auckland Geddes and Mr. J. H. Thomas are only clippings from the illustrated press. It may be that a miner is a complicated machine for cutting coal and voting on a ballot-paper. It may be that coal-owners are like the *petit bleu* arrangement, a system of vacuum tubes for whooshing Bradburys about from one to the other.

It may be that everybody delights in bits, in parts, that the public insists on noses, gaiters, white rabbits, bits of fluff, automata and gewgaws. If they do, then let 'em. *Chu Chin Chow* for ever!

In spite of them all: A People's Theatre. A People's Theatre shows men, and not parts. Not bits, nor bundles of bits. A whole bunch of rôles tied into one won't make an individual. Though gaiters perish, we will have men.

Although most miners may be pick-cum-shovel-cum-ballot implements, and no more, still among miners there must be two or three living individuals. The same among the masters. The majority are suction tubes for Bradburys. But in this Sodom of Industrialism there are surely ten men, all told. My poor little withered grain of mustard seed, I am half afraid to take you across to the seed-testing department!

And if there are men, there is A People's Theatre.

How many tragic situations did Goethe say were possible? Something like thirty-two. Which seems a lot. Anyhow, granted that men are men still, that not all of them are bits, parts, machine-sections, then we have added another tragic possibility to the list: the Strike situation. As yet no one tackles this situation. It is a sort of Medusa head, which turns—no, not to stone, but to sloppy treacle. Mr. Galsworthy had a peep, and sank down towards bathos.

Granted that men are still men, Labour *v.* Capitalism is a tragic struggle. If men are no more than implements, it is non-tragic and merely disastrous. In tragedy the man is more than his part. Hamlet is more than Prince of Denmark, Macbeth is more than murderer of Duncan. The man is caught in the wheels of his part, his fate, he may be torn asunder. He may be killed, but the resistant, integral soul in him is not destroyed. He comes through, though he dies. He goes through with his fate, though death swallows him. And it is in this facing of fate, this going right through with it, that tragedy lies. Tragedy is not disaster. It is a disaster when a cart-wheel goes over a frog, but it is not a tragedy. Tragedy is the working out of some immediate passional problem within the soul of man. If this passional problem and this working out be absent, then no disaster is a tragedy, not the hugest: not the death of ten million men. It is only a cart-wheel going over a frog. There must be a supreme *struggle*.

In Shakespeare's time it was the people *versus* king storm that was brewing. Majesty was about to have its head off. Come what might, Hamlet and Macbeth and Goneril and Regan had to see the business through.

Now a new wind is getting up. We call it Labour *versus* Capitalism.

We say it is a mere material struggle, a money-grabbing affair. But this is only one aspect of it. In so far as men are merely mechanical, the struggle is one which, though it may bring disaster and death to millions, is no more than accident, an accidental collision of forces. But in so far as men are men, the situation is tragic. It is not really the bone we are fighting for. We are fighting to have somebody's head off. The conflict is in pure, passional antagonism, turning upon the poles of belief. Majesty was only *hors d'œuvres* to this tragic repast.

So, the strike situation has this dual aspect. First it is a mechanico-material struggle, two mechanical forces pulling asunder from the central object, the bone. All it can result in is the pulling asunder of the fabric of civilization, and even of life, without any creative issue. It is no more than a frog under a cart-wheel. The mechanical forces, rolling on, roll over the body of life and squash it.

The second is the tragic aspect. According to this view, we see more than two dogs fighting for a bone, and life hopping under the Juggernaut wheel. The two dogs are making the bone a pretext for a fight with each other. That old bull-dog, the British capitalist, has got the bone in his teeth. That unsatisfied mongrel, Plebs, the proletariat, shivers with rage not so much at sight of the bone, as at sight of the great wrinkled jowl that holds it. There is the old dog, with his knowing look and his massive grip on the bone: and there is the insatiable mongrel, with his great splay paws. The one is all head and arrogance, the other all paws and grudge. The bone is only the pretext. A first condition of the being of Bully is that he shall hate the prowling great paws of Plebs, whilst Plebs by inherent nature goes mad at the sight of Bully's jowl. "Drop it!" cries Plebs. "Hands off!" growls Bully. It is hands against head, the shambling, servile body in a rage of insurrection at last against the wrinkled, heavy head.

Labour not only wants his debt. He wants his pound of flesh. It is a quandary. In our heart of hearts we must admit the debt. We must admit that it is long overdue. But this last condition! In vain we study our anatomy to see which part we can best spare.

Where is our Portia, to save us with a timely quibble? We've plenty of Portias. They've recited their heads off—"The quality of mercy is not strained." But the old Shylock of the proletariat persists. He pops up again, and says, "All right, I can't have my pound of flesh with the blood. But then you can't keep my pound of flesh with your blood—you owe it me. It is your business to deliver the goods. Deliver it then—with or without blood—deliver it." Then Portia scratches her head, and thinks again.

What's the solution? There is no solution. But still there is a choice. There's a choice between a mess and a tragedy. If Plebs and Bully hang on one to each end of the bone, and pull for grim life, they will at last tear the bone to atoms: in short, destroy the whole material substance of life, and so perish by accident, no better than a frog under the wheel of destiny. That may be a disaster, but it is only a mess for all that.

On the other hand, if they have a fight to fight they might really drop the bone. Instead of wrangling the bone to bits they might really go straight for one another. They are like hostile parties on board a ship, who both proceed to scuttle the ship so as to sink the other party. Down goes the ship with all the bally lot on board. A few survivors swim and squeal among the bubbles—and then silence.

It is too much to suppose that the combatants will ever drop the obvious old bone. But it is not too much to imagine that some men might acknowledge the bone to be merely a pretext, another hollow *casus belli*. If we really could know what we were fighting for, if we could deeply believe in what we were fighting for, then the struggle might have dignity, beauty, satisfaction for us. If it were a profound struggle that we were convinced would bring us to a new freedom, a new life, then it would be a creative activity, a creative activity in which death is a climax in the progression towards new being. And this is tragedy.

Therefore, if we could but comprehend or feel the tragedy in the great Labour struggle, the intrinsic tragedy of having to pass through death to birth, our souls would still know some happiness, the very happiness of creative suffering. Instead of which we pile accident on accident, we tear the fabric of our existence fibre by fibre, we confidently look forward to the time when the whole great structure will come down on our heads. Yet after all that, when we are squirming under the débris, we shall have no more faith or hope or satisfaction than we have now. We shall crawl from under one cart-wheel straight under another.

The essence of tragedy, which is creative crisis, is that a man should go through with his fate, and not dodge it and go bumping into an accident. And the whole business of life, at the great critical periods of mankind, is that men should accept and be one with their tragedy. Therefore we should open our hearts. For one thing, we should have a People's Theatre. Perhaps it would help us in this hour of confusion better than anything.

Preface to *Black Swans*

Difficult to write about *Black Swans*, when I have barely seen so much as the egg of the book. Yet I suppose the MS I did see in Western Australia may be considered the egg. It was a wild MS, climbing the mountain of impossibilities and improbabilities by leaps and bounds: a real rolling stone of an egg, no doubt.

There was Miss Skinner, in the house on the hills at the edge of the bush, in Western Australia, darting about rather vaguely in her white nurse's dress, with the nurse's white band over her head, looking after her convalescents who, mercifully, didn't need much looking after. Miss Skinner darting about on the brink of all the balances, and her partner, a wise, strong woman, sitting plumb at the centre of equilibrium.

Oh, and the ponderous manuscript, tangled, and simply crepitating with type-writer's mistakes, which I read with despair in that house in Western Australia. Such possibilities! And such impossibilities.

But the possibilities touched with magic. Always hovering over the borderline where probability merges into magic: then tumbling, like a bird gone too far out to sea, flopping and splashing into the wrong element, to drown soggily.

"Write," said I, like an old hand giving advice, "an Australian book about things you *actually* know, which you don't have to invent out of the ink-bottle."

Eighteen months later, when I was in Mexico and Miss Skinner in Australia, wandered in to me the MS called *The House of Ellis*. It was better than the first *Black Swans*, because it was pretty well about happenings in Australia. But tangled, gasping, and forever going under in the sea of incoherence. Such a queer, magical bird of imagination, always drowning itself.

What's to be done! One has a terrible feeling, in front of a MS that glimmers with imagination and chokes with incoherence. The authoress away in Australia, putting her hopes high. Myself in Mexico, too old a hand to put many hopes on the public or the critics or on anything mortal at all. Still, unwilling to play the hand-washing part.

I am not good at suggesting and criticizing. I did the only thing I knew well how to do: that is, I wrote the whole book over again, from start to finish, putting in and leaving out, yet keeping the main substance of Miss Skinner's work. Yet let me here make the confession that the last chapters and anything in the slightest bit "shocking," are, of course, my fault: not Molly Skinner's.

Miss Skinner had quite another conclusion. In her *House of Ellis*, which I turned into the *Boy in the Bush*, Monica went to the bad and disappeared, among the tears of the family. Jack set off to find her: got lost: and "came to" with Mary gazing lovingly upon him. In that instant, he knew he loved Mary far, far more than Monica. In fact, his love for Monica was a dead bluebottle. Mary and Jack happy ever after, virtue rewarded, *finale*!

Now I have my own ideas of morality. A young man who is supposed to love a young girl through years, with passion, and whose love just goes pop when she gets in a mess, bores me. He has no real integrity: and that, to my mind, is immorality.

At the same time, this Jack had always had a second "feeling" for Mary. Australia is a land which believes not at all in externally imposed authority. There is no limit to love. All right, there is no limit to love. The popular method would be for a hero, having got his Monica, and not having got his Mary, for whom he had a latent feeling all the time, suddenly to realize that he no longer "loved" Monica, but only Mary: then an "affair," Monica left in the lurch, sympathy streaming towards the virtuous, long-neglected Mary.

Public, popular morality seems to me a pig's business. If a man has ever cared for a woman enough to marry her, he always cares for her. And divorce is all bunk. Forgetting, as Miss Skinner's Jack forgot Monica, is all bunk. Once you care, and the connection is made, you keep the connection, if you are half a man.

But the further question, as to whether this one connection is final and exclusive, is up to us to settle. Largely a question of discipline. And since Australia is the most undisciplined country I have met, discipline won't settle the question there. Fall back on evasions and sentimentalism.

Discipline is a very good thing. Evasions and sentimentalism very bad.

I wonder very much how *Black Swans* has wound up. When I saw it, it was about a girl, a convict, and a Peter: Lettie, I think her name was, poised between the entirely praiseworthy Peter and the fascinating convict. But there the tale tumbled away into a sort of pirate-castaway-Swiss-Family-Robinson-Crusoe-Treasure-Island in the North West.

This "adventure" part was rather pointless. I suggested to Miss Skinner that she work out the Peter-Lettie-Convict combine on ordinary terra firma.

I believe she has done so in *Black Swans*.

She sailed off penniless, with a steerage ticket from Tremanitlo to England, the MS. of *Black Swans* in her bag, and hopes, heaven high! Ay-ay! anticipations! The *Boy in the Bush* was not yet out.

She arrived in London to be snubbed and treated as if she did not exist, and certainly *ought not* to exist, by the same-as-ever London literary people. Those that esteemed me, literairily, decided that *Mr.* Skinner was probably a myth, and didn't matter anyhow. Those that didn't esteem me declared that *Mr.* Skinner, if he existed, couldn't amount to anything, or he would never have made such a connection. Certainly I am a safe mark for the popular moralists to aim their slosh at. "Mr. Skinner" was buried before he went any further.

Of course Miss Skinner felt badly. But if Stafford put not his trust in Princes—or realized that he shouldn't have done—the first business of anybody who picks up a pen, even so unassuming a pen as Miss Skinner's now, is to put no trust in the literary rabble, nor in the rabble of the critics, nor in the vast rabble of the people. A writer should steer his aristocratic course through all the shoals and sewerage outlets of popular criticism, on to the high and empty seas where he finds his own way into the distance.

Poor Molly Skinner, she had a bad time. But two sorts of bad time. The first sort, of being informed she ought not to exist, and of having her *Black Swans* turned down. The second sort, when Old Edward Garnett tackled her. He saw her *Black Swans* floundering and flopping about, and went for them tooth and nail, like a rough-haired Yorkshire terrier. Poor old Molly Skinner, she saw the feathers of her birds flying like black snow, and the swans squawked as if they were at their last gasp. But old Edward twisted at them till they knew what's what.

I am dying to see *Black Swans* now, since Edward put their mistress through her paces. She is fleeing breathless back to Australia. I am laughing in the hot Mexican sun. Tonight is Christmas Eve, and who knows what sort of a child the Virgin is going to bring forth, this time!

V

Miscellaneous Pieces

A Britisher Has a Word with an Editor

In October's *Poetry*, the Editor tells what a real tea-party she had in Britain, among the poets: not a Bostonian one, either.

But she, alas, has to throw the dregs of her tea-cup in the faces of her hosts. She wonders whether British poets will have anything very essential to say, as long as the King remains, and the "oligarchic social system" continues. The poor King, casting a damper on poetry! And this about oligarchies is good, from an American.

"In England I found no such evidence of athletic sincerity in artistic experiment, of vitality and variety, and—yes!— (YES!!) beauty, in artistic achievement, as I get from the poets of our own land."

YANKEE DOODLE, KEEP IT UP.

As for that "worthless dude," George IV, what poet could possibly have flourished under his contemptible regime? Harriet, look in the history book, and see.

Oh what might not Milton have been, if he'd written under Calvin Coolidge!

Autobiographical Sketch

David Herbert Lawrence—born 11 Sept. 1885 in Eastwood, Nottingham, a small mining town in the Midlands—father a coal-miner, scarcely able to read or write—Mother from the bourgeoisie, the cultural element in the house (let them [*struck out*] read *Sons & Lovers*, the first part is all autobiography—you might send them a copy [*struck out*]).—Fourth of five children—two brothers oldest—then a sister, then D. H.—then another sister—always delicate health but strong constitution—went to elementary school & was just like anybody else of the miners' children—at age of twelve won a scholarship for Nottingham High School, considered best day school in England—purely bourgeois school—quite happy there, but the scholarship boys were a class apart—D. H. made a couple of bourgeois friendships, but they were odd fish,—he instinctively recoiled away from the bourgeoisie, regular sort—left school at 16—had a severe illness—made the acquaintance of Miriam and her family, who lived on a farm, and who really roused him to critcal & creative consciousness (see *Sons & Lovers*). Taught in a rough & fierce elementary school of mining boys: salary, first year, £5.—second year £10—third year £15—(from age of 17 to 21)—Next two years in Nottingham University, at first quite happy, then utterly bored.—Again the same feeling of boredom with the middle-classes, & recoil away from them instead of moving towards them & rising in the world. Took B.A. course, but dropped it; used to write bits of poems & patches of *The White Peacock* during lectures. These he wrote for Miriam, the girl on the farm, who was herself becoming a school-teacher. She thought it all wonderful—else, probably, he would never have written—His own family strictly "natural" looked on such performance as writing as "affectation." Therefore wrote in secret at home. Mother came upon a chapter of *White Peacock*—read it quizzically, & was amused. "But my boy, how do you know it was like that? You don't know—" She thought one ought to know—and she hoped her son, who was "clever," might one day be a professor or a clergyman or perhaps even a little Mr.

Gladstone. That would have been rising in the world—on the ladder. Flights of genius were nonsense—you had to be clever & rise in the world, step by step.—D. H. however recoiled away from the world, hated its ladder, & refused to rise. He had proper bourgeois aunts with "library" & "drawing-room" to their houses—but didn't like that either—preferred the powerful life in a miner's kitchen—& still more, the clatter of nailed boots in the little kitchen of Miriam's farm. Miriam was even poorer than he—but she loved poetry and consciousness and flights of fancy above all. So he wrote for her—still without any idea of becoming a literary man at all—looked on himself as just a school-teacher—& mostly hated school-teaching. Wrote *The White Peacock* in bits and snatches, between age of 19 and 24. Most of it written six or seven times.

At the age of twenty-three, left Nottingham college & went for the first time to London, to be a teacher in a boys' school in Croydon, £90. a year. Already the intense physical dissatisfaction with Miriam. Miriam read all his writings—she alone. His mother, whom he loved best on earth, he never spoke to, about his writing. It would have been a kind of "showing-off," or affectation. It was Miriam who sent his poems to Ford Madox Hueffer, who had just taken over *The English Review*. This was when D. H. was 24. Hueffer accepted, wrote to Lawrence, and was most kind and most friendly. Got Heinemann to accept the MS., a ragged & bulky mass, of *The White Peacock*—invited the school-teacher to lunch—introduced him to Edward Garnett—and Garnett became a generous and genuine friend. Hueffer & Garnett launched D. H. into the literary world. Garnett got Duckworth to accept the first book of poems: *Love Poems and Others*. When Lawrence was 25, *The White Peacock* appeared. But before the day of publication, his mother died—she just looked once at the advance copy, held it in her hand—

The death of his mother wiped out everything else—books published, or stories in magazines. It was the great crash, and the end of his youth. He went back to Croydon to the hated teaching—the £50 for *The White Peacock* paid the doctor etc for his mother.

Then a weary and bitter year—broke with Miriam—and again fell dangerously ill with pneumonia. Got slowly better. Was making a little money with stories, Austin Harrison, who had taken over *The English Review*, being à staunch supporter, and Garnett and Hueffer staunch backers. In May, 1912, went away suddenly with his present wife, of German birth, daughter of Baron Friedrich von Richthofen. They went to Metz, then Bavaria, then Italy—and the new phase had begun. He was 26—his youth was over—there came a great gap between him and it.

Was in Italy and Germany the greater part of the time between 1912 & 1914. In England during the period of the war—pretty well isolated. In 1915 *The Rainbow* was suppressed for immorality—and the sense of detachment from the bourgeois world, the world which controls press, publication and all, became almost complete. He had no interest in it, no desire to be at one with it. Anyhow the suppression of *The Rainbow* had proved it impossible. Henceforth he put away any idea of "success," of succeeding with the British bourgeois public, and stayed apart.

Left England in 1919, for Italy—had a house for two years in Taormina, Sicily. In 1920 was published in America *Women in Love*— which every publisher for four years had refused to accept, because of *The Rainbow* scandal. In Taormina wrote *The Lost Girl, Sea and Sardinia*, and most of *Aaron's Rod*. In 1922 sailed from Naples to Ceylon, and lived in Kandy for a while—then on to Australia for a time—in each case taking a house and settling down. Then sailed from Sydney to San Francisco, and went to Taos, in New Mexico, where he settled down again with his wife, near the Pueblo of the Indians. Next year he acquired a small ranch high up on the Rocky Mountains, looking west to Arizona. Here, and in Old Mexico, where he travelled and lived for about a year, he stayed till 1926, writing *St. Mawr* in New Mexico, and the final version of *The Plumed Serpent* down in Oaxaca in Old Mexico.

Came to England 1926—but cannot stand the climate. For the last two years has lived in a villa near Florence, where *Lady Chatterley's Lover* was written.

Introduction to *Memoirs of the Foreign Legion*

On a dark, wet, wintry evening in November, 1919, I arrived in Florence, having just got back to Italy for the first time since 1914. My wife was in Germany, gone to see her mother, also for the first time since that fatal year 1914. We were poor; who was going to bother to publish me and to pay for my writings, in 1918 and 1919? I landed in Italy with nine pounds in my pocket and about twelve pounds lying in the bank in London. Nothing more. My wife, I hoped, would arrive in Florence with two or three pounds remaining. We should have to go very softly, if we were to house ourselves in Italy for the winter. But after the desperate weariness of the war, one could not bother.

So I had written to N—— D—— to get me a cheap room somewhere in Florence, and to leave a note at Cook's. I deposited my bit of luggage at the station, and walked to Cook's in the Via Tornabuoni. Florence was strange to me: seemed grim and dark and rather awful on the cold November evening. There was a note from D——, who has never left me in the lurch. I went down the Lung 'Arno to the address he gave.

I had just passed the end of the Ponte Vecchio, and was watching the first lights of evening and the last light of day on the swollen river as I walked, when I heard D——'s voice:

"Isn't that Lawrence? Why of course it is, of course it is, beard and all! Well, how are you, eh? You got my note? Well now, my dear boy, you just go on to the Cavelotti—straight ahead, straight ahead—you've got the number. There's a room for you there. We shall be there in half an hour. Oh, let me introduce you to M——"

I had unconsciously seen the two men approaching, D—— tall and portly, the other man rather short and strutting. They were both buttoned up in their overcoats, and both had rather curly little hats. But D—— was decidedly shabby and a gentleman, with his wicked red face and tufted eyebrows. The other man was almost smart, all in grey, and he looked at first sight like an actor-manager, common. There was a touch of down-on-his-luck about him too. He looked at me, buttoned up in my old thick overcoat, and with my beard bushy and raggy because of my horror of entering a strange barber's shop, and he greeted me in

a rather fastidious voice, and a little patronizingly. I forgot to say I was
carrying a small hand-bag. But I realized at once that I ought, in this
little grey-sparrow man's eyes⸺he stuck his front out tubbily, like a
bird, and his legs seemed to perch behind him, as a bird's do⸺I ought
to be in a cab. But I wasn't. He eyed me in that shrewd and rather impertinent way of the world of actor-managers: cosmopolitan, knocking
shabbily round the world.

He looked a man of about forty, spruce and youngish in his deport-
ment, very pink-faced, and very clean, very natty, very alert, like a
sparrow painted to resemble a tom-tit. He was just the kind of man I
had never met: little smart man of the shabby world, very much on the
spot, don't you know.

"How much does it cost?" I asked D⸺, meaning the room.

"Oh, my dear fellow, a trifle. Ten francs a day. Third rate, tenth
rate, but not bad at the price. Pension terms of course—everything included—except wine."

"Oh no, not at all bad for the money," said M⸺. "Well now, shall
we be moving? You want the post office, D⸺?" His voice was precise and a little mincing, and it had an odd high squeak.

"I do," said D⸺.

"Well then come down here⸺" M⸺ turned to a dark little alley.

"Not at all," said D⸺. "We turn down by the bridge."

"This is quicker," said M⸺. He had a twang rather than an
accent in his speech—not definitely American.

He knew all the short cuts of Florence. Afterwards I found that he
knew all the short cuts in all the big towns of Europe.

I went on to the Cavelotti and waited in an awful plush and gilt
drawing-room, and was given at last a cup of weird muddy brown slush
called tea, and a bit of weird brown mush called jam on some bits of
bread. Then I was taken to my room. It was far off, on the third floor of
the big, ancient, deserted Florentine house. There I had a big and
lonely, stone-comfortless room looking on to the river. Fortunately it
was not very cold inside, and I didn't care. The adventure of being back
in Florence again after the years of war made one indifferent.

After an hour or so someone tapped. It was D⸺ coming in with his
grandiose air—now a bit shabby, but still very courtly.

"Why here you are—miles and miles from human habitation! I *told*
her to put you on the second floor, where we are. What does she mean
by it? Ring that bell. Ring it."

"No," said I, "I'm all right here."

"What!" cried D⸺. "In this Spitzbergen! Where's that bell?"

"Don't ring it," said I, who have a horror of chambermaids and explanations.

"Not ring it! Well you're a man, you are! Come on then. Come on down to my room. Come on. Have you had some tea—filthy muck they call tea here? I never drink it."

I went down to D——'s room on the lower floor. It was a littered mass of books and typewriter and papers: D—— was just finishing his novel. M—— was resting on the bed, in his shirt sleeves: a tubby, fresh-faced little man in a suit of grey, faced cloth bound at the edges with grey silk braid. He had light blue eyes, tired underneath, and crisp, curly, dark brown hair just grey at the temples. But everything was neat and even finicking about his person.

"Sit down! Sit down!" said D——, wheeling up a chair. "Have a whisky?"

"Whisky!" said I.

"Twenty-four francs a bottle—and a find at that," moaned D——. I must tell that the exchange was then about forty-five lire to the pound.

"Oh N——," said M——, "I didn't tell you. I was offered a bottle of 1913 Black and White for twenty-eight lire."

"Did you buy it?"

"No. It's your turn to buy a bottle."

"Twenty-eight francs—my dear fellow!" said D——, cocking up his eyebrows. "I shall have to starve myself to do it."

"Oh no you won't, you'll eat here just the same," said M——.

"Yes, and I'm starved to death. Starved to death by the muck—the absolute muck they call food here. I can't face twenty-eight francs, my dear chap—can't be done, on my honour."

"Well look here, N——. We'll both buy a bottle. And you can get the one at twenty-two, and I'll buy the one at twenty-eight."

So it always was, M—— indulged D——, and spoilt him in every way. And of course D—— wasn't grateful. *Au contraire!* And M——'s pale blue smallish round eyes, in his cockatoo-pink face, would harden to indignation occasionally.

The room was dreadful. D—— never opened the windows: didn't believe in opening windows. He believed that a certain amount of nitrogen—I should say a great amount—is beneficial. The queer smell of a bedroom which is slept in, worked in, lived in, smoked in, and in which men drink their whiskies, was something new to me. But I didn't care. One had got away from the war.

We drank our whiskies before dinner. M—— was rather yellow under the eyes, and irritable; even his pink fattish face went yellowish.

"Look here," said D——. "Didn't you say there was a turkey for dinner? What? Have you been to the kitchen to see what they're doing to it?"

"Yes," said M—— testily. "I forced them to prepare it to roast."

"With chestnuts—stuffed with chestnuts?" said D——.

"They *said* so," said M——.

"Oh, but go down and see that they're doing it. Yes, you've got to keep your eye on them, got to. The most awful howlers if you don't. You go now and see what they're up to." D—— used his most irresistible grand manner.

"It's too late," persisted M——, testy.

"It's *never* too late. You just run down and absolutely prevent them from boiling that bird in the old soup-water," said D——. "If you need force, fetch me."

M—— went. He was a great epicure, and knew how things should be cooked. But of course his irruptions into the kitchen roused considerable resentment, and he was getting quaky. However, he went. He came back to say the turkey was being roasted, but without chestnuts.

"What did I tell you! What did I tell you!" cried D——. "They are absolute——! If you don't hold them by the neck while they peel the chestnuts, they'll stuff the bird with old boots, to save themselves trouble. Of course you should have gone down sooner, M——."

Dinner was always late, so the whisky was usually two whiskies. Then we went down, and were merry in spite of all things. That is, D—— always grumbled about the food. There was one unfortunate youth who was boots and porter and waiter and all. He brought the big dish to D——, and D—— always poked and pushed among the portions, and grumbled frantically, sotto voce, in Italian to the youth Beppo, getting into a nervous frenzy. Then M—— called the waiter to himself, picked the nicest bits off the dish and gave them to D——, then helped himself.

The food was not good, but with D—— it was an obsession. With the waiter he was terrible—"Cos' è? Zuppa? Grazie. No niente per me. *No—No!*—Quest' acqua sporca non bevo io. I don't drink this dirty water. What—— What's that in it—a piece of dish clout? Oh holy Dio, I can't eat another thing this evening——"

And he yelled for more bread—bread being war rations and very limited in supply—so M—— in nervous distress gave him his piece, and D—— threw the crumb part on the floor, anywhere, and called for another litre. We always drank heavy dark red wine at three francs a litre. D—— drank two-thirds, M—— drank least. He loved his liquors, and did not care for wine. We were noisy and unabashed at table. The old Danish ladies at the other end of the room, and the rather impecunious young Duca and family not far off were not supposed to understand English. The Italians rather liked the noise, and the young signorina with the high-up yellow hair eyed us with profound interest. On we sailed, gay and noisy, D—— telling witty anecdotes and grumbling wildly and only half whimsically about the food. We sat on till most people had finished—then went up to more whisky—one more perhaps—in M——'s room.

When I came down in the morning I was called into M——'s room. He was like a little pontiff in a blue kimono-shaped dressing-gown with a broad border of reddish purple: the blue was a soft mid-blue, the material a dull silk. So he minced about, in demi-toilette. His room was very clean and neat, and slightly perfumed with essences. On his dressing-table stood many cut glass bottles and silver-topped bottles with essences and pomades and powders, and heaven knows what. A very elegant little prayer book lay by his bed—and a life of St. Benedict. For M—— was a Roman Catholic convert. All he had was expensive and finicking: thick leather silver-studded suit-cases standing near the wall, trouser-stretcher all nice, hair-brushes and clothes-brush with old ivory backs. I wondered over him and his niceties and little pomposities. He was a new bird to me.

For he wasn't at all just the common person he looked. He was queer and sensitive as a woman with D——, and patient and fastidious. And yet he *was* common, his very accent was common, and D—— despised him.

And M—— rather despised me because I did not spend money. I paid for a third of the wine we drank at dinner, and bought the third bottle of whisky we had during M——'s stay. After all, he only stayed three days. But I would not spend for myself. I had no money to spend, since I knew I must live and my wife must live.

"Oh," said M——. "Why, that's the very time to spend money, when you've got none. If you've got none, why try to save it? That's been my philosophy all my life; when you've got no money, you may just as well spend it. If you've got a good deal, that's the time to look after it." Then he laughed his queer little laugh, rather squeaky. These were his exact words.

"Precisely," said D——. "Spend when you've nothing to spend, my boy. Spent *hard* then."

"No," said I. "If I can help it, I will never let myself be penniless while I live. I mistrust the world too much."

"But if you're going to live in fear of the world," said M——, "what's the good of living at all? Might as well die."

I think I give his words almost verbatim. He had a certain impatience of me and of my presence. Yet we had some jolly times— mostly in one or other of their bedrooms, drinking a whisky and talking. We drank a bottle a day—I had very little, preferring the wine at lunch and dinner, which seemed delicious after the war famine. D—— would bring up the remains of the second litre in the evening, to go on with before the coffee came.

I arrived in Florence on the Wednesday or Thursday evening; I think Thursday. M—— was due to leave for Rome on the Saturday. I asked D—— who M—— was. "Oh, you never know what he's at. He was manager for Isadora Duncan for a long time—knows all the capitals of Europe: St. Petersburg, Moscow, Tiflis, Constantinople, Berlin, Paris—knows them as you and I know Florence. He's been mostly in that line—theatrical. Then a journalist. He edited the *Roman Review* till the war killed it. Oh, a many-sided sort of fellow."

"But how do you know him?" said I.

"I met him in Capri years and years ago—oh, sixteen years ago— and clean forgot all about him till somebody came to me one day in Rome and said: You're N—— D——. *I* didn't know who he was. But he'd never forgotten me. Seems to be smitten by me, somehow or other. All the better for me, ha-ha!—if he *likes* to run round for me. My dear fellow, I wouldn't prevent him, if it amuses him. Not for worlds."

And that was how it was. M—— ran D——'s errands, forced the other man to go to the tailor, to the dentist, and was almost a guardian angel to him.

"Look here!" cried D——. "I *can't* go to that damned tailor. Let the thing wait, I can't go."

"Oh yes. Now look here N——, if you don't get it done now while I'm here you'll never get it done. I made the appointment for three o'clock——"

"To hell with you! Details! Details! I can't stand it, I tell you."

D—— chafed and kicked, but went.

"A little fussy fellow," he said. "Oh yes, fussing about like a woman. Fussy, you know, fussy. I *can't stand* these fussy——" And D—— went off into improprieties.

Well, M—— ran round and arranged D——'s affairs and settled his little bills, and was so benevolent, and so impatient and nettled at the ungrateful way in which the benevolence was accepted. And D——

despised him all the time as a little busybody and an inferior. And I there between them just wondered. It seemed to me M—— would get very irritable and nervous at midday and before dinner, yellow round the eyes and played out. He wanted his whisky. He was tired after running round on a thousand errands and quests which I never understood. He always took his morning coffee at dawn, and was out to early Mass and pushing his affairs before eight o'clock in the morning. But what his affairs were I still do not know. Mass is all I am certain of.

However, it was his birthday on the Sunday, and D—— would not let him go. He had once said he would give a dinner for his birthday, and this he was not allowed to forget. It seemed to me M—— rather wanted to get out of it. But D—— was determined to have that dinner.

"You aren't going before you've given us that hare, don't you imagine it, my boy. I've got the smell of that hare in my imagination, and I've damned well got to set my teeth in it. Don't you imagine you're going without having produced that hare."

So poor M——, rather a victim, had to consent. We discussed what we should eat. It was decided the hare should have truffles, and a dish of champignons, and cauliflower, and zabaioni—and I forget what else. It was to be on Saturday evening. And M—— would leave on Sunday for Rome.

Early on the Saturday morning he went out, with the first daylight, to the old market, to get the hare and the mushrooms. He went himself because he was a connoisseur.

On the Saturday afternoon D—— took me wandering round to buy a birthday present.

"I shall have to buy him something—have to—have to——" he said fretfully. He only wanted to spend about five francs. We trailed over the Ponte Vecchio, looking at the jewellers' booths there. It was before the foreigners had come back, and things were still rather dusty and almost at pre-war prices. But we could see nothing for five francs except the little saint-medals. D—— wanted to buy one of those. It seemed to me infra dig. So at last coming down to the Mercato Nuovo we saw little bowls of Volterra marble, a natural amber colour, for four francs.

"Look, buy one of those," I said to D——, "and he can put his pins or studs or any trifle in, as he needs."

So we went in and bought one of the little bowls of Volterra marble.

M—— seemed so touched and pleased with the gift.

"Thank you a thousand times, N——," he said. "That's charming! That's exactly what I want."

The dinner was quite a success, and, poorly fed as we were at the pension, we stuffed ourselves tight on the mushrooms and the hare and the zabaioni, and drank ourselves tight with the good red wine which swung in its straw flask in the silver swing on the table. A flask has two and a quarter litres. We were four persons, and we drank almost two flasks. D—— made the waiter measure the remaining half-litre and take it off the bill. But good, good food, and cost about twelve francs a head the whole dinner.

Well, next day was nothing but bags and suit-cases in M——'s room, and the misery of departure with luggage. He went on the midnight train to Rome: first-class.

"I always travel first-class," he said, "and I always shall, while I can buy the ticket. Why should I go second? It's beastly enough to travel at all."

"My dear fellow, I came up third the last time I came from Rome," said D——. "Oh, not bad, not bad. Damned fatiguing journey anyhow."

So the little outsider was gone, and I was rather glad. I don't think he liked me. Yet one day he said to me at table:

"How lovely your hair is—such a lovely colour! What do you dye it with?"

I laughed, thinking he was laughing too. But no, he meant it.

"It's got no particular colour at all," I said, "so I couldn't dye it that!"

"It's a lovely colour," he said. And I think he didn't believe me, that I didn't dye it. It puzzled me, and it puzzles me still.

But he was gone. D—— moved into M——'s room, and asked me to come down to the room he himself was vacating. But I preferred to stay upstairs.

M—— was a fervent Catholic, taking the religion, alas, rather unctuously. He had entered the Church only a few years before. But he had a bishop for a god-father, and seemed to be very intimate with the upper clergy. He was very pleased and proud because he was a constant guest at the famous old monastery south of Rome. He talked of becoming a monk; a monk in that aristocratic and well-bred order. But he had not even begun his theological studies: or any studies of any sort. And D—— said he only chose the Benedictines because they lived better than any of the others.

But I had said to M—— that when my wife came and we moved south, I would like to visit the monastery some time, if I might. "Certainly," he said. "Come when I am there. I shall be there in about a month's time. Do come! Do be sure and come. It's a wonderful place —oh, wonderful. It will make a great impression on you. Do come. Do come. And I will tell Don Bernardo, who is my *greatest* friend, and who is guest-master, about you. So that if you wish to go when I am not there, write to Don Bernardo. But do come when I am there."

My wife and I were due to go into the mountains south of Rome, and stay there some months. Then I was to visit the big, noble monastery that stands on a bluff hill like a fortress crowning a great precipice, above the little town and the plain between the mountains. But it was so icy cold and snowy among the mountains, it was unbearable. We fled south again, to Naples, and to Capri. Passing, I saw the monastery crouching there above, world-famous, but it was impossible to call then.

I wrote and told M—— of my move. In Capri I had an answer from him. It had a wistful tone—and I don't know what made me think that he was in trouble, in monetary difficulty. But I felt it acutely—a kind of appeal. Yet he said nothing direct. And he wrote from an expensive hotel in Anzio, on the sea near Rome.

At the moment I had just received twenty pounds unexpected and joyful from America—a gift too. I hesitated for some time, because I felt unsure. Yet the curious appeal came out of the letter, though nothing was said. And I felt also I owed M—— that dinner, and I didn't want to owe him anything, since he despised me a little for being careful. So partly out of revenge, perhaps, and partly because I felt the strange wistfulness of him appealing to me, I sent him five pounds, saying perhaps I was mistaken in imagining him very hard up, but if so, he wasn't to be offended.

It is strange to me even now, how I knew he was appealing to me. Because it was all as vague as I say. Yet I felt it so strongly. He replied: "Your cheque has saved my life. Since I last saw you I have fallen down an abyss. But I will tell you when I see you. I shall be at the monastery in three days. Do come—and come alone." I have forgotten to say that he was a rabid woman-hater.

This was just after Christmas. I thought his "saved my life" and "fallen down an abyss" was just the American touch of "very, very ——." I wondered what on earth the abyss could be, and I decided it must be that he had lost his money or his hopes. It seemed to me that some of his old buoyant assurance came out again in this letter. But he was now very friendly, urging me to come to the monastery, and treating me with a curious little tenderness and protectiveness. He had a queer delicacy of his own, varying with a bounce and a commonness.

He was a common little bounder. And then he had this curious delicacy and tenderness and wistfulness.

I put off going north. I had another letter urging me—and it seemed to me that, rather assuredly, he was expecting more money. Rather cockily, as if he had a right to it. And that made me not want to give him any. Besides, as my wife said, what right had I to give away the little money we had, and we there stranded in the south of Italy with no resources if once we were spent up. And I have always been determined *never* to come to my last shilling—if I have to reduce my spending almost to nothingness. I have always been determined to keep a few pounds between me and the world.

I did not send any money. But I wanted to go to the monastery, so wrote and said I would come for two days. I always remember getting up in the black dark of the January morning, and making a little coffee on the spirit-lamp, and watching the clock, the big-faced, blue old clock on the campanile in the piazza in Capri, to see I wasn't late. The electric light in the piazza lit up the face of the campanile. And we were then a stone's throw away, high in the Palazzo Ferraro, opposite the bubbly roof of the little duomo. Strange dark winter morning, with the open sea beyond the roofs, seen through the side window, and the thin line of the lights of Naples twinkling far, far off.

At ten minutes to six I went down the smelly dark stone stairs of the old palazzo, out into the street. A few people were already hastening up the street to the terrace that looks over the sea to the bay of Naples. It was dark and cold. We slid down in the funicular to the shore, then in little boats were rowed out over the dark sea to the steamer that lay there showing her lights and hooting.

It was three long hours across the sea to Naples, with dawn coming slowly in the east, beyond Ischia, and flushing into lovely colour as our steamer pottered along the peninsula, calling at Massa and Sorrento and Piano. I always loved hanging over the side and watching the people come out in boats from the little places of the shore, that rose steep and beautiful. I love the movement of these watery Neapolitan people, and the naïve trustful way they clamber in and out the boats, and their softness, and their dark eyes. But when the steamer leaves the peninsula and begins to make away round Vesuvius to Naples, one is already tired, and cold, cold, cold in the wind that comes piercing from the snowcrests away there along Italy. Cold, and reduced to a kind of stony apathy by the time we come to the mole in Naples, at ten o'clock —or twenty past ten.

We were rather late, and I missed the train. I had to wait till two o'clock. And Naples is a hopeless town to spend three hours in. However, time passes. I remember I was calculating in my mind whether they had given me the right change at the ticket-window. They hadn't —and I hadn't counted in time. Thinking of this, I got in the Rome train. I had been there ten minutes when I heard a trumpet blow.

"Is this the Rome train?" I asked my fellow-traveller.

"Si."

"The express?"

"No, it is the slow train."

"It leaves?"

"At ten past two."

I almost jumped through the window. I flew down the platform.

"The diretto!" I cried to a porter.

"Parte! Eccolo là!" he said, pointing to a big train moving inevitably away.

I flew with wild feet across the various railway lines and seized the end of the train as it travelled. I had caught it. Perhaps if I had missed it fate would have been different. So I sat still for about three hours. Then I had arrived.

There is a long drive up the hill from the station to the monastery. The driver talked to me. It was evident he bore the monks no good will.

"Formerly," he said, "if you went up to the monastery you got a glass of wine and a plate of macaroni. But now they kick you out of the door."

"Do they?" I said. "It is hard to believe."

"They kick you out of the gate," he vociferated.

We twisted up and up the wild hillside, past the old castle of the town, past the last villa, between trees and rocks. We saw no one. The whole hill belongs to the monastery. At last at twilight we turned the corner of the oak wood and saw the monastery like a huge square fortress-palace of the sixteenth century crowning the near distance. Yes, and there was M—— just stepping through the huge old gateway and hastening down the slope to where the carriage must stop. He was bareheaded, and walking with his perky, busy little stride, seemed very much at home in the place. He looked up to me with a tender, intimate look as I got down from the carriage. Then he took my hand.

"So *very* glad to see you," he said. "I'm so *pleased* you've come."

And he looked into my eyes with that wistful, watchful tenderness rather like a woman who isn't quite sure of her lover. He had a certain charm in his manner; and an odd pompous touch with it at this moment, welcoming his guest at the gate of the vast monastery which reared above us from its buttresses in the rock, was rather becoming. His face was still pink, his eyes pale blue and sharp, but he looked greyer at the temples.

"Give me your bag," he said. "Yes do—and come along. Don Bernardo is just at Evensong, but he'll be here in a little while. Well now, tell me all the news."

"Wait," I said. "Lend me five francs to finish paying the driver— he has no change."

"Certainly, certainly," he said, giving the five francs.

I had no news—so asked him his.

"Oh, I have none either," he said. "Very short of money, that of course is *no* news." And he laughed his little laugh. "I'm so glad to be here," he continued. "The peace, and the rhythm of the life is so *beautiful!* I'm sure you'll love it."

We went up the slope under the big, tunnel-like entrance and were in the grassy courtyard, with the arched walk on the far sides, and one or two trees. It was like a grassy cloister, but still busy. Black monks were standing chatting, an old peasant was just driving two sheep from the cloister grass, and an old monk was darting into the little post-office which one recognized by the shield with the national arms over the doorway. From under the far arches came an old peasant carrying a two-handed saw.

And there was Don Bernardo, a tall monk in a black, well-shaped gown, young, good-looking, gentle, hastening forward with a quick smile. He was about my age, and his manner seemed fresh and subdued, as if he were still a student. One felt one was at college with one's college mates.

We went up the narrow stair and into the long, old, naked white corridor, high and arched. Don Bernardo had got the key of my room: two keys, one for the dark antechamber, one for the bedroom. A charming and elegant bedroom, with an engraving of English landscape, and outside the net curtain a balcony looking down on the garden, a narrow strip beneath the walls, and beyond, the clustered buildings of the farm, and the oak woods and arable fields of the hill summit: and beyond again, the gulf where the world's valley was, and all the mountains that stand in Italy on the plains as if God had just put them down ready made. The sun had already sunk, the snow on the mountains was full of a rosy glow, the valleys were full of shadow. One heard, far below, the trains shunting, the world clinking in the cold air.

"Isn't it wonderful! Ah, the most wonderful place on earth!" said

M———. "What now could you wish better than to end your days here? The peace, the beauty, the eternity of it." He paused and sighed. Then he put his hand on Don Bernardo's arm and smiled at him with that odd, rather wistful smirking tenderness that made him such a quaint creature in my eyes.

"But I'm going to enter the order. You're going to let me be a monk and be one of you, aren't you, Don Bernardo?"

"We will see," smiled Don Bernardo. "When you have begun your studies."

"It will take me two years," said M———. "I shall have to go to the college in Rome. When I have got the money for the fees———" He talked away, like a boy planning a new rôle.

"But I'm sure Lawrence would like to drink a cup of tea," said Don Bernardo. He spoke English as if it were his native language. "Shall I tell them to make it in the kitchen, or shall we go to your room?"

"Oh, we'll go to my room. How thoughtless of me! Do forgive me, won't you?" said M———, laying his hand gently on my arm. "I'm so awfully sorry, you know. But we get so excited and enchanted when we talk of the monastery. But come along, come along, it will be ready in a moment on the spirit-lamp."

We went down to the end of the high, white, naked corridor. M——— had a quite sumptuous room, with a curtained bed in one part, and under the window his writing-desk with papers and photographs, and nearby a sofa and an easy table, making a little sitting-room, while the bed and toilet things, pomades and bottles were all in the distance, in the shadow. Night was fallen. From the window one saw the world far below, like a pool the flat plain, a deep pool of darkness with little twinkling lights, and rows and bunches of light that were the railway station.

I drank my tea, M——— drank a little liqueur, Don Bernardo in his black winter robe sat and talked with us. At least he did very little talking. But he listened and smiled and put in a word or two as we talked, seated round the table on which stood the green-shaded electric lamp.

The monastery was cold as the tomb. Couched there on the top of its hill, it is not much below the winter snow-line. Now by the end of January all the summer heat is soaked out of the vast, ponderous stone walls, and they become masses of coldness cloaking around. There is no heating apparatus whatsoever—none. Save the fire in the kitchen, for cooking, nothing. Dead, silent, stone cold everywhere.

At seven we went down to dinner. Capri in the daytime was hot, so I had brought only a thin old dust-coat. M——— therefore made me wear a big coat of his own, a coat made of thick, smooth black cloth, and lined with black sealskin, and having a collar of silky black seal-skin. I can still remember the feel of the silky fur. It was queer to have him helping me solicitously into this coat, and buttoning it at the throat for me.

"Yes, it's a beautiful coat. Of course!" he said. "I hope you find it warm."

"Wonderful," said I. "I feel as warm as a millionaire."

"I'm so glad you do," he laughed.

"You don't mind my wearing your grand coat?" I said.

"Of course not! Of course not! It's a pleasure to me if it will keep you warm. We don't want to die of cold in the monastery, do we? That's one of the mortifications we will do our best to avoid. What? Don't you think? Yes, I think this coldness is going almost too far. I had that coat made in New York fifteen years ago. Of course in Italy ——" he said It'ly—"I've never worn it, so it is as good as new. And it's a beautiful coat, fur and cloth of the very best. *And* the tailor." He laughed a little, self-approving laugh. He liked to give the impression that he dealt with the *best* shops, don't you know, and stayed in the *best* hotels, etc. I grinned inside the coat, detesting best hotels, best shops, and best overcoats. So off we went, he in his grey overcoat and I in my sealskin millionaire monster, down the dim corridor to the guests' refec-tory. It was a bare room with a long white table. M—— and I sat at the near end. Further down was another man, perhaps the father of one of the boy students. There is a college attached to the monastery.

We sat in the icy room, muffled up in our overcoats. A lay-brother with a bulging forehead and queer, fixed eyes waited on us. He might easily have come from an old Italian picture. One of the adoring peasants. The food was abundant—but alas, it had got cold in the long cold transit from the kitchen. And it was roughly cooked, even if it was quite wholesome. Poor M—— did not eat much, but nervously nibbled his bread. I could tell the meals were a trial to him. He could not bear the cold food in that icy, empty refectory. And his phthisickiness offended the lay-brothers. I could see that his little pomposities and his "superior" behaviour and his long stay made them have that old monas-tic grudge against him, silent but very obstinate and effectual—the same now as six hundred years ago. We had a decanter of good red wine—but he did not care for much wine. He was glad to be peeling the cold orange which was dessert.

After dinner he took me down to see the church, creeping like two thieves down the dimness of the great, prison-cold white corridors, on the cold flag floors. Stone cold: the monks must have invented the term. These monks were at Compline. So we went by our two secret little selves into the tall dense nearly-darkness of the church. M——, knowing his way about here as in the cities, led me, poor wondering worldling, by the arm through the gulfs of the tomb-like place. He found the electric light switches inside the church, and stealthily made me a light as we went. We looked at the lily marble of the great floor, at the pillars, at the Benvenuto Cellini casket, at the really lovely pillars and slabs of different coloured marbles, all coloured marbles, yellow and grey and rose and green and lily white, veined and mottled and splashed: lovely, lovely stones—— And Benvenuto had used pieces of lapis lazuli, blue as cornflowers. Yes, yes, all very rich and wonderful.

We tiptoed about the dark church stealthily, from altar to altar, and M—— whispered ecstasies in my ear. Each time we passed before an altar, whether the high altar or the side chapels, he did a wonderful reverence, which he must have practised for hours, bowing waxily down and sinking till his one knee touched the pavement, then rising like a flower that rises and unfolds again, till he had skipped to my side and was playing cicerone once more. Always in his grey overcoat, and in whispers: me in the big black overcoat, millionairish. So we crept into the chancel and examined all the queer fat babies of the choir stalls, carved in wood and rolling on their little backs between monk's place and monk's place—queer things for the chanting monks to have between them, these shiny, polished, dark brown fat babies, all different, and all jolly and lusty. We looked at everything in the church—and then at everything in the ancient room at the side where surplices hang and monks can wash their hands.

Then we went down to the crypt, where the modern mosaics glow in wonderful colours, and sometimes in fascinating little fantastic trees and birds. But it was rather like a scene in the theatre, with M—— for the wizard and myself a sort of Parsifal in the New York coat. He switched on the lights, the gold mosaic of the vaulting glittered and bowed, the blue mosaic glowed out, the holy of holies gleamed theatrically, the stiff mosaic figures posed around us. To tell the truth I was glad to get back to the normal human room and sit on a sofa huddled in my overcoat, and look at photographs which M—— showed me: photographs of everywhere in Europe. Then he showed me a wonderful photograph of a picture of a lovely lady—asked me what I thought of it, and seemed to expect me to be struck to bits by the beauty. His almost sanctimonious expectation made me tell the truth, that I thought it just a bit cheap, trivial. And then he said, dramatic:

"That's my mother."

It looked so unlike anybody's mother, much less M——'s, that I was startled. I realized that she was his great stunt, and that I had put my foot in it. So I just held my tongue. Then I said, for I felt he was going to be silent forever:

"There are so few portraits, unless by the really great artists, that aren't a bit cheap. She must have been a beautiful woman."

"Yes, she *was*," he said curtly. And we dropped the subject.

He locked all his drawers *very* carefully, and kept the keys on a chain. He seemed to give the impression that he had a great many secrets, perhaps dangerous ones, locked up in the drawers of his writing-table there. And I always wonder what the secrets can be, that are able to be kept so tight under lock and key.

Don Bernardo tapped and entered. We all sat round and sipped a funny liqueur which I didn't like. M—— lamented that the bottle was finished. I asked him to order another and let me pay for it. So he said he would tell the postman to bring it up next day from the town. Don Bernardo sipped his tiny glass with the rest of us, and he told me, briefly, his story—and we talked politics till nearly midnight. Then I came out of the black overcoat and we went to bed.

In the morning a fat, smiling, nice old lay-brother brought me my water. It was a sunny day. I looked down on the farm cluster and the brown fields and the sere oak woods of the hill-crown, and the rocks and bushes savagely bordering it round. Beyond, the mountains with their snow were blue-glistery with sunshine, and seemed quite near, but across a sort of gulf. All was still and sunny. And the poignant grip of the past, the grandiose, violent past of the Middle Ages, when blood was strong and unquenched and life was flamboyant with splendours and horrible miseries, took hold of me till I could hardly bear it. It was really agony to me to be in the monastery and to see the old farm and the bullocks slowly working in the fields below, and the black pigs rooting among weeds, and to see a monk sitting on a parapet in the sun, and an old, old man in skin sandals and white bunched, swathed legs come driving an ass slowly to the monastery gate, slowly, with all that lingering nonchalance and wildness of the Middle Ages, and yet to know that I was myself, child of the present. It was so strange from M——'s window to look down on the plain and see the white road going straight past a mountain that stood like a loaf of sugar, the river meandering in loops, and the railway with glistening lines making a long black swoop across the flat and into the hills. To see trains come steaming, with white smoke flying. To see the station like a little harbour where trucks like shipping stood anchored in rows in the black bay of railway. To see trains stop in the station and tiny people swarming like flies! To see all this from the monastery, where the Middle Ages live on in a sort of agony, like Tithonus, and cannot die, this was almost a violation to my soul, made almost a wound.

Immediately after coffee we went down to Mass. It was celebrated in a small crypt chapel underground, because that was warmer. The twenty or so monks sat in their stalls, one monk officiating at the altar. It was quiet and simple, the monks sang sweetly and well, there was no organ. It seemed soon to pass by. M—— and I sat near the door. He was very devoted and scrupulous in his going up and down. I was an outsider. But it was pleasant—not too sacred. One felt the monks were very human in their likes and their jealousies. It was rather like a group of dons in the dons' room at Cambridge, a cluster of professors in any college. But during Mass they, of course, just sang their responses. Only I could tell some watched the officiating monk rather with ridi-cule—he was one of the ultra-punctilious sort, just like a don. And some boomed their responses with a grain of defiance against some brother monk who had earned dislike. It was human, and more like a university than anything. We went to Mass every morning, but I did not go to Evensong.

After Mass M—— took me round and showed me everything of the vast monastery. We went into the Bramante Courtyard, all stone, with its great well in the centre, and the colonnades of arches going round, full of sunshine, gay and Renaissance, a little bit ornate but still so jolly and gay, sunny pale stone waiting for the lively people, with the great flight of pale steps sweeping up to the doors of the church, waiting for gentlemen in scarlet trunk-hose, slender red legs, and ladies in brocade gowns, and page-boys with fluffed, golden hair. Splendid, sunny, gay Bramante Courtyard of lively stone. But empty. Empty of life. The gay red-legged gentry dead forever. And when pilgrimages do come and throng in, it is horrible artisan excursions from the great town, and the sordidness of industrialism.

We climbed the little watchtower that is now an observatory, and saw the vague and unshaven Don Giovanni among all his dust and instruments. M—— was very familiar and friendly, chattering in his quaint Italian, which was more wrong than any Italian I have ever heard spoken; very familiar and friendly, and a tiny bit deferential to the monks, and yet, and yet—rather patronizing. His little pomposity and patronizing tone coloured even his deferential yearning to be admitted to the monastery. The monks were rather brief with him.

They no doubt have their likes and dislikes greatly intensified by the monastic life.

We stood on the summit of the tower and looked at the world below: the town, the castle, the white roads coming straight as judgment out of the mountains north, from Rome, and piercing into the mountains south, toward Naples, traversing the flat, flat plain. Roads, railway, river, streams, a world in accurate and lively detail, with mountains sticking up abruptly and rockily, as the old painters painted it. I think there is no way of painting Italian landscape except that way —that started with Lorenzetti and ended with the sixteenth century.

We looked at the ancient cell away under the monastery, where all the sanctity started. We looked at the big library that belongs to the State, and at the smaller library that belongs still to the abbot. I was tired, cold, and sick among the books and illuminations. I could not bear it any more. I felt I must be outside, in the sun, and see the world below, and the way out.

That evening I said to M——:

"And what was the abyss, then?"

"Oh well, you know," he said, "it was a cheque which I made out at Anzio. There should have been money to meet it, in my bank in New York. But it appears the money had never been paid in by the people that owed it me. So there was I in a very nasty hole, an unmet cheque, and no money at all in Italy. I really had to escape here. It is an *absolute* secret that I am here, and it must be, till I can get this business settled. Of course I've written to America about it. But as you see, I'm in a very nasty hole. That five francs I gave you for the driver was the last penny I had in the world: absolutely the last penny. I haven't even anything to buy a cigarette or a stamp." And he laughed chirpily, as if it were a joke. But he didn't really think it a joke. Nor was it a joke.

I had come with only two hundred lire in my pocket, as I was waiting to change some money at the bank. Of this two hundred I had one hundred left or one hundred and twenty-five. I should need a hundred to get home. I could only give M—— the twenty-five, for the bottle of drink. He was rather crestfallen. But I didn't want to give him money this time: because he expected it.

However, we talked about his plans: how he was to earn something. He told me what he had written. And I cast over in my mind where he might get something published in London, wrote a couple of letters on his account, told him where I thought he had best send his material. There wasn't a great deal of hope, for his smaller journalistic articles seemed to me very self-conscious and poor. He had one about the monastery, which I thought he might sell because of the photographs.

That evening he first showed me the Legion manuscript. He had got it rather raggedly typed out. He had a typewriter, but felt he ought to have somebody to do his typing for him, as he hated it and did it unwillingly. That evening and when I went to bed and when I woke in the morning I read this manuscript. It did not seem very good—vague and diffuse where it shouldn't have been—lacking in sharp detail and definite event. And yet there was something in it that made me want it done properly. So we talked about it, and discussed it carefully, and he unwillingly promised to tackle it again. He was curious, always talking about his work, even always working, but never *properly* doing anything.

We walked out in the afternoon through the woods and across the rocky bit of moorland which covers most of the hill-top. We were going to the ruined convent which lies on the other brow of the monastery hill, abandoned and sad among the rocks and heath and thorny bushes. It was sunny and warm. A barefoot little boy was tending a cow and three goats and a pony, a barefoot little girl had five geese in charge. We came to the convent and looked in. The further part of the court-yard was still entire, the place was a sort of farm, two rooms occupied by a peasant-farmer. We climbed about the ruins. Some creature was crying—crying, crying, crying with a strange, inhuman persistence, leaving off and crying again. We listened and listened—the sharp, poignant crying. Almost it might have been a sharp-voiced baby. We scrambled about, looking. And at last outside a little cave-like place found a blind black puppy crawling miserably on the floor, unable to walk, and crying incessantly. We put it back in the little cave-like shed, and went away. The place was deserted save for the crying puppy.

On the road outside however was a man, a peasant, just drawing up to the arched convent gateway with an ass under a load of brushwood. He was thin and black and dirty. He took off his hat, and we told him of the puppy. He said the bitch-mother had gone off with his son with the sheep. Yes, she had been gone all day. Yes, she would be back at sunset. No, the puppy had not drunk all day. Yes, the little beast cried, but the mother would come back to him.

They were the old-world peasants still about the monastery, with the hard, small bony heads and deep-lined faces and utterly blank minds, crying their speech as crows cry, and living their lives as lizards among the rocks, blindly going on with the little job in hand, the present moment, cut off from all past and future, and having no idea and no sustained emotion, only that eternal will-to-live which makes a tortoise wake up once more in spring, and makes a grasshopper whistle on in the moonlight nights even of November. Only these peasants don't whistle much. The whistlers go to America. It is the hard, static, unhoping souls that persist in the old life. And still they stand back, as one passes them in the corridors of the great monastery, they press themselves back against the whitewashed walls of the still place, and drop their heads, as if some mystery were passing by, some God-mystery, the higher beings, which they must not look closely upon. So also this old peasant—he was not old, but deep-lined like a gnarled bough. He stood with his hat down in his hands as we spoke to him and answered the short, hard, insentient answers, as a tree might speak.

"The monks keep their peasants humble," I said to M——.

"Of course!" he said. "Don't you think they are quite right? Don't you think they should be humble?" And he bridled like a little turkey-cock on his hind legs.

"Well," I said, "if there's any occasion for humility, I do."

"Don't you think there is occasion?" he cried. "If there's one thing worse than another, it's this *equality* that has come into the world. Do you believe in it yourself?"

"No," I said. "I don't believe in equality. But the problem is, wherein does superiority lie."

"Oh," chirped M—— complacently. "It lies in many things. It lies in birth and in upbringing and so on, but it is chiefly in *mind*. Don't you think? Of course I don't mean that the physical qualities aren't *charming*. They are, and nobody appreciates them more than I do. Some of the peasants are *beautiful* creatures, perfectly beautiful. But that passes. And the mind endures."

I did not answer. M—— was not a man one talked far with. But I thought to myself, I *could* not accept M——'s superiority to the peasant. If I had really to live always under the same roof with either one of them, I would have chosen the peasant. If I had had to choose, I would have chosen the peasant. Not because the peasant was wonderful and stored with mystic qualities. No, I don't give much for the wonderful mystic qualities in peasants. Money is their mystery of mysteries, absolutely. No, if I chose the peasant it would be for what he *lacked* rather than for what he had. He lacked that complacent mentality that M—— was so proud of, he lacked all the trivial trash of glib talk and more glib thought, all the conceit of our shallow consciousness. For his mindlessness I would have chosen the peasant: and for his strong blood-presence. M—— wearied me with his facility and his readiness to rush into speech, and for the exhaustive nature of his presence. As if he had no strong blood in him to sustain him, only this modern parasitic lymph which cries for sympathy all the time.

"Don't you think yourself that you are superior to that peasant?" he asked me, rather ironically. He half expected me to say no.

"Yes, I do," I replied. "But I think most middle-class, most so-called educated people are inferior to the peasant. I do that."

"Of course," said M—— readily. "In their *hypocrisy*——" He was great against hypocrisy—especially the English sort.

"And if I think myself superior to the peasant, it is only that I feel myself like the growing tip, or one of the growing tips of the tree, and him like a piece of the hard, fixed tissue of the branch or trunk. We're part of the same tree: and it's the same sap," said I.

"Why, exactly! Exactly!" cried M——. "Of course! The Church would teach the same doctrine. We are all one in Christ—but between our souls and our duties there are great differences."

It is terrible to be agreed with, especially by a man like M——. All that one says, and means, turns to nothing.

"Yes," I persisted. "But it seems to me the so-called culture, education, the so-called leaders and leading-classes today, are only parasites —like a great flourishing bush of parasitic consciousness flourishing on top of the tree of life, and sapping it. The consciousness of today doesn't rise from the roots. It is just parasitic in the veins of life. And the middle and upper classes are just parasitic upon the body of life which still remains in the lower classes."

"What!" said M—— acidly. "Do you believe in the democratic lower classes?"

"Not a bit," said I.

"I should think not, indeed!" he cried complacently.

"No, I don't believe the lower classes can ever make life whole again, till they *do* become humble, like the old peasants, and yield themselves to real leaders. But not to great negators like Lloyd George or Lenin or Briand."

"Of course! of course!" he cried. "What you need is the Church in power again. The Church has a place for everybody."

"You don't think the Church belongs to the past?" I asked.

"Indeed I don't, or I shouldn't be here. No," he said sententiously, "the Church is eternal. It puts people in their proper place. It puts women down into *their* proper place, which is the first thing to be done——"

He had a great dislike of women, and was very acid about them. Not because of their sins, but because of their virtues: their economies, their philanthropies, their spiritualities. Oh, how he loathed women. He had been married, but the marriage had not been a success. He smarted still. Perhaps his wife had despised him, and he had not *quite* been able to defeat her contempt.

So, he loathed women, and wished for a world of men. "They talk about love between men and women," he said. "Why it's all a *fraud*. The woman is just taking all and giving nothing, and feeling sanctified about it. All she tries to do is to thwart a man in whatever he is doing. No, I have found my life in my *friendships*. Physical relationships are very attractive, of course, and one tries to keep them as decent and all that as one can. But one knows they will pass and be finished. But one's *mental* friendships last for ever."

"With me, on the contrary," said I. "If there is no profound blood-sympathy, I know the mental friendship is trash. If there is real, deep blood response, I will stick to that if I have to betray all the mental sympathies I ever made, or all the lasting spiritual loves I ever felt."

He looked at me, and his face seemed to fall. Round the eyes he was yellow and tired and nervous. He watched me for some time.

"Oh!" he said, in a queer tone, rather cold. "Well, my experience has been the opposite."

We were silent for some time.

"And you," I said, "even if you do manage to do all your studies and enter the monastery, do you think you will be satisfied?"

"If I can be so fortunate, I do really," he said. "Do you doubt it?"

"Yes," I said. "Your nature is worldly, more worldly than mine. Yet I should die if I had to stay up here."

"Why?" he asked, curiously.

"Oh, I don't know. The past, the past. The beautiful, the wonderful past, it seems to prey on my heart, I can't bear it."

He watched me closely.

"Really!" he said stoutly. "Do you feel like that? But don't you think it is a far preferable life up here than down there? Don't you think the past is far preferable to the future, with all this *socialismo* and these *communisti* and so on?"

We were seated, in the sunny afternoon, on the wild hill-top high above the world. Across the stretch of pale, dry, standing thistles that peopled the waste ground, and beyond the rocks was the ruined convent. Rocks rose behind us, the summit. Away on the left were the woods which hid us from the great monastery. This was the mountain top, the last foothold of the old world. Below we could see the plain, the straight white road, straight as a thought, and the more flexible black railway with the railway station. There swarmed the *ferrovieri* like ants. There was democracy, industrialism, socialism, the red flag of the communists and the red, white and green tricolor of the fascisti. That was another world. And how bitter, how barren a world! Barren like the black cinder-track of the railway, with its two steel lines.

And here above, sitting with the little stretch of pale, dry thistles around us, our back to a warm rock, we were in the Middle Ages. Both worlds were agony to me. But here, on the mountain top was worst: the past, the poignancy of the not-quite-dead past.

"I think one's got to go through with the life down there—get somewhere beyond it. One can't go back," I said to him.

"But do you call the monastery going back?" he said. "I don't. The peace, the eternity, the concern with things that matter. I consider it the happiest fate that could happen to me. Of course it means putting physical things aside. But when you've done that—why, it seems to me perfect."

"No," I said. "You're too worldly."

"But the monastery is worldly too. We're not Trappists. Why the monastery is one of the centres of the world—one of the most active centres."

"Maybe. But that impersonal activity, with the blood suppressed and going sour—no, it's too late. It is too abstract—political maybe——"

"I'm sorry you think so," he said, rising. "I don't."

"Well," I said. "You'll never be a monk here, M——. You see if you are."

"You don't think I shall?" he replied, turning to me. And there was a catch of relief in his voice. Really, the monastic state must have been like going to prison for him.

"You haven't a vocation," I said.

"I may not *seem* to have, but I hope I actually have."

"You haven't."

"Of course, if you're so sure," he laughed, putting his hand on my arm.

He seemed to understand so much, round about the questions that trouble one deepest. But the quick of the question he never felt. He had no real middle, no real centre bit to him. Yet, round and round about all the questions, he was so intelligent and sensitive.

We went slowly back. The peaks of those Italian mountains in the sunset, the extinguishing twinkle of the plain away below, as the sun declined and grew yellow; the intensely powerful mediæval spirit lingering on this wild hill summit, all the wonder of the mediæval past; and then the huge mossy stones in the wintry wood, that was once a sacred grove; the ancient path through the wood, that led from temple to temple on the hill summit, before Christ was born; and then the great Cyclopean wall one passes at the bend of the road, built even before the pagan temples; all this overcame me so powerfully this afternoon, that I was almost speechless. That hill-top must have been one of man's intense sacred places for three thousand years. And men die generation after generation, races die, but the new cult finds root in the old sacred place, and the quick spot of earth dies very slowly. Yet at last it too dies. But this quick spot is still not quite dead. The great monastery couchant there, half empty, but also not quite dead. And M—— and I walking across as the sun set yellow and the cold of the snow came into the air, back home to the monastery! And I feeling as if my heart had once more broken: I don't know why. And he feeling his fear of life, that haunted him, and his fear of his own self and its consequences, that never left him for long. And he seemed to walk close to me, very close. And we had neither of us anything more to say.

Don Bernardo was looking for us as we came up under the archway, he hatless in the cold evening, his black dress swinging voluminous. There were letters for M——. There was a small cheque for him from America—about fifty dollars—from some newspaper in the Middle West that had printed one of his articles. He had to talk with Don Bernardo about this.

I decided to go back the next day. I could not stay any longer. M—— was very disappointed, and begged me to remain. "I thought you would stay a week at least," he said. "Do stay over Sunday. Oh do!" But I couldn't, I didn't want to. I could see that his days were a torture to him—the long, cold days in that vast quiet building, with the strange and exhausting silence in the air, and the sense of the past preying on one, and the sense of the silent, suppressed scheming struggle of life going on still in the sacred place.

It was a cloudy morning. In the green courtyard the big Don Anselmo had just caught the little Don Lorenzo round the waist and was swinging him over a bush, like lads before school. The Prior was just hurrying somewhere, following his long fine nose. He bade me good-bye; pleasant, warm, jolly, with a touch of wistfulness in his deafness. I parted with real regret from Don Bernardo.

M—— was coming with me down the hill—not down the carriage road, but down the wide old paved path that swoops so wonderfully from the top of the hill to the bottom. It feels thousands of years old. M—— was quiet and friendly. We met Don Vincenzo, he who has the care of the land and crops, coming slowly, slowly uphill in his black cassock, treading slowly with his great thick boots. He was reading a little book. He saluted us as we passed. Lower down a strapping girl was watching three merino sheep among the bushes. One sheep came on its exquisite slender legs to smell of me, with that insatiable curiosity of a pecora. Her nose was silken and elegant as she reached it to sniff at me, and the yearning, wondering, inquisitive look in her eyes, made me realize that the Lamb of God must have been such a sheep as this.

M—— was miserable at my going. Not so much at my going, as at being left alone up there. We came to the foot of the hill, on to the town highroad. So we went into a little cave of a wine-kitchen to drink a glass of wine. M——chatted a little with the young woman. He chatted with everybody. She eyed us closely—and asked if we were from the monastery. We said we were. She seemed to have a little lurking antagonism round her nose, at the mention of the monastery. M—— paid for the wine—a franc. So we went out on the highroad, to part.

"Look," I said. "I can only give you twenty lire, because I shall need the rest for the journey——"

But he wouldn't take them. He looked at me wistfully. Then I went on down to the station, he turned away uphill. It was market in the town, and there were clusters of bullocks, and women cooking a little meal at a brazier under the trees, and goods spread out on the floor to sell, and sacks of beans and corn standing open, clustered round the trunks of the mulberry trees, and wagons with their shafts on the ground. The old peasants in their brown homespun frieze and skin sandals were watching for the world. And there again was the Middle Ages.

It began to rain, however. Suddenly it began to pour with rain, and my coat was wet through, and my trouser-legs. The train from Rome was late—I hoped not very late, or I should miss the boat. She came at last: and was full. I had to stand in the corridor. Then the man came to say dinner was served, so I luckily got a place and had my meal too. Sitting there in the dining-car, among the fat Neapolitans eating their macaroni, with the big glass windows steamed opaque and the rain beating outside, I let myself be carried away, away from the monastery, away from M——, away from everything.

At Naples there was a bit of sunshine again, and I had time to go on foot to the Immacolatella, where the little steamer lay. There on the steamer I sat in a bit of sunshine, and felt that again the world had come to an end for me, and again my heart was broken. The steamer seemed to be making its way away from the old world, that had come to another end in me.

It was after this I decided to go to Sicily. In February, only a few days after my return from the monastery, I was on the steamer for Palermo, and at dawn looking out on the wonderful coast of Sicily. Sicily, tall, forever rising up to her gem-like summits, all golden in dawn, and always glamorous, always hovering as if inaccessible, and yet so near, so distinct. Sicily unknown to me, and amethystine-glamorous in the Mediterranean dawn: like the dawn of our day, the wonder-morning of our epoch.

I had various letters from M———. He had told me to go to Girgenti. But I arrived in Girgenti when there was a strike of sulphur-miners, and they threw stones. So I did not want to live in Girgenti. M——— hated Taormina—he had been everywhere, tried everywhere, and was not, I found, in any good odour in most places. He wrote however saying he hoped I would like it. And later he sent the Legion manuscript. I thought it was good, and told him so. It was offered to publishers in London, but rejected.

In early April I went with my wife to Syracuse for a few days: lovely, lovely days, with the purple anemones blowing in the Sicilian fields, and Adonis-blood red on the little ledges, and the corn rising strong and green in the magical, malarial places, and Etna flowing now to the northward, still with her crown of snow. The lovely, lovely journey from Catania to Syracuse, in spring, winding round the blueness of that sea, where the tall pink asphodel was dying, and the yellow asphodel like a lily showing her silk. Lovely, lovely Sicily, the dawn-place, Europe's dawn, with Odysseus pushing his ship out of the shadows into the blue. Whatever had died for me, Sicily had then not died: dawn-lovely Sicily, and the Ionian sea.

We came back, and the world was lovely: our own house above the almond trees, and the sea in the cove below. Calabria glimmering like a changing opal away to the left, across the blue, bright straits and all the great blueness of the lovely dawn-sea in front, where the sun rose with a splendour like trumpets every morning, and me rejoicing like a madness in this dawn, day-dawn, life-dawn, the dawn which is Greece, which is me.

Well, into this lyricism suddenly crept the serpent. It was a lovely morning, still early. I heard a noise on the stairs from the lower terrace, and went to look. M—— on the stairs, looking up at me with a frightened face.

"Why!" I said. "Is it you?"

"Yes," he replied. "A terrible thing has happened."

He waited on the stairs, and I went down. Rather unwillingly, because I detest terrible things, and the people to whom they happen. So we leaned on the creeper-covered rail of the terrace, under festoons of creamy bignonia flowers, and looked at the pale blue, ethereal sea.

"When did you get back?" said he.

"Last evening."

"Oh! I came before. The contadini said they thought you would come yesterday evening. I've been here several days."

"Where are you staying?"

"At the San Domenico."

The San Domenico being then the most expensive hotel here, I thought he must have money. But I knew he wanted something of me.

"And are you staying some time?"

He paused a moment, and looked round cautiously.

"Is your wife there?" he asked, sotto voce.

"Yes, she's upstairs."

"Is there anyone who can hear?"

"No—only old Grazia down below, and she can't understand anyhow."

"Well," he said, stammering. "Let me tell you what's happened. I had to escape from the monastery. Don Bernardo had a telephone message from the town below, that the carabinieri were looking for an Americano—my name—— Of course you can guess how I felt, up there! Awful! Well——! I had to fly at a moment's notice. I just put two shirts in a handbag and went. I slipped down a path—or rather, it isn't a path—down the back of the hill. Ten minutes after Don Bernardo had the message I was running down the hill."

"But what did they want you for?" I asked dismayed.

"Well," he faltered. "I told you about the cheque at Anzio, didn't I? Well it seems the hotel people applied to the police. Anyhow," he added hastily, "I couldn't let myself be arrested up there, could I? So awful for the monastery!"

"Did they know then that you were in trouble?" I asked.

"Don Bernardo knew I had no money," he said. "Of course he had to know. Yes—he knew I was in *difficulty*. But, of course, he didn't know—well—*everything*." He laughed a little, comical laugh over the *everything,* as if he was just a little bit naughtily proud of it: most ruefully also.

"No," he continued, "that's what I'm most afraid of—that they'll find out everything at the monastery. Of course it's *dreadful*—the Americano, been staying there for months, and everything so nice and —, well you know how they are, they imagine every American is a millionaire, if not a multi-millionaire. And suddenly to be wanted by the police! Of course it's *dreadful*! Anything rather than a scandal at the monastery—anything. Oh, how awful it was! I can tell you, in that quarter of an hour, I sweated blood. Don Bernardo lent me two hundred lire of the monastery money—which he'd no business to do. And I escaped down the back of the hill, I walked to the next station up the line, and took the next train—the slow train—a few stations up towards Rome. And there I changed and caught the diretto for Sicily. I came straight to you—— Of course I was in *agony*: imagine it! I spent most of the time as far as Naples in the lavatory." He laughed his little jerky laugh.

"What class did you travel?"

"Second. All through the night. I arrived more dead than alive, not having had a meal for two days—only some sandwich stuff I bought on the platform."

"When did you come then?"

"I arrived on Saturday evening. I came out here on Sunday morning, and they told me you were away. Of course, imagine what it's like! I'm in torture every minute, in torture, of course. Why just imagine!" And he laughed his little laugh.

"But how much money have you got?"

"Oh—I've just got twenty-five francs and five soldi." He laughed as if it was rather a naughty joke.

"But," I said, "if you've got no money, why do you go to the San Domenico? How much do you pay there?"

"Fifty lire a day. Of course it's *ruinous*——"

"But at the Bristol you only pay twenty-five—and at Fichera's only twenty."

"Yes, I know you do," he said. "But I stayed at the Bristol once, and I loathed the place. Such an offensive manager. And I couldn't touch the food at Fichera's."

"But who's going to pay for the San Domenico, then?" I asked.

"Well, I thought," he said, "you know all those manuscripts of mine? Well, you think they're some good, don't you? Well, I thought if I made them over to you, and you did what you could with them and just kept me going till I can get a new start—or till I can get away——"

I looked across the sea: the lovely morning-blue sea towards Greece.

"Where do you want to get away to?" I said.

"To Egypt. I know a man in Alexandria who owns newspapers there. I'm sure if I could get over there he'd give me an editorship or something. And of course money will come. I've written to ——, who was my *greatest* friend, in London. He will send me something——"

"And what else do you expect?"

"Oh, my article on the monastery was accepted by *Land and Water* —thanks to you and your kindness, of course. I thought if I might stay very quietly with you, for a time, and write some things I'm wanting to do, and collect a little money—and then get away to Egypt——"

He looked up into my face, as if he were trying all he could on me. First thing I knew was that I could not have him in the house with me: and even if I could have done it, my wife never could.

"You've got a lovely place here, perfectly beautiful," he said. "Of course, if it had to be Taormina, you've chosen far the best place here. I like this side so much better than the Etna side. Etna always there and people raving about it gets on my nerves. And a *charming* house, *charming*."

He looked round the loggia and along the other terrace.

"Is it all yours?" he said.

"We don't use the ground floor. Come in here."

So we went into the salotta.

"Oh, what a beautiful room," he cried. "But perfectly palatial. Charming! Charming! *Much* the nicest house in Taormina."

"No," I said, "as a house it isn't very grand, though I like it for myself. It's just what I want. And I love the situation. But I'll go and tell my wife you are here."

"Will you?" he said, bridling nervously. "Of course I've never met your wife." And he laughed the nervous, naughty, jokey little laugh.

I left him, and ran upstairs to the kitchen. There was my wife, with wide eyes. She had been listening to catch the conversation. But M——'s voice was too hushed.

"M——!" said I softly. "The carabinieri wanted to arrest him at the monastery, so he has escaped here, and wants me to be responsible for him."

"Arrest him what for?"

"Debts, I suppose. Will you come down and speak to him?"

M—— of course was very charming with my wife. He kissed her

hand humbly, in the correct German fashion, and spoke with an air of reverence that infallibly gets a woman.

"Such a beautiful place you have here," he said, glancing through the open doors of the room, at the sea beyond. "So clever of you to find it."

"Lawrence found it," said she. "Well, and you are in all kinds of difficulty!"

"Yes, isn't it terrible!" he said, laughing as if it were a joke—rather a wry joke. "I felt dreadful at the monastery. So dreadful for them, if there was any sort of scandal. And after I'd been so well received there —and so much the Signor Americano—— Dreadful, don't you think?" He laughed again, like a naughty boy.

We had an engagement to lunch that morning. My wife was dressed, so I went to get ready. Then we told M—— we must go out, and he accompanied us to the village. I gave him just the hundred francs I had in my pocket, and he said could he come and see me that evening? I asked him to come next morning.

"You're so awfully kind," he said, simpering a little.

But by this time I wasn't feeling kind.

"He's quite nice," said my wife. "But he's rather an impossible little person. And you'll see, he'll be a nuisance. Whatever do you pick up such dreadful people for?"

"Nay," I said. "You can't accuse me of picking up dreadful people. He's the first. And even he isn't dreadful."

The next morning came a letter from Don Bernardo addressed to me, but only enclosing a letter to M——. So he was using my address. At ten o'clock he punctually appeared: slipping in as if to avoid notice. My wife would not see him, so I took him out on the terrace again.

"Isn't it beautiful here!" he said. "Oh, so beautiful! If only I had peace of mind. Of course I sweat blood every time anybody comes through the door. You are splendidly private out here."

"Yes," I said. "But M——, there isn't a room for you in the house. There isn't a spare room anyway. You'd better think of getting something cheaper in the village."

"But what can I get?" he snapped.

That rather took my breath away. Myself, I had never been near the San Domenico hotel. I knew I simply could not afford it.

"What made you go to the San Domenico in the first place?" I said. "The most expensive hotel in the place!"

"Oh, I'd stayed there for two months, and they knew me, and I knew they'd ask no questions. I knew they wouldn't ask for a deposit or anything."

"But nobody dreams of asking for a deposit," I said.

"Anyhow I shan't take my meals there. I shall just take coffee in the morning. I've had to eat there so far, because I was starved to death, and had no money to go out. But I had two meals in that little restaurant yesterday; disgusting food."

"And how much did that cost?"

"Oh fourteen francs and fifteen francs, with a quarter of wine—and such a poor meal!"

Now I was annoyed, knowing that I myself should have bought bread and cheese for one franc, and eaten it in my room. But also I realized that the modern creed says, if you sponge, sponge thoroughly: and also that every man has a "right to live," and that if he can manage to live well, no matter at whose expense, all credit to him. This is the kind of talk one accepts in one's slipshod moments; now it was actually tried on me, I didn't like it at all.

"But who's going to pay your bill at the San Domenico?" I said.

"I thought you'd advance me the money on those manuscripts."

"It's no good talking about the money on the manuscripts," I said. "I should have to give it to you. And as a matter of fact, I've got just sixty pounds in the bank in England, and about fifteen hundred lire here. My wife and I have got to live on that. We don't spend as much in a week as you spend in three days at the San Domenico. It's no good your thinking I can advance money on the manuscripts. I can't. If I was rich, I'd give you money. But I've got no money, and never have had any. Have you nobody you can go to?"

"I'm waiting to hear from ——. When I go back into the village, I'll telegraph to him," replied M——, a little crestfallen. "Of course I'm in torture night and day, or I wouldn't appeal to you like this. I know it's unpleasant for you——" and he put his hand on my arm and looked up beseechingly. "But what am I to do?"

"You must get out of the San Domenico," I said. "That's the first thing."

"Yes," he said, a little piqued now. "I know it is. I'm going to ask Pancrazio Melenga to let me have a room in his house. He knows me quite well—he's an awfully nice fellow. He'll do *anything* for me— *anything*. I was just going there yesterday afternoon when you were coming from Timeo. He was out, so I left word with his wife, who is a charming little person. If he has a room to spare, I know he will let me have it. And he's a *splendid* cook—splendid. By far the nicest food in Taormina."

"Well," I said. "If you settle with Melenga, I will pay your bill at the San Domenico, but I can't do any more. I simply can't."

"But what am I to *do*?" he snapped.

"I don't know," I said. "You must think."

"I came here," he said, "thinking you would help me. What am I to do, if you won't? I shouldn't have come to Taormina at all, save for you. Don't be unkind to me—don't speak so coldly to me——" He put his hand on my arm, and looked up at me with tears swimming in his eyes. Then he turned aside his face, overcome with tears. I looked away at the Ionian sea, feeling my blood turn to ice and the sea go black. I loathe scenes such as this.

"Did you telegraph to ——?" I said.

"Yes. I have no answer yet. I hope you don't mind—I gave your address for a reply."

"Oh," I said. "There's a letter for you from Don Bernardo."

He went pale. I was angry at his having used my address in this manner.

"Nothing further has happened at the monastery," he said. "They rang up from the Questura, from the police station, and Don Bernardo answered that the Americano had left for Rome. Of course I did take the train for Rome. And Don Bernardo wanted me to go to Rome. He advised me to do so. I didn't tell him I was here till I had got here. He thought I should have had more resources in Rome, and of course I should. I should certainly have gone there, if it hadn't been for *you here*——"

Well, I was getting tired and angry. I would not give him any more money at the moment. I promised, if he would leave the hotel I would pay his bill, but he must leave it at once. He went off to settle with Melenga. He asked again if he could come in the afternoon: I said I was going out.

He came nevertheless while I was out. This time my wife found him on the stairs. She was for hating him, of course. So she stood immovable on the top stair, and he stood two stairs lower, and he kissed her hand in utter humility. And he pleaded with her, and as he looked up to her on the stairs the tears ran down his face and he trembled with distress. And her spine crept up and down with distaste and discomfort. But he broke into a few phrases of touching German, and I know he broke down her reserve and she promised him all he wanted. This part she would never confess, though. Only she was shivering with revulsion and excitement and even a sense of power, when I came home.

That was why M—— appeared more impertinent than ever, next

morning. He had arranged to go to Melenga's house the following day, and to pay ten francs a day for his room, his meals extra. So that was something. He made a long tale about not eating any of his meals in the hotel now, but pretending he was invited out, and eating in the little restaurants where the food was so bad. And he had now only fifteen lire left in his pocket. But I was cold, and wouldn't give him any more. I said I would give him money next day, for his bill.

He had now another request, and a new tone.

"Won't you do *one more* thing for me?" he said. "Oh do! Do do this one thing for me. I want you to go to the monastery and bring away my important papers and some clothes and my important trinkets. I have made a list of the things here—and where you'll find them in my writing-table and in the chest of drawers. I don't think you'll have any trouble. Don Bernardo has the keys. He will open everything for you. And I beg you, *in the name of God*, don't let anybody else see the things. Not even Don Bernardo. Don't, whatever you do, let him see the papers and manuscripts you are bringing. If he sees them, there's an end to me at the monastery. I can *never* go back there. I am ruined in their eyes for ever. As it is—although Don Bernardo is the best person in the world and my dearest friend, still—you know what people are— especially monks. A little curious, don't you know, a little inquisitive. Well, let us hope for the best as far as that goes. But you will do this for me, won't you? I shall be so eternally grateful."

Now a journey to the monastery meant a terrible twenty hours in the train each way—all that awful journey through Calabria to Naples and northwards. It meant mixing myself up in this man's affairs. It meant appearing as his accomplice at the monastery. It meant travelling with all his "compromising" papers and his valuables. And all this time, I never knew what mischiefs he had really been up to, and I didn't trust him, not for one single second. He would tell me nothing save that Anzio hotel cheque. I knew that wasn't all, by any means. So I mistrusted him. And with a feeling of utter mistrust goes a feeling of contempt and dislike——And finally, it would have cost me at least ten pounds sterling, which I simply did not want to spend in waste.

"I don't want to do that," I said.

"Why not?" he asked, sharp, looking green. He had planned it all out.

"No, I don't want to."

"Oh, but I *can't* remain here as I am. I've got no *clothes*—I've got nothing to *wear*. I *must* have my things from the monastery. What can I do? What can I do? I came to you, if it hadn't been for you I should have gone to Rome. I came to you—Oh yes, you *will* go. You *will* go, won't you? You *will* go to the monastery for my things?" And again he put his hand on my arm, and the tears began to fall from his up-turned eyes. I turned my head aside. Never had the Ionian sea looked so sickening to me.

"I don't *want* to," said I.

"But you *will*! You will! You *will* go to the monastery for me, won't you? Everything else is no good if you won't. I've nothing to wear. I haven't got my manuscripts to work on, I can't do the things I am doing. Here I live in a sweat of anxiety. I try to work, and I can't settle. I can't do anything. It's dreadful. I shan't have a minute's peace till I have got those things from the monastery, till I know they can't get at my private papers. You will do this for me! You will, won't you? Please do! Oh please do!" And again tears.

And I with my bowels full of bitterness, loathing the thought of that journey there and back, on such an errand. Yet not quite sure that I ought to refuse. And he pleaded and struggled, and tried to bully me with tears and entreaty and reproach, to do his will. And I couldn't quite refuse. But neither could I agree.

At last I said:

"I don't want to go, and I tell you. I won't promise to go. And I won't say that I will not go. I won't say until tomorrow. Tomorrow I will tell you. Don't come to the house. I will be in the Corso at ten o'clock."

"I didn't doubt for a minute you would do this for me," he said. "Otherwise I should never have come to Taormina." As if he had done me an honour in coming to Taormina; and as if I had betrayed *him*.

"Well," I said. "If you make these messes you'll have to get out of them yourself. I don't know why you are *in* such a mess."

"Any man may make a mistake," he said sharply, as if correcting me.

"Yes, a *mistake*!" said I. "If it's a question of a mistake."

So once more he went, humbly, beseechingly, and yet, one could not help but feel, with all that terrible insolence of the humble. It is the humble, the wistful, the would-be-loving souls today who bully us with their charity-demanding insolence. They just make up their minds, these needful sympathetic souls, that one is there to do their will. Very good.

I decided in the day I would *not* go. Without reasoning it out, I knew I *really* didn't want to go. I plainly didn't want it. So I wouldn't go.

The morning came again hot and lovely. I set off to the village. But there was M—— watching for me on the path beyond the valley. He came forward and took my hand warmly, clingingly. I turned back, to remain in the country. We talked for a minute of his leaving the hotel—he was going that afternoon, he had asked for his bill. But he was waiting for the other answer.

"And I have decided," I said, "I won't go to the monastery."

"You won't." He looked at me. I saw how yellow he was round the eyes, and yellow under his reddish skin.

"No," I said.

And it was final. He knew it. We went some way in silence. I turned in at the garden gate. It was a lovely, lovely morning of hot sun. Butterflies were flapping over the rosemary hedges and over a few little red poppies, the young vines smelt sweet in flower, very sweet, the corn was tall and green, and there were still some wild, rose-red gladiolus flowers among the watery green of the wheat. M—— had accepted my refusal. I expected him to be angry. But no, he seemed quieter, wistfuller, and he seemed almost to love me for having refused him. I stood at a bend in the path. The sea was heavenly blue, rising up beyond the vines and olive leaves, lustrous pale lacquer blue as only the Ionian sea can be. Away at the brook below the women were washing, and one could hear the chock-chock-chock of linen beaten against the stones. I felt M—— then an intolerable weight and like a clot of dirt over everything.

"May I come in?" he said to me.

"No," I said. "Don't come to the house. My wife doesn't want it."

Even that he accepted without any offence, and seemed only to like me better for it. That was a puzzle to me. I told him I would leave a letter and a cheque for him at the bank in the Corso that afternoon.

I did so, writing a cheque for a few pounds, enough to cover his bill and leave a hundred lire or so over, and a letter to say I could *not* do any more, and I didn't want to see him any more.

So, there was an end of it for a moment. Yet I felt him looming in the village, waiting. I had rashly said I would go to tea with him to the villa of one of the Englishmen resident here, whose acquaintance I had not made. Alas, M—— kept me to the promise. As I came home he appealed to me again. He was rather insolent. What good to him, he said, were the few pounds I had given him? He had got a hundred and fifty lire left. What good was that? I realized it really was not a solution, and said nothing. Then he spoke of his plans for getting to Egypt.

The fare, he had found out, was thirty-five pounds. And where were thirty-five pounds coming from? Not from me.

I spent a week avoiding him, wondering what on earth the poor devil was doing, and yet *determined* he should not be a parasite on me. If I could have given him fifty pounds and sent him to Egypt to be a parasite on somebody else, I would have done so. Which is what we call charity. However, I couldn't.

My wife chafed, crying: "What have you done! We shall have him on our hands all our life. We can't let him starve. It is degrading, degrading, to have him hanging on to us."

"Yes," I said. "He must starve or work or something. I am not God who is responsible for him."

M—— was determined not to lose his status as a gentleman. In a way I sympathized with him. He would never be out at elbows. That is your modern rogue. He will not degenerate outwardly. Certain standards of a gentleman he *would* keep up: he would be well-dressed, he would be lavish with borrowed money, he would be as far as possible honourable in his small transactions of daily life. Well, very good. I sympathized with him to a certain degree. If he could find his own way out, well and good. Myself, I was not his way out.

Ten days passed. It was hot and I was going about the terrace in pyjamas and a big old straw hat, when suddenly, a Sicilian, handsome, in the prime of life, and in his best black suit, smiling at me and taking off his hat!

And could he speak to me. I threw away my straw hat, and we went into the salotta. He handed me a note.

"Il Signor M—— mi ha dato questa lettera per Lei!" he began, and I knew what was coming. Melenga had been a waiter in good hotels, had saved money, built himself a fine house which he let to foreigners. He was a pleasant fellow, and at his best now, because he was in a rage. I must repeat M——'s letter from memory—"Dear Lawrence, would you do me another kindness. *Land and Water* sent a cheque for seven guineas for the article on the monastery, and Don Bernardo forwarded this to me under Melenga's name. But unfortunately he made a mistake, and put Orazio instead of Pancrazio, so the post office would not deliver the letter, and have returned it to the monastery. This morning Melenga insulted me, and I cannot stay in his house another minute. Will you be so kind as to advance me these seven guineas, and I shall leave Taormina at once, for Malta."

I asked Melenga what had happened, and read him the letter. He was handsome in his rage, lifting his brows and suddenly smiling:

"Ma senta, Signore! Signor M—— has been in my house for ten days, and lived well, and eaten well, and drunk well, and I have not seen a single penny of his money. I go out in the morning and buy all the things, all he wants, and my wife cooks it, and he is very pleased, very pleased, has never eaten such good food in his life, and everything is splendid, splendid. And he never pays a penny. Not a penny. Says he is waiting for money from England, from America, from India. But the money never comes. And I am a poor man, Signore, I have a wife and child to keep. I have already spent three hundred lire for this Signor M——, and I never see a penny of it back. And he says the money is coming, it is coming—— But when? He never says he has got no money. He says he is expecting. Tomorrow—always tomorrow. It will come tonight, it will come tomorrow. This makes me in a rage. Till at last this morning I said to him I would bring nothing in, and he shouldn't have not so much as a drop of coffee in my house until he paid for it. It displeases me, Signore, to say such a thing. I have known Signor M—— for many years, and he has always had money, and always been pleasant, molto bravo, and also generous with his money. Si, lo so! And my wife, poverina, she cries and says if the man has no money he must eat. But he doesn't say he has no money. He says always it is coming, it is coming, today, tomorrow, today, tomorrow. E non viene mai niente. And this enrages me, Signore. So I said that to him this morning. And he said he wouldn't stay in my house, and that I had insulted him, and he sends me this letter to you, Signore, and says you will send him the money. Ecco come!"

Between his rage he smiled at me. One thing however I could see: he was not going to lose his money, M—— or no M——.

"Is it true that a letter came which the post would not deliver?" I asked him.

"Si signore, e vero. It came yesterday, addressed to me. And why, signore, why do his letters come addressed in my name? Why? Unless he has done something——?"

He looked at me enquiringly. I felt already mixed up in shady affairs.

"Yes," I said, "there is something. But I don't know exactly what. I don't ask, because I don't want to know in these affairs. It is better not to know."

"Gia! Gia! Molto meglio, signore. There will be something. There will be something happened that he had to escape from that monastery. And it will be some affair of the police."

"Yes, I think so," said I. "Money and the police. Probably debts. I don't ask. He is only an acquaintance of mine, not a friend."

"Sure it will be an affair of the police," he said with a grimace. "If not, why does he use my name! Why don't his letters come in his own name? Do you believe, signore, that he has any money? Do you think this money will come?"

"I'm sure he's *got* no money," I said. "Whether anybody will send him any I don't know."

The man watched me attentively.

"He's got nothing?" he said.

"No. At the present he's got nothing."

Then Pancrazio exploded on the sofa.

"Allora! Well then! Well then, why does he come to my house, why does he come and take a room in my house, and ask me to buy food, good food as for a gentleman who can pay, and a flask of wine, and everything, if he has no money? If he has no money, why does he come to Taormina? It is many years that he has been in Italy—ten years, fifteen years. And he has no money. Where has he had his money from before? Where?"

"From his writing, I suppose."

"Well then why doesn't he get money for his writing now? He writes. He writes, he works, he says it is for the big newspapers."

"It is difficult to sell things."

"Heh! then why doesn't he live on what he made before? He hasn't a soldo. He hasn't a penny—But how! How did he pay his bill at the San Domenico?"

"I had to lend him the money for that. He really hadn't a penny."

"You! You! Well then, he has been in Italy all these years. How is it he has nobody that he can ask for a hundred lire or two? Why does he come to you? Why? Why has he nobody in Rome, in Florence, anywhere?"

"I wonder that myself."

"Siccuro! He's been all these years here. And why doesn't he speak proper Italian? After all these years, and speaks all upside-down, it isn't Italian, an ugly confusion. Why? Why? He passes for a signore, for a man of education. And he comes to take the bread out of my mouth. And I have a wife and child, I am a poor man, I have nothing to eat myself if everything goes to a mezzo-signore like him. Nothing! He owes me now three hundred lire. But he will not leave my house, he will not leave Taormina till he has paid. I will go to the Prefettura, I will go to the Questura, to the police. I will not be swindled by such a mezzo-signore. What does he want to do? If he has no money, what does he want to do?"

"To go to Egypt where he says he can earn some," I replied briefly. But I was feeling bitter in the mouth. When the man called M—— a mezzo-signore, a half-gentleman, it was so true. And at the same time it was so cruel, and so rude. And Melenga—there I sat in my pyjamas and sandals—probably he would be calling me also a mezzo-signore, or a quarto-signore even. He was a Sicilian who feels he is being done out of his money—and that is saying everything.

"To Egypt! And who will pay for him to go? Who will give him money? But he must pay me first. He must pay me first."

"He says," I said, "that in the letter which went back to the monastery there was a cheque for seven pounds—some six hundred lire—and he asks me to send him this money, and when the letter is returned again I shall have the cheque that is in it."

Melenga watched me.

"Six hundred lire——" he said.

"Yes."

"Oh well then. If he pays me, he can stay——" he said; he almost added: "till the six hundred is finished." But he left it unspoken.

"But am I going to send the money? Am I sure that what he says is true?"

"I think it is true. I think it is true," said he. "The letter *did* come."

I thought for a while.

"First," I said, "I will write and ask him if it is quite true, and to give me a guarantee."

"Very well," said Melenga.

I wrote to M——, saying that if he could assure me that what he said about the seven guineas was quite correct, and if he would give me a note to the editor of *Land and Water*, saying that the cheque was to be paid to me, I would send the seven guineas.

Melenga was back in another half-hour. He brought a note which began:

"Dear Lawrence, I seem to be living in an atmosphere of suspicion. First Melenga this morning, and now you——" Those are the exact opening words. He went on to say that of course his word was true, and he enclosed a note to the editor, saying the seven guineas were to be transferred to me. He asked me please to send the money, as he could not stay another night at Melenga's house, but would leave for Catania, where, by the sale of some trinkets, he hoped to make some money and to see once more about a passage to Egypt. He had been to Catania once already—travelling *third class!*—but had failed to find any cargo boat that would take him to Alexandria. He would get away now to Malta. His things were being sent down to Syracuse from the monastery.

I wrote and said I hoped he would get safely away, and enclosed the cheque.

"This will be for six hundred lire," said Melenga.

"Yes," said I.

"Eh, va bene! If he pays the three hundred lire, he can stop in my house for thirty lire a day."

"He says he won't sleep in your house again."

"Ma! Let us see. If he likes to stay. He has always been a bravo signore. I have always liked him quite well. If he wishes to stay and pay me thirty lire a day——"

The man smiled at me rather greenly.

"I'm afraid he is offended," said I.

"Eh, va bene! Ma senta, Signore. When he was here before—you know I have this house of mine to let. And you know the English signorina goes away in the summer. Oh, very well. Says M——, he writes for a newspaper, he owns a newspaper, I don't know what, in Rome. He will put in an advertisement advertising my villa. And so I shall get somebody to take it. Very well. And he put in the advertisement. He sent me the paper and I saw it there. But no one came to take my villa. Va bene! But after a year, in the January, that is, came a bill for me for twenty-two lire to pay for it. Yes, I had to pay the twenty-two lire, for nothing—for the advertisement which Signore M—— put in the paper."

"Bah!" said I.

He shook hands with me and left. The next day he came after me in the street and said that M—— had departed the previous evening for Catania. As a matter of fact the post brought me a note of thanks from Catania. M—— was never indecent, and one could never dismiss him just as a scoundrel. He was not. He was one of these modern parasites who just assume their right to live and live well, leaving the payment to anybody who can, will, or must pay. The end is inevitably swindling.

There came also a letter from Rome, addressed to me. I opened it unthinking. It was for M——, from an Italian lawyer, stating that enquiry had been made about the writ against M——, and that it was for *qualche affaro di truffa*, some affair of swindling: that the lawyer had seen this, that and the other person, but nothing could be done. He regretted, etc., etc. I forwarded this letter to M—— at Syracuse, and hoped to God it was ended. Ah, I breathed free now he had gone.

But no. A friend who was with us dearly wanted to go to Malta. It is only about eighteen hours' journey from Taormina—easier than going to Naples. So our friend invited us to take the trip with her, as her guests. This was rather jolly. I calculated that M——, who had been gone a week or so, would easily have got to Malta. I had had a friendly letter from him from Syracuse, thanking me for the one I had forwarded, and enclosing an I.O.U. for the various sums of money he had had.

So, on a hot, hot Thursday, we were sitting in the train again running south, the four and a half hours' journey to Syracuse. And M—— dwindled now into the past. If we should see him! But no, it was impossible. After all the wretchedness of that affair we were in holiday spirits.

The train ran into Syracuse station. We sat on, to go the few yards further into the port. A tout climbed on the foot-board: were we going to Malta? Well, we couldn't. There was a strike of the steamers, we couldn't go. When would the steamer go? Who knows? Perhaps to-morrow.

We got down crestfallen. What should we do? There stood the express train about to start off back northwards. We could be home again that evening. But no, it would be too much of a fiasco. We let the train go, and trailed off into the town, to the Grand Hotel, which is an old Italian place just opposite the port. It is rather a dreary hotel—and many bloodstains of squashed mosquitoes on the bedroom walls. Ah, vile mosquitoes!

However, nothing to be done. Syracuse port is fascinating too, a tiny port with the little Sicilian ships having the slanting eyes painted on the prow, to see the way, and a coal boat from Cardiff, and one American and two Scandinavian steamers—no more. But there were two torpedo boats in the harbour, and it was like a festa, a strange, lousy festa.

Beautiful the round harbour where the Athenian ships came. And wonderful, beyond, the long sinuous sky-line of the long flat-topped table-land hills which run along the southern coast, so different from the peaky, pointed, bunched effect of many-tipped Sicily in the north. The sun went down behind that lovely, sinuous sky-line, the harbour water was gold and red, the people promenaded in thick streams under the pomegranate trees and hibiscus trees. Arabs in white burnouses and fat Turks in red and black alpaca long coats strolled also—waiting for the steamer.

Next day it was very hot. We went to the consul and the steamer agency. There was real hope that the brute of a steamer might actually sail that night. So we stayed on, and wandered round the town on the island, the old solid town, and sat in the church looking at the grand Greek columns embedded there in the walls.

When I came in to lunch the porter said there was a letter for me. Impossible! said I. But he brought me a note. Yes. M——! He was staying at the other hotel along the front. "Dear Lawrence, I saw you this morning, all three of you walking down the Via Nazionale, but you would not look at me. I have got my visés and everything ready. The strike of the steamboats has delayed me here. I am sweating blood. I have a last request to make of you. Can you let me have ninety lire, to make up what I need for my hotel bill? If I cannot have this I am lost. I hoped to find you at the hotel but the porter said you were out. I am at the Casa Politi, passing every half-hour in agony. If you can be so kind as to stretch your generosity to this last loan, of course I shall be eternally grateful. I can pay you back once I get to Malta——"

Well, here was a blow! The worst was that he thought I had cut him —a thing I wouldn't have done. So after luncheon behold me going through the terrific sun of that harbour front of Syracuse, an enormous and powerful sun, to the Casa Politi. The porter recognized me and looked enquiringly. M—— was out, and I said I would call again at four o'clock.

It happened we were in the town eating ices at four, so I didn't get to his hotel till half-past. He was out—gone to look for me. So I left a note saying I had not seen him in the Via Nazionale, that I had called twice, and that I should be in the Grand Hotel in the evening.

When we came in at seven, M—— in the hall, sitting the picture of misery and endurance. He took my hand in both his, and bowed to the women, who nodded and went upstairs. He and I went and sat in the empty lounge. Then he told me the trials he had had—how his luggage had come, and the station had charged him eighteen lire a day for deposit—how he had had to wait on at the hotel because of the ship— how he had tried to sell his trinkets, and had today parted with his opal sleevelinks—so that now he only wanted seventy, not ninety lire. I gave him a hundred note, and he looked into my eyes, his own eyes swimming with tears, and he said he was sweating blood.

Well, the steamer went that night. She was due to leave at ten. We went on board after dinner. We were going second class. And so, for once, was M——. It was only an eight hours' crossing, yet, in spite of all the blood he had sweated, he would not go third class. In a way I admired him for sticking to his principles. I should have gone third myself, out of shame of spending somebody else's money. He would not give way to such weakness. He knew that as far as the world goes, you're a first-class gentleman if you have a first-class ticket; if you have a third, no gentleman at all. It behoved him to be a gentleman. I understood his point, but the women were indignant. And I was just rather tired of him and his gentlemanliness.

It amused me very much to lean on the rail of the upper deck and watch the people coming on board—first going into the little customs house with their baggage, then scuffling up the gangway on board. The tall Arabs in their ghostly white woollen robes came carrying their sacks: they were going on to Tripoli. The fat Turk in his fez and long black alpaca coat with white drawers underneath came beaming up to the second class. There was a great row in the customs house: and then, simply running like a beetle with rage, there came on board a little Maltese or Greek fellow, followed by a tall lantern-jawed fellow: both seedy-looking scoundrels suckled in scoundrelism. They raved and nearly threw their arms away into the sea, talking wildly in some weird language with the fat Turk, who listened solemnly, away below on the deck. Then they rushed to somebody else. Of course, we were dying with curiosity. Thank heaven I heard men talking in Italian. It appears the two seedy fellows were trying to smuggle silver coin in small sacks and rolls out of the country. They were detected. But they declared they had a right to take it away, as it was foreign specie, English florins and half-crowns, and South American dollars and Spanish money. The customs-officers however detained the lot. The little enraged beetle of a fellow ran back and forth from the ship to the customs, from the customs to the ship, afraid to go without his money, afraid the ship would go without him.

At five minutes to ten, there came M——: very smart in his little grey overcoat and grey curly hat, walking very smart and erect and genteel, and followed by a porter with a barrow of luggage. They went into the customs, M—— in his grey suède gloves passing rapidly and smartly in, like the grandest gentleman on earth, and with his grey suède hands throwing open his luggage for inspection. From on board we could see the interior of the little customs shed.

Yes, he was through. Brisk, smart, superb, like the grandest little gentleman on earth, strutting because he was late, he crossed the bit of flagged pavement and came up the gangway, haughty as you can wish. The carabinieri were lounging by the foot of the gangway, fooling with one another. The little gentleman passed them with his nose in the air, came quickly on board, followed by his porter, and in a moment disappeared. After about five minutes the porter reappeared—a red-haired fellow, I knew him—he even saluted me from below, the brute. But M—— lay in hiding.

I trembled for him at every unusual stir. There on the quay stood the English consul with his bull-dog, and various elegant young officers with yellow on their uniforms, talking to elegant young Italian ladies in black hats with stiff ospreys and bunchy furs, and gangs of porters and hotel people and onlookers. Then came a tramp-tramp-tramp of a squad of soldiers in red fezzes and baggy grey trousers. Instead of coming on board they camped on the quay. I wondered if all these had come for poor M——. But apparently not.

So the time passed, till nearly midnight, when one of the elegant young lieutenants began to call the names of the soldiers: and the soldiers answered: and one after another filed on board with their kit. So, they were on board, on their way to Africa.

Now somebody called out—and the visitors began to leave the boat. Barefooted sailors and a boy ran to raise the gangway. The last visitor or official with a bunch of papers stepped off the gangway. People on shore began to wave handkerchiefs. The red-fezzed soldiers leaned like so many flower-pots over the lower rail. There was a calling of farewells. The ship was fading into the harbour, the people on shore seemed smaller, under the lamp, in the deep night—without one's knowing why.

So, we passed out of the harbour, passed the glittering lights of Ortygia, past the two lighthouses, into the open Mediterranean. The noise of a ship in the open sea! It was a still night, with stars, only a bit chill. And the ship churned through the water.

Suddenly, like a *revenant*, appeared M—— near us, leaning on the rail and looking back at the lights of Syracuse sinking already forlorn and little on the low darkness. I went to him.

"Well," he said, with his little smirk of a laugh. "Good-bye Italy!"

"Not a sad farewell either," said I.

"No, my word, not this time," he said. "But what an awful long time we were starting! A brutta mezz'ora for me, indeed. Oh, my word, I begin to breathe free for the first time since I left the monastery! How awful it's been! But of course, in Malta, I shall be all right. Don Bernardo has written to his friends there. They'll have everything ready for me that I want, and I can pay you back the money you so kindly lent me."

We talked for some time, leaning on the inner rail of the upper deck.

"Oh," he said, "there's Commander So-and-so, of the British fleet.

He's stationed in Malta. I made his acquaintance in the hotel. I hope we're going to be great friends in Malta. I hope I shall have an opportunity to introduce you to him. Well, I suppose you will want to be joining your ladies. So long, then. Oh, for tomorrow morning! I never longed so hard to be in the British Empire——" He laughed, and strutted away.

In a few minutes we three, leaning on the rail of the second-class upper deck, saw our little friend large as life on the first-class deck, smoking a cigar and chatting in an absolutely first-class-ticket manner with the above mentioned Commander. He pointed us out to the Commander, and we felt the first-class passengers were looking across at us second-class passengers with pleasant interest. The women went behind a canvas heap to laugh, I hid my face under my hat-brim to grin and watch. Larger than any first-class ticketer leaned our little friend on the first-class rail, and whiffed at his cigar. So *dégagé* and so genteel he could be. Only I noticed he wilted a little when the officers of the ship came near.

He was still on the first-class deck when we went down to sleep. In the morning I came up soon after dawn. It was a lovely summer Mediterranean morning, with the sun rising up in a gorgeous golden rage, and the sea so blue, so fairy blue, as the Mediterranean is in summer. We were approaching quite near to a rocky, pale yellow island with some vineyards, rising magical out of the swift blue sea into the morning radiance. The rocks were almost as pale as butter, the islands were like golden shadows loitering in the midst of the Mediterranean, lonely among all the blue.

M—— came up to my side.

"Isn't it lovely! Isn't it beautiful!" he said. "I love approaching these islands in the early morning." He had almost recovered his assurance, and the slight pomposity and patronizing tone I had first known in him. "In two hours I shall be free! Imagine it! Oh what a beautiful feeling!" I looked at him in the morning light. His face was a good deal broken by his last month's experience, older looking, and dragged. Now that the excitement was nearing its end, the tiredness began to tell on him. He was yellowish round the eyes, and the whites of his round, rather impudent blue eyes were discoloured.

Malta was drawing near. We saw the white fringe of the sea upon the yellow rocks, and a white road looping on the yellow rocky hillside. I thought of St. Paul, who must have been blown this way, must have struck the island from this side. Then we saw the heaped glitter of the square facets of houses, Valletta, splendid above the Mediterranean, and a tangle of shipping and Dreadnoughts and watch-towers in the beautiful, locked-in harbour.

We had to go down to have passports examined. The officials sat in the long saloon. It was a horrible squash and squeeze of the first- and second-class passengers. M—— was a little ahead of me. I saw the American eagle on his passport. Yes, he passed all right. Once more he was free. As he passed away he turned and gave a condescending affable nod to me and to the Commander, who was just behind me.

The ship was lying in Valletta harbour. I saw M——, quite superb and brisk now, ordering a porter with his luggage into a boat. The great rocks rose above us, yellow and carved, cut straight by man. On top were all the houses. We got at last into a boat and were rowed ashore. Strange to be on British soil and to hear English. We got a carriage and drove up the steep highroad through the cutting in the rock, up to the town. There, in the big square we had coffee, sitting out of doors. A military band went by playing splendidly in the bright, hot morning. The Maltese lounged about, and watched. Splendid the band, and the soldiers! One felt the splendour of the British Empire, let the world say what it likes. But alas, as one stayed on even in Malta, one felt the old lion had gone foolish and amiable. Foolish and amiable, with the weak amiability of old age.

We stayed in the Great Britain Hotel. Of course one could not be in Valletta for twenty-four hours without meeting M——. There he was, in the Strada Reale, strutting in a smart white duck suit, with a white piqué cravat. But alas, he had no white shoes: they had got lost or stolen. He had to wear black boots with his summer finery.

He was staying in an hotel a little further down our street, and he begged me to call and see him, he begged me to come to lunch. I promised and went. We went into his bedroom, and he rang for more sodas.

"How wonderful it is to be here!" he said brightly. "Don't you like it immensely? And oh, how wonderful to have a whisky and soda! Well now, say when."

He finished one bottle of Black and White, and opened another. The waiter, a good-looking Maltese fellow, appeared with two syphons. M—— was very much the signore with him, and at the same time very familiar: as I should imagine a rich Roman of the merchant class might have been with a pet slave. We had quite a nice lunch, and whisky and soda and a bottle of French wine. And M—— was the charming and attentive host.

After lunch we talked again of manuscripts and publishers and how he might make money. I wrote one or two letters for him. He was anxious to get something under way. And yet the trouble of these arrangements was almost too much for his nerves. His face looked broken and old, but not like an old man, like an old boy, and he was really very irritable.

For my own part I was soon tired of Malta, and would gladly have left after three days. But there was the strike of steamers still, we had to wait on. M—— professed to be enjoying himself hugely, making excursions every day, to St. Paul's Bay and to the other islands. He had also made various friends or acquaintances. Particularly two young men, Maltese, who were friends of Don Bernardo. He introduced me to these two young men: one Gabriel Mazzaiba and the other Salonia. They had small businesses down on the wharf. Salonia asked M—— to go for a drive in a motor-car round the island, and M—— pressed me to go too. Which I did. And swiftly, on a Saturday afternoon, we dodged about in the car upon that dreadful island, first to some fearful and stony bay, arid, treeless, desert, a bit of stony desert by the sea, with unhappy villas and a sordid, scrap-iron front: then away inland up long and dusty roads, across a bone-dry, bone-bare, hideous landscape. True, there was ripening corn, but this was all of a colour with the dust-yellow, bone-bare island. Malta is all a pale, softish, yellowish rock, just like bathbrick: this goes into fathomless dust. And the island is stark as a corpse, no trees, no bushes even: a fearful landscape, cultivated, and weary with ages of weariness, and old weary houses here and there.

We went to the old capital in the centre of the island, and this is interesting. The town stands on a bluff of hill in the middle of the dreariness, looking at Valletta in the distance, and the sea. The houses are all pale yellow, and tall, and silent, as if forsaken. There is a cathedral, too, and a fortress outlook over the sun-blazed, sun-dried, disheartening island. Then we dashed off to another village and climbed a church-dome that rises like a tall blister on the plain, with houses round and corn beyond and dust that has no glamour, stale, weary, like bone-dust, and thorn hedges sometimes, and some tin-like prickly pears. In the dusk we came round by St. Paul's Bay, back to Valletta.

The young men were very pleasant, very patriotic for Malta, very Catholic. We talked politics and a thousand things. M—— was gently patronizing, and seemed, no doubt, to the two Maltese a very elegant and travelled and wonderful gentleman. They, who had never seen even a wood, thought how wonderful a forest must be, and M—— talked to them of Russia and of Germany.

But I was glad to leave that bone-dry, hideous island. M—— begged

me to stay longer: but not for worlds! He was establishing himself
securely: was learning the Maltese language, and cultivating a thorough
acquaintance with the island. And he was going to establish himself.
Mazzaiba was exceedingly kind to him, helping him in every way. In
Rabato, the suburb of the old town—a quiet, forlorn little yellow street
—he found a tiny house of two rooms and a tiny garden. This would
cost five pounds a year. Mazzaiba lent the furniture—and when I left,
M—— was busily skipping back and forth from Rabato to Valletta,
arranging his little home, and very pleased with it. He was also being
very Maltese, and rather anti-British, as is essential, apparently, when
one is not a Britisher and finds oneself in any part of the British Empire.
M—— was very much the American gentleman.

Well, I was thankful to be home again and to know that he was
safely shut up in that beastly island. He wrote me letters, saying how
he loved it all, how he would go down to the sea—five or six miles' walk
—at dawn, and stay there all day, studying Maltese and writing for
the newspapers. The life was fascinating, the summer was blisteringly
hot, and the Maltese were *most* attractive, especially when they knew
you were not British. Such good-looking fellows, too, and do anything
you want. Wouldn't I come and spend a month?—I did not answer—
felt I had had enough. Came a postcard from M——: "I haven't had
a letter from you, nor any news at all. I am afraid you are ill, and feel
so anxious. Do write——" But no, I didn't want to write.

During August and September and half October we were away in the
north. I forgot my little friend: hoped he was gone out of my life. But
I had that fatal sinking feeling that he *hadn't* really gone out of it yet.

In the beginning of November a little letter from Don Bernardo—
did I know that M—— had committed suicide in Malta? Following
that, a scrubby Maltese newspaper, posted by Salonia, with a marked
notice: "The suicide of an American gentleman at Rabato. Yesterday
the American M—— M——, a well-built man in the prime of life, was
found dead in his bed in his house at Rabato. By the bedside was a
bottle containing poison. The deceased had evidently taken his life by
swallowing prussic acid. Mr. M—— had been staying for some months
on the island, studying the language and the conditions with a view to
writing a book. It is understood that financial difficulties were the cause
of this lamentable event."

Then Mazzaiba wrote asking me what I knew of M——, and saying
the latter had borrowed money which he, Mazzaiba, would like to
recover. I replied at once, and then received the following letter from

Salonia. "Valletta, 20 November, 1920. My dear Mr. Lawrence, some time back I mailed you our *Daily Malta Chronicle* which gave an account of the death of M——. I hope you have received same. As the statements therein given were very vague and not quite correct, please accept the latter part of this letter as a more correct version.

"The day before yesterday Mazzaiba received your letter which he gave me to read. As you may suppose we were very much astonished by its general purport. Mazzaiba will be writing to you in a few days, in the meantime I volunteered to give you the details you asked for.

"Mazzaiba and I have done all in our power to render M——'s stay here as easy and pleasant as possible from the time we first met him in your company at the Great Britain Hotel. [This is not correct. They were already quite friendly with M—— before that motor-drive, when I saw these two Maltese for the first time.] He lived in an embarrassed mood since then, and though we helped him as best we could both morally and financially he never confided to us his troubles. To this very day we cannot but look on his coming here and his stay amongst us, to say the least of the way he left us, as a huge farce wrapped up in mystery, a painful experience unsolicited by either of us and a cause of grief unrequited except by our own personal sense of duty towards a stranger.

"Mazzaiba out of mere respect did not tell me of his commitments towards M—— until about a month ago, and this he did in a most confidential and private manner merely to put me on my guard, thinking, and rightly, too, that M—— would be falling on me next time for funds; Mazzaiba having already given him about £55 and would not possibly commit himself any further. Of course, we found him all along a perfect gentleman. Naturally, he hated the very idea that we or anybody else in Malta should look upon him in any other light. He never asked directly, though Mazzaiba (later myself) was always quick enough to interpret rightly what he meant and obliged him forthwith.

"At this stage, to save the situation, he made up a scheme that the three of us should exploit the commercial possibilities in Morocco. It very nearly materialized, everything was ready, I was to go with him to Morocco, Mazzaiba was to take charge of affairs here and to dispose of transactions we initiated there. Fortunately, for lack of the necessary funds the idea had to be dropped, and there it ended, thank God, after a great deal of trouble I had in trying to set it well on foot.

"Last July, the Police, according to our law, advised him that he was either to find a surety or to deposit a sum of money with them as otherwise at the expiration of his three months' stay he would be compelled to leave the place. Money he had none, so he asked Mazzaiba to stand as surety. Mazzaiba could not as he was already guarantor for his alien cousins who were here at the time. Mazzaiba (not M——) asked me and I complied, thinking that the responsibility was just moral and only exacted as a matter of form.

"When, as stated before, Mazzaiba told me that M—— owed him £55 and that he owed his grocer and others at Notabile (the old town, of which Rabato is the suburb) over £10, I thought I might as well look up my guarantee and see if I was directly responsible for any debts he incurred here. The words of his declaration which I endorsed stated that 'I hereby solemnly promise that I will not be a burden to the inhabitants of these islands, etc.,' and deeming that unpaid debts to be more or less a burden, I decided to withdraw my guarantee, which I did on the 23rd ult. The reason I gave to the police was that he was outliving his income and that I did not intend to shoulder any financial responsibility in the matter. On the same day I wrote to him up at Notabile saying that for family reasons I was compelled to withdraw his surety. He took my letter in the sense implied and no way offended at my procedure.

"M——, in his resourceful way, knowing that he would with great difficulty find another guarantor, wrote at once to the police saying that he understood from Mr. Salonia that he (S) had withdrawn his guarantee, but as he (M) would be leaving the island in about three weeks' time (still intending to exploit Morocco) he begged the Commissioner to allow him this period of grace, without demanding a new surety. In fact he asked me to find him a cheap passage to Gib. in an ingoing tramp steamer. The police did not reply to his letter at all, no doubt they had everything ready and well thought out. He was alarmed in not receiving an acknowledgment, and, knowing full well what he imminently expected at the hands of the Italian police, he decided to prepare for the last act of his drama.

"We had not seen him for three or four days when he came to Mazzaiba's office on Wednesday, 3rd inst., in the forenoon. He stayed there for some time talking on general subjects and looking somewhat more excited than usual. He went up to town alone at noon as Mazzaiba went to Singlea. I was not with them in the morning, but in the afternoon about 4.30, whilst I was talking to Mazzaiba in his office, M—— again came in looking very excited, and, being closing time, we went up, the three of us, to town, and there left him in the company of a friend.

"On Thursday morning, 4th inst., at about 10 a.m., two detectives in plain clothes met him in a street at Notabile. One of them quite casually went up to him and said very civilly that the inspector of police wished to see him *re* a guarantee or something, and that he was to go with him to the police station. This was an excuse as the detective had about him a warrant for his arrest for frauding an hotel in Rome, and that he was to be extradited at the request of the authorities in Italy. M—— replied that as he was in his sandals he would dress up and go with them immediately, and, accompanying him to his house at No. 1 Strada S. Pietro, they allowed him to enter. He locked the door behind him, leaving them outside.

"A few minutes later he opened his bedroom window and dropped a letter addressed to Don Bernardo which he asked a boy in the street to post for him, and immediately closed the window again. One of the detectives picked up the letter and we do not know to this day if same was posted at all. Some time elapsed and he did not come out. The detectives were by this time very uneasy and as another police official came up they decided to burst open the door. As the door did not give way they got a ladder and climbed over the roof, and there they found M—— in his bedroom dying from poisoning, outstretched on his bed and a glass of water close by. A priest was immediately called in who had just time to administer Extreme Unction before he died at 11.45 a.m.

"At 8.0 a.m. the next day his body was admitted for examination at the Floriana Civil Hospital and death was certified to be from poisoning with hydrocyanic acid. His age was given as 44, being buried on his birthday (7th Novr.), with R. Catholic Rites at the expense of *His Friends in Malta.*

"Addenda: Contents of Don Bernardo's letter:—

"'I leave it to you and to Gabriel Mazzaiba to arrange my affairs. I cannot live any longer. Pray for me.'

"Document found on his writing-table:

"'In case of my unexpected death inform American consul.

"'I want to be buried first class, my wife will pay.

"'My little personal belongings to be delivered to my wife. (Address.)

"'My best friend here, Gabriel Mazzaiba, inform him. (Address.)

"'My literary executor N—— D——. (Address.)

"'All manuscripts and books for N—— D——. I leave my literary property to N—— D—— to whom half of the results are to accrue. The other half my debts are to be paid with:

"'Furniture etc. belong to Coleiro, Floriana.

"'Silver spoons etc. belong to Gabriel Mazzaiba. (Address.).'

"The American Consul is in charge of all his personal belongings. I am sure he will be pleased to give you any further details you may require. By the way, his wife refused to pay his burial expenses, but five of his friends in Malta undertook to give him a decent funeral. His mourners were: The consul, the vice-consul, Mr. A., an American citizen, Gabriel Mazzaiba and myself.

"Please convey to Mrs. Lawrence an expression of our sincere esteem and high regard and you will kindly accept equally our warmest respects, whilst soliciting any information you would care to pass on to us regarding the late M——. Believe me, My dear Mr. Lawrence, etc."

[Mrs. M—— refunded the burial expenses through the American consul about two months after her husband's death.]

When I had read this letter the world seemed to stand still for me. I knew that in my own soul I had said, "Yes, he must die if he cannot find his own way." But for all that, now I *realized* what it must have meant to be the hunted, desperate man: everything seemed to stand still. I could, by giving half my money, have saved his life. I had chosen not to save his life.

Now, after a year has gone by, I keep to my choice. I still would not save his life. I respect him for dying when he was cornered. And for this reason I feel still connected with him: still have this to discharge, to get his book published, and to give him his place, to present him just as he was as far as I knew him myself.

The worst thing I have against him, is that he abused the confidence, the kindness, and the generosity of unsuspecting people like Mazzaiba. He did not *want* to, perhaps. But he did it. And he leaves Mazzaiba swindled, distressed, confused, and feeling sold in the best part of himself. What next? What is one to feel towards one's strangers, after having known M——? It is this Judas treachery to *ask* for sympathy and for generosity, to take it when given—and then: "Sorry, but anybody may make a mistake!" It is this betraying with a kiss which makes me still say: "He should have died sooner." No, I would not help to keep him alive, not if I had to choose again. I would let him go over into death. He shall and should die, and so should all his sort: and so they will. There are so many kiss-giving Judases. He was not a criminal: he was obviously well intentioned: but a Judas every time, selling the good feeling he had tried to arouse, and had aroused, for any handful of silver he could get. A little loving vampire!

Yesterday arrived the manuscript of the Legion, from Malta. It is exactly two years since I read it first in the monastery. Then I was moved and rather horrified. Now I am chiefly amused; because in my mind's eye is the figure of M—— in the red trousers and the blue coat with lappets turned up, swinging like a little indignant pigeon across the drill yards and into the canteen of Bel-Abbès. He *is* so indignant, so righteously and morally indignant, and so funny. All the horrors of the actuality fade before the indignation, his little, tuppenny indignation.

Oh, M—— is a prime hypocrite. *How* loudly he rails against the *Boches*! *How* great his enthusiasm for the pure, the spiritual Allied cause. Just so long as he is in Africa, and it suits his purpose! His scorn for the German tendencies of the German legionaries: even Count de R. secretly leans towards Germany. "Blood is thicker than water," says our hero glibly. Some blood, thank God. Apparently not his own. For according to all showing he was, by blood, pure German: father and mother: even Hohenzollern blood !!! Pure German! Even his speech, his *mother-tongue*, was German and not English! And then the little mongrel!——!

But perhaps something happens to blood when once it has been taken to America.

And then, once he is in Valbonne, lo, a change! Where now is sacred France and the holy Allied Cause! Where is our hero's fervour? It is *worse than* Bel-Abbès! Yes, indeed, far less human, more hideously cold. One is driven by very rage to wonder if he was really a spy, a German spy whom Germany cast off because he was no good.

The little *gentleman*! God damn his white-blooded gentility. The legionaries must have been gentlemen, that they didn't kick him every day to the lavatory and back.

"You are a journalist?" said the colonel.

"No, a *littérateur*," said M—— perkily.

"That is something more?" said the Colonel.

Oh, I would have given a lot to have seen it and heard it. The *littérateur*! Well, I hope this book will establish his fame as such. I hope the editor, if it gets one, won't alter any more of the marvellously staggering sentences and the joyful French mistakes. The *littérateur*!—the impossible little pigeon!

But the Bel-Abbès part is alive and interesting. It should be read only by those who have the stomach. Ugly, foul—alas, it is no uglier and no fouler than the reality. M—— himself was near enough to being a scoundrel, thief, forger, etc., etc.—what lovely strings of names he hurls at them!—to be able to appreciate his company. He himself was such a liar, that he was not taken in. But his conceit as a gentleman *keeping up appearances* gave him a real standpoint from which to see the rest. The book is in its way a real creation. But I would hate it to be published and taken at its face value, with M—— as a spiritual dove among vultures of lust. Let us first put a pinch of salt on the tail of this dove. What he did do in the way of vice, even in Bel-Abbès, I never chose to ask him.

Yes, yes, he sings another note when he is planted right among the sacred Allies, with never a German near. Then the gorgeousness goes out of his indignation. He takes it off with the red trousers. Now he is just a sordid little figure in filthy corduroys. There is no vice to purple his indignation, the little holy liar. There is only sordidness and automatic, passionless, colourless awful mud. When all is said and done, mud, cold, hideous, foul, engulfing mud, up to the waist, this is the final symbol of the Great War. Hear some of the horrified young soldiers. They dare hardly speak of it yet.

The Valbonne part is worse, really, than the Bel-Abbès part. Passionless, barren, utterly, coldly foul and hopeless. The ghastly emptiness, and the slow mud-vortex, the brink of it.

Well, now M—— has gone himself. Yes, and he would be gone in the common mud and dust himself, if it were not that the blood still beats warm and hurt and kind in some few hearts. M—— "hinted" at Mazzaiba for money, in Malta, and Mazzaiba gave it to him, thinking him a man in distress. He thought him a gentleman, and lovable, and in trouble! And Mazzaiba—it isn't his real name, but there he is, real enough—still has this feeling of grief for M——. So much so that now he has had the remains taken from the public grave in Malta, and buried in his own, the Mazzaiba grave, so that they shall not be lost. For my part, I would have said that the sooner they mingled with the universal dust, the better. But one is glad to see a little genuine kindness and gentleness, even if it is wasted on the bones of that selfish little scamp of a M——. He despised his "physical friendships——" though he didn't forgo them. So why should anyone rescue his physique from the public grave?

But there you are—there was his power: to arouse affection and a certain tenderness in the hearts of others, for himself. And on this he traded. One sees the trick working all the way through the Legion book. God knows how much warm kindness, generosity, was showered on him during the course of his forty-odd years. And selfish little scamp, he took it as a greedy boy takes cakes off a dish, quickly, to make the most of his opportunity while it lasted. And the cake once eaten: *buona sera*! He patted his own little paunch and felt virtuous. Merely physical feeling, you see! He had a way of saying "physical"—a sort of American way, as if it were spelt "fisacal"—that made me want to kick him.

Not that he was mean, while he was about it. No, he would give very freely: even a little ostentatiously, always feeling that he was being a *liberal gentleman*. Ach, the liberality and the gentility he prided himself on! *Ecco!* And he gave a large tip, with a little winsome smile. But in his heart of hearts it was always himself he was thinking of, while he did it. Playing his rôle of the gentleman who was awfully *nice* to everybody: so long as they were nice to him, or so long as it served his advantage. Just private charity!

Well, poor devil, he is dead: which is all the better. He had his points, the courage of his own terrors, quick-wittedness, sensitiveness to certain things in his surroundings. I prefer him, scamp as he is, to the ordinary respectable person. He ran his risks: he *had* to be running risks with the police, apparently. And he poisoned himself rather than fall into their clutches. I like him for that. And I like him for the sharp and quick way he made use of every one of his opportunities to get out of that beastly army. There I admire him: a courageous isolated little devil, facing his risks, and like a good rat, *determined* not to be trapped. I won't forgive him for trading on the generosity of others, and so dropping poison into the heart of all warm-blooded faith. But I am glad after all that Mazzaiba has rescued his bones from the public grave. I wouldn't have done it myself, because I don't forgive him his "fisacal" impudence and parasitism. But I am glad Mazzaiba has done it. And, for my part, I will put his Legion book before the world if I can. Let him have his place in the world's consciousness.

Let him have his place, let his word be heard. He went through vile experiences: he looked them in the face, braved them through, and kept his manhood in spite of them. For manhood is a strange quality, to be found in human rats as well as in hot-blooded men. M—— carried the human consciousness through circumstances which would have been too much for me. I would have died rather than be so humiliated, I could never have borne it. Other men, I know, went through worse things in the war. But then, horrors, like pain, are their own anæsthetic. Men lose their normal consciousness, and go through in a sort of delirium. The bit of Stendhal which Dos Passos quotes in front of *Three Soldiers* is frighteningly true. There are certain things which are *so* bitter, *so* horrible, that the contemporaries just cannot know them, cannot contemplate them. So it is with a great deal of the late war. It was so foul, and humanity in Europe fell suddenly into such ignominy and inhuman ghastliness, that we shall *never* fully realize what it was. We just cannot bear it. We haven't the soul-strength to contemplate it.

And yet, humanity can only finally conquer by realizing. It is human destiny, since Man fell into consciousness and self-consciousness, that we can only go forward step by step through realization, full, bitter, conscious realization. This is true of all the great terrors and agonies and anguishes of life: sex, and war, and even crime. When Flaubert in his story—it is so long since I read it—makes his saint have to kiss the leper, and naked clasp the leprous awful body against his own, that is what we must at last do. It is the great command *Know Thyself*. We've got to *know* what sex is, let the sentimentalists wiggle as they like. We've got to know the greatest and most shattering human passions, let the puritans squeal as they like for screens. And we've got to know humanity's criminal tendency, look straight at humanity's great deeds of crime against the soul. We have to fold this horrible leper against our naked warmth: because life and the throbbing blood and the believing soul are greater even than leprosy. Knowledge, true knowledge is like vaccination. It prevents the continuing of ghastly moral disease.

And so it is with the war. Humanity in Europe fell horribly into a hatred of the living soul, in the war. There is no gainsaying it. We all fell. Let us not try to wriggle out of it. We fell into hideous depravity of hating the human soul; a purulent small-pox of the spirit we had. It was shameful, shameful, shameful, in every country and in all of us. Some tried to resist, and some didn't. But we were all drowned in shame. A purulent small-pox of the vicious spirit, vicious against the deep soul that pulses in the blood.

We haven't got over it. The small-pox sores are running yet in the spirit of mankind. And we have got to take this putrid spirit to our bosom. There's nothing else for it. Take the foul rotten spirit of mankind, full of the running sores of the war, to our bosom, and cleanse it there. Cleanse it not with blind love: ah no, that won't help. But with bitter and wincing realization. We have to take the disease into our consciousness and let it go through our soul, like some virus. We have got to realize. And then we can surpass.

M—— went where I could never go. He carried the human consciousness unbroken through circumstances I could not have borne. It is not heroism to rush on death. It is cowardice to accept a martyrdom today. That is the feeling one has at the end of Dos Passos' book. To let oneself be absolutely trapped? Never! I prefer M——. He drew himself out of the thing he loathed, despised, and feared. He fought it, for his own spirit and liberty. He fought it open-eyed. He went through. They were more publicly heroic, they won war medals. But the lonely terrified courage of the isolated spirit which grits its teeth and stares the horrors in the face and *will* not succumb to them, but fights its way through them, *knowing* that it must surpass them: this is the rarest courage. And this courage M—— had: and the man in the Dos Passos book didn't *quite* have it. And so, though M—— poisoned himself, and I would not wish him *not* to have poisoned himself: though as far as warm life goes, I don't forgive him; yet, as far as the eternal and unconquerable spirit of man goes, I am with him through eternity. I am grateful to him, he beat out for me boundaries of human experience which I could not have beaten out for myself. The *human* traitor he was. But he was not traitor to the spirit. In the great spirit of human consciousness he was a hero, little, quaking and heroic: a strange, quaking little star.

Even the dead ask only for *justice*: not for praise or exoneration. Who dares humiliate the dead with excuses for their living? I hope I may do M—— justice; and I hope his restless spirit may be appeased. I do not try to forgive. The living blood knows no forgiving. Only the overweening spirit takes on itself to dole out forgiveness. But Justice is a sacred human right. The overweening spirit pretends to perch above justice. But I am a man, not a spirit, and men with blood that throbs and throbs and throbs can only live at length by being just, can only die in peace if they have justice. Forgiveness gives the whimpering dead no rest. Only deep, true justice.

There is M——'s manuscript then, like a map of the lower places of mankind's activities. There is the war: foul, foul, unutterably foul. As foul as M—— says. Let us make up our minds about it.

It is the only help: to realize, *fully*, and then make up our minds. The war was *foul*. As long as I am a man, I say it and assert it, and further I say, as long as I am a man such a war shall never occur again. It shall not, and it shall not. All modern militarism is foul. It shall go. A man I am, and above machines, and it shall go, forever, because I have found it vile, vile, too vile ever to experience again. Cannons shall go. Never again shall trenches be dug. They *shall* not, for I am a man, and such things are within the power of man, to break and make. I have said it, and as long as blood beats in my veins, I mean it. Blood beats in the veins of many men who mean it as well as I.

Man perhaps *must* fight. Mars, the great god of war, will be a god forever. Very well. Then if fight you must, fight you shall, and without engines, without machines. Fight if you like, as the Roman fought, with swords and spears, or like the Red Indian, with bows and arrows and knives and war paint. But never again shall you fight with the foul, base, fearful, monstrous machines of war which man invented for the last war. You shall not. The diabolic mechanisms are man's, and I am a man. Therefore they are mine. And I smash them into oblivion. With every means in my power, *except* the means of these machines, I smash them into oblivion. I am at war! I, a man, am at war!—with these foul machines and contrivances that men have conjured up. Men have conjured them up. I, a man, will conjure them down again. Won't I? —but I will! I am not one man, I am many, I am most.

So much for the war! So much for M——'s manuscript. Let it be read. It is not this that will do harm, but sloppy sentiment and cant. Take the bitterness and cleanse the blood.

Now would you believe it, that little scamp M—— spent over a hundred pounds of borrowed money during his four months in Malta, when his expenses, he boasted to me, need not have been more than a pound a week, once he got into the little house in Notabile. That is, he spent at least seventy pounds too much. Heaven knows what he did with it, apart from "guzzling." And this hundred pounds must be paid back in Malta. Which it never will be, unless this manuscript pays it back. Pay the gentleman's last debts, if no others.

He had to be a gentleman. I didn't realize till after his death. I never suspected him of royal blood. But there you are, you never know where it will crop out. He was the grandson of an emperor. His mother was the illegitimate daughter of the German Kaiser: D—— says, of the old Kaiser Wilhelm I, Don Bernardo says, of Kaiser Frederick Wilhelm, father of the present ex-Kaiser. She was born in Berlin on the 31 October, 1845: and her portrait, by Paul, now hangs in a gallery in Rome. Apparently there had been some injustice against her in Berlin —for she seems once to have been in the highest society there, and to have attended at court. Perhaps she was discreetly banished by Wilhelm II, hence M——s hatred of that monarch. She lies buried in the Protestant Cemetery in Rome, where she died in 1912, with the words *Filia Regis* on her tomb. M—— adored her, and she him. Part of his failings one can *certainly* ascribe to the fact that he was an only son, an adored son, in whose veins the mother imagined only royal blood. And she must have thought him so beautiful, poor thing! Ah well, they are both dead. Let us be just and wish them Lethe.

M—— himself was born in New York, 7th November, 1876; so at least it says on his passport. He entered the Catholic Church in England in 1902. His father was a Mr. L—— M——, married to the mother in 1867.

So poor M—— had Hohenzollern blood in his veins: close kin to the ex-Kaiser William. Well, that itself excuses him a great deal: because of the cruel illusion of importance *manqué*, which it must have given him. He never breathed a word of this to me. Yet apparently it is accepted at the monastery, the great monastery which knows most European secrets of any political significance. And for myself, I believe it is true. And if he was a scamp and a treacherous little devil, he had also qualities of nerve and breeding undeniable. He faced his way through that Legion experience: royal nerves dragging themselves through the sewers, without giving way. But alas, for royal blood! Like most other blood, it has gradually gone white, during our spiritual era. Bunches of nerves! And whitish, slightly acid blood. And no bowels of deep compassion and kindliness. Only charity—a little more than kin, and less than kind.

Also—M——! Ich grüsse dich, in der Ewigkeit. Aber hier, im Herzblut, hast du Gift und Leid nachgelassen—to use your own romantic language.

VI

Reflections on the Death of a Porcupine

Note to "The Crown"

"*The Crown*" *was written in* 1915, *when the war was already twelve months old, and had gone pretty deep. John Middleton Murry said to me: "Let us do something."*

The doing consisted in starting a tiny monthly paper, which Murry called The Signature, *and in having weekly meetings somewhere in London—I have now no idea where it was—up a narrow stair-case over a green-grocer's shop: or a cobbler's shop. The only thing that made any impression on me was the room over the shop, in some old Dickensey part of London, and the old man downstairs.*

We scrubbed the room and colour-washed the walls and got a long table and some windsor chairs from the Caledonian market. And we used to make a good warm fire: it was dark autumn, in that unknown bit of London. Then on Thursday nights we had meetings of about a dozen people. We talked, but there was absolutely nothing in it. And the meetings didn't last two months.

The Signature *was printed by some little Jewish printer away in the east end. We sold it by subscription, half-a-crown for six copies. I don't know how many subscriptions there were: perhaps fifty. The helpless little brown magazine appeared three times, then we dropped it. The last three of the "Crown" essays were never printed.*

To me the venture meant nothing real: a little escapade. I can't believe in "doing things" like that. In a great issue like the war, there was nothing to be "done," in Murry's sense. There is still nothing to be "done." Probably not for many, many years will men start to "do" something. And even then, only after they have changed gradually, and deeply.

I knew then, and I know now, it is no use trying to do anything—I speak only for myself—publicly. It is no use trying merely to modify present forms. The whole great form of our era will have to go. And nothing will really send it down but the new shoots of life springing up and slowly bursting the foundations. And one can do nothing but fight tooth and nail to defend the new shoots of life from being crushed out, and let them grow. We can't make life. We can but fight for the life that grows in us.

So that, personally, little magazines mean nothing to me: nor groups, nor parties of people. I have no hankering after quick response, nor the effusive, semi-intimate back-chat of literary communion. So it was ridiculous to offer "The Crown" in a little six-penny pamphlet. I always felt ashamed, at the thought of the few who sent their half-crowns. Happily they were few; and they could read Murry. If one publishes in the ordinary way, people are not asked for their sixpences.

I alter "The Crown" only a very little. It says what I still believe. But it's no use for a five minutes' lunch.

The Crown

The Lion and the Unicorn
Were fighting for the Crown

What is it then, that they want, that they are forever rampant and unsatisfied, the king of beasts and the defender of virgins? What is this Crown that hovers between them, unattainable? Does either of them ever hope to get it?

But think of the king of beasts lying serene with the crown on his head! Instantly the unicorn prances from every heart. And at the thought of the lord of chastity with the crown ledged above his golden horn, lying in virgin lustre of sanctity, the lion springs out of his lair in every soul, roaring after his prey.

It is a strange and painful position, the king of beasts and the beast of purity, rampant forever on either side of the crown. Is it to be so for ever?

Who says lion?—who says unicorn? A lion, a lion!! Hi, a unicorn! Now they are at it, they have forgotten all about the crown. It is a greater thing to have an enemy than to have an object. The lion and the unicorn were fighting, it is no question any more of the crown. We know this, because when the lion beat the unicorn, he did not take the crown and put it on his head, and say, "Now Mr. Purity, I'm king." He drove the unicorn out of town, expelled him, obliterated him, expurgated him from the memory, exiled him from the kingdom. Instantly the town was all lion, there was no unicorn at all, no scent nor flavour of unicorn.

"Unicorn!" they said in the city. "That is a mythological beast that never existed."

There was no question any more of rivalry. The unicorn was erased from the annals of fact.

Why did the lion fight the unicorn? Why did the unicorn fight the lion? Why must the one obliterate the other? Was it the *raison d'être* of each of them, to obliterate the other?

But think, if the lion really destroyed, killed the unicorn: not merely drove him out of town, but annihilated him! Would not the lion at once expire, as if he had created a vacuum around himself? Is not the unicorn necessary to the very existence of the lion, is not each opposite kept in stable equilibrium by the opposition of the other?

This is a terrible position: to have for a *raison d'être* a purpose which, if once fulfilled, would of necessity entail the cessation from existence of both opponents. They would both cease to be, if either of them really won in the fight which is their sole reason for existing. This is a troublesome thought.

It makes us at once examine our own hearts. What do we find there? —a want, a need, a crying out, a divine discontent. Is it the lion, is it the unicorn?—one, or both? But certainly there is this crying aloud, this infant crying in the night, born into a blind want.

What do we find at the core of our hearts?—a want, a void, a hollow want. It is the lion that must needs fight the unicorn, the unicorn that must needs fight the lion. Supposing the lion refuses the obligation of his being, and says, "I won't fight, I'll just lie down. I'll be a lion couchant."

What *then* is the lion? A void, a hollow ache, a want. "What am I?" says the lion, as he lies with his head between his paws, or walks by the river feeding on raspberries, peacefully, like a unicorn. "I am a hollow void, my roaring is the resonance of a hollow drum, my strength is the power of the vacuum, drawing all things within itself."

Then he groans with horrible self-consciousness. After all, there is nothing for it but to set upon the unicorn, and so forget, forget, obtain the precious self-oblivion.

Thus are we, then, rounded upon a void, a hollow want, like the lion. And this want makes us draw all things into ourselves, to fill up the void. But it is a bottomless pit, this void. If ever it were filled, there would be a great cessation from being, of the whole universe.

Thus we portray ourselves in the field of the royal arms. The whole history is the fight, the whole *raison d'être*. For the whole field is occupied by the lion and the unicorn. These alone are the living occupants of the immortal and mortal field.

We have forgotten the Crown, which is the keystone of the fight. We are like the lion and the unicorn, we go on fighting underneath the Crown, entirely oblivious of its supremacy.

It is modest common sense for us to acknowledge, all of us, nowadays, that we are built round a void and hollow want which, if satisfied, would imply our collapse, our utter ceasing to be. Therefore we regard our craving with complacence, we feel the great aching of the Want, and we say, with conviction, "I know I exist, I know I am I, because I feel the divine discontent which is personal to me, and eternal, and present always in me."

That is because we are incomplete, we stand upon one side of the shield, or on the other. On the one side we are in darkness, our eyes gleam phosphorescent like cat's eyes. And with these phosphorescent gleaming eyes we look across at the opposite pure beast, and we say, "Yes, I am a lion, my *raison d'être* is to devour that unicorn, I am moulded upon an eternal void, a Want." Gleaming bright, we see ourselves reflected upon the surface of the darkness and we say: "I am the pure unicorn, it is for me to oppose and resist for ever that avid lion. If he ceased to exist, I should be supreme and unique and perfect. Therefore I will destroy him."

But the lion will not be destroyed. If he were, if he were swallowed into the belly of the unicorn, the unicorn would fly asunder into chaos.

This is like being a creature who walks by night, who says: "Men see by darkness, and in the darkness they have their being." Or like a creature that walks by day, and says: "Men live by the light."

We are enveloped in the darkness, like the lion: or like the unicorn, enveloped in the light.

For the womb is full of darkness, and also flooded with the strange white light of eternity. And we, the peoples of the world, we are enclosed within the womb of our era, we are there begotten and conceived, but not brought forth.

A myriad, myriad people, we roam in the belly of our era, seeking, seeking, wanting. And we seek and want deliverance. But we say we want to overcome the lion that shares with us this universal womb, the walls of which are shut, and have no window to inform us that we are in prison. We roam within the vast walls of the womb, unnourished now, because the time of our deliverance is ripe, even overpast, and the body of our era is lean and withered because of us, withered and inflexible.

We roam unnourished, moulded each of us around a core of want, a void. We stand in the darkness of the womb and we say: "Behold, there is the light, the white light of eternity, which we want." And we make war upon the lion of darkness, annihilate him, so that we may be free in the eternal light. Or else, suddenly, we admit ourselves the lion, and we rush rampant on the unicorn of chastity.

We stand in the light of Virginity, in the wholeness of our un-broached immortality, and we say: "Lo the darkness surrounds us, to envelop us. Let us resist the powers of darkness." Then like the bright and virgin unicorn we make war upon the ravening lion. Or we cry: "Ours is the strength and glory of the Creator, who precedes Creation, and all is unto us." So we open a ravening mouth, to swallow back all time has brought forth.

And there is no rest, no cessation from the conflict. For we are two opposites which exist by virtue of our inter-opposition. Remove the opposition and there is collapse, a sudden crumbling into universal nothingness.

The darkness, this has nourished us. The darkness, this is a vast infinite, an origin, a Source. The Beginning, this is the great sphere of darkness, the womb wherein the universe is begotten.

But this universal, infinite darkness conceives of its own opposite. If there is universal, infinite darkness, then there is universal, infinite light, for there cannot exist a specific infinite save by virtue of the opposite and equivalent specific infinite. So that if there be universal, infinite darkness in the beginning, there must be universal, infinite light in the end. And these are two relative halves.

Into the womb of the primary darkness enters the ray of ultimate light, and time is begotten, conceived, there is the beginning of the end. We are the beginning of the end. And there, within the womb, we ripen upon the beginning, till we become aware of the end.

We are fruit, we are an integral part of the tree. Till the time comes for us to fall, and we hang in suspense, realizing that we are an integral part of the vast beyond, which stretches under us and grasps us even before we drop into it.

We are the beginning, which has conceived us within its womb of darkness, and nourished us to the fulness of our growth. This is ours that we adhere to. This is our God, Jehovah, Zeus, the Father of Heaven, this that has conceived and created us, in the beginning, and brought us to the fulness of our strength.

And when we have come to the fulness of our strength, like lions which have been fed till they are full grown, then the strange necessity comes upon us, we must travel away, roam like falling fruit, fall from the initial darkness of the tree, of the cave which has reared us, into the eternal light of germination and begetting, the eternal light, shedding our darkness like the fruit that rots on the ground.

We travel across between the two great opposites of the Beginning and the End, the eternal night and everlasting day, and the transit is a stride taken, the night gives us up for the day to receive us. And what are we between the two?

But before the transit is accomplished, whilst we are yet like fruit heavy and ripe on the trees, we realize the delirious freedom of the end, the goal, and we cry: "Behold, I, who am here within the darkness, I am the light! I am the light, I am Unicorn, the beam of chastity. Behold, the beam of Virginity gleams within my loins, in this circumambient darkness. Behold, I am not the Beginning, I am the End. The End is universal light, the achieving again of infinite unblemished being, the infinite oneness of the Light, the escape from the infinite notbeing of the darkness."

All the time, these cries take place within the womb, these are the myriad unborn uttering themselves as they come towards maturity, cry after cry as the darkness develops itself over the sea of Light, and flesh is born, and limbs; cry after cry as the light develops within the darkness, and mind is born, and the consciousness of that which is outside my own flesh and limbs, and the desire for everlasting life grows more insistent.

These are the cries of the two adversaries, the two opposites.

First of all the flesh develops in splendour and glory out of the prolific darkness, begotten by the light it develops to a great triumph, till it dances naked in glory of itself, before the Ark, naked in glory of itself in the procession of heroes travelling towards the wise goddess, the white light, the Mind, the light which the vessel of living darkness has caught and captured within itself, and holds in triumph. The flesh of darkness triumphant circles round the treasure of light which it has enveloped, which it calls Mind, and this is the ecstasy, the dance before the Ark, the Bacchic delirium.

And then, within the womb, the light grows stronger and finds voice, it cries out: "Behold, I am free, I am not enveloped within this darkness. Behold, I am the everlasting light, the Eternity that stretches forward for ever, utterly the opposite of that darkness which departs backward, backward for ever. Come over to me, to the light, to the light that streams into the glorious eternity. For now the darkness is revoked for ever."

It is the voice of the unicorn crying in the wilderness, it is the Son of Man. And behold, in the fight, the unicorn beats the lion, and drives him out of town.

But all of this is within the Womb. The darkness builds up the warm shadow of the flesh in splendour and triumph, enclosing the light. This is the zenith of David and Solomon, and of Assyria and Egypt. Then the light, wrestling within the vessel, throws up a white gleam of universal love, which is St. Francis of Assisi, and Shelley.

Then each has reached its maximum of self-assertion. The flesh is made perfect within the womb, the spirit is at last made perfect also, within the womb. They are equally perfect, equally supreme, the one adhering to the infinite darkness of the beginning, the other adhering to the infinite light of the end.

Yet, within the womb, they are eternally opposite. Darkness stands over against light, light stands over against dark. The lion is reared against the unicorn, the unicorn is reared against the lion. One says, "Behold, the darkness which gave us birth is eternal and infinite: this we belong to." The other says, "We are of the light, which is everlasting and infinite."

And there is no reconciliation, save in negation. From the present, the stream flows in opposite directions, back to the past, on to the future. There are two goals, at opposite ends of time. There is the vast original dark out of which Creation issued, there is the Eternal light into which all mortality passes. And both are equally infinite, both are equally the goal, and both equally the beginning.

And we, fully equipped in flesh and spirit, fully built up of darkness, perfectly composed out of light, what are we but light and shadow lying together in opposition, or lion and unicorn fighting, the one to vanquish the other. This is our eternal life, in these two eternities which nullify each other. And we, between them both, what are we but nullity?

And this is because we see in part, always in part. We are enclosed within the womb, we are the seed from the loins of the eternal light, or we are the darkness which is enveloped by the body of the past, by our era.

Unless the sun were enveloped in the body of darkness, would a cast shadow run with me as I walk? Unless the night lay within the embrace of light, would the fish gleam phosphorescent in the sea, would the light break out of the black coals of the hearth, would the electricity gleam out of itself, suddenly declaring an opposite being?

Love and power, light and darkness, these are the temporary conquest of the one infinite by the other. In love, the Christian love, the End asserts itself supreme: in power, in strength like the lion's, the Beginning re-establishes itself unique. But when the opposition is complete on either side, then there is perfection. It is the perfect opposition of dark and light that brindles the tiger with gold flame and dark flame. It is the surcharge of darkness that opens the ravening mouth of the tiger, and drives his eyes to points of phosphorescence. It is the perfect balance of light and darkness that flickers in the stepping of a deer. But it is the conquered darkness that flares and palpitates in her eyes.

There are the two eternities fighting the fight of Creation, the light projecting itself into the darkness, the darkness enveloping herself within the embrace of light. And then there is the consummation of each in the other, the consummation of light in darkness and darkness in light, which is absolute: our bodies cast up like foam of two meeting waves, but foam which is absolute, complete, beyond the limitation of either infinity, consummate over both eternities. The direct opposites of the Beginning and the End, by their very directness, imply their own supreme relation. And this supreme relation is made absolute in the clash and the foam of the meeting waves. And the clash and the foam are the Crown, the Absolute.

The lion and the unicorn are not fighting for the Crown. They are fighting beneath it. And the Crown is upon their fight. If they made friends and lay down side by side, the Crown would fall on them both and kill them. If the lion really beat the unicorn, then the Crown pressing on the head of the king of beasts alone would destroy him. Which it has done and is doing. As it is destroying the unicorn who has achieved supremacy in another field.

So that now, in Europe, both the lion and the unicorn are gone mad, each with a crown tumbled on his bound-in head. And without rhyme or reason they tear themselves and each other, and the fight is no fight, it is a frenzy of blind things dashing themselves and each other to pieces.

Now the unicorn of virtue and virgin spontaneity has got the Crown slipped over the eyes, like a circle of utter light, and has gone mad with the extremity of light: whilst the lion of power and splendour, its own Crown of supreme night settled down upon it, roars in an agony of imprisoned darkness.

Now within the withered body of our era, within the husk of the past, the seed of light has come to supreme self-consciousness and has gone mad with the flare of eternal light in its eyes, whilst the fruit of darkness, unable to fall from the tree, has turned round towards the tree and is become mad, clinging faster upon the utter night whence it should have dropped away long ago.

For the stiffened, exhausted, inflexible loins of our era are too dry to give us forth in labour, the tree is withered, we are pent in, fastened, and now have turned round, some to the source of darkness, some to the source of light, and gone mad, purely given up to frenzy. For the dark has travelled to the light, and the light towards the dark. But when they reached the bound, neither could leap forth. The fruit could not fall from the tree, the lion just full grown could not get out of the cave, the unicorn could not enter the illimitable forest, the lily could not leap out of the darkness of her bulb straight into the sun. What then? The road was stopped. Whither then? Backward, back to the known eternity. There was a great, horrible huddle backwards. The process of birth had been arrested, the inflexible, withered loins of the mother-era were too old and set, the past was taut around us all. Then began chaos, the going asunder, the beginning of nothingness. Then we leaped back, by reflex from the bound and limit, back upon ourselves into madness.

There is a dark beyond the darkness of the womb, there is a light beyond the light of knowledge. There is the darkness of all the heavens for the seed of man to invest, and the light of all the heavens for the womb to receive. But we don't know it. How can the unborn within the womb know of the heavens outside; how can they?

How can they know of the tides beyond? On the one hand murmurs the utter, infinite sea of darkness, full of unconceived creation: on the other the infinite light stirs with eternal procreation. They are two seas which eternally attract and oppose each other, two tides which eternally advance to repel each other, which foam upon one another, as the ocean foams on the land, and the land rushes down into the sea.

And we, in the great movement, are begotten, conceived and brought forth, like the waves which meet and clash and burst up into foam, sending the foam like light, like shadow, into the zenith of the absolute, beyond the grasp of either eternity.

We are the foam and the foreshore, that which, between the oceans, is not, but that which supersedes the oceans in utter reality, and gleams in absolute Eternity.

The Beginning is-not, nor the eternity which lies behind us, save in part. Partial also is the eternity which lies in front. But that which is not partial, but whole, that which is not relative, but absolute, is the clash of the two into one, the foam of being thrown up into consummation.

It is the music which comes when the cymbals clash one upon the other: this is absolute and timeless. The cymbals swing back in one or the other direction of time, towards one or the other relative eternity. But absolute, timeless, beyond time or eternity, beyond space or infinity, is the music that was the consummation of the two cymbals in opposition.

It is that which comes when night clashes on day, the rainbow, the yellow and rose and blue and purple of dawn and sunset, which leaps out of the breaking of light upon darkness, of darkness upon light, absolute beyond day or night; the rainbow, the iridescence which is darkness at once and light, the two-in-one; the crown that binds them both.

It is the lovely body of foam that walks for ever between the two seas, perfect and consummate, the revealed consummation, the oneness that has taken being out of the two.

We say the foam is evanescent, the wind passes over it and it is gone —he who would save his life must lose it.

But if indeed the foam were-not, if the two seas fell apart, if the sea fell departed from the land, and the land from the sea, if the two halves, day and night, were ripped asunder, without attraction or opposition, what then? Then there would be between them nothingness, utter nothingness. Which is meaningless.

So that the foam and the iridescence, the music that comes from the cymbals, all formed things that come from perfect union in opposition, all beauty and all truth and being, all perfection, these are the be-all and the end-all, absolute, timeless, beyond time or eternity, beyond the Limit or the Infinite.

This lovely body of foam, this iris between the two floods, this music between the cymbals, this truth between the surge of facts, this supreme reason between conflicting desires, this holy spirit between the opposite divinities, this is the Absolute made visible between the two Infinities, the Timelessness into which are assumed the two Eternities.

It is wrong to try to make the lion lie down with the lamb. This is the supreme sin, the unforgivable blasphemy of which Christ spoke. This is the creating of nothingness, the bringing about, or the striving to bring about the nihil which is pure meaninglessness.

The great darkness of the lion must gather into itself the little, feeble darkness of the lamb. The great light of the lamb must absorb elsewhere, in the whole world, the small, weak light of the lion. The lamb indeed will inherit the world, rather than the lion. It is the triumph of the meek, but the meek, like the merciless, shall perish in their own triumph. Anything that *triumphs*, perishes. The consummation comes from perfect relatedness. To this a man may *win*. But he who triumphs, perishes.

The crown is upon the perfect balance of the fight, it is not the fruit of either victory. The crown is not prize of either combatant. It is the *raison d'être* of both. It is the absolute within the fight.

And those alone are evil, who say, "The lion shall lie down with the lamb, the eagle shall mate with the dove, the lion shall munch in the stable of the unicorn." For they blaspheme against the *raison d'être* of all life, they try to destroy the essential, intrinsic nature of God.

But it is the fight of opposites which is holy. The fight of like things is evil. For if a thing turn round upon itself in blind frenzy of destruction, this is to say: "The lamb shall roar like the lion, the dove strike down her prey like the eagle, and the unicorn shall devour the innocent virgin in her path." Which is precisely the equivalent blasphemy to the blasphemy of universal meekness, or peace.

And this, this last, is our blasphemy of the war. We would have the lamb roar like the lion, all doves turn into eagles.

2

The Lion beat the Unicorn
And drove him out of town

Life is a travelling to the edge of knowledge, then a leap taken. We cannot know beforehand. We are driven from behind, always as over the edge of the precipice.

It is a leap taken into the beyond, as a lark leaps into the sky, a fragment of earth which travels to be fused out, sublimated, in the shining of the heavens.

But it is not death. Death is neither here nor there. Death is a temporal, relative fact. In the absolute, it means nothing. The lark falls from the sky and goes running back to her nest. This is the ebb of the wave. The wave of earth flung up in spray, a lark, a cloud of larks, against the white wave of the sun. The spray of earth and the foam of heaven are one, consummated, a rainbow mid-way, a song. The larks return to earth, the rays go back to heaven. But these are only the shuttles that weave the iris, the song, mid-way, in absoluteness, timelessness.

Out of the dark, original flame issues a tiny green flicker, a weed coming alive. On the edge of the bright, ultimate, spiritual flame of the heavens is revealed a fragment of iris, a touch of green, a weed coming into being. The two flames surge and intermingle, casting up a crest of leaves and stems, their battlefield, their meeting-ground, their marriage bed, the embrace becomes closer, more unthinkably vivid, it leaps to climax, the battle grows fiercer, fiercer, intolerably, till there is the swoon, the climax, the consummation, the little yellow disk gleams absolute between heaven and earth, radiant of both eternities, framed in the two infinities. Which is a weed, a sow-thistle bursting into blossom. And we, the foreshore in whom the waves of dark and light are unequally seething, we can see this perfection, 'his absolute, as time opens to disclose it for a moment, like the Dove that hovered incandescent from heaven, before it is closed again in utter timelessness.

"But the wind passeth over it and is gone."

The wind passes over it and we are gone. It is time which blows in like a wind, closing up the clouds again upon the perfect gleam. It is the wind of time, out of either eternity, a wind which has a source and an issue, which swirls past the light of this absolute, like waves past a lighted buoy. For the light is not temporal nor eternal, but absolute. And we, who are temporal and eternal, at moments only we cease from our temporality. In these, our moments, we see the sow-thistle gleaming, light within darkness, darkness within light, consummated, we are with the song and the iris.

And then it is we, not the iris, not the song, who are blown away. We are blown for a moment against the yellow light of the window, the flower, then on again into the dark turmoil.

We have made a mistake. We are like travellers travelling in a train, who watch the country pass by and pass away; all of us who watch the sun setting, sliding down into extinction, we are mistaken. It is not the country which passes by and fades, it is not the sun which sinks to oblivion. Neither is it the flower that withers, nor the song that dies out.

It is we who are carried past in the seethe of mortality. The flower is timeless and beyond condition. It is we who are swept on in the condition of time. So we shall be swept as long as time lasts. Death is part of the story. But we have being also in timelessness, we shall become again absolute, as we have been absolute, as we are absolute.

We know that we are purely absolute. We know in the last issue we are absolved from all opposition. We know that in the process of life we are purely relative. But timelessness is our fate, and time is subordinate to our fate. But time is eternal.

And the life of man is like a flower that comes into blossom and passes away. In the beginning, the light touches the darkness, the darkness touches the light, and the two embrace. They embrace in opposition, only in their desire is their unanimity. There are two separate statements, the dark wants the light, and the light wants the dark. But these two statements are contained within the one: "They want each other." And this is the condition of absoluteness, this condition of their wanting each other, that which makes light and dark consummate even in opposition. The interrelation between them, this is constant and absolute, let it be called love or power or what it may. It is all the things that it can be called.

In the beginning, light touches darkness and darkness touches light. Then life has begun. The light enfolds and implicates and involves the dark, the dark receives and interpenetrates the light, they come nearer, they are more finely combined, till they burst into the crisis of oneness, the blossom, the utter being, the transcendent and timeless flame of the iris.

Then time passes on. Out of the swoon the waves ebb back, dark towards the dark, light towards the light. They ebb back and away, the leaves return unto the darkness of the earth, the quivering glimmer of substance returns into the light, the green of the last wavering iris disappears, the waves ebb apart, further, further, further.

Yet they never separate. The whole flood recedes, the tides are going to separate. And they separate entirely, save for one enfolded ripple, the tiny, silent, scarce-visible enfolded pools of the seeds. These lie potent, the meeting-ground, the well-head wherein the tides will surge again, when the turn comes.

This is the life of man. In him too the tide sweeps together towards the utter consummation, the consummation with the darkness, the consummation with the light, flesh and spirit, one culminating crisis, when man passes into timelessness and absoluteness.

The residue of imperfect fusion and unfulfilled desire remains, the child, the well-head where the tides will flow in again, the seed. The absolute relation is never fully revealed. It leaps to its maximum of revelation in the flower, the mature life. But some of it rolls aside, lies potent in the enfolded seed. My desire is fulfilled, I, as individual, am become timeless and absolute, perfect. But the whole desire of which I am part remains yet to be consummated. In me the two waves clash to perfect consummation. But immediately upon the clash come the next waves of the tide rippling in, the ripples, forerunners, which tinily meet and enfold each other, the seed, the unborn child. For we are all waves of the tide. But the tide contains all the waves.

It may happen that waves which meet and mingle come to no consummation, only a confusion and a swirl and a falling away again. These are the myriad lives of human beings which pass in confusion of nothingness, the uncreated lives. There are myriads of human lives that are not absolute nor timeless, myriads that just waver and toss temporarily, never become more than relative, never come into being. They have no being, no immortality. There are myriads of plants that never come to flower, but which perish away for ever, always separated in the fringe of time, never united, never consummated, never brought forth.

I know I am compound of two waves, I, who am temporal and mortal. When I am timeless and absolute, all duality has vanished. But whilst I am temporal and mortal, I am framed in the struggle and embrace of the two opposite waves of darkness and of light.

There is the wave of light in me which seeks the darkness, which has for its goal the Source and the Beginning, for its God the Almighty Creator to Whom is all power and glory. Thither the light of the seed of man struggles and aspires into the infinite darkness, the womb of all creation.

What way is it that leads me on to the Source, to the Beginning? It is the way of the blood, the way of power. Down the road of the blood, further and further into the darkness, I come to the Almighty God Who was in the beginning, is now, and ever shall be. I come to the Source of Power. I am received back into the utter darkness of the Creator, I am one again with Him.

This is a consummation, a becoming eternal. This is an arrival into eternity. But eternity is only relative.

I can become one with God, consummated into eternity, by taking the road down the senses into the utter darkness of power, till I am one with the darkness of initial power, beyond knowledge of any opposite.

It is thus, seeking consummation in the utter darkness, that I come to the woman in desire. She is the doorway, she is the gate to the dark eternity of power, the creator's power. When I put my hand on her, my heart beats with a passion of fear and ecstasy, for I touch my own passing away, my own ceasing-to-be, I apprehend my own consummation in a darkness which obliterates me in its infinity. My veins rock as if they were being destroyed, the blood takes fire on the edge of oblivion, and beats backward and forward. I resist, yet I am compelled; the woman resists, yet she is compelled. And we are the relative parts dominated by the strange compulsion of the absolute.

Gradually my veins relax their gates, gradually the rocking blood goes forward, quivers on the edge of oblivion, then yields itself up, passes into the borderland of oblivion. Oh, and then I would die, I would quickly die, to have all power, all life at once, to come instantly to pure, eternal oblivion, the source of life. But patience is fierce at the bottom of me; fierce, indomitable, abiding patience. So my blood goes forth in shock after shock of delirious passing-away, in shock after shock entering into consummation, till my soul is slipping its moorings, my mind, my will fuses down, I melt out and am gone into the eternal darkness, the primal creative darkness reigns, and I am not, and at last *I am*.

Shock after shock of ecstasy and the anguish of ecstasy, death after death of trespass into the unknown, till I fall down into the flame, I lapse into the intolerable flame, a pallid shadow I am transfused into the flux of unendurable darkness, and am gone. No spark nor vestige remains within the supreme dark flow of the flame, I am contributed again to the immortal source. I am with the dark Almighty of the beginning.

Till, new-created, I am thrown forth again on the shore of creation, warm and lustrous, goodly, new-born from the darkness out of which all time has issued.

And then, new-born on the knees of darkness, new-issued from the womb of creation, I open my eyes to the light and know the goal, the end, the light which stands over the end of the journey, the everlasting day, the oneness of the spirit.

The new journey, the new life has begun, the travelling to the opposite eternity, to the infinite light of the Spirit, the consummation in the Spirit.

My source and issue is in two eternities, I am founded in the two infinities. But absolute is the rainbow that goes between; the iris of my very being.

It may be, however, that the seed of light never propagates within the darkness, that the light in me is sterile, that I am never re-born within the womb, the Source, to be issued towards the opposite eternity.

It may be there is a great inequality, disproportion, within me, that I am nearly all darkness, like the night, with a few glimmers of cold light, moonlight, like the tiger with white eyes of reflected light brindled in the flame of darkness. Then I shall return again and again to the womb of darkness, avid, never satisfied, my spirit will fall unfertile into the womb, will never be conceived there, never brought forth. I shall know the one consummation, the one direction only, into the darkness. It will be with me for ever the almost, almost, almost, of satisfaction, of fulfilment. I shall know the one eternity, the one infinite, the one immortality, I shall have partial being; but never the whole, never the full. There is an infinite which does not know me. I am always relative, always partial, always, in the last issue, unconsummate.

The barren womb can never be satisfied, if the quick of darkness be sterile within it. But neither can the unfertile loins be satisfied, if the seed of light, of the spirit, be dead within them. They will return again and again and again to the womb of darkness, asking, asking, and never satisfied.

Then the unconsummated soul, unsatisfied, uncreated in part, will seek to make itself whole by bringing the whole world under its own order, will seek to make itself absolute and timeless by devouring its opposite. Adhering to the one eternity of darkness, it will seek to devour the eternity of light. Realizing the one infinite of the Source, it will endeavour to absorb into its oneness the opposite infinite of the Goal. This is the infinite with its tail in its mouth.

Consummated in one infinite, and one alone, this soul will assert the oneness of all things, that all things are one in the One Infinite of the Darkness, of the Source. One is one and all alone and ever more shall be so. This is the cry of the Soul consummated in one eternity only.

There is one eternity, one infinite, one God. "Thou shalt have no other god before me."

But why this Commandment, unless there were in truth another god, at least the equal of Jehovah?

Consummated in the darkness only, having not enough strength in the light, the partial soul cries out in a convulsion of insistence that the darkness alone is infinite and eternal, that all light is from the small, contained sources, the lamps lighted at will by the desire of the Creator, the sun, the moon and stars. These are the lamps and candles of the Almighty, which He blows out at will. These are little portions of special darkness, darkness transfigured, these lights.

There is one God, one Creator, one Almighty; there is one infinite and one eternity, it is the infinite and the eternity of the Source. There is One Way: it is the Way of the Law. There is one Life, the Life of Creation, there is one Goal, the Beginning, there is one immortality, the immortality of the great I Am. All is God, the One God. Those who deny this are to be stamped out, tortured, tortured for ever.

It is possible then to deny it?

Having declared the One God, then the partial soul, fulfilled of the darkness only, proceeds to establish this God on earth, to devour and obliterate all else.

Rising from the darkness of consummation in the flesh, with the woman, it seeks to establish its kingdom over all the world. It strides forth, the lord, the master, strong for mastery. It will dominate all, all, it will bring all under the rule of itself, of the One, the Darkness lighted with the lamps of its own choice.

This is the heroic tyrant, the fabulous king-warrior, like Sardanapolus or Caesar, like Saul even. These warrior kings seek to pass beyond all relatedness, to become absolute in might and power. And they fall inevitably. Their Judas is a David, a Brutus: the individual who knows something of both flames, but commits himself to neither. He holds himself, in his own ego, superior either to the creative dark power-flame, or the conscious love-flame. And so, he is the small man slaying the great. He is virtuous egoistic Brutus, or David: David slaying the preposterous Goliath, overthrowing the heroic Saul, taking Bathsheba and sending Uriah to death: David dancing naked before the Ark, asserting the oneness, his own oneness, the one infinity, *himself*, the egoistic God, I AM. And David never went in unto Michal any more, because she jeered at him. So that she was barren all her life.

But it was David who really was barren. Michal, when she mocked, mocked the sterility of David. For the spirit in him was blasted with unfertility; he could not become born again, he could not be conceived in the spirit. Michal, the womb of profound darkness, could not conceive to the overweak seed of David's spirit. David's seed was too impure, too feeble in sheer spirit, too egoistic, it bred and begot preponderant egoists. The flood of vanity set in after David, the lamps and candles began to gutter.

Power is sheer flame, and spirit is sheer flame, and between them is the clue of the Holy Ghost. But David put a false clue between them: the clue of his own ego, cunning and *triumphant*.

It is unfertility of spirit which sends man raging to the woman, and sends him raging away again, unsatisfied. It is not the woman's barrenness: it is his own. It is sterility in himself which makes a Don Juan.

And the course of the barren spirit is dogmatically to assert One God, One Way, One Glory, one exclusive salvation. And this One God is indeed God, this one Way is the way, but it is the way of egoism, and the One God is the reflection, inevitably, of the worshipper's ego.

This is the sham crown, which the victorious lion and the victorious unicorn alike puts on his own head. When either *triumphs*, the true crown disappears, and the triumphant puts a false crown on his own head: the crown of sterile egoism. The true Crown is above the fight itself, and above the embrace itself, not upon the brow of either fighter or lover. Or, if you like, in the true fight it shines equally upon the brow of the defeated and the winner. For sometimes, it is blessed to be beaten in a fight.

He who triumphs, perishes. As Caesar perished, and Napoleon. In the fight they were wonderful, and the power was with them. But when they would be supreme, sheer triumphers, exalted in their own ego, then they fell. Triumph is a false absolution, the winner salutes his enemy, and the light of victory is on *both* their brows, since both are consummated.

In the same way, Jesus triumphant perished. Any individual who will triumph, in love or in war, perishes. There is no triumph. There is but consummation in either case.

So Shelley also perishes. He wants to be love triumphant, as Napoleon wanted to be power triumphant. Both fell.

In both, there is the spuriousness of the *ego* trying to seize the Crown that belongs only to the consummation.

In the Roman "Triumph" itself lay the source of Rome's downfall. And in the arrogance of England's dispensation of Liberty in the world lies the downfall of England. When Liberty triumphs, as in Russia, where then is the British Empire? Where then is the British Lion, crowned *Fidei Defensor*, Defender of the Faith of Liberty and Love? When liberty needs no more defending, then the protective lion had better look out.

Take care of asserting any absolute, either of power or love, of empire or democracy. The moment power *triumphs*, it becomes spurious with sheer egoism, like Caesar and Napoleon. And the moment democracy triumphs, it too becomes hideous with egoism, like Russia now.

Either lion or unicorn, triumphant, turns into a sheer beast of prey. Foe it has none: only prey—or victims.

So we have seen in the world, every time that power has triumphed: every time the lion and the eagle have jammed the crown down on their heads. Now it will be given us to see democracy triumphant, the unicorn and the dove seizing the crown, and on the instant turning into beasts of prey.

The true crown is upon the consummation itself, not upon the triumph of one over another, neither in love nor in power. The ego is the false absolute. And the ego crowned with the crown is the monster and the tyrant, whether it represent one man, an Emperor, or a whole mass of people, a Demos. A million egos summed up under a crown are not *better* than one individual crowned ego. They are a million times worse.

3

The Flux of Corruption

The tiger blazed transcendent into immortal darkness. The unique phoenix of the desert grew up to maturity and wisdom. Sitting upon her tree, she was the only one of her kind in all creation, supreme, the zenith, the perfect aristocrat. She attained to perfection, eagle-like she rose in her nest and lifted her wings, surpassing the zenith of mortality; so she was translated into the flame of eternity, she became one with the fiery Origin.

It was not for her to sit tight, and assert her own tight ego. She was gone as she came.

In the nest was a little ash, a little flocculent grey dust wavering upon a blue-red, dying coal. The red coal stirred and gathered strength, gradually it grew white with heat, it shot forth sharp gold flames. It was the young phoenix within the nest, with curved beak growing hard and crystal, like a scimitar, and talons hardening into pure jewels.

Wherein, however, is the immortality, in the constant occupation of the nest, the widow's cruse, or in the surpassing of the phoenix? She goes gadding off into flame, into her consummation. In the flame she is timeless. But the ash within the nest lies in the restless hollow of time, shaken on the tall tree of the desert. It will rise to the same consummation, become absolute in flame.

In a low, shady bush, far off, on the other side of the world, where the rains are cold and the mists wrap the leaves in a chillness, the ring-dove presses low on the bough, while her mate sends forth the last ru-cuooo of peace. The mist darkens and ebbs-in in waves, the trees are melted away, all things pass into a universal oneness, with the last re-echoing dove, peace, all pure peace, ebbing in softer, softer waves to a universal stillness.

The dark blue tranquillity is universal and infinite, the doves are asleep in the sleeping boughs, all fruits are fallen and are silent and cold, all the leaves melt away into pure mist of darkness.

It is strange that, away on the other side of the world, the tiger gleams through the hot-purple darkness, and where the dawn comes crimson, the phoenix lifts her wings in a yawn like an over-sumptuous eagle, and passes into flame above the golden palpable fire of the desert.

Here are the opposing hosts of angels, the ruddy choirs, the upright, rushing flames, the lofty Cherubim that palpitate about the Presence, the Source; and then the tall, still angels soft and pearly as mist, who await round the Goal, the attendants that hover on the edge of the last Assumption.

And from the seed two travellers set forth, in opposite directions, the one concentrating towards the upper, ruddy, blazing sun, the zenith, the creative fire; the other towards the blue, cold silence, dividing itself and ever dividing itself till it is infinite in the universal darkness.

And at the summit, the zenith, there is a flash, a flame, as the traveller enters into infinity, there is a red splash as the poppy leaps into the upper, fiery eternity. And far below there is unthinkable silence as the roots ramify and divide and pass into the oneness of unutterable silence.

The flame is gone, the flower has leapt away, the fruit ripens and falls. Then dark ebbs back to dark, and light to light, hot to hot, and cold to cold. This is death and decay and corruption. And the worm, the maggot, these are the ministers of separation, these are the tiny clashing ripples that still ebb together, when the chief tide has set back, to flow utterly apart.

This is the terror and wonder of dark returning to dark, and of light returning to light, the two departing back to their Sources. This we cannot bear to think of. It is the temporal flux of corruption, as the flux together was the temporal flux of creation. The flux is temporal. It is only the perfect meeting, the perfect interpenetration into oneness, the kiss, the blow, the two-in-one, that is timeless and absolute.

And dark is not willing to return to dark till it has known the light, nor light to light till it has known the dark, till the two have been consummated into oneness. But the act of death may itself be a consummation, and life may be a state of negation.

It may be that our state of life is itself a denial of the consummation, a prevention, a negation; that this life is our nullification, our not-being.

It may be that the flower is held from the search of the light, and the roots from the dark, like a plant that is pot-bound. It may be that, as in the autumnal cabbage, the light and the dark are made prisoners in us, their opposition is overcome, the ultimate moving has ceased. We have forgotten our goal and our end. We have enclosed ourselves in our exfoliation, there are many little channels that run out into the sand.

This is evil, when that which is temporal and relative asserts itself eternal and absolute. This I, which I am, has no being save in timelessness. In my consummation, when that which came from the Beginning and that which came from the End are transfused into oneness, then I come into being, I have existence. Till then I am only a part of nature; I am not.

But as part of nature, as part of the flux, I have my instrumental identity, my inferior I, my self-conscious ego.

If I say that *I am*, this is false and evil. I am not. Among us all, how many have being?—too few. Our ready-made individuality, our identity is no more than an accidental cohesion in the flux of time. The cohesion will break down and utterly cease to be. The atoms will return into the flux of the universe. And that unit of cohesion which I was will vanish utterly. Matter is indestructible, spirit is indestructible. This of us remains, in any case, general in the flux. But the soul that has not come into being has no being for ever. The soul does not come into being at birth. The soul comes into being in the midst of life, just as the phoenix in her maturity becomes immortal in flame. That is not her perishing: it is her becoming absolute: a blossom of fire. If she did not pass into flame, *she* would never really exist. It is by her translation into fire that she is the phoenix. Otherwise she were only a bird, a transitory cohesion in the flux.

It is absurd to talk about all men being immortal, all having souls. Very few men have being at all. They perish utterly, as individuals. Their endurance afterwards is the endurance of Matter within the flux, non-individual: and spirit within the flux. Most men are just transitory natural phenomena. Whether they live or die does not matter: except in so far as every failure in the part is a failure in the whole. Their death is of no more matter than the cutting of a cabbage in the garden, an act utterly apart from grace.

They assert themselves as important, as absolute mortals. They are just liars. When one cuts a fat autumnal cabbage, one cuts off a lie, to boil it down in the pot.

They are all just fat lies, these people, these many people, these mortals. They are innumerable cabbages in the regulated cabbage plot. And our great men are no more than Mrs. Wiggs of the Cabbage Patch.

The cabbage is a nice fat lie. That is why we eat it. It is the business of the truthful to eat up the lies. A fatted cow is a lie, and a fat pig is a lie, and a fatted sheep is a lie, just the same: these sacrificial beasts, these lambs and calves, become fat lies when they are merely protected and fed full.

The cabbage is a lie because it asserts itself as a permanency, in the state wherein it finds itself. In the swirl of the Beginning and the End, stalk and leaves take place. But the stalk and leaves are only the swirl of the waves. Yet they say, they are absolute, they have achieved a permanent form. It is a lie. Their universal absolute is only the far-off dawning of the truth, the false dawn which in itself is nothing, nothing except in relation to that which comes after.

But they say, "We are the consummation and the reality, we are the fulfilment." This is pure amorphousness. Each one becomes a single, separate entity, a single separate nullity. Having started along the way to eternity, they say, "We are there, we have arrived," and they enclose themselves in the nullity of the falsehood.

And this is the state of man, when he falls into self-sufficiency, and asserts that his self-conscious ego is It. He falls into the condition of fine cabbages.

Then they are wealthy and fat. They go no further, so they become wealthy. All that great force which would carry them naked over the edge of time, into timelessness, into being, they convert into fatness, into having. And they are full of self-satisfaction. Having no being, they assert their artificial completeness, and the life within them becomes a will-to-have, which is the expression of the will-to-persist, in the temporary unit. Selfishness is the subjugating of all things to a false entity, and riches is the great flux over the edge of the bottomless pit, the falsity, the nullity. For where is the rich man who is not the very bottomless pit? Travel nearer, nearer, nearer to him, and one comes to the gap, the hole, the abyss where his soul should be. He is not. And to stop up his hollowness, he drags all things unto himself.

And what are we all, all of us, collectively, even the poorest, now, in this age? We are only potentially rich men. We are all alike. The distinction between rich and poor is purely accidental. Rich and poor alike are only, each one, a pit-head surrounding the bottomless pit. But the rich man, by pouring vast quantities of matter down his void, gives himself a more pleasant illusion of fulfilment than the poor man can get: that is all. Yet we would give our lives, every one of us, for this illusion.

There are no rich or poor, there are no masses and middle classes and aristocrats. There are myriads of framed gaps, people, and a few timeless fountains, men and women. That is all.

Myriads of framed gaps! Myriads of little egos, all wearing the crown of life! Myriads of little Humpty-Dumpties, self-satisfied emptinesses, all about to have a great fall.

The current ideal is to be a gap with a great heap of matter around it, which can be sent clattering down. The most sacred thing is to give all your having so that it can be put on the heaps that surround all the other bottomless pits. If you give away all your having, even your life, then, you are a bottomless pit with no sides to it. Which is infinite. So that to become infinite, give away all your having, even to your life. So that you will achieve immortality yourself. Like the heroes of the war, you will become the bottomless pit itself; but more than this, you will be contributing to the public good, you will be one of those who make blessed history: which means, you will be heaping goods upon the dwindling heaps of superfluity that surround these bottomless lives of the myriad people. If we poor can each of us hire a servant, then the servant will be like a stone tumbling always ahead of us down the bottomless pit. Which creates an almost perfect illusion of having a solid earth beneath us.

Long ago we agreed that we had fulfilled all purpose and that our only business was to look after other people. We said: "It is marvellous, we are really complete." If the regulation cabbage, hidebound and solid, could walk about on his stalk, he would be very much as we are. He would think of himself as we think of ourselves, he would talk, as we talk, of the public good.

But inside him, proper and fine, the heart would be knocking and urgent, the heart of the cabbage. Of course for a long time he would not hear it. His good, enveloping green leaves outside, the heap round the hole, would have closed upon him very early, like Wordsworth's "Shades of the prison house," very close and complete and gratifying.

But the heart would beat within him, beat and beat, grow louder and louder, till it was threshing the whole of his inside rotten, threshing him hollow, till his inside began to devour his consciousness.

Then he would say: "I must do something." Looking round he would see little dwindly cabbages struggling in the patch, and would say: "So much injustice, so much suffering and poverty in the world, it cannot be." Then he would set forth to make dwindly cabbages into proper, fine cabbages. So he would be a reformer.

He would kick, kick, kick against the conditions which make some cabbages poor and dwindly, most cabbages poorer and more dwindly than himself. He would but be kicking against the pricks.

But it is very profitable to kick against the pricks. It gives one a sensation, and saves one the necessity of bursting. If our reformers had not had the prickly wrongs of the poor to kick, so that they hurt their toes quite sorely, they might long ago have burst outwards from the enclosed form in which we have kept secure.

Let no one suffer, they have said. No mouse shall be caught by a cat, no mouse. It is a transgression. Every mouse shall become a pet, and every cat shall lap milk in peace, from the saucer of utter benevolence.

This is the millennium, the golden age that is to be, when all shall be domesticated, and the lion and the leopard and the hawk shall come to our door to lap milk and to peck the crumbs and no sound shall be heard but the lowing of fat cows and the baa-ing of fat sheep.

This is the Green Age that is to be, the age of the perfect cabbage. This was our hope and our fulfilment, for this, in this hope, we lived and we died.

So the virtuous, public-spirited ones have suffered bitterly from the aspect of their myriad more-or-less blighted neighbours, whom they love as themselves. They have lived and died to right the wrong conditions of social injustice.

Meanwhile the threshing has continued at the core of us, till our entrails are threshed rotten. We are a wincing mass of self-consciousness and corruption, within our plausible rind. The most unselfish, the most humanitarian of us all, he is the hollowest and fullest of rottenness. The more rotten we become, the more insistent and insane becomes our desire to ameliorate the conditions of our poorer, and maybe healthier neighbours.

Fools, vile fools! Why cannot we acknowledge and admit the horrible pulse and thresh of corruption within us? What is this self-consciousness that palpitates within us like a disease? What is it that threshes and threshes within us, drives us mad if we see a cat catch a sparrow?

We dare not know. Oh, we are convulsed with shame long before we come to the point. It is indecent beyond endurance to think of it.

Yet here let it be told. It was the living desire for immortality, for being, which urged us ceaselessly. It was the bud within the cabbage, threshing, threshing, threshing. And now, oh our convulsion of shame, when we must know this! We would rather die.

Yet it shall be made known. It was the struggling of the light and darkness within us, towards consummation, towards absoluteness, towards flowering. Oh, we shriek with anger of shame as the truth comes out: that the cabbage is rotten within because it wanted to straddle up into weakly fiery flower, wanted to straddle forth in a spire of ragged, yellow, inconsequential blossom.

Oh God, it is unendurable, this revelation, this disclosure, it is not to be borne. Our souls perish in an agony of self-conscious shame, we will not have it.

Yet had we listened, the hide-bound cabbage might have burst, might have opened apart, for a venturing forth of the tender, timid, ridiculous cluster of aspirations, that issue in little yellow tips of flame, the flowers naked in eternity, naked above the staring unborn crowd of amorphous entities, the cabbages: the myriad egos.

But the crowd of assertive egos, of tough entities, they were too strong, too many. Quickly they extinguished any shoot of tender immortality from among them, violently they adhered to the null rind and to the thresh of rottenness within.

Still the living desire beat and threshed at the heart of us, relentlessly. And still the fixed will of the temporal form we have so far attained, the static, mid-way form, triumphed in assertion.

Still the false I, the ego, held down the real, unborn I, which is a blossom with all a blossom's fragility.

Yet constantly the rising flower pushed and thrust at the belly and heart of us, thrashed and beat relentlessly. If it could not beat its way through into being, it must thrash us hollow. Let it do so then, we said. This also we enjoy, this being threshed rotten inside. This is sensationalism, reduction of the complex tissue back through rottenness to its elements. And this sensationalism, this reduction back, has become our very life, our only form of life at all. We enjoy it, it is our lust.

It became at last a collective activity, a war, when, within the great rind of virtue we thresh destruction further and further, till our whole civilization is like a great rind full of corruption, of breaking down, a mere shell threatened with collapse upon itself.

And the road of corruption leads back to one eternity. The activity of utter going apart has, in eternity, a result equivalent to the result of utter coming together. The tiger rises supreme, the last brindled flame upon the darkness; the deer melts away, a blood-stained shadow received into the utter pallor of light; each having leapt forward into eternity, at opposite extremes. Within the closed shell of the Christian conception, we lapse utterly back, through reduction, back to the Beginning. It is the triumph of death, of decomposition.

And the process is that of the serpent lying prone in the cold, watery fire of corruption, flickering with the flowing-apart of the two streams. His belly is white with the light flowing forth from him, his back is dark and brindled where the darkness returns to the Source. He is the ridge where the two floods flow apart. So in the orange-speckled belly of the newt, the light is taking leave of the darkness, and returning to the light; the imperious, demon-like crest is the flowing home of the darkness. He is the god within the flux of corruption, from him proceeds the great retrogression back to the Beginning and back to the End. These are our gods.

There are elsewhere the golden angels of the Kiss, the golden, fiery angels of strife, those that have being when we come together, as opposites, as complements coming to consummation. There is delight and triumph elsewhere, these angels sound their loud trumpets. Then men are like brands that have burst spontaneously into flame, the phoenix, the tiger, the glistening dove, the white-burning unicorn.

But here are only the angels that cleave asunder, terrible and invincible. With cold, irresistible hands they put us apart, they send like unto like, darkness unto darkness. They thrust the seas backward from embrace, backward from the locked strife. They set the cold phosphorescent flame of light flowing back to the light, and cold heavy darkness flowing back to the darkness. They are the absolute angels of corruption, they are the snake, the newt, the water-lily, as reflected from below.

I cease to be, my darkness lapses into utter, stone darkness, my light into a light that is keen and cold as frost.

This goes on within the rind. But the rind remains permanent, falsely absolute, my false absolute self, my self-conscious ego. Till the work of corruption is finished; then the rind also, the public form, the civilization, the established consciousness of mankind disappears as well in the mouth of the worm, taken unutterably asunder by the hands of the angels of separation. It ceases to be, all the civilization and all the consciousness, it passes utterly away, a temporary cohesion in the flux. It was this, this rind, this persistent temporary cohesion, that was evil, this alone was evil. And it destroys us all before itself is destroyed.

4

Within the Sepulchre

Within the womb of the established past, the light has entered the darkness, the future is conceived. It is conceived, the beginning of the end has taken place. Light is within the grip of darkness, darkness within the embrace of light, the Beginning and the End are closed upon one another.

They come nearer and nearer, till the oneness is full grown within the womb of the past, within the belly of Time, it must move out, must be brought forth, into timelessness.

But something withholds it. The pregnancy is accomplished, the hour of labour has come. Yet the labour does not begin. The loins of the past are withered, the young unborn is shut in.

All the time, within the womb, light has been travelling to the dark, the interfusion of the two into a oneness has continued. Now that it is fulfilled, it meets with some arrest. It is the dry walls of the womb which cannot relax.

There is a struggle. Then the darkness, having overcome the light, reaching the dead null wall of the womb, reacts into self-consciousness, and recoils upon itself. At the same time the light has surpassed its limit, become conscious, and starts in reflex to recoil upon itself. Thus the false I comes into being: the I which thinks itself supreme and infinite, and which is, in fact, a sick foetus shut up in the walls of an unrelaxed womb.

Here, at this moment when the birth pangs should begin, when the great opposition between the old and the young should take place, when the young should beat back the old body that surrounds it, and the old womb and loins should expel the young body, there is a deadlock. The two cannot fight apart. The walls of the old body are inflexible and insensible, the unborn does not know that there can be any travelling forth. It conceives itself as the whole universe, surrounded by dark nullity. It does not know that it is in prison. It believes itself to have filled up the whole of the universe, right to the extremes where is nothing but blank nullity.

It is tremendously conceited. It can only react upon itself. And the reaction can only take the form of self-consciousness. For the self is everything, universal, the surrounding womb is just the outer darkness in which that which *is*, exists. Therefore there remains either to die, to pass into the outer darkness, or to enter into self-knowledge.

So the unborn recoils upon itself, dark upon dark, light upon light. This is the horror of corruption begun already within the unborn, already dissolution and corruption set in before birth. And this is the triumph of the ego.

Mortality has usurped the Crown. The unborn, reacting upon the null walls of the womb, assumes that it has reached the limit of all space and all being. It concludes that its self is fulfilled, that all consummation is achieved. It takes for certain that itself has filled the whole of space and the whole of time.

And this is the glory of the ego.

There is no more fight to be fought, there is no more to be sought and embraced. All is fought and overcome, all is embraced and contained. It is all concluded, there is nothing remaining but the outer nothingness, the only activity is the reaction against the outer nothingness, into the achieved being of the self, all else is fulfilled and concluded. To die is merely to assume nothingness. The limit of all life is reached.

And this is the apotheosis of the ego.

So there is the great turning round upon the self, dark upon dark, light upon light, the flux of separation, corruption within the unborn. The tides which are set towards each other swirl back as from a promontory which intervenes. There has been no consummation. There can be no consummation. The only thing is to return, to go back—that which came from the Beginning to go back to the Beginning, that which came from the End to return to the End. In the return lies the fulfilment.

And this is the unconscious undoing of the ego.

That which we *are* is absolute. There is no adding to it, no superseding this accomplished self. It is final and universal. All that remains is thoroughly to explore it.

That is, to analyse it. Analysis presupposes a corpse.

It is at this crisis in the human history that tragic art appears again, that art becomes the only absolute, the only watchword among the people. This achieved self, which we are, is absolute and universal. There is nothing beyond. All that remains is to state this self, and the reactions upon this self, perfectly. And the perfect statement presumes to be art. It is aestheticism.

At this crisis there is a great cry of loneliness. Every man conceives himself as a complete unit surrounded by nullity. And he cannot bear it. Yet his pride is in this also. The greatest conceit of all is the cry of loneliness.

At this crisis, emotion turns into sentiment, and sentimentalism takes the place of feeling. The ego has no feeling, it has only sentiments. And the myriad egos sway in tides of sentimentalism.

But the *tacit* utterance of every man, when this state is reached, is "*Après moi le Déluge.*" And when the deluge begins to set in, there is profound secret satisfaction on every hand. For the ego in a man secretly hates every other ego. In a democracy where every little ego is crowned with the false crown of its own supremacy, every other ego is a false usurper, and nothing more. We can only tolerate those whose crowns are not yet manufactured, because they can't *afford* it.

And again, the supreme little ego in man hates an unconquered universe. We shall never rest till we have heaped tin cans on the North Pole and the South Pole, and put up barb-wire fences on the moon. Barb-wire fences are our sign of conquest. We have wreathed the world with them. The back of creation is broken. We have killed the mysteries and devoured the secrets. It all lies now within our skin, within the ego of humanity.

So circumscribed within the outer nullity, we give ourselves up to the flux of death, to analysis, to introspection, to mechanical war and destruction, to humanitarian absorption in the body politic, the poor, the birth-rate, the mortality of infants, like a man absorbed in his own flesh and members, looking for ever at himself. It is the continued activity of disintegration—disintegration, separating, setting apart, investigation, research, the resolution back to the original void.

All this goes on within the glassy, insentient, insensible envelope of nullity. And within this envelope, like the glassy insects within their rind, we imagine we fill the whole cosmos, that we contain within ourselves the whole of time, which shall tick forth from us as from a clock, now everlastingly.

We are capable of nothing but reduction within the envelope. Our every activity is the activity of disintegration, of corruption, of dissolution, whether it be our scientific research, our social activity—(the social activity is largely concerned with reducing all the parts contained within the envelope to an equality, so that there shall be no unequal pressure, tending to rupture the envelope, which is divine)—our art, or our anti-social activity, sensuality, sensationalism, crime, war. Everything alike contributes to the flux of death, to corruption, and liberates the static data of the consciousness.

Whatever single act is performed by any man now, in this condition, it is an act of reduction, disintegration. The scientist in his laboratory, the artist in his study, the statesman, the artisan, the sensualist obtaining keen gratification, every one of these is reducing down that which is himself to its simpler elements, reducing the compound back to its parts. It is the pure process of corruption in all of us. The activity of death is the only activity. It is like the decay of our flesh, and every new step in decay liberates a sensation, keen, momentarily gratifying, or a conscious knowledge of the parts that made a whole; knowledge equally gratifying.

It is like Dmitri Karamazov, who seeks and experiences sensation after sensation, reduction after reduction, till finally he is stripped utterly naked before the police, and the quick of him perishes. There *is* no more any physical or integral Dmitri Karamazov. That which is in the hospital, afterwards, is a conglomeration of qualities, strictly an idiot, a nullity.

And Dostoevsky has shown us perfectly the utter subjection of all human life to the flux of corruption. That is his theme, the theme of reduction through sensation after sensation, consciousness after consciousness, until nullity is reached, all complexity is broken down, an individual becomes an amorphous heap of elements, qualities.

There are the two types, the dark Dmitri Karamazov, or Rogozhin; and the Myshkin on the other hand. Dmitri Karamazov and Rogozhin will each of them plunge the flesh within the reducing agent, the woman, obtain the sensation and reduction within the flesh, add to the sensual experience, and progress towards utter dark disintegration, to nullity. Myshkin on the other hand will react upon the achieved consciousness or personality or ego of every one he meets, disintegrate this consciousness, this ego, and his own as well, obtaining the knowledge of the factors that made up the complexity of the consciousness, the ego, in the woman and in himself, reduce further and further back, till himself is a babbling idiot, a vessel full of disintegrated parts, and the woman is reduced to a nullity.

This is real death. The actual physical fact of death is part of the life-stream. It is an incidental point when the flux of light and dark has flowed sufficiently apart for the conjunction, which we call life, to disappear.

We live with the pure flux of death, it is part of us all the time. But our blossoming is transcendent, beyond death and life.

Only when we fall into egoism do we lose all chance of blossoming, and then the flux of corruption is the breath of our existence. From top to bottom, in the whole nation, we are engaged, fundamentally engaged in the process of reduction and dissolution. Our reward is sensational gratification in the flesh, or sensational gratification within the mind, the utter gratification we experience when we can pull apart the whole into its factors. This is the reward in scientific and introspective knowledge, this is the reward in the pleasure of cheap sensuality.

In each case, the experience remains as it were absolute. It is the statement of what is, or what was. And a statement of what *is*, is the absolute footstep in the progress backward towards the starting place, it is the *undoing* of a complete unit into the factors which previously went to making its oneness. It is the reduction of the iris back into its component waves.

There was the bliss when the iris came into being. There is now the bliss when the iris passes out of being, and the whole is torn apart. The secret of the whole is never captured. Certain data are captured. The secret escapes down the sensual, or the sensational, or intellectual, thrill of pleasure.

So there goes on reduction after reduction within the shell. And we, who find our utmost gratification in this process of reduction, this flux of corruption, this retrogression of death, we will preserve with might and main the glassy envelope, the insect rind, the tight-shut shell of the cabbage, the withered, null walls of the womb. For by virtue of this null envelope alone do we proceed uninterrupted in this process of gratifying reduction.

And this is utter evil, this secret, silent worship of the null envelope that preserves us intact for our gratification with the flux of corruption.

Intact within the null envelope, which we have come to worship as the preserver of this our life-activity of reduction, we re-act back upon what we are. We do not seek any more the consummation of union. We seek the consummation of reduction.

When a man seeks a woman in love, or in positive desire, he seeks a union, he seeks a consummation of himself with that which is not himself, light with dark, dark with light.

But within the glassy, null envelope of the enclosure, no union is sought, no union is possible; after a certain point, only reduction. Ego reacts upon ego only in friction. There are small egos, many small people, who have not reached the limit of the confines which we worship. They may still have small consummation in union. But all those who are strong and have travelled far have met and reacted from the nullity.

And then, when a man seeks a woman, he seeks not a consummation in union, but a frictional reduction. He seeks to plunge his compound flesh into the cold acid that will reduce him, in supreme sensual experience, down to his parts. This is Rogozhin seeking Nastasia Filippovna, Dmitri his Grushenka, or D'Annunzio in *Fuoco* seeking his Foscarina. This is more or less what happens when a soldier, maddened with lust of pure destructiveness, violently rapes the woman of his captivity. It is that he may destroy another being by the very act which is called the act of creation, or procreation. In the brute soldier it is cruelty-lust: as it was in the Red Indian. But when we come to civilized man, it is not so simple. His cruelty-lust is directed almost as much against himself as against his victim. He is destroying, reducing, breaking down that of himself which is within the envelope. He is immersing himself within a keen, fierce, terrible reducing agent. This is true of the hero in Edgar Allan Poe's tales, *Ligeia*, or *The Fall of the House of Usher*. The man seeks his own sensational reduction, but he disintegrates the woman even more, in the name of love. In the name of love, what horrors men perpetrate, and are applauded!

It is only in supreme crises that man reaches the supreme pitch of annihilation. The difference, however, is only a difference in degree, not in kind. The bank-clerk performs in a mild degree what Poe performed intensely and deathlily.

These are the men in whom the development is rather low, whose souls are coarsely compounded, so that the reduction is coarse, a sort of activity of coarse hate.

But the men of finer sensibility and finer development, sensuous or conscious, they must proceed more gradually and subtly and finely in the process of reduction. It is necessary for a finely compounded nature to reduce itself more finely, to know the subtle gratification of its own reduction.

A subtle nature like Myshkin's would find no pleasure of reduction in connection with Grushenka, scarcely any with Nastasia. He must proceed more delicately. He must give up his soul to the reduction. It is his mind, his conscious self he wants to reduce. He wants to dissolve it back. He wants to become infantile, like a child, to reduce and resolve back all the complexity of his consciousness, to the rudimentary condition of childhood. That is his ideal.

So he seeks mental contacts, mental re-actions. It is in his mental or conscious contacts that he seeks to obtain the gratification of self-reduction. He reaches his crisis in his monologue of self-analysis, self-dissolution, in the drawing-room scene where he falls in a fit.

And of course, all this reducing activity is draped in alluring sentimentalism. The most evil things in the world, today, are to be found under the chiffon folds of sentimentalism. Sentimentality is the garment of our vice. It covers viciousness as inevitably as greenness covers a bog.

With all our talk of advance, progress, we are all the time working backwards. Our heroines become younger and younger. In the movies, the heroine is becoming more and more childish, and touched with infantile idiocy. We cannot bear honest maturity. We want to reduce ourselves back, back to the *corruptive* state of childishness.

Now it is all very well for a child to be a child. But for a grown person to be slimily, pornographically reaching out for child-gratifications is disgusting. The same with the prevalent love of boys. It is the desire to be reduced back, reduced back, in our accomplished ego: always within the unshattered rind of our completeness and complacency, to go backwards, in sentimentalized disintegration, to the states of childhood.

And no matter *what* happens to us, now, we sentimentalize it and use it as a means of sensational reduction. Even the great war does not alter our civilization one iota, in its total nature. The form, the whole form, remains intact. Only inside the complete envelope we writhe with sensational experiences of death, hurt, horror, reduction.

The goodness of anything depends on the direction in which it is moving. Childhood, like a bud, striving and growing and struggling towards blossoming full maturity, is surely beautiful. But childhood as a *goal*, for which grown people aim: childishness futile and sentimental, for which men and women lust, and which always retreats when grasped, like the *ignis fatuus* of a poisonous marsh of corruption: this is disgusting.

While we live, we are balanced between the flux of life and the flux of death. All the while our bodies are being composed and decomposed. But while every man fully lives, all the time the two streams keep fusing into the third reality, of real creation. Every new gesture, every fresh smile of a child is a new emergence into creative being: a glimpse of the Holy Ghost.

But when grown people start grimacing with childishness, or lusting after child-gratifications, it is corruption pure and simple.

And the still clear look on an old face, and the stillness of old, withered hands, which have gathered the long repose of autumn, this is the purity of the two streams consummated, and the bloom, like autumn crocuses, of age.

But the painted, silly child-face that old women make nowadays: or the harpy's face that many have, lusting for the sensations of youth: the hard, voracious, selfish faces of old men, seeking their own ends, devouring the shoots of young life: this is vile.

While we live, we are balanced between the flux of life and the flux of death. But the real clue is the Holy Ghost, that moves us on into the state of blossoming. And each year the blossoming is different: from the delicate blue speedwells of childhood to the equally delicate, frail farewell flowers of old age: through all the poppies and sunflowers: year after year of difference.

While we live, we change, and our flowering is a constant change.

But once we fall into the state of egoism, we cannot change. The ego, the self-conscious ego remains fixed, a final envelope around us. And we are then safe inside the mundane egg of our own self-consciousness and self-esteem.

Safe we are! Safe as houses! Shut up like unborn chickens that cannot break the shell of the egg. That's how safe we are! And as we can't be born, we can only rot. That's how safe we are!

Safe within the everlasting walls of the egg-shell we have not the courage, nor the energy, to crack, we fall, like the shut-up chicken, into a pure flux of corruption, and the worms are our angels.

And mankind falls into the state of innumerable little worms bred within the unbroken shell: all clamouring for food, food, food, all feeding on the dead body of creation, all crying peace! peace! universal peace! brotherhood of man! Everything must be "universal," to the conquering worm. It is only *life* which is different.

5

The Nuptials of Death and the Attendant Vulture

To those who are in prison, whose being is prisoner within the walls of unliving fact, there are only two forms of triumph: the triumph of inertia, or the triumph of the Will. There is no flowering possible.

And the experience *en route* to either triumph, is the experience of sensationalism.

Stone walls need not a prison make: that is, not an *absolute* prison. If the great sun has shone into a man's soul, even prison-walls cannot blot it out. Yet prison-walls, unless they be a temporary shelter, are deadly things.

So, if we are imprisoned within walls of accomplished fact, experience, or knowledge, we are prisoned indeed. The living sun is shut out finally. A false sun, like a lamp, shines.

All absolutes are prison-walls. These "laws" which science has invented, like conservation of energy, indestructibility of matter, gravitation, the will-to-live, survival of the fittest: and even these absolute facts, like—the earth goes round the sun, or the doubtful atoms, electrons, or ether—they are all prison-walls, unless we realize that we don't know what they mean. We don't know what we mean, ultimately, by *conservation*, or *indestructibility*. Our atoms, electrons, ether, are caps that fit exceeding badly. And our will-to-live contains a germ of suicide, and our survival-of-the-fittest the germ of degeneracy. As for the earth going round the sun: it goes round as the blood goes round my body, absolutely mysteriously, with the rapidity and hesitation of life.

But the human ego, in its pettifogging arrogance, sets up these things for you as absolutes, and unless you kick hard and kick in time, they are your prison walls forever. Your spirit will be like a dead bee in a cell.

Once you are in prison, you have no experience left, save the experience of reduction, destruction going on inwardly. Your sentimentalism is only the smell of your own rottenness.

This reduction within the self is sensationalism. And sensationalism, of course, is progressive. You can't have your cake and eat it. To get a sensation, you eat your cake. That is, to get a sensation, you reduce down some part of your complex psyche, physical and psychic. You get a flash, as when you strike a match. But a match once struck can never be struck again. It is finished—sensationalism is an exhaustive process.

The resolving down is progressive. It can apparently go on *ad infinitum.* But in infinity it means what we call utter death, utter nothingness, opposites released from opposition, and from conjunction, till there *is* nothing left at all, only nullity itself.

Sensationalism progresses in the individual. This is the doom of it. This is the doom of egoistic sex. Egoistic sex-excitement means the reacting of the sexes against one another in a purely reducing activity. The reduction progresses. When I have finally reduced one complexity, one unit, I must proceed to the next, the lower. It is the progressive activity of dissolution within the soul.

And the climax of this progression is in perversity, degradation and death. But only the very powerful and energetic ego can go through all the phases of its own violent reduction. The ordinary crude soul, after having enjoyed the brief reduction in the sex, is finished there, blasé, empty. And alcohol is slow and crude, and opium is only for the imaginative, the somewhat spiritual nature. Then remain the opium-drugs, for a finisher, a last reducer.

There remains only the reduction of the contact with death. So that as the sex is exhausted, gradually, a keener desire, the desire for the touch of death follows on, in an intense nature. Then come the fatal drugs. Or else those equally fatal wars and revolutions which really create nothing at all, but destroy, and leave emptiness.

When a man is cleaving like a fly with spread arms upon the face of a rock, with infinite space beneath him, and he feels his foothold going, and he cries out to the men on the rope, and falls away, dangling into endless space, jerked back by the thin rope, then he perishes, he is fused in the reducing flame of death. He knows another keen anguish of reduction. What matters to that man, afterwards? Does any of the complex life of the world below matter? None. All that is left is the triumph of his will in having gone so far and recovered. And all that lies ahead is another risk, another slip, another agony of the fall, or a demonish triumph of the will. And the *final* consummation of such a man is the last fall of all, the few horrible seconds whilst he drops, like a meteorite, to extinction. This is his final and utter satisfaction, the smash of extinction at the bottom.

But even this man is not a pure egoist. This man still has his soul open to the mystery of the mountains, he still feels the passion of the *contact* with death.

If he wins, however, in the contest: if his will triumphs in the test: then there is danger of his falling into final egoism, the more-or-less inert complacency of a self-satisfied old man.

The soul is still alive, while it has passion: any sort of passion, even for the brush with death, or for the final and utter reduction. And in the brush with death it may be released again into positive life. A man may be sufficiently released by a fall on the rope and the dangling for a few minutes of agony, in space. That may finally reduce his soul to its elements, set it free and child-like, and break-down that egoistic entity which has developed upon it from the past. The near touch of death may be a release into life; if only it will break the egoistic will, and release that other flow.

But if a man, having fallen very near to death, gets up at length and says: "I did it! It's my triumph! I beat the mountains that time!" —then, of course, his ego has only pulled itself in triumph out of the menace, and the individual will go on more egoistic and barrenly complacent.

If a man says: "I fell! But the unseen goodness helped me, when I struggled for life, and so I was saved"—then this man will go on in life unimprisoned, the channels of his heart open, and passion still flowing through him.

But if the brush with death only gave the brilliant sensational thrill of fear, followed immediately, by the *gamin* exultance: "Yah! I got myself out all right!"—then the ego continues intact, having enjoyed the sensation, and remaining vulgarly triumphant in the power of the Will. And it will continue inert and complacent till the next thrill.

So it is with war. Whoever goes to war in his own might alone, will, even if he come out victorious, come out barren: a barren triumpher, whose strength is in inertia. A man must do his own utmost: but even then, the final stroke will be delivered, or the final strength will be given from the unseen, and the man must feel it. If he doesn't feel it, he will be an inert victor, or equally inert vanquished, complacent and sterile in either case.

There must be a certain faith. And that means an ultimate reliance on that which is beyond our will, and not contained in our ego.

We have gone to war. For a hundred years we have been piling up safety upon safety, we have grown enormously within the shell of our civilization, we have rounded off our own ego and grown almost complacent about our own triumphs of will. Till we come to a point where sex seems exhausted, and passion falls flat. When even criticism and analysis now only fatigue the mind and weary the soul.

Then we gradually, gradually formulate the desire: Oh, give us the brush with death, and let us see if we can win out all right!

We go into a war like this in order to get once more the final reduction under the touch of death. That the death is so inhuman, cold, mechanical, sordid, the giving of the body to the grip of cold, stagnant mud and stagnant water, whilst one awaits for some falling death, the knowledge of the gas clouds that may lacerate and reduce the lungs to a heaving mass, this, this sort of self-inflicted Sadism, brings almost a final satisfaction to our civilized and still passionate men.

Almost! And when it is over, and we have won out, shall we be released into a new lease of life? Or shall we only extend our dreary lease of egoism and complacency? Shall we know the barren triumph of the will?—or the equally barren triumph inertia, helplessness, barren irresponsibility.

And still, as far as there is any passion in the war, it is a passion for the embrace with death. The desire to deal death and to take death. The enemy is the bride, whose body we will reduce with rapture of agony and wounds. We are the bridegroom, engaged with him in the long, voluptuous embrace, the giving of agony, the rising and rising of the slow unwilling transport of misery, the soaking-in of day after day of wet mud, in penetration of the heavy, sordid, unendurable cold, on and on to the climax, the laceration of the blade, like a frost through the tissue, blasting it.

This is the desire and the consummation, this is the war. But at length, we shall be satisfied, at length we shall have consummation. Then the war will end. And what then?

It is not really a question of victories or defeats. It is a question of fulfilment, and release from the old prison-house of a dead form. The war is one bout in the terrific, horrible labour, our civilization labouring in child-birth, and unable to bring forth.

How will it end? Will there be a release, a relaxation of the horrible walls, and a real issuing, a birth?

Or will it end in nothing, all the agony going to stiffen the old form deader, to enclose the unborn more helplessly and drearily.

It may easily be. For behind us all, in the war, stand the old and the elderly, complacent with egoism, bent on maintaining the old form. Oh, they are the monkey grinning with anxiety and anticipation, behind us, waiting for the burnt young cat to pull the chestnut out of the fire. And in the end, they will thrill with the triumph of their egoistic will, and harden harder still with vulture-like inertia, rapacious inertia.

In sex, we have plunged the quick of creation deep into the cold flux of reduction, corruption, till the quick is extinguished. In war we have plunged the whole quick of the living, sentient body into a cold, cold flux. Much has died and much will die. But if the whole quick dies, and there remain only the material, mechanical unquickened tissue, acting at the bidding of the mechanical will, and the sterile ego triumphant, then it is a poor tale, a barrenly poor tale.

I have seen a soldier at the seaside who was maimed. One leg was only a small stump, with the trouser folded back on it. He was a handsome man of about thirty, finely built. His face was sun-browned, and extraordinarily beautiful, still, with a strange placidity, something like perfection, abstract, complete. He had known his consummation. It seemed he could never desire corruption or reduction again, he had had his satisfaction of death. He was become almost impersonal, a simple abstraction, all his personality loosed and undone. He was now like a babe just born, new to begin life. Yet in a sense, still-born. The newness and candour, like a flower just unloosed, was something strange and rare in him. Yet unloosed, curiously, into the light of death.

So he came forward down the pier, in the sunshine, slowly on his crutches. Behind, the sea was milk-white and vague, as if full of ghosts, and silent, except when a long white wave plunged to silence out of the smooth, milky silence of the sea, coming from very far out of the ghostly stillness.

The maimed soldier, strong and handsome, with some of the frail candour of a newly-wakened child in his face, came slowly down the pier on his crutches, looking at everybody who looked at him. He was naïve like a child, wondering. The people stared at him with a sort of fascination. So he was rather vain, rather proud, like a vain child.

He did not know he was maimed, it had not entered his consciousness. His soul, so clean and new and fine, could not conceive of such a thing. He was rather vain and slightly ostentatious, not as a man with a wound, a trophy, more as a child who is conspicuous among envious elders.

The women particularly were fascinated. They could not look away from him. The strange abstraction of horror and death was so perfect in his face, like the horror of birth on a new-born infant, that they were almost hysterical. They gravitated towards him, helplessly, they could not move away from him.

They wanted him, they wanted him so badly, that they were almost beside themselves. They wanted his consummation, his perfect completeness in horror and death. They too wanted the consummation. They followed him, they made excuses to talk to him. And he, strange, abstract, glowing still from the consummation of destruction and pain and horror, like a bridegroom just come from the bride, seemed to glow before the women, to give off a strange, unearthly radiance, which was like an embrace, a most poignant embrace to their souls.

But still his eyes were looking, looking, looking for someone who was not eager for him, to know him, to devour him, like women round a perfect child. He had not realized yet what all the attention meant, which he received. He was so strong in his new birth. And he was looking for his own kind, for the living, the new-born, round about. But he was surrounded by greedy, voracious people, like birds seeking the death in him, pecking at the death in him.

It was horrible, rather sinister, the women round the man, there on the pier stretched from the still, sunny land over the white sea, noiseless and inhuman.

The spirit of destruction is divine, when it breaks the ego and opens the soul to the wide heavens. In corruption there is divinity. Aphrodite is, on one side, the great goddess of destruction in sex, Dionysus in the spirit. Moloch and some gods of Egypt are gods also of the knowledge of death. In the soft and shiny voluptuousness of decay, in the marshy chill heat of reptiles, there is the sign of the Godhead. It is the activity of departure. And departure is the opposite equivalent of coming together; decay, corruption, destruction, breaking down is the opposite equivalent of creation. In infinite going-apart there is revealed again the pure absolute, the absolute relation: this time truly as a Ghost: the ghost of what was.

We who live, we can only live or die. And when, like the maimed soldier on the pier with the white sea behind, when we have come right back into life, and the wonder of death fades off our faces again, what then?

Shall we go on with wide, careless eyes and the faint astonished smile waiting all our lives for the accomplished death? Waiting for death finally? And continuing the sensational reduction process? Or shall we fade into a dry empty egoism? Which will the maimed soldier do? He cannot remain as he is, clear and peaceful.

Are we really doomed, and smiling with the wonder of doom?

Even if we are, we need not say: "It is finished." It is never finished. That is one time when Jesus spoke a fatal half-truth, in his *Consummatum Est*! Death consummates nothing. It can but abruptly close the individual life. But Life itself, and even the forms men have given it, will persist and persist. There is no consummation into death. Death leaves still further deaths.

Leonardo knew this: he knew the strange endlessness of the flux of corruption. It is Mona Lisa's ironic smile. Even Michael Angelo knew it. It is in his *Leda and the Swan*. For the swan is one of the symbols of divine corruption with its reptile feet buried in the ooze and mud, its voluptuous form yielding and embracing the ooze of water, its beauty white and cold and terrifying, like the dead beauty of the moon, like the water-lily, the sacred lotus, its neck and head like the snake, it is for us a flame of the cold white fire of flux, the phosphorescence of corruption, the salt, cold burning of the sea which corrodes all it touches, coldly reduces every sun-built form to ash, to the original elements. This is the beauty of the swan, the lotus, the snake, this cold white salty fire of infinite reduction. And there was some suggestion of this in the Christ of the early Christians, the Christ who was the Fish.

So that, when Leonardo and Michael Angelo represent Leda in the embrace of the swan, they are painting mankind in the clasp of the divine flux of corruption, the singing death. Mankind *turned back*, to cold, bygone consummations.

When the swan first rose out of the marshes, it was a glory of creation. But when we turn back, to seek its consummation again, it is a fearful flower of corruption.

And corruption, like growth, is only divine when it is pure, when all is given up to it. If it be experienced as a controlled activity within an intact whole, this is vile. When the cabbage flourishes round a hollow rottenness, this is vile. When corruption goes on within the living womb, this is unthinkable. The chicken dead in the egg is an abomination. We cannot subject a divine process to a static will, not without blasphemy and loathsomeness. The static will must be subject to the process of reduction, also. For the pure absolute, the Holy Ghost, lies also in the relationship which is made manifest by the departure, the departure *ad infinitum*, of the opposing elements.

Corruption will at last break down for us the deadened forms, and release us into the infinity. But the static ego, with its will-to-persist, neutralizes both life and death, and utterly defies the Holy Ghost. The unpardonable sin!

It is possible for this static will, this vile rind of nothingness, to triumph for a long while over the divine relation in the flux, to assert an absolute nullity of static form.

This we do who preserve intact our complete null concept of life, as an envelope around this flux of destruction, the war. The whole concept and form of life remains absolute and static, around the gigantic but contained seething of the fight. It is the rottenness seething within the cabbage, corruption within the old, fixed body. The cabbage does not relax, the body is not broken open. The reduction is sealed and contained.

That is our attitude now. It is the attitude of the women who flutter round and peck at death in us. This is the carrion process set in, the process of obscenity, the baboon, the vulture in us.

In so far as we fight to remain ideally intact, in so far as we seek to give and to have the experience of death, so that we may remain unchanged in our whole conscious form, may preserve the static entity of our conception, around the fight, we are obscene. We are like vultures and obscene insects.

We may give ourselves utterly to destruction. Then our conscious forms are destroyed along with us, and something new must arise. But we may not have corruption within ourselves as sensationalism, our skin and outer form intact. To destroy life for the preserving of a static, rigid form, a shell, a glassy envelope, this is the lugubrious activity of the men who fight to save democracy and to end all fighting. The fight itself is divine, the relation betrayed in the fight is absolute. But the glassy envelope of the established concept is only a foul nullity.

Destruction and Creation are the two relative absolutes between the opposing infinities. Life is in both. Life may even, for a while be almost entirely in one, or almost entirely in the other. The end of either oneness is death. For life is really in the two, the absolute is the pure relation, which is both.

If we have our fill of destruction, then we shall turn again to creation. We shall need to live again, and live hard, for once our great civilized form is broken, and we are at last born into the open sky, we shall have a whole new universe to grow up into, and to find relations with. The future will open its delicate, dawning æons in front of us, unfathomable.

But let us watch that we do not preserve an enveloping falsity around our destructive activity, some nullity of virtue and self-righteousness, some conceit of the "general good" and the salvation of the world by bringing it all within our own conceived whole form. This is the utter lie and obscenity. The ego, like Humpty Dumpty, sitting for ever on the wall.

The vulture was once, perhaps, an eagle. It became a supreme strong bird, almost like the phoenix. But at a certain point, it said: "I am It." And then it proceeded to preserve its own static form crystal about the flux of corruption, fixed, absolute as a crystal, about the horrible seethe of corruption. Then the eagle became a vulture.

And the dog, through cowardice, arrested itself at a certain point and became domestic, or a hyæna, preserving a glassy, fixed form about a voracious seethe of corruption.

And the baboon, almost a man, or almost a high beast, arrested himself and became obscene, a grey, hoary rind closed upon an activity of strong corruption.

And the louse, in its little glassy envelope, brings everything into the corrupting pot of its little belly.

And these are all perfectly-arrested egoists, asserting themselves static and foul, triumphant in inertia and in will.

Let us watch that we do not turn either into carrion or into carrion eaters. Let us watch that we do not become, in the vulgar triumph of our will, and the obscene inertia of our ego, vultures who feed on putrescence. The lust for death, for pain, for torture, is even then better than this fatal triumph of inertia and the egoistic will. Anything is better than that. The Red Indians, full of Sadism and self-torture and death, destroyed themselves. But the eagle, when it gets stuck and can know no more blossoming turns into a vulture with a naked head, and becomes carrion-foul.

There must always be some balance between the passion for destruction and the passion for creation, in every living activity; for in the race to destruction we can utterly destroy the vital quick of our being, leave us amorphous, undistinguished, vegetable; and in the race for creation we can lose ourselves in mere production, and pile ourselves over with dead null monstrosities of obsolete form. All birth comes with the reduction of old tissue. But the reduction is not the birth. That is the fallacy of all of us, who represent the old tissue now. In this fallacy we go careering down the slope in our voluptuousness of death and horror, careering into oblivion, like Hippolytus trammelled up and borne away in the traces of his maddened horses.

Who says that the spirit of destruction will outrun itself? Not till the driver be annihilated. Then the destructive career will run itself out.

And then what?

But neither destruction nor production is, in itself, evil. The danger lies in the fall into egoism, which neutralizes both. When destruction and production alike are mechanical, meaningless.

The race of destruction may outrun itself. But still the form may remain intact, the old imprisoning laws. Only those who have not travelled to the confines will be left, the mean, the average, the labourers, the slaves: all of them little crowned egos.

Still the ancient mummy will have the people within its belly. There they will be slaves: not to the enemy, but to themselves, the concept established about them: being slaves, they will be happy enclosed within the tomb-like belly of a concept, like gold-fish in a bowl, which think themselves the centre of the universe.

This is like the vultures of the mountains. They have kept the form and height of eagles. But their souls have turned into the souls of slaves and carrion eaters. Their size, their strength, their supremacy of the mountains, remains intact. But they have become carrion eaters.

This is the tomb, the whited sepulchre, this very form, this liberty, this ideal for which we are fighting. The Germans are fighting for another sepulchre. Theirs is the sepulchre of the Eagle become vulture, ours is the sepulchre of the lion become dog: soon to become hyæna.

But we would have our own sepulchre, in which we shall dwell secure when the rage of destruction is over. Let it be the sepulchre of the dog or the vulture, the sepulchre of democracy or aristocracy, what does it matter! Inside it, the worms will jig the same jazzy dances, and heave and struggle to get hold of vast and vaster stores of carrion, or its equivalent, gold.

The carrion birds, aristocrats, sit up high and remote, on the sterile rocks of the old absolute, the obscene heads gripped hard and small, like knots of stone clenched upon themselves for ever. The carrion dogs and hyænas of the old, arid, democratic absolute, prowl among the bare stones of the common earth, in numbers, their loins cringing, their heads sharpened to stone.

Those who will hold power, afterwards, they will sit on their rocks and heights of unutterable morality, which have become foul through the course of ages, like vultures upon the unchangeable mountain-tops. The fixed, existing form will persist for ever beneath them, about them, they will have become the spirit incarnate of the fixed form of life. They will eat carrion, having become a static hunger for keen putrescence. This alone will support the incarnation of hoary fixity which they are. And beside the carrion they will fight the multitudes of hoary, obscene dogs, which also persist. It is the mortal form become null and fixed and enduring, glassy, horrible, beyond life and death, beyond consummation, the awful, stony nullity. It is timeless, almost as the rainbow.

But it is not utterly timeless. It is only unthinkably slow, static in its passing away, perpetuated.

Its very aspect of timelessness is a fraud.

What is evil?—not death, nor the blood-devouring Moloch, but this spirit of perpetuation and apparent timelessness, this obscenity which holds the great carrion birds, and the carrion dogs. The tiger, the hawk, the weasel, are beautiful things to me; and as they strike the dove and the hare, that is the will of God, it is a consummation, a bringing together of two extremes, a making perfect one from the duality.

But the baboon, and the hyæna, the vulture, the condor, and the carrion crow, these fill me with fear and horror. These are the highly developed life-forms, now arrested, petrified, frozen falsely, timeless. The baboon was almost as man, the hyæna as the lion: the vulture and the condor are greater than the eagle, the carrion crow is stronger than the hawk. And these obscene beasts are not ashamed. They are stark and static, they are not mixed. Their will is hoary, ageless. Before us, the Egyptians have known them and worshipped them.

The baboon, with his intelligence and his unthinkable loins, the cunning hyæna with his cringing, stricken loins, these are the static form of one achieved ego, the egoistic Christian, the democratic, the unselfish. The vulture, with her naked neck and naked, small stony head, this is the static form of the other achieved ego, the eagle, the Self, aristocratic, lordly, pagan.

It is unthinkable and unendurable. Yet we are drawn more and more in this direction. After the supreme intelligence, the baboon, after the supreme pride, the vulture. The millionaire: the international financier: the bankers of this world. The baboons, the hyænas, the vultures.

The snake is the spirit of the great corruptive principle, the festering cold of the marsh. This is how he seems, as we look back. We revolt from him, but we share the same life and tide of life as he. He struggles as we struggle, he enjoys the sun, he comes to the water to drink, he curls up, hides himself to sleep. And under the low skies of the far past æons, he emerged a king out of chaos, a long beam of new life. But the vulture looms out in sleep like a rock, invincible within the hoary, static form, invincible against the flux of both eternities.

One day there was a loud, terrible scream from the garden, tearing the soul. Oh, and it was a snake lying on the warm garden bed, and in his teeth the leg of a frog, a frog spread out, screaming with horror. We ran near. The snake glanced at us sharply, holding fast to the frog, trying to get further hold. In so trying, it let the frog escape, which leaped, convulsed, away. Then the snake slid noiselessly under cover, sullenly, never looking at us again.

We were all white with fear. But why? In the world of twilight as in the world of light, one beast shall devour another. The world of corruption has its stages, where the lower shall devour the higher, *ad infinitum*.

So a snake, also, devours the fascinated bird, the little, static bird with its tiny skull. Yet is there no great reptile that shall swallow the vulture?

As yet, the vulture is beyond life or change. It stands hard, immune within the principle of corruption, and the principle of creation, unbreakable. It is kept static by the fire of putrescence, which makes the void within balance the void without. It is a changeless tomb wherein the latter stages of corruption take place, counteracting perfectly the action of life. Life devours death to keep the static nullity of the form.

So the ragged, grey-and-black vulture sits hulked, motionless, like a hoary, foul piece of living rock, its naked head and neck sunk in, only the curved beak protruding, the naked eyelids lowered. Motionless, beyond life, it sits on the sterile heights.

It does not sleep, it stays utterly static. When it spreads its great wings and floats down the air, still it is static, still this is the sleep, a dream-floating. When it rips up carrion and swallows it, it is still the same dream-motion, static, beyond the inglutination. The naked, obscene head is always fast locked, like stone.

It is this naked, obscene head of a bird, sleep-locked, a petrified knot of sleep, that I cannot bear to think of. When I think of it, I neither live nor die, I am petrified into foulness. The knot of volition, the will knotted upon a perpetuated moment, will not now be unloosed for ever. It will remain hoary, unchanging, timeless. Till it disappears, suddenly. Amid all the flux of time, of the two eternities, this head remains unbroken in a cold, riveted sleep. But one day it will be broken.

I am set utterly against this small, naked, stone-clinched head, it is a foul vision I want to wipe away. But I am set utterly also against the loathsome, cringing, imprisoned loins of the hyæna, that cringe down the hind legs of the beast with their static weight. Again the static will has knotted into riveted, endless nullity, but here upon the loins. In the vulture, the head is turned to stone, the fire is in the talons and the beak. In the hoary, glassy hyæna, the loins are turned to stone, heavy, sinking down to earth, almost dragged along, the fire is in the white eyes, and in the fangs. The hyæna can scarcely see and hear the living world; it draws back on to the stony fixity of its own loins, draws back upon its own nullity, sightless save for carrion. The vulture can neither see nor hear the living world, it is one supreme glance, the glance in search of carrion, its own absolute quenching, beyond which is nothing.

This is the end, and beyond the end. This is beyond the beginning and the end. Here the beginning and the end are revoked. The vulture, revoking the end, the end petrified upon the beginning, is a nullity. The hyæna, the beginning petrified beneath the end, is a nullity. This is beyond the beginning and the end, this is aristocracy gone beyond aristocracy, the I gone beyond the I; the other is democracy gone beyond democracy, the not-me surpassed upon itself.

This is the changelessness of the kingdoms of the earth, null, unthinkable.

This is the last state into which man may fall, in the triumph of will and the triumph of inertia, the state of the animated sepulchre.

6

To Be, and to Be Different

Behind me there is time stretching back for ever, on to the unthinkable beginnings, infinitely. And this is eternity. Ahead of me, where I do not know, there is time stretching on infinitely, to eternity. These are the two eternities.

We cannot say they are one and the same. They are two and utterly different. If I look at the eternity ahead, my back is towards the other eternity, this latter is forgotten, it *is* not. Which is the Christian attitude. If I look at the eternity behind, back to the source, then there is for me one eternity, one only. And this is the pagan eternity, the eternity of Pan. This is the eternity some of us are veering round to, in private life, during the past few years.

The two eternities are *not* one eternity. It is only by denying the very meaning of speech itself that we can argue them into oneness. They are two, relative to one another.

They are only *one* in their mutual relation, which relation is timeless and absolute. The eternities are temporal and relative. But their relation is constant, absolute without mitigation.

The motion of the eternities is dual: they flow together, and they flow apart, they flow for ever towards union, they start back for ever in opposition, to flow for ever back to the issue, back into the unthinkable future, back into the unthinkable past.

We have known both directions. The Pagan, aristocratic, lordly, sensuous, has declared the Eternity of the Origin, the Christian, humble, spiritual, unselfish, democratic, has declared the Eternity of the Issue, the End. We have heard both declarations, we have seen each great ideal fulfilled, as far as is possible, at this time, on earth. And now we say: "There is no eternity, there is no infinite, there is no God, there is no immortality."

And all the time we know we are cutting off our nose to spite our face. Without God, without some sort of immortality, not necessarily life-everlasting, but without *something* absolute, we are nothing. Yet now, in our spitefulness of self-frustration, we would rather be nothing than listen to our own being.

God is not the one infinite, nor the other, our immortality is not in the original eternity, neither in the ultimate eternity. God is the utter relation between the two eternities, He is in the flowing together and the flowing apart.

This utter relation is timeless, absolute and perfect. It is in the Beginning and the End, just the same. Whether it be revealed or not, it is the same. It is the Unrevealed God: what Jesus called the Holy Ghost.

My immortality is not from the beginning, in my endless ancestry. Nor is it on ahead in life everlasting. My life comes to me from the great Creator, the Beginner. And my spirit runs towards the Comforter, the Goal far ahead. But I, what am I between?

These two halves I always am. But I am never *myself* until they are consummated into a spark of oneness, the gleam of the Holy Ghost. And in this spark is my immortality, my non-mortal being, that which is not swept away down either direction of time.

I am not immortal till I have achieved immortality. And immortality is not a question of time, of everlasting life. It is a question of consummate being. Most men die and perish away, unconsummated, unachieved. It is not easy to achieve immortality, to win a consummate being. It is supremely difficult. It means undaunted suffering and undaunted enjoyment, both. And when a man has reached his ultimate of enjoyment and his ultimate of suffering, *both*, then he knows the two eternities, then he is made absolute, like the iris, created out of the two. Then he is immortal. It is not a question of time. It is a question of being. It is not a question of submission, submitting to the divine grace: it is a question of submitting to the divine grace, in suffering and self-obliteration, and it is a question of conquering by divine grace, as the tiger leaps on the trembling deer, in utter satisfaction of the Self, in complete fulfilment of desire. The fulfilment is dual. And having known the dual fulfilment, then within the fulfilled soul is established the divine relation, the Holy Spirit dwells there, the soul has achieved immortality, it has attained to absolute being.

So the body of man is begotten and born in an ecstasy of delight and of suffering. It is a flame kindled between the opposing confluent elements of the air. It is the battle-ground and marriage-bed of the two invisible hosts. It flames up to its full strength, and is consummate, perfect, absolute, the human body. It is a revelation of God, it is the foam-burst of the two waves, it is the iris of the two eternities. It is a flame, flapping and travelling in the winds of mortality.

Then the pressure of the dark and the light relaxes, the flame sinks. We watch the slow departure, till only the wick glows. Then there is the dead body, cold, rigid, perfect in its absolute form, the revelation of the consummation of the flux, a perfect jet of foam that has fallen and is vanishing away. The two waves are fast going asunder, the snow-wreath melts, corruption's quick fire is burning in the achieved revelation.

We cannot bear it, that the body should decay. We cover it up, we cannot bear it. It is the revelation of God, it is the most holy of all revealed things. And it melts into slow putrescence.

We cannot bear it. We wish above all to preserve this achieved and perfect form, this revelation of God. And despair comes over us when it passes away. "*Sic transit*," we say, in agony.

The perfect form was not achieved in time, but in timelessness. It does not belong to today or tomorrow, or to eternity. It just *is*.

It is we who pass away, we and the whole flux of the two eternities, these pass. This is the eternal flux. But the God-quick, which is the constant within the flux, this is neither temporal nor eternal, it is truly timeless. And this perfect body was a revelation of the timeless God, timeless as He. If we, in our mortality, are temporal, if we are part of the flux of the eternities, then we swirl away in our living flux, the flesh decomposes and is lost.

But all the time, whether in the glad warm confluence of creation or in the cold flowing-apart of corruption, the same quick remains absolute and timeless, the revelation is in God, timeless. This alone of mortality does not belong to the passing away, this consummation, this revelation of God within the body, or within the soul. This revelation of God *is* God. But we who live, we are of the flux, we belong to the two eternities.

Only perpetuation is a sin. The perfect relation is perfect. But it is therefore timeless. And we must not think to tie a knot in Time, and thus to make the consummation temporal or eternal. The consummation is timeless, and we belong to Time, in our process of living.

Only Matter is a very slow flux, the waves ebbing slowly apart. So we engrave the beloved image on the slow, slow wave. We have the image in marble, or in pictured colour.

This is art, this transferring to a slow flux the form that was attained at the maximum of confluence between the two quick waves. This is art, the revelation of a pure, an absolute relation between the two eternities.

Matter is a slow, big wave flowing back to the Origin. And Spirit is a slow, infinite wave flowing back to the Goal, the ultimate Future. On the slow wave of matter and spirit, on marble or bronze or colour or air, and on the consciousness, we imprint a perfect revelation, and this is art: whether it reveal the relation in creation or in corruption, it is the same, it is a revelation of God: whether it be Piero della Francesca or Leonardo da Vinci, the *garçon qui pisse* or Phidias, or Christ or Rabelais. Because the revelation is imprinted on stone or granite, on the slow, last-receding wave, therefore it remains with us for a long, long time, like the sculptures of Egypt. But it is all the time slowly passing away, unhindered, in its own time.

It passes away, but it is not in any sense lost. Our souls are established upon all the revelations, upon all the timeless achieved relationships, as the seed contains a convoluted memory of all the revelation in the plant it represents. The flower is the burning of God in the bush: the flame of the Holy Ghost: the actual Presence of accomplished oneness, accomplished out of twoness. The true God is *created* every time a pure relationship, or a consummation out of twoness into oneness takes place. So that the poppy flower is God come red out of the poppy-plant. And a man, if he win to a sheer fusion in himself of all the manifold creation, a pure relation, a sheer gleam of oneness out of manyness, then this man is God created where before God was uncreated. He is the Holy Ghost in tissue of flame and flesh, whereas before, the Holy Ghost was but Ghost. It is true of a man as it is true of a dandelion or of a tiger or of a dove. Each creature, by some mystery, achieved a consummation in itself of all the wandering sky and sinking earth, and leaped into the other kingdom, where flowers are, of the gleaming Ghost. So it is for ever. The two waves of Time flow in from the eternities, towards a meeting, a consummation. And the meeting, the consummation, is heaven, is absolute. All the while, as long as time lasts, the shock of the two waves passed into oneness, there is a new heaven. All the while, heaven is created from the flux of time, the galaxies between the night. And we too may be heavenly bodies, however we swirl back in the flux. When we have surged into being, when we have caught fire with friction, we are the immortals of heaven, the invisible stars that make the galaxy of night, no matter how the skies are tossed about. We can forget, but we cannot cease to be. Life nor death makes any difference, once we *are*.

For ever the kingdom of Heaven is established more perfectly, more beautifully, between the flux of the two eternities.

One by one, in our consummation, we pass, a new star, into the galaxy that arches between the nightfall and the dawn, one by one, like the bushes in the desert, we take fire with God, and burn timelessly: and within the flame is heaven that has come to pass. Every flower that comes out, every bird that sings, every hawk that drops like a blade on her prey, every tiger flashing his paws, every serpent hissing out poison, every dove bubbling in the leaves, this is timeless heaven established from the flood, in this we have our form and our being. Every night new Heaven may ripple into being, every era a new Cycle of God may take place.

But it is all timeless. The error of errors is to try to keep heaven fixed and rocking like a boat anchored within the flux of time. Then there is sure to be shipwreck: "*Die Wellen verschlingen am Ende Schiffer und Kahn.*" From the flux of time Heaven takes place in timelessness. The flux must go on.

This is sin, this tying the knot in Time, this anchoring the ark of eternal truth upon the waters. There is no ark, there is no eternal system, there is no rock of eternal truth. In Time and in Eternity all is flux. Only in the other dimension, which is not the time-space dimension, is there Heaven. We can no more *stay* in this heaven than the flower can stay on its stem. We come and go.

So the body that came into being and walked transfigured in heavenliness must lie down and fuse away in the slow fire of corruption. Time swirls away, out of sight of the heavenliness. Heaven is not here nor there nor anywhere. Heaven is in the other dimension. In the young, in the unborn, this kingdom of Heaven which was revealed and has passed away is established; of this Heaven the young and the unborn have their being. And if in us the Heaven be not revealed, if there be no transfiguration, no consummation, then the infants cry in the night, in want, void, strong want.

This is evil, this desire for constancy, for fixity in the temporal world. This is the denial of the absolute good, the revocation of the Kingdom of Heaven.

We cannot know God, in terms of the permanent, temporal world; we cannot. We can only know the *revelation* of God in the physical world. And the revelation of God is God. But it vanishes as the rainbow. The revelation is a condition in the whole flux of time. When this condition has passed away, the revelation is no more revealed. It has gone. And then God is gone, except to memory, a remembering of a critical moment within the flux. But there is no revelation of God in memory. Memory is not truth. Memory is persistence, perpetuation of a momentary cohesion in the flux. God is gone, until next time. But the next time will come. And then again we shall *see* God, and once more, it will be different. It is always different.

And we are all, now, living on the stale memory of a revelation of God. Which is purely a repetitive and temporal thing. But it contains us, it is our prison.

Whereas, there is nothing for a man to do but to behold God, and to become God. It is no good living on memory. When the flower opens, see him, don't remember him. When the sun shines, be him, and then cease again.

So we seek war, death, to kill this memory within us. We hate this imprisoning memory so much, we will kill the whole world rather than remain in prison to it. But why do we not create a new revelation of God, instead of seeking merely the destruction of the old revelations? We do this, because we are cowards. We say, "The great revelation cannot be destroyed, but I, who am a failure, I can be destroyed." So we destroy the individual stones rather than decide to pull down the whole edifice. The edifice must stand, but the individual bricks must sacrifice themselves. So carefully we remove single lives from the edifice, and we destroy these single lives, carefully supporting the edifice in the weakened place.

And the soldier says: "I die for my God and my Country." When, as a matter of fact, in his death his God and his country are so much destroyed.

But we must always lie, always convert our action to a lie. We know that we are living in a state of falsity, that all our social and religious form is dead, a crystallized lie. Yet we say: "We will die for our social and religious form."

In truth, we proceed to die because the whole frame of our life is a falsity, and we know that, if we die sufficiently, the whole frame and form and edifice will collapse upon itself. But it were much better to pull it down and have a great clear space, than to have it collapse on top of us. For we shall be like Samson, buried among the ruins.

And moreover, if we are like Samson, trying to pull the temple down, we must remember that the next generation will be nonetheless slaves, sightless, in Gaza, at the mill. And they will be by no means eager to commit suicide by bringing more temple beams down with a bang on their heads. They will say: "It is a very nice temple, quite weather-tight. What's wrong with it?" They will be near enough to extinction to be very canny and cautious about imperilling themselves.

No, if we are to break through, it must be in the strength of life bubbling inside us. The chicken does not break the shell out of animosity against the shell. It bursts out in its blind desire to move under a greater heavens.

And so must we. We must burst out, and move under a greater heavens. As the chicken bursts out, and has a whole new universe to get into relationship with.

Our universe is not much more than a mannerism with us now. If we break through, we shall find, that man is not man, as he seems to be, nor woman woman. The present seeming is a ridiculous travesty. And even the sun is not the sun as it appears to be. It is something tingling with magnificence.

And then starts the one glorious activity of man: the getting himself into a new relationship with a new heaven and a new earth. Oh, if we knew, the earth is everything and the sun is everything that we have missed knowing. But if we persist in our attitude of parasites on the body of earth and sun, the earth and the sun will be mere victims on which we feed our louse-like complacency for a long time yet: we, a myriad myriad little egos, five billion feeding like one.

The thing in itself! Why, I never yet met a man who was anything but what he had been *told* to be. Let a man be a man-in-himself, and then he can begin to talk about the *Ding an Sich*. Men may be utterly different from the things they now seem. And then they will behold, to their astonishment, that the sun is absolutely different from the thing they now see, and that they call "sun."

The Novel

Somebody says the novel is doomed. Somebody else says it is the green bay tree getting greener. Everybody says something, so why shouldn't I!

Mr. Santayana sees the modern novel expiring because it is getting so thin; which means, Mr. Santayana is bored.

I am rather bored myself. It becomes harder and harder to read the *whole* of any modern novel. One reads a bit, and knows the rest; or else one doesn't want to know any more.

This is sad. But again, I don't think it's the novel's fault. Rather the novelists'.

You can put anything you like in a novel. So why do people *always* go on putting the same thing? Why is the *vol au vent* always chicken! Chicken *vol au vents* may be the rage. But who sickens first shouts first for something else.

The novel is a great discovery: far greater than Galileo's telescope or somebody else's wireless. The novel is the highest form of human expression so far attained. Why? Because it is so incapable of the absolute.

In a novel, everything is relative to everything else, if that novel is art at all. There may be didactic bits, but they aren't the novel. And the author may have didactic "purpose" up his sleeve. Indeed most great novelists have, as Tolstoi had his Christian-socialism, and Hardy his pessimism, and Flaubert his intellectual desperation. But even a didactic purpose so wicked as Tolstoi's or Flaubert's cannot put to death the novel.

You can tell me, Flaubert had a "philosophy", not "purpose". But what is a novelist's philosophy but a purpose on a rather higher level? And since every novelist who amounts to anything has a philosophy— even Balzac—any novel of importance has a purpose. If only the "purpose" be large enough, and not at outs with the passional inspiration.

Vronsky sinned, did he? But also the sinning was a consummation devoutly to be wished. The novel makes that obvious: in spite of old Leo Tolstoi. And the would-be-pious Prince in *Resurrection* is a muff, with his piety that nobody wants or believes in.

There you have the greatness of the novel itself. It won't *let* you tell didactic lies, and put them over. Nobody in the world is anything but delighted when Vronsky gets Anna Karénina. Then what about the sin?—Why, when you look at it, all the tragedy comes from Vronsky's and Anna's fear of *society*. The monster was social, not phallic at all. They couldn't live in the pride of their sincere passion, and spit in Mother Grundy's eye. And that, that cowardice, was the real "sin". The novel makes it obvious, and knocks all old Leo's teeth out. "As an officer I am still useful. But as a man, I am a ruin," says Vronsky—or words to that effect. Well what a skunk, collapsing as a man and a male, and remaining merely as a social instrument; an "officer", God love us!—merely because people at the opera turn backs on him! As if people's backs weren't preferable to their faces, anyhow!

And old Leo tries to make out it was all because of the phallic sin. Old liar! Because where would any of Leo's books be, without the phallic splendour? And then to blame the column of blood, which really gave him all his life riches! The Judas! Cringe to a mangy, bloodless Society, and try to dress up that dirty old Mother Grundy in a new bonnet and face-powder of Christian-Socialism. Brothers indeed! Sons of a castrated Father!

The novel itself gives Vronsky a kick in the behind, and knocks old Leo's teeth out, and leaves us to learn.

It is such a bore that nearly all great novelists have a didactic purpose, otherwise a philosophy, directly opposite to their passional inspiration. In their passional inspiration, they are all phallic worshippers. From Balzac to Hardy, it is so. Nay, from Apuleius to E. M. Forster. Yet all of them, when it comes to their philosophy, or what they think-they-are, they are all crucified Jesuses. What a bore! And what a burden for the novel to carry!

But the novel has carried it. Several thousands of thousands of lamentable crucifixions of self-heroes and self-heroines. Even the silly duplicity of *Resurrection*, and the wickeder duplicity of Salammbô, with that flayed phallic Matho, tortured upon the Cross of a gilt Princess.

You can't fool the novel. Even with man crucified upon a woman: his "dear cross". The novel will show you how dear she was: dear at any price. And it will leave you with a bad taste of disgust against these heroes who *turn* their women into a "dear cross", and *ask* for their own crucifixion.

You can fool pretty nearly every other medium. You can make a poem pietistic, and still it will be a poem. You can write *Hamlet* in drama: if you wrote him in a novel, he'd be half comic, or a trifle suspicious: a suspicious character, like Dostoevsky's Idiot. Somehow, you sweep the ground a bit too clear in the poem or the drama, and you let the human Word fly a bit too freely. Now in a novel there's always a tom-cat, a black tom-cat that pounces on the white dove of the Word, if the dove doesn't watch it; and there is a banana-skin to trip on; and you know there is a water-closet on the premises. All these things help to keep the balance.

If, in Plato's *Dialogues*, somebody had suddenly stood on his head and given smooth Plato a kick in the wind, and set the whole school in an uproar, then Plato would have been put into a much truer relation to the universe. Or if, in the midst of the *Timaeus*, Plato had only paused to say: "And now, my dear Cleon—(or whoever it was)—I have a bellyache, and must retreat to the privy: this too is part of the Eternal Idea of man," then we never need have fallen so low as Freud.

And if, when Jesus told the rich man to take all he had and give it to the poor, the rich man had replied: "*All right, old sport! You are poor, aren't you? Come on, I'll give you a fortune. Come on!*" Then a great deal of snivelling and mistakenness would have been spared us all, and we might never have produced a Marx and a Lenin. If only Jesus had *accepted* the fortune!

Yes, it's a pity of pities that Matthew, Mark, Luke, and John didn't write straight novels. They did write novels; but a bit crooked. The *Evangels* are wonderful novels, by authors "with a purpose". Pity there's so much Sermon-on-the-Mounting.

> Matthew, Mark, Luke, and John
> Went to bed with their breeches on!—

as every child knows. Ah, if only they'd taken them off!

Greater novels, to my mind, are the books of the Old Testament, Genesis, Exodus, Samuel, Kings, by authors whose purpose was so big, it didn't quarrel with their passionate inspiration. The purpose and the inspiration were almost one. Why, in the name of everything bad, the two ever should have got separated, is a mystery! But in the modern novel they are hopelessly divorced. When there *is* any inspiration there, to be divorced from.

This, then, is what is the matter with the modern novel. The modern novelist is possessed, hag-ridden, by such a stale old "purpose", or idea-of-himself, that his inspiration succumbs. Of course he denies having any didactic purpose at all: because a purpose is supposed to be like catarrh, something to be ashamed of. But he's got it. They've all got it: the same snivelling purpose.

They're all little Jesuses in their own eyes, and their "purpose" is to prove it. Oh Lord!—*Lord Jim! Sylvestre Bonnard! If Winter Comes! Main Street! Ulysses! Pan!* They are all pathetic or sympathetic or antipathetic little Jesuses *accomplis* or *manqués*. And there is a heroine who is always "pure", usually, nowadays, on the muck-heap! Like the Green Hatted Woman. She is all the time at the feet of Jesus, though her behaviour there may be misleading. Heaven knows what the Saviour really makes of it: whether she's a Green Hat or a Constant Nymph (eighteen months of constancy, and her heart failed), or any of the rest of 'em. They are all, heroes and heroines, novelists and she-novelists, little Jesuses or Jesusesses. They may be wallowing in the mire: but then didn't Jesus harrow Hell! *A la bonne heure!*

Oh, they are all novelists with an idea of themselves! Which is a "purpose", with a vengeance! For what a weary, false, sickening idea it is nowadays! The novel gives them away. They can't fool the novel.

Now really, it's time we left *off* insulting the novel any further. If your purpose is to prove your own Jesus qualifications, and the thin stream of your inspiration is "sin", then dry up, for the interest is dead. *Life as it is!* What's the good of pretending that the lives of a set of tuppenny Green Hats and Constant Nymphs is Life-as-it-is, when the novel itself proves that all it amounts to is life as it is isn't life, but a sort of everlasting and intricate and boring habit: of Jesus peccant and *Jesusa peccante.*

These wearisome sickening little personal novels! After all, they aren't novels at all. In every great novel, who is the hero all the time? Not any of the characters, but some unnamed and nameless flame behind them all. Just as God is the pivotal interest in the books of the Old Testament. But just a trifle too intimate, too *frère et cochon*, there. In the great novel, the felt but unknown flame stands behind all the characters, and in their words and gestures there is a flicker of the presence. If you are *too personal, too human*, the flicker fades out, leaving you with something awfully lifelike, and as lifeless as most people are.

We have to choose between the quick and the dead. The quick is God-flame, in everything. And the dead is dead. In this room where I write, there is a little table that is dead: it doesn't even weakly exist. And there is a ridiculous little iron stove, which for some unknown reason is quick. And there is an iron wardrobe trunk, which for some still more mysterious reason is quick. And there are several books, whose mere corpus is dead, utterly dead and non-existent. And there is a sleeping cat, very quick. And a glass lamp, alas, is dead.

What makes the difference? *Quién sabe!* But difference there is. And I *know* it.

And the sum and source of all quickness we will call God. And the sum and total of all deadness we may call human.

And if one tries to find out wherein the quickness of the quick lies, it is in a certain weird relationship between that which is quick and—I don't know; perhaps all the rest of things. It seems to consist in an odd sort of fluid, changing, grotesque or beautiful relatedness. That silly iron stove somehow *belongs*. Whereas this thin-shanked table doesn't belong. It is a mere disconnected lump, like a cut-off finger.

And now we see the great, great merits of the novel. It can't exist without being "quick". The ordinary unquick novel, even if it be a best seller, disappears into absolute nothingness, the dead burying their dead with surprising speed. For even the dead like to be tickled. But the next minute, they've forgotten both the tickling and the tickler.

Secondly, the novel contains no didactic absolute. All that is quick, and all that is said and done by the quick, is in some way godly. So that Vronsky's taking Anna Karenina we must count godly, since it is quick. And that Prince in *Resurrection*, following the convict girl, we must count dead. The convict train is quick and alive. But that would-be-expiatory Prince is as dead as lumber.

The novel itself lays down these laws for us, and we spend our time evading them. The man in the novel must be "quick". And this means one thing, among a host of unknown meaning: it means he must have a quick relatedness to all the other things in the novel: snow, bed-bugs, sunshine, the phallus, trains, silk-hats, cats, sorrow, people, food, diphtheria, fuchsias, stars, ideas, God, tooth-paste, lightning, and toilet-paper. He must be in quick relation to all these things. What he says and does must be relative to them all.

And this is why Pierre, for example, in *War and Peace*, is more dull and less quick than Prince André. Pierre is quite nicely related to ideas, tooth-paste, God, people, foods, trains, silk-hats, sorrow, diphtheria, stars. But his relation to snow and sunshine, cats, lightning and the phallus, fuchsias and toilet-paper, is sluggish and mussy. He's not quick enough.

The really quick, Tolstoi loved to kill them off or muss them over. Like a true Bolshevist. One can't help feeling Natasha is rather mussy and unfresh, married to that Pierre.

Pierre was what we call "so human." Which means "so limited." Men clotting together into social masses in order to limit their individual liabilities: this is humanity. And this is Pierre. And this is Tolstoi, the philosopher with a very nauseating Christian-brotherhood idea of himself. Why limit man to a Christian-brotherhood? I myself, I could belong to the sweetest Christian-brotherhood one day, and ride after Attila with a raw beefsteak for my saddle-cloth, to see the red cock crow in flame over all Christendom, next day.

And that is man! That, really, was Tolstoi. That, even, was Lenin, God in the machine of Christian-brotherhood, that hashes men up into social sausage-meat.

Damn all absolutes. Oh damn, damn, damn all absolutes! I tell you, no absolute is going to make the lion lie down with the lamb: unless, like the limerick, the lamb is inside.

> They returned from the ride
> With lamb Leo inside
> And a smile on the face of the tiger!
> Sing fol-di-lol-lol!
> Fol-di-lol-lol!
> Fol-di-lol-ol-di-lol-olly!

For man, there is neither absolute nor absolution. Such things should be left to monsters like the right-angled triangle, which does only exist in the ideal consciousness. A man can't have a square on his hypotenuse, let him try as he may.

Ay! Ay! Ay!—Man handing out absolutes to man, as if we were all books of geometry with axioms, postulates and definitions in front. God with a pair of compasses! Moses with a set square! Man a geometric bifurcation, not even a radish!

Holy Moses!

"Honour thy father and thy mother!" That's awfully cute! But supposing they are not honourable? How then, Moses?

Voice of thunder from Sinai: "*Pretend to honour them!*"

"Love thy neighbour as thyself."

Alas, my neighbour happens to be mean and detestable.

Voice of the lambent Dove, cooing: "*Put it over him, that you love him.*"

Talk about the cunning of serpents! I never saw even a serpent kissing his instinctive enemy.

Pfui! I wouldn't blacken my mouth, kissing my neighbour, who, I repeat, to me is mean and detestable.

Dove, go home!

The Goat and Compasses, indeed!

Everything is relative. Every Commandment that ever issued out of the mouth of God or man, is strictly relative: adhering to the particular time, place and circumstance.

And this is the beauty of the novel; everything is true in its own relationship, and no further.

For the relatedness and interrelatedness of all things flows and changes and trembles like a stream, and like a fish in the stream the characters in the novel swim and drift and float and turn belly-up when they're dead.

So, if a character in a novel wants two wives—or three—or thirty: well, that is true of that man, at that time, in that circumstance. It may be true of other men, elsewhere and elsewhen. But to infer that all men at all times want two, three, or thirty wives; or that the novelist himself is advocating furious polygamy; is just imbecility.

It has been just as imbecile to infer that, because Dante worshipped a remote Beatrice, every man, all men, should go worshipping remote Beatrices.

And that wouldn't have been so bad, if Dante had put the thing in its true light. Why do we slur over the actual fact that Dante had a cosy bifurcated wife in his bed, and a family of lusty little Dantinos? Petrarch, with his Laura in the distance, had *twelve* little legitimate Petrarchs of his own, between his knees. Yet all we hear is *Laura! Laura! Beatrice! Beatrice! Distance! Distance!*

What bunk! Why didn't Dante and Petrarch chant in chorus:

> Oh be my spiritual concubine
>   Beatrice! ⎱
>   Laura!   ⎰
> My old girl's got several babies that are mine,
> But *thou* be my spiritual concubine,
>   Beatrice! ⎱
>   Laura!   ⎰

Then there would have been an honest relation between all the bunch. Nobody grudges the gents their spiritual concubines. But keeping a wife and family—twelve children—up one's sleeve, has always been recognized as a dirty trick.

Which reveals how *immoral* the absolute is! Invariably keeping some vital fact dark! Dishonourable!

Here we come upon the third essential quality of the novel. Unlike the essay, the poem, the drama, the book of philosophy, or the scientific treatise: all of which may beg the question, when they don't downright filch it; the novel inherently is and must be:

1. Quick.
2. Interrelated in all its parts, vitally, organically.

3. Honourable.

I call Dante's *Commedia* slightly dishonourable, with never a mention of the cosy bifurcated wife, and the kids. And *War and Peace* I call downright dishonourable, with that fat, diluted Pierre for a hero, stuck up as preferable and desirable, when everybody knows that he *wasn't* attractive, even to Tolstoi.

Of course Tolstoi, being a great creative artist, was true to his characters. But being a man with a philosophy, he wasn't true to his *own character*.

Character is a curious thing. It is the flame of a man, which burns brighter or dimmer, bluer or yellower or redder, rising or sinking or flaring according to the draughts of circumstance and the changing air of life, changing itself continually, yet remaining one single, separate flame, flickering in a strange world: unless it be blown out at last by too much adversity.

If Tolstoi had looked into the flame of his own belly, he would have seen that he didn't really like the fat, fuzzy Pierre, who was a poor tool, after all. But Tolstoi was a personality even more than a character. And a personality is a self-conscious *I am*: being all that is left in us of a once-almighty Personal God. So being a personality and almighty *I am*, Leo proceeded deliberately to lionize that Pierre, who was a domestic sort of house-dog.

Doesn't anybody call that dishonourable on Leo's part? He might just as well have been true to *himself*! But no! His self-conscious personality was superior to his own belly and knees, so he thought he'd improve on himself, by creeping inside the skin of a lamb; the doddering old lion that he was! Leo! Léon!

Secretly, Leo worshipped the human male, man as a column of rapacious and living blood. He could hardly meet three lusty, roisterous young guardsmen in the street, without crying with envy: and ten minutes later, fulminating on them black oblivion and annihilation, utmost moral thunder-bolts.

How boring, in a great man! And how boring, in a great nation like Russia, to let its old-Adam manhood be so improved upon by these reformers, who all feel themselves short of something, and therefore live by spite, that at last there's nothing left but a lot of shells of men, improving themselves steadily emptier and emptier, till they rattle with words and formulae, as if they'd swallowed the whole encyclopædia of socialism.

But wait! There is life in the Russians. Something new and strange will emerge out of their weird transmogrification into Bolshevists.

When the lion swallows the lamb, fluff and all, he usually gets a pain, and there's a rumpus. But when the lion tries to force himself down the throat of the huge and popular lamb—a nasty old sheep, really—then it's a phenomenon. Old Leo did it: wedged himself bit by bit down the throat of woolly Russia. And now out of the mouth of the bolshevist lambkin still waves an angry, mistaken, tufted leonine tail, like an agitated exlamation mark.

Meanwhile it's a deadlock.

But what a dishonourable thing for that claw-biting little Leo to do! And in his novels you see him at it. So that the papery lips of *Resurrection* whisper: "*Alas! I would have been a novel. But Leo spoiled me.*"

Count Tolstoi had that last weakness of a great man: he wanted the absolute: the absolute of love, if you like to call it that. Talk about the "last infirmity of noble minds"! It's a perfect epidemic of senility. He wanted to *be* absolute: a universal brother. Leo was too tight for Tolstoi. He wanted to puff, and puff, and puff, till he became Universal Brotherhood itself, the great gooseberry of our globe.

Then pop went Leo! And from the bits sprang up bolshevists.

It's all bunk. No man can be absolute. No man can be absolutely good or absolutely right, nor absolutely lovable, nor absolutely beloved, nor absolutely loving. Even Jesus, the paragon, was only relatively good and relatively right. Judas could take him by the nose.

No god, that men can conceive of, could possibly be absolute or absolutely right. All the gods that men ever discovered are still God: and they contradict one another and fly down one another's throats, marvellously. Yet they are *all* God: the incalculable Pan.

It is rather nice, to know what a lot of gods there are, and have been, and will be, and that they are all of them God all the while. Each of them utters an absolute: which, in the ears of all the rest of them, falls flat. This makes even eternity lively.

But man, poor man, bobbing like a cork in the stream of time, must hitch himself to some absolute star of righteousness overhead. So he throws out his line, and hooks on. Only to find, after a while, that his star is slowly falling: till it drops into the stream of time with a fizzle, and there's *another* absolute star gone out.

Then we scan the heavens afresh.

As for the babe of love, we're simply tired of changing its napkins. Put the brat down, and let it learn to run about, and manage its own little breeches.

But it's nice to think that all the gods are God all the while. And if a god only genuinely feels to you like God, then it *is* God. But if it doesn't feel quite, quite altogether like God to you, then wait awhile, and you'll hear him fizzle.

The novel knows all this, irrevocably. "My dear," it kindly says, "one God is relative to another god, until he gets into a machine; and then it's a case for the traffic cop!"

"But what am I to do!" cries the despairing novelist. "From Amon and Ra to Mrs. Eddy, from Ashtaroth and Jupiter to Annie Besant, I don't know where I am."

"Oh yes you do, my dear!" replies the novel. "You are where you are, so you needn't hitch yourself on to the skirts either of Ashtaroth or Eddy. If you meet them, say *how-do-you-do*! to them quite courteously. But don't hook on, or I shall turn you down."

"Refrain from hooking on!" says the novel.

"But be honourable among the host!" he adds.

Honour! Why, the gods are like the rainbow, all colours and shades. Since light itself is invisible, a manifestation has got to be pink or black or blue or white or yellow or vermilion, or "tinted".

You may be a theosophist, and then you will cry: *Avaunt! Thou dark-red aura! Away!!!—Oh come! Thou pale-blue or thou primrose aura, come!*

This you may cry if you are a theosophist. And if you put a theosophist in a novel, he or she may cry *avaunt*! to the heart's content.

But a theosophist cannot be a novelist, as a trumpet cannot be a regimental band. A theosophist, or a Christian, or a Holy Roller, may be *contained* in a novelist. But a novelist may not put up a fence. The wind bloweth where it listeth, and auras will be red when they want to.

As a matter of fact, only the Holy Ghost knows truly what righteousness is. And heaven only knows what the Holy Ghost is! But it sounds all right. So the Holy Ghost hovers among the flames, from the red to the blue and the black to the yellow, putting brand to brand and flame to flame, as the wind changes, and life travels in flame from the unseen to the unseen, men will never know how or why. Only travel it must, and not die down in nasty fumes.

And the honour, which the novel demands of you, is only that you shall be true to the flame that leaps in you. When that Prince in *Resurrection* so cruelly betrayed and abandoned the girl, at the beginning of her life, he betrayed and wetted on the flame of his own manhood. When, later, he bullied her with his repentant benevolence, he again betrayed and slobbered upon the flame of his waning manhood, till in the end his manhood is extinct, and he's just a lump of half-alive elderly meat.

It's the oldest Pan-mystery. God is the flame-life in all the universe; multifarious, multifarious flames, all colours and beauties and pains and sombrenesses. Whichever flame flames in your manhood, that is you, for the time being. It is your manhood, don't make water on it, says the novel. A man's manhood is to honour the flames in him, and to know that none of them is absolute: even a flame is only relative.

But see old Leo Tolstoi wetting on the flame. As if even his wet were absolute!

Sex is flame, too, the novel announces. Flame burning against every absolute, even against the phallic. For sex is so much more than phallic, and so much deeper than functional desire. The flame of sex singes your absolute, and cruelly scorches your ego. What, will you assert your ego in the universe? Wait till the flames of sex leap at you like striped tigers.

> They returned from the ride
> With the lady inside,
> And a smile on the face of the tiger.

You will play with sex, will you! You will tickle yourself with sex as with an ice-cold drink from a soda-fountain! You will pet your best girl, will you, and spoon with her, and titillate yourself and her, and do as you like with your sex?

Wait! Only wait till the flame you have dribbled on flies back at you; later! Only wait!

Sex is a life-flame, a dark one, reserved and mostly invisible. It is a deep reserve in a man, one of the core-flames of his manhood.

What, would you play with it? Would you make it cheap and nasty!

Buy a king-cobra, and try playing with that.

Sex is even a majestic reserve in the sun.

Oh, give me the novel! Let me hear what the novel says.

As for the novelist, he is usually a dribbling liar.

Him with His Tail in His Mouth

Answer a fool according to his folly, philosophy ditto.

Solemnity is a sign of fraud.

Religion and philosophy both have the same dual purpose: to get at the beginning of things, and at the goal of things. They have both decided that the serpent has got his tail in his mouth, and that the end is one with the beginning.

It seems to me time someone gave that serpent of eternity another dummy to suck.

They've all decided that the beginning of all things is the life-stream itself, energy, ether, libido, not to mention the Sanskrit joys of Purusha, Pradhana, Kala.

Having postulated the serpent of the beginning, now see all the heroes from Moses and Plato to Bergson, wrestling with him might and main, to push his tail into his mouth.

Jehovah creates man in his Own Image, according to His Own Will. If man behaves according to the ready-made Will of God, formulated in a bunch of somewhat unsavoury commandments, then lucky man will be received into the bosom of Jehovah.

Man isn't very keen. And that is Sin, original and perpetual.

Then Plato discovers how lovely the intellectual idea is: in fact, the only perfection is ideal.

But the old dragon of creation, who fathered us all, didn't have an idea in his head.

Plato was prepared. He popped the Logos into the mouth of the dragon, and the serpent of eternity was rounded off. The old dragon, ugly and venomous, wore yet the precious jewel of the Platonic idea in his head. Unable to find the dragon wholesale, modern philosophy sets up a retail shop. You can't lay salt on the old scoundrel's tail, because, of course, he's got it in his mouth, according to postulate. He doesn't seem to be sprawling in his old lair, across the heavens. In fact, he appears to have vamoosed. Perhaps, instead of being one big old boy, he is really an infinite number of little tiny boys: atoms, electrons, units of force or energy, tiny little birds all spinning with their tails in their

beaks. Just the same in detail as in the gross. Nothing will come out of
the egg that isn't in it. Evolution sings away at the same old song. Out
of the amœba, or some such old-fashioned entity, the dragon of evolved
life stretches himself enormous and more enormous, only, at last, to return each time, and put his tail into his own mouth, and be an amœba
once more. The amœba, or the electron, or whatever it may lately be—
the rose would be just as scentless—is the constant, from which all
manifest living creation starts out, and to which it all returns.

There was a time when man was not, nor monkey, nor cow, nor cat-
fish. But the amœba (or the electron, or the atom, or whatever it is)
always was and always will be.

> Boom! tiddy-ra-ta! Boom!
> Boom! tiddy-ra-ta! Boom!

How do you know? How does anyone know, what always was or
wasn't? Bunk of geology, and strata, and all that, biology or evolution.

> One, two, three four five,
> Catch a little fish alive.
> Six, seven, eight nine ten,
> I have let him go again . . .

Bunk of beginnings and of ends, and heads and tails. Why does man
always want to know so damned much? Or rather, so damned little? If
he can't draw a ring round creation, and fasten the serpent's tail into its
mouth with the padlock of one final clinching idea, then creation can
go to hell, as far as man is concerned.

There is such a thing as life, or life energy. We know, because we've
got it, or had it. It isn't a constant. It comes and it goes. But we *want* it.

This I think is incontestable.

More than anything else in the world, we want to have life, and life-
energy abundant in us. We think if we eat yeast, vitamins and pro-
teins, we're sure of it. We're had. We diddle ourselves for the million
millionth time.

What we want is life, and life-energy inside us. Where it comes from,
or what it is, we don't know, and never shall. It is the capital X of all
our knowledge.

But we want it, we must have it. It is the all in all.

This we know, now, for good and all: that which is good, and moral,
is that which brings into us a stronger, deeper flow of life and life-
energy: evil is that which impairs the life-flow.

But man's difficulty is, that he can't have life for the asking. "He asked life of Thee, and Thou gavest it him: even length of days for ever and ever." There's a pretty motto for the tomb!

It isn't length of days for ever and ever that a man wants. It is strong life within himself, while he lives.

But how to get it? You may be as healthy as a cow, and yet have fear inside you, because your life is not enough.

We know, really, that we can't have life for the asking, nor find it by seeking, nor get it by striving. The river flows into us from behind and below. We must turn our backs to it, and go ahead. The faster we go ahead, the stronger the river rushes into us. The moment we turn round to embrace the river of life, it ebbs away, and we see nothing but a stony fiumara.

We must go ahead.

But which way is ahead?

We don't know.

We only know that, continuing in the way we are going, the river of life flows feebler and feebler in us, and we lose all sense of vital direction. We begin to talk about vitamins. We become idiotic. We cunningly prepare our own suicide.

This is the philosophic problem: to find the way ahead.

Allons!—there is no road before us.

Plato said that ahead, ahead was the perfect Idea, gleaming in the brow of the dragon.

We have pretty well caught up with the perfect Idea, and we find it a sort of vast, white, polished tombstone.

If the mouth of the serpent is the open grave, into which the tail disappears, then three cheers for the Logos, and down she goes.

We children of a later Pa, know that Life is real, Life is earnest, and the Grave is not its Goal.

Let us side-step.

All goals become graves.

Every goal is a grave, when you get there.

Well, I came out of an egg-cell, like an amœba, and I go into the grave. I can't help it. It's not my fault, and it's not my business.

I don't want eternal life, nor length of days for ever and ever. Nothing so long drawn out.

I give up all that sort of stuff.

Yet while I live, I want to live. Death, no doubt, solves its own problems. Let Life solve the problem of living.

> Teach me to live that so I may
> Rise glorious at the Judgment Day.

I have no desire to rise glorious at any Judgment Day, when the serpent finally chokes himself with his own tail.

> Teach me to live that I may
> Go gaily on from day to day.

Nay, in all the world, I feel the life-urge weakening. It may be there are too many people alive. I feel it is because there is too much automatic consciousness and self-consciousness in the world.

We can't live by loving life, alone. Life is like a capricious mistress: the more you woo her the more she despises you. You have to get up and go to something more interesting. Then she'll pelt after you.

Life is the river, darkly sparkling, that enters into us from behind, when we set our faces towards the unknown. Towards some goal!!!

But there is no eternal goal. Every attempt to find an eternal goal puts the tail of the serpent into his mouth again, whereby he chokes himself in one more last gasp.

What is there then, if there is no eternal goal?

By itself, the river of life just gets nowhere. It sinks into the sand.

The river of life follows the living. If the living don't get anywhere, the river of life doesn't. The old serpent lays him down and goes into a torpor, instead of dancing at our heels and sending the life-sparks up our legs and spine, as we travel.

So we've got to get somewhere.

Is there no goal?

"Oh man! on your four legs, your two, and your three, where are you going?"—says the Sphinx.

"I'm just going to say *How-do-you-do?* to Susan," replies the man. And he passes without a scratch.

When the cock crows, he says "*How-do-you-do?*"

"*How-do-you-do Peter? How-do-you-do? old liar!*"

"*How-do-you-do, Oh Sun!*"

A challenge and a greeting.

We live in a multiple universe. I am a chick that absolutely refuses to chirp inside the monistic egg. See me walk forth, with a bit of egg-shell sticking to my tail!

When the cuckoo, the cow, and the coffee-plant chipped the Mundane Egg, at various points, they stepped out, and immediately set off in different directions. Not different directions of space and time, but different directions in creation: within the fourth dimension. The cuckoo went cuckoo-wards, the cow went cow-wise, and the coffee-plant started coffing. Three very distinct roads across the fourth dimension.

The cow was dumb, and the cuckoo too.
They went their ways, as creatures do,
Till they chanced to meet, in the Lord's green Zoo.

The bird gave a cluck, the cow gave a coo,
At the sight of each other the pair of them flew
Into tantrums, and started their hullabaloo.

They startled creation; and when they were through
Each said to the other: till I came across you
I wasn't aware of the things I could do!

Cuckoo!
Moo!
Cuckoo!

And this, I hold, is the true history of evolution.

The Greeks made equilibrium their goal. Equilibrium is hardly a goal to travel towards. Yet it's something to attain. You travel in the fourth dimension, not in yards and miles, like the eternal serpent.

Equilibrium argues either a dualistic or a pluralistic universe. The Greeks, being sane, were pantheists and pluralists, and so am I.

Creation is a fourth dimension, and in it there are all sorts of things, gods and what-not. That brown hen, scratching with her hind leg in such common fashion, is a sort of goddess in the creative dimension. Of course, if you stay outside the fourth dimension, and try to measure creation in length, breadth and height, you've set yourself the difficult task of measuring up the Monad, the Mundane Egg. Which is a game, like any other. The solution is, of course (let me whisper): *put his tail in his mouth!*

Once you realize that, willy nilly, you're *inside* the Monad, you give it up. You're inside it and you always will be. Therefore, Jonah, sit still in the whale's belly, and have a look round. For you'll *never* measure the whale, since you're inside him.

And then you see it's a fourth dimension, with all sorts of gods and goddesses in it. That brown hen, who, being a Rhode Island Red, is big and stuffy like plush-upholstery, is, of course, a goddess in her own rights. If I myself had to make a poem to her, I should begin:

Oh my flat-footed plush armchair
So commonly scratching in the yard—!

But this poem would only reveal my own limitations.

Because Flat-foot is the favourite of the white leghorn cock, and he shakes the tid-bit for her with a most wooing noise, and when she lays an egg, he bristles like a double white poppy, and rushes to meet her, as she flounders down from the chicken-house, and his echo of her *I've-laid-an-egg* cackle is rich and resonant. Every pine-tree on the mountains hears him:

$$\left.\begin{array}{l} \text{She's} \\ \text{I've} \end{array}\right\} \textit{laid an egg!}$$

$$\left.\begin{array}{l} \text{She's} \\ \text{I've} \end{array}\right\} \textit{laid an egg!}$$

And his poem would be:

> Oh you who make me feel so good, when you sit next me on the perch
> At night! (temporarily, of course!)
> Oh you who make my feathers bristle with the vanity of life!
> Oh you whose cackle makes my throat go off like a rocket!
> Oh you who walk so slowly, and make me feel swifter
> Than my boss!
> Oh you who bend your head down, and move in the under
> Circle, while I prance in the upper!
> Oh you, come! come! come! for here is a bit of fat from
> The roast veal; I am shaking it for you.

In the fourth dimension, in the creative world, we live in a pluralistic universe, full of gods and strange gods and unknown gods; a universe where that Rhode Island Red hen is a goddess in her own right and the white cock is a god indisputable, with a little red ring on his leg: which the boss put there.

Why? Why, I mean, is he a god?

Because he is something that nothing else is. Certainly he is something that I am not.

And she is something that neither he is nor I am.

When she scratches and finds a bug in the earth, she seems fairly to gobble down the monad of all monads; and when she lays, she certainly thinks she's put the Mundane Egg in the nest.

Just part of her naïve nature!

As for the goal, which doesn't exist, but which we are always coming back to: well, it doesn't spatially, or temporally, or eternally exist: but in the fourth dimension, it does.

What the Greeks called equilibrium: what I call relationship. Equilibrium is just a bit mechanical. It became very mechanical with the Greeks: an intellectual nail put through it.

I don't *want* to be "good" or "righteous"—and I won't even be "virtuous", unless "vir" means a man, and "vis" means the life-river.

But I *do* want to be alive. And to be alive, I must have a goal in the *creative*, not the *spatial* universe.

I want, in the Greek sense, an equilibrium between me and the rest of the universe. That is, I want a relationship between me and the brown hen.

The Greek equilibrium took too much for granted. The Greek never asked the brown hen, nor the horse, nor the swan, if it would kindly be equilibrated with him. He took it for granted that hen and horse would be only too delighted.

You can't take it for granted. That brown hen is extraordinarily callous to my god-like presence. She doesn't even choose to know me to nod to. If I've got to strike a balance between us, I've got to work at it.

But that is what I want: that she shall nod to me, with a *"Howdy!"* —and I shall nod to her, more politely: *"How-do-you-do, Flat-foot?"* And between us there shall exist the third thing, the *connaissance*. That is the goal.

I shall not betray myself nor my own life-passion for her. When she walks into my bedroom and makes droppings in my shoes, I shall chase her with disgust, and she will flutter and squawk. And I shall not ask her to be human for my sake.

That is the mistake the Greeks made. They talked about equilibrium, and then, when they wanted to equilibrate themselves with a horse, or an ox, or an acanthus, then horse, ox, and acanthus had to become nine-tenths human, to accommodate them. Call that equilibrium?

As a matter of fact, we don't call it equilibrium, we call it anthropomorphism. And anthropomorphism is a bore. Too much anthropos makes the world a dull hole.

So Greek sculpture tends to become a bore. If it's a horse, it's an anthropomorphized horse. If it's a Praxiteles *Hermes*, it's a Hermes so Praxitelized, that it begins sugarily to bore us.

Equilibrium, in its very best sense—in the sense the Greeks *originally* meant it—stands for the strange spark that flies between two creatures, two things that are equilibrated, or in living relationship. It is a goal: to come to that state when the spark will fly from me to Flatfoot, the brown hen, and from her to me.

I shall leave off addressing her: *"Oh my flatfooted plush arm-chair!"* I realize that is only impertinent anthropomorphism on my part. She might as well address me: *"Oh my skin-flappy split pole!"* Which would be like her impudence. Skin-flappy, of course, would refer to my blue shirt and baggy cord trousers. How would *she* know I don't grow them like a loose skin!

In the early Greeks, the spark between man and man, stranger and stranger, man and woman, stranger and strangeress, was alive and vivid. Even those Doric Apollos.

In the Egyptians, the spark between man and the living universe remains alight for ever in those early, silent, motionless statues of Pharaohs. They say it is the statue of the soul of the man. But what is the soul of a man, except *that* in him which is himself alone, suspended in immediate relationship to the sum of things? Not isolated or cut off. The Greeks began the cutting apart business. And Rodin's remerging was only an intellectual tacking on again.

The serpent hasn't got his tail in his mouth. He is on the alert, with lifted head like a listening, sparky flower. The Egyptians knew.

But when the oldest Egyptians carve a hawk or a Sekhet-cat, or paint birds or oxen or people: and when the Assyrians carve a she-lion: and when the cavemen drew the charging bison, or the reindeer, in the caves of Altamira: or when the Hindoo paints geese or elephants or lotus in the great caves of India whose name I forget—Ajanta!—then how marvellous it is! How marvellous is the living relationship between man and his object! be it man or woman, bird, beast, flower or rock or rain: the exquisite frail moment of pure conjunction, which, in the fourth dimension, is timeless. An Egyptian hawk, a Chinese painting of a camel, an Assyrian sculpture of a lion, an African fetish idol of a woman pregnant, an Aztec rattlesnake, an early Greek Apollo, a caveman's paintings of a Prehistoric mammoth, on and on, how perfect the timeless moments between man and the other Pan-creatures of this earth of ours!

And by the way, speaking of cave-men, how did those prognathous semi-apes of Altamira come to depict so delicately, so beautifully, a female bison charging, with swinging udder, or deer stooping feeding, or an antediluvian mammoth deep in contemplation. It is art on a pure, high level, beautiful as Plato, far, far more "civilized" than Burne Jones. Hadn't somebody better write Mr. Wells' History backwards, to prove how we've degenerated, in our stupid visionlessness, since the cave-men?

The pictures in the cave represent moments of purity which are the quick of civilization. The pure relation between the cave-man and the deer: fifty per cent man, and fifty per cent bison, or mammoth, or deer. It is not ninety-nine per cent man, and one per cent horse: as in a Raphael horse. Or hundred per cent fool, as when F. G. Watts sculpts a bronze horse and calls it Physical Energy.

If it is to be life, then it is fifty per cent me, fifty per cent thee: and the third thing, the spark, which springs from out of the balance, is timeless. Jesus, who saw it a bit vaguely, called it the Holy Ghost.

Between man and woman, fifty per cent man and fifty per cent woman: then the pure spark. Either this, or less than nothing.

As for ideal relationships, and pure love, you might as well start to water tin pansies with carbolic acid (which is pure enough, in the antiseptic sense) in order to get the Garden of Paradise.

Blessed Are the Powerful

The reign of love is passing, and the reign of power is coming again.

The day of popular democracy is nearly done. Already we are entering the twilight, towards the night that is at hand.

Before the darkness comes, it is as well to take our directions.

It is time to enquire into the nature of power, so that we do not crassly blunder into a new era: or fall down the gulf of anarchy, in the dark, as we cross the borders.

We have a confused idea, that *will* and power are somehow identical. We think we can have a will-to-power.

A will-to-power seems to work out as bullying. And bullying is something despicable and detestable.

Tyranny, too, which seems to us the apotheosis of power, is detestable.

It comes from our mistaken idea of power. It comes from the ancient mistake, old as Moses, of confusing power with *will*. The *power* of God, and the *will* of God, we have imagined identical. We need only think for a moment, and we can see the vastness of difference between the two.

The Jews, in Moses' time, and again particularly in the time of the Kings, came to look upon Jehovah as the apotheosis of arbitrary *will*. This is the root of a very great deal of evil; an old, old root.

Will is no more than an attribute of the ego. It is, as it were, the accelerator of the engine: or the instrument which increases the pressure. A man may have a strong will, an iron will, as we say, and yet be a stupid mechanical instrument, useful simply as an instrument, without any *power* at all.

An instrument, even an iron one, has no power. The power has to be put into it. This is true of men with iron wills, just the same.

The Jews made the mistake of deifying Will, the ethical Will of God. The Germans again made the mistake of deifying the egoistic Will of Man: the will-to-power.

There is a certain inherent stupidity in apotheosized Will, and a consequent inevitable inferiority in the devotees thereof. They all have an inferiority complex.

Because power is not in the least like Will. Power comes to us, we know not how, from beyond. Whereas our will is our own.

When a man prides himself on something that is just in himself, part of his own ego, he falls into conceit, and conceit carries an inferiority complex as its shadow.

If a man, or a race, or a nation is to be anything at all, he must have the generosity to admit that his strength comes to him from beyond. It is not his own, self-generated. It comes as electricity comes, out of nowhere into somewhere.

It is no good trying to intellectualize about it. All attempts to argue and intellectualize merely strangle the passages of the heart. We wish to keep our hearts open. Therefore we brush aside argument and intellectual haggling.

The intellect is one of the most curious instruments of the psyche. But, like the will, it is only an instrument. And it works only under pressure of the will.

By willing and by intellectualizing we have done all we can, for the time being. We only exhaust ourselves, and lose our lives—that is, our livingness, our power to live—by any further straining of the will and the intellect. It is time to take our hands off the throttle: knowing well enough what we are about, and choosing our course of action with a steady heart.

To take one's hand off the throttle is not the same as to let go the reins.

Man lives to live, and for no other reason. And life is not mere length of days. Many people hang on, and hang on, into a corrupt old age, just because they have *not* lived, and therefore cannot let go.

We must live. And to live, life must be in us. It must come to us, the power of life, and we must not try to get a strangle-hold upon it. From beyond comes to us the life, the power to live, and we must wisely keep our hearts open.

But the life will not come *unless* we live. That is the whole point. "To him that hath shall be given." To him that hath life shall be given life: on condition, of course, that he lives.

And again, life does not mean length of days. Poor old Queen Victoria had length of days. But Emily Brontë had life. She died of it.

And again "living" doesn't mean just doing certain things: running after women, or digging a garden, or working an engine, or becoming a member of Parliament. Just because, for Lord Byron, to sleep with a "crowned head" was life itself, it doesn't follow that it will be life for *me* to sleep with a crowned head, or even a head uncrowned.

Sleeping with heads is no joke, anyhow. And living won't even consist in jazzing or motoring or going to Wembley, just because most folks do it. Living consists in doing what you really, vitally want to do: what the *life* in you wants to do, not what your ego imagines you want to do. And to find out *how* the life in you wants to be lived, and to live it, is terribly difficult. Somebody has to give us a clue.

And this is the real *exercise* of power.

That settles two points. First, power is life rushing in to us. Second, the exercise of power is the setting of life in motion.

And this is very far from *Will*.

It you want a dictator, whether it is Lenin, or Mussolini, or Primo de Rivera, ask, not whether he can set money in circulation, but if he can set life in motion, by dictating to his people.

Now, although we hate to admit it, Lenin did set life a good deal in motion, for the Russian proletariat. The Russian proletariat was like a child that had been kept under too much. So it was dying to be free. It was crazy to keep house for itself.

Now, like a child, it is keeping house for itself, without Papa or Mama to interfere. And naturally it enjoys it. For the time it's a game.

But for us, English or American or French or German people, it would not be a game. We have more or less kept house for ourselves for a long time, and it's not very thrilling after years of it.

So a Lenin wouldn't do us any good. He wouldn't set any life going in us at all.

The Gallic and Latin blood isn't thrilled about keeping house, any-how. It wants Glory, or else ᴸɹoꞁƐ. Glory on horse-back, or Glory up-set. If there was any Glory to upset, either in France or Italy or Spain, then communism might flourish. But since there isn't even a spark of Glory to blow out—Alfonso! Victor Emmanuel! Poincaré!—what's the good of blowing?

So they set up a little harmless Glory in baggy trousers—Papa Musso-lini—or a bit of fat, self-loving but amiable elder-brother Glory in General de Rivera: and they call it power. And the democratic world holds up its hands, and moans: *"Dictators! Tyranny!"* While the conservative world cheers loudly, and cries: *"The Man! The Man! El hombre! L'uomo! L'homme! Hooray!!!"*

Bunk!

We want life. And we want the power of life. We want to feel the power of life in ourselves.

We're sick of being soft, and amiable, and harmless. We're sick to

death of even enjoying ourselves. We're a bit ashamed of our own existence. Or if we aren't we ought to be.

But what then? Shall we exclaim, in a fat voice: "*Aha! Power!
Glory! Force! The Man!*"—and proceed to set up a harmless Mussolini, or a fat Rivera? Well, let us, if we want to. Only it won't make
the slightest difference to our real living. Except it's probably a good
thing to have the press—the newpaper press—crushed under the up-to-
date rubber heel of a tyrannous but harmless dictator.

We won't speak of poor old Hindenburg. Except, why didn't they set
up his wooden statue with all the nails knocked into it, for a President?
For surely they drove *something* in, with those nails!

We had a harmless dictator, in Mr. Lloyd George. Better go ahead
with the Houses of Representatives, than have another shot in that
direction.

Power! How can there be power in politics, when politics is money?

Money is power, they say. Is it? Money is to power what margarine
is to butter: a nasty substitute.

No, power is something you've got to respect, even revere, before you
can have it. It isn't bossing, or bullying, hiring a manservant or Sal-
vationizing your social inferior, issuing loud orders and getting your
own way, doing your opponent down. That isn't power.

Power is *pouvoir*: to be able to.

Might: the ability to make: to bring about that which may be.

And where are we to get Power, or Might, or Glory, or Honour, or
Wisdom?

Out of Lloyd George, or Lenin, or Mussolini, or Rivera, or anything
else political?

Bah! It has to be in the people, before it can come out in politics.

Do we *want* Power, Might, Glory, Honour, and Wisdom?

If we do, we'd better start to get them, each man for himself.

But if we don't, we'd better continue our lick-spittling course of being as happy, as happy as Kings.

> The world is so full of a number of things
> We ought all to be happy, as happy as Kings.

Which Kings, might we ask? Better be careful!

Myself I want Power. But I don't want to boss anybody.

I want Honour. But I don't see any existing nation or government
that could give it me.

I want Glory. But heaven save me from mankind.

I want Might. But perhaps I've got it.

The first thing, of course, is to open one's heart to the source of Power, and Might, and Glory, and Honour. It just depends, which gates of one's heart one opens. You can open the humble gate, or the proud gate. Or you can open both, and see what comes.

Best open both, and take the responsibility. But set a guard at each gate, to keep out the liars, the snivellers, the mongrel and the greedy.

However smart we be, however rich and clever or loving or charitable or spiritual or impeccable, it doesn't help us at all. The real power comes in to us from beyond. Life enters us from behind, where we are sightless, and from below, where we do not understand.

And unless we yield to the beyond, and take our power and might and honour and glory from the unseen, from the unknown, we shall continue empty. We may have length of days. But an empty tin-can lasts longer than Alexander lived.

So, anomalous as it may sound, if we want power, we must put aside our own will, and our own conceit, and *accept* power, from the beyond.

And having admitted the power from the beyond into us, we must abide by it, and not traduce it. Courage, discipline, inward isolation, these are the conditions upon which power will abide in us.

And between brave people there will be the communion of power, prior to the communion of love. The communion of power does not exclude the communion of love. It includes it. The communion of love is only a part of the greater communion of power.

Power is the supreme quality of God and man: the power to cause, the power to create, the power to make, the power to do, the power to destroy. And then, between those things which are created or made, love is the supreme binding relationship. And between those who, with a single impulse, set out passionately to destroy what must be destroyed, joy flies like electric sparks, within the communion of power.

Love is simply and purely a relationship, and in a pure relationship there can be nothing but equality; or at least equipoise.

But Power is more than a relationship. It is like electricity, it has different degrees. Men are powerful or powerless, more or less: we know not how or why. But it is so. And the communion of power will always be a communion in inequality.

In the end, as in the beginning, it is always Power that rules the world! There *must be* rule. And only Power can rule. Love cannot, should not, does not seek to. The statement that love rules the camp, the court, the grove, is a lie; and the fact that such love has to rhyme with "grove", proves it. Power rules and will always rule. Because it was

Power that created us all. The act of love itself is an act of power, original as original sin. The power is given us.

As soon as there is an *act*, even in love, it is power. Love itself is purely a relationship.

But in an age that, like ours, has lost the mystery of power, and the reverence for power, a false power is substituted: the power of money. This is a power based on the force of human envy and greed, nothing more. So nations naturally become more envious and greedy every day. While individuals ooze away in a cowardice that they call love. They call it love, and peace, and charity, and benevolence, when it is mere cowardice. Collectively they are hideously greedy and envious.

True power, as distinct from the spurious power, which is merely the force of certain human vices directed and intensified by the human will: true power never belongs to us. It is given us, from the beyond.

Even the simplest form of power, physical strength, is not our own, to do as we like with. As Samson found.

But power is given differently, in varying degrees and varying kind to different people. It always was so, it always will be so. There will never be equality in power. There will always be unending inequality.

Nowadays, when the only power is the power of human greed and envy, the greatest men in the world are men like Mr. Ford, who can satisfy the modern lust, we can call it nothing else, for owning a motor-car: or men like the great financiers, who can soar on wings of greed to uncanny heights, and even can spiritualize greed.

They talk about "equal opportunity": but it is bunk, ridiculous bunk. It is the old fable of the fox asking the stork to dinner. All the food is to be served in a shallow dish, levelled to perfect equality, and you get what you can.

If you're a fox, like the born financier, you get a bellyful and more. If you're a stork, or a flamingo, or even a *man*, you have the food gobbled from under your nose, and you go comparatively empty.

Is the fox, then, or the financier, the highest animal in creation? Bah!

Humanity never bunked itself so thoroughly as with the bunk of equality, even qualified down to "equal opportunity".

In living life, we are all born with different powers, and different degrees of power: some higher, some lower. The only thing to do is honourably to accept it, and to live in the communion of power. Is it not better to serve a man in whom power lives, than to clamour for equality with Mr. Motor-car Ford, or Mr. Shady Stinnes? Pfui! to your equality with such men! It gives me gooseflesh.

How much better it must have been to be a colonel under Napoleon than to be a Marshal Foch! Oh! how much better it must have been, to live in terror of Peter the Great—who was great—than to be a member of the proletariat under Comrade Lenin: or even to *be* Comrade Lenin: though even he was greatish, far greater than any extant millionaire.

Power is beyond us. Either it is given us from the unknown, or we have not got it. And better to touch it in another than never to know it. Better be a Russian and shoot oneself out of sheer terror of Peter the Great's displeasure, than to live like a well-to-do American, and never know the mystery of Power at all. Live in blank sterility.

For Power is the first and greatest of all mysteries. It is the mystery that is behind all our being, even behind all our existence. Even the phallic erection is a first blind movement of power. Love is said to call the power into motion: but it is probably the reverse: that the slumbering *power* calls love into being.

Power is manifold. There is physical strength, like Samson's. There is racial power, like David's or Mahomet's. There is mental power, like that of Socrates, and ethical power, like that of Moses, and spiritual power, like Jesus' or like Buddha's, and mechanical power, like that of Stephenson, or military power, like Napoleon's, or political power, like Pitt's. These are all true manifestations of power, coming out of the unknown.

Unlike the millionaire power, which comes out of the known forces of human greed and envy.

Power puts something new into the world. It may be Edison's gramophone, or Newton's Law or Cæsar's Rome or Jesus' Christianity, or even Attila's charred ruins and emptied spaces. Something new displaces something old, and sometimes room has to be cleared beforehand.

Then power is obvious. Power is much more obvious in its destructive than in its constructive activity. A tree falls with a crash. It grew without a sound.

Yet true destructive power is power just the same as constructive. Even Attila, the Scourge of God, who helped to scourge the Roman world out of existence, was great with power. He was the scourge of *God*: not the scourge of the League of Nations, hired and paid in cash.

If it must be a scourge, let it be a scourge of God. But let it be power, the old divine power. The moment the divine power manifests itself, it is right: whether it be Attila or Napoleon or George Washington. But Lloyd George, and Woodrow Wilson, and Lenin, they never had the right smell. They never even roused real fear: no real passion. Whereas a manifestation of real power arouses passion, and always will.

Time it should again.

Blessed are the powerful, for theirs is the kingdom of earth.

... Love Was Once a Little Boy

Collapse, as often as not, is the result of persisting in an old attitude towards some important relationship, which, in the course of time, has changed its nature.

Love itself is a relationship, which changes as all things change, save abstractions. If you want something really more durable than diamonds you must be content with eternal truths like "twice two are four".

Love is a relationship between things that live, holding them together in a sort of unison. There are other vital relationships. But love is this special one.

In every living thing there is the desire, for love, or for the relationship of unison with the rest of things. That a tree should desire to develop itself between the power of the sun, and the opposite pull of the earth's centre, and to balance itself between the four winds of heaven, and to unfold itself between the rain and the shine, to have roots and feelers in blue heaven and innermost earth, both, this is a manifestation of love: a knitting together of the diverse cosmos into a oneness, a tree.

At the same time, the tree must most powerfully exert itself and defend itself, to maintain its own integrity against the rest of things.

So that love, as a desire, is balanced against the opposite desire, to maintain the integrity of the individual self.

Hate is not the opposite of love. The real opposite of love is individuality.

We live in the age of individuality, we call ourselves the servants of love. That is to say, we enact a perpetual paradox.

Take the love of a man and a woman, today. As sure as you start with a case of "true love" between them, you end with a terrific struggle and conflict of the two opposing egos or individualities. It is nobody's fault: it is the inevitable result of trying to snatch an intensified individuality out of the mutual flame.

Love, as a relationship of unison, means and must mean, *to some extent*, the sinking of the individuality. Woman for centuries was expected to sink her individuality into that of her husband and family.

Nowadays the tendency is to insist that a man shall sink his individuality into his job, or his business, primarily, and secondarily into his wife and family.

At the same time, education and the public voice urge man and woman into intenser individualism. The sacrifice takes the old symbolic form of throwing a few grains of incense on the altar. A certain amount of time, labour, money, emotion are sacrificed on the altar of love, by man and woman: especially emotion. But each calculates the sacrifice. And man and woman alike, each saves his individual ego, her individual ego, intact, as far as possible, in the scrimmage of love. Most of our talk about love is cant, and bunk. The treasure of treasures to man and woman today is his own, or her own ego. And this ego, each hopes it will flourish like a salamander in the flame of love and passion. Which it well may: but for the fact that there are two salamanders in the same flame, and they fight till the flame goes out. Then they become grey cold lizards of the vulgar ego.

It is much easier, of course, when there *is* no flame. Then there is no serious fight.

You can't worship love and individuality in the same breath. Love is a mutual relationship, like a flame between wax and air. If either wax or air insists on getting its own way, or getting its own back too much, the flame goes out and the unison disappears. At the same time, if one yields itself up to the other entirely, there is a guttering mess. You have to balance love and individuality, and actually sacrifice a portion of each.

You have to have some sort of balance.

The Greeks said equilibrium. But whereas you can quite nicely balance a pound of butter against a pound of cheese, it is quite another matter to balance a rose and a ruby. Still more difficult is it to put male man in one scale and female woman in the other, and equilibrate that little pair of opposites.

Unless, of course, you abstract them. It's easy enough to balance a citizen against a citizeness, a Christian against a Christian, a spirit against a spirit, or a soul against a soul. There's a formula for each case. Liberty, Equality, Fraternity, etc., etc.

But the moment you put young Tom in one scale, and young Kate in the other: why, not God Himself has succeeded as yet in striking a nice level balance. Probably doesn't intend to, ever.

Probably it's one of the things that are most fascinating because they are *nearly* possible, yet absolutely impossible. Still, a miss is better than a mile. You can at least draw blood.

How can I equilibrate myself with my black cow Susan? I call her daily at six o'clock. And sometimes she comes. But sometimes, again, she doesn't, and I have to hunt her away among the timber. Possibly she is lying peacefully in cowy inertia, like a black Hindu statue, among the oak-scrub. Then she rises with a sighing heave. My calling was a mere nothing against the black stillness of her cowy passivity.

Or possibly she is away down in the bottom corner, lowing *sotto voce* and blindly to some far-off, inaccessible bull. Then when I call at her, and approach, she screws round her tail and flings her sharp, elastic haunch in the air with a kick and a flick, and plunges off like a buck rabbit, or like a black demon among the pine trees, her udder swinging like a chime of bells. Or possibly the coyotes have been howling in the night along the top fence. And then I call in vain. It's a question of saddling a horse and sifting the bottom timber. And there at last the horse suddenly winces, starts: and with a certain pang of fear I too catch sight of something black and motionless and alive, and terribly silent, among the tree-trunks. It is Susan, her ears apart, standing like some spider suspended motionless by a thread, from the web of the eternal silence. The strange faculty she has, cow-given, of becoming a suspended ghost, hidden in the very crevices of the atmosphere! It is something in her *will*. It is her tarnhelm. And then, she doesn't know me. If I am afoot, she knows my voice, but not the advancing me, in a blue shirt and cord trousers. She waits, suspended by the thread, till I come close. Then she reaches forward her nose, to smell. She smells my hand: gives a little snort, exhaling her breath, with a kind of contempt, turns, and ambles up towards the homestead, perfectly assured. If I am on horse-back, although she knows the grey horse perfectly well, at the same time she *doesn't* know what it is. She waits till the wicked Azul, who is a born cow-punching pony, advances mischievously at her. Then round she swings, as if on the blast of some sudden wind, and with her ears back, her head rather down, her black back curved, up she goes, through the timber, with surprising, swimming swiftness. And the Azul, snorting with jolly mischief, dashes after her, and when she is safely in her milking place, still she watches with her great black eyes as I dismount. And she has to smell my hand before the cowy peace of being milked enters her blood. Till then, there is something *roaring* in the chaos of her universe. When her cowy peace comes, then her universe is silent, and like the sea with an even tide, without sail or smoke: nothing.

That is Susan, my black cow.

And how am I going to equilibrate myself with her? Or even, if you prefer the word, to get in harmony with her?

Equilibrium? Harmony? with that black blossom! Try it!

She doesn't even know me. If I put on a pair of white trousers, she wheels away as if the devil was on her back. I have to go behind her, talk to her, stroke her, and let her smell my hand; and smell the white trousers. She doesn't know they are trousers. She doesn't know that I am a gentleman on two feet. Not she. Something mysterious happens in her blood and her being, when she smells me and my nice white trousers.

Yet she knows me, too. She likes to linger, while one talks to her. She knows quite well she makes me mad when she swings her tail in my face. So sometimes she swings it, just on purpose: and looks at me out of the black corner of her great, pure-black eye, when I yell at her. And when I find her, away down the timber, when she is a ghost, and lost to the world, like a spider dangling in the void of chaos, then she is relieved. She comes to, out of a sort of trance, and is relieved, trotting up home with a queer, jerky cowy gladness. But she is never *really* glad, as the horses are. There is always a certain untouched chaos in her.

Where she is when she's *in* the trance, heaven only knows.

That's Susan! I have a certain relation to her. But that she and I are in equilibrium, or in harmony, I would never guarantee while the world stands. As for her individuality being in balance with mine, one can only feel the great blank of the gulf.

Yet a relationship there is. She knows my touch and she goes very still and peaceful, being milked. I, too, I know her smell and her warmth and her feel. And I share some of her cowy silence, when I milk her. There *is* a sort of relation between us. And this relation is part of the mystery of love: the individuality on each side, mine and Susan's, suspended in the relationship.

> Cow Susan by the forest's rim
> A black-eyed Susan was to him
> And nothing more—

One understands Wordsworth and the primrose and the yokel. The yokel had no relation at all—or next to none—with the primrose. Wordsworth gathered it into his own bosom and made it part of his own nature. "I, William, am also a yellow primrose blossoming on a bank." This, we must assert, is an impertinence on William's part. He ousts the primrose from its own individuality. He doesn't allow it to call its soul its own. It must be identical with *his* soul. Because, of course, by begging the question, there is but One Soul in the universe.

This is bunk. A primrose has its own peculiar primrosy identity, and all the oversouling in the world won't melt it into a Williamish oneness. Neither will the yokel's remarking: "Nay, boy, that's nothing. It's only a primrose!"—turn the primrose into nothing. The primrose will neither be assimilated nor annihilated, and Boundless Love breaks on the rock of one more flower. It has its own individuality, which it opens with lovely naïveté to sky and wind and William and yokel, bee and beetle alike. It *is* itself. But its very floweriness is a kind of communion with all things: the love unison.

In this lies the eternal absurdity of Wordsworth's lines. His own behaviour, primrosely, was as foolish as the yokel's.

> A primrose by the river's brim
> A yellow primrose was to him
>   And nothing more—
>
> A primrose by the river's brim
> A yellow primrose was to him
>   And a great deal more—
>
> A primrose by the river's brim
> Lit up its pallid yellow glim
>   Upon the floor—
>
> And watched old Father William trim
> His course beside the river's brim
>   And trembled sore—
>
> The yokel, going for a swim
> Had very nearly trod on him
>   An hour before.
>
> And now the poet's fingers slim
> Were reaching out to pluck at him
>   And hurt him more.
>
> Oh gentlemen, hark to my hymn!
> To be a primrose is my whim
>   Upon the floor,
>   And nothing more.
>
> The sky is with me, and the dim
> Earth clasps my roots. Your shadows skim
>   My face once more. . . .
>   Leave me therefore
>   Upon the floor;
>   Say *au revoir* . . . . .

Ah William! The "something more" that the primrose was to you, was yourself in the mirror. And if the yokel actually got as far as beholding a "yellow primrose", he got far enough.

You see it is not so easy even for a poet to equilibrate himself even with a mere primrose. He didn't leave it with a soul of its own. It had to have his soul. And nature had to be sweet and pure, Williamish. Sweet-Williamish at that! Anthropomorphized! Anthropomorphism, that allows nothing to call its soul its own, save anthropos: and only a special brand, even of him!

Poetry can tell alluring lies, when we let our feelings, or our ego, run away with us.

And we must always beware of romance: of people who love nature, or flowers, or dogs, or babies, or pure adventure. It means they are getting into a love-swing where everything is easy and nothing opposes their egoism. Nature, babies, dogs are *so* lovable, because they can't answer back. The primrose, alas! couldn't pipe up and say: "Hey! Bill! get off the barrow!"

That's the best of men and women. There's bound to be a lot of back chat. You can *Lucy Gray* your woman as hard as you like, one day she's bound to come back at you: "Who are *you* when you're at home?"

A man isn't going to spread his own ego over a woman, as he has done over nature and primroses, and dogs, or horses, or babies, or "the people", or the proletariat or the poor-and-needy. The old hen takes the cock by the beard, and says: "*That's me, mind you!*"

Man is an individual, and woman is an individual. Which sounds easy.

But it's not as easy as it seems. These two individuals are as different as chalk and cheese. True, a pound of chalk weighs as much as a pound of cheese. But the proof of the pudding is in the eating, not the scales.

That is to say, you can announce that men and women should be equal and *are* equal. All right. Put them in the scales.

Alas! my wife is about twenty pounds heavier than I am.

Nothing to do but to abstract. *L'homme est né libre:* with a napkin round his little tail.

Nevertheless, I am a citizen, my wife is a citizeness: I can vote, she can vote, I can be sent to prison, she can be sent to prison, I can have a passport, she can have a passport, I can be an author, she can be an authoress. Ooray! OO-bloomin-ray!

You see, we are both British subjects. Everybody bow!

Subjects! Subjects! Subjects!

Madame is already shaking herself like a wet hen.

But yes, my dear! we are both subjects. And as subjects, we enjoy a lovely equality, liberty, my dear! Equality! Fraternity or Sorority! my dear!

Aren't you pleased?

But it's no use talking to a wet hen. That "subject" was a cold douche.

As subjects, men and women may be equal.

But as objects, it's another pair of shoes. Where, I ask you, is the equality between an arrow and a horseshoe? or a serpent and a squash-blossom? Find me the equation that equates the cock and the hen.

You can't.

As inhabitants of my backyard, as loyal subjects of my *rancho*, they, the cock and the hen, are equal. When he gets wheat, she gets wheat. When sour milk is put out, it is as much for him as for her. She is just as free to go where she likes as he is. And if she likes to crow at sunrise, she may. There is no law against it. And he can lay an egg, if the fit takes him. Absolutely nothing forbids.

Isn't that equality? If it isn't, what is?

Even then, they're two very different objects.

As equals, they are just a couple of barnyard fowls, clucking! generalized!

But dear me, when he comes prancing up with his red beard shaking, and his eye gleaming, and she comes slowly pottering after, with her nose to the ground, they're two very different objects. You never think of equality: or of inequality, for that matter. They're a cock and a hen, and you accept them as such.

You don't think of them as equals, or as unequals. But you think of them *together*.

Wherein, then, lies the togetherness?

Would you call it love?

I wouldn't.

Their two egos are absolutely separate. He's a cock, she's a hen. He never thinks of her for a moment, as if she were a cock like himself; and she never thinks for a moment that he is a hen like herself. I never hear anything in her squawk which would seem to say: "*Aren't I a fowl as much as you are, you brute!*" Whereas I always hear women shrieking at their men: "Aren't I a human being as much as you are?"

It seems beside the point.

I always answer my spouse, with sweet reasonableness: "My dear, we are both British Subjects. What can I say more, on the score of equality? You are a British Subject as much as I am."

Curiously, she hates to have it put that way. She wants to be a human being as much as I am. But absolutely and honestly, I don't know what a human being is. Whereas I do know what a British Subject is. It can be defined.

And I can see how a *Civis Romanum*, or a British Subject can be free, whether it's he or she. The he-ness or the she-ness doesn't matter. But how a *man* can consider himself free, I don't know. Any more than a cock-robin or a dandelion.

Imagine a dandelion suddenly hissing: "*I am free and I will be free!*" Then wriggling on his root like a snake with his tail pegged down!

What a horrifying sight!

So it is when a man, with two legs and a penis, a belly and a mouth begins to shout about being free. One wants to ask: which bit do you refer to?

There's a cock and there's the hen, and their two egos or individualities seem to stay apart without friction. They never coo at one another, nor hold each other's hand. I never see her sitting on his lap and being petted. True, sometimes he calls for her to come and eat a titbit. And sometimes he dashes at her and walks over her for a moment. She doesn't seem to mind. I never hear her squawking: "*Don't you think you can walk over me!*"

Yet she's by no means downtrodden. She's just herself, and seems to have a good time: and she doesn't like it if he is missing.

So there is this peculiar togetherness about them. You can't call it love. It would be too ridiculous.

What then?

As far as I can see, it is desire. And the desire has a fluctuating intensity, but it is always there. His desire is always towards her, even when he has absolutely forgotten her. And by the way she puts her feet down, I can see she always walks in her plumes of desirableness, even when she's going broody.

The mystery about her, is her strange undying desirableness. You can see it in every step she takes. She is desirable. And this is the breath of her life.

It is the same with Susan. The queer cowy mystery of her is her changeless cowy desirableness. She is far, alas, from any bull. She never even remotely dreams of a bull, save at rare and brief periods. Yet her whole being and motion is that of being desirable: or else fractious. It seems to unite her with the very air, and the plants and trees. Even to the sky and the trees and the grass and the running stream, she is subtly, delicately and *purely* desirable, in cowy desirability. It is her cowy mystery. Then her fractiousness is the fireworks of her desirableness.

To me she is fractious, tiresome, and a faggot. Yet the subtle desirableness is in her, for me. As it is in a brown hen, or even a sow. It is like a peculiar charm: the creature's femaleness, her desirableness. It is her sex, no doubt: but so subtle as to have nothing to do with function. It is a mystery, like a delicate flame. It would be false to call it love, because love complicates the ego. The ego is always concerned in love. But in the frail, subtle desirousness of the true male, towards everything female, and the equally frail, indescribable desirability of every female for every male, lies the real clue to the equating, or the *relating*, of things which otherwise are incommensurable.

And this, this desire, is the reality which is inside love. The ego itself plays a false part in it. The individual is like a deep pool, or tarn, in the mountains, fed from beneath by unseen springs, and having no obvious inlet or outlet. The springs which feed the individual at the depths are sources of power, power from the unknown. But it is not until the stream of desire overflows and goes running downhill into the open world, that the individual has his further, secondary existence.

Now we have imagined love to be something absolute and personal. It is neither. In its essence, love is no more than the stream of clear and unmuddied, subtle desire which flows from person to person, creature to creature, thing to thing. The moment this stream of delicate but potent desire dries up, the love has dried up, and the joy of life has dried up. It's no good trying to turn on the tap. Desire is either flowing, or gone, and the love with it, and the life too.

This subtle streaming of desire is beyond the control of the ego. The ego says: "This is *my* love, to do as I like with! This is *my* desire, given me for my own pleasure."

But the ego deceives itself. The individual cannot possess the love which he himself feels. Neither should he be entirely possessed by it. Neither man nor woman should sacrifice individuality to love, nor love to individuality.

If we lose desire out of our life, we become empty vessels. But if we break our own integrity, we become a squalid mess, like a jar of honey dropped and smashed.

The individual has nothing, really, to do with love. That is, his individuality hasn't. Out of the deep silence of his individuality runs the stream of desire, into the open squash-blossom of the world. And the stream of desire may meet and mingle with the stream from a woman. But it is never *himself* that meets and mingles with *herself*: any more than two lakes, whose waters meet to make one river, in the distance, meet in themselves.

The two individuals stay apart, for ever and ever. But the two streams of desire, like the Blue Nile and the White Nile, from the mountains one and from the low hot lake the other, meet and at length mix their strange and alien waters, to make a Nilus Flux.

See then the childish mistake we have made, about love. We have *insisted* that the two individualities should "fit". We have insisted that the "love" between man and woman must be "perfect". What on earth that means, is a mystery. What would a perfect Nilus Flux be? —one that never overflowed its banks? or one that always overflowed its banks? or one that had exactly the same overflow every year, to a hair's-breadth?

My dear, it is absurd. Perfect love is an absurdity. As for casting out fear, you'd better be careful. For fear, like curses and chickens, will also come home to roost.

Perfect love, I suppose, means that a married man and woman never contradict one another, and that they both of them always feel the same thing at the same moment, and kiss one another on the strength of it. What blarney! It means, I suppose, that they are absolutely intimate: this precious intimacy that lovers insist on. They tell each other *everything*: and if she puts on chiffon knickers, he ties the strings for her: and if he blows his nose, she holds the hanky.

Pfui! Is anything so loathsome as intimacy, especially the married sort, or the sort that "lovers" indulge in!

It's a mistake and ends in disaster. Why? Because the individualities of men and women are incommensurable, and they will no more meet than the mountains of Abyssinia will meet with Lake Victoria Nyanza. It is far more important to keep them distinct than to join them. If they are to join, they will join in the third land where the two streams of desire meet.

Of course, as citizen and citizeness, as two persons, even as two spirits, man and woman can be equal and intimate. But this is their outer, more general or common selves. The individual man himself, and the individual woman herself, this is another pair of shoes.

It is a pity that we have insisted on putting all our eggs in one basket: calling love the basket, and ourselves the eggs. It is a pity we have insisted on being individuals only in the communistic, semi-abstract or generalized sense: as voters, money-owners, "free" men and women: free in so far as we are all alike, and individuals in so far as we are commensurable integers.

By turning ourselves into integers: every man to himself and every woman to herself a Number One; an infinite number of Number Ones;

we have destroyed ourselves as desirous or desirable individuals, and broken the inward sources of our power, and flooded all mankind into one dreary marsh where the rivers of desire lie dead with everything else, except a stagnant unity.

It is a pity of pities women have learned to think like men. Any husband will say, "*They haven't.*" But they have: they've all learned to think like some other beastly man, who is not their husband. Our education goes on and on, on and on, making the sexes alike, destroying the original individuality of the blood, to substitute for it this dreary individuality of the ego, the Number One. Out of the ego streams neither Blue Nile nor White Nile. The infinite number of little human egos makes a mosquito marsh, where nothing happens except buzzing and biting, ooze and degeneration.

And they call this marsh, with its poisonous will-o'-the-wisps, and its clouds of mosquitoes, *democracy*, and the reign of love!!

You can have it.

I am a man, and the Mountains of Abyssinia, and my Blue Nile flows towards the desert. There should be a woman somewhere far South, like a great lake, sending forth her White Nile towards the desert, too: and the rivers will meet among the Slopes of the World, somewhere.

But alas, every woman I've ever met spends her time saying she's as good as any man, if not better, and she can beat him at his own game. So Lake Victoria Nyanza gets up on end, and declares it's the Mountains of Abyssinia, and the Mountains of Abyssinia fall flat and cry: "*You're all that, and more, my dear!*"—and between them, you're bogged.

I give it up.

But at any rate it's nice to know *what's* wrong, since wrong it is.

If we were men, if we were women, our individualities would be lone and a bit mysterious, like tarns, and fed with power, male power, female power, from underneath, invisibly. And from us the streams of desire would flow out in the eternal glimmering adventure, to meet in some unknown desert.

Mais nous avons changé tout cela.

I'll bet the yokel, even then, was more himself, and the stream of his desire was stronger and more gurgling, than William Wordsworth's. For a long time the yokel retains his own integrity, and his own real stream of desire flows from him. Once you break this, and turn him, who was a yokel, into still another Number One, an assertive newspaper-parcel of an ego, you've done it!

But don't, dear, darling reader, when I say "desire", immediately conclude that I mean a jungleful of rampaging Don Juans and raping buck niggers. When I say that a woman should be eternally desirable, *don't* say that I mean every man should want to sleep with her, the instant he sets eyes on her.

On the contrary. Don Juan was only Don Juan because he *had* no real desire. He had broken his own integrity, and was a mess to start with. No stream of desire, with a course of its own, flowed from him. He was a marsh in himself. He mashed and trampled everything up, and desired no woman, so he ran after every one of them, with an itch instead of a steady flame. And tortured by his own itch, he inflamed his itch more and more. That's Don Juan, the man who *couldn't* desire a woman. He shouldn't have tried. He should have gone into a monastery at fifteen.

As for the yokel, his little stream may have flowed out of commonplace little hills, and been ready to mingle with the streams of any easy, puddly little yokeless. But what does it matter! And men are far less promiscuous, even then, than we like to pretend. It's Don Juanery, sex-in-the-head, no real desire, which leads to profligacy or squalid promiscuity. The yokel usually met desire with desire: which is all right: and sufficiently rare to ensure the moral balance.

Desire is a living stream. If we gave free rein, or a free course, to our living flow of desire, we shouldn't go far wrong. It's quite different from giving a free rein to an itching, prurient imagination. That is our vileness.

The living stream of sexual desire itself does not often, in any man, find its object, its confluent, the stream of desire in a woman into which it can flow. The two streams flow together, spontaneously, not often, in the life of any man or woman. Mostly, men and women alike rush into a sort of prostitution, because our idiotic civilization has never learned to hold in reverence the true desire-stream. We force our desire from our ego: and this is deadly.

Desire itself is a pure thing, like sunshine, or fire, or rain. It is desire that makes the whole world living to me, keeps me in the flow connected. It is my flow of desire that makes me move as the birds and animals move through the sunshine and the night, in a kind of accomplished innocence, not shut outside of the natural paradise. For life is a kind of Paradise, even to my horse Azul, though he doesn't get his own way in it, by any means, and is sometimes in a real temper about it. Sometimes he even gets a bellyache, with wet alfalfa. But even the bellyache is part of the natural paradise. Not like human *ennui*.

So a man can go forth in desire, even to the primroses. But let him refrain from falling all over the poor blossom, as William did. Or trying to incorporate it in his own ego, which is a sort of lust. Nasty anthropomorphic lust.

Everything that exists, even a stone, has two sides to its nature. It fiercely maintains its own individuality, its own solidity. And it reaches forth from itself in the subtlest flow of desire.

It fiercely resists all inroads. At the same time it sinks down in the curious weight, or flow, of that desire which we call gravitation. And imperceptibly, through the course of ages, it flows into delicate combination with the air and sun and rain.

At one time, men worshipped stones: symbolically, no doubt, because of their mysterious durability, their power of hardness, resistance, their strength of remaining unchanged. Yet even then, worshipping man did not rest till he had erected the stone into a pillar, a menhir, symbol of the eternal desire, as the phallus itself is but a symbol.

And we, men and women, are the same as stones: the powerful resistance and cohesiveness of our individuality is countered by the mysterious flow of desire, from us and towards us.

It is the same with the worlds, the stars, the suns. All is alive, in its own degree. And the centripetal force of spinning earth is the force of earth's individuality: and the centrifugal force is the force of desire. Earth's immense centripetal energy, almost passion, balanced against her furious centrifugal force, holds her suspended between her moon and her sun, in a dynamic equilibrium.

So instead of the Greek: *Know thyself!* we shall have to say to every man: *"Be Thyself! Be Desirous!"*—and to every woman: *"Be Thyself! Be Desirable!"*

Be Thyself! does not mean *Assert thy ego!* It means, be true to your own integrity, as man, as woman: let your heart stay open, to receive the mysterious inflow of power from the unknown: know that the power comes to you from beyond, it is not generated by your own will: therefore all the time, be watchful, and reverential towards the mysterious coming of power into you.

Be Thyself! is the grand cry of individualism. But individualism makes the mistake of considering an individual as a fixed entity: a little windmill that spins without shifting ground or changing its own nature. And this is nonsense. When power enters us, it does not just move us mechanically. It changes us. When the unseen wind blows, it blows upon us, and through us. It carries us like a ship on a sea. And it roars to flame in us, like a draught in a fierce fire. Or like a dandelion **in flower.**

What is the difference between a dandelion and a windmill?

Heap on more wood!

Even the Nirvanists consider man as a fixed entity, a changeless ego, which is capable of nothing, ultimately, but remerging into the infinite. A little windmill that can turn faster and faster, till it becomes actually invisible, and nothing remains in nothingness, except a blur and a faint hum.

I am not a windmill. I am not even an ego. I am a man.

I am myself, and I remain myself only by the grace of the powers that enter me, from the unseen, and make me forever newly myself.

And I am myself, also, by the grace of the desire that flows from me and consummates me with the other unknown, the invisible, tangible creation.

The powers that enter me fluctuate and ebb. And the desire that goes forth from me waxes and wanes. Sometimes it is weak, and I am almost isolated. Sometimes it is strong, and I am almost carried away.

But supposing the cult of Individualism, Liberty, Freedom, and so forth, has landed me in the state of egoism, the state so prettily and nauseously described by Henley in his *Invictus*: which, after all, is but the yelp of a house-dog, a domesticated creature with an inferiority complex!

> It matters not how strait the gate,
> How charged with punishment the scroll:
> I am the master of my fate!
> I am the captain of my soul!

Are you, old boy? Then why hippety-hop?

He was a cripple at that!

As a matter of fact, it is the slave's bravado! The modern slave is he who does not receive his powers from the unseen, and give reverence, but who thinks he is his own little boss. Only a slave would take the trouble to shout: "*I am free!*" That is to say, to shout it in the face of the open heavens. In the face of men, and their institutions and prisons. Yes-yes! But in the face of the open heavens I would be ashamed to talk about freedom. I have no life, no real power, unless it will come to me. And I accomplish nothing, not even my own fulfilled existence, unless I go forth, delicately, desirous, and find the mating of my desire; even if it be only the sky itself, and trees, and the cow Susan, and the inexpressible consolation of a statue of an Egyptian Pharaoh, or the Old Testament, or even three rubies. These answer my desire with fulfilment. What bunk then to talk about being master of my fate! when my fate depends upon these things:—not to mention the unseen reality that sends strength, or life, into me, without which I am a gourd rattle.

The ego, the little conscious ego that I am, that doll-like entity, that mannikin made in ridiculous likeness of the Adam which I am: am I going to allow that that is *all of me?* And shout about it?

Of course, if I am nothing but an ego, and woman is nothing but another ego, then there is really no vital difference between us. Two little dolls of conscious entities, squeaking when you squeeze them. And with a tiny bit of an extraneous appendage to mark which is which.

"Woman is just the same as man," loudly said the political speaker, "save for a very little difference."

"Three cheers for the very little difference!" says a vulgar voice from the crowd.

But that's a chestnut.

> Quick! Sharp! On the alert!
> Let every gentleman put on his shirt!
> And be *quick* if you please!
> Let every lady put on her chemise!

Though nowadays, a lady's chemise won't save her face.

In or out her chemise, however, doesn't make much difference to the modern woman. She's a finished-off ego, an assertive conscious entity, cut off like a doll from any mystery. And her nudity is about as interesting as a doll's. If you can *be* interested in the nudity of a doll, then jazz on, jazz on!

The same with the men. No matter how they pull their shirts off they never arrive at their own nakedness. They have none. They can only be undressed. Naked they cannot be. Without their clothes on, they are like a dismantled street-car without its advertisements: sort of public article that doesn't refer to anything.

The ego! Anthropomorphism! Love! What it works out to in the end is that even anthropos disappears, and leaves a sawdust mannikin wondrously jazzing.

"My little sisters, the birds!" says Francis of Assisi.

"*Whew!*" goes the blackbird.

"Listen to me, my little sisters, you birds!"

"*Whew!*" goes the blackbird. "I'm a cock, mister!"

Love! What's the good of woman who isn't desirable, even though she's as pretty as paint, and the waves in her hair are as permanent as the pyramids!

He buried his face in her permanent wave, and cried: "Help! Get me out!"

Individualism! Read the advertisements! "Jew-jew's hats give a man that individual touch he so much desires. No man could lack individuality in Poppem's pyjamas." Poor devil! If he was left to his own skin, where would he be!

Pop goes the weasel!

Reflections on the Death of a Porcupine

There are many bare places on the little pine trees, towards the top, where the porcupines have gnawed the bark away and left the white flesh showing. And some trees are dying from the top.

Everyone says porcupines should be killed; the Indians, Mexicans, Americans all say the same.

At full moon a month ago, when I went down the long clearing in the brilliant moonlight, through the poor dry herbage a big porcupine began to waddle away from me, towards the trees and the darkness. The animal had raised all its hairs and bristles, so that by the light of the moon it seemd to have a tall, swaying, moonlit aureole arching its back as it went. That seemed curiously fearsome, as if the animal were emitting itself demon-like on the air.

It waddled very slowly, with its white spiky spoon-tail steering flat, behind the round bear-like mound of its back. It had a lumbering, beetle's, squalid motion, unpleasant. I followed it into the darkness of the timber, and there, squat like a great tick, it began scrapily to creep up a pine-trunk. It was very like a great aureoled tick, a bug, struggling up.

I stood near and watched, disliking the presence of the creature. It is a duty to kill the things. But the dislike of killing him was greater than the dislike of him. So I watched him climb.

And he watched me. When he had got nearly the height of a man, all his long hairs swaying with a bristling gleam like an aureole, he hesitated, and slithered down. Evidently he had decided, either that I was harmless, or else that it was risky to go up any further, when I could knock him off so easily with a pole. So he slithered podgily down again, and waddled away with the same bestial, stupid motion of that white-spiky repulsive spoon-tail. He was as big as a middle-sized pig: or more like a bear.

I let him go. He was repugnant. He made a certain squalor in the moonlight of the Rocky Mountains. As all savagery has a touch of squalor, that makes one a little sick at the stomach. And anyhow, it seemed almost more squalid to pick up a pine-bough and push him over, hit him and kill him.

A few days later, on a hot, motionless morning when the pine-trees put out their bristles in stealthy, hard assertion; and I was not in a good temper, because Black-eyed Susan, the cow, had disappeared into the timber, and I had had to ride hunting her, so it was nearly nine o'clock before she was milked: Madame came in suddenly out of the sunlight, saying: "I got such a shock! There are two strange dogs, and one of them has got the most awful beard, all round his nose."

She was frightened, like a child, at something unnatural.

"Beard! Porcupine quills, probably! He's been after a porcupine."

"Ah!" she cried in relief. "Very likely! Very likely!"—then with a change of tone; "Poor thing, will they hurt him?"

"They will. I wonder when he came."

"I heard dogs bark in the night."

"Did you? Why didn't you say so? I should have known Susan was hiding—"

The ranch is lonely, there is no sound in the night, save the innumerable noises of the night, that you can't put your finger on; cosmic noises in the far deeps of the sky, and of the earth.

I went out. And in the full blaze of sunlight in the field, stood two dogs, a black-and-white, and a big, bushy, rather handsome sandy-red dog, of the collie type. And sure enough, this latter did look queer and a bit horrifying, his whole muzzle set round with white spines, like some ghastly growth; like an unnatural beard.

The black-and-white dog made off as I went through the fence. But the red dog whimpered and hesitated, and moved on hot bricks. He was fat and in good condition. I thought he might belong to some shepherds herding sheep in the forest ranges, among the mountains.

He waited while I went up to him, wagging his tail and whimpering, and ducking his head, and dancing. He daren't rub his nose with his paws any more: it hurt too much. I patted his head and looked at his nose, and he whimpered loudly.

He must have had thirty quills, or more, sticking out of his nose, all the way round: the white, ugly ends of the quills protruding an inch, sometimes more, sometimes less, from his already swollen, blood-puffed muzzle.

The porcupines here have quills only two or three inches long. But they are devilish; and a dog will die if he does not get them pulled out. Because they work further and further in, and will sometimes emerge through the skin away in some unexpected place.

Then the fun began. I got him in the yard: and he drank up the whole half-gallon of the chickens' sour milk. Then I started pulling out the quills. He was a big, bushy, handsome dog, but his nerve was gone, and every time I got a quill out, he gave a yelp. Some long quills were fairly easy. But the shorter ones, near his lips, were deep in, and hard to get hold of, and hard to pull out when you did get hold of them. And with every one that came out, came a little spurt of blood and another yelp and writhe.

The dog wanted the quills out: but his nerve was gone. Every time he saw my hand coming to his nose, he jerked his head away. I quieted him, and stealthily managed to jerk out another quill, with the blood all over my fingers. But with every one that came out, he grew more tiresome. I tried and tried and tried to get hold of another quill, and he jerked and jerked, and writhed and whimpered, and ran under the porch floor.

It was a curiously unpleasant, nerve-trying job. The day was blazing hot. The dog came out and I struggled with him again for an hour or more. Then we blindfolded him. But either he smelled my hand approaching his nose, or some weird instinct told him. He jerked his head, this way, that way, up, down, sideways, roundwise, as one's fingers came slowly, slowly, to seize a quill.

The quills on his lips and chin were deep in, only about a quarter of an inch of white stub protruding from the swollen, blood-oozed, festering black skin. It was very difficult to jerk them out.

We let him lie for an interval, hidden in the quiet cool place under the porch floor. After half an hour, he crept out again. We got a rope round his nose, behind the bristles, and one held while the other got the stubs with the pliers. But it was too trying. If a quill came out, the dog's yelp startled every nerve. And he was frightened of the pain, it was impossible to hold his head still any longer.

After struggling for two hours, and extracting some twenty quills, I gave up. It was impossible to quiet the creature, and I had had enough. His nose on the top was clear: a punctured, puffy, blood-darkened mess; and his lips were clear. But just on his round little chin, where the few white hairs are, was still a bunch of white quills, eight or nine, deep in.

We let him go, and he dived under the porch, and there he lay invisible: save for the end of his bushy, foxy tail, which moved when we came near. Towards noon he emerged, ate up the chicken-food, and stood with that doggish look of dejection, and fear, and friendliness, and greediness, wagging his tail.

But I had had enough.

"Go home!" I said. "Go home! Go home to your master, and let him finish for you."

He would not go. So I led him across the blazing hot clearing, in the way I thought he should go. He followed a hundred yards, then stood motionless in the blazing sun. He was not going to leave the place.

And I! I simply did not want him.

So I picked up a stone. He dropped his tail, and swerved towards the house. I knew what he was going to do. He was going to dive under the porch, and there stick, haunting the place.

I dropped my stone, and found a good stick under the cedar tree. Already in the heat was that sting-like biting of electricity, the thunder gathering in the sheer sunshine, without a cloud, and making one's whole body feel dislocated.

I could not bear to have that dog around any more. Going quietly to him, I suddenly gave him one hard hit with the stick, crying: "Go home!" He turned quickly, and the end of the stick caught him on his sore nose. With a fierce yelp, he went off like a wolf, downhill, like a flash, gone. And I stood in the field full of pangs of regret, at having hit him, unintentionally, on his sore nose.

But he was gone.

And then the present moon came, and again the night was clear. But in the interval there had been heavy thunder-rains, the ditch was running with bright water across the field, and the night, so fair, had not the terrific, mirror-like brilliancy, touched with terror, so startling bright, of the moon in the last days of June.

We were alone on the ranch. Madame went out into the clear night, just before retiring. The stream ran in a cord of silver across the field, in the straight line where I had taken the irrigation ditch. The pine tree in front of the house threw a black shadow. The mountain slope came down to the fence, wild and alert.

"Come!" said she excitedly. "There is a big porcupine drinking at the ditch. I thought at first it was a bear."

When I got out he had gone. But among the grasses and the coming wild sunflowers, under the moon, I saw his greyish halo, like a pallid living bush, moving over the field, in the distance, in the moonlit *clair-obscur*.

We got through the fence, and following, soon caught him up. There he lumbered, with his white spoon-tail spiked with bristles, steering behind almost as if he were moving backwards, and this was his head. His long, long hairs above the quills quivering with a dim grey gleam, like a bush.

And again I disliked him.

"Should one kill him?"

She hesitated. Then with a sort of disgust:

"Yes!"

I went back to the house, and got the little twenty-two rifle. Now never in my life had I shot at any live thing: I never wanted to. I always felt guns very repugnant: sinister, mean. With difficulty I had fired once or twice at a target: but resented doing even so much. Other people could shoot if they wanted to. Myself, individually, it was repugnant to me even to try.

But something slowly hardens in a man's soul. And I knew now it had hardened in mine. I found the gun, and with rather trembling hands got it loaded. Then I pulled back the trigger and followed the porcupine. It was still lumbering through the grass. Coming near, I aimed.

The trigger stuck. I pressed the little catch with a safety-pin I found in my pocket, and released the trigger. Then we followed the porcupine. He was still lumbering towards the trees. I went sideways on, stood quite near to him, and fired, in the clear-dark of the moonlight.

And as usual I aimed too high. He turned, went scuttling back whence he had come.

I got another shell in place, and followed. This time I fired full into the mound of his round back, below the glistening grey halo. He seemed to stumble on to his hidden nose, and struggled a few strides, ducking his head under like a hedgehog.

"He's not dead yet! Oh, fire again!" cried Madame.

I fired, but the gun was empty.

So I ran quickly, for a cedar pole. The porcupine was lying still, with subsiding halo. He stirred faintly. So I turned him and hit him hard over the nose; or where, in the dark, his nose should have been. And it was done. He was dead.

And in the moonlight, I looked down on the first creature I had ever shot.

"Does it seem mean?" I asked aloud, doubtful.

Again Madame hesitated. Then: "No!" she said resentfully.

And I felt she was right. Things like the porcupine, one must be able to shoot them, if they get in one's way.

One must be able to shoot. I, myself, must be able to shoot, and to kill.

For me, this is a *volta face*. I have always preferred to walk round my porcupine, rather than kill it.

Now, I know it's no good walking round. One must kill.

I buried him in the adobe hole. But some animal dug down and ate him; for two days later there lay the spines and bones spread out, with the long skeletons of the porcupine-hands.

The only nice thing about him—or her, for I believe it was a female, by the dugs on her belly—were the feet. They were like longish, alert black hands, paw-hands. That is why a porcupine's tracks in the snow look almost as if a child had gone by, leaving naked little human foot-prints, like a little boy.

So, he is gone: or she is gone. But there is another one, bigger and blacker-looking, among the west timber. That too is to be shot. It is part of the business of ranching: even when it's only a little half-aban-doned ranch like this one.

Wherever man establishes himself, upon the earth, he has to fight for his place against the lower orders of life. Food, the basis of existence, has to be fought for even by the most idyllic of farmers. You plant, and you protect your growing crop with a gun. Food, food, how strangely it relates man with the animal and vegetable world! How important it is! And how fierce is the fight that goes on around it.

The same when one skins a rabbit, and takes out the inside, one realizes what an enormous part of the animal, comparatively, is intes-tinal, what a big part of him is just for food-apparatus; for *living on* other organisms.

And when one watches the horses in the big field, their noses to the ground, bite-bite-biting at the grass, and stepping absorbedly on, and bite-bite-biting without ever lifting their noses, cropping off the grass, the young shoots of alfalfa, the dandelions, with a blind, relentless, un-wearied persistence, one's whole life pauses. One suddenly realizes again how all creatures devour, and *must* devour the lower forms of life.

So Susan, swinging across the field, snatches off the tops of the little wild sunflowers as if she were mowing. And down they go, down her black throat. And when she stands in her cowy oblivion chewing her cud, with her lower jaw swinging peacefully, and I am milking her, suddenly the camomiley smell of her breath, as she glances round with glaring, smoke-blue eyes, makes me realize it is the sunflowers that are her ball of cud. Sunflowers! And they will go to making her glistening black hide, and the thick cream on her milk.

And the chickens, when they see a great black beetle, that the Mexi-cans call a *toro*, floating past, they are after it in a rush. And if it settles, instantly the brown hen stabs it with her beak. It is a great beetle two or three inches long: but in a second it is in the crop of the chicken. Gone!

And Timsy, the cat, as she spies on the chipmunks, crouches in another sort of oblivion, soft, and still. The chipmunks come to drink the milk from the chickens' bowl. Two of them met at the bowl. They were little squirrely things with stripes down their backs. They sat up in front of one another, lifting their inquisitive little noses and humping their backs. Then each put its two little hands on the other's shoulders, they reared up, gazing into each other's faces; and finally they put their two little noses together, in a sort of kiss.

But Miss Timsy can't stand this. In a soft, white-and-yellow leap she is after them. They skip, with the darting jerks of chipmunks, to the wood-heap, and with one soft, high-leaping sideways bound Timsy goes through the air. Her snow-flake of a paw comes down on one of the chipmunks. She looks at it for a second. It squirms. Swiftly and triumphantly she puts her two flowery little white paws on it, legs straight out in front of her, back arched, gazing concentratedly yet whimsically. Chipmunk does not stir. She takes it softly in her mouth, where it dangles softly, like a lady's tippet. And with a proud, prancing motion the Timsy sets off towards the house, her white little feet hardly touching the ground.

But she gets shooed away. We refuse to loan her the sitting-room any more, for her gladiatorial displays. If the chippy must be "butchered to make a Timsy holiday", it shall be outside. Disappointed, but still high-stepping, the Timsy sets off towards the clay oven by the shed.

There she lays the chippy gently down, and soft as a little white cloud lays one small paw on its striped back. Chippy does not move. Soft as thistle-down she raises her paw a tiny, tiny bit, to release him.

And all of a sudden, with an elastic jerk, he darts from under the white release of her paw. And instantly, she is up in the air and down she comes on him, with the forward thrusting bolts of her white paws. Both creatures are motionless.

Then she takes him softly in her mouth again, and looks round, to see if she can slip into the house. She cannot. So she trots towards the wood-pile.

It is a game, and it is pretty. Chippy escapes into the wood-pile, and she softly, softly reconnoitres among the faggots.

Of all the animals, there is no denying it, the Timsy is the most pretty, the most fine. It is not her mere *corpus* that is beautiful; it is her bloom of aliveness. Her "infinite variety"; the soft, snow-flakey lightness of her, and at the same time her lean, heavy ferocity. I had never realized the latter, till I was lying in bed one day moving my toe, unconsciously, under the bedclothes. Suddenly a terrific blow struck my foot. The Timsy had sprung out of nowhere, with a hurling, steely force, thud upon the bedclothes where the toe was moving. It was as if someone had aimed a sudden blow, vindictive and unerring.

"Timsy!"

She looked at me with the vacant, feline glare of her hunting eyes. It is not even ferocity. It is the dilation of the strange, vacant arrogance of power. The power is in her.

And so it is. Life moves in circles of power and of vividness, and each circle of life only maintains its orbit upon the subjection of some lower circle. If the lower cycles of life are not *mastered*, there can be no higher cycle.

In nature, one creature devours another, and this is an essential part of all existence and of all being. It is not something to lament over, nor something to try to reform. The Buddhist who refuses to take life is really ridiculous, since if he eats only two grains of rice per day, it is two grains of life. We did not make creation, *we* are not the authors of the universe. And if we see that the whole of creation is established upon the fact that one life devours another life, one cycle of existence can only come into existence through the subjugating of another cycle of existence, then what is the good of trying to pretend that it is not so? The only thing to do is to realize what is higher, and what is lower, in the cycles of existence.

It is nonsense to declare that there *is* no higher and lower. We know full well that the dandelion belongs to a higher cycle of existence than the hartstongue fern, that the ant's is a higher form of existence than the dandelion's, that the thrush is higher than the ant, that Timsy the cat is higher than the thrush, and that I, a man, am higher than Timsy.

What do we mean by higher? Strictly, we mean more alive. More vividly alive. The ant is more vividly alive than the pine-tree. We know it, there is no trying to refute it. It is all very well saying that they are both alive in two different ways, and therefore they are incomparable, incommensurable. This is also true.

But one truth does not displace another. Even apparently contradictory truths do not displace one another. Logic is far too coarse to make the subtle distinctions life demands.

Truly, it is futile to compare an ant with a great pine-tree, in the absolute. Yet as far as *existence* is concerned, they are not only placed in comparison to one another, they are occasionally pitted against one another. And if it comes to a contest, the little ant will devour the life of the huge tree. If it comes to a contest.

And, in the cycles of *existence*, this is the test. From the lowest form of existence to the highest, the test question is: *Can thy neighbour finally overcome thee?*

If he can, then he belongs to a higher cycle of existence.

This is the truth behind the survival of the fittest. Every cycle of existence is established upon the overcoming of the lower cycles of existence. The real question is, wherein does *fitness* lie? Fitness for what? Fit merely to survive? That which is only fit to survive will survive only to supply food or contribute in some way to the existence of a higher form of life, which is able to do more than survive, which can really *vive*, live.

Life is more vivid in the dandelion than in the green fern, or than in a palm tree.

Life is more vivid in a snake than in a butterfly.

Life is more vivid in a wren than in an alligator.

Life is more vivid in a cat than in an ostrich.

Life is more vivid in the Mexican who drives the wagon than in the two horses in the wagon.

Life is more vivid in me than in the Mexican who drives the wagon for me.

We are speaking in terms of *existence:* that is, in terms of species, race, or type.

The dandelion can take hold of the land, the palm tree is driven into a corner, with the fern.

The snake can devour the fiercest insect.

The fierce bird can destroy the greatest reptile.

The great cat can destroy the greatest bird.

The man can destroy the horse, or any animal.

One race of man can subjugate and rule another race.

All this in terms of *existence*. As far as existence goes, that life-species is the highest which can devour, or destroy, or subjugate every other life-species against which it is pitted in contest.

This is a law. There is no escaping this law. Anyone, or any race, trying to escape it will fall a victim: will fall into subjugation.

But let us insist and insist again, we are talking now of existence, of species, of types, of races, of nations, not of single individuals, nor of *beings*. The dandelion in full flower, a little sun bristling with sun-rays on the green earth, is a nonpareil, a nonsuch. Foolish, foolish, foolish to compare it to anything else on earth. It is itself incomparable and unique.

But that is the fourth dimension, of *being*. It is in the fourth dimension, nowhere else.

Because, in the time-space dimension, any man may tread on the yellow sun-mirror, and it is gone. Any cow may swallow it. Any bunch of ants may annihilate it.

This brings us to the inexorable law of life.

1. Any creature that attains to its own fullness of being, its own *living* self, becomes unique, a nonpareil. It has its place in the fourth dimension, the heaven of existence, and there it is perfect, it is beyond comparison.

2. At the same time, every creature exists in time and space. And in time and space it exists relatively to all other existence, and can never be absolved. Its existence impinges on other existences, and is itself impinged upon. And in the struggle for existence, if an effort on the part of any one type or species or order of life can finally destroy the other species, then the destroyer is of a more vital cycle of existence than the one destroyed. (When speaking of existence we always speak in types, species, not individuals. Species exist. But even an individual dandelion has *being*.)

3. The force which we call *vitality*, and which is the determining factor in the struggle for existence, is, however, derived also from the fourth dimension. That is to say, the ultimate source of all vitality is in that other dimension, or region, where the dandelion blooms, and which men have called heaven, and which now they call the fourth dimension: which is only a way of saying that it is not to be reckoned in terms of space and time.

4. The primary way, in our existence, to get vitality, is to absorb it from living creatures lower than ourselves. It is thus transformed into a new and higher creation. (There are many ways of absorbing: devouring food is one way, love is often another. The best way is a pure relationship, which includes the *being* on each side, and which allows the transfer to take place in a living flow, enhancing the life in both beings.)

5. No creature is fully itself till it is, like the dandelion, opened in the bloom of pure relationship to the sun, the entire living cosmos.

So we still find ourselves in the tangle of existence and being, a tangle which man has never been able to get out of, except by sacrificing the one to the other.

Sacrifice is useless.

The clue to all existence is being. But you can't have being without existence, any more than you can have the dandelion flower without the leaves and the long tap root.

Being is *not* ideal, as Plato would have it: nor spiritual. It is a transcendent form of existence, and as much material as existence is. Only the matter suddenly enters the fourth dimension.

All existence is dual, and surging towards a consummation into being. In the seed of the dandelion, as it floats with its little umbrella of hairs, sits the Holy Ghost in tiny compass. The Holy Ghost is that which holds the light and the dark, the day and the night, the wet and the sunny, united in one little clue. There it sits, in the seed of the dandelion.

The seed falls to earth. The Holy Ghost rouses, saying: *"Come!"* And out of the sky come the rays of the sun, and out of earth come dampness and dark and the death-stuff. They are called in, like those bidden to a feast. The sun sits down at the hearth, inside the seed; and the dark, damp death-returner sits on the opposite side, with the host between. And the host says to them: *"Come! Be merry together!"* So the sun looks with desirous curiosity on the dark face of the earth, and the dark damp one looks with wonder on the bright face of the other, who comes from the sun. And the host says: *"Here you are at home! Lift me up, between you, that I may cease to be a Ghost. For it longs me to look out, it longs me to dance with the dancers."*

So the sun in the seed, and the earthy one in the seed take hands, and laugh, and begin to dance. And their dancing is like a fire kindled, a bonfire with leaping flame. And the treading of their feet is like the running of little streams, down into the earth. So from the dance of the sun-in-the-seed with the earthy death-returner, green little flames of leaves shoot up, and hard little trickles of roots strike down. And the host laughs, and says: *"I am being lifted up! Dance harder! Oh wrestle, you two, like wonderful wrestlers, neither of which can win."* So sun-in-the-seed and the death-returner, who is earthy, dance faster and faster and the leaves rising greener begin to dance in a ring above-ground, fiercely overwhelming any outsider, in a whirl of swords and lions' teeth. And the earthy one wrestles, wrestles with the sun-in-the-seed, so the long roots reach down like arms of a fighter gripping the power of earth, and strangles all intruders, strangling any intruder mercilessly. Till the two fall in one strange embrace, and from the centre the long flower-stem lifts like a phallus, budded with a bud. And out of the bud the voice of the Holy Ghost is heard crying: *"I am lifted up! Lo! I am lifted up! I am here!"* So the bud opens, and there is the flower poised in the very middle of the universe, with a ring of green swords below, to guard it, and the octopus, arms deep in earth, drinking and threatening. So the Holy Ghost, being a dandelion flower, looks round, and says: "*Lo! I am yellow! I believe the sun has lent me his body! Lo! I am sappy with golden, bitter blood! I believe death out of the damp black earth has lent me his blood! I am incarnate! I like my incarnation! But this is not all. I will keep this incarnation. It is good! But oh! if I can win to another incarnation, who knows how wonderful it will be! This one will have to give place. This one can help to create the next.*"

So the Holy Ghost leaves the clue of himself behind, in the seed, and wanders forth in the comparative chaos of our universe, seeking another incarnation.

And this will go on for ever. Man, as yet, is less than half grown. Even his flower-stem has not appeared yet. He is all leaves and roots, without any clue put forth. No sign of bud anywhere.

Either he will have to start budding, or he will be forsaken of the Holy Ghost: abandoned as a failure in creation, as the ichthyosaurus was abandoned. Being abandoned means losing his vitality. The sun and the earth-dark will cease rushing together in him. Already it is ceasing. To men, the sun is becoming stale, and the earth sterile. But the sun itself will never become stale, nor the earth barren. It is only that the *clue* is missing inside men. They are like flowerless, seedless fat cabbages, nothing inside.

Vitality depends upon the clue of the Holy Ghost inside a creature, a man, a nation, a race. When the clue goes, the vitality goes. And the Holy Ghost seeks for ever a new incarnation, and subordinates the old to the new. You will know that any creature or race is still alive with the Holy Ghost, when it can subordinate the lower creatures or races, and assimilate them into a new incarnation.

No man, or creature, or race can have vivid vitality unless it be moving towards a blossoming: and the most powerful is that which moves towards the as-yet-unknown blossom.

Blossoming means the establishing of a pure, *new* relationship with all the cosmos. This is the state of heaven. And it is the state of a flower, a cobra, a jenny-wren in spring, a man when he knows himself royal and crowned with the sun, with his feet gripping the core of the earth.

This too is the fourth dimension: this state, this mysterious other reality of things in a perfected relationship. It is into this perfected relationship that every straight line curves, as if to some core, passing out of the time-space dimension.

But any man, creature, or race moving towards blossoming will have to draw immense supplies of vitality from men, or creatures below, passionate strength. And he will have to accomplish a perfected relation with all things.

There will be conquest, always. But the aim of conquest is a perfect relation of conquerors with conquered, for a new blossoming. Freedom is illusory. Sacrifice is illusory. Almightiness is illusory. Freedom, sacrifice, almightiness, these are all human side-tracks, cul-de-sacs, bunk. All that is real is the overwhelmingness of a new inspirational command, a new relationship with all things.

Heaven is always there. No achieved consummation is lost. Procreation goes on for ever, to support the achieved revelation. But the torch of revelation itself is handed on. And this is all important.

Everything living wants to procreate more living things.

But more important than this is the fact that every revelation is a torch held out, to kindle new revelations. As the dandelion holds out the sun to me, saying: "*Can you take it!*"

Every gleam of heaven that is shown—like a dandelion flower, or a green beetle—quivers with strange passion to kindle a new gleam, never yet beheld. This is not self-sacrifice: it is self-contribution: in which the highest happiness lies.

The torch of existence is handed on, in the womb of procreation.

And the torch of revelation is handed on, by every living thing, from the protococcus to a brave man or a beautiful woman, handed to whomsoever can take it. He who can take it has power beyond all the rest.

The cycle of procreation exists purely for the keeping alight of the torch of perfection, in any species: the torch being the dandelion in blossom, the tree in full leaf, the peacock in all his plumage, the cobra in all his colour, the frog at full leap, woman in all the mystery of her fathomless desirableness, man in the fulness of his power: every creature become its pure self.

One cycle of perfection urges to kindle another cycle, as yet unknown.

And with the kindling from the torch of revelation comes the inrush of vitality, and the need to consume and *consummate* the lower cycles of existence, into a new thing. This consuming and this consummating means conquest, and fearless mastery. Freedom lies in the honourable yielding towards the new flame, and the honourable mastery of that which shall be new, over that which must yield. As I must master my horses, which are in a lower cycle of existence. And they, they are relieved and *happy* to serve. If I turn them loose into the mountain ranges, to run wild till they die, the thrill of real happiness is gone out of their lives.

Every lower order seeks in some measure to serve a higher order: and rebels against being conquered.

It is always conquest, and it always will be conquest. If the conquered be an old, declining race, they will have handed on their torch to the conqueror: who will burn his fingers badly, if he is too flippant. And if the conquered be a barbaric race, they will consume the fire of the conqueror, and leave him flameless, unless he watch it. But it is always conquest, conquered and conqueror, for ever. The Kingdom of heaven is the Kingdom of conquerors, who can serve the conquest for ever, after their own conquest is made.

In heaven, in the perfected relation, is peace: in the fourth dimension. But there is getting there. And that, for ever, is the process of conquest.

When the rose blossomed, then the great Conquest was made by the Vegetable Kingdom. But even this conqueror of conquerors, the rose, had to lend himself towards the caterpillar and the butterfly of a later conquest. A conqueror, but tributary to the later conquest.

There is no such thing as equality. In the kingdom of heaven, in the fourth dimension, each soul that achieves a perfect relationship with the cosmos, from its own centre, is perfect, and incomparable. It has no superior. It is a conqueror, and incomparable.

But every man, in the struggle of conquest towards his own consummation, must master the inferior cycles of life, and never relinquish his mastery. Also, if there be men beyond him, moving on to a newer consummation than his own, he must yield to their greater demand, and serve their greater mystery, and so be faithful to the kingdom of heaven which is within him, which is gained by conquest and by loyal service.

Any man who achieves his own being will, like the dandelion or the butterfly, pass into that other dimension which we call the fourth, and the old people called heaven. It is the state of perfected relationship. And here a man will have his peace for ever: whether he serve or command, in the process of living.

But even this entails his faithful allegiance to the kingdom of heaven, which must be for ever and for ever extended, as creation conquers chaos. So that my perfection will but serve a perfection which still lies ahead, unrevealed and unconceived, and beyond my own.

We have tried to build walls round the kingdom of heaven: but it's no good. It's only the cabbage rotting inside.

Our last wall is the golden wall of money. This is a fatal wall. It cuts us off from life, from vitality, from the alive sun and the alive earth, as *nothing* can. Nothing, not even the most fanatical dogmas of an iron-bound religion, can insulate us from the inrush of life and inspiration, as money can.

We are losing vitality: losing it rapidly. Unless we seize the torch of inspiration, and drop our moneybags, the moneyless will be kindled by the flame of flames, and they will consume us like old rags.

We are losing vitality, owing to money and money-standards. The torch in the hands of the moneyless will set our house on fire, and burn us to death, like sheep in a flaming corral.

Aristocracy

Everything in the world is relative to everything else. And every living thing is related to every other living thing.

But creation moves in cycles, and in degrees. There is higher and lower, in the cycles of creation, and greater and less, in the degree of life.

Each thing that attains to purity in its own cycle of existence is pure and is itself, and, in its purity, is beyond compare.

But in relation to other things, it is either higher or lower, of greater or less degree.

We have to admit that a daisy is more highly developed than a fern, even if it be a tree-fern. The daisy belongs to a higher order of life. That is, the daisy is more alive. The fern more torpid.

And a bee is more alive than a daisy: of a higher order of life. The daisy, pure as it is in its own being, yet, when compared with the bee, is limited in its being.

And birds are higher than bees: more alive. And mammals are higher than birds. And man is the highest, most developed, most conscious, most *alive* of the mammals: master of them all.

But even within the species, there is a difference. The nightingale is higher, purer, even more alive, more subtly, delicately alive, than the sparrow. And the parrot is more highly developed, or more alive, than the pigeon.

Among men, the difference in *being* is infinite. And it is a difference in degree as well as in kind. One man *is*, in himself, more, more alive, more of a man, than another. One man has greater being than another, a purer manhood, a more vivid livingness. The difference is infinite.

And, seeing that the inferiors are vastly more numerous than the superiors, when Jesus came, the inferiors, who are by no means the meek that they *should* be, set out to inherit the earth.

Jesus, in a world of arrogant Pharisees and egoistic Romans, thought that purity and poverty were one. It was a fatal mistake. Purity is often enough poor. But poverty is only too rarely pure. Poverty too often is only the result of *natural* poorness, poorness in courage, poorness in living vitality, poorness in manhood: poor life, poor character. Now the poor in life are the most impure, the most easily degenerate.

But the few men rich in life and pure in heart read purity into poverty, and Christianity started. "Charity suffereth long, and is kind. Charity envieth not. Charity vaunteth not itself, is not puffed up."

They are the words of a noble manhood.

There happened what was bound to happen: the men with pure hearts left the scramble for money and power to the impure.

Still the great appeal: "The Kingdom of Heaven is within you," acted powerfully on the hearts of the poor, who were still full of life. The rich were more active, but less alive. The poor still wanted, most of all, the Kingdom of Heaven.

Until the pure men began to mistrust the figurative Kingdom of Heaven: "Not much Kingdom of Heaven for a hungry man," they said.

This was a mistake, and a fall into impurity. For even if I die of hunger, the Kingdom of Heaven is within me, and I am within it, if I truly choose.

But once the pure man said this: "*Not much Kingdom of Heaven for a hungry man,*" the Soul began to die out of men.

By the old creed, every soul was equal in the sight of God. By the new creed, everybody should be equal in the sight of men. And being equal meant having equal possessions. And possessions were reckoned in terms of money.

So that money became the one absolute. And man figures as a money-possessor and a money-getter. The absolute, the God, the Kingdom of Heaven itself, became money; hard, hard cash. "The Kingdom of Heaven is within you" now means "The money is in your pocket." "Then shall thy peace be as a river" now means "Then shall thy investments bring thee a safe and ample income."

"*L'homme est né libre*" means "He is born without a sou." "*Et on le trouve partout enchaîné*" means "He wears breeches, and must fill his pockets."

So now there is a new (a new-old) aristocracy, completely unmysterious and scientific: the aristocracy of money. Have you a million *gold?* (for heaven's sake, the gold standard!). Then you are a *king.* Have you five hundred thousand? Then you are a lord.

"In my country, we're *all* kings and queens," as the American lady said, being a bit sick of certain British snobbery. She was quite right: they are all potential kings and queens. But until they come into their kingdom—five hundred thousand dollars minimum—they might just as well be commoners.

Yet even still, there is *natural* aristocracy.

Aristocracy of birth is bunk, when a Kaiser Wilhelm and an Emperor Franz-Josef and a Czar Nicholas is all that noble birth will do for you.

Yet the whole of life is established on a natural aristocracy. An aristocracy of money. (Oh, for God's sake, the gold standard!)

But a millionaire can do without birth, whereas birth cannot do without dollars. So, by the all-prevailing law of pragmatism, the dollar has it.

What then does *natural* aristocracy consist in?

It's not just brains! the mind is an instrument, and the *savant*, the professor, the scientist, has been looked upon since the Ptolemies as a sort of upper servant. And justly. The millionaire has brains too: so does a modern President or Prime Minister. They all belong to the class of upper servants. They serve, forsooth, the public.

> Ca, Ca, Caliban!
> Get a new master, be a new man.

What does a natural aristocracy consist in? Count Keyserling says: "Not in what a man can *do*, but what he *is*." Unfortunately what a man *is*, is measured by what he can do, even in nature. A nightingale, being a nightingale, can sing: which a sparrow can't. If you *are* something you'll *do* something, *ipso facto*.

The question is what *kind* of thing can a man do? Can he put more life into us, and release in us the fountains of our vitality? Or can he only help to feed us, and give us money or amusement.

The providing of food, money, and amusement belongs, truly, to the servant class.

The providing of *life* belongs to the aristocrat. If a man, whether by thought or action, makes *life*, he is an aristocrat. So Cæsar and Cicero are both strictly aristocrats. Lacking these two, the first century B.C. would have been far less vital, less vividly alive. And Antony, who seemed so much more vital, robust and robustious, was, when we look at it, comparatively unimportant. Cæsar and Cicero lit the flame.

How? It is easier asked than answered.

But one thing they did, whatever else: they put men into a new relation with the universe. Cæsar opened Gaul, Germany and Britain, and let the gleam of ice and snow, the shagginess of the north, the mystery of the menhir and the mistletoe in upon the rather stuffy soul of Rome, and of the Orient. And Cicero was discovering the moral nature of man, as citizen chiefly, and so putting man in new relation to man.

But Cæsar was greater than Cicero. He put man in new relation to ice and sun.

Only Cæsar was, perhaps, also too much an egoist; he never knew the mysteries he moved amongst. But Cæsar was great *beyond* morality.

Man's life consists in a connection with all things in the universe. Whoever can establish, or initiate, a new connection between mankind and the circumambient universe is, in his own degree, a saviour. Because mankind is always exhausting its human possibilities, always degenerating into repetition, torpor, *ennui*, lifelessness. When *ennui* sets in, it is a sign that human vitality is waning, and the human connection with the universe is gone stale.

Then he who comes to make a new revelation, a new connection, whether he be soldier, statesman, poet, philosopher, artist, he is a saviour.

When George Stephenson invented the locomotive engine, he provided a *means of communication*, but he didn't alter in the slightest man's *vital* relation to the universe. But Galileo and Newton, *discoverers*, not inventors, they made a big difference. And the energy released in mankind because of them was enormous. The same is true of Peter the Great, Frederick the Great, and Napoleon. The same is true of Voltaire, Shelley, Wordsworth, Byron, Rousseau. They established a *new* connection between mankind and the universe, and the result was a vast release of energy. The *sun* was reborn to man, so was the moon.

To man, the very sun goes stale, becomes a habit. Comes a saviour, a seer, and the very sun dances new in heaven.

That is because the *sun* is always *sun beyond sun beyond sun*. The sun is every sun that ever has been, Helios or Mithras, the sun of China or of Brahma, or of Peru or of Mexico: great gorgeous suns, besides which our puny "envelope of incandescent gas" is a smoky candlewick.

It is our fault. When man becomes stale and paltry, his sun is the mere stuff that our sun is. When man is great and splendid, the sun of China and Mithras blazes over him and gives him, not radiant energy in the form of heat and light, but life, life, life!

The world is to us what we take from it. The sun is to us what we take from it. And if we are puny, it is because we take punily from the superb sun.

Man is great according as his relation to the living universe is vast and vital.

Men are related to men: including women: and this, of course, is very

important. But one would think it were everything. One would think, to
read modern books, that the life of any tuppenny bank-clerk was more
important than sun, moon, and stars; and to read the pert drivel of the
critics, one would be led to imagine that every three-farthing whipper-
snapper who lifts up his voice in approval or censure were the thrice-
greatest Hermes speaking in judgment out of the mysteries.

This is the democratic age of cheap clap-trap, and it sits in jackdaw
judgment on all greatness.

And this is the result of making, in our own conceit, man the measure
of the universe. Don't you be taken in. The universe, so vast and profound, measures man up very accurately, for the yelping mongrel with
his tail between his legs, that he is. And the great sun, and the moon,
with a smile will soon start dropping the mongrel down the vast refuse-
pit of oblivion. Oh, the universe has a terrible hole in the middle of it,
an oubliette for all of you, whipper-snappering mongrels.

Man, of course, being measure of the universe, is measured only
against man. Has, of course, vital relationship only with his own cheap
little species. Hence the cheap little twaddler he has become.

In the great ages, man had vital relation with man, with woman: and
beyond that, with the cow, the lion, the bull, the cat, the eagle, the
beetle, the serpent. And beyond these, with narcissus and anemone,
mistletoe and oak-tree, myrtle, olive, and lotus. And beyond these with
humus and slanting water, cloud-towers and rainbow and the sweeping
sun-limbs. And beyond that, with sun, and moon, the living night and
the living day.

Do you imagine the great realities, even the ram of Amon, are only
symbols of something human? Do you imagine the great symbols, the
dragon, the snake, the bull, only refer to bits, qualities or attributes of
little man? It is puerile. The puerilty, the puppyish conceit of modern
white humanity is almost funny.

Amon, the great ram, do you think he doesn't stand alone in the universe, without your permission, oh cheap little man? Because he's
there, do you think *you* bred him, out of your own almightiness, you
cheap-jack?

Amon, the great ram! Mithras, the great bull! The mistletoe on the
tree. Do you think, you stuffy little human fool sitting in a chair and
wearing lambs-wool underwear and eating your mutton and beef under
the Christmas decoration, do you think then that Amon, Mithras,
Mistletoe, and the whole Tree of Life were just invented to contribute
to your complacency?

You fool! You dyspeptic fool, with your indigestion tablets! You can eat your mutton and your beef, and buy sixpenn'orth of the golden bough, till your belly turns sour, you fool. Do you think, because you keep a fat castrated cat, the moon is upon your knees? Do you think, in your woollen underwear, you are clothed in the might of Amon?

You idiot! You cheap-jack idiot!

Was not the ram created before you were, you twaddler? Did he not come in might out of chaos? And is he not still clothed in might? To you, he is mutton. Your wonderful perspicacity relates you to him just that far. But any farther, he is—well, wool.

Don't you see, idiot and fool, that you have *lost* the ram out of your life entirely, and it is one great connection gone, one great life-flow broken? Don't you see you are so much the emptier, mutton-stuffed and wool-wadded, but lifeless, lifeless.

And the oak-tree, the slow great oak-tree, isn't he alive? Doesn't he live where you don't live, with a vast silence you shall never, never penetrate, though you chop him into kindling shred from shred? He is alive with life such as you have not got and will never have. And in so far as he is a vast, powerful, silent life, you should worship him.

You should seek a living relation with him. Didn't the old Englishman have a living, vital relation to the oak-tree, a *mystic* relation? Yes, mystic! Didn't the red-faced old Admirals who *made* England have a living relation in *sacredness* with the oak-tree which was their ship, their ark? The last living vibration and power in pure connection, between man and tree, coming down from the Druids.

And all you can do now is to twiddle-twaddle about golden boughs, because you are empty, empty, empty, hollow, deficient, and cardboardy.

Do you think the tree is not, now and for ever, sacred and fearsome? The trees have turned against you, fools, and you are running in imbecility to your own destruction.

Do you think the bull is at your disposal, you zenith of creation? Why, I tell you, the blood of the bull is indeed your poison. Your veins are bursting, with beef. You may well turn vegetarian. But even milk is bull's blood: or Hathor's.

My cow Susan is at my disposal indeed. But when I see her suddenly emerging, jet-black, sliding through the gate of her little corral into the open sun, does not my heart stand still, and cry out, in some long-forgotten tongue, salutation to the fearsome one? Is not even now my life widened and deepened in connection with her life, throbbing with the other pulse, of the bull's blood?

Is not this my life, this throbbing of the bull's blood in my blood?

And as the white cock calls in the doorway, who calls? Merely a barnyard rooster, worth a dollar-and-a-half. But listen! Under the old dawns of creation the Holy Ghost, the Mediator, shouts aloud in the twilight. And every time I hear him, a fountain of vitality gushes up in my body. It is life.

So it is! Degree after degree after degree widens out the relation between man and his universe, till it reaches the sun and the night.

The impulse of existence, of course, is to *devour* all the lower orders of life. So man now looks upon the white cock, the cow, the ram, as good to eat.

But *living* and having *being* means the relatedness between me and all things. In so far as I am I, a being who is proud and in place, I have a connection with my circumambient universe, and I know my place. When the white cock crows, I do not hear myself, or some anthropomorphic conceit, crowing. I hear the not-me, the voice of the Holy Ghost. And when I see the hard, solid, longish green cones thrusting up at blue heaven from the high bluish tips of the balsam pine, I say: "Behold! Look at the strong, fertile silence of the thrusting tree! God is in the bush like a clenched dark fist, or a thrust phallus."

So it is with every natural thing. It has a vital relation with all other natural things. Only the machine is absolved from vital relation. It is based on the mystery of neuters. The neutralizing of one great natural force against another makes mechanical power. Makes the engine's wheels go round.

Does the earth go round like a wheel, in the same way? No! In the living, balanced, hovering flight of the earth, there is a strange leaning, an unstatic equilibrium, a balance that is non-balance. This is owing to the relativity of earth, moon, and sun, a vital, even sentient relatedness, never perpendicular: nothing neutral or neuter.

Every natural thing has its own living relation to every other natural thing. So the tiger, striped in gold and black, lies and stretches his limbs in perfection between all that the day is, and all that is night. He has a by-the-way relatedness with trees, soil, water, man, cobras, deer, ants, and of course the she-tiger. Of all these he is reckless as Cæsar was. When he stretches himself superbly, he stretches himself between the living day and the living night, the vast inexhaustible duality of creation. And he is the fanged and brindled Holy Ghost, with ice-shining whiskers.

The same with man. His life consists in a relation with all things: stone, earth, trees, flowers, water, insects, fishes, birds, creatures, sun, rainbow, children, women, other men. But his greatest and final relation is with the sun, the sun of suns: and with the night, which is moon and dark and stars. In the last great connections, he lifts his body speechless to the sun, and, the same body, but so different, to the moon and the stars, and the spaces between the stars.

Sun! Yes, the actual sun! That which blazes in the day! Which scientists call a sphere of blazing gas—what a lot of human gas there is, which has never been set ablaze!—and which the Greeks call Helios!

The sun, I tell you, is alive, and more alive than I am, or a tree is. It may have blazing gas, as I have hair, and a tree has leaves. But I tell you, it is the Holy Ghost in full raiment, shaking and walking, and alive as a tiger is, only more so, in the sky.

And when I can turn my body to the sun, and say: "Sun! Sun!" and we meet—then I am come finally into my own. For the universe of day, finally, is the sun. And when the day of the sun is my day too, I am a lord of all the world.

And at night, when the silence of the moon, and the stars, and the spaces between the stars, is the silence of me too, then I am come into my own by night. For night is a vast untellable life, and the Holy Ghost starry, beheld as we only behold night on earth.

In his ultimate and surpassing relation, man is given only to that which he can never describe or account for; the sun, as it is alive, and the living night.

A man's supreme moment of active life is when he looks up and is with the sun, and is with the sun as a woman is with child. The actual yellow sun of morning.

This makes man a lord, an aristocrat of life.

And the supreme moment of quiescent life is when a man looks up into the night, and is gone into the night, so the night is like a woman with child, bearing him. And this a man has to himself.

The true aristocrat is the man who has passed all the relationships and has met the sun, and the sun is with him as a diadem.

Cæsar was like this. He passed through the great relationships, with ruthlessness, and came to the sun. And he became a sun-man. But he was too unconscious. He was not aware that the sun for ever was beyond him, and that only in his *relation* to the sun was he deified. He wanted to be God.

Alexander was wiser. He placed himself a god among men. But when blood flowed from a wound in him, he said, "Look! It is the blood of a man like other men."

The sun makes man a lord: an aristocrat: almost a deity. But in his consummation with night and the moon, man knows for ever his own passing away.

But no man is man in all his splendour till he passes further than every relationship: further than mankind and womankind, in the last leap to the sun, to the night. The man who can touch both sun and night, as the woman touched the garment of Jesus, becomes a lord and a saviour, in his own kind. With the sun he has his final and ultimate relationship, beyond man or woman, or anything human or created. And in this final relation is he most intensely alive, surpassing.

Every creature at its zenith surpasses creation and is alone in the face of the sun, and the night: the sun that lives, and the night that lives and survives. Then we pass beyond every other relationship, and every other relationship, even the intensest passion of love, sinks into subordination and obscurity. Indeed, every relationship, even that of purest love, is only an approach nearer and nearer to a man's last consummation with the sun, with the moon or night. And in the consummation with the sun, even love is left behind.

He who has the sun in his face, in his body, he is the pure aristocrat. He who has the sun in his breast, and the moon in his belly, he is the first: the aristocrat of aristocrats, supreme in the aristocracy of life.

Because he is *most alive*.

Being alive constitutes an aristocracy which there is no getting beyond. He who is most alive, intrinsically, is King, whether men admit it or not. In the face of the sun.

Life rises in circles, in degrees. The most living is the highest. And the lower shall serve the higher, if there is to be any life among men.

More life! More *vivid* life! Not more safe cabbages, or meaningless masses of people.

Perhaps Dostoevsky was more vividly alive than Plato: culminating a more vivid life circle, and giving the clue towards a higher circle still. But the clue *hidden*, as it always is hidden, in every revelation, underneath what is stated.

All creation contributes, and must contribute, to this: towards the achieving of a vaster, vivider cycle of life. That is the goal of living. He who gets nearer the sun is leader, the aristocrat of aristocrats. Or he who, like Dostoevsky, gets nearest the moon of our not-being.

There is, of course, the power of mere conservatism and inertia. Deserts made the cactus thorny. But the cactus still is a rose of roses.

Whereas a sort of cowardice made the porcupine spiny. There is a difference between the cowardice of inertia, which now governs the democratic masses, particularly the capitalist masses: and the conservative fighting spirit which saved the cactus in the middle of the desert.

The democratic mass, capitalist and proletariat alike, are a vast, sluggish, ghastily greedy porcupine, lumbering with inertia. Even Bolshevism is the same porcupine: nothing but greed and inertia.

The cactus had a rose to fight for. But what has democracy to fight for, against the living elements, except money, money, money!

The world is stuck solid inside an achieved form, and bristling with a myriad spines, to protect its hulking body as it feeds: gnawing the bark of the young tree of Life, and killing it from the top downwards. Leaving its spines to fester and fester in the nose of the gay dog.

The actual porcupine, in spite of legend, cannot shoot its quills. But mankind, the porcupine out-pigging the porcupine, can stick quills into the face of the sun.

Bah! Enough of the squalor of democratic humanity. It is time to begin to recognize the aristocracy of the sun. The children of the sun shall be lords of the earth.

There will form a new aristocracy, irrespective of nationality, of men who have reached the sun. Men of the sun, whether Chinese or Hottentot, or Nordic, or Hindu, or Eskimo, if they touch the sun in the heavens, are lords of the earth. And together they will form the aristocracy of the world. And in the coming era they will rule the world; a confraternity of the living sun, making the embers of financial internationalism and industrial internationalism pale upon the hearth of the earth.

VII

A Propos of
Lady Chatterley's Lover

A Propos of *Lady Chatterley's Lover*

Owing to the existence of various pirated editions of *Lady Chatterley's Lover*, I brought out in 1929 a cheap popular edition, produced in France and offered to the public at sixty francs, hoping at least to meet the European demand. The pirates, in the United States certainly, were prompt and busy. The first stolen edition was being sold in New York almost within a month of the arrival in America of the first genuine copies from Florence. It was a facsimile of the original, produced by the photographic method, and was sold, even by reliable booksellers, to the unsuspecting public as if it were the original first edition. The price was usually fifteen dollars, whereas the price of the original was ten dollars: and the purchaser was left in fond ignorance of the fraud.

This gallant attempt was followed by others. I am told there was still another facsimile edition produced in New York or Philadelphia: and I myself possess a filthy-looking book bound in a dull orange cloth, with green label, smearily produced by photography, and containing my signature forged by the little boy of the piratical family. It was when this edition appeared in London, from New York, towards the end of 1928, and was offered to the public at thirty shillings, that I put out from Florence my little second edition of two hundred copies, which I offered at a guinea. I had wanted to save it for a year or more, but had to launch it against the dirty orange pirate. But the number was too small. The orange pirate persisted.

Then I have had in my hand a very funereal volume, bound in black and elongated to look like a bible or long hymn-book, gloomy. This time the pirate was not only sober, but earnest. He has not one, but two title-pages, and on each is a vignette representing the American Eagle, with six stars round his head and lightning splashing from his paw, all surrounded by a laurel wreath in honour of his latest exploit in literary robbery. Altogether it is a sinister volume—like Captain Kidd with his face blackened, reading a sermon to those about to walk the plank. Why the pirate should have elongated the page, by adding a false page-heading, I don't know. The effect is peculiarly depressing, sinisterly high-brow. For of course this book also was produced by the photographic process. The signature anyhow is omitted. And I am told this lugubrious tome sells for ten, twenty, thirty, and fifty dollars, according to the whim of the bookseller and the gullibility of the purchaser.

That makes three pirated editions in the United States for certain. I have heard mentioned the report of a fourth, another facsimile of the original. But since I haven't seen it, I want not to believe in it.

There is, however, the European pirated edition of fifteen hundred, produced by a Paris firm of booksellers, and stamped *Imprimé en Allemagne*: Printed in Germany. Whether printed in Germany or not, it was certainly printed, not photographed, for some of the spelling errors of the original are corrected. And it is a very respectable volume, a very close replica of the original, but lacking the signature and it gives itself away also by the green-and-yellow silk edge of the backbinding. This edition is sold to the trade at one hundred francs, and offered to the public at three hundred, four hundred, five hundred francs. Very unscrupulous booksellers are said to have forged the signature and offered the book as the original signed edition. Let us hope it is not true. But it all sounds very black against the "trade". Still there is some relief. Certain booksellers will not handle the pirated edition at all. Both sentimental and business scruples prevent them. Others handle it, but not very warmly. And apparently they would all rather handle the authorized edition. So that sentiment does genuinely enter in, against the pirates, even if not strong enough to keep them out altogether.

None of these pirated editions has received any sort of authorization from me, and from none of them have I received a penny. A semi-repentant bookseller of New York did, however, send me some dollars which were, he said, my 10% royalty on all copies sold in his shop. "I know," he wrote, "it is but a drop in the bucket." He meant, of course, a drop out of the bucket. And since, for a drop, it was quite a nice little sum, what a beautiful bucketful there must have been for the pirates!

I received a belated offer from the European pirates, who found the booksellers stiff-necked, offering me a royalty on all copies sold in the past as well as the future, if I would authorize their edition. Well, I thought to myself, in a world of: Do him or you will be done by him, —why not?—When it came to the point, however, pride rebelled. It is understood that Judas is always ready with a kiss. But that I should have to kiss him back—!

So I managed to get published the little cheap French edition, photographed down from the original, and offered at sixty francs. English publishers urge me to make an expurgated edition, promising large returns, perhaps even a little bucket, one of those children's sea-side pails!—and insisting that I should show the public that here is a fine novel, apart from all "purple" and all "words". So I begin to be tempted and start in to expurgate. But impossible! I might as well try to clip my own nose into shape with scissors. The book bleeds.

And in spite of all antagonism, I put forth this novel as an honest, healthy book, necessary for us today. The words that shock so much at first don't shock at all after a while. Is this because the mind is depraved by habit? Not a bit. It is that the words merely shocked the eye, they never shocked the mind at all. People without minds may go on being shocked, but they don't matter. People with minds realize that they aren't shocked, and never really were: and they experience a sense of relief.

And that is the whole point. We are today, as human beings, evolved and cultured far beyond the taboos which are inherent in our culture. This is a very important fact to realize. Probably, to the Crusaders, mere words were potent and evocative to a degree we can't realize. The evocative power of the so-called obscene words must have been very dangerous to the dim-minded, obscure, violent natures of the Middle Ages, and perhaps is still too strong for slow-minded, half-evoked lower natures today. But real culture makes us give to a word only those mental and imaginative reactions which belong to the mind, and saves us from violent and indiscriminate physical reactions which may wreck social decency. In the past, man was too weak-minded, or crude-minded, to contemplate his own physical body and physical functions, without getting all messed up with physical reactions that overpowered him. It is no longer so. Culture and civilization have taught us to separate the reactions. We now know the act does not necessarily follow on the thought. In fact, thought and action, word and deed, are two separate forms of consciousness, two separate lives which we lead. We need, very sincerely, to keep a connection. But while we think, we do not act, and while we act we do not think. The great necessity is that we should act according to our thoughts, and think according to our acts. But while we are in thought we cannot really act, and while we are in action we cannot really think. The two conditions, of thought and action, are mutually exclusive. Yet they should be related in harmony.

And this is the real point of this book. I want men and women to be able to think sex, fully, completely, honestly and cleanly.

Even if we can't act sexually to our complete satisfaction, let us at least think sexually, complete and clear. All this talk of young girls and virginity, like a blank white sheet on which nothing is written, is pure nonsense. A young girl and a young boy is a tormented tangle, a seething confusion of sexual feelings and sexual thoughts which only the years will disentangle. Years of honest thoughts of sex, and years of struggling action in sex will bring us at last where we want to get, to our real and accomplished chastity, our completeness, when our sexual act and our sexual thought are in harmony, and the one does not interfere with the other.

Far be it from me to suggest that all women should go running after gamekeepers for lovers. Far be it from me to suggest that they should be running after anybody. A great many men and women today are happiest when they abstain and stay sexually apart, quite clean: and at the same time, when they understand and realize sex more fully. Ours is the day of realization rather than action. There has been so much action in the past, especially sexual action, a wearying repetition over and over, without a corresponding thought, a corresponding realization. Now our business is to realize sex. Today the full conscious realization of sex is even more important than the act itself. After centuries of obfuscation, the mind demands to know and know fully. The body is a good deal in abeyance, really. When people act in sex, nowadays, they are half the time acting up. They do it because they think it is expected of them. Whereas as a matter of fact it is the mind which is interested, and the body has to be provoked. The reason being that our ancestors have so assiduously acted sex without ever thinking it or realizing it, that now the act tends to be mechanical, dull and disappointing, and only fresh mental realization will freshen up the experience.

The mind has to catch up, in sex: indeed, in all the physical acts. Mentally, we lag behind in our sexual thought, in a dimness, a lurking, grovelling fear which belongs to our raw, somewhat bestial ancestors. In this one respect, sexual and physical, we have left the mind unevolved. Now we have to catch up, and make a balance between the consciousness of the body's sensations and experiences, and these sensations and experiences themselves. Balance up the consciousness of the act, and the act itself. Get the two in harmony. It means having a proper reverence for sex, and a proper awe of the body's strange experience. It means being able to use the so-called obscene words, because these are a natural part of the mind's consciousness of the body. Obscenity only comes in when the mind despises and fears the body, and the body hates and resists the mind.

When we read of the case of Colonel Barker, we see what is the matter. Colonel Barker was a woman who masqueraded as a man. The "Colonel" married a wife, and lived five years with her in "conjugal happiness". And the poor wife thought all the time she was married normally and happily to a real husband. The revelation at the end is beyond all thought cruel for the poor woman. The situation is monstrous. Yet there are thousands of women today who might be so deceived, and go on being deceived. Why? Because they know nothing, they can't think sexually at all; they are morons in this respect. It is better to give all girls this book, at the age of seventeen.

The same with the case of the venerable schoolmaster and clergyman, for years utterly "holy and good": and at the age of sixty-five, tried in the police courts for assaulting little girls. This happens at the moment when the Home Secretary, himself growing elderly, is most loudly demanding and enforcing a mealy-mouthed silence about sexual matters. Doesn't the experience of that other elderly, most righteous and "pure" gentleman, make him pause at all?

But so it is. The mind has an old grovelling fear of the body and the body's potencies. It is the mind we have to liberate, to civilize on these points. The mind's terror of the body has probably driven more men mad than ever could be counted. The insanity of a great mind like Swift's is at least partly traceable to this cause. In the poem to his mistress Celia, which has the maddened refrain "But— Celia, Celia, Celia s***s," (the word rhymes with spits), we see what can happen to a great mind when it falls into panic. A great wit like Swift could not see how ridiculous he made himself. Of course Celia s***s! Who doesn't? And how much worse if she didn't. It is hopeless. And then think of poor Celia, made to feel iniquitous about her proper natural function, by her "lover". It is monstrous. And it comes from having taboo words, and from not keeping the mind sufficiently developed in physical and sexual consciousness.

In contrast to the puritan hush! hush!, which produces the sexual moron, we have the modern young jazzy and high-brow person who has gone one better, and won't be hushed in any respect, and just "does as she likes". From fearing the body, and denying its existence, the advanced young go to the other extreme and treat it as a sort of toy to be played with, a slightly nasty toy, but still you can get some fun out of it, before it lets you down. These young people scoff at the importance of sex, take it like a cocktail, and flout their elders with it. These young ones are advanced and superior. They despise a book like *Lady Chatterley's Lover*. It is much too simple and ordinary for them.

The naughty words they care nothing about, and the attitude to love they find old-fashioned. Why make a fuss about it? Take it like a cocktail! The book, they say, shows the mentality of a boy of fourteen. But perhaps the mentality of a boy of fourteen, who still has a little natural awe and proper fear in fact of sex, is more wholesome than the mentality of the young cocktaily person who has no respect for anything and whose mind has nothing to do but play with the toys of life, sex being one of the chief toys, and who loses his mind in the process. Heliogabulus, indeed!

So, between the stale grey puritan who is likely to fall into sexual indecency in advanced age, and the smart jazzy person of the young world, who says: "We can do anything. If we can think a thing we can do it," and then the low uncultured person with a dirty mind, who looks for dirt—this book has hardly a space to turn in. But to them all I say the same: Keep your perversions if you like them—your perversion of puritanism, your perversion of smart licentiousness, your perversion of a dirty mind. But I stick to my book and my position: Life is only bearable when the mind and body are in harmony, and there is a natural balance between them, and each has a natural respect for the other.

And it is obvious, there is no balance and no harmony now. The body is at the best the tool of the mind, at the worst, the toy. The business man keeps himself "fit", that is, keeps his body in good working order, for the sake of his business, and the usual young person who spends much time on keeping fit does so as a rule out of self-conscious self-absorption, narcissism. The mind has a stereotyped set of ideas and "feelings", and the body is made to act up, like a trained dog: to beg for sugar, whether it wants sugar or whether it doesn't, to shake hands when it would dearly like to snap the hand it has to shake. The body of men and women today is just a trained dog. And of no one is this more true than of the free and emancipated young. Above all, their bodies are the bodies of trained dogs. And because the dog is trained to do things the old-fashioned dog never did, they call themselves free, full of real life, the real thing.

But they know perfectly well it is false. Just as the business man knows, somewhere, that he's all wrong. Men and women aren't really dogs: they only look like it and behave like it. Somewhere inside there is a great chagrin and a gnawing discontent. The body is, in its spontaneous natural self, dead or paralysed. It has only the secondary life of a circus dog, acting up and showing off: and then collapsing.

What life could it have, of itself? The body's life is the life of sensations and emotions. The body feels real hunger, real thirst, real joy in the sun or the snow, real pleasure in the smell of roses or the look of a lilac bush; real anger, real sorrow, real love, real tenderness, real warmth, real passion, real hate, real grief. All the emotions belong to the body, and are only recognized by the mind. We may hear the most sorrowful piece of news, and only feel a mental excitement. Then, hours after, perhaps in sleep, the awareness may reach the bodily centres, and true grief wrings the heart.

How different they are, mental feelings and real feelings. Today, many people live and die without having had any real feelings—though they have had a "rich emotional life" apparently, having showed strong mental feeling. But it is all counterfeit. In magic, one of the so-called "occult" pictures represents a man standing, apparently, before a flat table mirror, which reflects him from the waist to the head, so that you have the man from head to waist, then his reflection downwards from waist to head again. And whatever it may mean in magic, it means what we are today, creatures whose active emotional self has no real existence, but is all reflected downwards from the mind. Our education from the start has *taught* us a certain range of emotions, what to feel and what not to feel, and how to feel the feelings we allow ourselves to feel. All the rest is just non-existent. The vulgar criticism of any new good book is: Of course nobody ever felt like that!—People allow themselves to feel a certain number of finished feelings. So it was in the last century. This feeling only what you allow yourselves to feel at last kills all capacity for feeling, and in the higher emotional range you feel nothing at all. This has come to pass in our present century. The higher emotions are strictly dead. They have to be faked.

And by higher emotions we mean love in all its manifestations, from genuine desire to tender love, love of our fellowmen, and love of God: we mean love, joy, delight, hope, true indignant anger, passionate sense of justice and injustice, truth and untruth, honour and dishonour, and real belief in *anything*: for belief is a profound emotion that has the mind's connivance. All these things, today, are more or less dead. We have in their place the loud and sentimental counterfeit of all such emotion.

Never was an age more sentimental, more devoid of real feeling, more exaggerated in false feeling, than our own. Sentimentality and counterfeit feeling have become a sort of game, everybody trying to outdo his neighbour. The radio and the film are mere counterfeit emotion all the time, the current press and literature the same. People wallow in emotion: counterfeit emotion. They lap it up: they live in it and on it. They ooze with it.

And at times, they seem to get on very well with it all. And then, more and more, they break down. They go to pieces. You can fool yourself for a long time about your own feelings. But not forever. The body itself hits back at you, and hits back remorselessly in the end.

As for other people—you can fool most people all the time, and all people most of the time, but not all people all the time, with false feelings. A young couple fall in counterfeit love, and fool themselves and each other completely. But, alas, counterfeit love is good cake but bad bread. It produces a fearful emotional indigestion. Then you get a modern marriage, and a still more modern separation.

The trouble with counterfeit emotion is that nobody is really happy, nobody is really contented, nobody has any peace. Everybody keeps on rushing to get away from the counterfeit emotion which is in themselves worst of all. They rush from the false feelings of Peter to the false feelings of Adrian, from the counterfeit emotions of Margaret to those of Virginia, from film to radio, from Eastbourne to Brighton, and the more it changes the more it is the same thing.

Above all things love is a counterfeit feeling today. Here, above all things, the young will tell you, is the greatest swindle. That is, if you take it seriously. Love is all right if you take it lightly, as an amusement. But if you begin taking it seriously you are let down with a crash.

There are, the young women say, no *real* men to love. And there are, the young men say, no *real* girls to fall in love with. So they go on falling in love with unreal ones, on either side; which means, if you can't have real feelings, you've got to have counterfeit ones: since some feelings you've *got* to have: like falling in love. There are still some young people who would *like* to have real feelings, and they are bewildered to death to know why they can't. Especially in love.

But especially in love, only counterfeit emotions exist nowadays. We have all been taught to mistrust everybody emotionally, from parents downwards, or upwards. Don't trust *anybody* with your real emotions: if you've got any: that is the slogan of today. Trust them with your money, even, but *never* with your feelings. They are bound to trample on them.

I believe there has never been an age of greater mistrust between persons than ours today: under a superficial but quite genuine social trust. Very few of my friends would pick my pocket, or let me sit on a chair where I might hurt myself. But practically all my friends would turn my real emotions to ridicule. They can't help it; it's the spirit of the day. So there goes love, and there goes friendship: for each implies a fundamental emotional sympathy. And hence, counterfeit love, which there is no escaping.

And with counterfeit emotions there is no real sex at all. Sex is the one thing you cannot really swindle; and it is the centre of the worst swindling of all, emotional swindling. Once come down to sex, and the emotional swindle must collapse. But in all the approaches to sex, the emotional swindle intensifies more and more. Till you get there. Then collapse.

Sex lashes out against counterfeit emotion, and is ruthless, devastating against false love. The peculiar hatred of people who have not loved one another, but who have pretended to, even perhaps have imagined they really did love, is one of the phenomena of our time. The phenomenon, of course, belongs to all time. But today it is almost universal. People who thought they loved one another dearly, dearly, and went on for years, ideal: lo! suddenly the most profound and vivid hatred appears. If it doesn't come out fairly young, it saves itself till the happy couple are nearing fifty, the time of the great sexual change—and then —cataclysm!

Nothing is more startling. Nothing is more staggering, in our age, than the intensity of the hatred people, men and women, feel for one another when they have once "loved" one another. It breaks out in the most extraordinary ways. And when you know people intimately, it is almost universal. It is the charwoman as much as the mistress, and the duchess as much as the policeman's wife.

And it would be too horrible, if one did not remember that in all of them, men and women alike, it is the organic reaction against counterfeit love. All love today is counterfeit. It is a stereotyped thing. All the young know just how they ought to feel and how they ought to behave, in love. And they feel and they behave like that. And it is counterfeit love. So that revenge will come back at them, tenfold. The sex, the very sexual organism in man and woman alike accumulates a deadly and desperate rage, after a certain amount of counterfeit love has been palmed off on it, even if itself has given nothing but counterfeit love. The element of counterfeit in love at last maddens, or else kills, sex, the deepest sex in the individual. But perhaps it would be safe to say that it *always* enrages the inner sex, even if at last it kills it. There is always the period of rage. And the strange thing is, the worst offenders in the counterfeit-love game fall into the greatest rage. Those whose love has been a bit sincere are always gentler, even though they have been most swindled.

Now the real tragedy is here: that we are none of us all of a piece, none of us *all* counterfeit, or *all* true love. And in many a marriage, in among the counterfeit there flickers a little flame of the true thing, on both sides. The tragedy is, that in an age peculiarly conscious of counterfeit, peculiarly suspicious of substitute and swindle in emotion, particularly sexual emotion, the rage and mistrust against the counterfeit element is likely to overwhelm and extinguish the small, true flame of real loving communion, which might have made two lives happy. Herein lies the danger of harping only on the counterfeit and the swindle of emotion, as most "advanced" writers do. Though they do it, of course, to counterbalance the hugely greater swindle of the sentimental "sweet" writers.

Perhaps I shall have given some notion of my feeling about sex, for which I have been so monotonously abused. When a "serious" young man said to me the other day: "I can't believe in the regeneration of England by sex, you know," I could only say, "I'm sure you can't." He had no sex anyhow: poor, self-conscious, uneasy, narcissus-monk as he was. And he didn't know what it meant, to have any. To him, people only had minds, or no minds, mostly no minds, so they were only there to be gibed at, and he wandered round ineffectively seeking for gibes or for truth, tight shut in inside his own ego.

Now when brilliant young people like this talk to me about sex: or scorn to: I say nothing. There is nothing to say. But I feel a terrible weariness. To them, sex means just plainly and simply, a lady's underclothing, and the fumbling therewith. They have read all the love literature, *Anna Karenina*, all the rest, and looked at statues and pictures of Aphrodite, all very laudable. Yet when it comes to actuality, to today, sex means to them meaningless young women and expensive underthings. Whether they are young men from Oxford, or workingmen, it is the same. The story from the modish summer-resort, where city ladies take up with young mountaineer "dancing partners" for a season—or less—is typical. It was end of September, the summer visitors had almost all gone. Young John, the young mountain farmer, had said goodbye to his "lady" from the capital, and was lounging about alone. "Ho, John! you'll be missing your lady!" "Nay!" he said. "Only she had such nice underclothes."

That is all sex means to them: just the trimmings. The regeneration of England with that? Good God! Poor England, she will have to regenerate the sex in her young people, before they do any regenerating of her. It isn't England that needs regeneration, it is her young.

They accuse me of barbarism. I want to drag England down to the level of savages. But it is this crude stupidity, deadness, about sex which I find barbaric and savage. The man who finds a woman's underclothing the most exciting part about her is a savage. Savages are like that.

We read of the woman-savage who wore three overcoats on top of one another to excite her man: and did it. That ghastly crudity of seeing in sex nothing but a functional act and a certain fumbling with clothes is, in my opinion, a low degree of barbarism, savagery. And as far as sex goes, our white civilization is crude, barbaric, and uglily savage: especially England and America.

Witness Bernard Shaw, one of the greatest exponents of our civilization. He says clothes arouse sex and lack of clothes tends to kill sex— speaking of muffled-up women or our present bare-armed and bare-legged sisters: and scoffs at the Pope for wanting to cover women up; saying that the last person in the world to know anything about sex is the Chief Priest of Europe: and that the one person to ask about it would be the chief Prostitute of Europe, if there were such a person.

Here we see the flippancy and vulgarity of our chief thinkers, at least. The half-naked women of today certainly do not rouse much sexual feeling in the muffled-up men of today—who don't rouse much sexual feeling in the women, either.—But why? Why does the bare woman of today rouse so much less sexual feeling than the muffled-up woman of Mr. Shaw's muffled-up eighties? It would be silly to make it a question of mere muffling.

When a woman's sex is in itself dynamic and alive, then it is a power in itself, beyond her reason. And of itself it emits its peculiar spell, drawing men in the first delight of desire. And the woman has to protect herself, hide herself as much as possible. She veils herself in timidity and modesty, because her sex is a power in itself, exposing her to the desire of men. If a woman in whom sex was alive and positive were to expose her naked flesh as women do today, then men would go mad for her. As David was mad for Bathsheba.

But when a woman's sex has lost its dynamic call, and is in a sense dead or static, then the woman *wants* to attract men, for the simple reason that she finds she no longer does attract them. So all the activity that used to be unconscious and delightful becomes conscious and repellent. The woman exposes her flesh more and more, and the more she exposes, the more men are sexually repelled by her. But let us not forget that the men are *socially* thrilled, while sexually repelled. The two things are opposites, today. Socially, men like the gesture of the half-naked woman, half-naked in the street. It is *chic*, it is a declaration of defiance and independence, it is modern, it is free, it is popular because it is strictly a-sexual, or anti-sexual. Neither men nor women *want* to feel real desire, today. They want the counterfeit, mental substitute.

But we are very mixed, all of us, and creatures of many diverse and often opposing desires. The very men who encourage women to be most daring and sexless complain most bitterly of the sexlessness of women. The same with women. The women who adore men so tremendously for their social smartness and sexlessness as males, hate them most bitterly for not being "men". In public, *en masse*, and socially, everybody today wants counterfeit sex. But at certain hours in their lives, all individuals hate counterfeit sex with deadly and maddened hate, and those who have dealt it out most perhaps have the wildest hate of it, in the other person—or persons.

The girls of today could muffle themselves up to the eyes, wear crinolines and chignons and all the rest, and though they would not, perhaps, have the peculiar hardening effect on the hearts of men that our half-naked women truly have, neither would they exert any more real sexual attraction. If there is no sex to muffle up, it's no good muffling. Or not much good. Man is often willing to be deceived—for a time— even by muffled-up nothingness.

The point is, when women are sexually alive and quivering and helplessly attractive, beyond their will, then they always cover themselves, and drape themselves with clothes, gracefully. The extravagance of 1880 bustles and such things was only a forewarning of approaching sexlessness.

While sex is a power in itself, women try all kinds of fascinating disguise, and men flaunt. When the Pope insists that women shall cover their naked flesh in church, it is not sex he is opposing, but the sexless tricks of female immodesty. The Pope, and the priests, conclude that the flaunting of naked women's flesh in street and church produces a bad, "unholy" state of mind both in men and women. And they are right. But not because the exposure arouses sexual desire: it doesn't, or very rarely: even Mr. Shaw knows that. But when women's flesh arouses no sort of desire, something is specially wrong! Something is sadly wrong. For the naked arms of women today arouse a feeling of flippancy, cynicism and vulgarity which is indeed the very last feeling to go to church with, if you have any respect for the Church. The bare arms of women in an Italian church are really a mark of disrespect, given the tradition.

The Catholic Church, especially in the south, is neither anti-sexual, like the northern Churches, nor a-sexual, like Mr. Shaw and such social thinkers. The Catholic Church recognizes sex, and makes of marriage a sacrament based on the sexual communion, for the purpose of procreation. But procreation in the south is not the bare and scientific fact, and act, that it is in the north. The act of procreation is still charged with all the sensual mystery and importance of the old past. The man is potential creator, and in this has his splendour. All of which has been stripped away by the northern Churches and the Shavian logical triviality.

But all this which has gone in the north, the Church has tried to keep in the south, knowing that it is of basic importance in life. The sense of being a potential creator and law-giver, as father and husband, is perhaps essential to the day-by-day life of a man, if he is to live full and satisfied. The sense of the eternality of marriage is perhaps necessary to the inward peace, both of men and women. Even if it carry a sense of doom, it is necessary. The Catholic Church does not spend its time reminding the people that in heaven there is no marrying nor giving in marriage. It insists: if you marry, you marry for ever! And the people accept the decree, the doom and the dignity of it. To the priest, sex is the clue to marriage and marriage is the clue to the daily life of the people and the Church is the clue to the greater life.

So that sexual lure in itself is not deadly to the Church. Much more deadly is the anti-sexual defiance of bare arms and flippancy, "freedom", cynicism, irreverence. Sex may be obscene in church, or blasphemous, but never cynical and atheist. Potentially, the bare arms of women today are cynical, atheist, in the dangerous, vulgar form of atheism. Naturally the Church is against it. The Chief Priest of Europe knows more about sex than Mr. Shaw does, anyhow, because he knows more about the essential nature of the human being. Traditionally, he has a thousand years' experience. Mr. Shaw jumped up in a day. And Mr. Shaw, as a dramatist, has jumped up to play tricks with the counterfeit sex of the modern public. No doubt he can do it. So can the cheapest film. But it is equally obvious that he *cannot* touch the deeper sex of the real individual, whose existence he hardly seems to suspect.

And, as a parallel to himself, Mr. Shaw suggests that the Chief Prostitute of Europe would be the one to consult about sex, not the Chief Priest. The parallel is just. The Chief Prostitute of Europe would know truly as much about sex as Mr. Shaw himself does. Which is, not much. Just like Mr. Shaw, the Chief Prostitute of Europe would know an immense amount about the counterfeit sex of men, the shoddy thing that is worked by tricks. And just like him, she would know nothing at all about the real sex in a man, that has the rhythm of the seasons and the years, the crisis of the winter solstice and the passion of Easter. This the Chief Prostitute would know nothing about, positively, because to be a prostitute she would have to have lost it. But even then, she would know more than Mr. Shaw. She would know that the profound, rhythmic sex of a man's inward life *existed*. She would know, because time and again she would have been up against it. All the literature of the world shows the prostitute's ultimate impotence in sex, her inability to keep a man, her rage against the profound instinct of fidelity in a man, which is, as shown by world-history, just a little deeper and more powerful than his instinct of faithless sexual promiscuity. All the literature of the world shows how profound is the instinct of fidelity in both man and woman, how men and women both hanker restlessly after the satisfaction of this instinct, and fret at their own inability to find the real mode of fidelity. The instinct of fidelity is perhaps the deepest instinct in the great complex we call sex. Where there is real sex there is the underlying passion for fidelity. And the prostitute knows this, because she is up against it. She can only keep men who have no real sex, the counterfeits: and these she despises. The men with real sex leave her inevitably, as unable to satisfy their real desire.

The Chief Prostitute knows so much. So does the Pope, if he troubles to think of it, for it is all in the traditional consciousness of the Church. But the Chief Dramatist knows nothing of it. He has a curious blank in his make-up. To him, all sex is infidelity and only infidelity is sex. Marriage is sexless, null. Sex is only manifested in infidelity, and the queen of sex is the chief prostitute. If sex crops up in marriage, it is because one party falls in love with somebody else, and wants to be unfaithful. Infidelity is sex, and prostitutes know all about it. Wives know nothing and are nothing, in that respect.

This is the teaching of the Chief Dramatists and Chief Thinkers of our generation. And the vulgar public agrees with them entirely. Sex is a thing you don't have except to be naughty with. Apart from naughtiness, that is, apart from infidelity and fornication, sex doesn't exist. Our chief thinkers, ending in the flippantly cock-sure Mr. Shaw, have taught this trash so thoroughly, that it has almost become a fact. Sex is almost non-existent, apart from the counterfeit forms of prostitution and shallow fornication. And marriage is empty, hollow.

Now this question of sex and marriage is of paramount importance. Our social life is established on marriage, and marriage, the sociologists say, is established upon property. Marriage has been found the best method of conserving property and stimulating production. Which is all there is to it.

But is it? We are just in the throes of a great revolt against marriage, a passionate revolt against its ties and restrictions. In fact, at least three-quarters of the unhappiness of modern life could be laid at the door of marriage. There are few married people today, and few unmarried, who have not felt an intense and vivid hatred against marriage itself, marriage as an institution and an imposition upon human life. Far greater than the revolt against governments is this revolt against marriage.

And everybody, pretty well, takes it for granted that as soon as we can find a possible way out of it, marriage will be abolished. The Soviet abolishes marriage: or did. If new "modern" states spring up, they will almost certainly follow suit. They will try to find some social substitute for marriage, and abolish the hated yoke of conjugality. State support of motherhood, state support of children, and independence of women. It is on the programme of every great scheme of reform. And it means, of course, the abolition of marriage.

The only question to ask ourselves is, do we really want it? Do we want the absolute independence of women, State support of motherhood and of children, and consequent doing away with the necessity of marriage? Do we want it? Because all that matters is that men and women shall do what they *really* want to do. Though here, as everywhere, we must remember that man has a double set of desires, the shallow and the profound, the personal, superficial, temporary desires, and the inner, impersonal, great desires that are fulfilled in long periods of time. The desires of the moment are easy to recognize, but the others, the deeper ones, are difficult. It is the business of our Chief Thinkers to tell us of our deeper desires, not to keep shrilling our little desires in our ears.

Now the Church is established upon a recognition of some, at least, of the greatest and deepest desires in man, desires that take years, or a life-time, or even centuries to fulfil. And the Church, celibate as its priesthood may be, built as it may be upon the lonely rock of Peter, or of Paul, really rests upon the indissolubility of marriage. Make marriage in any serious degree unstable, dissoluble, destroy the permanency of marriage, and the Church falls. Witness the enormous decline of the Church of England.

The reason being that the Church is established upon the element of *union* in mankind. And the first element of union in the Christian world is the marriage-tie. The marriage-tie, the marriage bond, take it which way you like, is the fundamental connecting link in Christian society. Break it, and you will have to go back to the overwhelming dominance of the State, which existed before the Christian era. The Roman State was all-powerful, the Roman Fathers represented the State, the Roman family was the father's estate, held more or less in fee for the State itself. It was the same in Greece, with not so much feeling for the *permanence* of property, but rather a dazzling splash of the moment's possessions. The family was much more insecure in Greece than in Rome.

But, in either case, the family was the man, as representing the State. There are States where the family is the woman: or there have been. There are States where the family hardly exists, priest States where the priestly control is everything, even functioning as family control. Then there is the Soviet State, where again family is not supposed to exist, and the State controls every individual direct, mechanically, as the great religious States, such as early Egypt, may have controlled every individual direct, through priestly surveillance and ritual.

Now the question is, do we want to go back, or forward, to any of these forms of State control? Do we want to be like the Romans under the Empire, or even under the Republic? Do we want to be, as far as our family and our freedom is concerned, like the Greek citizens of a City State in Hellas? Do we want to imagine ourselves in the strange priest-controlled, ritual-fulfilled condition of the earlier Egyptians? Do we want to be bullied by a Soviet?

For my part, I have to say NO! every time. And having said it, we have to come back and consider the famous saying, that perhaps the greatest contribution to the social life of man made by Christianity is—marriage. Christianity brought marriage into the world: marriage as we know it. Christianity established the little autonomy of the family within the greater rule of the State. Christianity made marriage in some respects inviolate, not to be violated by the State. It is marriage, per-haps, which has given man the best of his freedom, given him his little kingdom of his own within the big kingdom of the State, given him his foothold of independence on which to stand and resist an unjust State. Man and wife, a king and queen with one or two subjects, and a few square yards of territory of their own: this, really, is marriage. It is a true freedom because it is a true fulfilment, for man, woman, and children.

Do we, then, want to break marriage? If we do break it, it means we all fall to a far greater extent under the direct sway of the State. Do we want to fall under the direct sway of the State, any State? For my part, I don't.

And the Church created marriage by making it a sacrament, a sacra-ment of man and woman united in the sex communion, and never to be separated, except by death. And even when separated by death, still not freed from the marriage. Marriage, as far as the individual went, eternal. Marriage, making one complete body out of two incomplete ones, and providing for the complex development of the man's soul and the woman's soul in unison, throughout a life-time. Marriage sacred and inviolable, the great way of earthly fulfilment for man and woman, in unison, under the spiritual rule of the Church.

This is Christianity's great contribution to the life of man, and it is only too easily overlooked. Is it, or is it not, a great step in the direction of life-fulfilment, for men and women? Is it, or is it not? Is marriage a great help to the fulfilment of man and woman, or is it a frustration? It is a very important question indeed, and every man and woman must answer it.

If we are to take the Nonconformist, protestant idea of ourselves: that we are all isolated individual souls, and our supreme business is to save our own souls; then marriage surely is a hindrance. If I am only out to save my own soul, I'd better leave marriage alone. As the monks and hermits knew. But also, if I am only out to save other people's souls, I had also best leave marriage alone, as the apostles knew, and the preaching saints.

But supposing I am neither bent on saving my own soul nor other people's souls? Supposing Salvation seems incomprehensible to me, as I confess it does. "Being saved" seems to me just jargon, the jargon of self-conceit. Supposing, then, that I cannot see this Saviour and Salvation stuff, supposing that I see the soul as something which must be developed and fulfilled throughout a life-time, sustained and nourished, developed and further fulfilled, to the very end; what then?

Then I realize that marriage, or something like it, is essential, and that the Old Church knew best the enduring needs of man, beyond the spasmodic needs of today and yesterday. The Church established marriage for life, for the fulfilment of the soul's living life, not postponing it till the after-death.

The old Church knew that life is here our portion, to be lived, to be lived in fulfilment. The stern rule of Benedict, the wild flights of Francis of Assisi, these were coruscations in the steady heaven of the Church. The rhythm of life itself was preserved by the Church hour by hour, day by day, season by season, year by year, epoch by epoch, down among the people, and the wild coruscations were accommodated to this permanent rhythm. We feel it, in the south, in the country, when we hear the jangle of the bells at dawn, at noon, at sunset, marking the hours with the sound of mass or prayers. It is the rhythm of the daily sun. We feel it in the festivals, the processions, Christmas, the Three Kings, Easter, Pentecost, St. John's Day, All Saints, All Souls.

This is the wheeling of the year, the movement of the sun through solstice and equinox, the coming of the seasons, the going of the seasons.
And it is the inward rhythm of man and woman, too, the sadness of
Lent, the delight of Easter, the wonder of Pentecost, the fires of St.
John, the candles on the graves of All Souls, the lit-up tree of Christmas, all representing kindled rhythmic emotions in the souls of men and
women. And men experience the great rhythm of emotion man-wise,
women experience it woman-wise, and in the unison of men and
women it is complete.

Augustine said that God created the universe new every day: and to
the living, emotional soul, this is true. Every dawn dawns upon an
entirely new universe, every Easter lights up an entirely new glory of a
new world opening in utterly new flower. And the soul of man and
the soul of woman is new in the same way, with the infinite delight of
life and the evernewness of life. So a man and a woman are new to one
another throughout a life-time, in the rhythm of marriage that matches
the rhythm of the year.

Sex is the balance of male and female in the universe, the attraction,
the repulsion, the transit of neutrality, the new attraction, the new repulsion, always different, always new. The long neuter spell of Lent,
when the blood is low, and the delight of the Easter kiss, the sexual
revel of spring, the passion of mid-summer, the slow recoil, revolt, and
grief of autumn, greyness again, then the sharp stimulus of winter of
the long nights. Sex goes through the rhythm of the year, in man and
woman, ceaselessly changing: the rhythm of the sun in his relation to
the earth. Oh, what a catastrophe for man when he cut himself off
from the rhythm of the year, from his unison with the sun and the
earth. Oh, what a catastrophe, what a maiming of love when it was
made a personal, merely personal feeling, taken away from the rising
and the setting of the sun, and cut off from the magic connection of the
solstice and the equinox! This is what is the matter with us. We are
bleeding at the roots, because we are cut off from the earth and sun
and stars, and love is a grinning mockery, because, poor blossom, we
plucked it from its stem on the tree of Life, and expected it to keep on
blooming in our civilized vase on the table.

Marriage is the clue to human life, but there is no marriage apart
from the wheeling sun and the nodding earth, from the straying of the
planets and the magnificence of the fixed stars. Is not a man different,
utterly different, at dawn from what he is at sunset? and a woman too?
And does not the changing harmony and discord of their variation
make the secret music of life?

And is it not so throughout life? A man is different at thirty, at forty, at fifty, at sixty, at seventy: and the woman at his side is different. But is there not some strange conjunction in their differences? Is there not some peculiar harmony, through youth, the period of child-birth, the period of florescence and young children, the period of the woman's change of life, painful yet also a renewal, the period of waning passion but mellowing delight of affection, the dim, unequal period of the approach of death, when the man and woman look at one another with the dim apprehension of separation that is not really a separation: is there not, throughout it all, some unseen, unknown interplay of balance, harmony, completion, like some soundless symphony which moves with a rhythm from phase to phase, so different, so very different in the various movements, and yet one symphony, made out of the soundless singing of two strange and incompatible lives, a man's and a woman's?

This is marriage, the mystery of marriage, marriage which fulfils itself here, in this life. We may well believe that in heaven there is no marrying or giving in marriage. All this has to be fulfilled here, and if it is not fulfilled here, it will never be fulfilled. The great saints only live, even Jesus only lives to add a new fulfilment and a new beauty to the permanent sacrament of marriage.

But—and this *but* crashes through our heart like a bullet—marriage is no marriage that is not basically and permanently phallic, and that is not linked up with the sun and the earth, the moon and the fixed stars and the planets, in the rhythm of days, in the rhythm of months, in the rhythm of quarters, of years, of decades and of centuries. Marriage is no marriage that is not a correspondence of blood. For the blood is the substance of the soul, and of the deepest consciousness. It is by blood that we are: and it is by the heart and the liver that we live and move and have our being. In the blood, knowing and being, or feeling, are one and undivided: no serpent and no apple has caused a split. So that only when the conjunction is of the blood, is marriage truly marriage. The blood of man and the blood of woman are two eternally different streams, that can never be mingled. Even scientifically we know it. But therefore they are the two rivers that encircle the whole of life, and in marriage the circle is complete, and in sex the two rivers touch and renew one another, without ever commingling or confusing. We know it. The phallus is a column of blood that fills the valley of blood of a woman. The great river of male blood touches to its depths the great river of female blood—yet neither breaks its bounds. It is the deepest of all communions, as all the religions, in practice, know. And it is one of the greatest mysteries, in fact, the greatest, as almost every initiation shows, showing the supreme achievement of the mystic marriage.

And this is the meaning of the sexual act: this Communion, this touching on one another of the two rivers, Euphrates and Tigris—to use old jargon—and the enclosing of the land of Mesopotamia, where Paradise was, or the Park of Eden, where man had his beginning. This is marriage, this circuit of the two rivers, this communion of the two blood-streams, this, and nothing else: as all the religions know.

Two rivers of blood, are man and wife, two distinct eternal streams, that have the power of touching and communing and so renewing, making new one another, without any breaking of the subtle confines, any confusing or commingling. And the phallus is the connecting-link between the two rivers, that establishes the two streams in a oneness, and gives out of their duality a single circuit, forever. And this, this oneness gradually accomplished throughout a life-time in twoness, is the highest achievement of time or eternity. From it all things human spring, children and beauty and well-made things; all the true creations of humanity. And all we know of the will of God is that He wishes this, this oneness, to take place, fulfilled over a lifetime, this oneness within the great dual blood-stream of humanity.

Man dies, and woman dies, and perhaps separate the souls go back to the Creator. Who knows? But we know that the oneness of the blood-stream of man and woman in marriage completes the universe, as far as humanity is concerned, completes the streaming of the sun and the flowing of the stars.

There is, of course, the counterpart to all this, the counterfeit. There is counterfeit marriage, like nearly all marriage today. Modern people are just personalities, and modern marriage takes place when two people are "thrilled" by each other's personality: when they have the same tastes in furniture or books or sport or amusement, when they love "talking" to one another, when they admire one another's "minds". Now this, this affinity of mind and personality is an excellent basis of friendship between the sexes, but a disastrous basis for marriage. Because marriage inevitably starts the sex-activity, and the sex-activity is, and always was and will be, in some way hostile to the mental, *personal* relationship between man and woman. It is almost an axiom that the marriage of two *personalities* will end in a startling physical hatred. People who are personally devoted to one another at first end by hating one another with a hate which they cannot account for, which they try to hide, for it makes them ashamed, and which is nonetheless only too painfully obvious, especially to one another. In people of strong individual feeling the irritation that accumulates in marriage increases only too often to a point of rage that is close akin to madness. And, apparently, all without reason.

But the real reason is, that the exclusive sympathy of nerves and mind and personal interest is, alas, hostile to blood-sympathy, in the sexes. The modern cult of personality is excellent for friendship between the sexes, and fatal for marriage. On the whole, it would be better if modern people didn't marry. They could remain so much more true to what they are, to their own personality.

But marriage or no marriage, the fatal thing happens. If you have only known personal sympathy and personal love, then rage and hatred will sooner or later take possession of the soul, because of the frustration and denial of blood-sympathy, blood-contact. In celibacy, the denial is withering and souring, but in marriage, the denial produces a sort of rage. And we can no more avoid this, nowadays, than we can avoid thunderstorms. It is part of the phenomenon of the psyche. The important point is that sex itself comes to subserve the personality and the personal "love" entirely, without ever giving sexual satisfaction or fulfilment. In fact, there is probably far more sexual activity in a "personal" marriage than in a blood-marriage. Woman sighs for a perpetual lover: and in the personal marriage, relatively, she gets him. And how she comes to hate him, with his never-ending desire, which never gets anywhere or fulfils anything!

It is a mistake I have made, talking of sex I have always inferred that sex meant blood-sympathy and blood-contact. Technically this is so. But as a matter of fact, nearly all modern sex is a pure matter of nerves, cold and bloodless. This is personal sex. And this white, cold, nervous, "poetic" personal sex, which is practically all the sex that moderns know, has a very peculiar physiological effect, as well as psychological. The two bloodstreams are brought into contact, in man and woman, just the same as in the urge of blood-passion and blood-desire. But whereas the contact in the urge of blood-desire is positive, making a newness in the blood, in the insistence of this nervous, personal desire the blood-contact becomes frictional and destructive, there is a resultant whitening and impoverishment of the blood. Personal or nervous or spiritual sex is destructive to the blood, has a katabolistic activity, whereas coition in warm blood-desire is an activity of metabolism. The katabolism of "nervous" sex-activity may produce for a time a sort of ecstasy and a heightening of consciousness. But this, like the effect of alcohol or drugs, is the result of the decomposition of certain corpuscles in the blood, and is a process of impoverishment. This is one of the many reasons for the failure of energy in modern people; sexual activity, which ought to be refreshing and renewing, becomes exhaustive and debilitating. So that when the young man fails to believe in the regeneration of England by sex, I am constrained to agree with him. Since modern sex is practically all personal and nervous, and, in effect, exhaustive, disintegrative. The disintegrative effect of modern sex-activity is undeniable. It is only less fatal than the disintegrative effect of masturbation, which is more deadly still.

So that at last I begin to see the point of my critics' abuse of my exalting of sex. They only know one form of sex: in fact, to them there *is* only one form of sex: the nervous, personal, disintegrative sort, the "white" sex. And this, of course, is something to be flowery and false about, but nothing to be very hopeful about. I quite agree. And I quite agree, we can have no hope of the regeneration of England from such sort of sex.

At the same time, I cannot see any hope of regeneration for a sexless England. An England that has lost its sex seems to me nothing to feel very hopeful about. And nobody feels very hopeful about it. Though I may have been a fool for insisting on sex where the current sort of sex is just what I *don't* mean and *don't* want, still I can't go back on it all and believe in the regeneration of England by pure sexlessness. A sexless England!—it doesn't ring very hopeful, to me.

And the other, the warm blood-sex that establishes the living and re-vitalizing connection between man and woman, how are we to get that back? I don't know. Yet get it back we must: or the younger ones must, or we are all lost. For the bridge to the future is the phallus, and there's the end of it. But not the poor, nervous counterfeit phallus of modern "nervous" love. Not that.

For the new impulse to life will never come without blood-contact; the true, positive blood-contact, not the nervous negative reaction. And the essential blood-contact is between man and woman, always has been so, always will be. The contact of positive sex. The homosexual contacts are secondary, even if not merely substitutes of exasperated reaction from the utterly unsatisfactory nervous sex between men and women.

If England is to be regenerated—to use the phrase of the young man who seemed to think there was need of *regeneration*—the very word is his—then it will be by the arising of a new blood-contact, a new touch, and a new marriage. It will be a phallic rather than a sexual regeneration. For the phallus is only the great old symbol of godly vitality in a man, and of immediate contact.

It will also be a renewal of marriage: the true phallic marriage. And, still further, it will be marriage set again in relationship to the rhythmic cosmos. The rhythm of the cosmos is something we cannot get away from, without bitterly impoverishing our lives. The Early Christians tried to kill the old pagan rhythm of cosmic ritual, and to some extent succeeded. They killed the planets and the zodiac, perhaps because astrology had already become debased to fortune-telling. They wanted to kill the festivals of the year. But the Church, which knows that man doth not live by man alone, but by the sun and moon and earth in their revolutions, restored the sacred days and feasts almost as the pagans had them, and the Christian peasants went on very much as the pagan peasants had gone, with the sunrise pause for worship, and the sunset, and noon, the three great daily moments of the sun: then the new holy-day, one in the ancient seven-cycle: then Easter and the dying and rising of God, Pentecost, Midsummer Fire, the November dead and the spirits of the grave, then Christmas, then Three Kings. For centuries the mass of people lived in this rhythm, under the Church. And it is down in the mass that the roots of religion are eternal. When the mass of a people loses the religious rhythm, that people is dead, without hope. But Protestantism came and gave a great blow to the religious and ritualistic rhythm of the year, in human life. Nonconformity *almost* finished the deed. Now you have a poor, blind, disconnected people with nothing but politics and bank-holidays to satisfy the eternal human need of living in ritual adjustment to the cosmos in its revolutions, in eternal submission to the greater laws. And marriage, being one of the greater necessities, has suffered the same from the loss of the sway of the greater laws, the cosmic rhythms which should sway life always. Mankind has got to get back to the rhythm of the cosmos, and the permanence of marriage.

All this is post-script, or afterthought, to my novel, *Lady Chatterley's Lover*. Man has little needs and deeper needs. We have fallen into the mistake of living from our little needs till we have almost lost our deeper needs in a sort of madness. There is a little morality, which concerns persons and the little needs of man: and this, alas, is the morality we live by. But there is a deeper morality, which concerns all womanhood, all manhood, and nations, and races, and classes of men. This greater morality affects the destiny of mankind over long stretches of time, applies to man's greater needs, and is often in conflict with the little morality of the little needs. The tragic consciousness has taught us, even, that one of the greater needs of man is a knowledge and experience of death; every man needs to know death in his own body. But the greater consciousness of the pre-tragic and post-tragic epochs teaches us—though we have not yet reached the post-tragic epoch—that the greatest need of man is the renewal forever of the complete rhythm of life and death, the rhythm of the sun's year, the body's year of a lifetime, and the greater year of the stars, the soul's year of immortality. This is our need, our imperative need. It is a need of the mind and soul, body, spirit and sex: all. It is no use asking for a Word to fulfil such a need. No Word, no Logos, no Utterance will ever do it. The Word is uttered, most of it: we need only pay true attention. But who will call us to the Deed, the great Deed of the Seasons and the year, the Deed of the soul's cycle, the Deed of a woman's life at one with a man's, the little Deed the moon's wandering, the bigger Deed of the sun's, and the biggest, of the great still stars? It is the *Deed* of life we have now to learn: we are supposed to have learnt the Word, but, alas, look at us. Word-perfect we may be, but Deed-demented. Let us prepare now for the death of our present "little" life, and the re-emergence in a bigger life, in touch with the moving cosmos.

It is a question, practically, of relationship. We *must* get back into relation, vivid and nourishing relation to the cosmos and the universe. The way is through daily ritual, and the re-awakening. We *must* once more practise the ritual of dawn and noon and sunset, the ritual of the kindling fire and pouring water, the ritual of the first breath, and the last. This is an affair of the individual and the household, a ritual of day. The ritual of the moon in her phases, of the morning star and the evening star is for men and women separate. Then the ritual of the seasons, with the Drama and the Passion of the soul embodied in procession and dance, this is for the community, an act of men and women, a whole community, in togetherness. And the ritual of the great events in the year of stars is for nations and whole peoples. To these rituals we must return: or we must evolve them to suit our needs. For the truth is, we are perishing for lack of fulfilment of our greater needs, we are cut off from the great sources of our inward nourishment and renewal, sources which flow eternally in the universe. Vitally, the human race is dying. It is like a great uprooted tree, with its roots in the air. We must plant ourselves again in the universe.

It means a return to ancient forms. But we shall have to create these forms again, and it is more difficult than the preaching of an evangel. The Gospel came to tell us we were all saved. We look at the world today and realize that humanity, alas, instead of being saved from sin, whatever that may be, is almost completely lost, lost to life, and near to nullity and extermination. We have to go back, a long way, before the idealist conceptions began, before Plato, before the tragic idea of life arose, to get on to our feet again. For the gospel of salvation through the Ideals and escape from the body coincided with the tragic conception of human life. Salvation and tragedy are the same thing, and they are now both beside the point.

Back, before the idealist religions and philosophies arose and started man on the great excursion of tragedy. The last three thousand years of mankind have been an excursion into ideals, bodilessness, and tragedy and now the excursion is over. And it is like the end of a tragedy in the theatre. The stage is strewn with dead bodies, worse still, with meaningless bodies, and the curtain comes down.

But in life, the curtain never comes down on the scene. There the dead bodies lie, and the inert ones, and somebody has to clear them away, somebody has to carry on. It is the day after. Today is already the day after the end of the tragic and idealist epoch. Utmost inertia falls on the remaining protagonists. Yet we have to carry on.

Now we have to re-establish the great relationships which the grand idealists, with their underlying pessimism, their belief that life is nothing but futile conflict, to be avoided even unto death, destroyed for us. Buddha, Plato, Jesus, they were all three utter pessimists as regards life, teaching that the only happiness lay in abstracting oneself from life, the daily, yearly, seasonal life of birth and death and fruition, and in living in the "immutable" or eternal spirit. But now, after almost three thousand years, now that we are almost abstracted entirely from the rhythmic life of the seasons, birth and death and fruition, now we realize that such abstraction is neither bliss nor liberation, but nullity. It brings null inertia. And the great saviours and teachers only cut us off from life. It was the tragic *excursus*.

The universe is dead for us, and how is it to come to life again? "Knowledge" has killed the sun, making it a ball of gas, with spots; "knowledge" has killed the moon, it is a dead little earth fretted with extinct craters as with smallpox; the machine has killed the earth for us, making it a surface, more or less bumpy, that you travel over. How, out of all this, are we to get back the grand orbs of the soul's heavens, that fill us with unspeakable joy? How are we to get back Apollo, and Attis, Demeter, Persephone, and the halls of Dis? How even see the star Hesperus, or Betelguese?

We've got to get them back, for they are the world our soul, our greater consciousness, lives in. The world of reason and science, the moon, a dead lump of earth, the sun, so much gas with spots: this is the dry and sterile little world the abstracted mind inhabits. The world of our little consciousness, which we know in our pettifogging *apartness*. This is how we know the world when we know it apart from ourselves, in the mean separateness of everything. When we know the world in togetherness with ourselves, we know the earth hyacinthine or Plutonic, we know the moon gives us our body as delight upon us, or steals it away, we know the purring of the great gold lion of the sun, who licks us like a lioness her cubs, making us bold, or else, like the red, angry lion, dashes at us with open claws. There are many ways of knowing, there are many sorts of knowledge. But the two ways of knowing, for man, are knowing in terms of apartness, which is mental, rational, scientific, and knowing in terms of togetherness, which is religious and poetic. The Christian religion lost, in Protestantism finally, the togetherness with the universe, the togetherness of the body, the sex, the emotions, the passions, with the earth and sun and stars.

But relationship is threefold. First, there is the relation to the living universe. Then comes the relation of man to woman. Then comes the relation of man to man. And each is a blood-relationship, not mere spirit or mind. We have abstracted the universe into Matter and Force, we have abstracted men and women into separate personalities—personalities being isolated units, incapable of togetherness—so that all three great relationships are bodiless, dead.

None, however, is quite so dead as the man-to-man relationship. I think, if we came to analyse to the last what men feel about one another today, we should find that every man feels every other man as a menace. It is a curious thing, but the more mental and ideal men are, the more they seem to feel the bodily presence of any other man a menace, a menace, as it were, to their very being. Every man that comes near me threatens my very existence: nay, more, my very being.

This is the ugly fact which underlies our civilization. As the advertisement of one of the war novels said, it is an epic of "friendship and hope, mud and blood", which means, of course, that the friendship and hope must end in mud and blood.

When the great crusade against sex and the body started in full blast with Plato, it was a crusade for "ideals", and for this "spiritual" knowledge in apartness. Sex is the great unifier. In its big, slower vibration it is the warmth of heart which makes people happy together, in togetherness. The idealist philosophies and religions set out deliberately to kill this. And they did it. Now they have done it. The last great ebullition of friendship and hope was squashed out in mud and blood. Now men are all separate little entities. While "kindness" is the glib order of the day—everybody *must* be "kind"—underneath this "kindness" we find a coldness of heart, a lack of heart, a callousness, that is very dreary. Every man *is* a menace to every other man.

Men only know one another in menace. Individualism has triumphed. If I am a sheer individual, then every other being, every other man especially, is over against me as a menace to me. This is the peculiarity of our society today. We are all extremely sweet and "nice" to one another, because we merely fear one another.

The sense of isolation, followed by the sense of menace and of fear, is bound to arise as the feeling of oneness and community with our fellow-men declines, and the feeling of individualism and personality, which is existence in isolation, increases. The so-called "cultured" classes are the first to develop "personality" and individualism, and the first to fall into this state of unconscious menace and fear. The working-classes retain the old blood-warmth of oneness and togetherness some decades longer. Then they lose it too. And then class-consciousness becomes rampant, and class-hate. Class-hate and class-consciousness are only a sign that the old togetherness, the old blood-warmth has collapsed, and every man is really aware of himself in apartness. Then we have these hostile groupings of men for the sake of opposition, strife. Civil strife becomes a necessary condition of self-assertion.

This, again, is the tragedy of social life today. In the old England, the curious blood-connection held the classes together. The squires might be arrogant, violent, bullying and unjust, yet in some ways they were *at one* with the people, part of the same blood-stream. We feel it in Defoe or Fielding. And then, in the mean Jane Austen, it is gone. Already this old maid typifies "personality" instead of character, the sharp knowing in apartness instead of knowing in togetherness, and she is, to my feeling, thoroughly unpleasant, English in the bad, mean, snobbish sense of the word, just as Fielding is English in the good, generous sense.

So, in *Lady Chatterley's Lover* we have a man, Sir Clifford, who is purely a personality, having lost entirely all connection with his fellow-men and women, except those of usage. All warmth is gone entirely, the hearth is cold, the heart does not humanly exist. He is a pure product of our civilization, but he is the death of the great humanity of the world. He is kind by rule, but he does not know what warm sympathy means. He is what he is. And he loses the woman of his choice.

The other man still has the warmth of a man, but he is being hunted down, destroyed. Even it is a question if the woman who turns to him will really stand by him and his vital meaning.

I have been asked many times if I intentionally made Clifford paralysed, if it is symbolic. And literary friends say, it would have been better to have left him whole and potent, and to have made the woman leave him nevertheless.

As to whether the "symbolism" is intentional—I don't know. Certainly not in the beginning, when Clifford was created. When I created Clifford and Connie, I had no idea what they were or why they were. They just came, pretty much as they are. But the novel was written, from start to finish, three times. And when I read the first version, I recognized that the lameness of Clifford was symbolic of the paralysis, the deeper emotional or passional paralysis, of most men of his sort and class today. I realized that it was perhaps taking an unfair advantage of Connie, to paralyse him technically. It made it so much more vulgar of her to leave him. Yet the story came as it did, by itself, so I left it alone. Whether we call it symbolism or not, it is, in the sense of its happening, inevitable.

And these notes, which I write now almost two years after the novel was finished, are not intended to explain or expound anything: only to give the emotional beliefs which perhaps are necessary as a background to the book. It is so obviously a book written in defiance of convention that perhaps some reason should be offered for the attitude of defiance: since the silly desire to *épater le bourgeois*, to bewilder the commonplace person, is not worth entertaining. If I use the taboo words, there is a reason. We shall never free the phallic reality from the "uplift" taint till we give it its own phallic language, and use the obscene words. The greatest blasphemy of all against the phallic reality is this "lifting it to a higher plane". Likewise, if the lady marries the gamekeeper— she hasn't done it yet—it is not class-spite, but in spite of class.

Finally, there are the correspondents who complain that I describe the pirated editions—some of them—but not the original. The original first edition, issued in Florence, is bound in hard covers, dullish mulberry-red paper with my phoenix (symbol of immortality, the bird rising new from the nest of flames) printed in black on the cover, and a white paper label on the back. The paper is good, creamy hand-rolled Italian paper, but the print, though nice, is ordinary, and the binding is just the usual binding of a little Florentine shop. There is no expert bookmaking in it: yet it is a pleasant volume, much more so than many far "superior" books.

And if there are many spelling errors—there are—it is because the book was set up in a little Italian printing shop, such a family affair, in which nobody knew one word of English. They none of them knew any

English at all, so they were spared all blushes: and the proofs were terrible. The printer would do fairly well for a few pages, then he would go drunk, or something. And then the words danced weird and *macabre*, but not English. So that if still some of the hosts of errors exist, it is a mercy they are not more.

Then one paper wrote pitying the poor printer who was deceived into printing the book. Not deceived at all. A white-moustached little man who has just married a second wife, he was told: Now the book contains such-and-such words, in English, and it describes certain things. Don't you print it if you think it will get you into trouble!— "What does it describe?" he asked. And when told, he said, with the short indifference of a Florentine: "O! *ma*! but we do it every day!" —And it seemed, to him, to settle the matter entirely. Since it was nothing political or out of the way, there was nothing to think about. Everyday concerns, commonplace.

But it was a struggle, and the wonder is the book came out as well as it did. There was just enough type to set up a half of it: so the half was set up, the thousand copies were printed and, as a measure of caution, the two hundred on ordinary paper, the little second edition, as well: then the type was distributed, and the second half set up.

Then came the struggle of delivery. The book was stopped by the American customs almost at once. Fortunately in England there was a delay. So that practically the whole edition—at least eight hundred copies, surely—must have gone to England.

Then came the storms of vulgar vituperation. But they were inevitable. "But we do it every day," says a little Italian printer. "Monstrous and horrible!" shrieks a section of the British press. "Thank you for a really sexual book about sex, at last. I am so tired of a-sexual books," says one of the most distinguished citizens of Florence to me—an Italian. "I don't know—I don't know—if it's not a bit too strong," says a timid Florentine critic—an Italian. "Listen, Signor Lawrence, you find it really necessary to *say* it?" I told him I did, and he pondered.— "Well, one of them was a brainy vamp, and the other was a sexual moron," said an American woman, referring to the two men in the book—"so I'm afraid Connie had a poor choice—*as usual!*"

VIII

Assorted Articles

The "Jeune Fille" Wants to Know

If you are a writer, nothing is more confusing than the difference between the things you have to say and the things you are allowed to print. Talking to an intelligent girl, the famous "*jeune fille*" who is the excuse for the great Hush! Hush! in print, you find, not that you have to winnow your words and leave out all the essentials, but that she, the innocent girl in question, is flinging all sorts of fierce questions at your head, in all sorts of shameless language, demanding all sorts of impossible answers. You think to yourself: "My heaven, *this* is the innocent young thing on whose behalf books are suppressed!" And you wonder: "How on earth am I to answer her?"

You decide the only way to answer her is straight-forward. She smells an evasion in an instant, and despises you for it. She is no fool, this innocent maiden. Far from it. And she loathes an evasion. Talking to her father in the sanctum of his study, you have to winnow your words and watch your step, the old boy is so nervous, so tremulous lest anything be said that should hurt his feelings. But once away in the draw-ing-room or the garden, the innocent maiden looks at you anxiously, and it is all you can do to prevent her saying crudely, "Please don't be annoyed with daddy. You see, he *is* like that, and we have to put up with him"—or else from blurting out, "Daddy's an old fool, but he *is* a dear, isn't he?"

It is a queer reversal of the Victorian order. Father winces and bridles and trembles in his study or his library, and the innocent maiden knocks you flat with her outspokenness in the conservatory. And you have to admit that she is the man of the two; of the three, maybe. Especially when she says, rather sternly, "I hope you didn't let daddy see what you thought of him!" "But what *do* I think of him?" I gasp. "Oh, it's fairly obvious!" she replies coolly, and dismisses the point.

I admit the young are a little younger than I am; or a little older, which is it? I really haven't spent my years cultivating prunes and prisms, yet, confronted with a young thing of twenty-two, I often find myself with a prune-stone in my mouth, and I don't know what to do with it.

"Why *is* daddy like that?" she says, and there is genuine pain in the question. "Like what?" you ask. "Oh, you know what I mean! Like a baby ostrich with its head in the sand! It only makes his rear so much the more conspicuous. And it's a pity, because he's awfully intelligent in other ways."

Now, what is man to answer? "*Why* are they like that?" she insists. "Who?" say I. "Men!" she says; "men like daddy!" "I suppose it's a sort of funk," say I. "*Exactly!*" she pounces on me like a panther. "But what is there to be in a funk about?"

I have to confess I don't know. "Of course not!" she says. "There's nothing at all to be in a funk about. So why can't we make him see it?"

When the younger generation, usually the feminine half of it in her early twenties, starts firing off Whys? at me, I give in. Anything crosses her in the least—and she takes aim at it with the deadly little pistol of her inquiring spirit, and says "*Why?*" She is a deadly shot: Billy the Kid is nothing to her; she hits the nail on the head every time. "Now, why can't I talk like a sensible human being to daddy?" "I suppose he thinks it is a little early for you to be quite so sensible," say I mildly. "Cheek! What *cheek* of him to think he can measure out the amount of sense I ought to have!" she cries. "Why does he think it?"

Why indeed? But once you start whying, there's no end to it. A hundred years ago, a few reformers piped up timorously, "Why is man so infinitely superior to woman?" And on the slow years came the whisper "He isn't!" Then the poor padded young of those days roused up. "Why are fathers *always* in the right?" And the end of the century confessed that they weren't. Since then, the innocent maiden has ceased to be anæmic; all maidens were more or less anæmic thirty years ago; and though she is no less innocent, but probably more so, than her stuffy grandmother or mother before her, there isn't a thing she hasn't shot her Why? at, or her Wherefore?—the innocent maiden of today. And digging implements are called by their bare, their barest names. "Why should daddy put his foot down upon love? He's been a prize muff at it himself, judging from mother."

It's terrible, if all the sanctifications have to sit there like celluloid Aunt Sallies, while the young take pot shots at them. A real straight Why? aimed by sweet-and-twenty goes clean through them. Nothing but celluloid! and looking so important! Really, *why* . . . ?

The answer seems to be, bogey! The elderly today seem to be ridden by a bogey, they grovel before the fetish of human wickedness. Every young man is out to "ruin" every young maiden. Bogey! The young maiden knows a thing or two about that. She's not quite the raw egg she's supposed to be, in the first place. And as for most young men, they're only too nice, and it would grieve them bitterly to "ruin" any young maid, even if they knew exactly how to set about it. Of which the young maiden is perfectly aware, and "Why can't daddy see it?" He can, really. But he is so wedded to his bogey, that once the young man's back is turned, the old boy can see in the young boy nothing but a danger, a danger to my daughter! Wickedness in other people is an *idée fixe* of the elderly. "Ah, my boy, you will find that in life every man's hand is against you!" As a matter of fact, my boy finds nothing of the sort. Every man has to struggle for himself, true. But most people are willing to give a bit of help where they can. The world may really be a bogey. But that isn't because individuals are wicked villains. At least ninety-nine per cent of individuals in this country, and in any other country as far as we have ever seen, are perfectly decent people who have a certain amount of struggle to get along, but who don't want to do anybody any harm, if they can help it.

This seems to be the general experience of the young, and so they can't appreciate the bogey of human wickedness which seems to dominate the minds of the old, in their relation to the succeeding generation. The young ask "What, exactly, is this bogey, this wickedness we are to be shielded from?" And the old only reply, "Of course, there is no danger to *us*. But to you, who are young and inexperienced . . . !"

And the young, naturally, see nothing but pure hypocrisy. They have no desire to be shielded. If the bogey exists, they would like to set eyes on him, to take the measure of this famous "wickedness." But since they never come across it, since they find meanness and emptiness the worst crimes, they decide that the bogey doesn't and never did exist, that he is an invention of the elderly spirit, the last stupid stick with which the old can beat the young and feel self-justified. "Of course, it's perfectly hopeless with mother and daddy, one has to treat them like mental infants," say the young. But the mother sententiously reiterates, "I don't mind, as far as I am concerned. But I have to protect my children."

Protect, that is, some artificial children that only exist in parental imagination, from a bogey that likewise has no existence outside that imagination, and thereby derive a great sense of parental authority, importance and justification.

The danger for the young is that they will question everything out of

existence, so that nothing is left. But that is no reason to stop questioning. The old lies must be questioned out of existence, even at a certain
loss of things worth having. When everything is questioned out of existence, then the real fun will begin putting the right things back. But
nothing is any good till the old lies are got rid of.

Laura Philippine

When you find two almonds in one shell, that's a Philippine. So when Philippa Homes had twins she called them Laura Philippine and Philip Joseph. And she went on calling them Laura Philippine and Philip Joseph till it fixed, and they are it to this day, and Laura Philippine is twenty.

She is quite a lovely girl, tall and white-skinned, but except when she's dancing, or driving a car, or riding a horse, she's languid. Having had what is called a good education, she drawls in slang. She has rather wonderful blue eyes, asleep rather than sleepy, with the oddest red-gold lashes coming down over them; close, red-gold lashes. You notice the lashes because most of the daytime she doesn't trouble to raise them.

At about half-past eleven in the morning you suddenly come across her reclining on a lounge in the drawing-room, smoking a cigarette, showing several yards of good leg and turning over a periodical without looking at it.

"Hello, Laura Philippine, just got up?"

"This minute."

"How are you?"

"Same."

And she's nothing more to say. She turns over the periodical without looking at it, lights another cigarette, and time, since it can't help it, passes. At half-past twelve you find her in the hall in an elegant wrap, and a nut of a little blue hat, looking as if she might possibly be drifting out of doors to commit suicide in some half-delicious fashion.

"Where are you going, Laura Philippine?"

"Out."

"Where's that?"

"Oh, meet some of the boys—"

"Well, lunch is half-past one—"

But she is gone, with a completeness that makes it seem impossible she will ever come back. Yet back she comes, about two, when we are peeling our apple. She is the image of freshness, in her bit of a putty-coloured frock, her reddish petals of hair clinging down over her ears, her cheeks pink by nature, till she almost powders them out of spite, her long white limbs almost too languid to move, and her queer fiery eye-lashes down over her dark blue eyes.

"I told her not to serve me soup till I came."

"And I told her to serve it when she served us. Lunch is half-past one."

Laura Philippine sits down in front of her soup, which Philippa always has for lunch, out of spite. The parlourmaid comes in again.

"I won't have soup," says Laura Philippine. "What else is there?" And when she is told, she replies: "I won't take that either. I'll just take salad, and will you find me something to eat with it?"

The parlourmaid looks at Philippa, and Philippa says:

"I suppose you'd better bring the galantine."

So Laura Philippine, with pure indifference, eats galantine and salad, and drinks burgundy, which almost shows ruddy as it goes down her white throat.

"Did you find the boys?" I ask.

"Oh, quite."

"Did you drink cocktails?"

"Not before lunch. Gin and bitters."

I got no more out of her. But we went out in the afternoon in the car. As we went through Windsor Park, I said:

"It is rather lovely, isn't it?"

"Oh, quite!"

"But you don't look at it."

"What am I to look at it for?"

"Pleasure."

"No pleasure to me."

She looked at nothing—unless it might be at a well-dressed woman. She was interested in nothing: unless it were the boys, just at meal-times.

So she came with Philippa to Rome.

"Doing the sights of Italy with your mother, are you?" said I.

"Mother'll have a swell time taking me to see sights."

Mother did. Laura Philippine just smoked cigarettes and lowered her reddish-gold lashes over her dark blue eyes, and said languidly: Is that so? We drove down to Ostia over the Campagna. Oh, look, Laura Philippine, there are still a few buffaloes! Laura Philippine knocked cigarette ash over the other side of the car in order not to look, and said

yes! Look at the old fortifications of Ostia, Laura Philippine!—Yes,
I've seen 'em!—We came to the sea, got out of the car and walked on
to the shingle shore. Call that the sea? said Laura Philippine. I said
I did: the Mediterranean, at least. Is it always that way? Why, it must
have something the matter with it!—And Laura Philippine reclined on
the shingle, lit another cigarette, and was gone into a special void of
her own, leaving the sea to take care of itself. Where shall we have tea,
Laura Philippine?—Oh, anywhere!—At the Castle of the Cæsars?—
Suit me all right!—If one had said in the cemetery, she would have
answered the same.

She appeared at dinner looking very, very modern.

"Where are you going tonight, Laura Philippine?"

"There's a dance at the Hotel de Russie."

"But you're not going alone."

"Oh, I shan't be alone. I know a whole crowd of 'em."

"But does your mother let you go off like that?"

"My mother! Imagine if she had to come along!" Laura Philippine was animated. Her red-gold lashes lifted, her dark blue eyes
flashed.

"Do you Charleston?" she said. It was the day before yesterday,
when people still said it. And she started wriggling in the middle of the
drawing-room. She was flushed, animated, flashing, a weird sort of
Bacchanal on the hills of Rome, wriggling there, and her white teeth
showing in an odd little smile.

She was gone for good again. But next day about lunch-time, there
she was, lying down, faintly haunted by the last vestiges of life, otherwise quite passed out.—Have a good time?—Yes!—What time did
you get home?—About four. Dance all night?—Yes! Isn't it too much
for you?—Not a bit. If I could dance all day as well, I might keep going. It's this leaving off that does me in.—And she lapsed out.

One day Philippa said to her: "Show him your poems. Yes, let him
see them. He won't think you a fool."

They were really nice poems, like little sighs. They were poems to
yellow leaves, then to a grey kitten, then to a certain boy. They were
ghostly wisps of verse, somehow touching and wistful. You should care
for somebody, Laura Philippine, said I.—Oh, come! Not that old bait!
she replied.—But you've got to live, said I.—I know it! she said. Why
mention it?—But you're only twenty. Think of your future. The only
single thing you care about is jazz.—Exactly. But what are boys for,
'xcept to jazz with?—Quite! But what about when you're thirty, and
forty?—and fifty?—I suppose they'll invent new dances all the time,

she said mildly. I see old birds trotting like old foxes, so why shouldn't I, if I'm ninety?—But you'll wear out, said I.—Not if anybody's a good dancer, and will wind me up, she said.—But are you happy? said I.—Mother's always saying that. Why should anybody on earth want to be happy? I say to mother: *Show* me somebody happy, then! And she shows me some guy, or some bright young thing, and gets mad when I say: See the pretty monkey! I'm not happy, thank God, because I'm not anything. Why should I be?

Sex versus Loveliness

It is a pity that *sex* is such an ugly little word. An ugly little word, and really almost incomprehensible. What *is* sex, after all? The more we think about it the less we know.

Science says it is an instinct; but what is an instinct? Apparently an instinct is an old, old habit that has become ingrained. But a habit, however old, has to have a beginning. And there is really no beginning to sex. Where life is, there it is. So sex is no "habit" that has been formed.

Again, they talk of sex as an appetite, like hunger. An appetite; but for what? An appetite for propagation? It is rather absurd. They say a peacock puts on all his fine feathers to dazzle the peahen into letting him satisfy his appetite for propagation. But why should the peahen not put on fine feathers, to dazzle the peacock, and satisfy *her* desire for propagation? She has surely quite as great a desire for eggs and chickens as he has. We cannot believe that her sex-urge is so weak that she needs all that blue splendour of feathers to rouse her. Not at all.

As for me, I never even saw a peahen so much as look at her lord's bronze and blue glory. I don't believe she ever sees it. I don't believe for a moment that she knows the difference between bronze, blue, brown or green.

If I had ever seen a peahen gazing with rapt attention on her lord's flamboyancy, I might believe that he had put on all those feathers just to "attract" her. But she never looks at him. Only she seems to get a little perky when he shudders all his quills at her, like a storm in the trees. Then she does seem to notice, just casually, his presence.

These theories of sex are amazing. A peacock puts on his glory for the sake of a wall-eyed peahen who never looks at him. Imagine a scientist being so naïve as to credit the peahen with a profound, dynamic appreciation of a peacock's colour and pattern. Oh, highly æsthetic peahen!

And a nightingale sings to attract his female. Which is mighty curious, seeing he sings his best when courtship and honeymoon are over and the female is no longer concerned with him at all, but with the young. Well, then, if he doesn't sing to attract her, he must sing to distract her and amuse her while she's sitting.

How delightful, how naïve theories are! But there is a hidden will behind them all. There is a hidden will behind all theories of sex, implacable. And that is the will to deny, to wipe out the mystery of beauty.

Because beauty is a mystery. You can neither eat it nor make flannel out of it. Well, then, says science, it is just a trick to catch the female and induce her to propagate. How naïve! As if the female needed inducing. She will propagate in the dark, even—so where, then, is the beauty trick?

Science has a mysterious hatred of beauty, because it doesn't fit in the cause-and-effect chain. And society has a mysterious hatred of sex, because it perpetually interferes with the nice money-making schemes of social man. So the two hatreds made a combine, and sex and beauty are mere propagation appetite.

Now sex and beauty are one thing, like flame and fire. If you hate sex you hate beauty. If you love *living* beauty, you have a reverence for sex. Of course you can love old, dead beauty and hate sex. But to love living beauty you must have a reverence for sex.

Sex and beauty are inseparable, like life and consciousness. And the intelligence which goes with sex and beauty, and arises out of sex and beauty, is intuition. The great disaster of our civilization is the morbid hatred of sex. What, for example, could show a more poisoned hatred of sex than Freudian psycho-analysis?—which carries with it a morbid fear of beauty, "alive" beauty, and which causes the atrophy of our intuitive faculty and our intuitive self.

The deep psychic disease of modern men and women is the diseased, atrophied condition of the intuitive faculties. There is a whole world of life that we might know and enjoy by intuition, and by intuition alone. This is denied us, because we deny sex and beauty, the source of the intuitive life and of the insouciance which is so lovely in free animals and in plants.

Sex is the root of which intuition is the foliage and beauty the flower. Why is a woman lovely, if ever, in her twenties? It is the time when sex rises softly to her face, as a rose to the top of a rose bush.

And the appeal is the appeal of beauty. We deny it wherever we can. We try to make the beauty as shallow and trashy as possible. But, first and foremost, sex appeal is the appeal of beauty.

Now beauty is a thing about which we are so uneducated we can hardly speak of it. We try to pretend it is a fixed arrangement: straight nose, large eyes, etc. We think a lovely woman must look like Lilian Gish, a handsome man must look like Rudolph Valentino. So we *think*.

In actual life we behave quite differently. We say: "She's quite beautiful, but I don't care for her." Which shows we are using the word *beautiful* all wrong. We should say: "She has the stereotyped attributes of beauty, but she is not beautiful to me."

Beauty is an *experience*, nothing else. It is not a fixed pattern or an arrangement of features. It is something *felt*, a glow or a communicated sense of fineness. What ails us is that our sense of beauty is so bruised and blunted, we miss all the best.

But to stick to the films—there is a greater essential beauty in Charlie Chaplin's odd face than ever there was in Valentino's. There is a bit of true beauty in Chaplin's brows and eyes, a gleam of something pure.

But our sense of beauty is so bruised and clumsy, we don't see it, and don't know it when we do see it. We can only see the blatantly obvious, like the so-called beauty of Rudolph Valentino, which only pleases because it satisfies some ready-made notion of handsomeness.

But the plainest person can look beautiful, can *be* beautiful. It only needs the fire of sex to rise delicately to change an ugly face to a lovely one. That is really sex appeal: the communicating of a sense of beauty.

And in the reverse way, no one can be quite so repellent as a really pretty woman. That is, since beauty is a question of experience, not of concrete form, no one can be as acutely ugly as a really pretty woman. When the sex-glow is missing, and she moves in ugly coldness, how hideous she seems, and all the worse for her externals of prettiness.

What sex is, we don't know, but it must be some sort of fire. For it always communicates a sense of warmth, of glow. And when the glow becomes a pure shine, then we feel the sense of beauty.

But the communicating of the warmth, the glow of sex, is true sex appeal. We all have the fire of sex slumbering or burning inside us. If we live to be ninety, it is still there. Or, if it dies, we become one of those ghastly living corpses which are unfortunately becoming more numerous in the world.

Nothing is more ugly than a human being in whom the fire of sex has gone out. You get a nasty clayey creature whom everybody wants to avoid.

But while we are fully alive, the fire of sex smoulders or burns in us. In youth it flickers and shines; in age it glows softer and stiller, but there it is. We have some control over it; but only partial control. That is why society hates it.

While ever it lives, the fire of sex, which is the source of beauty and anger, burns in us beyond our understanding. Like actual fire, while it lives it will burn our fingers if we touch it carelessly. And so social man, who only wants to be "safe," hates the fire of sex.

Luckily, not many men succeed in being merely social men. The fire of the old Adam smoulders. And one of the qualities of fire is that it calls to fire. Sex-fire here kindles sex-fire there. It may only rouse the smoulder into a soft glow. It may call up a sharp flicker. Or rouse a flame; and then flame leans to flame, and starts a blaze.

Whenever the sex-fire glows through, it will kindle an answer somewhere or other. It may only kindle a sense of warmth and optimism. Then you say: "I like that girl; she's a real good sort." It may kindle a glow that makes the world look kindlier, and life feel better. Then you say: "She's an attractive woman. I like her."

Or she may rouse a flame that lights up her own face first, before it lights up the universe. Then you say: "She's a lovely woman. She looks lovely to me."

It takes a rare woman to rouse a real sense of loveliness. It is not that a woman is born beautiful. We say that to escape our own poor, bruised, clumsy understanding of beauty. There have been thousands and thousands of women quite as good-looking as Diane de Poitiers, or Mrs. Langtry, or any of the famous ones. There are today thousands and thousands of superbly good-looking women. But oh, how few lovely women!

And why? Because of the failure of their sex appeal. A good-looking woman becomes lovely when the fire of sex rouses pure and fine in her and flickers through her face and touches the fire in me.

Then she becomes a lovely woman to me, then she is in the living flesh a lovely woman: not a mere photograph of one. And how lovely a lovely woman! But, alas! how rare! How bitterly rare in a world full of unusually handsome girls and women!

Handsome, good-looking, but not lovely, not beautiful. Handsome and good-looking women are the women with good features and the right hair. But a lovely woman is an experience. It is a question of communicated fire. It is a question of sex appeal in our poor, dilapidated modern phraseology. Sex appeal applied to Diane de Poitiers, or even, in the lovely hours, to one's wife—why, it is a libel and a slander in itself. Nowadays, however, instead of the fire of loveliness, it is sex appeal. The two are the same thing, I suppose, but on vastly different levels.

The business man's pretty and devoted secretary is still chiefly valuable because of her sex appeal. Which does not imply "immoral relations" in the slightest.

Even today a girl with a bit of generosity likes to feel she is helping a man if the man will take her help. And this desire that he shall take her help is her sex appeal. It is the genuine fire, if of a very mediocre heat.

Still, it serves to keep the world of "business" alive. Probably, but for the introduction of the lady secretary into the business man's office, the business man would have collapsed entirely by now. She calls up the sacred fire in her and she communicates it to her boss. He feels an added flow of energy and optimism, and—business flourishes.

There is, of course, the other side of sex appeal. It can be the destruction of the one appealed to. When a woman starts using her sex appeal to her own advantage it is usually a bad moment for some poor devil. But this side of sex appeal has been overworked lately, so it is not nearly as dangerous as it was.

The sex-appealing courtesans who ruined so many men in Balzac no longer find it smooth running. Men have grown canny. They fight shy even of the emotional vamp. In fact, men are inclined to think they smell a rat the moment they feel the touch of feminine sex appeal today.

Which is a pity, for sex appeal is only a dirty name for a bit of life-flame. No man works so well and so successfully as when some woman has kindled a little fire in his veins. No woman does her housework with real joy unless she is in love—and a woman may go on being quietly in love for fifty years almost without knowing it.

If only our civilization had taught us how to let sex appeal flow properly and subtly, how to keep the fire of sex clear and alive, flickering or glowing or blazing in all its varying degrees of strength and communication, we might, all of us, have lived all our lives in love, which means we should be kindled and full of zest in all kinds of ways and for all kinds of things. . . .

Whereas, what a lot of dead ash there is in life now.

Insouciance

My balcony is on the east side of the hotel, and my neighbours on the right are a Frenchman, white-haired, and his white-haired wife; my neighbours on the left are two little white-haired English ladies. And we are all mortally shy of one another.

When I peep out of my room in the morning and see the matronly French lady in a purple silk wrapper, standing like the captain on the bridge surveying the morning, I pop in again before she can see me. And whenever I emerge during the day, I am aware of the two little white-haired ladies popping back like two white rabbits, so that literally I only see the whisk of their skirt-hems.

This afternoon being hot and thundery, I woke up suddenly and went out on the balcony barefoot. There I sat serenely contemplating the world, and ignoring the two bundles of feet of the two little ladies which protruded from their open doorways, upon the end of the two *chaises longues*. A hot, still afternoon! the lake shining rather glassy away below, the mountains rather sulky, the greenness very green, all a little silent and lurid, and two mowers mowing with scythes, downhill just near: *slush! slush!* sound the scythe-strokes.

The two little ladies become aware of my presence. I become aware of a certain agitation in the two bundles of feet wrapped in two discreet steamer rugs and protruding on the end of two *chaises longues* from the pair of doorways upon the balcony next me. One bundle of feet suddenly disappears; so does the other. Silence!

Then lo! with odd sliding suddenness a little white-haired lady in grey silk, with round blue eyes, emerges and looks straight at me, and remarks that it is pleasant now. A little cooler, say I, with false amiability. She quite agrees, and we speak of the men mowing; how plainly one hears the long breaths of the scythes!

By now we are *tête-à-tête*. We speak of cherries, strawberries, and the promise of the vine crop. This somehow leads to Italy, and to Signor Mussolini. Before I know where I am, the little white-haired lady has swept me off my balcony, away from the glassy lake, the veiled mountains, the two men mowing, and the cherry trees, away into the troubled ether of international politics.

I am not allowed to sit like a dandelion on my own stem. The little lady in a breath blows me abroad. And I was so pleasantly musing over the two men mowing: the young one, with long legs in bright blue cotton trousers, and with bare black head, swinging so lightly downhill, and the other, in black trousers, rather stout in front, and wearing a new straw hat of the boater variety, coming rather stiffly after, crunching the end of his stroke with a certain violent effort.

I was watching the curiously different motions of the two men, the young thin one in bright blue trousers, the elderly fat one in shabby black trousers that stick out in front, the different amount of effort in their mowing, the lack of grace in the elderly one, his jerky advance, the unpleasant effect of the new "boater" on his head—and I tried to interest the little lady.

But it meant nothing to her. The mowers, the mountains, the cherry trees, the lake, all the things that were *actually* there, she didn't care about. They even seemed to scare her off the balcony. But she held her ground, and instead of herself being scared away, she snatched me up like some ogress, and swept me off into the empty desert spaces of right and wrong, politics, Fascism and the rest.

The worst ogress couldn't have treated me more villainously. I don't care about right and wrong, politics, Fascism, abstract liberty or anything else of the sort. I want to look at the mowers, and wonder why fatness, elderliness and black trousers should inevitably wear a new straw hat of the boater variety, move in stiff jerks, shove the end of the scythe-stroke with a certain violence, and win my hearty disapproval, as contrasted with the young long thinness, bright blue cotton trousers, a bare black head, and a pretty lifting movement at the end of the scythe-stroke.

Why do modern people almost invariably ignore the things that are actually present to them? Why, having come out from England to find mountains, lakes, scythe-mowers and cherry trees, does the little blue-eyed lady resolutely close her blue eyes to them all, now she's got them, and gaze away to Signor Mussolini, whom she hasn't got, and to Fascism, which is invisible anyhow? Why isn't she content to be where she is? Why can't she be happy with what she's got? Why must she *care*?

I see now why her round blue eyes are so round, so noticeably round. It is because she "cares." She is haunted by that mysterious bugbear of "caring." For everything on earth that doesn't concern her she "cares." She cares terribly because far-off, invisible, hypothetical Italians wear black shirts, but she doesn't care a rap that one elderly mower whose stroke she can hear, wears black trousers instead of bright blue cotton ones. Now if she would descend from the balcony and climb the grassy slope and say to the fat mower: "*Cher monsieur, pourquoi portez-vous les pantalons noirs?* Why, oh, why do you wear black trousers?"—then I should say: What an on-the-spot little lady!—But since she only torments me with international politics, I can only remark: What a tiresome off-the-spot old woman!

They care! They simply are eaten up with caring. They are so busy caring about Fascism or Leagues of Nations or whether France is right or whether Marriage is threatened, that they never know where they are. They certainly never live on the spot where they are. They inhabit abstract space, the desert void of politics, principles, right and wrong, and so forth. They are doomed to be abstract. Talking to them is like trying to have a human relationship with the letter x in algebra.

There simply is a deadly breach between actual living and this abstract caring. What is actual living? It is a question mostly of direct contact. There was a direct sensuous contact between me, the lake, the mountains, cherry trees, mowers, and a certain invisible but noisy chaffinch in a clipped lime tree. All this was cut off by the fatal shears of that abstract word Fascism, and the little old lady next door was the Atropos who cut the thread of my actual life this afternoon. She beheaded me, and flung my head into abstract space. Then we are supposed to love our neighbours!

When it comes to living, we live through our instincts and our intuitions. Instinct makes me run from little over-earnest ladies; instinct makes me sniff the lime blossom and reach for the darkest cherry. But it is intuition which makes me feel the uncanny glassiness of the lake this afternoon, the sulkiness of the mountains, the vividness of near green in thunder-sun, the young man in bright blue trousers lightly tossing the grass from the scythe, the elderly man in a boater stiffly shoving his scythe-strokes, both of them sweating in the silence of the intense light.

Give Her a Pattern

The real trouble about women is that they must always go on trying to adapt themselves to men's theories of women, as they always have done. When a woman is thoroughly herself, she is being what her type of man wants her to be. When a woman is hysterical it's because she doesn't quite know what to be, which pattern to follow, which man's picture of woman to live up to.

For, of course, just as there are many men in the world, there are many masculine theories of what women should be. But men run to type, and it is the type, not the individual, that produces the theory, or "ideal" of woman. Those very grasping gentry, the Romans, produced a theory or ideal of the matron, which fitted in very nicely with the Roman property lust. "Cæsar's wife should be above suspicion."— So Cæsar's wife kindly proceeded to be above it, no matter how far below it the Cæsar fell. Later gentlemen like Nero produced the "fast" theory of woman, and later ladies were fast enough for everybody. Dante arrived with a chaste and untouched Beatrice, and chaste and untouched Beatrices began to march self-importantly through the centuries. The Renaissance discovered the learned woman, and learned women buzzed mildly into verse and prose. Dickens invented the child-wife, so child-wives have swarmed ever since. He also fished out his version of the chaste Beatrice, a chaste but marriageable Agnes. George Eliot imitated this pattern, and it became confirmed. The noble woman, the pure spouse, the devoted mother took the field, and was simply worked to death. Our own poor mothers were this sort. So we younger men, having been a bit frightened of our noble mothers, tended to revert to the child-wife. We weren't very inventive. Only the child-wife must be a boyish little thing—that was the new touch we added. Because young men are definitely frightened of the real female. She's too risky a quantity. She is too untidy, like David's Dora. No, let her be a boyish little thing, it's safer. So a boyish little thing she is.

There are, of course, other types. Capable men produce the capable woman ideal. Doctors produce the capable nurse. Business men produce the capable secretary. And so you get all sorts. You can produce the masculine sense of honour (whatever that highly mysterious quantity may be) in women, if you want to.

There is, also, the eternal secret ideal of men—the prostitute. Lots of women live up to this idea: just because men want them to.

And so, poor woman, destiny makes away with her. It isn't that she hasn't got a mind—she has. She's got everything that man has. The only difference is that she asks for a pattern. Give me a pattern to follow! That will always be woman's cry. Unless of course she has already chosen her pattern quite young, then she will declare she is herself absolutely, and no man's idea of women has any influence over her.

Now the real tragedy is not that women ask and must ask for a pattern of womanhood. The tragedy is not, even, that men give them such abominable patterns, child-wives, little-boy-baby-face girls, perfect secretaries, noble spouses, self-sacrificing mothers, pure women who bring forth children in virgin coldness, prostitutes who just make themselves low, to please the men; all the atrocious patterns of womanhood that men have supplied to woman; patterns all perverted from any real natural fulness of a human being. Man is willing to accept woman as an equal, as a man in skirts, as an angel, a devil, a baby-face, a machine, an instrument, a bosom, a womb, a pair of legs, a servant, an encyclopædia, an ideal or an obscenity; the one thing he won't accept her as is a human being, a real human being of the feminine sex.

And, of course, women love living up to strange patterns, weird patterns—the more uncanny the better. What could be more uncanny than the present pattern of the Eton-boy girl with flower-like artificial complexion? It is just weird. And for its very weirdness women like living up to it. What can be more gruesome than the little-boy-baby-face pattern? Yet the girls take it on with avidity.

But even that isn't the real root of the tragedy. The absurdity, and often, as in the Dante-Beatrice business, the inhuman nastiness of the pattern—for Beatrice had to go on being chaste and untouched all her life, according to Dante's pattern, while Dante had a cosy wife and kids at home—even that isn't the worst of it. The worst of it is, as soon as a woman has really lived up to the man's pattern, the man dislikes her for it. There is intense secret dislike for the Eton-young-man girl, among the boys, now that she is actually produced. Of course, she's very nice to show in public, absolutely the thing. But the very young men who have brought about her production detest her in private and in their private hearts are appalled by her.

When it comes to marrying, the pattern goes all to pieces. The boy marries the Eton-boy girl, and instantly he hates the *type*. Instantly his mind begins to play hysterically with all the other types, noble Agneses, chaste Beatrices, clinging Doras and lurid *filles de joie*. He is in a wild welter of confusion. Whatever pattern the poor woman tries to live up to; he'll want another. And that's the condition of modern marriage.

Modern woman isn't really a fool. But modern man is. That seems to me the only plain way of putting it. The modern man is a fool, and the modern young man a prize fool. He makes a greater mess of his women than men have ever made. Because he absolutely doesn't know *what* he wants her to be. We shall see the changes in the woman-pattern follow one another fast and furious now, because the young men hysterically don't know what they want. Two years hence women may be in crinolines—there was a pattern for you!—or a bead flap, like naked negresses in mid-Africa—or they may be wearing brass armour, or the uniform of the Horse Guards. They may be anything. Because the young men are off their heads, and don't know what they want.

The women aren't fools, but they *must* live up to some pattern or other. They *know* the men are fools. They don't really respect the pattern. Yet a pattern they must have, or they can't exist.

Women are not fools. They have their own logic, even if it's not the masculine sort. Women have the logic of emotion, men have the logic of reason. The two are complementary and mostly in opposition. But the woman's logic of emotion is no less real and inexorable than the man's logic of reason. It only works differently.

And the woman never really loses it. She may spend years living up to a masculine pattern. But in the end, the strange and terrible logic of emotion will work out the smashing of that pattern, if it has not been emotionally satisfactory. This is the partial explanation of the astonishing changes in women. For years they go on being chaste Beatrices or child-wives. Then on a sudden—bash! The chaste Beatrice becomes something quite different, the child-wife becomes a roaring lioness! The pattern didn't suffice, emotionally.

Whereas men are fools. They are based on a logic of reason, or are supposed to be. And then they go and behave, especially with regard to women, in a more-than-feminine unreasonableness. They spend years training up the little-boy-baby-face type, till they've got her perfect. Then the moment they marry her, they want something else. Oh, beware, young women, of the young men who adore you! The moment they've got you they'll want something utterly different. The moment they marry the little-boy-baby face, instantly they begin to pine for the noble Agnes, pure and majestic, or the infinite mother with deep bosom of consolation, or the perfect business woman, or the lurid prostitute on black silk sheets: or, most idiotic of all, a combination of all the lot of them at once. And that is the logic of reason! When it comes to women, modern men are idiots. They don't know what they want, and so they never want, permanently, what they get. They want a cream cake that is at the same time ham and eggs and at the same time porridge. They are fools. If only women weren't bound by fate to play up to them!

For the fact of life is that women *must* play up to man's pattern. And she only gives her best to a man when he gives her a satisfactory pattern to play up to. But today, with a stock of ready-made, worn-out idiotic patterns to live up to, what can women give to men but the trashy side of their emotions? What could a woman possibly give to a man who wanted her to be a boy-baby face? What could she possibly give him but the dribblings of an idiot?—And, because women aren't fools, and aren't fooled even for very long at a time, she gives him some nasty cruel digs with her claws, and makes him cry for mother dear!— abruptly changing his pattern.

Bah! men are fools. If they want anything from women, let them give women a decent, satisfying idea of womanhood—not these trick patterns of washed-out idiots.

Do Women Change?

They tell of all the things that are going to happen in the future—babies bred in bottle, all the love-nonsense cut out, women indistinguishable from men. But it seems to me bosh. We like to imagine we are something very new on the face of the earth. But it seems to me we flatter ourselves. Motor-cars and aeroplanes are something novel, if not something new—one could draw a distinction. But the people in them are merely people, and not many steps up, if any, it seems to me, from the people who went in litters or palanquins or chariots, or who walked on foot from Egypt to Jordan, in the days of Moses. Humanity seems to have an infinite capacity for remaining the same—that is, human.

Of course, there are all kinds of ways of being human; but I expect almost every possible kind is alive and kicking today. There are little Cleopatras and Zenobias and Semiramises and Judiths and Ruths, and even Mother Eves, today just the same as in all the endless yesterdays. Circumstances make them little Cleopatras and little Semiramises instead of big ones, because our age goes in for quantity regardless of quality. But sophisticated people are sophisticated people, no matter whether it is Egypt or Atlantis. And sophisticated people are pretty well all alike. All that varies is the proportion of "modern" people to all the other unmodern sorts, the sophisticated to the unsophisticated. And today there is a huge majority of sophisticated people. And they are probably very little different from all the other sophisticated people of all the other civilizations, since man was man.

And women are just part of the human show. They aren't something apart. They aren't something new on the face of the earth, like the loganberry or artificial silk. Women are as sophisticated as men, anyhow, and they were never anything but women, and they are nothing but women today, whatever they may think of themselves. They say the modern woman is a new type. But is she? I expect, in fact I am sure, there have been lots of women like ours in the past, and if you'd been married to one of them, you wouldn't have found her any different from your present wife. Women are women. They only have phases. In Rome, in Syracuse, in Athens, in Thebes, more than two or three thousand years ago, there was the bob-haired, painted, perfumed Miss and Mrs. of today, and she inspired almost exactly the feelings that our painted and perfumed Misses and Mrses. inspire in the men.

I saw a joke in a German paper—a modern young man and a modern young woman leaning on an hotel balcony at night, overlooking the sea. *He:* "See the stars sinking down over the dark restless ocean!" *She:* "Cut it out! My room number is 32!"

That is supposed to be very modern: the very modern woman. But I believe women in Capri under Tiberias said *"Cut it out"* to their Roman and Campanian lovers in just the same way. And women in Alexandria in Cleopatra's time. Certain phases of history are "modern." As the wheel of history goes round women become "modern," then they become unmodern again. The Roman women of the late Empire were most decidedly "modern"—so were the women of Ptolemaic Egypt. True modern cut-it-out women. Only the hotels were run differently.

Modernity or modernism isn't something we've just invented. It's something that comes at the end of civilizations. Just as leaves in autumn are yellow, so the women at the end of every known civilization—Roman, Greek, Egyptian, etc.—have been modern. They were smart, they were *chic*, they said cut-it-out, and they did as they jolly well pleased.

And then, after all, how deep does modernness go? Even in a woman? You give her a run for her money; and if you don't give it her, she takes it. The sign of modernness in a woman is that she says: Oh, cut it out, boy!—So the boy cuts it out—all the stars and ocean stuff.— My room number's thirty-two!—Come to the point!

But the point, when you come to it, is a very bare little place, a very meagre little affair. It's extraordinary how meagre the point is once you've come to it. It's not much better than a full-stop. So the modern girl comes to the point brutally and repeatedly, to find that her life is a series of full-stops, then a mere string of dots. Cut it out, boy! ... When she comes to dot number one thousand, she's getting about tired of dots, and of the plain point she's come to. The point is all too plain and too obvious. It is so pointed that it is pointless. Following the series of dots comes a blank—a dead blank. There's nothing left to cut out. Blank-eye!

Then the thoroughly modern girl begins to moan: Oh, boy, do put something in again!—And the thoroughly modern boy, having cut it out so thoroughly that it will never grow again, tunes up with: I can't give you anything but love, Baby!—And the thoroughly modern girl accepts it with unction. She knows it's nothing but a most crestfallen echo from the sentimental past. But when you've cut everything out so that it will never grow again, you are thankful even for echoes from a sentimental past. And so the game begins again. Having cut it out, and brought it down to brass tacks, you find brass tacks are the last thing you want to lie down on.—Oh, boy, aren't you going to do something about it?—And the boy, having cut it all out so that it won't grow again, has no other bright inspiration but to turn the brass tacks round, when lo, they become the brass-headed nails that go around Victorian plush furniture. And there they are, the hyper-modern two.

No, women don't change. They only go through a rather regular series of phases. They are first the slave; then the obedient helpmeet; then the respected spouse; then the noble matron; then the splendid woman and citizen; then the independent female; then the modern girl, oh, cut-it-out, boy! And when the boy has cut it all out, the mills of God grind on, and having nothing else to grind, they grind the cut-it-out girl down, down, down—back to—we don't know where—but probably to the slave once more, and the whole cycle starts afresh, on and on, till in the course of a thousand years or two we come once more to the really "modern" girl. Oh, cut it out, boy!

A lead-pencil has a point, an argument may have a point, remarks may be pointed, and a man who wants to borrow five pounds from you only comes to the point when he asks you for the fiver. Lots of things have points: especially weapons. But where is the point to life? Where is the point to love? Where, if it comes to the point, is the point to a bunch of violets? There is no point. Life and love are life and love, a bunch of violets is a bunch of violets, and to drag in the idea of a point is to ruin everything. Live and let live, love and let love, flower and fade, and follow the natural curve, which flows on, pointless.

Now women used to understand this better than men. Men, who were keen on weapons, which all have points, used to insist on putting points to life and love. But women used to know better. They used to know that life is a flow, a soft curving flow, a flowing together and a flowing apart and a flowing together again, in a long subtle motion that has no full-stops and no points, even if there are rough places. Women used to see themselves as a softly flowing stream of attraction and desire and beauty, soft quiet rivers of energy and peace. Then suddenly the idea changes. They see themselves as isolated things, independent females, instruments, instruments for love, instruments for work, instruments for politics, instruments for pleasure, this, that and the other. And as instruments they become pointed and they want everything, even a small child, even love itself, to have a point. When women start coming to the point, they don't hesitate. They pick a daisy, and they say: There must be a point to this daisy, and I'm going to get at it.—So they start pulling off the white petals, till there are none left. Then they pull away the yellow bits of the centre, and come to a mere green part, still without having come to the point. Then in disgust they tear the green base of the flower across, and say: I call that a fool flower. It had no point to it!

Life is not a question of points, but a question of flow. It's the *flow* that matters. If you come to think of it, a daisy even is like a little river flowing, that never for an instant stops. From the time when the tiny knob of a bud appears down among the leaves, during the slow rising up a stem, the slow swelling and pushing out the white petal-tips from the green, to the full round daisy, white and gold and gay, that opens and shuts through a few dawns, a few nights, poised on the summit of her stem, then silently shrivels and mysteriously disappears—there is no stop, no halt, it is a perpetual little streaming of a gay little life out into full radiance and delicate shrivelling, like a perfect little fountain that flows and flows, and shoots away at last into the invisible, even then without any stop.

So it is with life, and especially with love. There is no point. There is nothing you can cut out, except falsity, which isn't love or life. But the love itself is a flow, two little streams of feeling, one from the woman, one from the man, that flow and flow and never stop, and sometimes they twinkle with stars, sometimes they chafe, but still they flow on, intermingling; and if they rise to a floweriness like a daisy, that is part of the flow; and they will inevitably die down again, which is also part of a flow. And one relationship may produce many flowerinesses, as a daisy plant produces many daisies; but they will all die down again as the summer passes, though the green plant itself need not die. If flowers didn't fade they wouldn't be flowers, they'd be artificial things. But there are roots to faded flowers and in the root the flow continues and continues. And only the flow matters; live and let live, love and let love. There is no point to love.

Ownership

The question of the possession of property, I read somewhere lately, has now become a religious question. On the other hand, the religious people assert that the possession of property can never be a religious question, because in his religious soul a man is indifferent to property either way. I only care about property, money, possessions of any sort, when I have no religion in me. As soon as real religion enters, out goes my interest in the things of this world.

This, I consider, is hard lines on a man; since I must spend the best part of my day earning my living and acquiring a modicum of possession, I must acknowledge myself a religionless wretch most of my time: or else I must be a possessionless beggar and a parasite on industrious men.

There is something wrong with the arrangement. Work is supposed to be sacred, wages are slightly contemptible and mundane, and a savings bank account is distinctly irreligious, as far as pure religion goes. Where are we, quite?

No getting away from it, there is something rather mean about saving money. But still more fatal is the disaster of having no money at all, when you need it.

The trouble about this property business, money, possessions, is that we are most of us exceedingly and excruciatingly bored by it. Our fathers got a great thrill out of making money, building their own houses, providing for their old age and laying by something for their children. Children inherit their father's leavings; they never inherit their father's and mother's thrill; never more than the tail end of it: a point to which parents are consistently blind. If my father was thrilled by saving up, I shall be thrilled by blowing my last shilling. If my father gave all he had to the poor, I shall quite enjoy making things pleasant for my own little self. If my father wasted, I shall probably economize. Unless, of course, my father was a jolly waster.

But fathers for the last fifty years have been saving up, building their own houses, acquiring neat little properties, leaving small inheritances to their children, and preaching the sanctity of work. And they have pretty well worn it all out. The young don't believe in the sanctity of work, they are bored by the thought of saving up for their children. If they do build themselves a little house, they are tired of it in ten minutes. They want a car to run around in, and money to spend; but possessions, as possessions, are simply a bore to them. What's the fun owning things, anyway, unless you can do something with them?

So that the young are approaching the religious indifference to property, out of sheer boredom.

But being bored by property doesn't solve the problem. Because, no matter how bored you may be, you've got to live, and to do so you have to earn a living, and you have to own a certain amount of property. If you have wife and children, the earning and the property are a serious matter. So, many young men today drive themselves along in work and business, feeling a distinct inner boredom with it all, and bemoaning a thankless existence.

What's to be done about it? Why, nothing, all in a hurry. The thing to do is to face the situation. A young man today says to himself: I'm bored! I'm bored by making money slowly and meagrely, I'm bored at the thought of owning my own little bit. Why haven't I a maiden aunt who'll die and leave me a thousand a year? Why can't I marry a rich wife? Why doesn't somebody set me up for life? Why . . . ?

This seems to be peculiarly the attitude of the young Englishman. He truly doesn't want much, it's not riches he's after. All he wants, he says, is independence. By which he means, not real independence at all, but freedom from the bore of having to make a living.

To make a living was to our fathers and grandfathers an adventure; to us it is no more an adventure, it is a bore. And the situation is serious. Because, after all, it is change in feelings which makes changes in the world.

When it says in *The Times:* The question of the possession of property has now become a religious question—it does not mean that the question whether I shall own my little six-roomed house or not has become a religious question. It is a vague hint at national ownership. It is becoming a religious question with us now, whether the nation or whether private individuals shall own the land and the industries. This is what is hinted at.

And perhaps national or private ownership is indeed becoming a religious question. But if so, like the question of a man and his own little house, it is becoming religious not because of our passionate interest in it, but because of our deadly indifference. Religion must be indifferent to the question of ownership, and we are, *au fond*, indifferent. Most

men are inwardly utterly bored by the problem of individual ownership or national ownership; and therefore, at this point, they are inwardly utterly religious.

Ownership altogether has lost its point, its vitality. We are bored
by ownership, public or private, national or individual. Even though we
may hang on like grim death to what we've got, if somebody wants to
snatch it—and the instinct is perfectly normal and healthy—still, for
all that, we are inwardly bored by the whole business of ownership.
And the sooner we realize it, the better. It saves us from the bogey of
Bolshevism.

If we could come to a fair unanimity on this point—the point that
ownership is boring, making money is boring, earning a living is a
bore—then we could wriggle out of a lot of the boredom. Take the
land, for example. Nobody really wants it, when it comes to the point.
Neither does anybody really want the coal mines. Even the nation
doesn't want them. The men of the nation are fed stiff with mines and
land and wages.

Why not hand it all over to the women? To the women of Britain!
The modern excessive need of money is a female need. Why not hand
over to the women the means of making the money which they, the
women, mostly need? Men must admit themselves flummoxed. If we
handed over to the women the means of making money, perhaps there
might be a big drop in the feminine need of money. Which, after all, is
the straight road to salvation.

Master in His Own House

We still are ruled too much by ready-made phrases. Take, for example: A man must be master in his own house. There's a good old maxim; we all believe it in theory. Every little boy sees himself a future master in his own house. He grows up with the idea well fixed. So naturally, when his time comes and he finds, as he does pretty often, that he's *not* master in his own house, his nose is conventionally out of joint. He says: These overbearing modern women, they insist on bossing the show, and they're absolutely in the wrong.

What we have to beware of is mass thinking. The idea that a man must be master in his own house is just a mass idea. No man really thinks it for himself. He accepts it *en bloc*, as a member of the mass. He is born, so to speak, tightly swaddled up in it, like a lamb in its wool. In fact, we are born so woolly and swaddled up in mass ideas that we hardly get a chance to move, to make a real move of our own. We just bleat foolishly out of a mass of woolly cloud, our mass-ideas and we get no further. A man must be master in his own house. Feed the brute. An Englishman's home is his castle. Two servants are better than one. Happy is the bride who has her own little car in her own little garage. It is the duty of a husband to give his wife what she wants. It is the duty of a wife to say "Yes, darling!" to her husband; all these are mass ideas, often contradicting one another, but always effective. If you want to silence a man, or a woman, effectively, trot out a mass idea. The poor sheep is at once mum.

Now the thing to do with a mass idea is to individualize it. Instead of massively asserting: A man must be master in his own house, the gentleman in question should particularize and say: I, Jim, must be master in my own house, The Rosebud, or The Doves' Nest, over my wife, Julia.—And as soon as you make it personal, and drag it to earth, you will feel a qualm about it. You can storm over the breakfast coffee: A man must be master in his own house! But it takes much more courage to say: My name's Jim, and I must be master in this house, The Rosebud, over you, Julia, my spouse!—This is bringing things to an issue. And things are rarely so brought. The lord and master fumes with a mass idea, and the spouse and helpmeet fumes with a mass resentment, and their mingled fumings make a nice mess of The Rosebud.

As a matter of fact, when Jim begins to look into his own heart, and also to look The Rosebud, which is his own house, firmly in the eye, he finds—O shattering discovery!—that he has very little desire to be master in The Rosebud. On the contrary, the idea rather nauseates him. And when he looks at Julia calmly pouring the coffee, he finds, if he's the usual Jim, that his desire to be master over that young dame is curiously non-existent.

And there's the difference between a mass idea and real individual thinking. A man must be master in his own house. But Jim finds the idea of being master in The Rosebud rather feeble, and the idea of being master over the cool Julia somehow doesn't inspire him. He doesn't really care whether The Rosebud has pink bows on the curtains or not. And he doesn't care really what Julia does with her day, while he's away at his job. He wants her to amuse herself and not bother him.— That is, if he's the ordinary Jim.

So that man being master in his own house falls flat when the man is indifferent to his mastery. And that's the worst of mass ideas: they remain, like fossils, when the life that animated them is dead. The problem of a man being master in his own house is today no problem, really, because the man is helplessly indifferent about it. He feels mere indifference; only now and then he may spout up the mass idea, and make an unreal fume which does a lot of harm.

We may take it for granted, that wherever woman bosses the show, it is because man doesn't want to. It is not rapacity and pushing on the woman's part. It is indifference on the man's. Men don't really care. Wherever they *do* care, there is no question of the intrusion of women. Men really care still about engineering and mechanical pursuits, so there is very little intrusion of women there. But men are sadly indifferent to clerking pursuits, and journalistic pursuits, and even to parliamentary pursuits. So women flood in to fill the vacuums. If we get a House of Commons filled with women Members, it will be purely and simply for the reason that men, energetic men, are indifferent; they don't care any more about being Members of Parliament and making laws.

Indifference is a strange thing. It lies there under all the mass thinking and the mass activity, like a gap in the foundations. We still make a great fuss about Parliament—and underneath, most men are indifferent to Parliament. All the fuss about a home of your own and a wife of your own: and underneath, the men are only too often indifferent to the house and the wife both. They are only too willing for the wife to do the bossing and the caring, so that they need neither care nor boss.

Indifference is not the same as insouciance. Insouciance means not caring about things that don't concern you; it also means not being pinched by anxiety. But indifference is inability to care; it is the result of a certain deadness or numbness. And it is nearly always accompanied by the pinch of anxiety. Men who can't care any more, feel anxious about it. They have no insouciance. They are thankful if the woman will care. And at the same time they resent the women's caring and running the show.

The trouble is not in the women's bossiness, but in the men's indifference. This indifference is the real malady of the day. It is a deadness, an inability to care about anything. And it is always pinched by anxiety.

And whence does the indifference arise? It arises from having cared too much, from having cared about the wrong thing, in the immediate past. If there is a growing indifference to politics on the part of men, it is because men have cared far too much about politics. If Jim is really indifferent to his little home, The Rosebud, if he leaves it all to Julia, that is because his father and grandfather cared far too much about their little homes, made them a bit nauseating. If men don't care very vitally about their jobs, nowadays, and leave them to women, it is because our fathers and grandfathers considered the job sacrosanct—which it isn't—and so wore out the natural feeling for it, till it became repulsive.

Men leave the field to women, when men become inwardly indifferent to the field. What the women take over is really an abandoned battle. They don't pick up the tools and weapons of men till men let them drop.

And then men, gnawed by the anxiety of their own very indifference, blame women and start reiterating like parrots such mass ideas as: "Man must be master in his own house."

Matriarchy

Whether they are aware of it or not, the men of today are a little afraid of the women of today; and especially the younger men. They not only see themselves in the minority, overwhelmed by numbers, but they feel themselves swamped by the strange unloosed energy of the silk-legged hordes. Women, women everywhere, and all of them on the warpath! The poor young male keeps up a jaunty front, but his masculine soul quakes. Women, women everywhere, silk-legged hosts that are up and doing, and no gainsaying them. They settle like silky locusts on all the jobs, they occupy the offices and the playing-fields like immensely active ants, they buzz round the coloured lights of pleasure in amazing bare-armed swarms, and the rather dazed young male is, naturally, a bit scared. Tommy may not be scared of his own individual Elsie, but when he sees her with her scores of female "pals," let him bluff as he may, he is frightened.

Being frightened, he begins to announce: Man must be master again! —The *must* is all very well. Tommy may be master of his own little Elsie in the stronghold of his own little home. But when she sets off in the morning to her job, and joins the hosts of her petticoatless, silk-legged "pals," who is going to master her? Not Tommy!

It's not a question of petticoat rule. Petticoats no longer exist. The unsheathed silky legs of the modern female are petticoatless, and the modern young woman is not going to spend her life managing some little husband. She is not interested. And as soon as a problem ceases to contain interest, it ceases to be a problem. So that petticoat rule, which was such a problem for our fathers and grandfathers, is for us nothing. Elsie is not interested.

No, the modern young man is not afraid of being petticoat-ruled. His fear lies deeper. He is afraid of being swamped, turned into a mere accessory of bare-limbed, swooping woman; swamped by her numbers, swamped by her devouring energy. He talks rather bitterly about rule of women, monstrous regiment of women, and about matriarchy, and, rather feebly, about man being master again. He knows perfectly well that he will never be master again. John Knox could live to see the head of his monstrous regiment of women, and the head of Mary of Scotland, just chopped off. But you can't chop off the head of the modern woman. As leave try to chop the head off a swarm of locusts. Woman has emerged, and you can't put her back again. And she's not going back of her own accord, not if she knows it.

So we are in for the monstrous rule of women, and a matriarchy. A matriarchy! This seems the last word of horror to the shuddering male. What it means, exactly, is not defined. But it rings with the hollow sound of man's subordination to woman. Woman cracks the whip, and the poor trained dog of a man jumps through the hoop. Nightmare!

Matriarchy, according to the dictionary, means mother-rule. The mother the head of the family. The children inherit the mother's name. The property is bequeathed from mother to daughter, with a small allowance for the sons. The wife, no doubt, swears to love and cherish her husband, and the husband swears to honour and obey his spouse.— It doesn't sound so very different from what already is: except that when Tommy Smith marries Elsie Jones, he becomes Mr. Jones; quite right, too, nine cases out of ten.

And this is the matriarchy we are drifting into. No good trying to stem the tide. Woman is in flood.

But in this matter of matriarchy, let us not be abstract. Men and women will always be men and women. There is nothing new under the sun, not even matriarchy. Matriarchies have been and will be. And what about them, in living actuality?—It is said that in the ancient dawn of history there was nothing but matriarchy: children took the mother's name, belonged to the mother's clan, and the man was nameless. There is supposed to be a matriarchy today among the Berbers of the Sahara, and in Southern India, and one or two other rather dim places.

Yet, if you look at photographs of Berbers, the men look most jaunty and cocky, with their spears, and the terrible matriarchal women look as if they did most of the work. It seems to have been so in the remote past. Under the matriarchal system that preceded the patriarchal system of Father Abraham, the men seem to have been lively sports, hunting and dancing and fighting, while the women did the drudgery and minded the brats.

Courage! Perhaps a matriarchy isn't so bad, after all. A woman deserves to possess her own children and have them called by her name. As for the household furniture and the bit of money in the bank, it seems naturally hers.

Far from being a thing to dread, matriarchy is a solution to our weary social problem. Take the Pueblo Indians of the Arizona desert. They still have a sort of matriarchy. The man marries into the woman's clan, and passes into *her* family house. His corn supply goes to *her* tribe. His children are the children of *her* tribe, and take *her* name, so to speak. Everything that comes into the house is hers, *her* property. The man has no claim on the house, which belongs to her clan, nor to anything within the house. The Indian woman's home is *her* castle.

So! And what about the man, in this dread matriarchy? Is he the slave of the woman? By no means. Marriage, with him, is a secondary consideration, a minor event. His first duty is not to his wife and children—they belong to the clan. His first duty is to the tribe. The man is first and foremost an active, religious member of the tribe. Secondarily, he is son or husband or father.

The real life of the man is not spent in his own little home, daddy in the bosom of the family, wheeling the perambulator on Sundays. His life is passed mainly in the khiva, the great underground religious meeting-house where only the males assemble, where the sacred practices of the tribe are carried on; then also he is away hunting, or performing the sacred rites on the mountains, or he works in the fields. But he spends only certain months of the year in his wife's house, sleeping there. The rest he spends chiefly in the great khiva, where he sleeps and lives, along with the men, under the tuition of the old men of the tribe.

The Indian is profoundly religious. To him, life itself is religion: whether planting corn or reaping it, scalping an enemy or begetting a child; even washing his long black hair is a religious act. And he believes that only by the whole united effort of the tribe, day in, day out, year in, year out, in sheer religious attention and practice, can the tribe be kept vitally alive. Of course, the religion is pagan, savage, and to our idea unmoral. But religion it is, and it is his charge.

Then the children. When the boys reach the age of twelve or thirteen, they are taken from the mother and given into the charge of the old men. They live now in the khiva, or they are taken to the sacred camps on the mountains, to be initiated into manhood. Now their home is the khiva, the great sacred meeting-house underground. They may go and eat in their mother's house, but they live and sleep with the men.

And this is ancient matriarchy. And this is the instinctive form that society takes, even now. It seems to be a social instinct to send boys away to school at the age of thirteen, to be initiated into manhood. It is a social instinct in a man to leave his wife and children safe in the home, while he goes out and foregathers with other men, to fulfil his deeper social necessities. There is the club and the public-house, poor substitutes for the sacred khiva, no doubt, and yet absolutely necessary to most men. It is in the clubs and public-houses that men have really educated one another, by immediate contact, discussed politics and ideas, and made history. It is in the clubs and public-houses that men have tried to satisfy their deeper social instincts and intuitions. To satisfy his deeper social instincts and intuitions, a man must be able to get away from his family, and from women altogether, and foregather in the communion of men.

Of late years, however, the family has got hold of a man, and begun to destroy him. When a man is clutched by his family, his deeper social instincts and intuitions are all thwarted, he becomes a negative thing. Then the woman, perforce, becomes positive, and breaks loose into the world.

Let us drift back to matriarchy. Let the woman take the children and give them her name—it's a wise child that knows its own father. Let the woman take the property—what has a man to do with inheriting or bequeathing a grandfather's clock! Let the women form themselves into a great clan, for the preservation of themselves and their children. It is nothing but just.

And so, let men get free again, free from the tight littleness of family and family possessions. Give woman her full independence, and with it, the full responsibility of her independence. That is the only way to satisfy women once more: give them their full independence and full self-responsibility as mothers and heads of the family. When the children take the mother's name, the mother will look after the name all right.

And give the men a new foregathering ground, where they can meet and satisfy their deep social needs, profound social cravings which can only be satisfied apart from women. It is absolutely necessary to find some way of satisfying these ultimate social cravings in men, which are deep as religion in a man. It is necessary for the life of society, to keep us organically vital, to save us from the mess of industrial chaos and industrial revolt.

Cocksure Women and Hensure Men

It seems to me there are two aspects to women. There is the demure and the dauntless. Men have loved to dwell, in fiction at least, on the demure maiden whose inevitable reply is: Oh, yes, if you please, kind sir! The demure maiden, the demure spouse, the demure mother—this is still the ideal. A few maidens, mistresses and mothers *are* demure. A few pretend to be. But the vast majority are not. And they don't pretend to be. We don't expect a girl skilfully driving her car to be demure, we expect her to be dauntless. What good would demure and maidenly Members of Parliament be, inevitably responding: Oh, yes, if you please, kind sir!—Though of course there are masculine members of that kidney.—And a demure telephone girl? Or even a demure stenographer? Demureness, to be sure, is outwardly becoming, it is an outward mark of femininity, like bobbed hair. But it goes with inward dauntlessness. The girl who has got to make her way in life has got to be dauntless, and if she has a pretty, demure manner with it, then lucky girl. She kills two birds with two stones.

With the two kinds of femininity go two kinds of confidence: There are the women who are cocksure, and the women who are hensure. A really up-to-date woman is a cocksure woman. She doesn't have a doubt nor a qualm. She is the modern type. Whereas the old-fashioned demure woman was sure as a hen is sure, that is, without knowing anything about it. She went quietly and busily clucking around, laying the eggs and mothering the chickens in a kind of anxious dream that still was full of sureness. But not mental sureness. Her sureness was a physical condition, very soothing, but a condition out of which she could easily be startled or frightened.

It is quite amusing to see the two kinds of sureness in chickens. The cockerel is, naturally, cocksure. He crows because he is *certain* it is day. Then the hen peeps out from under her wing. He marches to the door of the hen-house and pokes out his head assertively: *Ah ha! daylight, of course, just as I said!*—and he majestically steps down the chicken ladder towards *terra firma*, knowing that the hens will step cautiously after him, drawn by his confidence. So after him, cautiously, step the hens. He crows again: *Ha-ha! here we are!*—It is indisputable, and the hens accept it entirely. He marches towards the house. From the house a person ought to appear, scattering corn. Why does the person not appear? The cock will see to it. He is cocksure. He gives a loud crow in the doorway, and the person appears. The hens are suitably impressed but immediately devote all their henny consciousness to the scattered corn, pecking absorbedly, while the cock runs and fusses, cocksure that he is responsible for it all.

So the day goes on. The cock finds a tit-bit, and loudly calls the hens. They scuffle up in henny surety, and gobble the tit-bit. But when they find a juicy morsel for themselves, they devour it in silence, hensure. Unless, of course, there are little chicks, when they most anxiously call the brood. But in her own dim surety, the hen is really much surer than the cock, in a different way. She marches off to lay her egg, she secures obstinately the nest she wants, she lays her egg at last, then steps forth again with prancing confidence, and gives that most assured of all sounds, the hensure cackle of a bird who has laid her egg. The cock, who is never so sure about anything as the hen is about the egg she has laid, immediately starts to cackle like the female of his species. He is pining to be hensure, for hensure is so much surer than cocksure.

Nevertheless, cocksure is boss. When the chicken-hawk appears in the sky, loud are the cockerel's calls of alarm. Then the hens scuffle under the verandah, the cock ruffles his feathers on guard. The hens are numb with fear, they say: Alas, there is no health in us! How wonderful to be a cock so bold!—And they huddle, numbed. But their very numbness is hensurety.

Just as the cock can cackle, however, as if he had laid the egg, so can the hen bird crow. She can more or less assume his cocksureness. And yet she is never so easy, cocksure, as she used to be when she was hensure. Cocksure, she is cocksure, but uneasy. Hensure, she trembles, but is easy.

It seems to me just the same in the vast human farmyard. Only nowadays all the cocks are cackling and pretending to lay eggs, and all the hens are crowing and pretending to call the sun out of bed. If women today are cocksure, men are hensure. Men are timid, tremulous, rather soft and submissive, easy in their very henlike tremulousness. They only want to be spoken to gently. So the women step forth with a good loud *cock-a-doodle-do!*

The tragedy about cocksure women is that they are more cocky, in their assurance, than the cock himself. They never realize that when the cock gives his loud crow in the morning, he listens acutely afterwards, to hear if some other wretch of a cock dare crow defiance, challenge. To the cock, there is always defiance, challenge, danger and death on the clear air; or the possibility thereof.

But alas, when the hen crows, she listens for no defiance or challenge. When she says *cock-a-doodle-do!* then it is unanswerable. The cock listens for an answer, alert. But the hen knows she is unanswerable. *Cock-a-doodle-do!* and there it is, take it or leave it!

And it is this that makes the cocksureness of women so dangerous, so devastating. It is really out of scheme, it is not in relation to the rest of things. So we have the tragedy of cocksure women. They find, so often, that instead of having laid an egg, they have laid a vote, or an empty ink-bottle, or some other absolutely unhatchable object, which means nothing to them.

It is the tragedy of the modern woman. She becomes cocksure, she puts all her passion and energy and years of her life into some effort or assertion, without ever listening for the denial which she ought to take into count. She is cocksure, but she is a hen all the time. Frightened of her own henny self, she rushes to mad lengths about votes, or welfare, or sports, or business: she is marvellous, out-manning the man. But alas, it is all fundamentally disconnected. It is all an attitude, and one day the attitude will become a weird cramp, a pain, and then it will collapse. And when it has collapsed, and she looks at the eggs she has laid, votes, or miles of typewriting, years of business efficiency—suddenly, because she is a hen and not a cock, all she has done will turn into pure nothingness to her. Suddenly it all falls out of relation to her basic henny self, and she realizes she has lost her life. The lovely henny surety, the hensureness which is the real bliss of every female, has been denied her: she had never had it. Having lived her life with such utmost strenuousness and cocksureness, she has missed her life altogether. Nothingness!

Is England Still a Man's Country?

They, that is men, Englishmen, get up and ask if England is still a man's country. The only answer is, it would be if there were any men in it. For what makes a man's country, do you imagine? Is it the landscape or the number of pubs or the rate of wages or the size of boots? Is it the fact that the women say: I obey you, my lord? If the men of England *feel* that England is no longer a man's country—for apparently it was so not long ago—then it isn't. And if it isn't a man's country, then what in heaven's name is it?

The men will say, it's a woman's country. The women will immediately reply: I *don't* think!—And so it's nobody's country. Poor England! The men say it's no longer a man's country, it has fallen into the hands of the women. The women give a shout of scorn, and say *Not half!*—and proceed to demonstrate that England would be a very different place if it *were* a woman's country—my word, a changed shop altogether. And between the two of them, men and women, Old England rubs her eyes and says: Where am I? What am I? Am I at all? In short, do I exist?—And there's never a man or a woman takes the trouble to answer, they're all so busy blaming one another.

If England is not a man's country, it isn't a woman's country either. That's obvious. Women didn't make England. And women don't run England today, in spite of the fact that nine-tenths of the voices on the telephone are female voices. Women today, wherever they are, show up; and they pipe up. They are heard and they are seen. No denying it. And it seems to get on the men's nerves. Quite! But that doesn't prove that the women own England and run England. They don't. They occupy, on the whole, rather inferior jobs, which they embellish with flowered voile and artificial silk stockings and a number of airs and graces, and they are apt to be a drain on a man's cigarettes. What then? Is this the cormorant devouring England, gobbling it up under the eyes of the squeaking herring-gulls of men? Do the men envy the women these rather inferior jobs? Or do they envy them the flowered voile and the silk stockings which decorate the jobs? Or is it the airs and graces they begrudge them, or the cigarettes?—that England is no more a man's country!

"When my father and my mother forsake me, then the Lord will take me up." I suppose that's how poor old England feels today. The men have certainly forsaken her. They pretend the women have usurped the land, so the men need do no more about it. Which is very comfortable for the men. Very soft and nice and comfortable. Which is what the men of today want. No responsibility.

Soft and nice and comfortable! Soft jobs, nice wives, comfortable homes—that is supposed to be England today. And Englishmen are quite startled if you suggest that it might require more to make a real England.—What more could England be, they say, than soft and nice and comfortable?—And then they blame the women for being hard and unkind and uncomfortable, and usurping England.

England, we are told, has always been a fighting country, though never a military country. That is a *cliché*. But it seems true. The Englishman hated being bossed or bullied. So he hated being a soldier or a marine, because as such he was bossed and bullied. And when he felt anything or anybody coming to boss or to bully him, he got up and prepared to place his fist in the eye of the boss and bully. Which is a real man's spirit, and the only spirit that makes a country a man's country.

Nowadays, alas, a change has come over all that. The Englishman only wants to be soft and nice and comfortable, and to have no real responsibility, not even for his own freedom and independence. He's got all the political freedom he can manage, and so he cares nothing about it. He even won't mind if it's taken from him again, after his forefathers fought so hard for it. He's got political freedom, so he cares nothing about it; which is a bit despicable, after all.

He's got political freedom, but he hasn't got economical freedom. There's the rub. And the modern man feels it not right. He feels he *ought* to have an income. A man's parents *ought* to leave him a sufficient independent income, and if they don't, he bears them a lifelong grudge.—And worse still, he has to do a job.

Now this is the disaster that has happened to almost every Englishman—he's got to do a job. All day long and every day, all his life, he is condemned to a job. There's no getting away from it. Very few men can inherit a fortune or marry a fortune. A job!—That is the great inevitable. That is the boss and the bully. That is the treadmill. The job! Men secretly and silently hate the job today. They push it over to the women. Then they loudly and openly abuse the women for having taken it. And they ask: Is England a man's country? Or is it nothing but a dog-gone women's show?

The answer is obvious. When a man wants a plum off a plum tree, he climbs up and gets it. But if he won't face the climb, and stands under the tree with his mouth open, waiting for the plum to fall into it; and if while he stands waiting, he sees a woman picking up a few plums that he wasn't smart enough even to pick up; and if he then begins to yell that the women have snatched away all the plums from the impoverished men, then what are we to think of him?

If men find they've got political freedom only to realize most disastrously their economic enslavement, they'd better do something about it. It's no good despising their political freedom—that is ridiculous, for political freedom is a supremely valuable thing. And it's no good blaming the women. Women, poor things, have to live, just as much as men do. It's no good whining that England is no more a man's country.

It will be a man's country the instant there are men in it. And men will be men the instant they tackle their insuperable difficulty. The insuperable difficulty, the unsolvable problem, are only insuperable and unsolvable because men can't make up their minds to tackle them. The insuperable difficulty to modern man is economic bondage. Slavery! Well, history is the long account of the abolishing of endless forms of slavery, none of which we ever want back again. Now we've got a new form of slavery. If every man who feels the burden of it determined ultimately to abolish it, using all his wits and powers and accepting no ready-made formula—then England would be a man's country, sure as eggs.

Dull London

It begins the moment you set foot ashore, the moment you step off the boat's gangway. The heart suddenly, yet vaguely, sinks. It is no lurch of fear. Quite the contrary. It is as if the life-urge failed, and the heart dimly sank. You trail past the benevolent policeman and the inoffensive passport officials, through the fussy and somehow foolish customs—we don't *really* think it matters if somebody smuggles in two pairs of false-silk stockings—and we get into the poky but inoffensive train, with poky but utterly inoffensive people, and we have a cup of inoffensive tea from a nice inoffensive boy, and we run through small, poky but nice and inoffensive country, till we are landed in the big but unexciting station of Victoria, when an inoffensive porter puts us into an inoffensive taxi and we are driven through the crowded yet strangely dull streets of London to the cosy yet strangely poky and dull place where we are going to stay. And the first half-hour in London, after some years abroad, is really a plunge of misery. The strange, the grey and uncanny, almost deathly sense of *dullness* is overwhelming. Of course, you get over it after a while, and admit that you exaggerated. You get into the rhythm of London again, and you tell yourself that it is *not* dull. And yet you are haunted, all the time, sleeping or waking, with the uncanny feeling: It is dull! It is all dull! This life here is one vast complex of dullness! I am dull! I am being dulled! My spirit is being dulled! My life is dulling down to London dullness.

This is the nightmare that haunts you the first few weeks of London. No doubt if you stay longer you get over it, and find London as thrilling as Paris or Rome or New York. But the climate is against me. I cannot stay long enough. With pinched and wondering gaze, the morning of departure, I look out of the taxi upon the strange dullness of London's arousing; a sort of death; and hope and life only return when I get my seat in the boat-train, and I hear all the Good-byes! Good-bye! Good-bye! Thank God to say Good-bye!

Now to feel like this about one's native land is terrible. I am sure I am an exceptional, or at least an exaggerated case. Yet it seems to me most of my fellow-countrymen have the pinched, slightly pathetic look in their faces, the vague, wondering realization: It is dull! It is always essentially dull! My life is dull!

Of course, England is the easiest country in the world, easy, easy and nice. Everybody is nice, and everybody is easy. The English people on the whole are surely the *nicest* people in the world, and everybody makes everything so easy for everybody else, and there is almost nothing to resist at all. But this very easiness and this very niceness become at last a nightmare. It is as if the whole air were impregnated with chloroform or some other pervasive anæsthetic, that makes everything easy and nice, and takes the edge off everything, whether nice or nasty. As you inhale the drug of easiness and niceness, your vitality begins to sink. Perhaps not your physical vitality, but something else: the vivid flame of your individual life. England can afford to be so free and individual because no individual flame of life is sharp and vivid. It is just mildly warm and safe. You couldn't burn your fingers at it. Nice, safe, easy: the whole ideal. And yet under all the easiness is a gnawing uneasiness, as in a drug-taker.

It used not to be so. Twenty years ago London was to me thrilling, thrilling, thrilling, the vast and roaring heart of all adventure. It was not only the heart of the world, it was the heart of the world's living adventure. How wonderful the Strand, the Bank, Charing Cross at night, Hyde Park in the morning!

True, I am now twenty years older. Yet I have not lost my sense of adventure. But now all the adventure seems to me crushed out of London. The traffic is too heavy! It used to be going somewhere, on an adventure. Now it only rolls massively and overwhelmingly, going nowhere, only dully and enormously *going*. There is no adventure at the end of the 'buses' journey. The 'bus lapses into an inertia of dullness, then dully starts again. The traffic of London used to roar with the mystery of man's adventure on the seas of life, like a vast sea-shell, murmuring a thrilling, half-comprehensible story. Now it booms like monotonous, far-off guns, in a monotony of crushing something, crushing the earth, crushing out life, crushing everything dead.

And what does one do, in London? I, not having a job to attend to, lounge round and gaze in bleak wonder on the ceaseless dullness. Or I have luncheons and dinners with friends, and talk. Now my deepest private dread of London is my dread of this talk. I spend most of my days abroad, saying little, or with a bit of chatter and a silence again. But in London I feel like a spider whose thread has been caught by somebody, and is being drawn out of him, so he must spin, spin, spin, and all to no purpose. He is not even spinning his own web, for his own reasons.

So it is in London, at luncheon, dinner or tea. I don't want to talk. I don't mean to talk. Yet the talk is drawn out of me, endlessly. And the others talk, endlessly also. It is ceaseless, it is intoxicating, it is the only real occupation of us who do not jazz. And it is purely futile. It is quite as bad as ever the Russians were: talk for talk's sake, without the very faintest intention of a result in action. Utter inaction and storms of talk. That again is London to me. And the sense of abject futility in it all only deepens the sense of abject dullness, so all there is to do is to go away.

Red Trousers

A man wrote to me, in answer to my article in which I complained of London dullness: "Dear Sir,—Have you ever paused to consider that the cause of our dullness is the cigarette? This is the tubular white ant which is sapping our civilization."

Now this man, at least, is not entirely dull. He is out on a crusade, a crusade against the "tubular white ant," from which he wants to rescue our holy civilization. And whatever else a crusader may be, he is not, to himself at least, dull. He is inspired with a mission, and on the march, which, perhaps, is better than sitting still and being inert.

But, after all, a crusade may turn out ultimately dull, like the crusade of Votes for Women, or teetotalism, or even the Salvation Army. When you've got the vote, it is dull. When people are merely teetotal, it is merely dull. When the Salvation Army has saved you, you may really feel duller than when you weren't saved. Or, of course, you may not.

So that there are two sides to a crusade. The good side is the activity. There was a thrill in the Votes for Women processions, even in the sight of suffragettes being marched off by stout and semi-indignant policemen. When I hear the tambourine clashing, and see the poke bonnets of the Salvation Army lasses and the funny scarlet of the men, and hear the piercing music of "Marching to Zion" or "Throw Out the Lifeline," then I am invariably thrilled. Here is a crusade, of a sort, here is spunk! And even in the denunciative "tubular white ants" of my correspondent there is a certain pep, a certain "go."

But the bad side of these crusades is the disillusion when the mission is fulfilled. Take the cigarette and dullness. Which causes which? Does dullness cause the cigarette, or the cigarette the dullness? Apparently it is a vicious circle: each causes the other. But at the very beginning, dullness causes the cigarette, after which the cigarette may cause more dullness, or may not, as the case may be. Anyhow, that is not my crusade, because it isn't really interesting.

What is really the point is that a crusade is a sovereign remedy against dullness, but you'd better watch out that the end of the crusade isn't a greater dullness still. Nothing is such fun as a crusade, it is the adventure of adventures. But it is no good setting out grandly to rescue some Zion from the clutch of the infidel, if you're not going to care a button about the Zion when you've rescued it.

That's the trouble with most of our modern crusades, like Votes or Socialism or politics, freedom of little nations, and the rest. In the flush of youth, I believed in Socialism, because I thought it would be thrilling and delightful. Now I no longer believe very deeply in Socialism, because I am afraid it might be dull, duller even than what we've got now. In the past, it seemed wildly thrilling to think of a free Poland, or a free Bohemia. Now we have a painful suspicion that free Czecho-Slovakia is possibly duller than when it was an Austrian province.

What we want is life, first and foremost: to live, and to know that we are living. And you can't have life without adventure of some sort. There are two sorts of adventure: the hair's-breadth escape sort, and the more inward sort. The hair's-breadth escape sort is nearly used up, though of course small boys still climb trees, and there is speeding on the roads, the traffic danger, aeroplanes, and the North Pole. But this is meagre, compared to the wild old days when the Turk held Jerusalem, and the world was flat.

What remains is the vast field of social adventure. In the ancient recipe, the three antidotes for dullness or boredom are sleep, drink, and travel. It is rather feeble. From sleep you wake up, from drink you become sober, and from travel you come home again. And then where are you? No, the two sovereign remedies for dullness are love or a crusade.

But love is a thing you can do nothing about. It's like the weather. Whereas a crusade can be carefully considered. When the Salvation Army march out with drum and brass to pitch a stand at the street corner, they are on a crusade, and full of adventure, though they run no risk except that of ridicule. Probably they get more out of life than those who ridicule them: and that's the chief point.

Yet, still, we can't all join the Salvation Army; there'd be nobody to save. And we sadly need a crusade. What are we going to do about it? Politics, Socialism, preaching of any sort: we feel there's not much in it. It is going to make greater dullness in the end. There is money, that is an adventure to a certain degree. But it is an adventure within definite limits, very definite limits. Besides, it is for his leisure that man needs a crusade.

Women, of course, are still thrilling in the last stages of their emancipation crusade. Votes, short skirts, unlimited leg, Eton crop, the cigarette, and see you damned first; these are the citadels captured by women, along with endless "jobs." Women, for a little while longer, have enough to thrill them in the triumphs of the emancipation crusade.

But the men, what are they going to do? The world of adventure is pretty well used up, especially for a man who has a wage to earn. He gets a little tired of being spoon-fed on wireless, cinema, and newspaper, sitting an inert lump while entertainment or information is poured into him. He wants to *do* something.

And what is there to be done? Thousands of things—and nothing. Golf, jazz, motoring—hobbies. But what we want is a crusade.

Find us a crusade. It is apparently impossible. There is no formula.

The thing to do is to decide that there is no crusade or holy war feasible at this moment and to treat life more as a joke, but a good joke, a jolly joke. That would freshen us up a lot. Our flippant world takes life with a stupid seriousness. Witness the serious mock-morality of the film and the wireless, the spurious earnestness poured out. What a bore!

It is time we treated life as a joke again, as they did in the really great periods like the Renaissance. Then the young men swaggered down the street with one leg bright red, one leg bright yellow, doublet of puce velvet and yellow feather in silk cap.

Now that is the line to take. Start with externals, and proceed to internals, and treat life as a good joke. If a dozen men would stroll down the Strand and Piccadilly tomorrow, wearing tight scarlet trousers fitting the leg, gay little orange-brown jackets and bright green hats, then the revolution against dullness which we need so much would have begun. And, of course, those dozen men would be considerably braver, really, than Captain Nobile or the other arctic venturers. It is not particularly brave to do something the public wants you to do. But it takes a lot of courage to sail gaily, in brave feathers, right in the teeth of a dreary convention.

The State of Funk

What is the matter with the English, that they are so scared of everything? They are in a state of blue funk, and they behave like a lot of mice when somebody stamps on the floor. They are terrified about money, finance, about ships, about war, about work, about Labour, about Bolshevism, and funniest of all, they are scared stiff of the printed word. Now this is a very strange and humiliating state of mind, in a people which has always been so dauntless. And, for the nation, it is a very dangerous state of mind. When a people falls into a state of funk, then God help it. Because mass funk leads some time or other to mass panic, and then—one can only repeat, God help us.

There is, of course, a certain excuse for fear. The time of change is upon us. The need for change has taken hold of us. We are changing, we have got to change, and we can no more help it than leaves can help going yellow and coming loose in autumn, or than bulbs can help shoving their little green spikes out of the ground in spring. We are changing, we are in the throes of change, and the change will be a great one. Instinctively, we feel it. Intuitively, we know it. And we are frightened. Because change hurts. And also, in the periods of serious transition, everything is uncertain, and living things are most vulnerable.

But what of it? Granted all the pains and dangers and uncertainties, there is no excuse for falling into a state of funk. If we come to think of it, every child that is begotten and born is a seed of change, a danger to its mother, at childbirth a great pain, and after birth, a new responsibility, a new change. If we feel in a state of funk about it, we should cease having children altogether. *If* we fall into a state of funk, indeed, the best thing is to have no children. But why fall into a state of funk?

Why not look things in the face like men, and like women? A woman who is going to have a child says to herself: Yes, I feel uncomfortable, sometimes I feel wretched, and I have a time of pain and danger ahead of me. But I have a good chance of coming through all right, especially if I am intelligent, and I bring a new life into the world. Somewhere I feel hopeful, even happy. So I must take the sour with the sweet. There is no birth without birth-pangs.

It is the business of men, of course, to take the same attitude towards the birth of new conditions, new ideas, new emotions. And sorry to say, most modern men don't. They fall into a state of funk. We all of us know that ahead of us lies a great social change, a great social readjustment. A few men look it in the face and try to realize what will be best. We none of us *know* what will be best. There is no ready-made solution. Ready-made solutions are almost the greatest danger of all. A change is a slow flux, which must happen bit by bit. And it must *happen*. You can't drive it like a steam engine. But all the time you can be alert and intelligent about it, and watch for the next step, and watch for the direction of the main trend. Patience, alertness, intelligence, and a human goodwill and fearlessness, that is what you want in a time of change. Not funk.

Now England is on the brink of great changes, radical changes. Within the next fifty years the whole framework of our social life will be altered, will be greatly modified. The old world of our grandfathers is disappearing like thawing snow, and is as likely to cause a flood. What the world of our grandchildren will be, fifty years hence, we don't know. But in its social form it will be very different from our world of today. We've got to change. And in our power to change, in our capacity to make new intelligent adaptation to new conditions, in our readiness to admit and fulfil new needs, to give expression to new desires and new feelings, lies our hope and our health. Courage is the great word. Funk spells sheer disaster.

There is a great change coming, bound to come. The whole money arrangement will undergo a change: what, I don't know. The whole industrial system will undergo a change. Work will be different and pay will be different. The owning of property will be different. Class will be different, and human relations will be modified and perhaps simplified. If we are intelligent, alert and undaunted, then life will be much better, more generous, more spontaneous, more vital, less basely materialistic. If we fall into a state of funk, impotence and persecution, then things may be very much worse than they are now. It is up to us. It is up to men to be men. While men are courageous and willing to change, nothing terribly bad can happen. But once men fall into a state of funk, with the inevitable accompaniment of bullying and repression, then only bad things can happen. To be firm is one thing. But bullying is another. And bullying of any sort whatsoever can have nothing but disastrous results. And when the mass falls into a state of funk, and you have mass bullying, then catastrophe is near.

Change in the whole social system is inevitable not merely because conditions change—though partly for that reason—but because people themselves change. We change, you and I, we change and change vitally, as the years go on. New feelings arise in us, old values depreciate, new values arise. Things we thought we wanted most intensely we realize we don't care about. The things we built our lives on crumble and disappear, and the process is painful. But it is not tragic. A tadpole that has so gaily waved its tail in the water must feel very sick when the tail begins to drop off and little legs begin to sprout. The tail was its dearest, gayest, most active member, all its little life was in its tail. And now the tail must go. It seems rough on the tadpole; but the little green frog in the grass is a new gem, after all.

As a novelist, I feel it is the change inside the individual which is my real concern. The great social change interests me and troubles me, but it is not my field. I know a change is coming—and I know we must have a more generous, more human system based on the life values and not on the money values. That I know. But what steps to take I don't know. Other men know better.

My field is to know the feelings inside a man, and to make new feelings conscious. What really torments civilized people is that they are full of feelings they know nothing about; they can't realize them, they can't fulfil them, they can't *live* them. And so they are tortured. It is like having energy you can't use—it destroys you. And feelings are a form of vital energy.

I am convinced that the majority of people today have good, generous feelings which they can never know, never experience, because of some fear, some repression. I do not believe that people would be villains, thieves, murderers and sexual criminals if they were freed from legal restraint. On the contrary, I think the vast majority would be much more generous, good-hearted and decent if they felt they dared be. I am convinced that people want to be more decent, more good-hearted than our social system of money and grab allows them to be. The awful fight for money, into which we are all forced, hurts our good nature more than we can bear. I am sure this is true of a vast number of people.

And the same is true of our sexual feelings; only worse. There, we start all wrong. Consciously, there is supposed to be no such thing as sex in the human being. As far as possible, we never speak of it, never mention it, never, if we can help it, even think of it. It is disturbing. It is—somehow—wrong.

The whole trouble with sex is that we daren't speak of it and think of it naturally. We are not secretly sexual villains. We are not secretly sexually depraved. We are just human beings with living sex. We are all right, if we had not this unaccountable and disastrous *fear* of sex. I know, when I was a lad of eighteen, I used to remember with shame and rage in the morning the sexual thoughts and desires I had had the night before. Shame, and rage, and terror lest anybody else should have to know. And I *hated* the self that I had been, the night before.

Most boys are like that, and it is, of course, utterly wrong. The boy that had excited sexual thoughts and feelings was the living, warm-hearted, passionate me. The boy that in the morning remembered these feelings with such fear, shame and rage was the social mental me: perhaps a little priggish, and certainly in a state of funk. But the two were divided against one another. A boy divided against himself; a girl divided against herself; a people divided against itself; it is a disastrous condition.

And it was a long time before I was able to say to myself: I am *not* going to be ashamed of my sexual thoughts and desires, they are me myself, they are part of my life. I am going to accept myself sexually as I accept myself mentally and spiritually, and know that I am one time one thing, one time another, but I am always myself. My sex is me as my mind is me, and nobody will make me feel shame about it.

It is long since I came to that decision. But I remember how much freer I felt, how much warmer and more sympathetic towards people. I had no longer anything to hide from them, no longer anything to be in a funk about, lest they should find it out. My sex was me, like my mind and my spirit. And the other man's sex was him, as his mind was him, and his spirit was him. And the woman's sex was her, as her mind and spirit were herself too. And once this quiet admission is made, it is wonderful how much deeper and more real the human sympathy flows. And it is wonderful how difficult the admission is to make, for man or woman: the tacit, natural admission, that allows the natural warm flow of the blood-sympathy, without repression and holding back.

I remember when I was a very young man I was enraged when with a woman, if I was reminded of her sexual actuality. I only wanted to be aware of her personality, her mind and spirit. The other had to be fiercely shut out. Some part of the natural sympathy for a woman had to be shut away, cut off. There was a mutilation in the relationship all the time.

Now, in spite of the hostility of society, I have learned a little better. Now I know that a woman is her sexual self too, and I can feel the normal sex sympathy with her. And this silent sympathy is utterly different from desire or anything rampant or lurid. If I can really sympathize with a woman in her sexual self, it is just a form of warmheartedness and compassionateness, the most natural life-flow in the world. And it may be a woman of seventy-five, or a child of two, it is the same. But our civilization, with its horrible fear and funk and repression and bullying, has almost destroyed the natural flow of common sympathy between men and men, and men and women.

And it is this that I want to restore into life: just the natural warm flow of common sympathy between man and man, man and woman. Many people hate it, of course. Many men hate it that one should tacitly take them for sexual, physical men instead of mere social and mental personalities. Many women hate it the same. Some, the worst, are in a state of rabid funk. The papers call me "lurid"; and a "dirty-minded fellow." One woman, evidently a woman of education and means, wrote to me out of the blue: "You, who are a mixture of the missing-link and the chimpanzee, etc."—and told me my name stank in men's nostrils: though, since she was Mrs. Something or other, she might have said women's nostrils.—And these people think they are being perfectly well-bred and perfectly "right." They are safe inside the convention, which also agrees that we are sexless creatures and social beings merely, cold and bossy and assertive, cowards safe inside a convention.

Now I am one of the least lurid mortals, and I don't at all mind being likened to a·chimpanzee. If there is one thing I don't like it is cheap and promiscuous sex. If there is one thing I insist on it is that sex is a delicate, vulnerable, vital thing that you mustn't fool with. If there is one thing I deplore it is heartless sex. Sex must be a real flow, a real flow of sympathy, generous and warm, and not a trick thing, or a moment's excitation, or a mere bit of bullying.

And if I write a book about the sex relations of a man and a woman, it is not because I want all men and women to begin having indiscriminate lovers and love affairs, off the reel. All this horrid scramble of love affairs and prostitution is only part of the funk, bravado and *doing it on purpose*. And bravado and *doing it on purpose* is just as unpleasant and hurtful as repression, just as much a sign of secret fear.

What you have to do is to get out of the state of funk, sex funk. And to do so, you've got to be perfectly decent, and you have to accept sex fully in the consciousness. Accept sex in the consciousness, and let the normal physical awareness come back, between you and other people. Be tacitly and simply aware of the sexual being in every man and woman, child and animal; and unless the man or woman is a bully, be sympathetically aware. It is the most important thing just now, this gentle physical awareness. It keeps us tender and alive at a moment when the great danger is to go brittle, hard, and in some way dead.

Accept the sexual, physical being of yourself, and of every other creature. Don't be afraid of it. Don't be afraid of the physical functions. Don't be afraid of the so-called obscene words. There is nothing wrong with the words. It is your fear that makes them bad, your needless fear. It is your fear which cuts you off physically even from your nearest and dearest. And when men and women are physically cut off, they become at last dangerous, bullying, cruel. Conquer the fear of sex, and restore the natural flow. Restore even the so-called obscene words, which are part of the natural flow. If you don't, if you don't put back a bit of the old warmth into life, there is savage disaster ahead.

The Risen Lord

> The risen lord, the risen lord
> has risen in the flesh,
> and treads the earth to feel the soil
> though his feet are still nesh.*

The Churches loudly assert: We preach Christ crucified!—But in so doing, they preach only half of the Passion, and do only half their duty. The Creed says: "Was crucified, dead, and buried . . . the third day He rose again from the dead." And again, "I believe in the resurrection of the body . . ." So that to preach Christ Crucified is to preach half the truth. It is the business of the Church to preach Christ born among men—which is Christmas; Christ crucified, which is Good Friday; and Christ Risen, which is Easter. And after Easter, till November and All Saints, and till Annunciation, the year belongs to the Risen Lord: that is, all the full-flowering spring, all summer, and the autumn of wheat and fruit, all belong to Christ Risen.

But the Churches insist on Christ Crucified, and rob us of the blossom and fruit of the year. The Catholic Church, which has given us our images, has given us the Christ-child, in the lap of woman, and again, Christ Crucified: then the Mass, the mystery of atonement through sacrifice. Yet all this is really preparatory, these are the preparatory stages of the real living religion. The Christ-child, enthroned in the lap of the Mother, is obviously only a preparatory image, to prepare us for Christ the Man. Yet a vast mass of Christians stick there.

What we have to remember is that the great religious images are only images of our own experiences, or of our own state of mind and soul. In the Catholic countries, where the Madonna-and-Child image overwhelms everything else, the man visions himself all the time as a child, a Christ-child, standing on the lap of a virgin mother. Before the war, if an Italian hurt himself, or suddenly fell into distress, his immediate cry was: *O mamma mia! mamma mia!—Oh, mother, mother!—*The same was true of many Englishmen. And what does this mean? It means that the man sees himself as a child, the innocent saviour-child enthroned on the lap of the all-pitying virgin mother. He lives

* Nesh, now *dialect*, meaning tender, sensitive. Eds.

according to this image of himself—the image of the guileless "good" child sheltered in the arms of an all-sheltering mother—until the image breaks in his heart.

And during the war, this image broke in the hearts of most men, though not in the hearts of their women. During the war, the man who suffered most bitterly suffered beyond the help of wife or mother, and no wife nor mother nor sister nor any beloved could save him from the guns. This fact went home in his heart, and broke the image of mother and Christ-child, and left in its place the image of Christ crucified.

It was not so, of course, for the woman. The image did not break for her. She visioned herself still as the all-pitying, all-sheltering Madonna, on whose lap the man was enthroned, as in the old pictures, like a Christ-child. And naturally the woman did not want to abandon this vision of herself. It gave her her greatest significance; and the greatest power. Break the image, and her significance and her power were gone. But the men came back from the war and denied the image —for them it was broken. So she fought to maintain it, the great vision of man, the Christ-child, enthroned in the lap of the all-pitying virginal woman. And she fought in vain, though not without disastrous result.

For the vision of the all-pitying and all-helpful Madonna was shattered in the hearts of men, during the war. The all-pitying and all-helpful Woman actually did not, whether she could or not, prevent the guns from blowing to pieces the men who called upon her. So her image collapsed, and with it the image of the Christ-child. For the man who went through the war the resultant image inevitably was Christ Crucified, Christ tortured on the Cross. And Christ Crucified is essentially womanless.

True, many of the elderly men who never went through the war still insist on the Christ-child business, and most of the elderly women insist on their benevolent Madonna supremacy. But it is in vain. The guns broke the image in the hearts of middle-aged men, and the young were born, or are come to real consciousness, after the image was already smashed.

So there we are! We have three great image-divisions among men and women today. We have the old and the elderly, who never were exposed to the guns, still fatuously maintaining that man is the Christ-child and woman the infallible safeguard from all evil and all danger. It is fatuous, because it absolutely didn't work. Then we have the men of middle age, who were all tortured and virtually put to death by the war. They accept Christ Crucified as their image, are essentially womanless, and take the great cry: *Consummatum est!—It is finished!*

—as their last word.—Thirdly, we have the young, who never went through the war. They have no illusions about it, however, and the death-cry of their elder generation: *It is finished!* rings cold through their blood. They cannot answer. They cannot even scoff. It is no joke, and never will be a joke.

And yet, neither of the great images is *their* image. They cannot accept the child-and-mother position which the old buffers still pose in. They cannot accept the Christ Crucified finality of the generations immediately ahead. For they, the young, came into the field of life after the death-cry *Consummatum est!* had rung through the world, and while the body, so to speak, was being put into the tomb. By the time the young came on to the stage, Calvary was empty, the tombs were closed, the women had lost for ever the Christ-child and the virgin savour, and it was altogether the day after, cold, bleak, empty, blank, meaningless, almost silly.

The young came into life, and found everything finished. Everywhere the empty crosses, everywhere the closed tombs, everywhere the man-less, bitter or over-assertive woman, everywhere the closed grey disillusion of Christ Crucified, dead, and buried, those grey empty days between Good Friday and Easter.

And the Churches, instead of preaching the Risen Lord, go on preaching the Christ-child and Christ Crucified. Now man cannot live without some vision of himself. But still less can he live with a vision that is not true to his inner experience and inner feeling. And the vision of Christ-child and Christ Crucified are both untrue to the inner experience and feeling of the young. They don't feel that way. They show the greatest forbearance and tolerance of their elders, for whom the two images *are* livingly true. But for the post-war young, neither the Christ-child nor Christ Crucified means much.

I doubt whether the Protestant Churches, which supported the war, will ever have the faith and the power of life to take the great step onwards, and preach Christ Risen. The Catholic Church might. In the countries of the Mediterranean, Easter has always been the greatest of the holy days, the gladdest and holiest, not Christmas, the birth of the Child. Easter, Christ Risen, the Risen Lord, this, to the old faith, is still the first day in the year. The Easter festivities are the most joyful, the Easter processions the finest, the Easter ceremonies the most splendid. In Sicily the women take into church the saucers of growing corn, the green blades rising tender and slim like green light, in little pools, filling round the altar. It is Adonis. It is the re-born year. It is Christ Risen. It is the Risen Lord. And in the warm south still a great joy floods the hearts of the people on Easter Sunday. They feel it, they feel it everywhere. The Lord is risen. The Lord of the rising wheat and the plum blossoms is warm and kind upon earth again, after having been done to death by the evil and the jealous ones.

The Roman Catholic Church may still unfold this part of the Passion fully, and make men happy again. For Resurrection is indeed the consummation of all the passion. Not even Atonement, the being at one with Christ through partaking in His sacrifice, consummates the Passion finally. For even after Atonement men still must live, and must go forward with the vision. After we share in the body of Christ, we rise with Him in the body. And that is the final vision that has been blurred to all the Churches.

Christ risen in the flesh! We must accept the image complete, if we accept it at all. We must take the mystery in its fulness and in fact. It is only the image of our own experience. Christ rises, when He rises from the dead, in the flesh, not merely as spirit. He rises with hands and feet, as Thomas knew for certain: and if with hands and feet, then with lips and stomach and genitals of a man. Christ risen, and risen in the whole of His flesh, not with some left out.

Christ risen in the full flesh! What for? It is here the gospels are all vague and faltering, and the Churches leave us in the lurch. Christ risen in the flesh in order to lurk obscurely for six weeks on earth, then be taken vaguely up into heaven in a cloud? Flesh, solid flesh, feet and bowels and teeth and eyes of a man, taken up into heaven in a cloud, and never put down again?

It is the only part of the great mystery which is all wrong. The virgin birth, the baptism, the temptation, the teaching, Gethsemane, the betrayal, the crucifixion, the burial and the resurrection, these are all true according to our inward experience. They are what men and women go through, in their different ways. But floated up into heaven as flesh-and-blood, and never set down again—this nothing in all our experience will ever confirm. If aeroplanes take us up, they bring us down, or let us down. Flesh and blood belong to the earth, and only to the earth. We know it.

And Jesus was risen flesh-and-blood. He rose a man on earth to live on earth. The greatest test was still before Him: His life as a man on earth. Hitherto He had been a sacred child, a teacher, a messiah, but never a full man. Now, risen from the dead, He rises to be a man on earth, and live His life of the flesh, the great life, among other men. This is the image of our inward state today.

This is the image of the young: the Risen Lord. The teaching is over, the crucifixion is over, the sacrifice is made, the salvation is accomplished. Now comes the true life, man living his full life on earth, as flowers live their full life, without rhyme or reason except the magnificence of coming forth into fulness.

If Jesus rose from the dead in triumph, a man on earth triumphant in renewed flesh, triumphant over the mechanical anti-life convention of Jewish priests, Roman despotism, and universal money-lust; triumphant above all over His own self-absorption, self-consciousness, self-importance; triumphant and free as a man in full flesh and full, final experience, even the accomplished acceptance of His own death; a man at last full and free in flesh and soul, a man at one with death: then He rose to become at one with life, to live the great life of the flesh and the soul together, as peonies or foxes do, in their lesser way. If Jesus rose as a full man, in full flesh and soul, then He rose to take a woman to Himself, to live with her, and to know the tenderness and blossoming of the twoness with her; He who had been hitherto so limited to His oneness, or His universality, which is the same thing. If Jesus rose in the full flesh, He rose to know the tenderness of a woman, and the great pleasure of her, and to have children by her. He rose to know the responsibility and the peculiar delight of children, and also the exasperation and nuisance of them. If Jesus rose as a full man, in the flesh, He rose to have friends, to have a man-friend whom He would hold sometimes to His breast, in strong affection, and who would be dearer to Him than a brother, just out of the sheer mystery of sympathy. And how much more wonderful, this, than having disciples! If Jesus rose a full man in the flesh, He rose to do His share in the world's work, something He really liked doing. And if He remembered His first life, it would neither be teaching nor preaching, but probably carpentering again, with joy, among the shavings. If Jesus rose a full man in the flesh, He rose to continue His fight with the hard-boiled conventionalists like Roman judges and Jewish priests and money-makers of every sort. But this time, it would no longer be the fight of self-sacrifice that would end in crucifixion. This time it would be a freed man fighting to shelter the rose of life from being trampled on by the pigs. This time, if Satan attempted temptation in the wilderness, the Risen Lord would answer: Satan, your silly temptations no longer tempt me. Luckily, I have died to that sort of self-importance and self-conceit. But let me tell you something, old man! Your name's Satan, isn't it? And your name is Mammon? You are the selfish hog that's got hold of all the world, aren't you? Well, look here, my boy, I'm going to take it all from you, so don't worry. The world and the power and the riches thereof, I'm going to take them all from you, Satan or Mammon or whatever your name is. Because you don't know how to use them. The earth is the Lord's, and the fulness thereof, and it's going to be. Men have risen from the dead and learned not to be so greedy and self-important. We left most of that behind in the late tomb. Men have risen beyond you, Mammon, they are your risen lords. And so, you hook-nosed, glisten-eyed, ugly, money-smelling anachronism, you've got to get out. Men have not died and risen again for nothing. Whom do you think the earth belongs to, you stale old rat? The earth is the Lord's and is given to the men who have died and had the power to rise again. The earth is given to the men who have risen from the dead, risen, you old grabber, and when did you ever rise? Never! So go you down to oblivion, and give your place to the risen men, and the women of the risen men. For man has been dispossessed of the full earth and the earth's fulness long enough. And the poor women, they have been shoved about manless and meaningless long enough. The earth is the Lord's and the fulness thereof, and I, the Risen Lord, am here to take possession. For now I am fully a man, and free above all from my own self-importance. I want life, and the pure contact with life. What are riches, and glory, and honour, and might, and power, to me who have died and lost my self-importance? That's why I am going to take them all from you, Mammon, because I care nothing about them. I am going to destroy all your values, Mammon; all your money values and conceit values, I am going to destroy them all.

Because only life is lovely, and you, Mammon, prevent life. I love to see a squirrel peep round a tree; and left to you, Mammon, there will soon be no squirrels to peep. I love to hear a man singing a song to himself, and if it is an old, improper song, about the fun between lads and girls, I like it all the better. But you, beastly mealy-mouthed Mammon, you would arrest any lad that sings a gay song. I love the movement of life, and the beauty of life, O Mammon, since I am risen, I love the beauty of life intensely; columbine flowers, for example, the way they dangle, or the delicate way a young girl sits and wonders, or the rage with which a man turns and kicks a fool dog that suddenly attacks him—beautiful that, the swift fierce turn and lunge of a kick, then the quivering pause for the next attack; or even the slightly silly glow that comes over some men as they are getting tipsy—it still is a glow, beautiful; or the swift look a woman fetches me, when she would really like me to go off with her, but she is troubled; or the real compassion I saw a woman express for a man who slipped and wrenched his foot: life, the beauty, the beauty of life! But that which is anti-life,

Mammon, like you, and money, and machines, and prostitution, and all that tangled mass of self-importance and greediness and self-conscious conceit which adds up to Mammon, I hate it. I hate it, Mammon, I hate you and am going to push you off the face of the earth, Mammon, you great mob-thing, fatal to men.

Enslaved by Civilization

The one thing men have not learned to do is to stick up for their own instinctive feelings, against the things they are taught. The trouble is, we are all caught young. Little boys are trundled off to school at the age of five, and immediately the game begins, the game of enslaving the small chap. He is delivered over into the hands of schoolmistresses, young maids, middle-aged maids, and old maids, and they pounce on him, and with absolute confidence in their own powers, their own *rightness*, and their own superiority, they begin to "form" the poor little devil. Nobody questions for a moment the powers of these women to mould the life of a young man. The Jesuits say: Give me a child till he is seven, and I will answer for him for the rest of his life.—Well, schoolmistresses are not as clever as Jesuits, and certainly not as clear as to what they are about, but they do the trick, nevertheless. They make the little boy into an incipient man, the man of today.

Now I ask you, do you really think that schoolmistresses are qualified to form the foundations of a *man*? They are almost all excellent women, and filled with the best of motives. And they have all passed some little exam. or other. But what, in the name of heaven, qualifies them to be the makers of men? They are all maids: young maids, middling maids, or old maids. They none of them know anything about men: that is to say, they are not *supposed* to know anything about men. What knowledge they have must be surreptitious. They certainly know nothing about manhood. Manhood, in the eyes of the school-mistress, and especially the elderly schoolmistress, is something un-called-for and unpleasant. Men, in the pleasant opinions of school-mistresses, are mostly grown-up babies. Haven't the babies all been through the mistress's hands, and aren't the men almost identically the same?

Well, it may be so! It may be that men nowadays are all grown-up babies. But if they are, it is because they were delivered over in their tenderest years, poor little devils, to absolute petticoat rule; mothers first, then schoolmistresses. But the mother very quickly yields to the schoolmistress. It is amazing what reverence ordinary women have for the excellent old-maid mistress of the infants' school. What the mistress says is gospel. Kings are no more kings by divine right, but queens are queens and mistresses, mistresses straight from God. It is amazing. It is fetish-worship. And the fetish is goodness.

"Oh, but Miss Teacher is so *good*, she's awfully *good*," say the approving mothers, in luscious voices. "Now, Johnny, you must mind what Miss Teacher says, she knows what is best for you. You must always listen to her!"

Poor Johnny, poor little devil! On the very first day it is: "Now, Johnny dear, you must sit like a good little boy, like all the other good little boys." And when he can't stand it, it is: "Oh, Johnny dear, I wouldn't cry if I were you. Look at all the other good little boys, they don't cry, do they, dear? Be a good little boy, and teacher will give you a teddy-bear to play with. Would Johnny like a teddy-bear to play with? There, don't cry! Look at all the other good little boys. They are learning to write—to write! Wouldn't Johnny like to be a good little boy, and learn to write?"

As a matter of fact, Johnny wouldn't. At the bottom of his heart, he doesn't in the least want to be a good little boy and learn to write. But she comes it over him. Dear teacher, she starts him off in the way he must go, poor little slave. And once started, he goes on wheels, being a good little boy like all the other good little boys. School is a very elaborate railway system where good little boys are taught to run upon good lines till they are shunted off into life, at the age of fourteen, sixteen, or whatever it is. And by that age the running-on-lines habit it absolutely fixed. The good big boy merely turns off one set of rails on to another. And it is so easy, running on rails; he never realizes that he is a slave to the rails he runs on. Good boy!

Now the funny thing is that nobody, not even the most conscientious father, ever questions the absolute rightness of these school-marms. It is all for dear little Johnny's own good. And these school-marms know absolutely what Johnny's own good is. It is being a good little boy like all the other good little boys.

But to be a good little boy like all the other good little boys is to be at last a slave, or at least an automaton, running on wheels. It means that dear little Johnny is going to have all his own individual manhood nipped out of him, carefully plucked out, every time it shows a little peep. Nothing is more insidiously clever than an old maid's fingers at picking off the little shoots of manhood as they sprout out from a growing boy, and turning him into that neutral object, a good little boy. It is a subtle, loving form of mutilation, and mothers absolutely believe in it. "Oh, but I *want* him to be a good boy!" She fails to remember how bored she gets with her good-boy husband. Good boys are very nice to mothers and schoolmistresses. But as men, they make a wishy-washy nation.

Of course, nobody wants Johnny to be a bad little boy. One would like him to be just a boy, with no adjective at all. But that is impossible. At the very best schools, where there is most "freedom," the subtle, silent *compulsion* towards goodness is perhaps strongest. Children are all silently, steadily, relentlessly bullied into being good. They grow up good. And then they are no good.

For what does goodness mean? It means, in the end, being like everybody else, and not having a soul to call your own. Certainly you mustn't have a feeling to call your own. You must be good, and feel exactly what is expected of you, which is just what other people feel. Which means that in the end you feel nothing at all, all your feeling has been killed out of you. And all that is left is the artificial stock emotion which comes out with the morning papers.

I think I belong to the first generation of Englishmen that was really broken in. My father's generation, at least among the miners where I was brought up, was still wild. But then my father had never been to anything more serious than a dame's school, and the dame, Miss Hight,* had never succeeded in making him a good little boy. She had barely succeeded in making him able to write his name. As for his feelings, they had escaped her clutches entirely: as they escaped the clutches of his mother. The country was still open. He fled away from the women and rackapelted with his own gang. And to the end of his days his idea of life was to escape over the fringe of virtue and drink beer and perhaps poach an occasional rabbit.

But the boys of my generation were caught in time. We were sent at the ripe age of five to Board-schools, British schools, national schools, and though there was far less of the Johnny dear business, and no teddy-bear, we were forced to knuckle under. We were forced on to the rails. I went to the Board-school. Most of us, practically all, were miners' sons. The bulk were going to be miners themselves. And we all hated school.

I shall never forget the anguish with which I wept the first day. I was captured. I was roped in. The other boys felt the same. They hated school because they felt captives there. They hated the masters because they felt them as jailers. They hated even learning to read and write. The endless refrain was: "When I go down pit you'll see what ——

* Her name was actually Miss Eyte. Eds.

sums I'll do." That was what they waited for: to go down pit, to escape, to be men. To escape into the wild warrens of the pit, to get off the narrow lines of school.

The schoolmaster was an excellent, irascible old man with a white beard. My mother had the greatest respect for him. I remember he flew into a rage with me because I did not want to admit my first name, which is David. "David! David!" he raved. "David is the name of a great and good man. You don't like the name of David? You don't like the name of David!" He was purple with indignation. But I had an unreasonable dislike of the name David, and still have, and he couldn't force me into liking it. But he wanted to.

And there it was. David was the name of a great and good man, so I was to be *forced* to like it. If my first name had been Ananias or Ahab, I should have been excused. But David! no! My father, luckily, didn't know the difference between David and Davy of the safety-lamp.

But the old schoolmaster gradually got us under. There were occasional violent thrashings. But what really did the trick was not the thrashing, but the steady, persistent pressure of: Honest, decent lads behave in my way, and no other.—And he got the lads under. Because he was so absolutely sure he was right, and because mothers and fathers all agreed he was right, he managed pretty well to tame the uncouth colliery lads during the six or seven years he was responsible for them. They were the first generation to be really tamed.

With what result? They went down pit, but even pit was no more the happy subterranean warren it used to be. Down pit everything was made to run on lines, too, new lines, up-to-date lines; and the men became ever less men, more mere instruments. They married, and they made what the women of my mother's generation always prayed for, good husbands. But as soon as the men were good husbands, the women were a tiresome, difficult, unsatisfied lot of wives, so there you are! Without knowing it, they missed the old wildness, and were bored.

The last time I was back in the Midlands was during the great coal strike. The men of my age, the men just over forty, were there, standing derelict, pale, silent, with nothing to say, nothing to do, nothing to feel, and great hideous policemen from God-knows-where waiting in gangs to keep them on the lines. Alas, there was no need. The men of my generation were broken in; they'll stay on the lines and rust there. For wives, schoolmasters and employers of labour it is perhaps very nice to have men well broken in. But for a nation, for England, it is a disaster.

Men Must Work and Women as Well

Supposing that circumstances go on pretty much in the same way they're going on in now, then men and women will go on pretty much in the same way they are now going on in. There is always an element of change, we know. But change is of two sorts: the next step, or a jump in another direction. The next step is called progress. If our society continues its course of gay progress along the given lines, then men and women will do the same: always along the given lines.

So what is important in that case is not so much men and women, but the given lines. The railway train doesn't matter particularly in itself. What matters is where it is going to. If I want to go to Crewe, then a train to Bedford is supremely uninteresting to me, no matter how full it may be. It will only arouse a secondary and temporal interest if it happens to have an accident.

And there you are with men and women today. They are not particularly interesting, and they are not, in themselves, particularly important. All the thousands and millions of bowler hats and neat handbags that go bobbing to business every day may represent so many immortal souls, but somehow we feel that is not for us to say. The clergyman is paid to tickle our vanity in these matters. What all the bowler hats and neat handbags represent to you and me and to each other is business, my dear, and a job.

So that, granted the present stream of progress towards better business and better jobs continues, the point is, not to consider the men and women bobbing in the stream, any more than you consider the drops of water in the Thames—but where the stream is flowing. Where is the stream flowing, indeed, the stream of progress? Everybody hopes, of course, it is flowing towards bigger business and better jobs. And what does that mean, again, to the man under the bowler hat and the woman who clutches the satchel?

It means, of course, more money, more congenial labours, and fewer hours. It means freedom from all irksome tasks. It means, apart from the few necessary hours of highly paid and congenial labour, that men and women shall have nothing to do except enjoy themselves. No beastly housework for the women, no beastly homework for the men. Free! free to enjoy themselves. More films, more motor-cars, more dances, more golf, more tennis and more getting completely away from yourself. And the goal of life is enjoyment.

Now if men and women want these things with sufficient intensity, they may really get them, and go on getting them. While the game is worth the candle, men and women will go on playing the game. And it seems today as if the motor-car, the film, the radio and the jazz were worth the candle. This being so, progress will continue from business to bigger business, and from job to better job. This is, in very simple terms, the plan of the universe laid down by the great magnates of industry like Mr. Ford. And they know what they are talking about.

But—and the "but" is a very big one—it is not easy to turn business into bigger business, and it is sometimes *impossible* to turn uncongenial jobs into congenial ones. This is where science really leaves us in the lurch, and calculation collapses. Perhaps in Mr. Ford's super-factory of motor-cars all jobs may be made abstract and congenial. But the woman whose cook falls foul of the kitchen range, heated with coal, every day, hates that coal range herself even more darkly than the cook hates it. Yet many housewives can't afford electric cooking. And if everyone could, it still doesn't make housework entirely congenial. All the inventions of modern science fail to make housework anything but uncongenial to the modern woman, be she mistress or servantmaid. Now the only decent way to get something done is to get it done by somebody who quite likes doing it. In the past, cooks really enjoyed cooking and housemaids enjoyed scrubbing. Those days are over; like master, like man, and still more so, like mistress, like maid. Mistress loathes scrubbing; in two generations, maid loathes scrubbing. But scrubbing must be done. At what price?—raise the price. The price is raised, the scrubbing goes a little better. But after a while, the loathing of scrubbing becomes again paramount in the kitchenmaid's breast, and then ensues a general state of tension, and a general outcry: Is it worth it? Is it really worth it?

What applies to scrubbing applies to all labour that cannot be mechanized or abstracted. A girl will slave over shorthand and typing for a pittance because it is not muscular work. A girl will not do housework well, not for a good wage. Why? Because, for some mysterious or obvious reason, the modern woman and the modern man hate physical work. Ask your husband to peel the potatoes, and earn his deep resentment. Ask your wife to wash your socks, and earn the same. There is still a certain thrill about "mental" and purely mechanical work like attending a machine. But actual labour has become to us, with our education, abhorrent.

And it is here that science has not kept pace with human demand. It is here that progress is fatally threatened. There is an enormous, insistent demand on the part of the human being that mere labour, such as scrubbing, hewing and loading coal, navvying, the crude work that is the basis of all labour, shall be done away with. Even washing dishes. Science hasn't even learned how to wash dishes for us yet. The mistress who feels so intensely bitter about her maid who will not wash the dishes properly does so because she herself so loathes washing them. Science has rather left us in the lurch in these humble but basic matters. Before babies are conveniently bred in bottles, let the scientist find a *hey presto!* trick for turning dirty teacups into clean ones; since it is upon science we depend for our continued progress.

Progress, then, which proceeds so smoothly, and depends on science, does not proceed as rapidly as human feelings change. Beef-steaks are beef-steaks still, though all except the eating is horrible to us. A great deal must be done about a beef-steak besides the eating of it. And this great deal is done, we have to face the fact, unwillingly. When the mistress loathes trimming and grilling a beef-steak, or paring potatoes, or wringing the washing, the maid will likewise loathe these things, and do them at last unwillingly, and with a certain amount of resentment.

The one thing we don't sufficiently consider, in considering the march of human progress, is also the very dangerous march of human feeling that goes on at the same time and not always parallel. The change in human feeling! And one of the greatest changes that has ever taken place in man and woman is this revulsion from physical effort, physical labour and physical contact, which has taken place within the last thirty years. This change hits woman even harder than man, for she has always had to keep the immediate physical side going. And now it is repellent to her—just as nearly all physical activity is repellent to modern man. The film, the radio, the gramophone were all invented because physical effort and physical contact have become repulsive to man and woman alike. The aim is to abstract as far as possible. And science is our only help. And science still can't wash the dinner-things or darn socks, or even mend the fire. Electric heaters or central heating, of course! But that's not all.

What, then, is the result? In the abstract we sail ahead to bigger business and better jobs and babies bred in bottles and food in tabloid form. But meanwhile science hasn't rescued us from beef-steaks and dish-washing, heavy labour and howling babies. There is a great hitch. And owing to the great hitch, a great menace to progress. Because every day mankind hates the business of beef-steaks and dish-washing, heavy labour and howling babies more bitterly.

The housewife is full of resentment—she can't help it. The young husband is full of resentment—he can't help it, when he has to plant potatoes to eke out the family income. The housemaid is full of resentment, the navvy is full of resentment, the collier is full of resentment, and the collier's wife is full of resentment, because her man can't earn a proper wage. Resentment grows as the strange fastidiousness of modern men and women increases. Resentment, resentment, resentment—because the basis of life is still brutally physical, and that has become repulsive to us. Mr. Ford, being in his own way a genius, has realized that what the modern workman wants, just like the modern gentleman, is abstraction. The modern workman doesn't *want* to be "interested" in his job. He wants to be as little interested, as nearly perfectly mechanical as possible. This is the great will of the people, and there is no gainsaying it. It is precisely the same in woman as in man. Woman demands an electric cooker because it makes no call on her attention or her "interest" at all. It is almost a pure abstraction, a few switches, and no physical contact, no *dirt*, which is the inevitable result of physical contact, at all. If only we could make housework a real abstraction, a matter of turning switches and guiding a machine, the housewife would again be more or less content. But it can't quite be done, even in America.

And the resentment is enormous. The resentment against *eating*, in the breast of modern woman who has to prepare food, is profound. Why all this work and bother about *mere eating?* Why, indeed? Because neither science nor evolution has kept up with the change in human feeling, and beef-steaks are beef-steaks still, no matter how detestable they may have become to the people who have to prepare them. The loathsome fuss of food continues, and will continue, in spite of all talk about tabloids. The loathsome digging of coal out of the earth, by half-naked men, continues, deep underneath Mr. Ford's super-factories. There it is, and there it will be, and you can't get away from it. While men quite enjoyed hewing coal, which they did, and while women really enjoyed cooking, even with a coal range, which they did—then all was well. But suppose society *en bloc* comes to hate the thought of sweating cooking over a hot range, or sweating hacking at a coal-seam, then what are you to do? You have to ask, or to demand that a large section of society shall do something they have come to hate doing, and which you would hate to do yourself. What then? Resentment and ill-feeling!

Social life means all classes of people living more or less harmoniously together. And private life means men and women, man and woman living together more or less congenially. If there is serious discord between the social classes, then society is threatened with confusion. If there is serious discord betwen man and woman, then the individual, and that means practically everybody, is threatened with internal confusion and unhappiness.

Now it is quite easy to keep the working classes in harmonious working order, so long as you don't ask them to do work they simply do not want to do. The board-schools, however, did the fatal deed. They said to the boys: Work is noble, but what you want is to *get on*, you don't want to stick down a coal-mine all your life. Rise up, and do *clean* work! become a school-teacher or a clerk, not a common collier.

This is sound board-school education, and is in keeping with all the noblest social ideals of the last century. Unfortunately it entirely overlooks the unpleasant effect of such teaching on those who *cannot* get on, and who must perforce stick down a coal-mine all their lives. And these, in the board-school of a mining district, are at least 90 per cent of the boys; it must be so. So that 90 per cent of these board-school scholars are deliberately taught, at school, to be malcontents, taught to despise themselves for not having "got on," for not having "got out of the pit," for sticking down all their lives doing "dirty work" and being "common colliers." Naturally, every collier, doomed himself, wants to get his boys out of the pit, to be gentlemen. And since this again is *impossible* in 90 per cent of the cases, the number of "gentlemen," or clerks and school-teachers, being strictly proportionate to the number of colliers, there comes again the sour disillusion. So that by the third generation you have exactly what you've got today, the young malcontent collier. He has been deliberately produced by modern education coupled with modern conditions, and is logically, inevitably and naturally what he is: a malcontent collier. According to all the accepted teaching, he ought to have risen and bettered himself: equal opportunity, you know. And he hasn't risen and bettered himself. Therefore he is more or less a failure in his own eyes even. He is doomed to do dirty work. He is a malcontent. Now even Mr. Ford can't make coal-mines clean and shiny and abstract. Coal won't be abstracted. Even a Soviet can't do it. A coal-mine remains a hole in the black earth, where blackened men hew and shovel and sweat. You can't abstract it, or make it an affair of pulling levers, and, what is even worse, you can't abandon it, you can't do away with it. There it is, and it has got to be. Mr. Ford forgets that his clean and pure and harmonious super-factory, where men only pull shining levers or turn bright handles, has all had to be grossly mined and smelted before it could come into existence. Mr. Ford's is one of the various heavens of industry. But these heavens rest on various hells of labour, always did and always will. Science rather leaves us in the lurch in these matters. Science is supposed to remove these hells for us. And—it doesn't. Not at all!

If you had never taught the blackened men down in the various hells that they *were* in hell, and made them despise themselves for being there—a *common* collier, a *low* labourer—the mischief could never have developed so rapidly. But now we have it, all society resting on a labour basis of smouldering resentment. And the collier's question: How would *you* like to be a collier?—is unanswerable. We know perfectly well we should dislike it intensely.—At the same time, my father, who never went to a Board-school, quite liked it. But he has been improved on. Progress! Human feeling has changed, changed rapidly and radically. And science has not changed conditions to fit.

What is to be done? We all loathe brute physical labour. We all think it is horrible to have to do it. We consider those that actually do it low and vile, and we have told them so, for fifty years, urging them to get away from it and "better themselves," which would be very nice, if everybody *could* get on, and brute labour could be abandoned, as, scientifically, it ought to be. But actually, not at all. We are forced to go on forcing a very large proportion of society to remain "unbettered," "low and common," "common colliers, common labourers," since a very large portion of humanity must still spend its life labouring, now and in the future, science having let us down in this respect. You can't teach mankind to "better himself" unless you'll better the gross earth to fit him. And the gross earth remains what it was, and man its slave. For neither science nor evolution shows any signs of saving us from our gross necessities. The labouring masses are and will be, even if all else is swept away: because they must be. They represent the gross necessity of man, which science has failed to save us from.

So then, what? The only thing that remains to be done is to make labour as likeable as possible, and try to teach the labouring masses to like it: which, given the trend of modern feeling, not only sounds, but is, fatuous. Mankind *en bloc* gets more fastidious and more "nice" every day. Every day it loathes dirty work more deeply. And every day the whole pressure of social consciousness works towards making everybody more fastidious, more "nice," more refined, and more unfit for dirty work. Before you make all humanity unfit for dirty work, you should first remove the necessity for dirty work.

But such being the condition of men and women with regard to work —a condition of repulsion in the breasts of men and women for the work that has got to be done—what about private life, the relation between man and woman? How does the new fastidiousness and nicety of mankind affect this?

Profoundly! The revulsion from physical labour, physical effort, physical contact has struck a death-blow at marriage and home-life. In the great trend of the times, a woman cannot save herself from the universal dislike of housework, housekeeping, rearing children and keeping a home going. Women make the most unselfish efforts in this direction, because it is generally expected of them. But this cannot remove the *instinctive* dislike of preparing meals and scouring saucepans, cleaning baby's bottles or darning the man's underwear, which a large majority of women feel today. It is something which there is no denying, a real physical dislike of doing these things. Many women school themselves and are excellent housewives, physically disliking it all the time. And this, though admirable, is wearing. It is an exhaustive process, with many ill results.

Can it be possible that women actually ever did like scouring saucepans and cleaning the range?—I believe some few women still do. I believe that twenty years ago, even, the majority of women enjoyed it. But what, then, has happened? Can human instincts really change?

They can, and in the most amazing fashion. And this is the great problem for the sociologist: the violent change in human instinct, especially in women. Woman's instinct used to be all for home, shelter, the protection of the man, and the happiness of running her own house. Now it is all against. Woman *thinks* she wants a lovely little home of her own, but her instinct is all against it, when it means matrimony. She *thinks* she wants a man of her own, but her instinct is dead against having him around all the time. She would like him on a long string, that she can let out or pull in, as she feels inclined. But she just doesn't want him inevitably and insidiously there all the time—not even every evening—not even for week-ends, if it's got to be a fixture. She wants him to be merely intermittent in her landscape, even if he is always present in her soul, and she writes him the most intimate letters every day. All well and good! But her instinct is against him, against his permanent and perpetual physical presence. She doesn't want to feel his presence as something material, unavoidable and permanent. It goes dead against her grain, it upsets her instinct. She loves him, she loves, even, being faithful to him. But she doesn't want him substantially around. She doesn't want his actual physical presence—except in snatches. What she *really* loves is the thought of him, the idea of him, the *distant* communion with him—varied with snatches of actually being together, like little festivals, which we are more or less glad when they are over.

Now a great many modern girls feel like this, even when they force themselves to behave in the conventional side-by-side fashion. And a great many men feel the same—though perhaps not so acutely as the women. Young couples may force themselves to be conventional husbands and wives, but the strain is often cruel, and the result often disastrous.

Now then we see the trend of our civilization, in terms of human feeling and human relation. It is, and there is no denying it, towards a greater and greater abstraction from the physical, towards a further and further physical separateness between men and women, and between individual and individual. Young men and women today are together all the time, it will be argued. Yes, but they are together as good sports, good chaps, in strange independence of one another, intimate one moment, strangers the next, hands-off! all the time and as little connected as the bits in a kaleidoscope.

The young have the fastidiousness, the nicety, the revulsion from the physical, intensified. To the girl today, a man whose physical presence she is aware of, especially a bit *heavily* aware of, is or becomes really abhorrent. She wants to fly away from him to the uttermost ends of the earth. And as soon as women or girls get a bit female physical, young men's nerves go all to pieces. The sexes can't stand one another. They adore one another as spiritual or personal creatures, all talk and wit and back-chat, or jazz and motor-cars and machines, or tennis and swimming—even sitting in bathing-suits all day on a beach. But this is all peculiarly non-physical, a flaunting of the body in its non-physical, merely optical aspect. So much nudity, fifty years ago, would have made man and woman quiver through and through. Now, not at all! People flaunt their bodies to show how unphysical they are. The more the girls are not desired, the more they uncover themselves.

And this means, when we analyse it out, repulsion. The young are, in a subtle way, physically repulsive to one another, the girl to the man and the man to the girl. And they rather enjoy the feeling of repulsion, it is a sort of contest. It is as if the young girl said to the young man today: I rather like you, you know. You are so thrillingly repulsive to me.—And as if the young man replied: Same here!—There may be of course, an intense bodiless sort of affection between young men and women. But as soon as either becomes a positive physical presence to the other, immediately there is repulsion.

And marriages based on the thrill of physical repulsion, as so many are today, even when coupled with mental "adoring" or real wistful, bodiless affection, are in the long run—not so very long, either—catastrophic. There you have it, the great "spirituality," the great "betterment" or refinement; the great fastidiousness; the great "niceness" of feeling; when a girl must be a flat, thin, bodiless stick, and a boy a correct mannequin, each of them abstracted towards real caricature. What does it all amount to? What is its motive force?

What it amounts to, really, is physical repulsion. The great spirituality of our age means that we are all physically repulsive to one another. The great advance in refinement of feeling and squeamish fastidiousness means that we hate the *physical* existence of anybody and everybody, even ourselves. The amazing move into abstraction on the part of the whole of humanity—the film, the radio, the gramophone—means that we loathe the physical element in our amusements, we don't *want* the physical contact, we want to get away from it. We don't *want* to look at flesh and blood people—we want to watch their shadows on a screen. We don't *want* to hear their actual voices: only transmitted through a machine. We must get away from the physical.

The vast mass of the lower classes—and this is most extraordinary—are even more grossly abstracted, if we may use the term, than the educated classes. The uglier sort of working man today truly has no body and no real feelings at all. He eats the most wretched food, because taste has left him, he only *sees* his meal, he never *really* eats it. He drinks his beer by idea, he no longer tastes it at all. This must be so, or the food and beer could not be as bad as they are. And as for his relation to his women—his poor women—they are pegs to hang clothes on, and there's an end of them. It is a horrible state of feelingless depravity, atrophy of the senses.

But under it all, as ever, as everywhere, vibrates the one great impulse of our civilization, physical recoil from every other being and from every form of physical existence. Recoil, recoil, recoil. Revulsion, revulsion, revulsion. Repulsion, repulsion, repulsion. This is the rhythm that underlies our social activity, everywhere, with regard to physical existence.

Now we are all basically and permanently physical. So is the earth, so even is the air. What then is going to be the result of all this recoil and repulsion, which our civilization has deliberately fostered?

The result is really only one and the same: some form of collective social madness. Russia, being a very physical country, was in a frantic state of physical recoil and "spirituality" twenty years ago. We can look on the revolution, really, as nothing but a great outburst of anti-physical insanity; we can look on Soviet Russia as nothing but a logical state of society established in anti-physical insanity.—Physical and material are, of course, not the same; in fact, they are subtly opposite. The machine is absolutely material, and absolutely anti-physical—as even our fingers know. And the Soviet is established on the image of the machine, "pure" materialism. The Soviet hates the real physical body far more deeply than it hates Capital. It mixes it up with the bourgeois. But it sees very little danger in it, since all western civilization is now mechanized, materialized and ready for an outburst of insanity which shall throw us all into some purely machine-driven unity of lunatics.

What about it, then? What about it, men and women? The only thing to do is to get your bodies back, men and women. A great part of society is irreparably lost: abstracted into non-physical, mechanical entities whose motive power is still recoil, revulsion, repulsion, hate, and, ultimately, blind destruction. The driving force *underneath* our society remains the same: recoil, revulsion, hate. And let this force once run out of hand, and we know what to expect. It is not only in the working class. The well-to-do classes are just as full of the driving force of recoil, revulsion, which ultimately becomes hate. The force is universal in our spiritual civilization. Let it once run out of hand, and then—

It only remains for some men and women, individuals, to try to get back their bodies and preserve the other flow of warmth, affection and physical unison. There is nothing else to do.

Autobiographical Sketch

They ask me: "Did you find it very hard to get on and to become a success?" And I have to admit that if I can be said to have got on, and if I can be called a success, then I *did not* find it hard.

I never starved in a garret, nor waited in anguish for the post to bring me an answer from editor or publisher, nor did I struggle in sweat and blood to bring forth mighty works, nor did I ever wake up and find myself famous.

I was a poor boy. I *ought* to have wrestled in the fell clutch of circumstance, and undergone the bludgeonings of chance before I became a writer with a very modest income and a very questionable reputation. But I didn't. It all happened by itself and without any groans from me.

It seems a pity. Because I was undoubtedly a poor boy of the working classes, with no apparent future in front of me. But after all, what am I now?

I was born among the working classes and brought up among them. My father was a collier, and only a collier, nothing praiseworthy about him. He wasn't even respectable, in so far as he got drunk rather frequently, never went near a chapel, and was usually rather rude to his little immediate bosses at the pit.

He practically never had a good stall all the time he was a butty, because he was always saying tiresome and foolish things about the men just above him in control at the mine. He offended them all, almost on purpose, so how could he expect them to favour him? Yet he grumbled when they didn't.

My mother was, I suppose, superior. She came from town, and belonged really to the lower bourgeoisie. She spoke King's English, without an accent, and never in her life could even imitate a sentence of the dialect which my father spoke, and which we children spoke out of doors.

She wrote a fine Italian hand, and a clever and amusing letter when she felt like it. And as she grew older she read novels again, and got terribly impatient with *Diana of the Crossways* and terribly thrilled by *East Lynne*.

But she was a working man's wife, and nothing else, in her shabby little black bonnet and her shrewd, clear, "different" face. And she was very much respected, just as my father was not respected. Her nature was quick and sensitive, and perhaps really superior. But she was down, right down in the working class, among the mass of poorer colliers' wives.

I was a delicate pale brat with a snuffy nose, whom most people treated quite gently as just an ordinary delicate little lad. When I was twelve I got a county council scholarship, twelve pounds a year, and went to Nottingham High School.

After leaving school I was a clerk for three months, then had a very serious pneumonia illness, in my seventeenth year, that damaged my health for life.

A year later I became a school-teacher, and after three years' savage teaching of collier lads I went to take the "normal" course in Nottingham University.

As I was glad to leave school, I was glad to leave college. It had meant mere disillusion, instead of the living contact of men. From college I went down to Croydon, near London, to teach in a new elementary school at a hundred pounds a year.

It was while I was at Croydon, when I was twenty-three, that the girl who had been the chief friend of my youth, and who was herself a school-teacher in a mining village at home, copied out some of my poems, and without telling me, sent them to the *English Review*, which had just had a glorious re-birth under Ford Madox Hueffer.

Hueffer was most kind. He printed the poems, and asked me to come and see him. The girl had launched me, so easily, on my literary career, like a princess cutting a thread, launching a ship.

I had been tussling away for four years, getting out *The White Peacock* in inchoate bits, from the underground of my consciousness. I must have written most of it five or six times, but only in intervals, never as a task or a divine labour, or in the groans of parturition.

I would dash at it, do a bit, show it to the girl; she always admired it; then realize afterwards it wasn't what I wanted, and have another dash. But at Croydon I had worked at it fairly steadily, in the evenings after school.

Anyhow, it was done, after four or five years' spasmodic effort. Hueffer asked at once to see the manuscript. He read it immediately, with the greatest cheery sort of kindness and bluff. And in his queer voice, when we were in an omnibus in London, he shouted in my ear: "It's got every fault that the English novel can have."

Just then the English novel was supposed to have so many faults, in comparison with the French, that it was hardly allowed to exist at all. "But," shouted Hueffer in the 'bus, "you've got GENIUS."

This made me want to laugh, it sounded so comical. In the early days they were always telling me I had got genius, as if to console me for not having their own incomparable advantages.

But Hueffer didn't mean that. I always thought he had a bit of genius himself. Anyhow, he sent the MS. of *The White Peacock* to William Heinemann, who accepted it at once, and made me alter only four little lines whose omission would now make anybody smile. I was to have £50 when the book was published.

Meanwhile Hueffer printed more poems and some stories of mine in the *English Review*, and people read them and told me so, to my embarrassment and anger. I hated being an author, in people's eyes. Especially as I was a teacher.

When I was twenty-five my mother died, and two months later *The White Peacock* was published, but it meant nothing to me. I went on teaching for another year, and then again a bad pneumonia illness intervened. When I got better I did not go back to school. I lived henceforward on my scanty literary earnings.

It is seventeen years since I gave up teaching and started to live an independent life of the pen. I have never starved, and never even felt poor, though my income for the first ten years was no better, and often worse, than it would have been if I had remained an elementary school-teacher.

But when one has been born poor a very little money can be enough. Now my father would think I am rich, if nobody else does. And my mother would think I have risen in the world, even if I don't think so.

But something is wrong, either with me or with the world, or with both of us. I have gone far and met people, of all sorts and all conditions, and many whom I have genuinely liked and esteemed.

People, *personally*, have nearly always been friendly. Of critics we will not speak, they are different fauna from people. And I have *wanted* to feel truly friendly with some, at least, of my fellow-men.

Yet I have never quite succeeded. Whether I get on *in* the world is a question; but I certainly don't get on very well *with* the world. And whether I am a worldly success or not I really don't know. But I feel, somehow, not much of a human success.

By which I mean that I don't feel there is any very cordial or fundamental contact between me and society, or me and other people.

There is a breach. And my contact is with something that is non-human, non-vocal.

I used to think it had something to do with the oldness and the worn-outness of Europe. Having tried other places, I know that is not so. Europe is, perhaps, the least worn-out of the continents, because it is the most lived in. A place that is lived in lives.

It is since coming back from America that I ask myself seriously: Why is there so little contact between myself and the people whom I know? Why has the contact no vital meaning?

And if I write the question down, and try to write the answer down, it is because I feel it is a question that troubles many men.

The answer, as far as I can see, has something to do with class. Class makes a gulf, across which all the best human flow is lost. It is not exactly the triumph of the middle classes that has made the deadness, but the triumph of the middle-class *thing*.

As a man from the working class, I feel that the middle class cut off some of my vital vibration when I am with them. I admit them charming and educated and good people often enough. *But they just stop some part of me from working.* Some part has to be left out.

Then why don't I live with my working people? Because their vibration is limited in another direction. They are narrow, but still fairly deep and passionate, whereas the middle class is broad and shallow and passionless. Quite passionless. At the best they substitute affection, which is the great middle-class positive emotion.

But the working class is narrow in outlook, in prejudice, and narrow in intelligence. This again makes a prison. One can belong absolutely to no class.

Yet I find, here in Italy, for example, that I live in a certain silent contact with the peasants who work the land of this villa. I am not intimate with them, hardly speak to them save to say good day. And they are not working for me; I am not their *padrone*.

Yet it is they, really, who form my *ambiente*, and it is from them that the human flow comes to me. I don't want to live with them in their cottages; that would be a sort of prison. But I want them to be there, about the place, their lives going on along with mine, and in relation to mine. I don't idealize them. Enough of that folly! It is worse than setting school-children to express themselves in self-conscious twaddle. I don't expect them to make any millennium here on earth, neither now nor in the future. But I want to live near them, because their life still flows.

And now I know, more or less, why I cannot follow in the footsteps even of Barrie or of Wells, who both came from the common people also and are both such a success. Now I know why I cannot rise in the world and become even a little popular and rich.

I cannot make the transfer from my own class into the middle class. I cannot, not for anything in the world, forfeit my passional consciousness and my old blood-affinity with my fellow-men and the animals and the land, for that other thin, spurious mental conceit which is all that is left of the mental consciousness once it has made itself exclusive.

Hymns in a Man's Life

Nothing is more difficult than to determine what a child takes in, and does not take in, of its environment and its teaching. This fact is brought home to me by the hymns which I learned as a child, and never forgot. They mean to me almost more than the finest poetry, and they have for me a more permanent value, somehow or other.

It is almost shameful to confess that the poems which have meant most to me, like Wordsworth's "Ode to Immortality" and Keats's Odes, and pieces of *Macbeth* or *As You Like It* or *Midsummer Night's Dream*, and Goethe's lyrics, such as "Über allen Gipfeln ist Ruh," and Verlaine's "Ayant poussé la porte qui chancelle"—all these lovely poems which after all give the ultimate shape to one's life; all these lovely poems woven deep into a man's consciousness, are still not woven so deep in me as the rather banal Nonconformist hymns that penetrated through and through my childhood.

> Each gentle dove
> And sighing bough
> That makes the eve
> So fair to me
> Has something far
> Diviner now
> To draw me back
> To Galilee.
> O Galilee, sweet Galilee
> Where Jesus loved so much to be,
> O Galilee, sweet Galilee,
> Come sing thy songs again to me!

To me the word Galilee has a wonderful sound. The Lake of Galilee! I don't want to know where it is. I never want to go to Palestine. Galilee is one of those lovely, glamorous worlds, not places, that exist in the golden haze of a child's half-formed imagination. And in my man's imagination it is just the same. It has been left untouched. With regard to the hymns which had such a profound influence on my childish consciousness, there has been no crystallizing out, no dwindling into actuality, no hardening into the commonplace. They are the same to my man's experience as they were to me nearly forty years ago.

The moon, perhaps, has shrunken a little. One has been forced to learn about orbits, eclipses, relative distances, dead worlds, craters of the moon, and so on. The crescent at evening still startles the soul with its delicate flashing. But the mind works automatically and says: "Ah, she is in her first quarter. She is all there, in spite of the fact that we see only this slim blade. The earth's shadow is over her." And, willy-nilly, the intrusion of the mental processes dims the brilliance, the magic of the first apperception.

It is the same with all things. The sheer delight of a child's apperception is based on *wonder*; and deny it as we may, knowledge and wonder counteract one another. So that as knowledge increases wonder decreases. We say again: Familiarity breeds contempt. So that as we grow older, and become more familiar with phenomena, we become more contemptuous of them. But that is only partly true. It has taken some races of men thousands of years to become contemptuous of the moon, and to the Hindu the cow is still wondrous. It is not familiarity that breeds contempt: it is the assumption of knowledge. Anybody who looks at the moon and says, "I know all about that poor orb," is, of course, bored by the moon.

Now the great and fatal fruit of our civilization, which is a civilization based on knowledge, and hostile to experience, is boredom. All our wonderful education and learning is producing a grand sum-total of boredom. Modern people are inwardly thoroughly bored. Do as they may, they are bored.

They are bored because they experience nothing. And they experience nothing because the wonder has gone out of them. And when the wonder has gone out of a man he is dead. He is henceforth only an insect.

When all comes to all, the most precious element in life is wonder. Love is a great emotion, and power is power. But both love and power are based on wonder. Love without wonder is a sensational affair, and power without wonder is mere force and compulsion. The one universal element in consciousness which is fundamental to life is the element of wonder. You cannot help feeling it in a bean as it starts to grow and pulls itself out of its jacket. You cannot help feeling it in the glisten of the nucleus of the amœba. You recognize it, willy-nilly, in an ant busily tugging at a straw; in a rook, as it walks the frosty grass.

They all have their own obstinate will. But also they all live with a sense of wonder. Plant consciousness, insect consciousness, fish consciousness, all are related by one permanent element, which we may call the religious element inherent in all life, even in a flea: the sense of wonder. That is our sixth sense. And it is the *natural* religious sense.

Somebody says that mystery is nothing, because mystery is something you don't know, and what you don't know is nothing to you. But there is more than one way of knowing.

Even the real scientist works in the sense of wonder. The pity is, when he comes out of his laboratory he puts aside his wonder along with his apparatus, and tries to make it all perfectly didactic. Science in its true condition of wonder is as religious as any religion. But didactic science is as dead and boring as dogmatic religion. Both are wonderless and productive of boredom, endless boredom.

Now we come back to the hymns. They live and glisten in the depths of the man's consciousness in undimmed wonder, because they have not been subjected to any criticism or analysis. By the time I was sixteen I had criticized and got over the Christian dogma.

It was quite easy for me; my immediate forebears had already done it for me. Salvation, heaven, Virgin birth, miracles, even the Christian dogmas of right and wrong—one soon got them adjusted. I never could really worry about them. Heaven is one of the instinctive dreams. Right and wrong is something you can't dogmatize about; it's not so easy. As for my soul, I simply don't and never did understand how I could "save" it. One can save one's pennies. But how can one save one's soul? One can only *live* one's soul. The business is to live, really alive. And this needs wonder.

So that the miracle of the loaves and fishes is just as good to me now as when I was a child. I don't care whether it is historically a fact or not. What does it matter? It is part of the genuine wonder. The same with all the religious teaching I had as a child, *apart* from the didacticism and sentimentalism. I am eternally grateful for the wonder with which it filled my childhood.

> Sun of my soul, thou Saviour dear,
> It is not night if Thou be near—

That was the last hymn at the board-school. It did not mean to me any Christian dogma or any salvation. Just the words, "Sun of my soul, thou Saviour dear," penetrated me with wonder and the mystery of twilight. At another time the last hymn was:

> Fair waved the golden corn
> In Canaan's pleasant land—

And again I loved "Canaan's pleasant land." The wonder of "Canaan," which could never be localized.

I think it was good to be brought up a Protestant: and among Protestants, a Nonconformist, and among Nonconformists, a Congregationalist. Which sounds pharisaic. But I should have missed bitterly a direct knowledge of the Bible, and a direct relation to Galilee and Canaan, Moab and Kedron, those places that never existed on earth. And in the Church of England one would hardly have escaped those snobbish hierarchies of class, which spoil so much for a child. And the Primitive Methodists, when I was a boy, were always having "revivals" and being "saved," and I always had a horror of being saved.

So, altogether, I am grateful to my "Congregational" upbringing. The Congregationalists are the oldest Nonconformists, descendants of the Oliver Cromwell Independents. They still had the Puritan tradition of no ritual. But they avoided the personal emotionalism which one found among the Methodists when I was a boy.

I liked our chapel, which was tall and full of light, and yet still; and colour-washed pale green and blue, with a bit of lotus pattern. And over the organ-loft, "O worship the Lord in the beauty of holiness," in big letters.

That was a favourite hymn, too:

> O worship the Lord, in the beauty of holiness,
>   Bow down before Him, His glory proclaim;
> With gold of obedience and incense of lowliness
>   Kneel and adore Him, the Lord is His name.

I don't know what the "beauty of holiness" is exactly. It easily becomes cant, or nonsense. But if you don't think about it—and why should you?—it has a magic. The same with the whole verse. It is rather bad, really, "gold of obedience" and "incense of lowliness." But in me, to the music, it still produces a sense of splendour.

I am always glad we had the Bristol hymn-book, not Moody and Sankey. And I am glad our Scotch minister on the whole avoided sentimental messes such as "Lead, Kindly Light," or even "Abide with Me." He had a healthy preference for healthy hymns.

> At even, ere the sun was set,
>   The sick, O Lord, around Thee lay.
> Oh, in what divers pains they met!
>   Oh, in what joy they went away!

And often we had "Fight the good fight with all thy might."

In Sunday School I am eternally grateful to old Mr. Remington,* with his round white beard and his ferocity. He made us sing! And he loved the martial hymns:

---

* His name was actually Rimmington. Eds.

Sound the battle-cry,
See, the foe is nigh.
Raise the standard high
For the Lord.

The ghastly sentimentalism that came like a leprosy over religion had not yet got hold of our colliery village. I remember when I was in Class II in the Sunday School, when I was about seven, a woman teacher trying to harrow us about the Crucifixion. And she kept saying: "And aren't you sorry for Jesus? Aren't you sorry?" And most of the children wept. I believe I shed a crocodile tear or two, but very vivid is my memory of saying to myself: "I don't *really* care a bit." And I could never go back on it. I never *cared* about the Crucifixion, one way or another. Yet the *wonder* of it penetrated very deep in me.

Thirty-six years ago men, even Sunday School teachers, still believed in the fight for life and the fun of it. "Hold the fort, for I am coming." It was far, far from any militarism or gun-fighting. But it was the battle-cry of a stout soul, and a fine thing too.

Stand up, stand up for Jesus,
Ye soldiers of the Lord.

Here is the clue to the ordinary Englishman—in the Nonconformist hymns.

Making Pictures

One has to eat one's own words. I remember I used to assert, perhaps I even wrote it: Everything that can possibly be painted has been painted, every brush-stroke that can possibly be laid on canvas has been laid on. The visual arts are at a dead end. Then suddenly, at the age of forty, I begin painting myself and am fascinated.

Still, going through the Paris picture shops this year of grace, and seeing the Dufys and Chiricos, etc., and the Japanese Ito with his wish-wash nudes with pearl-button eyes, the same weariness comes over one. They are all so would-be, they make such efforts. They at least have nothing to paint. In the midst of them a graceful Fricsz flower-piece, or a blotting-paper Laurencin, seems a masterpiece. At least here is a bit of *natural* expression in paint. Trivial enough, when compared to the big painters, but still, as far as they go, real.

What about myself, then! What am I doing, bursting into paint? I am a writer, I ought to stick to ink. I have found my medium of expression; why, at the age of forty, should I suddenly want to try another?

Things happen, and we have no choice. If Maria Huxley hadn't come rolling up to our house near Florence with four rather large canvases, one of which she had busted, and presented them to me because they had been abandoned in her house, I might never have started in on a real picture in my life. But those nice stretched canvases were too tempting. We had been painting doors and window-frames in the house, so there was a little stock of oil, turps and colour in powder, such as one buys from an Italian drogheria. There were several brushes for house-painting. There was a canvas on which the unknown owner had made a start—mud-grey, with the beginnings of a red-haired man. It was a grimy and ugly beginning, and the young man who had made it had wisely gone no further. He certainly had had no inner compulsion: nothing in him, as far as paint was concerned, or if there was anything in him, it had stayed in, and only a bit of the mud-grey "group" had come out.

So for the sheer fun of covering a surface and obliterating that mud-grey, I sat on the floor with the canvas propped against a chair—and with my house-paint brushes and colours in little casseroles, I disappeared into that canvas. It is to me the most exciting moment—when you have a blank canvas and a big brush full of wet colour, and you plunge. It is just like diving into a pond—then you start frantically to swim. So far as I am concerned, it is like swimming in a baffling current and being rather frightened and very thrilled, gasping and striking out for all you're worth. The knowing eye watches sharp as a needle; but the picture comes clean out of instinct, intuition and sheer physical action. Once the instinct and intuition gets into the brush-tip, the picture *happens*, if it is to be a picture at all.

At least, so my first picture happened—the one I have called "A Holy Family." In a couple of hours there it all was, man, woman, child, blue shirt, red shawl, pale room—all in the rough, but, as far as I am concerned, a picture. The struggling comes later. But the picture itself comes in the first rush, or not at all. It is only when the picture has come into being that one can struggle and make it *grow* to completion.

Ours is an excessively conscious age. We *know* so much, we feel so little. I have lived enough among painters and around studios to have had all the theories—and how contradictory they are—rammed down my throat. A man has to have a gizzard like an ostrich to digest all the brass-tacks and wire nails of modern art theories. Perhaps all the theories, the utterly indigestible theories, like nails in an ostrich's gizzard, do indeed help to grind small and make digestible all the emotional and æsthetic pabulum that lies in an artist's soul. But they can serve no other purpose. Not even corrective. The modern theories of art make real pictures impossible. You only get these expositions, critical ventures in paint, and fantastic negations. And the bit of fantasy that may lie in the negation—as in a Dufy or a Chirico—is just the bit that has escaped theory and perhaps saves the picture. Theorize, theorize all you like—but when you start to paint, shut your theoretic eyes and go for it with instinct and intuition.

Myself, I have always loved pictures, the pictorial art. I never went to an art school, I have had only one real lesson in painting in all my life. But of course I was thoroughly drilled in "drawing," the solid-geometry sort, and the plaster-cast sort, and the pin-wire sort. I think the solid-geometry sort, with all the elementary laws of perspective, was valuable. But the pin-wire sort and the plaster-cast light-and-shade sort was harmful. Plaster-casts and pin-wire outlines were always so repulsive to me, I quite early decided I "couldn't draw." I couldn't draw, so I could never do anything on my own. When I did paint jugs of flowers or bread and potatoes, or cottages in a lane, copying from Nature, the result wasn't very thrilling. Nature was more or less of a plaster-cast to me—those plaster-cast heads of Minerva or figures of Dying Gladiators which so unnerved me as a youth. The "object," be it what it might, was always slightly repulsive to me once I sat down in front of it, to paint it. So, of course, I decided I couldn't really paint. Perhaps I can't. But I verily believe I can make pictures, which is to me all that matters in this respect. The art of painting consists in making pictures—and so many artists accomplish canvases without coming within miles of painting a picture.

I learnt to paint from copying other pictures—usually reproductions, sometimes even photographs. When I was a boy, how I concentrated over it! Copying some perfectly worthless scene reproduction in some magazine. I worked with almost dry water-colour, stroke by stroke, covering half a square-inch at a time, each square-inch perfect and completed, proceeding in a kind of mosaic advance, with no idea at all of laying on a broad wash. Hours and hours of intense concentration, inch by inch progress, in a method entirely wrong—and yet those copies of mine managed, when they were finished, to have a certain something that delighted me: a certain glow of life, which was beauty to me. A picture lives with the life you put into it. If you put no *life* into it—no thrill, no concentration of delight or exaltation of visual discovery— then the picture is dead, like so many canvases, no matter how much thorough and scientific work is put into it. Even if you only copy a purely banal reproduction of an old bridge, some sort of keen, delighted awareness of the old bridge or of its atmosphere, or the image it has kindled inside you, can go over on to the paper and give a certain touch of life to a banal conception.

It needs a certain purity of spirit to be an artist, of any sort. The motto which should be written over every School of Art is: "Blessed are the pure in spirit, for theirs is the kingdom of heaven." But by "pure in spirit" we mean pure in spirit. An artist may be a profligate and, from the social point of view, a scoundrel. But if he can paint a nude woman, or a couple of apples, so that they are a living image, then he was pure in spirit, and, for the time being, his was the kingdom of heaven. This is the beginning of all art, visual or literary or musical: be pure in spirit. It isn't the same as goodness. It is much more difficult and nearer the divine. The divine isn't only good, it is all things.

One may see the divine in natural objects; I saw it today, in the frail, lovely little camellia flowers on long stems, here on the bushy and splendid flower-stalls of the Ramblas in Barcelona. They were different from the usual fat camellias, more like gardenias, poised delicately, and I saw them like a vision. So now, I could paint them. But if I had bought a handful, and started in to paint them "from nature," then I should have lost them. By staring at them I should have lost them. I have learnt by experience. It is personal experience only. Some men can only get at a vision by staring themselves blind, as it were: like Cézanne; but staring kills my vision. That's why I could never "draw" at school. One was supposed to draw what one stared at.

The only thing one can look into, stare into, and see only vision, is the vision itself: the visionary image. That is why I am glad I never had any training but the self-imposed training of copying other men's pictures. As I grew more ambitious, I copied Leader's landscapes, and Frank Brangwyn's cartoon-like pictures, then Peter de Wint and Girtin water-colours. I can never be sufficiently grateful for the series of English water-colour painters, published by the *Studio* in eight parts, when I was a youth. I had only six of the eight parts, but they were invaluable to me. I copied them with the greatest joy, and found some of them extremely difficult. Surely I put as much labour into copying from those water-colour reproductions as most modern art students put into all their years of study. And I had enormous profit from it. I not only acquired a considerable technical skill in handling water-colour— let any man try copying the English water-colour artists, from Paul Sandby and Peter de Wint and Girtin, up to Frank Brangwyn and the impressionists like Brabazon, and he will see how much skill he requires —but also I developed my visionary awareness. And I believe one can only develop one's visionary awareness by close contact with the vision itself: that is, by knowing pictures, real vision pictures, and by dwelling on them, and really dwelling in them. It is a great delight, to dwell in a picture. But it needs a purity of spirit, a sloughing of vulgar sensation and vulgar interest, and above all, vulgar contact, that few people know how to perform. Oh, if art schools only taught that! If, instead of saying: This drawing is wrong, incorrect, badly drawn, etc., they would say: Isn't this in bad taste? isn't it insensitive? isn't that an insentient curve with none of the delicate awareness of life in it?—But art is treated all wrong. It is treated as if it were a science, which it is not. Art is a form of religion, minus the Ten Commandment business, which is sociological. Art is a form of supremely delicate awareness and atonement—meaning at-oneness, the state of being at one with the object. But is the great atonement in delight?—for I can never look on art save as a form of delight.

All my life I have from time to time gone back to paint, because it

gave me a form of delight that words can never give. Perhaps the joy in
words goes deeper and is for that reason more unconscious. The *conscious* delight is certainly stronger in paint. I have gone back to paint
for real pleasure—and by paint I mean copying, copying either in oils
or waters. I think the greatest pleasure I ever got came from copying
Fra Angelico's "Flight into Egypt" and Lorenzetti's big picture of the
Thebaid, in each case working from photographs and putting in my
own colour; or perhaps even more a Carpaccio picture in Venice. Then
I *really* learned what life, what powerful life has been put into every
curve, every motion of a great picture. Purity of spirit, sensitive awareness, intense eagerness to portray an inward vision, how it all comes.
The English water-colours are frail in comparison—and the French and
the Flemings are shallow. The great Rembrandt I never tried to copy,
though I loved him intensely, even more than I do now; and Rubens I
never tried, though I always liked him so much, only he seemed so
spread out. But I have copied Peter de Hooch, and Vandyck, and others
that I forget. Yet none of them gave me the deep thrill of the Italians,
Carpaccio, or the lovely "Death of Procris" in the National Gallery, or that "Wedding" with the scarlet legs, in the Uffizi, or a Giotto
from Padua. I must have made many copies in my day, and got endless joy out of them.

Then suddenly, by having a blank canvas, I discovered I could make
a picture myself. That is the point, to make a picture on a blank canvas.
And I was forty before I had the real courage to try. Then it became
an orgy, making pictures.

I have learnt now not to work from objects, not to have models, not
to have a technique. Sometimes, for a water-colour, I have worked
direct from a model. But it always spoils the *picture*. I can only use a
model when the picture is already made; then I can look at the model
to get some detail which the vision failed me with, or to modify something which I *feel* is unsatisfactory and I don't know why. Then a
model may give a suggestion. But at the beginning, a model only spoils
the picture. The picture must all come out of the artist's inside, awareness of forms and figures. We can call it memory, but it is more than
memory. It is the image as it lives in the consciousness, alive like a
vision, but unknown. I believe many people have, in their consciousness, living images that would give them the greatest joy to bring out.
But they don't know how to go about it. And teaching only hinders
them.

To me, a picture has delight in it, or it isn't a picture. The saddest
pictures of Piero della Francesca or Sodoma or Goya, have still that

indescribable delight that goes with the real picture. Modern critics talk a lot about ugliness, but I never saw a real picture that seemed to me ugly. The theme may be ugly, there may be a terrifying, distressing, almost repulsive quality, as in El Greco. Yet it is all, in some strange way, swept up in the delight of a picture. No artist, even the gloomiest, ever painted a picture without the curious delight in image-making.

Pictures on the Walls

Whether wall pictures are or are not an essential part of interior decoration in the home seems to be considered debatable. Yet since there is scarcely one house in a thousand which doesn't have them, we may easily conclude that they are, in spite of the snobbism which pretends to prefer blank walls. The human race loves pictures. Barbarians or civilized, we are all alike, we straightway go to look at a picture if there is a picture to look at. And there are very few of us who wouldn't love to have a perfectly fascinating work hanging in our room, that we could go on looking at, if we could afford it. Instead, unfortunately, as a rule we have only some mediocre thing left over from the past, that hangs on the wall just because we've got it, and it must go somewhere. If only people would be firm about it, and rigorously burn *all* insignificant pictures, frames as well, how much more freely we should breathe indoors. If only people would go round their walls every ten years and say, Now, what about that oil-painting, what about that reproduction, what about that photograph? What do they mean? What do we get from them? Have they any point? Are they worth keeping? —the answer would almost invariably be No. And then what? Shall we say, Oh, let them stay! They've been there ten years, we might as well leave them!—But that is sheer inertia and death to any freshness in the home. A woman might as well say: I've worn this hat for a year, so I may as well go on wearing it for a few more years.—A house, a home, is only a greater garment, and just as we feel we must renew our clothes and have fresh ones, so we should renew our homes and make them in keeping. Spring cleaning isn't enough. Why do fashions in clothes change? Because, really, we ourselves change, in the slow metamorphosis of time. If we imagine ourselves now in the clothes we wore six years ago, we shall see that it is impossible. We are, in some way, different persons now, and our clothes express our different personality.

And so should the home. It should change with us, as we change. Not so quickly as our clothes change, because it is not so close in contact. More slowly, but just as inevitably, the home should change around us.

And the change should be more rapid in the more decorative scheme of the room: pictures, curtains, cushions; and slower in the solid furniture. Some furniture may satisfy us for a lifetime. Some may be quite unsuitable after ten years. But certain it is that the cushions and curtains and pictures will begin to be stale after a couple of years. And staleness in the home is stifling and oppressive to the spirit. It is a woman's business to see to it. In England especially we live so much indoors that our interiors must live, must change, must have their seasons of fading and renewing, must come alive to fit the new moods, the new sensations, the new selves that come to pass in us with the changing years. Dead and dull permanency in the home, dreary sameness, is a form of inertia, and very harmful to the modern nature, which is in a state of flux, sensitive to its surroundings far more than we really know.

And, do as we may, the pictures in a room are in some way the key to the atmosphere of a room. Put up grey photogravures, and a certain greyness will dominate in the air, no matter if your cushions be daffodils. Put up Baxter prints, and for a time you will have charm; after that, a certain stuffiness will ensue. Pictures are strange things. Most of them die as sure as flowers die, and, once dead, they hang on the wall as stale as brown withered bouquets. The reason lies in ourselves. When we buy a picture because we like it, then the picture responds fresh to some living feeling in us. But feelings change: quicker or slower. If our feeling for the picture was superficial, it wears away quickly—and quickly the picture is nothing but a dead rag hanging on the wall. On the other hands, if we can see a little deeper, we shall buy a picture that will at least last us a year or two, and give a certain fresh joy all the time, like a living flower. We may even find something that will last us a lifetime. If we found a masterpiece, it would last many lifetimes. But there are not many masterpieces of any sort in this world.

The fact remains there are pictures of every sort, and people of every sort to be pleased by them; and there is, perhaps, a limit to the length of time that even a masterpiece will please mankind. Raphael now occasionally bores us, after several centuries, and Michael Angelo begins to.

But we needn't bother about Raphael or Michael Angelo, who keep up their fresh interest for centuries. Our concern is rather with pictures that may be dead rags in six months, all the fresh feeling for them gone. If we think of Landseer, or Alma Tadema, we see how even traditional connoisseurs like Dukes of Devonshire paid large sums for momentary masterpieces that now hang on the ducal walls as dead and ridiculous rags. Only a very uneducated person nowadays would want to put those two Landseer dogs, "Dignity and Impudence," on the drawing-room wall. Yet they pleased immensely in their day. And the interest was sustained, perhaps, for twenty years. But after twenty years it has become a humiliation to keep them hanging on the walls of Chatsworth or wherever they hang. They should be burnt, of course. They only make an intolerable stuffiness wherever they are, and remind us of the shallowness of our taste.

And if this is true of "Dignity and Impudence" or Millais' "Bubbles," which have a great deal of technical skill in them, how much more true is it of cheap photogravures, which have none. Familiarity wears a picture out. Since Whistler's portrait of his mother was used for advertisement, it has lost most of its appeal, and become for most people a worn-out picture, a dead rag. And once a picture has been really popular, and then died into staleness, it never revives again. It is dead for ever. The only thing is to burn it.

Which applies very forcibly to photogravures and other such machine pictures. They may have fascinated the young bride twenty years ago. They may even have gone on fascinating her for six months or two years. But at the end of that time they are almost certainly dead, and the bride's pleasure in them can only be a reminiscent sentimental pleasure, or that rather vulgar satisfaction in them as pieces of property. It is fatal to look on pictures as pieces of property. Pictures are like flowers, that fade away sooner or later, and die, and must be thrown in the dustbin and burnt. It is true of all pictures. Even the beloved Giorgione will one day die to human interest—but he is still very lovely, after almost five centuries, still a fresh flower. But when at last he is dead, as so many pictures are that hang on honoured walls, let us hope he will be burnt. Let us hope he won't still be regarded as a piece of valuable property, worth huge sums, like lots of dead-as-doornails canvases today.

If only we could get rid of the idea of "property" in the arts! The arts exist to give us pleasure or joy. A yellow cushion gives us pleasure. The moment it ceases to do so, take it away, have done with it, give us another.—Which we do, and so cushions remain fresh and interesting, and the manufacturers manufacture continually new, fresh, fascinating fabrics. The natural demand causes a healthy supply.

In pictures it is just the opposite. A picture, instead of being regarded, like a flower or a cushion, as something that must be fresh and fragrant with attraction, is looked on as solid property. We may spend ten shillings on a bunch of roses, and throw away the dead stalks without thinking we have thrown away ten shillings. We may spend two guineas on the cover of a lovely cushion, and strip it off and discard it the moment it is stale, without for a moment lamenting the two guineas. We know where we are. We paid for æsthetic pleasure, and we have had it. Lucky for us that money can buy roses or lovely embroidery.—Yet if we pay two pounds for some picture, and are tired of it after a year, we can no more burn that picture than we can set the house on fire. It is uneducated folly on our part. We *ought* to burn the picture, so that we can have real, fresh pleasure in a different one, as in fresh flowers and fresh cushions. In every school it is taught: Never leave stale flowers in a vase. Throw them away!—So it should be taught: Never leave stale pictures on the wall. Burn them! The value of a picture lies in the æsthetic emotion it brings, exactly as if it were a flower. The æsthetic emotion dead, the picture is a piece of ugly litter.

Which belies the tedious dictum that a picture should be part of the architectural whole, built into the room, as it were. This is fallacy. A picture is decoration, not architecture. The room exists to shelter us and house us, the picture exists only to please us, to give us certain emotions. Of course, there can be harmony or disharmony between the pictures and the whole *ensemble* of a room. But in any room in the world you could carry out dozens of different schemes of decoration, at different times, and to harmonize with each scheme of decoration there are hundreds of different pictures. The built-in theory is all wrong. A picture in a room is the gardenia in my buttonhole. If the tailor "built" a permanent and irremovable gardenia in my morning-coat buttonhole, I should be done in.

Then there is the young school which thinks pictures should be kept in stacks like books in a library, and looked at for half an hour or so at a time, as we turn over the leaves of a book of reproductions. But this again entirely disregards the real psychology of pictures. It is true the great trashy mass of pictures are exhausted in half an hour. But then why keep them in a stack, why keep them at all? On the other hand, if I had a Renoir nude, or a good Fricsz flower-study, or even a Brabazon water-colour, I should want to keep it at least a year or two, and hang it up in a chosen place, to live with it and get all the fragrance out of it. And if I had the Titian "Adam and Eve," from the Prado, I should want to have it hanging in my room all my life, to look at: because I know it would give me a subtle rejoicing all my life, and would make my life delightful. And if I had some Picassos I should want to keep them about six months, and some Braques I should like to have for about a year: then, probably, I should be through with them. But I would not want a Romney even for a day.

And so it varies, with the individual and with the picture, and so it should be allowed to vary. But at present it is not allowed to vary. We all have to stare at the dead rags our fathers and mothers hung on the walls, just because they are *property.*

But let us change it. Let us refuse to have our vision filled with dust and nullity of dead pictures in the home. Let there be a grand conflagration of dead "art," immolation of canvas and paper, oil-colours, water-colours, photographs and all, a grand clearance.

Then what? Then ask Harrods about it. Don't for heaven's sake go and spend twenty guineas on another picture that will have to hang on the wall till the end of time just because it cost twenty guineas. Go to Harrods and ask them what about their Circulating Picture scheme. They have a circulating library—or other people have—huge circulating libraries. People hire books till they have assimilated their content. Why not the same with pictures?

Why should not Harrods have a great "library" of pictures? Why not have a great "pictuary," where we can go and choose a picture? There would be men in charge who knew about pictures, just as librarians know about books. We subscribe, we pay a certain deposit, and our pictures are sent home to us, to keep for one year, for two, for ten, as we wish: at any rate, till we have got all the joy out of them, and want a change.

In the pictuary you can have everything except machine-made rubbish that is not worth having. You can have big supplies of modern art, fresh from the artists, etchings, engravings, drawings, paintings; you can have the lovely new colour reproductions that most of us can't afford to buy; you can have frames to suit. And here you can choose, choose what will give you real joy and will suit your home for the time being.

There are few, very few great artists in any age. But there are hundreds and hundreds of men and women with genuine artistic talent and beautiful artistic feeling, who produce quite lovely works that are never seen. They are lovely works—not immortal, not masterpieces, not "great"; yet they are lovely, and will keep their loveliness a certain number of years; after which they will die, and the time will have come to destroy them.

Now it is a tragedy that all these pictures with their temporary loveliness should be condemned to a premature dust-heap. For that is what they are. Contemporary art belongs to contemporary society. Society at large *needs* the pictures of its contemporaries, just as it needs the books. Modern people read modern books. But they hang up pictures that belong to no age whatever, and have no life, and have no meaning, but are mere blotches of deadness on the walls.

The living moment is everything. And in pictures we never experience it. It is useless asking the public to "see" Matisse or Picasso or Braque. They will never see more than an odd horrific canvas, anyhow. But does the modern public read James Joyce or Marcel Proust? It does not. It reads the great host of more congenial and more intelligible contemporary writers. And so the modern public is more or less up-to-date and on the spot about the general run of modern books. It is conscious of the literature of its day, moderately awake and intelligent in that respect.

But of the pictures and drawings of its day it is blankly unaware. The general public feels itself a hopeless ignoramus when confronted with modern works of art. It has no clue to the whole unnatural business of modern art, and is just hostile. Even those who are tentatively attracted are uneasy, and they dare never *buy*. Prices are comparatively high, and you may so easily be let in for a dud. So the whole thing is a deadlock.

Now the only way to keep the public in touch with art is to let it get hold of works of art. It was just the same with books. In the old five-guinea and two-guinea days there was no public for literature, except the squire class. The great reading public came into being with the lending library. And the great picture-loving public would come into being with the lending pictuary. The public *wants* pictures hard enough. But it simply can't get them.

And this will continue so long as a picture is regarded as a piece of property, and not as a source of æsthetic emotion, of sheer pleasure, as a flower is. The great public was utterly deprived of books till books ceased to be looked on as lumps of real estate, and came to be regarded as something belonging to the mind and consciousness, a spiritual instead of a gross material property. Today, if I say: "Doughty's 'Arabia Deserta' is a favourite book of mine," then the man I say it to won't reply: "Yes, I own a copy," he will say: "Yes, I have read it." In the eighteenth century he would probably have replied: "I have a fine example *in folio* in my library," and the sense of "property" would have overwhelmed any sense of literary delight.

The cheapening of books freed them from the gross property valuation and released their true spiritual value. Something of the same must happen for pictures. The public wants and needs badly all the real æsthetic stimulus it can get. And it knows it. When books were made available, the vast reading public sprang into being almost at once. And a vast picture-loving public would arise, once the public could get at the pictures, personally.

There are thousands of quite lovely pictures, not masterpieces, of course, but with real beauty, *which belong to today*, and which remain stacked dustily and hopelessly in corners of artists' studios, going stale. It is a great shame. The public wants them, but it never sees them; and if it does see an occasional few, it daren't buy, especially as "art" is high-priced, for it feels incompetent to judge. At the same time, the unhappy, work-glutted artists of today want above all things to let the public have their works. And these works are, we insist, an essential part of the education and emotional experience of the modern mind. It is necessary that adults should *know* them, as they know modern books. It is necessary that children should be familiar with them, in the constant stream of creation. Our æsthetic education is become immensely important, since it is so immensely neglected.

And there we are, the pictures going to dust, for they don't keep their freshness, any more than books or flowers or silks, beyond a certain time; yet their freshness now is the breath of life to us, since it means hours and days of delight. And the public is pining for the pictures, but daren't buy, because of the money-property complex. And the artist is pining to let the public have them, but daren't make himself cheap. And so the thing is an *impasse*, simple state of frustration.

Now for Messrs. Harrods and their lending library—or pictuary—of modern works of art. Or, better still, an Artists' Co-operative Society, to supply pictures on loan or purchase, to the great public. Today nobody buys pictures, except as a speculation. If a man pays a hundred pounds for a canvas, he does it in the secret belief that that canvas will be worth a thousand pounds in a few years' time.

The whole attitude is disgusting. The reading public only asks of a book that it shall be entertaining, it doesn't give a hang as to whether the book will be considered a great book five years hence. The great public wants to be entertained and, sometimes, delighted, and literature exists to supply the demand. Now there is a great deal of delight in even a very minor picture, produced by an artist who has delicate artistic feeling and some skill, even if he be not wildly original. There are hundreds and hundreds of perfectly obscure pictures stuck away in corners of studios, which would, I know, give me a real delight if they were hung in my room for a year. After a while they would go stale; but not nearly as quickly as a bunch of lilac, which yet I love and set with pleasure on the table. As a tree puts beauty into a flower that will fade, so all the hosts of minor artists, one way and another, put beauty and delight into their pictures, that likewise will not last beyond their rhythmic season. But it is a wicked shame and waste that nearly all these pictures, with their modicum of beauty and their power of giving delight, should just be taken from the easel to be laid on the dust-heap, while a beauty-starved public doesn't even get a look at them. It is all very well saying the public should buy. A picture is cheap at twenty pounds, and very cheap at ten pounds, and "given away" at five pounds. And the public is not only shy, it has a complex about buying any picture that hasn't at least the chance of turning out a masterpiece of ultimate extraordinary value.

It is all nonsensical and futile. The only way now is for the hosts of small artists to club together and form an Artists' Co-operative Society, with proper business intelligence and business energy, to supply the public with pictures on the public's own terms. Or for the shrewd business men of the world to take the matter up and make a profitable concern of it, as publishers have made a profitable concern of publishing books.

On Being a Man

Man is a thought-adventurer.

Which isn't the same as saying that man has intellect. In intellect there is skill, and tricks. To the intellect the terms are given, as the chessmen and rules of the game are given in chess. Real thought is an experience. It begins as a change in the blood, a slow convulsion and revolution in the body itself. It ends as a new piece of awareness, a new reality in mental consciousness.

On this account, thought is an adventure, and not a practice. In order to think, man must risk himself. He must risk himself doubly. First, he must go forth and meet life in the body. Then he must face the result in his mind.

It is bad enough going out like a little David to meet the giant of life bodily. Take the war as an example of that. It is still harder, and bitterer, after a great encounter with life, to sit down and face out the result. Take the war again. Many men went out and faced the fight. Who dared to face his own self afterwards?

The risk is double, because man is double. Each of us has two selves. First is this body which is vulnerable and never quite within our control. The body with its irrational sympathies and desires and passions, its peculiar direct communication, defying the mind. And second is the conscious ego, the self I KNOW I am.

The self that lives in my body I can never finally know. It has such strange attractions, and revulsions, and it lets me in for so much irrational suffering, real torment, and occasional frightening delight. The me that is in my body is a strange animal to me, and often a very trying one. My body is like a jungle in which dwells an unseen me, like a black panther in the night, whose two eyes glare green through my dreams, and, if a shadow falls, through my waking day.

Then there is this other me, that is fair-faced and reasonable and sensible and complex and full of good intentions. The known me, which can be seen and appreciated. I say of myself: "Yes, I know I am impatient and rather intolerant in ideas. But in the ordinary way of life I am quite easy and really rather kindly. My kindliness makes me sometimes a bit false. But then I don't believe in mechanical honesty. There is an honesty of the feelings, of the sensibilities, as well as of the mind. If a man is lying to me, and I know it, it is a matter of choice whether I tell him so or not. If it would only damage his real feelings, and my own, then it would be *emotionally* dishonest to call him a liar to his face. I would rather be a bit mentally dishonest, and pretend to swallow the lie."

This is the known me, having a talk with itself. It sees a reason for everything it does and feels. It has a certain unchanging belief in its own good intentions. It tries to steer a sensible and harmless course among all the other people and "personalities" around itself.

To this known me, everything exists as a term of knowledge. A man is what I know he is. England is what I know it to be. I am what I know I am. And Bishop Berkeley is absolutely right: things only exist in our own consciousness. To the known me, nothing exists beyond what I know. True, I am always adding to the things I know. But this is because, in my opinion, knowledge begets knowledge. Not because anything has entered *from the outside*. There *is* no outside. There is only more knowledge to be added.

If I sit in the train and a man enters my compartment, he is already, in a great measure, known to me. He is, in the first place, A Man, and I know what that is. Then, he is old. And Old, I know what that means. Then he is English and middle class, and so on, and so on. And I know it all.

There remains a tiny bit that is not known to me. He is a stranger. As a personality I don't yet know him. I glance at him quickly. It is a very small adventure, still an adventure in knowledge, a combination of certain qualities grouped in a certain way. At a glance I know as much about him as I want to know. It is finished, the adventure is over.

This is the adventure of knowing. People go to Spain, and "know" Spain. People study entomology, and "know" insects. People meet Lenin and "know" Lenin. Lots of people "know" me.

And this is how we live. We proceed from what we know already to what we know next. If we don't know the Shah of Persia, we think we have only to call at the palace in Teheran to accomplish the feat. If we don't know much about the moon, we have only to get the latest book on that orb, and we shall be *au courant*.

We know we know all about it, really. *Connu! Connu!* Remains only the fascinating little game of *understanding*, putting two and two together and being real little gods in the machine.

All this is the adventure of knowing and understanding. But it isn't the thought-adventure.

The thought-adventure starts in the blood, not in the mind. If an Arab or a Negro or even a Jew sits down next to me in the train, I cannot proceed so glibly with my knowing. It is not enough for me to glance at a black face and say: He is a Negro. As he sits next to me, there is a faint uneasy movement in my blood. A strange vibration comes from him, which causes a slight disturbance in my own vibration. There is a slight odour in my nostrils. And above all, even if I shut my eyes, there is a strange *presence* in contact with me.

I now can no longer proceed from what I am and what I know I am, to what I know him to be. I am not a nigger and so I can't quite know a nigger, and I can never fully "understand" him.

What then? It's an *impasse*.

Then, I have three courses open. I can just plank down the word Nigger, and having labelled him, finish with him! Or I can try to track him down in terms of my own knowledge. That is, understand him as I understand any other individual.

Or I can do a third thing. I can admit that my blood is disturbed, that something comes from him and interferes with my normal vibration. Admitting so much, I can either put up a resistance and insulate myself. Or I can allow the disturbance to continue, because, after all, there is some peculiar alien sympathy between us.

In almost every case, of course, the nigger among white men will insulate himself, and not let his black aura reach the white neighbours. If I find myself in a train full of niggers, I shall no doubt do the same.

But apart from this, I shall admit a certain strange and incalculable reaction between me and him. This reaction causes a slight but unmistakable change in the vibration of my blood and nerves. This slight change in my blood develops in dreams and unconsciousness till, if I allow it, it struggles forward into light as a new bit of realization, a new term of consciousness.

Take the much commoner case of men and women. A man, proceeding from his known self, likes a woman because she is in sympathy with what he knows. He feels that he and she know one another. They marry. And then the fun begins. In so far as they know one another they can proceed from their known selves, they are as right as ninepence. Loving couple, etc. But the moment there is real blood contact, as likely as not a strange discord enters in. She is not what he thought her. He is not what she thought him. It is the other, primary or bodily self—appearing, very often like a black demon, out of the fair creature who was erst the beloved.

The man who before marriage seemed everything that is delightful, after marriage begins to come out in his true colours, a son of the old and rather hateful Adam. And she, who was an angel of loveliness and desirability, gradually emerges as an almost fiendlike daughter of the snake-frequenting Eve.

What has happened?

It is the invariable crucifixion. The Cross, as we know, stands for the body, for the dark self which lives in the body. And on the Cross of this bodily self is crucified the self which I know I am, my so-called *real* self. The Cross, as an ancient symbol, has an inevitable phallic reference. But it is far deeper than sex. It is the self which darkly inhabits our blood and bone, and for which the ithyphallus is but a symbol. This self which lives darkly in my blood and bone is my *alter ego*, my other self, the homunculus, the second one of the Kabiri, the second of the Twins, the Gemini. And the sacred black stone at Mecca stands for this: the dark self that dwells in the blood of a man and of a woman. Phallic if you like. But much more than phallic. And on this cross of division in the whole self is crucified the Christ. We are all crucified on it.

Marriage is the great puzzle of our day. It is our sphinx-riddle. Solve it, or to be torn to bits, is the decree.

We marry from the known self, taking the woman as an extension of our knowledge—an extension of our known self. And then, almost invariably, comes the jolt and the crucifixion. The woman of the known self is fair and lovely. But the woman of the dark blood looks, to man, most malignant and horrific. In the same way, the fair daytime man of courtship days leaves nothing to be desired. But the husband, horrified by the serpent-advised Eve of the blood, obtuse and arrogant in his Adam obstinacy, is an enemy pure and simple.

Solve the puzzle. The quickest way is for the wife to smother the serpent-advised Eve which is in her, and for the man to talk himself out of his old arrogant Adam. Then they make a fair and above-board combination, called a successful marriage.

But Nemesis is on our track. The husband forfeits his arrogance, the wife has her children and her way to herself. But lo, the son of one woman is husband to the woman of the next generation! And oh, women, beware the mother's boy! Or else the wife forfeits the old serpent-advised Eve from her nature and becomes the instrument of the man. And then, oh, young husband of the next generation, prepare for the daughter's revenge.

What's to be done?

The thought-adventure! We've got to take ourselves as we are, not as

we know ourselves to be. I am the son of the old red-earth Adam, with
a black touchstone at the centre of me. And all the fair words in the
world won't alter it. Woman is the strange serpent-communing Eve,
inalterable. We are a strange pair, who meet, but never mingle. I came,
in the bath of birth, out of a mother. But I arose the old Adam, with the
black old stone at the core of me. She had a father who begot her, but
the column of her is pure enigmatic Eve.

In spite of all the things I know about her, in spite of my knowing
her so well, the serpent knows her better still. And in spite of my fair
words, and my goodly pretences, she runs up against the black stone of
Adam which is in the middle of me.

Know thyself means knowing at last that you *can't* know yourself. I
can't know the Adam of red-earth which is me. It will always do things
to me, beyond my knowledge. Neither can I know the serpent-listen-
ing Eve which is the woman, beneath all her modern glibness. I have
to take her at that. And we have to meet as I meet a jaguar between
the trees in the mountains, and advance, and touch, and risk it. When
man and woman *actually* meet, there is always terrible risk to both
of them. Risk for her, lest her womanhood be damaged by the hard
dark stone which is unchangeable in his soul. Risk for him, lest the
serpent drag him down, coiled round his neck, and kissing him with
poison.

There is always risk, for him and for her. Take the risk, make the adventure. Suffer and enjoy the change in the blood. And, if you are a
man, slowly, slowly make the great experience of realizing. The final
adventure and experience of realization, if you are man. Fully conscious
realization. If you are a woman, the strange, slumbrous serpentine realization, which knows without thinking.

But with man, it is a thought-adventure. He risks his body and blood.
He withdraws and touches the black stone of his inner conscience. And
in a new adventure he dares take thought. He dares take thought for
what he has done and what has happened to him. And daring to take
thought, he ventures on, and realizes at last.

To be a man! To risk your body and your blood first, and then to
risk your mind. All the time, to risk your known self, and become
once more a self you could never have known or expected.

To be man, instead of being a mere personality. Today men don't
risk their blood and bone. They go forth, panoplied in their own idea of
themselves. Whatever they do, they perform it all in the full armour of
their own idea of themselves. Their unknown bodily self is never for one
moment unsheathed. All the time, the only protagonist is the known

ego, the self-conscious ego. And the dark self in the mysterious labyrinth of the body is cased in a tight armour of cowardly repression.

Men marry and commit all their adulteries from the head. All that happens to them, all their reactions, all their experiences, happen only in the head. To the unknown man in them nothing happens. He remains shut up in armour, lest he might be hurt and give pain. And inside the armour he goes quite deranged.

All the suffering today is psychic: it happens in the mind. The red Adam only suffers the slow torture of compression and derangement. A man's wife is a mental thing, a known thing to him. The old Adam in him never sees her. She is just a thing of his own conscious ego. And not for one moment does he risk himself under the strange snake-infested bushes of her extraordinary Paradise. He is afraid.

He becomes extraordinarily clever and agile in his self-conscious panoply. With his mind he can dart about among the emotions as if he really felt something. It is all a lie, he feels nothing. He is just tricking you. He becomes extraordinarily acute at recognizing real feelings from false ones, knowing for certain the falsity of his own. He has always the touchstone of his own conscious falseness against which to test the reality or the falseness of others. And he is always exposing falseness in others. But not for the sake of liberating the real Adam and Eve. On the contrary. He is more terrified even than the ordinary frightened man in the street, of the real Adam and Eve. He is a greater coward still. But his greater cowardice makes him strive to appear a greater man. He denounces falsity in order to triumph in his own greater falsity. He praises the real thing in order to establish his own superiority even to the real thing. He must, must, must be superior. Because he knows himself absolutely and unspeakably and irremediably false. His spurious emotions are more like the real thing than genuine emotions, and they have, for a time, greater effect. But all the time, somewhere, he knows they are false.

And this is his one point of power. Instead of having inside him, like the Adam of red earth, that heavy and immutable black stone which is the eternal touchstone of false and true, good and evil, he has this awful little tombstone of the knowledge of his own falsity. And in this ghastly little white tombstone which he erects to himself lies his peculiar infallibility among a false and mental people.

That's the widdishins way of being a man. To know so absolutely that you are *not* a man, that you dare almost anything on the strength of it. You dare anything, except being a man. So intense and final is the modern white man's conviction, his internal conviction, that he is *not* a man, that he dares anything on earth except be a man. There his courage drops to its grave. He daren't be a man: the old Adam of red earth, with the black touchstone at the middle of him.

He knows he's not a man. Hence his creed of harmlessness. He knows he is not a man of living red earth, to live onward through strange weather into new springtime. He knows there is extinction ahead: for nothing but extinction lies in wait for the conscious ego. Hence his creed of harmlessness, of relentless kindness. A little less than kin, and more than kind. There should be no danger in life *at all*, even no friction. This he asserts, while all the time he is slowly, malignantly undermining the tree of life.

On Human Destiny

Man is a domesticated animal that must think. His thinking makes him a little lower than the angels. And his domestication makes him, at times, a little lower than the monkey.

It is no use retorting that most men *don't* think. It is quite true, most men don't have any original thoughts. Most men, perhaps, are incapable of original thought, or original thinking. This doesn't alter the fact that they are all the time, all men, all the time, thinking. Man cannot even sleep with a blank mind. The mind refuses to be blank. The millstones of the brain grind on while the stream of life runs. And they grind on the grist of whatever ideas the mind contains.

The ideas may be old and ground to powder already. No matter. The mill of the mind grinds on, grinds the old grist over and over and over again. The blackest savage in Africa is the same, in this respect, as the whitest Member of Parliament in Westminster. His risk of death, his woman, his hunger, his chieftain, his lust, his immeasurable fear, all these are fixed ideas in the mind of the black African savage. They are ideas based on certain sensual reactions in the black breast and bowels, that is true. They are nonetheless ideas, however "primitive." And the difference between a primitive idea and a civilized one is not very great. It is remarkable how little change there is in man's rudimentary ideas.

Nowadays we like to talk about spontaneity, spontaneous feeling, spontaneous passion, spontaneous emotion. But our very spontaneity is just an idea. All our modern spontaneity is fathered in the mind, gestated in self-consciousness.

Since man became a domesticated, thinking animal, long, long ago, a little lower than the angels, he long, long ago left off being a wild instinctive animal. If he ever was such, which I don't believe. In my opinion, the most prognathous cave-man was an ideal beast. He ground on his crude, obstinate ideas. He was no more like the wild deer or the jaguar among the mountains than we are. He ground his ideas in the slow ponderous mill of his heavy cranium.

Man is never spontaneous, as we imagine the thrushes or the sparrow-hawk, for example, to be spontaneous. No matter how wild, how savage, how apparently untamed the savage may be, Dyak or Hottentot, you may be sure he is grinding upon his own fixed, peculiar ideas, and he's no more spontaneous than a London 'bus conductor: probably not as much.

The simple innocent child of nature does not exist. If there be an occasional violet by a mossy stone in the human sense, a Wordsworthian Lucy, it is because her vitality is rather low, and her simple nature is very near a simpleton's. You may, like Yeats, admire the simpleton, and call him God's Fool. But for me the village idiot is a cold egg.

No, no, let man be as primitive as primitive can be, he still has a mind. Give him at the same time a certain passion in his nature, and between his passion and his mind he'll beget himself ideas, ideas more or less good, more or less monstrous, but whether good or monstrous, absolute.

The savage grinds on his fetish or totem or taboo ideas even more fixedly and fatally than we on our love and salvation and making-good ideas.

Let us dismiss the innocent child of nature. He does not exist, never did, never will, and never could. No matter at what level man may be, he still has a mind, he has also passions. And the mind and the passions between them beget the scorpion brood of ideas. Or, if you like, call it the angelic hosts of the ideal.

Let us accept our own destiny. Man *can't* live by instinct, because he's got a mind. The serpent, with a crushed head, learned to brood along his spine, and take poison in his mouth. He has a strange sapience. But even he doesn't have ideas. Man has a mind and ideas, so it is just puerile to sigh for innocence and naïve spontaneity. Man is never spontaneous. Even children aren't spontaneous, not at all. It is only that their few and very dominant young ideas don't make logical associations. A child's ideas are ideas hard enough, but they hang together in a comical way, and the emotion that rises jumbles them ludicrously.

Ideas are born from a marriage between mind and emotion. But surely, you will say, it is possible for emotions to run free, without the dead hand of the ideal mind upon them.

It is impossible. Because, since man ate the apple and became endowed with mind, or mental consciousness, the human emotions are like a wedded wife; lacking a husband she is only a partial thing. The emotions cannot be "free." You can let your emotions run loose, if you like. You can let them run absolutely "wild." But their wildness and their looseness are a very shoddy affair. They leave nothing but boredom afterwards.

Emotions by themselves become just a nuisance. The mind by itself becomes just a sterile thing, making everything sterile. So what's to be done?

You've got to marry the pair of them. Apart, they are no good. The emotions that have not the approval and inspiration of the mind are just hysterics. The mind without the approval and inspiration of the emotions is just a dry stick, a dead tree, no good for anything unless to make a rod to beat and bully somebody with.

So, taking the human psyche, we have this simple trinity: the emotions, the mind, and then the children of this venerable pair, ideas. Man is controlled by his own ideas: there's no doubt about that.

Let us argue it once more. A pair of emancipated lovers are going to get away from the abhorred old ideal suasion. They're just going to fulfil their lives. That's all there is to it. They're just going to live their lives.

And then look at them! They do all the things that they know people do, when they are "living their own lives." They play up to their own ideas of being naughty instead of their ideas of good. And then what? It's the same old treadmill. They are just enacting the same set of ideas, only in the widdishins direction, being naughty instead of being good, treading the old circle in the opposite direction, and going round in the same old mill, even if in a reversed direction.

A man goes to a *cocotte*. And what of it? He does the same thing he does with his wife, but in the reverse direction. He just does everything naughtily instead of from his good self. It's a terrible relief perhaps, at first, to get away from his good self. But after a little while he realizes, rather drearily, that he's only going round in the same old treadmill, in the reversed direction. The Prince Consort turned us giddy with goodness, plodding round and round in the earnest mill. King Edward drove us giddy with naughtiness, trotting round and round in the same mill, in the opposite direction. So that the Georgian era finds us flummoxed, because we know the whole cycle back and forth.

At the centre is the same emotional idea. You fall in love with a woman, you marry her, you have bliss, you have children, you devote yourself to your family and to the service of mankind, and you live a happy life. Or, same idea but in the widdishins direction, you fall in love with a woman, you don't marry her, you live with her under the rose and enjoy yourself in spite of society; you leave your wife to swallow her tears or spleen, as the case may be; you spend the dowry of your daughters, you waste your substance, and you squander as much of mankind's heaped-up corn as you can.

The ass goes one way, and threshes out the corn from the chaff. The ass goes the other way and kicks the corn into the mud. At the centre is the same idea: love, service, self-sacrifice, productivity. It just depends upon which way round you run.

So there you are, poor man! All you can do is to run round like an ass, either in one direction or another, round the fixed pole of a certain central idea, in the track of a number of smaller, peripheral ideas. This idea of love, these peripheral ideals of service, marriage, increase, etc.

Even the vulgarist self-seeker trots in the same tracks and gets the same reactions, minus the thrill of the centralized passion.

What's to be done? What is being done?

The ring is being tightened. Russia was a complication of mixed ideas, old barbaric ideas of divine kingship, of irresponsible power, of sacred servility, conflicting with modern ideas of equality, serviceableness, productivity, etc. This complication had to be cleaned up. Russia was a great and bewildering but at the same time fascinating circus, with her splendours and miseries and brutalities and mystery. *Il faut changer tout cela.* So modern men have changed it. And the bewildering, fascinating circus of human anomalies is to be turned into a productive threshing-floor, an ideal treadmill. The treadmill of the one accomplished idea.

What's to be done? Man is an ideal animal: an idea-making animal. In spite of all his ideas, he remains an animal, often a little lower than the monkey. And in spite of all his animal nature, he can only act in fulfilment of disembodied ideas. What's to be done?

That too is quite simple. Man is not pot-bound in his ideas. Then let him burst the pot that contains him. Ideally he is pot-bound. His roots are choked, squeezed, and the life is leaving him, like a plant that is pot-bound and is gradually going sapless.

Break the pot, then.

But it's no good waiting for the slow accumulation of circumstance to break the pot. That's what men are doing today. They know the pot's got to break. They know our civilization has got to smash, sooner or later. So they say: "Let it! But let me live my life first!"

Which is all very well, but it's a coward's attitude. They say glibly: "Oh, well, every civilization must fall at last. Look at Rome!" Very good, look at Rome. And what do you see? A mass of "civilized" so-called Romans, airing their *laissez-faire* and *laissez-aller* sentiments.

And a number of barbarians, Huns, etc., coming down to wipe them out, and expending themselves in the effort.

What of it, the Dark Ages? What about the Dark Ages, when the fields of Italy ran wild as the wild wastes of the undiscovered world, and wolves and bears roamed in the streets of the grey city of Lyons?

Very nice! But what else? Look at the other tiny bit of a truth. Rome was pot-bound, the pot was smashed to atoms, and the highly developed Roman tree of life lay on its side and died. But not before a new young seed had germinated. There in the spilt soil, small, humble, almost indiscernible, was the little tree of Christianity. In the howling wilderness of slaughter and debacle, tiny monasteries of monks, too obscure and poor to plunder, kept the eternal light of man's undying effort at consciousness alive. A few poor bishops wandering through the chaos, linking up the courage of these men of thought and prayer. A scattered, tiny minority of men who had found a new way to God, to the life-source, glad to get again into touch with the Great God, glad to know the way and to keep the knowledge burningly alive.

That is the essential history of the Dark Ages, when Rome fell. We talk as if the flame of human courage and perspicacity had, in this time, gone out entirely, and that it miraculously popped into life again, out of nowhere, later on. Fusion of races, new barbaric blood, etc. Blarney! The fact of the matter is, the exquisite courage of brave men goes on in an unbroken continuity, even if sometimes the thread of flame becomes very thin. The exquisite delicate light of ever-renewed human consciousness is never blown out. The lights of great cities go out, and there is howling darkness to all appearance. But always, since men began, the light of the pure, God-knowing human consciousness has kept alight; sometimes, as in the Dark Ages, tiny but perfect flames of purest God-knowledge here and there; sometimes, as in our precious Victorian era, a huge and rather ghastly glare of human "understanding." But the light never goes out.

And that's the human destiny. The light shall never go out till the last day. The light of the human adventure into consciousness, which is, essentially, the light of human God-knowledge.

And human God-knowledge waxes and wanes, fed, as it were, from different oil. Man is a strange vessel. He has a thousand different essential oils in him, to keep the light of consciousness fed. Yet, apparently, he can only draw on one source at a time. And when the source he has been drawing on dries up, he has a bad time sinking a new well of oil, or guttering to extinction.

So it was in Roman times. The great old pagan fire of knowledge gradually died, its sources dried up. Then Jesus started a new, strange little flicker.

Today, the long light of Christianity is guttering to go out and we have to get at new resources in ourselves.

It is no use waiting for the debacle. It's no use saying: "Well, I didn't make the world, so it isn't up to me to mend it. Time and the event must do the business."—Time and the event will do nothing. Men are worse after a great debacle than before. The Russians who have "escaped" from the horrors of the revolution are most of them extinguished as human beings. The real manly dignity has gone, all that remains is a collapsed human creature saying to himself: "Look at me! I am alive. I can actually eat more sausage."

Debacles don't save men. In nearly every case, during the horrors of a catastrophe the light of integrity and human pride is extinguished in the soul of the man or the woman involved, and there is left a painful, unmanned creature, a thing of shame, incapable any more. It is the great danger of debacles, especially in times of unbelief like these. Men lack the faith and courage to keep their souls alert, kindled and unbroken. Afterwards there is a great smouldering of shamed life.

Man, poor, conscious, forever-animal man, has a very stern destiny, from which he is never allowed to escape. It is his destiny that he must move on and on, in the thought-adventure. He is a thought-adventurer, and adventure he must. The moment he builds himself a house and begins to think he can sit still in his knowledge, his soul becomes deranged, and he begins to pull down the house over his own head.

Man is now house-bound. Human consciousness today is too small, too tight to let us live and act naturally. Our dominant idea, instead of being a pole-star, is a millstone round our necks, strangling us. Old tablets of stone.

That is part of our destiny. As a thinking being, man is destined to seek God and to form some conception of Life. And since the invisible God *cannot* be conceived, and since Life is always more than any idea, behold, from the human conception of God and of Life, a great deal of necessity is left out. And this God whom we have left out and this Life that we have shut out from our living, must in the end turn against us and rend us. It is our destiny.

Nothing will alter it. When the Unknown God whom we ignore turns savagely to rend us, from the darkness of oblivion, and when the Life that we exclude from our living turns to poison and madness in our veins, then there is only one thing left to do. We have to struggle down to the heart of things, where the everlasting flame is, and kindle ourselves another beam of light. In short, we have to make another bitter adventure in pulsating thought, far, far to the one central pole of energy. We have to germinate inside us, between our undaunted mind and our reckless, genuine passions, a new germ. The germ of a new idea. A new germ of God-knowledge, or Life-knowledge. But a new germ.

And this germ will expand and grow, and flourish to a great tree, maybe. And in the end die again. Die like all the other human trees of knowledge.

But what does that matter? We walk in strides, we live by days and nights. A tree slowly rises to a great height, and quickly falls to dust. There is a long life-day for the individual. Then a very dark, spacious death-room——

I live and I die. I ask no other. Whatever proceeds from me lives and dies. I am glad, too. God is eternal, but my idea of Him is my own, and perishable. Everything human, human knowledge, human faith, human emotions, all perishes. And that is very good; if it were not so, everything would turn to cast-iron. There is too much of this cast-iron of permanence today.

Because I know the tree will ultimately die, shall I therefore refrain from planting a seed? Bah! it would be conceited cowardice on my part. I love the little sprout and the weak little seedling. I love the thin sapling, and the first fruit, and the falling of the first fruit. I love the great tree in its splendour. And I am glad that at last, at the very last, the great tree will go hollow, and fall on its side with a crash, and the little ants will run through it, and it will disappear like a ghost back into the humus.

It is the cycle of all things created, thank God. Because, given courage, it saves even eternity from staleness.

Man fights for a new conception of life and God, as he fights to plant seeds in the spring: because he knows that is the only way to harvest. If after harvest there is winter again, what does it matter? It is just seasonable.

But you have to fight even to plant seed. To plant seed you've got to kill a great deal of weeds and break much ground.

Notes

I. Stories and Sketches

A Prelude
One of three stories submitted by Lawrence for a Christmas competition held by the *Nottinghamshire Guardian* in 1907, "A Prelude" first appeared in the *Guardian* for 7 December 1907. It was later reprinted with the original illustrations in facsimile in the *Nottinghamshire Weekly Guardian* for 10 December 1949 and separately published by the Merle Press, Thames Ditton, Surrey, 1949.

A Fly in the Ointment
Although included in *Young Lorenzo, The Early Life of D. H. Lawrence*, as a previously unpublished story, "A Fly in the Ointment" appeared in the *New Statesman* for 13 August 1913.

Lessford's Rabbits
Previously unpublished. From a typescript in the possession of Harry T. Moore.

A Lesson on a Tortoise
Previously unpublished. From a typescript in the possession of Harry T. Moore.

A Chapel among the Mountains
Previously published in *Love among the Haystacks and Other Pieces*. London, 1930.

A Hay Hut among the Mountains
Previously published in *Love among the Haystacks and Other Pieces*. London, 1930.

Once
Previously published in *Love among the Haystacks and Other Pieces*. London, 1930.

The Thimble
First published in *Seven Arts* for March 1917, "The Thimble" was later rewritten as "The Ladybird".

The Mortal Coil
   First published in *Seven Arts* for July 1917.
Delilah and Mr. Bircumshaw
   First published in *The Virginia Quarterly Review* for Spring, 1940.
Prologue to *Women in Love*
   The "Prologue" is part of an early version of *Women in Love* which Lawrence discarded. Published in *The Texas Quarterly* for Spring, 1963.
Mr. Noon
   Originally published in *A Modern Lover*, "Mr. Noon" has not appeared elsewhere.

II. Translation

The Gentleman from San Francisco
   This story originally appeared in *The Gentleman from San Francisco and Other Stories*, by I. A. Bunin. The other stories in the book were translated from the Russian by S. S. Koteliansky and Leonard Woolf. Although Lawrence's name was not mentioned on the title page, an erratum slip was laid in afterwards which named Lawrence as Koteliansky's collaborator for the translation of the title story.

III. Essays

Rachel Annand Taylor
   First published in *Young Lorenzo, The Early Life of D. H. Lawrence*. Florence, 1932.
Art and the Individual
   First published as "Early Work" in *Young Lorenzo, The Early Life of D. H. Lawrence*. Florence, 1932.
The Two Principles
   Originally published as a part of the series on American literature, "The Two Principles" first appeared in the *English Review* for June 1919. Although not included by Lawrence in *Studies in Classic American Literature*, it was published in *The Symbolic Meaning*, edited by Armin Arnold, 1962.
Certain Americans and An Englishman
   First appeared in the *New York Times Magazine* for 24 December 1922.

[Germans and English]

Never before published in English, this essay appeared as "Tedeschi e Inglese" in *La Cultura* for November 1934. Apparently designed for publication in *Insel Almanac*, the piece was translated from German to Italian for its *La Cultura* publication. It is similar to the essay "Germans and Latins" collected in *Phoenix*.

On Coming Home

Previously unpublished. From a manuscript in the D. H. Lawrence Collection at the University of Texas.

[Return to Bestwood]

Previously unpublished. From a manuscript in the library of the University of Cincinnati.

IV. Reviews and Introductions

A Review of *The Oxford Book of German Verse*

This review appeared in the *English Review* for January 1912. It was discovered by Armin Arnold who included it in his book *D. H. Lawrence and German Literature*. Montreal, 1963.

A Review of *The Minnesingers*

First appeared in the *English Review* for January 1912, and collected in *D. H. Lawrence and German Literature*. Montreal, 1963.

A Review of *The Book of Revelation*

Originally published under the pseudonym L. H. Davidson, this review appeared in *The Adelphi* for April 1924. It was identified by Mr. W. Forster of London, whose discovery was confirmed in a letter from John Middleton Murry in 1953.

Foreword to *Women in Love*

Apparently designed as a preface to the American edition of *Women in Love*, this foreword was separately published as *D. H. Lawrence's Unpublished Foreword to Women in Love*, San Francisco, 1936. It was included as an introduction to the Random House Modern Library edition of *Women in Love*.

Introduction to *Little Novels of Sicily*

This introduction appeared in the American edition of *Little Novels of Sicily*. New York, 1925. It is about a page longer than the introduction included in the first English edition, London, 1925.

Introduction to *Mastro-don Gesualdo*

This introduction was first published in the Jonathan Cape *Traveller's Library* edition of Mastro-don Gesualdo, London, 1928.

This is a different essay from that published under the same title in *Phoenix*.

Preface to *Touch and Go*

From the separately published English and American editions of the play.

Preface to *Black Swans*

Previously unpublished. From a manuscript in the University of Texas Library.

V. Miscellaneous pieces

A Britisher Has a Word with an Editor

This short essay first appeared in *Palms* for Christmas 1923 and was later collected in Vol. II of Edward Nehls' *D. H. Lawrence: A Composite Biography*.

Autobiographical Sketch

This autobiographical sketch was written for the Curtis Brown Agency. Edward Nehls published it for the first time in Vol. III of *D. H. Lawrence: A Composite Biography*.

Introduction to *Memoirs of the Foreign Legion*

Originally published as the Introduction to *Memoirs of the Foreign Legion* by Maurice Magnus. London, 1924.

VI. *Reflections on the Death of a Porcupine*

Of the essays in this book, *Reflections on the Death of a Porcupine*, Philadelphia, 1925, "The Novel", "Him with His Tail in His Mouth", "Blessed Are the Powerful", "Love Was Once a Little Boy", "Reflections on the Death of a Porcupine" and "Aristocracy" were previously unpublished.

The Crown

First published in *The Signature* for 4 October, 18 October, and 4 November 1915.

... Love Was Once a Little Boy

An excerpt from this essay appeared in *The Laughing Horse*, Number 15, for March–July 1928 as "Susan the Cow."

VII. A Propos of *Lady Chatterley's Lover*

First published as a book by Mandrake Press, London, 1930.

VIII. *Assorted Articles*

This collection of essays by D. H. Lawrence, most of which were previously published in newspapers, appeared as *Assorted Articles*. London, 1930.

The "Jeune Fille" Wants to Know
First appeared in the *Evening News* for 8 May 1928 as "When She Asks Why?"
Laura Philippine
First appeared in *T. P.'s Weekly* for 7 July 1928.
Sex versus Loveliness
First appeared in the *Sunday Dispatch* for 25 November 1928 as "Sex Locked Out."
Insouciance
First appeared in the *Evening News* for 12 July 1928 as "Over-Earnest Ladies."
Give Her a Pattern
First appeared in the *Daily Express* for 19 June 1929 as "The Real Trouble About Women."
Do Women Change?
First appeared in the *Sunday Dispatch* for 28 April 1929 as "Women Don't Change."
Ownership
Master in His Own House
First appeared in the *Evening News* for 2 August 1928.
Matriarchy
First appeared in the *Evening News* for 5 October 1928 as "If Women Were Supreme."
Cocksure Women and Hensure Men
First appeared in the *Forum* for January 1929.
Is England Still a Man's Country?
First appeared in the *Daily Express* for 29 November 1928.
Dull London
First appeared in the *Evening News* for 3 September 1928.
Red Trousers
First appeared in the *Evening News* for 27 September 1928 as "Oh! For a New Crusade."
The State of Funk
The Risen Lord
First appeared in *Everyman* for 3 October 1929.

Enslaved by Civilization
> First appeared in *Vanity Fair* for September 1929 as "The Manufacture of Good Little Boys."

Men Must Work and Women as Well
> First appeared in the *Star Review* for November 1929 as "Men and Women."

Autobiographical Sketch
> First appeared in the *Sunday Dispatch* for 17 February 1929 as "Myself Revealed."

Hymns in a Man's Life
> First appeared in the *Evening News* for 13 October 1928.

Making Pictures
> First appeared in *Creative Art* for July 1929.

Pictures on the Walls
> First appeared in *Vanity Fair* for December 1929 as "Dead Pictures on the Wall."

On Being a Man
> First appeared in *Vanity Fair* for June 1924.

On Human Destiny
> First appeared in the *Adelphi* for March 1924.

INDEX